Also by Madeline Hunter

BY
ARRANGEMENT

MADELINE
HUNTER

Bantam Books
New York Toronto London Sydney Auckland

BY ARRANGEMENT
A Bantam Book

PUBLISHING HISTORY

Bantam mass market edition published June 2000
Bantam mass market special edition / August 2004
Bantam mass market reissue / June 2006

Published by Bantam Dell
A Division of Random House, Inc.
New York, New York

Bantam Books and the rooster colophon are registered trademarks
of Random House, Inc.

ISBN-13: 978-0-553-58772-2
ISBN-10: 0-553-58772-2

Printed in the United States of America
Published simultaneously in the United States and Canada

www.bantamdell.com

OPM   10   9   8   7   6   5   4   3   2

FOR PAM,
WHO KNOWS WHY

BY ARRANGEMENT

CHAPTER 1

IF YOUR BROTHER finds out about this, I'll be lucky to walk away with my manhood, let alone my head," Thomas said.

The moon's pale light threw shadows on the walls of the shops that lined the street. Ominous movements to the right and left occasionally caught Christiana's attention, but she didn't fear footpads or nightwalkers tonight. Thomas Holland, one of the Queen's knights, rode alongside her, and the glow from his torch displayed his long sword. Christiana expected no challenges from anyone who might see them in the city out after the curfew.

"He will never know, I promise you. No one will," she reassured him.

Thomas worried with good reason. If her brother Morvan found out that Thomas had helped her sneak out of Westminster after dark, there would be hell to pay. She would take all of the blame on herself if they were discovered, though. After all, she could hardly get into any more trouble than she was in right now.

"This merchant you need to see must be rich, if he doesn't live above his shop," Thomas mused. "Not my business to pry, my lady, but this be a peculiar time to be visiting, and on the sly at that. I trust that it is not a lover I bring you to. The King himself will gut me if it is."

She would have laughed at his suggestion, except that her frantic emotions had left her too sick to enjoy the dreadful joke. "Not a lover, and I come now because it is the only time I can be sure of finding him at home," she said, hoping that he would not ask for more explanation. It had taken all of her guile to slip away for this clandestine visit, and she had none to spare for inventing another lie.

The last day had been one of the worst in her life, and one of the longest. Had it only been last evening that she had met with Queen Philippa and been told of the King's decision to accept a marriage offer for her? Every moment since had been an eternity of hellish panic and outrage.

She was not opposed to marriage. In fact, at eighteen she was past the age when most girls wed. But this offer had not come from Stephen Percy, the knight to whom she had given her heart. Nor had it been made by some other knight or lord, as befitted the daughter of Hugh Fitzwaryn and a girl from a family of ancient nobility.

Nay, King Edward had decided to marry her to David de Abyndon, whom she had never met.

A common merchant.

A common, *old* merchant, according to her guardian, Lady Idonia, who remembered buying silks from Master David the mercer in her youth.

It was the King's way of punishing her. Since her parents' deaths she had been his ward and lived at court with his eldest daughter, Isabele, and his young cousin Joan of Kent. When he had learned about Stephen, he must have flown into a rage to have taken such drastic revenge on her.

Stephen. Handsome, blond Stephen. Her heart ached for him. His secret attentions had brought the sun into her sheltered, lonely life. He was the first man to dare to pay court to her. Morvan had threatened to kill any man who wooed her before a betrothal. Her brother's size and skill at arms had proven a depressingly effective deterrent to a love match, just as her lack of a dowry had precluded one secured by property. Other girls at court had admirers, but not her. Until Stephen.

This marriage would be a harsh retribution for what had occurred on that bed before Idonia had found them together. And not one that she planned to accept. Nor would this old merchant want it when he learned how the King was using him.

She and Thomas followed the blond head of the apprentice whom they had woken from his bed in the mercer's shop. The young man had agreed to guide them to his master's house. He led them up the lane away from the Cheap and then over toward the Guildhall before stopping at a gate and rapping lightly. The heavy door swung back and a huge body filled it.

The gate guard held a torch in one massive hand. He was the tallest person Christiana had ever seen, and thick as a tree. Whitish blond hair flowed down his shoulders.

He spoke in a voice accented with the lilting tones of Sweden. "Andrew, is that you? What the hell are you doing here? The constables catch you out after curfew again . . ."

"These two came to the shop, Sieg. I had to show them the way, didn't I?"

The torch pointed out so that Sieg could scrutinize them. "He be expecting you, but I was told it was two men," he said warily. "*Ja*, well, follow me. I'll put you in the solar and tell him you are here."

Thomas turned to her. "I will go up with you," he whispered. "If anything happens . . ."

"I must do this alone. There is no danger for me here."

Thomas did not like it. "I see a courtyard beyond this gate. I will wait there. Be quick, and yell if you need me."

She followed the mountain called Sieg. Doors gave out on either side of a short passage, and she realized that this was a building with a gate cut into its bottom level. They crossed the courtyard and entered a hall set at right angles to the first. She caught the impression of benches and tables as they filed through, turning finally into yet another wing that faced the first across the courtyard. Here a narrow staircase led to a second level.

Sieg opened a door off the top landing and gestured. "You can wait here. Master David be abed, so it might take a while."

She raised a hand to halt him. "I didn't expect to disturb him. I can come another time."

"I was told to wake him when you came."

That was the second time that this man had suggested that they expected her. "I think that you've made a mistake . . ." she began, but Sieg was already out the door.

The solar was quite large, and a low fire burned in the hearth at one end. The furniture appeared as little more than heavy shadows in the moonlight filtering through a bank of pointed arched windows along the far wall. She strolled over to those windows and fingered the rippled glazing and lead tracery. Glass. Lots of it, and very expensive. This Master David had done well over the years selling his cloths and vanities.

It didn't surprise her. She knew that some of the London merchants were as rich as landed lords and that a few had even become lords through their wealth. The mayor of London was always treated like a peer of the realm at important court functions, and the families that supplied the aldermen had a very high status too. London's merchants, with their royal charter of freedoms, were a proud and influential group of men, jealous of their prerogatives and rights. Edward negotiated and consulted with London much as he did with his barons.

Sieg returned and built up the fire. He took a rush and lit several candles on a table nearby before he left. Christiana stayed near the windows, away from the light in her shadowed corner.

A door set in the wall beside the hearth opened, and a man walked through. He paused, looking around the chamber. His eyes found her shadow near the windows, and he walked forward a few steps.

The light from the hearth illuminated him. She took in the tall, lean frame, the golden brown hair, the planes of a handsome face.

Humiliation swept her. They had come to the wrong place!

"My lady?" The voice was a quiet baritone. A beautiful voice. Its very timbre pulled you in and made you want to listen to what it said even if it spoke nonsense.

She searched for the words to form an apology.

"You have something for me?" he encouraged.

Perhaps she could leave without this man knowing just who had made a fool of herself tonight.

"I am sorry. There has been a mistake," she said. "We seem to have come to the wrong house."

"Whom do you seek?"

"Master David the mercer."

"I am he."

"I think it is a different David. I was told that he is . . . older."

"I am David the mercer, and there is no other. If you have brought something for me . . ."

Christiana wanted to disappear. She would kill Idonia! Her kindly old merchant was a man of no more than thirty years.

He had stopped in mid-sentence, and she saw him realize that she was not whom he expected either. He took another few steps toward her. "Perhaps if you would tell me why you seek me . . ."

Young or old, it made no difference. She was here now and she would tell her story. This man would not like playing the fool for the King no matter what his age.

"My name is Christiana Fitzwaryn."

They stood in a long silence broken only by crackle of the new logs on the fire.

"You had only to send word and I would have come to you. In fact, I was told that the Queen would introduce us at the castle tomorrow," he finally said.

She knew then for sure that there had been no mistake.

"I wanted to speak with you privately."

His head tilted back a bit. "Then come and sit yourself, Lady Christiana, and say what you need to say."

Three good-sized chairs stood near the fire, all with backs and arms. Suppressing an instinct to bolt from the room, she took the middle one. It was too big for her, and even when she perched on the edge, her feet dangled. She felt the same way that she had last night with the Queen, like a child waiting to be chastised. She reached up and pushed down the hood of her cloak.

A movement beside her brought David de Abyndon into the chair on her left. He angled it away so that he faced her. Close here, in the glow of the fire, she could see him clearly.

Her eyes fell on expertly crafted brown high boots, and long, well-shaped legs in brown hose. Her gaze drifted up to a beautiful masculine hand, long-fingered and traced with elegant veins, resting on the front edge of the chair's arm. The red wool pourpoint was completely unadorned by embroidery or jewels, and yet, even in the dancing light of the fire, she could tell that the fabric and workmanship were of the best quality and very expensive. She paused a moment, studying the richly carved chair on which he sat and the birds and vines decorating it.

Finally, there was no place else to look but at his face.

Dark blue eyes the color of lapis lazuli examined her as closely as she did him. They seemed friendly enough eyes, even expressive eyes, but she found it disconcerting that she could not interpret the thoughts and reactions in them. What was reflected there? Amusement? Curiosity? Boredom? They were beautifully set under low arched brows, and the bones around them, indeed all of the bones of his face, looked perfectly formed and regularly fitted, as if some master craftsman of great skill had carefully chosen each one and placed it just so. A straight nose led to a straight wide mouth. Golden brown hair, full and a little shorter than this year's fashion, was parted at the center and feathered carelessly over his temples and down his chiseled cheeks and jaw to his shirt collar.

David de Abyndon, warden of the mercers' company and merchant of London, was a very handsome man. Almost beautiful, but a vague hardness around the eyes and mouth kept that from being so.

A shrewd scrutiny veiled his lapis eyes, and she suddenly felt very self-conscious. It had been impolite of her to examine him so obviously, of course, but he was older and should know better than to do the same.

"Don't you want to remove your cloak? It is warm here," that quiet voice asked.

The idea of removing her cloak unaccountably horrified her. She was sure that she would feel naked without it. In fact, she pulled it a bit closer in response.

His faint smile reappeared. It made him appear amiable, but revealed nothing.

She cleared her throat. "I was told that . . . that you were . . ."

"Older."

"Aye."

"No doubt someone confused me with my dead master and partner, David Constantyn. The business was his before mine."

"No doubt."

The silence stretched. He sat there calmly, watching her. She sensed an inexplicable presence emanating from him. The air around him possessed a tension or intensity that she couldn't define. She began to feel very uncomfortable. Then she remembered that she had come here to talk to him and that he was waiting patiently for her to do so.

"I need to speak with you about something very important."

"I am glad to hear it."

She glanced over, startled. "What?"

"I'm glad to hear that it is something important. I would not like to think that you traveled London's streets at night for something frivolous."

He was subtly either scolding her or teasing her. She couldn't tell which.

"I am not alone. A knight awaits in the courtyard," she said pointedly.

"It was kind of him to indulge you."

Not teasing. Scolding.

That annoyed her enough that she collected her thoughts quickly. She was beginning to think that she didn't like this man much. He made her feel very vulnerable. She sensed something proud and aloof in him too, and that annoyed her even further. She had been expecting an elderly man who would treat her with a certain deference because of their difference in degrees. There was absolutely no deference in this man.

"Master David, I have come to ask you to withdraw your offer of marriage."

He glanced to the fire, then his gaze returned to her. One lean, muscular leg crossed the other, and he settled comfortably back in his chair. An unreadable expression appeared in his eyes, and the faint smile formed again.

"Why would I want to do that, my lady?"

He didn't seem the least bit surprised or angry. Perhaps this meeting would go as planned after all.

"Master David, I am sure that you are the good and honorable man that the King assumes. But this offer was accepted without my consent."

He looked at her impassively. "And?"

"And?" she repeated, a little stunned.

"My lady, that is an excellent reason for you to withdraw, but not me. Express your will to the King or the bishop and it is over. But your consent or lack of it is not my affair."

"It is not so simple. Perhaps amongst you people it is, but I am a ward of the King. He has spoken for me. To defy him on this . . ."

"The church will not marry an unwilling woman, even if a King has made the match. I, on the other hand, have given my consent and cannot withdraw it. There is no reason to, as I have said."

His calm lack of reaction irked her. "Well, then, let me explain my position more clearly and perhaps you will have your reason. I do not give my consent because I am in love with another man."

Absolutely nothing changed in his face or eyes. She might have told him that she was flawed by a wart on her leg.

"No doubt an excellent reason to refuse your consent in your view, Christiana. But again, it is not my affair."

She couldn't believe his bland acceptance of this. Had he no pride? No heart? "You cannot want to marry a woman who loves another," she blurted out.

"I expect it happens all the time. England is full of marriages made under these circumstances. In the long run, it is not such a serious matter."

Oh, dear saints, she thought. A man who believed in practical marriages. Just her luck. But then, he was a merchant.

"It may not be a serious matter amongst you people," she tried explaining, "but marriages based on love have become desired—"

"That is the second time that you have said that, my lady. Do not say it again." His voice was still quiet, his face still impassive, but a note of command echoed nonetheless.

"Said what?"

" 'You people.' You have used the phrase twice now."

"I meant nothing by it."

"You meant everything by it. But we will discuss that another day."

He had flustered and distracted her with this second scolding. She sought the strand of her argument. He found it for her.

"My lady, I am sure a young girl thinks that she needs to marry the man whom she thinks that she loves. But your emotions are a short-term problem. You will get over this. Marriage is a long-term investment. All will work out in the end."

He spoke to her as if she were a child, and as dispassionately as if they discussed a shipment of wool. It had been a mistake to think that she could appeal to his sympathy. He was a tradesman, after all, and to him life was probably just one big ledger sheet of expenses and profits.

Well, maybe he would understand things better if he saw the potential cost to his pride.

"This is not just a short-term infatuation on my part, Master David. I am not some little girl," she said. "I pledged myself to this man."

"You both privately pledged your troth?"

It could be done that way. She could lie. She desperately wanted to, and felt sorely tempted, but such a lie could have dire consequences, and very public ones, and she wasn't that brave. "Not formally," she said, hoping to leave a bit of ambiguity there.

He at least seemed moderately interested now. "Has this man offered for you?"

"His family sent him home from court before he could settle it."

"He is some boy whom his family controls?"

She had to remember with whom she spoke. "A family's will may seem a minor issue for a man such as you, but he is part of a powerful family up north. One does not defy kinship so easily. Still, when he hears of this betrothal, I am sure that he will come back."

"So, Christiana, you are saying that this man said that he wanted to marry you but left without settling for you."

That seemed a rather bald way to put it.

"Aye."

He smiled again. "Ah."

She really resented that "Ah." Her annoyance made her bold. She leaned toward him, feeling her jaw harden with repressed anger. "Master David, let me be blunt. I have given myself to this man."

Finally a reaction besides that impassive indifference. His head went back a fraction and he studied her from beneath lowered lids.

"Then be blunt, my lady. Exactly what do you mean by that?"

She threw up her hands in exasperation. "We made love together. Is that blunt enough for you? We went to bed together. In fact, we were found in bed together. Your offer was only accepted so that the Queen could hush up any scandal and keep my brother from forcing a marriage that my lover's family does not want."

She thought that she saw a flash of anger beneath those lids.

"You were discovered thus and this man left you to face it alone? Your devotion to this paragon of chivalry is impressive."

His assessment of Stephen was like a slap in her face. "How dare such as you criticize—"

"You are doing it again."

"Doing what?" she snapped.

" 'Such as you.' Twice now. Another phrase that you might avoid. For prudence' sake." He paused. "Who is this man?"

"I have sworn not to tell," she said stiffly. "My brother . . . Besides, as you have said, it is none of your affair."

He rose, uncoiling himself with an elegant movement, and went to stand by the hearth. The lines beneath the pourpoint suggested a lean, hard body. He was quite tall.

Not quite as tall as Morvan, but taller than most. She found his presence unsettling. Merchants were supposed to be skinny or portly men in fur hats.

He gazed at the flames. "Are you with child?" he asked.

The notion astounded her. She hadn't thought of that. But perhaps the Queen had. She looked at him vacantly. He turned and saw the expression.

"Do you know the signs?" he asked softly.

She shook her head.

"Have you had your flux since you were last with him?"

She blushed and nodded. In fact, it had come today.

He turned back to the fire.

She wondered what he thought about as he studied those tongues of heat. She stayed silent, letting him weigh however he valued these things, praying that she had succeeded, hoping that he indeed had a merchant's soul and would be repelled by accepting used goods.

Finally she couldn't wait any longer.

"So, you will go to the King and withdraw this offer?" she asked hopefully.

He glanced over his shoulder at her. "I think not."

Her heart sank.

"Young girls make mistakes," he added.

"This was no mistake," she said forcefully. "If you do not withdraw, you will end up looking a fool. He will come for me, if not before the betrothal, then after. When he comes, I will go with him."

He did not look at her, but his quiet, beautiful voice drifted over the space between them. "What makes you think that I will let you?"

"You will not be able to stop me. He is a knight, and skilled at arms . . ."

"There are more effective weapons in this world than

steel, Christiana." He turned. "As I said earlier, you are always free to go to the bishop and declare your lack of consent to this marriage. But I will not withdraw now."

"An honorable man would not expect me to face the King's wrath," she said bitterly.

"An honorable man would not ruin a girl at her request. If I withdraw, it will displease the King, whom I have no wish to anger. At the least I will need a good reason. Should I use the one that you have given me? Should I repudiate you because you are not a virgin? It is the only way."

She dropped her eyes. The panicked desolation of the last day returned to engulf her.

She sensed a movement and then David de Abyndon stood in front of her. A strong, gentle hand lifted her chin until she looked up into his handsome face. It seemed to her that those blue eyes read her soul and her mind and saw right into her. Even Lady Idonia's hawklike inspections had not been so thorough and successful. Nor so oddly mesmerizing.

That intensity that flowed from him surrounded her. She became very aware of his rough fingers on her chin. His thumb stretched and brushed her jaw, and something tingled in her neck.

"If he comes for you before the wedding, I will step aside," he said. "I will not contest an annulment of the betrothal. But I must tell you, girl, that I know men and I do not think that he will come, although you are well worth what it would cost him."

"You do not know *him*."

"Nay, I do not. And I am not so old that I can't be surprised." He smiled down at her. A real smile, she realized. The first one of the evening. A wonderful smile, actually. His hand fell away. Her skin felt warm where he had touched her.

She stood up. "I must go. My escort will grow impatient."

He walked with her to the door. "I will come and see you in a few days."

She felt sick at heart. He was making her go through with the farce of this betrothal, and it would complicate things horribly. She had no desire to play this role any more than necessary.

"Please do not. There is no point."

He turned and looked at her as he opened the door and led her to the steps. "As you wish, Christiana."

She saw Thomas's shadowy form in the courtyard, and flew to him as soon as they exited the hall. She glanced back to the doorway where David stood watching.

Thomas began guiding her to the portal. "Did you accomplish what you needed?"

"Aye," she lied. Thomas did not know about the betrothal. It had not been announced yet, and she had hoped that it never would be. Master David's stubbornness meant that now things were going to become very difficult. She would have to find some other way to stop this betrothal, or at least this marriage.

David watched her cross the courtyard, her nobility obvious in her posture and graceful walk. A very odd stillness began claiming him, and her movements slowed as if time grew sluggish. An eerie internal silence spread until it blocked out all sound. In an isolated world connected to the one in the yard but separate from it by invisible degrees, he began observing her in an abstract way.

He had felt this before several times in his life, and was stunned to find himself having the experience now. All the same, he did nothing to stop the sensation and did not question the importance of what was happening.

He recognized the silence that permeated him as the inaudible sound of Fortune turning her capricious wheel and changing his life in ways that he could only dimly foresee. Unlike most men, he did not fear the unpredictable coincidences that revealed Fortune's willfulness, for he had thus far been one of her favorite children.

Christiana Fitzwaryn of Harclow. The caves of Harclow. There was an elegant balance in this particular coincidence.

The gate closed behind her and time abruptly righted itself. He contemplated the implications of this girl's visit.

He had understood King Edward's desire to hide the payment for the exclusive trading license that he was buying. If word got out about it, other merchants would be jealous. He had himself suggested several other ways to conceal the arrangement, but they involved staggered payments, and the King, desperate for coin to finance his French war, wanted the entire sum now. Edward's solution of giving him a noble wife and disguising the payment as a bride price had created a host of problems, though, not the least of which was the possibility that the girl would not suit him.

His vision turned inward and he saw Christiana's black hair and pale skin and lovely face. Her dark eyes sparkled like black diamonds. She was not especially small, but her elegance gave the impression of delicacy, even frailty. The first sight of her in the fire glow had made his breath catch the way it always did when he came upon an object or view of distinctive beauty.

Her visit had announced unanticipated complications, but it had resolved one question most clearly. Christiana Fitzwaryn would suit him very well indeed.

He had been stunned when the King had chosen the daughter of Hugh Fitzwaryn to be the bride in this scheme, and had pointed out that she was too far above him. Even the huge bride price that everyone would think he was paying did not bridge their difference in degrees.

The King had brushed it aside. *We will put it about that you saw her and wanted her and paid me a fortune to have her.* Well, now he knew the reason for the King's choice of Christiana. A quick marriage for the girl would snuff out any flames of scandal regarding her and her lover.

It was good to know the truth. He did not like playing the pawn in another man's game. Usually he was the one who moved the pieces.

He walked across the courtyard to Sieg.

"It is done then?" the Swede asked as he turned to enter his chamber off the passageway.

"It was not them."

"The hell you say!"

David laughed. "Go to sleep. I doubt that they will come tonight."

"I hope not. There's more visitors here at night than the day, as it is." Sieg paused. "What about Lady Alicia's guard?"

David glanced to the end of the building, and the glow of a candle through a window. "He knows to stay there. I will bring her to him later."

He turned to leave, then stopped. "Sieg, tomorrow I want you to find the name of a man for me. He is a knight, and his family is from the north country. An important family."

"Not much to go on. There be dozens . . ."

"He left Westminster recently. I would guess in the last day or so."

"That makes it easier."

"His name, Sieg. And what you can learn about him."

CHAPTER 2

CHRISTIANA SPENT a desperate night trying to figure out how to save herself. By morning she could find no course of action except writing to Stephen, bribing a royal messenger to carry the letter north, and praying that he received it quickly. But the betrothal was in a week, too soon for Stephen to get that letter and come for her.

The only solution was to speak with the King. She would not refuse the marriage outright, but would let him know that she did not welcome it. Perhaps, at the very least, she could convince him to delay the betrothal.

Steeling her resolve, she left the apartment that she shared with Isabele and Joan under Idonia's watchful eyes, and made her way through the castle to the room where the King met with petitioners. When she arrived, its anteroom had already filled with people. She gave her name to the clerk who sat by the door, and hoped that her place in the household would put her ahead of some of the others.

Some benches lined one wall. An older knight gave up his place, and she settled down. The standing crowd walled her in while she concentrated on planning her request.

As she waited and pondered, the outer door opened and a page entered, followed by her brother Morvan. She saw his dark head disappear into the King's chamber.

The King was going to tell him about the match now. What would her proud brother say? How would he react?

She had her answer very soon. Within minutes the measured rumble of a raised voice leaked through wall that separated the anteroom from the chamber. She knew that it was Edward who had lost his temper, because Morvan's worst anger always manifested itself quietly and coldly.

She had to leave immediately. With the King enraged, there could be no benefit in speaking with him today, and when Morvan left that room, she did not want him to see her sitting here.

She was rising to leave when Morvan hurried out, his black eyes flashing and his handsome face frozen into a mask of fury. He strode to the corridor like a man headed for battle.

She still needed to leave, but she dared not follow him. He might have stopped in the passageways leading here.

She glanced around the anteroom. Another door on a side wall gave out to a private corridor that connected Edward's chambers and rooms. It led to an exterior stairway, and there were rumors that secret guests, diplomats, and sometimes women came to him this way. Without it ever being formally declared off limits, everyone knew that it meant trouble to be found there. Even the Queen did not use that passageway.

She pushed through the crowd. She would slip away and no one would know that she had even come.

Opening the small door a crack, she slid through. The passageway stretched along the exterior wall of the castle lit by good-sized windows set into shallow alcoves. She scurried toward the end opposite the one with the staircase.

The sound of a door opening behind her sent her darting into one of the alcoves. Pressing into the corner, she prayed that whoever had entered the passageway would go in the other direction. She sighed with relief as she heard footsteps walking away.

Then, to her horror, more steps started coming quickly toward her from the direction in which she had been heading. Crushing herself into the alcove's shallow corner, she gritted her teeth and waited for discovery.

A shortish middle-aged man with gray hair and beard, sumptuously dressed like a diplomat, hurried by. He did not notice her, because he fixed all of his attention on the space ahead of him. It seemed that he tried to make his own footsteps fall more softly than normal.

"*Pardon. Attendez,*" she heard him whisper loudly.

The other steps stopped. She heard the men meet.

They began speaking in low tones but their words carried easily to her ears. Both spoke Parisian French, the kind taught to her by the tutors, and not the corrupted dialect used casually by the English courtiers.

"If you are found here, it will go badly for you," the other man said. His voice sounded very low, little more than a whisper, but the words reached her just the same.

"A necessary risk. I needed to know if what I had heard of you was true."

"And what did you hear?"

"That you can help us."

"You have the wrong man."

"I do not think so. I followed you here. You have the access, as I was told."

"If you want what I think you want, you have the wrong man."

"At least hear me out."

"Nay."

The men began walking away. The voices receded.

"It will be worth your while," the first man said.

"There is nothing that you have that I want."

"How do you know if you don't listen?"

"You are a fool to speak to me of this here. I do not deal with fools."

The voices and footsteps continued to grow fainter. Christiana listened until their sound disappeared down the stairway. Lifting her hem, she ran back to her chamber.

She was sitting on her bed in Isabele's anteroom, fretting over whether to approach the King another day, when Morvan came storming into the chamber still furious from his meeting with the King.

He stomped around and ranted with dangerous anger. Rarely had she seen him like this, and keeping him from doing something rash became her primary concern. She felt guilty calming and soothing him, since she knew that everything was her fault and he, of course, did not. Morvan laid all of the blame on the King and the merchant.

"This mercer did not even have the decency to speak with me first," Morvan spat out, his black eyes flashing sparks as he strode around. He was a big man, taller than most, and he filled the space. "He went directly to the King! The presumptions of those damn merchants is ever galling, but this is an outrage."

"Perhaps he didn't know how it is done with us," she

said. She needed him calm and rational. If they thought about this together, they might have some ideas.

"It is the same with every degree, sister. Would this man have gone to his mayor to offer for some skinner's daughter?"

"Well, he did it this way, and the King agreed. We are stuck with that part."

"Aye, Edward agreed." He suddenly stopped his furious stride and stared bleakly into the hearth. "This is a bad sign, Christiana. It means that the King has indeed forgotten."

Her heart went out to him. She walked over and embraced him and forgot her own disappointment and problems. She had been so selfishly concerned with her own pride that she hadn't seen the bigger implications of this marriage.

Fleeting, vague memories of another life filtered into her exhausted mind. Memories of Harclow and happiness. Images of war and death. The echo of gnawing hunger and relentless fear during siege. And finally, clearly and distinctly, she had the picture of Morvan, ten years old but tall already, walking bravely through the castle gate to surrender to the enemy. He had fully expected to be killed. Over the years, she came to believe that God had moved that Scottish lord to spare him so that she herself would not be totally alone.

When they had fled Harclow and gone to young King Edward and told him of Hugh Fitzwaryn's death and the loss of the estate, Edward had blamed himself for not bringing relief fast enough. Their father had been one of his friends and supporters on the Scottish marches, and in front of Morvan and their dying mother Edward had sworn to avenge his friend and return the family lands to them.

That had been eleven years ago. For a long while thereafter, Morvan had assumed that once he earned his spurs the King would fulfill that oath. But he had been a knight for two years now, and it had become clear that Edward planned no aggressive campaigns on the Scottish borders. The army sent there every year was involved in little more than a holding action. All of the King's attention had become focused on France.

And now this. Agreeing to marry her to this merchant was a tacit admission on the King's part that he would never help Morvan reclaim Harclow. The ancient nobility of the Fitzwaryn family would be meaningless in a generation.

No wonder the Percys did not want one of their young men marrying her. But Stephen's love would be stronger than such petty concerns of politics property. And once they were married, she hoped that the Percy family would help Morvan, since he would be tied to their kinship through her.

The chance of that had always increased Stephen's appeal. The redemption of their family honor should not rest entirely on Morvan's shoulders. It was her duty to marry a man who would give her brother a good alliance.

Morvan pulled away. "The King said the betrothal is to be Saturday. I do not understand the haste."

She could hardly confide to her strict older brother that the haste was to make sure that her lover could not interfere. And maybe also to avert Morvan's anger. If he learned what had happened with Stephen, he would undoubtedly demand satisfaction through a duel. King Edward probably wanted to avoid the trouble with the Percy family that such a challenge would create.

Her attempts at soothing him failed. The storm broke in his expression again. He left as furiously as he had entered. "Do not worry, sister. I will deal with this merchant."

✦   ✦   ✦

David stood at the door of his shop watching his two young apprentices, Michael and Roger, carry the muslin-wrapped silks and furs out to the transport wagon. A long, gaily decorated box on wheels, the wagon held seats for the ladies and had windows piercing its sides. Princess Isabele sat at one of the openings.

The arrival of Lady Idonia and Lady Joan and Princess Isabele today had amused him and awed the apprentices. The ladies ostensibly came to choose cloth for the cotehardie and surcoat that Isabele would wear at Christiana's wedding, but the princess was not his patron. The news of the betrothal had just spread at Westminster, and he knew that in reality Christiana's friends had come to inspect him.

They had almost been disappointed, since he hadn't arrived until they were preparing to leave. His business extended far beyond the walls of this shop now, and he left the daily workings of it to Andrew. He smiled at the memory of tiny Lady Idonia throwing her body between Isabele and Sieg when he and the Swede had entered the shop, as if she sought to save the girl from Viking ravishment.

The boys handed their packages in to Lady Idonia. They peered into the wagon one last time as it pulled away surrounded by five mounted guards.

They had a lot to peer at, David thought, glancing at the crowd of onlookers that had formed on the lane when the wagon drew up. A princess and the famous Lady Joan, Fair Maid of Kent, cousin to the King. Members of the royal family rarely visited the tradesmen's shops. It was customary to bring goods to them instead.

Christiana had not come, of course. He wondered what ruse she had used to avoid it. He was sending a gift back to her with Idonia, however, a red cloak lined with black fur which the tailor George who worked upstairs had sewn at his bidding. The one that she had worn to his house four nights ago looked to be several years old and a handspan too short. Being the King's ward clearly did not mean that she lived in luxury.

She would probably feel guilty accepting his gift. In that brief time in his solar, he had learned much about her character and she had impressed him favorably. Her beauty had impressed him even more. The memory of those bright eyes and that pale skin had not been far from his mind since her visit.

She waited for her lover. How long would she wait?

Unlike most men, he liked women and understood them. He certainly understood the pain Christiana felt. After all, he had lived eighteen years near a similar anguish. Was he fated now to spend the rest of his life in its shadow again? Was that to be the price this time of Fortune's favor? This girl seemed stronger and prouder than that.

He had briefly lost awareness of the street, but its movements and colors reclaimed his attention. He pushed away from the doorjamb. As he turned to enter the building he noticed a man walking up the lane from the Cheap, wearing livery that he recognized. He waited for the man to reach him.

"David de Abyndon?" the messenger asked.

"Aye."

A folded piece of parchment was handed over. David read the note. He had expected this letter. In fact, he had been waiting for the meeting it requested for over ten years. Better to finish it quickly. Betrothal and marriage probably had a way of complicating things like this.

He turned to the messenger. "Tell her I cannot see her this week. Next Tuesday afternoon. She should come to my house."

He entered the shop. Michael and Roger were closing

the front shutters, and Andrew came in with cloth from the back room.

"I put the tallies from Lady Idonia and Lady Joan up in the counting room," Andrew said as he settled his burden down.

David clapped a hand on his shoulder. "So. A whole afternoon with the Fair Joan. Your friends will buy you ale for a month to hear your story."

Andrew smiled roguishly. "I was just thinking the same thing. She *is* very fair. As is Lady Christiana Fitzwaryn. I have seen them together in the city. You might have told us about this betrothal. It was very awkward finding out from them."

The boys stopped and listened. Sieg stood by the door.

"It was just decided."

They all waited silently.

"Let us close and go home. I'll explain all there."

Explain what, though? Not the truth. No one would ever learn that, not even Christiana. He would have to come up with a good story fast.

They were almost ready to leave when the sounds of a horse stopping in the lane came through the shutters. Michael ran over and peered out the door. "A King's knight," he said. "The same one who came looking for you this morning, David."

David knew who this would be. "All of you go back to the house. You too, Sieg. I will take care of this."

The door opened and a tall, dark-haired young man entered. He paused in the threshold and looked around. He wore the King's livery and a long sword hung from his knight's belt. Bright black eyes, so like those others but brittle with a colder light, came to rest on David.

The apprentices filed out around the big man, clearly

impressed with his size and bearing. Sieg glanced meaningfully at David. David shook his head and Sieg left too.

"I am Christiana's brother Morvan," the knight said
when they were finally alone.

"I know who you are."

"Do you? I thought that perhaps you mistakenly
thought that she had no kin."

David waited. He would let this brother make his
objections. He would not assume that he knew what they
would be, for there was much to object to.

"I thought that we should meet," Sir Morvan said,
walking down the passageway. "I wanted to see the man
who buys a wife like she is some horse."

David thought about the two hours he had spent this
morning with one of the King's clerks drawing up the
marriage contract. It had been impossible to keep out the
terms of the supposed bride price completely, because
only Edward and he knew its real purpose. Still, David had
tried, and finally negotiated only a reference to its amount
involving a complicated formula based on the price of last
year's wool exports. Only someone very interested would
ever bother to make the calculations.

Morvan must have been shown the contract for
approval and not missed that particular clause.

"The King insisted on the bride price, as in the old
days. I would have been happy to pay nothing."

Morvan studied him. "If she were not my sister, I
might find that amusing. You go to a lot of trouble to
marry a woman whom you do not know."

"It happens all of the time."

"Aye. If the dowry is satisfactory."

"I have no need of a dowry."

"So I am told. Nor are you much in need of a woman
to warm your bed, from what I hear. So why do you pay a
fortune for my sister?"

David had to admit that it was a damn good question. He realized that he shouldn't underestimate this young man. Morvan had been asking about him, just as David had been asking about Morvan. Perhaps the King's proposed explanation would work. *We will put it about that you saw her and wanted her and paid a fortune to have her.* Not, he suspected, that a man lusting after his sister would appeal much to this young knight.

"I saw her several times and asked about her. The King was receptive to my inquiries."

"So you offered for her just on seeing her?"

"I have these whims sometimes. They almost always work out. As far as the rest, the lack of dowry and the payment, things just developed as they often do in such negotiations." It sounded almost plausible. It had better. He had nothing else to offer.

Morvan considered him. "That would make sense if you were a fool, but I do not think that you are. I think that you are an upstart who seeks to buy status among his people through this marriage, and who sees his children raised above their natural degree through their mother's nobility."

Another plausible explanation. But if Morvan had spoken with the right people, he would know just how wrong it was.

"You are Christiana's brother, and are thus unaware of just how foolish she might make a man who is otherwise not a fool," David said.

A fire flashed in the young man's dark eyes. Nay, he did not like the idea of a man lusting after his sister.

"I will not permit this marriage. I will not see Christiana tied to a common tradesman, no matter what his wealth. She is not a brood mare to be purchased to ennoble a bastard's bloodline. She does not want this either."

David ignored the insults, barely, except to note that Morvan had been checking up on him quite thoroughly. "She and I have already spoken of that. She knows that I will not withdraw. I have no reason to."

"Let me give you a reason, then. Go to the King and say that the lady has a brother who has threatened you with bodily harm unless you withdraw. Explain that you did not anticipate that when you made this offer."

"And what of the King's displeasure with you if I say this?"

"If need be, my sword can serve another man."

"And if I don't do this?"

"The threat is not an idle one."

David studied his resolute expression. An intelligent man, and probably an honest one. "Do you know why your sister does not consent to this marriage?"

"That is obvious, isn't it?"

So Morvan did not know about Sir Stephen. She had claimed that he didn't, but he may have discovered it nonetheless and been planning to force things with Percy.

"Is it?"

"She is the daughter of a baron. This marriage is an insult to her."

David fought down a sudden profound irritation. He had long ago become almost immune to such comments, and to the assumptions of superiority that they revealed. But he had accepted more from this man in the last few minutes than he normally swallowed from anyone. He leaned against the wall and folded his arms and met Morvan's fiery eyes.

"Will you withdraw?"

"I think not."

Morvan looked him up and down. "You wear a dagger. Do you use a sword?"

"Not well."

"Then you had best practice."

"You plan to kill me over this?"

"I cannot stop this betrothal, but I will stop the wedding. A month hence, if you have not left London or annulled the match, we will meet."

Anger seeped into David's head. He almost never lost control anymore, but he was in danger of it now. "Send word of when and where. I will be there."

He knew that Morvan's own cold fury matched his own. But he also saw the surprise that the threat had been met with anger and not fear.

"We will see if you come," Morvan said with a slow smile. "I think that time will show that you are like most of your breed. Rich in gold but without honor."

"And you are like too many knights these days. Rich in pompous arrogance but without land or value," David replied sharply. It was unworthy of him, but he had had enough.

Morvan's eyes flashed dangerously. He pivoted on his heel and walked the twenty paces to the door. "My sister is not for you, merchant. You have a month to undo this."

Something snapped. As Morvan disappeared into the street, David uncoiled himself with a fluid, tense movement. His hand went to his hip, and a long steel dagger flew down the passageway, imbedding itself into the doorjamb directly behind the spot where Morvan Fitzwaryn's neck had just been.

A blond head moved in the open door's twilight, and Sieg bent into the threshold. He glanced at David and then turned and yanked the still-quivering dagger out of its target. He came down the passageway.

"I suppose that it is still early to congratulate you on this marriage."

David took the dagger and sheathed it. The worst of his anger had flown with the knife. "You heard."

"*Ja.*"

"I told you to leave."

"His sword and face told me to stay. I thought that I would have the chance to repay my debt today."

David ignored him and began walking away.

"Do you want us to take care of him? The girl need never know. There be all of these rivers around. A man could fall in."

"Nay."

"The sword is not your weapon."

"It will not come to that."

"You are sure? He looked determined."

"I am sure."

They walked up the lane toward the house. Sieg kept looking over at him. Finally the Swede spoke. "It is an odd time to be getting married."

"Aye." And it was. Any number of carefully cultivated fields were awaiting harvesting in the next few months.

"It could make things harder," Sieg said.

"I've thought of that."

"You could put the wedding off until next winter. November maybe. All should be settled by then."

David shook his head. He realized that he was not inclined to give her lover a whole year to come back. He also already knew that he had no intention of waiting that long to take the beautiful Christiana Fitzwaryn to his bed. "Nay. It will be safer to have her at the house."

"And if there are problems . . ."

"Then the girl is doubly blessed. She gets rid of a husband whom she does not want and becomes a rich widow."

✦   ✦   ✦

A fine cold mist shrouded the Strand as the little party rode up its length. John Constantyn sat straight and proud on his horse, his fur-trimmed and bejeweled velvet robe barely covered by the bright blue cloak thrown back over his shoulders. He glanced at David's own unadorned and austere blue pourpoint.

"Thank God you at least wore that chain," John said, grinning. "They might mistake you for some gentry squire otherwise. Under the circumstances you might have fancied yourself up some, just this once. It is an odd statement that you make with your garments, David."

David would like to claim that he made no statement at all with his clothes, that their plainness merely reflected his taste, but he knew that wasn't entirely true. Refusing to compete in the nobility's game of luxury was, he supposed, a tacit repudiation of the nobleman's assumption of superior worth.

He felt the heavy gold chain on his chest, arching from shoulder to shoulder. He had even worn this with reluctance, and finally put it on only for Christiana's sake. Her friends would know its value. He would not make this day any harder for her than it promised to be already.

"You should have seen your uncle Gilbert's face when I told him what I would be doing today," John said. "By God, it was rich. Right there outside the Guildhall, I asked him if he would attend, aware that he knew nothing of it. I made him worm the details out of me bit by bit, too. At least twenty of the wardens must have overheard." John's hearty laugh echoed down the Strand. " 'Aye, Gilbert,' I said, 'didn't you know? The daughter of the famous Hugh Fitzwaryn. By the king's pleasure, no less. In the royal chapel with the royal family in attendance.' His face looked the color of ash before I was done."

David smiled at the thought of Gilbert's expression when he learned that David would marry a baron's daughter. It was the first time that this betrothal had given him any pleasure.

He hadn't spoken to any of the Abyndons since he was a youth and had fully realized what they had done to his mother. He also refused to trade with them, and never sold them any of the goods that he imported. It was a childish revenge, but the only one open to him right now. Eventually the chance would come to plant that particular field in a more appropriate way.

John smiled more soberly. "Would that my brother could see this."

Aye, David thought. *But it is just as well that he cannot.* He thought a moment about his dead master and partner, the man who had probably saved him from a life in the alleys. A good man, David Constantyn, whose faith in his young apprentice had made them both rich and permitted David to become the man he was today. He had loved his master more than a son does a father.

It was out of respect and love that he had bided his time and waited. Waited for his master's death before planting those fields that waited to be harvested now. *Better that he is not here, for there is much that honest man wouldn't like*, David thought. *But then, he was shrewd, and might not be so surprised. He probably knew what he had in me.*

They rode through the town of Westminster to the castle and buildings that housed the court and the government. David led the way to the royal chapel.

People milled around outside its doors. The King's approach caused no commotion or even much attention. Edward and Philippa led their children and their closest retainers in for the daily mass. David had no trouble locating Christiana in the group, because she wore the red cloak. Her eyes did not seek him out as she silently between Joan and Lady Idonia.

A page had reserved space for David behind the royal family. At the other end of his row stood the rigid form of Morvan Fitzwaryn. In front of him Christiana focused her attention on the priest at the altar, not once turning her head.

The mass was brief and after it the priest came down from the altar and called Christiana and himself forward. Christiana, her cloak still on to ward off the chill in the chapel, went to her brother, then the two of them joined David in front of the priest. He looked over at her and saw a vacant expression in her eyes as she trained her gaze on a spot somewhere in the distance. She looked noble and calm and emotionally void.

Morvan took her hand and placed it in David's. It felt incredibly small and soft. One slight tremble shook her arm, and then they listened to the priest's prayer before pledging their troth. She recited the words like a school lesson, her expressionless chant suggesting that they held no meaning, if indeed she even heard them.

She turned for the betrothal kiss, lifting her face dutifully but keeping her eyes downcast. David felt an odd combination of sympathy and annoyance.

In the law of the church and the realm, she belonged to him now, but she had carefully managed not to see or acknowledge him since her arrival. It had been subtle, and he knew that she had done it for her own sake and to control her own pain. She had not deliberately tried to insult him. He simply didn't matter. He doubted that anyone but Morvan had even noticed.

He suspected that Christiana sought to turn this betrothal into a dream so that she could wake when her lover came and find that it had conveniently never really happened. That he understood this girl did not mean, however, that he felt inclined to indulge her illusions with the dutiful kiss that she now offered and expected.

He did not care that the King and Queen stood nearby, nor that the angry brother watched. This was solely between him and her.

He stepped close to her and laid his hand on her cheek. A small tremor awoke beneath his touch.

The hood of her cloak still rested atop her head, hiding her hair. He could tell that she wore it unbound, a symbol of virginity, as was traditional for the ceremony. With his other hand he pushed the hood away. The thick black locks cascaded down her back, and his hand followed until he embraced her.

"Look at me, Christiana," he commanded quietly.

The black lashes fluttered. The creamy lids rose slowly. Two diamonds flashed startled alertness and fear.

He lowered his head and tasted the soft sweetness of her trembling lips.

CHAPTER 3

CHRISTIANA STUDIED THE chessboard propped on the chest between her and Joan. She shifted a pawn.

Joan quickly took one of her knights. "You are playing badly today," she said.

They sat by a window in Isabele's bedchamber. The princess had gone to visit a friend in another part of Westminster, and Lady Idonia had accompanied her.

Christiana tried to concentrate on the game and not think about her betrothal three days earlier. In particular she worked hard not to reflect on David de Abyndon, but his intense eyes and warm touch kept intruding on her memory in a distressing way. He had handled the ceremony and dinner very kindly, almost sympathetically. With one stunning exception.

"You never told me what it was like getting betrothed," Joan said.

Christiana shrugged. "I don't remember much. I was most unsettled."

Joan tossed her blond curls and her eyes twinkled. "What was the kiss like? It looked like a wonderful kiss."

Christiana stared at the chessmen scattered on the board. She had been working especially hard not to think about that kiss.

What should she say to Joan? What *could* she say? How could she explain that only the most necessary part of her had paid attention to either the mass or the pledge? That she had deliberately dulled her mind so that she would get through the morning without panicking. That she had filled her heart with Stephen and the trust and knowledge of his love, and that the whole scene in the church had only been a restless dream that would quickly fade.

Until there had been that hand on her face in a gesture of intimacy, forcing her awake as surely as a shake during the night. A voice commanding her to look reality in the face. An embrace and a kiss of masterful possession.

What was that kiss like? Confusing. Frightening. Longer than necessary. Long enough to make clear that one of them intended to treat this betrothal seriously.

The sensation of a streak of warmth flowing through her body licked at her memory. She shifted restlessly and forced all of her attention on the chess game.

Aye, she did not want to think or talk about that kiss very much at all. "It was nice enough."

At least that part of this travesty was over. Now she had only to wait for Stephen to come.

"Have you ever been kissed before?" Joan asked.

Christiana wished that she could confide in her friend, but Joan was a notorious gossip. It had, of course, crossed her mind that if Joan did gossip, and Morvan learned about Stephen, then maybe her brother would encourage the Percys to change their mind. She had immediately felt guilty for that unworthy thought. After all, she didn't want

Stephen offering for her at the point of a sword. That wouldn't be necessary anyway.

The memory of Stephen's mouth crushing hers fluttered in her mind. David's kiss hadn't been at all like that, but then they had been standing in a church in front of a king and a priest. Still . . . nay, she didn't want to think about that kiss. "I have been kissed before. Frankly, didn't like it. I think that I am one of those women who doesn't."

Joan's expression contained a touch of pity. "He is very handsome," she said after a pause. "If you have to marry a merchant, he may as well be a rich and handsome one."

Christiana knew that Joan echoed the opinion of the whole court. *Poor Christiana. A sweet girl. Too bad about the King giving her to a common merchant, but at least he is rich and handsome.* It reminded her of the encouraging sympathy offered to a maimed knight. *Too bad that you will never walk right again, but at least you are not dead.*

"Lady Elizabeth buys from him, you know," Joan added very casually. "And Lady Agnes and a few others."

Joan always managed to find out such things. In the last week she had probably learned all there was to know in Westminster about David de Abyndon. She would drop tidbits like this here and there as it suited her.

"They prefer to go to his shop, which is quite wonderful. You really should have come with us, Christiana. He brings in silks from Italy and as far away as India. There are tailors there too. The women who use him treat him like a secret and will go nowhere else. Lady Agnes says that Lady Elizabeth's whole white and silver style was his idea. I'm surprised that you never saw him before this happened if Elizabeth is one of his patrons."

Lady Elizabeth, a widow, had been a special friend of Morvan's for a number of months a year ago. She was at least ten years older than him but exquisitely beautiful. Her most notable features were her prematurely white hair and her translucent white skin. Court rumors had predicted a marriage, but then Elizabeth had accepted the offer of an elderly lord and suddenly her friendship with Morvan had cooled.

For two years now, Elizabeth had affected a highly personal style that enhanced her unique beauty. She wore only white and silvery grays. Even her jewels were reset in silver.

"Isabele is convinced that he will make you work for him," Joan giggled. "Idonia has explained that wealthy merchants don't do that, but Isabele sees the women working in the shops and thinks that you will have to as well."

Dear saints, Morvan would kill her to protect the family honor before he swallowed *that*. "It is your move, Joan," she said, deciding that it was time to end the subject.

A page entered a short time later. "My lady, your husband is in the hall and bids you to attend on him," he said to her.

She stared at the boy as if he had spoken gibberish. "Is that the message as he sent it?"

"Aye, my lady."

"I do not much like this message," she said to Joan.

"It sounds common enough to me."

"He is not my husband yet."

"Oh, Christiana, you know that betrothed couples are often referred to as husband and wife. Saturday was the first part of the ceremony, and the wedding is the conclusion. It is half done."

Not for me, she wanted to shout. *And this man knows it.*

She also didn't like, not one bit, being "bidden" to do anything by David de Abyndon. When Morvan put her hand in David's, it was symbolic of handing over authority and responsibility, but under the circumstances of this particular betrothal, that was meaningless too.

She turned to the page. "Tell my betrothed that I regret that I cannot attend on him this morning. I am grateful that he has visited, but I am not well. Tell him that I have a headache and am feeling dizzy."

"I hope that you know what you are doing," Joan said.

More to the point was the importance that David know what she was doing. She had told him that they would not see each other, and if he mistakenly thought that she meant only before the betrothal, then this should clarify it. She had no intention of explaining to Stephen when he came that she had been playing out this farce more than necessary.

A short while later their door flew open and the page reappeared, red faced and winded from running.

"My lady, your hus . . . that man is coming here."

"Coming here!"

"Aye. I handed him over to another page and sent them the long way, but he will be here soon."

She looked desperately at Joan as the page left.

"I thought that you knew what you were doing," Joan said, laughing.

She jumped up. "Help me. Quickly." She ran into the bedchamber's anteroom and threw back the coverlet on her bed. "Tuck me in and close the curtains. Try not to let any of my gown show."

"This isn't going to work." Joan giggled as she poked the coverlet around her neck and sides.

"Tell him that I am resting and send him away."

Joan grinned and pulled the curtains.

Christiana lay absolutely still in the dark shadows of the bed. She could hear Joan walking around, humming a melody. She felt a little ridiculous doing this, but something deep inside her said that she should not see this man again.

Even though her curtains muffled the sounds, she heard the boots walking into the room.

"Master David!" Joan cried brightly.

"Lady Joan. You, at least, appear to be well."

Christiana sighed. This man's quiet, beautiful voice had a talent for putting a lot of meaning into simple words without so much as changing its inflection. It was very clear that he knew that she lied about being ill, but then she had counted on him seeing that. She just hadn't counted on him coming to confront her and thus forcing her to pretend that she hadn't lied.

"Indeed I am very well, David. And you?"

"Well enough, my lady. Although I find myself recently more short of temper than is normal."

"No doubt it is something that you ate."

"No doubt."

Boots paced across the floor. "I am told that Christiana is ill."

"Aye. She is resting, David, and really should not be disturbed."

"What is the malady?"

"It was really quite frightening. When she awoke this morning she was overcome with dizziness. She almost fell. We put her right back to bed, of course, and that seems to help. She could be abed for days, even weeks."

Don't overdo it. Christiana prompted silently.

"It sounds most serious," David said. "Such an illness is not to be taken lightly. Perhaps I should pay the abbey monks to say masses on her behalf."

"We are very worried, but I trust all will be well soon. We will be sure to send word to you when she is better."

"Is this her bed? I will see her before I go."

"I really don't think that will be wise, David," Joan said hurriedly. "The light seems to make it worse."

A clever touch, Christiana thought approvingly.

But not clever enough. "I will be quick."

Even with her eyes closed, Christiana saw the light flood over her as the curtains were pushed back.

She gasped as he took her firmly by the waist, lifted her up, and dropped her on her back.

She lowered her lids as if the light hurt them, and moaned for effect. She hoped that she looked suitably pale and ill.

David gave her hip a gentle whack, gesturing for her to move over. Biting back her indignation, she scooted a little and he sat on the edge of the bed.

"Well, Christiana, I am very concerned. A headache and dizziness. You seem to have a serious illness indeed."

That hardness around his mouth seemed a bit more pronounced. Something in his expression suggested that he was capable of being the exact opposite of the kindly merchant whom she had first expected.

He rubbed her cheek with the backs of his fingers. "No fever. All the same, I think that we should have a physician see you at once."

"I am sure that isn't necessary." She tried to make her voice a little weak but not too much so. "I am feeling better, and I am sure that this will pass."

He ignored her. "I will have to ask around and see which of the ones at court are any good. Some of these physicians immediately want to bleed the patient, and that is so painful. We would like to avoid it if possible, don't you think?"

She had been bled once when she was eleven. She thought that avoiding it was an excellent idea.

"On the other hand, headaches and dizziness are probably caused by the humors that require it."

"I really find that I am feeling much better. The light doesn't bother me at all now."

"The idea of being bled always makes one feel better, my girl, but it doesn't last. However, if you think that you are recovering a little for now, I would really prefer to get you dressed and take you to see a Saracen physician whom I know in Southwark. He is an expert in ladies' illnesses, and treats all of the whores in the Stews. He is very skilled."

"A Saracen! A whores' physician!" She completely forgot to make her voice weak at all.

"Aye. Trained in Alexandria. Saracen physicians are much better than Christians. We are barbarians in comparison."

"I assure you that going to Southwark is not needed, David. Truly, I am feeling enormously better. Quite myself, in fact. I am confident that I am completely cured."

He smiled slowly. "Are you? That is good news. However, you must be sure to let me know if these spells return. I will be sure to get you to a physician immediately. I am responsible for you now, and would not have your health neglected."

She glared at him. This "husband" who had "bid her attend on him" was reminding her of his rights and warning her not to play this game again. She could think of nicer ways to have made the point without threatening to have her arm cut open.

He rose. Apparently his oblique scolding was finished, and Christiana felt confident that he would leave. She glanced at Joan triumphantly.

David looked down at her. "The day is fair. Perhaps all that you need is some fresh air to clear your head."

"I'm not at all sure . . ."

His gaze lit on the closest ambry. "Are your things in here? We will get you dressed and I will take you out for a while."

She narrowed her eyes at David's handsome face. One farce after another. She couldn't claim to be too dizzy to go out but also too well to see a physician. He had cleverly, elegantly manipulated her ruse against her.

"I am already dressed," she announced, throwing back the coverlet and sitting up, admitting defeat.

"So you are," he said quietly, coming toward her with a vague smile on his face and her old cloak in his hand. "What a disappointment. I was looking forward to that part."

That smile made her very uncomfortable. She would admit defeat, but not surrender. "Unfortunately," she said regretfully, "I cannot go with you. It is a rule. None of us can be with a man alone."

Joan nodded her head vigorously in support.

"Lady Idonia is gone, and unfortunately Joan has to meet with her brother soon," she added.

Joan continued nodding even though she had no such plans.

"It is a most serious prohibition," she emphasized. "As you can imagine, the consequences for disobeying are dire."

"Dire," Joan echoed helpfully.

David gave them both a look that indicated he thought that consequences had not been nearly dire enough for the two of them over the years.

"I might risk it, except that the Queen is most strict and . . ." She threw up her hands.

David flipped the cloak out and around her shoulders. He bent to pin the brooch under her neck. His closeness, and his hands working near her body, made her yet more uncomfortable.

"I am not just a man, I am your betrothed. What is the worst that can happen? If I ravish you, it simply means that the marriage is finalized that much earlier. Perhaps they would thank me for taking you off their hands. Besides, it is for me to punish your future bad behavior and not Lady Idonia and the Queen."

He was talking to her like a child again. In fact, he was dressing her like a child. Furthermore, this was his second reference to *that*, and she really could do without his innuendos. They prodded at something inside her that she didn't want to think about. Since they insinuated a familiarity that simply wasn't going to develop, she thought that it would be nice if they didn't even jest about it.

This merchant's presumptions indicated that he was taking his betrothal rights far too seriously. She did not want to be alone with David de Abyndon any longer than necessary, and she had ruined the chance of getting Joan to come with them. While he put on his own cloak, she caught Joan's attention.

Idonia, she mouthed.

She stood up to leave. With a smooth movement David bent and scooped her into his arms. She cried a startled "Oh!" and stared at him.

"I can walk." She fumed when he laughed.

"There are steps. If you get dizzy again, you might fall and break your neck."

"It is more likely that you will drop me."

"Nonsense. You are very light."

"Oh, dear saints," she groaned, letting her head fall back in exasperation. "Well, at least go down the back stairs to the entrance there. I don't want the whole court to see this."

As he carried her out, she turned her head and looked desperately back at Joan.

Send Idonia, she mouthed again.

He set her down at the back entrance that led to a small courtyard beneath Isabele's windows.

"There are some benches here and the sun is warm against that wall," she suggested. "Let us sit here."

"I think that we would prefer to take a ride."

Idonia would never find them and rescue her then. "*I* would prefer to sit here."

"Soon the shadows will move over that wall, and then you will get chilled. A ride in the sun will be better."

Walking beside him around the corner of the manor, she wondered if all men got so willful after one got betrothed to them. Would Stephen stop speaking pretty words when they were married? Was that just something done beforehand to lure women? The chansons weren't much help with this question. The couples in those romantic songs were never married. She immediately felt guilty for equating Stephen with this merchant. Stephen was a chivalrous knight, and poetry and romance flowed in his blood.

David took the reins of his horse from the young groom who had been holding them.

"I will send for a mount from the stables," she said.

"You will ride with me. One of the problems with being dizzy is that you cannot ride a horse unattended for a while." He lifted her up to the front of the saddle and swung up behind her.

She had never sat on a horse with a man before. The perch up front was a little precarious, especially if one leaned forward as she strained to do. This promised to be backbreaking and her mood did not improve.

They rode out the castle gate and turned upriver. The road grew deserted once they moved away from the castle and town. A few carts straggled past, and in the river an occasional barge drifted by. They were less than two miles from London's wall, but suddenly a world away.

They rode in silence for about a quarter of a mile. Christiana focused her attention on avoiding any contact with the man a hair's breadth behind her. Her back ached from the effort.

Suddenly and without warning, David pushed the horse to a faster walk. That did it. The gait threw her backward against his chest and shoulders. His arm slid around her waist. She tensed in surprise as that peculiar intensity flowed and embraced her more surely than his arm.

She noticed the solidity of his support and became acutely aware of his arm resting lightly across her waist. She looked down at the beautiful masculine hand gently holding her, and felt the soft pressure of his fingers as he steadied her. There was something tantalizing about his warmth along her back.

The oddest tremor swept through her. She tensed again.

"Are you afraid of me, Christiana?" he asked.

His face was very close to her head, and his voice barely louder than a whisper. His breath drifted over her temple, carrying his words. The warm sound mixed with the warm air and caressed her as surely as if fingers had touched her. Despite that warmth, a chill trembled down her neck and back. A very peculiar chill.

"Of course not."

"You act as if you are."

He had noticed the tremors, she thought, a little horrified but not sure why.

"I am a bit cold is all."

In response he drew the edges of his own cloak around her.

He seemed closer now. She could feel the muscles of his chest all along her back. His breath grazed her hair, making her scalp tingle. He was virtually a stranger, and the subtle intimacy of being cocooned inside his cloak with him did make her a little fearful now, but of what she couldn't say. She squirmed to let him know that she wanted him to let go.

He did not release her. Instead he bent his body over hers. Soft hair brushed against her cheek before he turned his head to kiss her neck.

The heat of his lips against her skin produced an incredible shock. He kissed her again, increasing the pressure, and the warmth of that mouth penetrated her skin, flowed down her neck and arms, and streaked through her chest and belly. The pure physicality of the sensation stunned her.

His arm pulled her tighter. His lips moved up her neck. Quivering, delicious tremors coursed through her. He nipped lightly along the edge of her ear. A hollow tension exploded, shaking her, and she gasped.

The sound woke her from the sensual daze. She turned her head away from his mouth. "Now I am afraid of you," she said.

"That was not fear."

She pushed against his arm. "I want to get down. This familiarity is wrong."

"We are betrothed."

"Not really."

"Very really."

"Not in my mind, and you know it. I want to get down. Now. I want to walk for a while."

He stopped the horse and swung off. She braced herself for his anger as she turned to be lifted down, but he only smiled and fell into step beside her.

Even walking apart from him, she could still feel the pull of that unsettling intimacy. This man had made her feel uncomfortable and vulnerable from the first time she had seen him, and it wasn't getting any better.

She felt an urgent need to banish the last few minutes from their memories, and took refuge in conversation to do so.

"Lady Idonia told me that the Abyndons are an aldermanic family in London."

"My uncle Stephen was an alderman about ten years ago, at the time that he died. I have an uncle Gilbert who would like to be."

"He did not come Saturday."

"We are estranged."

"And your parents did not come. Are they dead or are you estranged from them too?"

He didn't answer right away. "They did not tell you much about me, did they? My mother is dead. I do not know my father. Abyndon is my mother's name."

He was a bastard. Of all of the topics to choose for conversation, this had probably been the worst.

"Your brother knows of this," he added.

"It is a common thing. He would not find it worthwhile to comment upon it to me." That was a courteous lie, of course. It wasn't *that* common.

"Is there anything else you want to know about me?"

She thought a moment. "How old are you?"

"Twenty-nine."

"And you were an apprentice until twenty-five?"

"Actually, twenty-four."

"So how did you get so rich so fast?"

He laughed a little. A nice laugh. Quiet. "It is a long story."

"Not too long, if you are only twenty-nine."

He laughed again. "My master, David Constantyn, bought his goods from traders who came to England. Italians mostly, from Genoa and Venice. When I was about Andrew's age, twenty, I convinced him to send me to Flanders to purchase some wool directly. The prices at which we sell are regulated, so the only way to make more profit is to buy more cheaply."

"Your trip was successful?"

"Very much so. We did that for a year. Then, one day he came to me and agreed on another idea I had proposed. He gave me a large amount of money to try my luck elsewhere. I was gone for three years, and visited many of the ports around the Inland Sea. I sent back goods, became friends with men who became our agents, and established a trading network. We had a large advantage after that."

He told his tale as if men did this all of the time, but of course they did not and even a girl like her knew it. "You were still his apprentice then?"

"In the eyes of law. But he had been more like a father to me for years. As soon as I received the city's freedom and citizenship, he made me his partner. He was a widower and had no children, and left me his property upon his death. His wealth went to charity and for prayers for his soul."

She hadn't thought of a merchant as an adventurer. In her world only a knight errant or crusader might wander thus. "Where are some of the places that you traveled to?"

"I went by ship down the coast of the Aquitane and Castile and into the Inland Sea through the Pillars of Hercules. Then along the coast of the Dark Continent first."

"Saracen lands!"

"One must trade with Saracens to get anything from the East."

"It must have been dangerous."

"Only once. In Egypt. I stayed too long there. The ports welcome traders and depend on them. No one wants to discourage commerce by killing merchants. After Egypt, I went up to Tripoli and Constantinople, then sailed to Genoa. I came back through France."

She pictured the maps of the Inland Sea that she had seen. She imagined him riding through deserts and passing over the Alps. She glanced at the daggers he wore. One was a decorative eating tool, but the other was large and lethal looking.

"It still sounds dangerous. And very risky." Actually it sounded wonderfully exciting and adventurous.

"The risk was real enough, but mostly financial. David Constantyn was probably a bit of a fool to agree to it. Only as I see Andrew approaching the same age do I see the faith that he had."

"Will you have Andrew do as you did?"

"Nay. But I will send him to Genoa soon, where the agents send their goods for shipment here. I need a man there, I think, so that I do not have to travel down every other year."

There were many Florentine bankers and Italian traders in London, and tales of that sunny land had filtered through the court over the years. She felt a little envious of Andrew. The idea of spending her years embroidering in one of Stephen's drafty castles suddenly seemed very dull.

"I came to speak with you about something, Christiana," he said. "I was at Westminster to discuss the wedding. The spring and early summer are out of the question. There will be times when I will be out of London unexpectedly."

Spring and summer were the times when many trading fairs were held. Presumably he would need to attend some.

"Next fall, then," she offered. "October or November."

"I think not. Before Lent. The end of February."

"Five weeks hence! That is too soon!"

"How so?"

She glared at him. They had been having such a nice talk, too. He knew "how so." She marched on a little quicker, her gaze fixed on the road ahead.

He kept up by simply lengthening his stride. Finally his quiet voice flowed around her. "I said that I would step aside if this man comes, but you cannot expect me to arrange my life for his convenience. If he wants you, he will be here very soon."

She turned on him. "You are conceited and arrogant and I hate you. You are deliberately doing this to make things difficult for me."

"Nay. I only seek to avoid difficulties for myself that might complicate my business affairs. Five weeks is enough time for a man to decide that he wants a woman. I made my decision in a matter of days. A man in love should be even quicker."

He didn't think that Stephen would come, and now he had created a test for him. How dare he claim to know the heart of a chivalrous knight! How dare he compare himself to him! Stephen was as different from this mercer as a destrier from a palfrey. The same animal, but different breeds with different duties.

"Five weeks, my lady," he repeated firmly. He glanced up at the sun. "Now we must ride back. I have a meeting this afternoon."

He brought up the horse and lifted her up. She kept

her back very straight all of the way home to West-minster.

In the back courtyard they found Lady Idonia sitting by the wall. She rose at once and came toward them.

David dismounted and brought Christiana down. He turned to the guardian. "You decided to take some air, too, my lady? The day is fair, is it not?"

Lady Idonia did her best. "You should not have taken Christiana out with her illness. Her dizziness was most severe."

David slung an arm around Christiana's shoulders. It was a casual gesture, but it very effectively kept her from bolting. "Your solicitous concern for my betrothed moves me, my lady. But I have something to say to Christiana in private. Perhaps you would wait inside the entrance for her."

Idonia flustered in response to this blunt dismissal, glanced sharply at Christiana, and stomped off.

David dropped his arm and turned to her. "I will visit you next week."

Stephen would come soon, but not that soon. She really did not want to spend more time with David. It felt like a betrayal of her love. "That is not necessary," she said.

"It may not be necessary, but for your sake it is prudent. You expect your lover to come, but what if he does not?"

"He will come."

"And if not?"

His insistence irritated her. "What of it?"

"Then in five weeks you wed me, my girl. Just in case, shouldn't we spend this time getting to know one another? It is what betrothals are for."

But I am not really betrothed, she thought, eyeing him obstinately. *Not in my heart or mind.*

"Christiana, if you do not want to meet again until the wedding, that is how it will be. Yet think about it, girl. Going to bed with a stranger will not bother me at all, but you may find the experience distressing."

Her mouth fell open in shock at this blunt reminder of the marriage bed. Memories of herself with Stephen flew rapidly through her mind. He had not been a stranger, and she quickly relived the shock of his ferocious passion, the crushing insistence of his kisses, the almost horrible intimacy of his hand on her nakedness.

She stared up at David de Abyndon, noting the frank and open way that he watched her. It was cruel of him to make her think about this and face the possible conclusion of this betrothal. All the same, her mind involuntarily began to substitute him for Stephen in those memories. She was appalled that it had no trouble doing so and that the strange feelings that he summoned tried to attach themselves to the ghostlike fantasy. She shook those thoughts away. The whole notion was indeed distressing. And very frightening.

Five weeks.

"Am I supposed to wait upstairs for you to come and 'bid me to attend'?" she asked sarcastically.

"Let us say that I will come on Mondays. If I cannot, I will send word. If you are ill again, send a message to me."

She nodded and turned toward the door. She wanted to be done with this man today. She wanted to cleanse her mind of what it had just imagined.

He caught her arm and pulled her back. With gentle but firm movements he clasped her in an embrace.

A surging desperation claimed her. She remembered the betrothal ceremony and she knew, she just knew, that it was vital, essential, that he not kiss her again. She struggled against his arms and almost cried out for Idonia. As his head bent to hers, she twisted to avoid him.

His lips found hers anyway and connected with a grazing brush that wasn't even a kiss. She felt that same, warm soothing lightness again and again on her cheek and brow and neck. In spite of her love for Stephen, in spite of her anger at this man's intrusion into her life, she calmed beneath the repeated caress of his mouth as ripples of sensation flowed through her. Her awareness dulled to everything but those compelling feelings.

When he finally stopped, she wasn't struggling anymore. A little dazed, she looked up at him. The perfect planes of his face appeared tighter than usual, and he looked in her eyes with a commanding gaze that seemed to speak a language that she didn't understand. She knew that he was going to kiss her and that she should get away, but when he lowered his mouth to hers, she couldn't resist at all.

It was a beautiful kiss, full of warmth and promise. It deepened slowly and he held her head in one hand, the other arm lifting her into it. The waves of sensation flowed higher and stronger, carrying her toward a delicious oblivion.

He released the pressure on her mouth and took one lip, then the other, gently between his teeth. A sharper warmth shot down the center of her body. It was a stunning quiver of pleasurable discomfort that seemed to reach completely through her. Less gently, he kissed each pulse point on her neck, and it happened again and again, each time stronger, the compelling discomfort growing.

He lifted his head and looked down at her, his mouth set in a hard line with the lips slightly parted. He looked gloriously handsome like that.

"You make me forget myself," he said, his fingers stretching through her hair.

Their surroundings slowly intruded. Her position,

arching acceptingly into his embrace, suddenly became apparent, too.

Horrified, she abruptly disentangled herself. He let her go. With a very red face she hurried to the door.

Lady Idonia waited there. She looked up sharply. " 'Send Idonia to save me,' " she mimicked. "I sat out there almost an hour, worried for you, although why I don't know, since you are marrying the man. Then you return and what do I see? Keep that up, girl, and there will be no need for a wedding at all."

Christiana blushed deeper. A profound sense of guilt swept through her. She loved Stephen. How could she be so faithless? How could she let this man kiss her like that? Even if he forced her to it, how could she let those feelings undo her so outrageously?

She followed Idonia up the stairs, more confused and frightened than she had been on her betrothal day. This was wrong. She must never let it happen again. She must be sure that she was never again alone with this merchant.

At the second-level landing, she paused and looked out the small window to the courtyard below. David was just mounting his horse to leave. As he began riding away, a movement at the end of the courtyard caught her attention. A man stepped away from the building and toward David's approaching horse.

David stopped and spoke with the man for a moment, then made to move on. But the man followed alongside, speaking and gesturing. Finally David dismounted. He tied his reins to a post and disappeared behind the building, following the man.

Christiana frowned. They had been some distance away, but she felt sure that she recognized the man. He was the French-speaking diplomat who had passed her alcove in the King's passageway the morning after she had met David.

CHAPTER 4

DAVID STOOD AT the threshold between the solar and the bedchamber and studied the woman whom Sieg had just brought upstairs. She was still an attractive lady, but thirteen years take their toll on anyone. He hadn't realized back then how young she must have been. No more than twenty-five at the time, he would judge now. Still, he would remember her anywhere.

She hadn't noticed him, and he watched her glide around the solar, fingering the carving on the chairs and examining the tapestry on the wall. She touched the glazing in the windows much as Christiana had done that first night.

He would not think about Christiana now. If he did, he suspected that he might not go through with this. He had already spent more time the last week thinking of those diamond eyes than about the carefully planned harvest of justice that he would reap this afternoon. The last thing he wanted now was the thought of a good woman making him weak with a bad one.

The woman's face looked paler than her hands, and he could tell that she used wheat flour to make it so. An artful touch of paint flushed her cheeks and colored her lips. If he gave a damn, he would find a kind way to tell her that the coloring was a bit too strong for the honey hair that had begun to dull with age. He suspected that this was one of those women who looks in the mirror a lot but never really sees what is reflected there.

He shifted his weight silently but it drew her attention anyway. Amber cat eyes turned and regarded him. He saw the brief scrutiny and then the slow relief. *Aye,* he thought, *if this woman whores for a man, she prefers him young and handsome.* She continued looking at him and he noticed the total absence of recognition.

"David de Abyndon?" she asked. Her eyes narrowed and a thin smile stretched her mouth.

"Lady Catherine. I'm sorry that I could not see you sooner."

She misunderstood and, flattered, smiled more naturally.

He gestured and she joined him at the doorway. When she saw it was a bedchamber, she glanced at him, reproving him for his lack of subtlety.

She entered slowly and again she took in the details of the room, calculating their value. Time and again her gaze rested on the large tub set before the hearth. It had been brought in by the servants before David dismissed all of them for the afternoon. If they wondered why he wanted it here and not in the wardrobe where it belonged, they hadn't said so.

It had been filled with water, and more water was heating by the hearth. David lifted the buckets and poured them into the tub.

She watched him with amusement. "Perhaps I came too early."

"This is for you."

"You thought that I would be unclean?"

You are so unclean that all of the water in the world would not cleanse you. "Nay. But I remember how much you enjoy baths and sought to indulge you."

She frowned and looked at him more closely. A spark of memory tried to catch flame, but he watched it die.

"My husband assumed . . ."

"I know what your husband assumed. But we do it this way or not at all." He leaned against the hearth wall and waited.

A little flustered, but not too much so, she began to remove her clothing. She carefully folded the bejeweled surcoat and placed it on the nearby stool. The beautiful cotehardie followed. Rich fabrics. He had no trouble calculating how many of her husband's debts were devoted to her wardrobe.

She untied her garters and peeled off her hose. He noted her lack of embarrassment. He was by far not the first stranger she had stripped for.

The shift dropped to the floor and she looked at him boldly. He gestured to the tub and she stepped in with clear irritation.

She settled down. She was childless and her body was still youthful. Her full breasts bobbed in the high water.

"Well?" she asked.

"Your husband sent you here to ask something of me. To negotiate for him, did he not?"

She gestured with exasperation at the tub.

David smiled. "I only do this to give you every advantage, my lady. I remember that you negotiate best when you are thus."

Again that scrutiny. Again the flame of recognition that died before it caught fire. She became all business.

"My husband says that you have bought up all of his debts."

The man had amassed debts to merchants and bankers over the last few years. When he had resorted to borrowing from one to pay another, when the financial market in London had realized that he tottered on the edge of ruin, David had bought the loans at a deep discount. He had not even gone looking for today's justice. It had simply fallen into his lap, one of Fortune's many gifts to him.

"He needs time to repay them."

"They are long overdue, as I have explained to him."

"He thought that you might be more reasonable with me. I have come to ask for an extension. The properties have been less productive of late, but that should improve."

"They are less productive because they are neglected and mismanaged. Already the ones that I hold have improved."

"The loans were made with the promise that the property you hold now would be returned to us."

"Only if the loans are repaid." He paused. "I think that we might be able to work something out about the loans and the property, however. Is there anything else that you require?"

Her face lightened. It was going better than she thought it would. "Aye. We need a further loan. A small one. As a bridge until things work out."

This husband placed a high value indeed on his wife's favors. "You are asking me to throw good money after bad."

"You will be repaid in full."

"Madam, your husband gambles. You are extravagant. Both vices are rarely conquered. I will consider the extension of the old loans, but in truth you will never repay them. Why would I now give you more?"

She looked at him boldly and a small smile formed on her tinted lips. Slowly, expertly, she shifted in the tub so that he had a full view of her body.

The years fell away. He was in another chamber standing in front of a younger woman. She was a frequent visitor to the shop, but when she had come this day, David Constantyn had not been in. She bought expensive cloths and paid with a tally as was the habit of such women, but then insisted that the young apprentice deliver the goods that afternoon to her manor in Hampstead where the tally would be made good.

He had gone. Like others before him, he had innocently ridden the five miles north to Hampstead.

She had received him in her chamber, lying in a tub much as she did now. Pretending to ignore his presence, she had demanded that her servants open and examine the purchases while he waited. All the while she had bathed herself, slowly and languidly, occasionally looking at him with a challenging stare that dared him to react to her nakedness.

He did not. He was randy enough at sixteen and not inexperienced, but he held his body in check. At first his dismay and shock helped him. His knowledge of females consisted of the happy servant girls with whom coupling was a form of joyful play. Instinctively he knew that this woman was nothing like that and that she tempted him to something other than pleasure.

But as she continued displaying herself, it was anger that kept him in control. He turned away from her. He did not like playing the mouse to this cat woman. He resented her using her position and degree to humiliate him.

Finally he could tell that she grew angry too. She addressed him directly and began to renegotiate the price of the goods. She pursued the subject a long while, refusing to pay the whole tally, demanding his attention. Finally, he had to look at her, and as he did she raised one leg to the side of the tub and exposed herself.

He lost control then, but not in the way that she expected. He let his face show what he thought, but it was not the desire she demanded. He looked down at her and let her see his utter disgust before he walked out.

He had almost reached the road before her men came and dragged him back. They tied him to a metal ring set in the trunk of an oak tree in the garden. Before the lash fell, he looked over his shoulder and saw her honey hair at a window.

"You do not remember me," he said. "But then, there were a number of us, why would you remember one?"

Over the years, they had found each other, the boys now grown to men whom she had ensnared in her web. The woman's unhealthy appetite was not discussed openly, but it was not unknown. It was why David Constantyn had never let his apprentices serve her or deliver goods.

But he was the one who had not played her game as she wanted it, and so the lash fell harder on him than those others whose only crime had been to show the lust that she demanded and then punished while she watched from her bower window. He had been flogged once in Egypt, but it was this first time that had scarred his back. His youth had been beaten out of him that day.

He regarded her impassively, watching her study him hard. This time the spark of memory caught hold and her eyes flamed with recognition. Her gaze slowly swept the room as she calculated her danger. She collected herself.

"You were compensated," she said coolly.

Aye, he had been compensated. When he staggered back home and his master saw his condition, that good man had done what no other master or father had done. Going to the city courts the next day, he petitioned against this woman and forced the mayor to address the issue. After a long while, the husband had been made to pay fifty pounds. David had refused to touch the money.

"The others were not. And it is not a debt that money settles anyway."

She glared at him angrily before calming herself. She glanced at the bed and then eyed him with a question.

"Aye, that too. But if you want this extension, I have other terms. I will extend the loans in return for the Hampstead manor and property, and for one hour of your time."

"The Hampstead lands belong to me, not my husband. They were not pledged as surety for any loans."

"I know that they are yours. In return for them, however, I will in fact forgive the loans, not just extend them." He smiled. "See how well you negotiate? Already I have conceded much more than I had planned."

He saw her weighing certain ruin against the property. If he called the loans, she would have to sell it anyway.

"Why do you want that house? Why not another? Are you going to burn it or something?"

"Nay. We merchants are very practical people. We rarely destroy property. It is a very beautiful house and I have admired it. I will have need of a country home near London soon. I hold no grudge against a building."

"And the hour of my time?"

"That is for the other debt. You will go to a place that I tell you. There a man will flog you just as you watched others flogged for your pleasure. Ten lashes."

Her eyes flew open in shock. He noted her reaction with relief. Those who took pleasure in pain often went both ways, and he did not want her to get perverse enjoyment out of this.

"I didn't realize that we had so much in common," she finally said.

"We have nothing in common. I will not be there, although some of the others might be. They will be told of this and may want to see it. I would demand your husband do it, as he should have long ago, but he knows what he has in you, and if he started he might not stop. It is justice we seek, not revenge or your husband's satisfaction."

She abruptly rose from the tub. She stepped out and began to dry herself. Her hurried, angry movements gradually slowed, however, and the expression on her face changed. He saw her considering, calculating, planning the final negotiation that, if executed well enough, might change everything.

He realized with surprise that he had totally lost interest in taking her humiliation any further.

He removed a small purse from the front of his pourpoint. It contained exactly the difference between the value of the loans and the Hampstead property. He dropped the purse on top of her garments. "It is the money that you seek but not a loan. That would be bad business. However, I always pay for my whores whether I use them or not."

He walked to the door. "A week hence, madam. The time and place will be sent to you. Afterward husband can contact me about settling the loans and property."

Her voice, harsh and ugly, ripped across the chamber. "There will be a new debt to settle after this, you bastard son of a whore!"

He paused. Justice, not revenge, he reminded himself. Still . . .

"Fifteen lashes, I think now, my lady. The last five for the insult to my mother."

He strode out through the solar and hall and left the house.

✦   ✦   ✦

The sky had clouded over and a light snow was falling by the time David reined in his horse outside the tavern. To his right, along the Southwark docks, small craft of all types bobbed. Stretched out in front of them rose the small houses where the prostitutes of the Stews plied their trade. Even at night these docks would be full, for the city discouraged crossing the river after dark and it was traditional for these women to have their customers stay until dawn.

The rude tavern was dark and musty with river damp. David let his eyes adjust, and then walked to a corner table.

"You are late," the man sitting there said.

David slid onto the bench. "Oliver, you are the most punctual whoremonger I have ever met."

Oliver passed him a cup of ale, drank some of his own, and wiped his black mustache and beard on his sleeve. "I am a busy man, David. Time is money."

"Your woman's time is money, Oliver, not yours. How is Anne?"

Oliver shrugged. "She doesn't like the winter. The nights are too long in her opinion."

She would probably move to Cock Lane soon. It was right outside the city wall and the women there worked differently than here in Southwark. But then, they also had to deal with the city laws. Southwark, across the Thames from London, was a town apart and close to lawless.

He looked at Oliver's wiry thin body and long black hair. They had known each other since boyhood, when they had played and scrapped in the streets and alleys together. On occasion during those carefree days, they had met danger side by side. But then Oliver's poor family had moved up to Hull and David had been plucked from those alleys and sent to school and into trade.

They had met again when Oliver returned to London several years ago. David had recognized at once that he had found a man whom he could trust. Like Sieg, Oliver might do a criminal's deeds sometimes, but he lived by a code of loyalty and fairness that would put most knights to shame. Since then, they had again on occasion met danger side by side.

The decision for Anne to become a prostitute had simply been the easiest of several choices available to them when they had come back to London. Anne had already decided that the winter nights were too long when he had met them a short while later. Still, she probably earned three times as much on her back than she and Oliver could together through honest labor. The odd jobs Oliver did for him and others helped some.

He wondered how he was going to explain Oliver and Anne to Christiana. Sieg's story would be strange enough when she finally realized that he wasn't a typical servant.

"Has he spoken to you?" Oliver asked.

"Twice. The last time just this morning."

"I have followed him like you said. He spoke to a ship's master yesterday. I think that he will sail back soon."

"He will need to. I expect that he will seek me out one more time, though, and delay his trip until I will talk to him at length. He has only felt me out so far, and has not achieved what he came for."

"You think that it is set, then?"

"I think so. I refused him, but I left the door open."

Oliver shook his head. "I am not convinced. His actions have been very normal. He goes to merchants and other places of business. That is all."

"His offer to me has been subtle so far but unmistakable. He appears to be a merchant because he is one. Except for the letter for Edward and his mission with me, he is here for trade. It is the whole point. Whenever

I go to France or Flanders, I go for trade, too." He stretched out his legs beneath the table. "Speaking of which, tell Albin that I will need to go over in about a week or so."

"Running from your duel?" Oliver asked with a grin.

"Before that. After he talks with me but before my wedding. I want to sail along the coast."

"You are pushing things, my friend," Oliver said, laughing. "Wait until after you marry this princess. Tempt fate and you might find yourself caught in bad seas for a week and miss the ceremony. That will take some explaining, I'll warrant."

David looked away. Sieg had been right. It was a bad time to be getting married. Oliver was right, too. He should wait until after the wedding to sail the coast. But it needed to be done soon, and he had no intention of leaving Christiana for a while after she came to him. This girl, and the growing desire he felt for her, were complicating things.

Her eyes were faceted jewels full of bright reflections. A man could lose his soul in eyes like that.

For one thing, he had begun to lose interest in these subtle and dangerous plans that he had laid and in which Oliver played a role. He had finally admitted that to himself as he rode over here today, and had been astonished to discover it. After all, he had been slowly planting this particular field for almost two years. A piece of information here, a deliberate slip there. It had worked because people like himself were quick to notice mistakes and weakness and potential advantage, and he knew that he dealt with a man very much like himself. In fact, matching wits with him should be a pleasure in itself, and the final justice much more satisfying than the rather thin contentment he had felt with Lady Catherine today.

Instead, he was losing interest and even considering cutting things short just as they reached the critical moves. His own plans and Edward's had become so intertwined that he had pondered at length whether it would be possible to extricate one from the other. That he even considered such a thing had to do with Christiana. She had him thinking of the future more than the past. He already felt responsibility for her. He considered far too often what it would mean for her if in the end he lost this game.

He had changed his testament so that she would be a wealthy widow if something went wrong. Funds would be on account with Florentine bankers too. When the time came, he would give Sieg and Oliver instructions for getting her out of the country if that became necessary. But all of that would never compensate her if he failed.

Her gestures were full of elegance and poise, her hands and arms beautifully angled like a dancer's. It was the way that she moved that made her appear fragile.

She still expected that her lover would come for her. He didn't doubt her resolve on that for one moment.

Stephen Percy. Learning the man's name and something of his character had been easy enough, but the knowledge only confirmed David's initial instincts about the affair. Christiana was in for a bad disappointment.

That her heart would break soon went without saying, but when would she see the truth behind illusions? Two weeks? A month? Never? The last possible. A girl's first love could be a blind thing, and she was convinced that she was in love with this man. Accepting the truth could well be impossible. God knew he had seen that before.

So young Percy doesn't come for her. Then what? A marriage full of cold duty? He smiled thinly at the thought. He knew well what happened in such unions. The men found mistresses quickly or spent too many nights with the prostitutes on Cock Lane. The more honest wives absorbed themselves with religion or their children.

And the braver and bolder women . . . well, they eventually found their ways to the beds of men like David de Abyndon.

He felt her thin, lithe body against his. He sensed her responses to him, and her fear of them. A tremor flowed through her and into him, and he had wanted to kiss her again and again.

He had enough experience to recognize the possibilities which those tremors had revealed. But then, he had already sensed them that night in his solar.

In his memory's eye he saw her sparkling eyes and pale skin and the wide mouth that he couldn't see without wanting to kiss. He imagined her walking toward him, naked and inviting, that beautiful face and mouth finally turned up willingly to his.

But then her image grew hazy and dim, and another woman's face replaced it. Gaunt and tired, this face was beautiful too despite its weariness. Resting on a pillow with golden brown hair encircling it like a halo, its eyes were finally closed to disappointment and disillusion.

The image fell away and he could see the entire chamber with its flickering candles and the white sheets on the bed. Clothes hung on pegs along a wall and a fire burned too hotly in the hearth. And sitting on the bed, his graying head buried in that lifeless breast, bent the anguished figure of David Constantyn.

He hadn't realized until then how much the man had loved her. At night when the house was dark, did he go to her? Did she go to him? Had she slept with him? God, but he hoped so.

He firmly set aside consideration of the risks that had meant nothing before he met Christiana.

For both of them, then, he thought.

"If you refuse this merchant, do you think the other will come?" Oliver asked.

"He will come," David said. "I would come. Keep your ears and those of your listeners open, Oliver. Not just for that, by the way. Stay around the pilgrims' taverns. I seek news from Northumberland."

"Any particular news?"

"There is a knight named Stephen Percy. If he comes to Westminster, I want to know right away. Or if you hear anything else about that family."

Oliver raised an eyebrow. "And if this man comes?"

David saw the look and knew at once that Sieg had already told Oliver of his interest in Sir Stephen. No doubt they guessed that he had something to do with Christiana.

He remembered Sieg's offer to deal with Morvan, and knew that Oliver was making the same suggestion now. It was not in their natures to do such things, but out of friendship for him they would do them anyway. Their loyalty could be burdensome at times. He had enough trouble battling his own inclinations without having to worry about the souls of the men who served him.

He thought about his promise to step aside. It had been a moment of weakness while gazing at a lovely face. His eye for beauty drove him from one bad bargain to another sometimes, especially when he negotiated for something that he wanted to keep for himself. Fortunately, Percy would not return and test his honesty to that promise. All the same . . .

"Just let me know at once," he said. "I will decide then."

CHAPTER 5

CHRISTIANA REMAINED FIRM in her decision not to be alone again with David. The next Monday she insisted that they sit in the garden, where Lady Idonia just happened to find and join them. It was a pleasant visit as he entertained them with stories from his travels.

During dinner a few days later, Sir Walter Manny stopped by her table. Sir Walter was one of the Queen's men from Philippa's native land of Hainault. During their conversation he mentioned that he knew David and had even introduced him to the King two years ago when Edward had a letter for the mayor of Ghent and David was planning a trip to Flanders.

"Are you saying that David delivered the letter for the King?" she asked.

"It is done all the time, my lady. Why send a messenger if a trusted merchant makes the trip? Sometimes it is even better this way, especially if you do not want to draw attention to the communication. For example, everyone knows that there is currently a Flemish trader in

Westminster who is partial to the French alliance of the Count of Flanders, unlike his fellow burghers who support England. We just assume that he might have brought a private letter from the Count to our King. A formal exchange would be awkward since they are adversaries, but still negotiations occur." He scanned the hall and pointed. "There he is with Lady Catherine. His name is Frans van Horlst."

Christiana looked to where a gray-haired man fawned over Catherine. It was her "diplomat," the one she had seen speak with David that first Tuesday after the betrothal.

And then, out of the corner of her mind came another memory, of the first time that she had seen that man in the King's private corridor. Two voices speaking Parisian French. One soft and low and barely a whisper.

David? The voice had been too quiet to tell. He knew the King well enough to offer for the daughter of Hugh Fitzwaryn, and yet no one had ever seen him around court. The access of that private passageway would explain that contradiction. Had it been David there that day? If so, what was he to the King that he entered and left by that special route? And what had Frans van Horlst wanted of him?

"Do you know if David still performs such favors for the King?"

Sir Walter shrugged. "I suggested him that once and introduced them. Whether the relationship continued I cannot say."

"How did you come to know my betrothed?"

Sir Walter grinned and bent his fair head conspiratorially. "You no doubt know that he is an accomplished musician? Taught himself, too."

She nodded dutifully, although she didn't know that at all.

"We both belong to the Pui," he confided.

The Pui was one of many secret fraternities in London. The only thing truly secret about it was the date and location of its annual meetings. Besides drinking all night, the men of the Pui performed songs that they had composed, and one of the songs was chosen to be "crowned." Sometimes when a jongleur played a new chanson, one might hear references to it being from the Pui.

"Has he played the lute for you? His preferred instrument is that ancient Celtic harp of his, but it often doesn't suit the songs and so he has had to learn the lute. Still, two years ago he beat me out for the crown, and I still swear it was only because of the novelty of that damned harp," Walter said.

Christiana suddenly thought of the perfect way to be the exact opposite of alone with David that upcoming Monday. She confessed that her dear betrothed had never had the chance to play for her. Would Sir Walter be willing to help remedy the situation?

When David arrived Monday morning, she greeted him happily. She even smiled when he kissed her.

"I have called for a mount from the stables for you," he said. "We will go to my house for dinner. You should meet the servants, and the boys need to get to know you."

The last thing she wanted was to go to his house and meet the people involved in his life. They would be greeting her as their future mistress, while she would know that she would never see them again.

"Let us go out through the hall," she suggested. "I need to see if Morvan is there. I have something to tell him."

Of course Morvan wasn't there as she knew he wouldn't be. But Sir Walter was, sitting in a corner surrounded by seven young girls. He sang a plucky love song as he played his lute, raising his eyebrows comically at the more romantic parts. The girls giggled at his exaggerated expressions.

"David!" he called, breaking off his playing as they crossed the hall.

"Walter," David greeted him warmly. He glanced down at the girls sitting on the floor. "I see that you are living an Englishman's fantasy."

The girls turned and assessed him. Christiana watched them react to his handsome face. They were all unmarried and younger than her.

"I am trying out a new lute," Walter explained, holding up the instrument. He gestured to another on the bench beside him. "But I think that I prefer the old one."

"It is always thus at first," David said. He took Christiana's arm and began to guide her away.

Christiana glared at Walter.

"Let us see how they sound together, David," Walter said quickly.

The girls clapped their hands in encouragement. David looked at Walter. He looked at the second lute. He looked at Christiana.

She smiled and tried to make her expression glitter like Joan's. She let her eyes plead a little.

With a sigh of resignation he stepped through the girls and sat beside Walter, taking the lute on his lap. Walter mumbled something and they both began playing a song about spring.

They played a long while, until the hall began filling for dinner. Whenever David attempted to finish, the girls would whine and cajole. There came a point when Christiana could tell that he had given up, that he knew that he was trapped for the duration. After that he even enjoyed himself, trading jokes with Walter and finally singing a song on his own.

It was a love song that she had never heard before. The melody was lyrical and slow and a little sad. Christiana closed her eyes and felt her own sadness stirred by it.

Her thoughts turned to Stephen and the melancholy swelled. She lost track of the next few songs as her heart and worry dwelled on him. Then the girls moved around her and she became alert again. The merry group broke up and Walter insisted that David dine with him. David accepted and then helped her to her feet. Briefly he looked at her, then smiled and shook his head in amusement.

They did not go to his house. She did not meet the people there. More importantly, they were not alone all day. When she finally returned to Isabele's apartment, Idonia and Joan had returned, and so his departing kiss was as light and discreet as his greeting.

Christiana stepped out of the silvery pink wedding gown and handed it to the tailor, who managed adroitly not to see her standing in her shift.

This marriage business did wonders for a girl's wardrobe. She could not feel excited about this new cotehardie, however. The cost made her feel guilty because she knew that it would never be worn. It would be in extremely poor taste to run off with Stephen in defiance of the Queen but still take the gown that the Queen had purchased.

What really bothered her about this gown, however, was its relentless progress toward completion. These fittings had become unwelcome but unavoidable reminders that time kept passing far too quickly. Half of the five weeks had passed, and still she had no word from Stephen Percy.

A servant helped her into her plain purple cotehardie

and blue surcoat. She sent the woman off to find Joan while she slipped on some low boots.

It was Friday, almost three weeks since her betrothal, and she would be seeing David this afternoon instead of next Monday because he would be out of the city then. They were going to the horse fair and races at Smithfield, which she thought might be fun.

Before they got there, however, she had a thing to two to say to Master David de Abyndon.

David rode into Westminster flanked by Sieg and Andrew.

Sieg was frowning. "Now, if pretty young Joan comes out with her, I leave and Andrew stays," he said. "But if the little bit of fire from hell, that Lady Idonia, shows up, it's the other way around."

"I'm afraid so, Sieg," David said. On his left Andrew smirked.

Sieg frowned some more. "And whoever stays is to distract the other female so she's not in the way."

David nodded. He had used Christiana's own lie about the Queen insisting that the girls not be alone with men to explain his need of Sieg and Andrew today. He was almost thirty years old, but this girl had reduced him to games that he'd given up at eighteen. She had avoided being alone with him since that first Tuesday and had been very clever about it. He was amused and not annoyed, but then he was growing fascinated with her and would probably excuse anything.

Their mutual attraction simply did not fit in with her plans. Her response to his kiss and embrace had badly frightened her. She acted as confused and inexperienced as an untouched virgin. That effect of innocence had charmed him almost as much as her quick passion had enflamed him.

He could avoid this game. Eventually, soon in fact, she would be his. But he found himself picturing those eyes and tasting those lips in his memory far too often for complete retreat. Besides, he did not want her rebuilding her defenses too well. He didn't relish the notion of having to choose between continence or rape on his wedding night.

"The problem as I see it," Sieg continued, "is what if Lady Idonia won't be distracted? She's like a lioness protecting her cubs."

"Hell, Sieg, you're three times her size, for heaven's sake," Andrew muttered. "Just pick her up under your arm and walk off with her."

Sieg's frown disappeared. "*Ja*? That was how I did it back home, of course, but I thought that here in England . . ."

"Andrew is jesting, Sieg."

The frown returned. "Oh. *Ja*."

David had agreed to meet Christiana in the back courtyard. She and Joan stood by two horses being held by grooms. Sieg turned his horse away and David slipped a delighted Andrew some coins. "Keep Lady Joan busy at the races and the stalls."

The grooms got the girls mounted. Christiana looked meaningfully in Andrew's direction.

"He will ride with us. He needs to see a man at the fair for me," David explained.

She seemed to accept that, and they rode together in silence. By the time that they reached the Strand, Joan and Andrew were four horse lengths ahead and Christiana didn't seem to mind.

"People have been talking about you," she said at last. David got the impression that she had waited for exactly the moment when Joan was too far ahead to hear what she said.

"People?"

"At court. Talking about you. Us. Everything."

"It was bound to happen, Christiana."

"Not these things. They weren't bound to be talked about because they are very unusual."

"You needn't turn to the court gossips. I will tell you anything you want to know."

She raised her eyebrows. "Will you? Well, first of all, some ladies have spoken to me on your behalf. Told me how wonderful you are."

"Which ladies?" he asked cautiously.

"Lady Elizabeth for one."

That surprised him. He and Elizabeth had an old friendship, but it was not her style to interfere in such things. "I am honored if Lady Elizabeth speaks well of me."

"And Alicia."

Hell.

Christiana's face was a picture of careful indifference. "Are you Lady Alicia's lover?"

"Did she say that?"

"Nay. There was something in the way that she spoke, however."

When he had offered to tell her anything, this was not what he had in mind. "I do not think that we want to pursue this, do you? I did not press you for the names of your lovers. You should not ask me for mine."

She twisted toward him abruptly. "Lovers! How dare you suggest that I have had lovers! I told you of one man."

"You told me of a current man. There may have been others, but as I said, I have been open-minded and not asked."

"Of course there were no others!"

"There is no of course to it. But it matters not." He

smiled inwardly at her dismay. "Christiana, I am almost thirty years old and I have not been a monk. I do not plan on being unfaithful to you. However, if our marriage is cold, I imagine that I will do as men have always done and find warmth elsewhere."

He had deliberately broached a topic that she would not want to talk about. As he expected, she had no response. So much for Lady Alicia. She would change the subject now. He waited.

"That is the least of what I have heard," she said.

"Somehow I thought so."

Her lids lowered. "Did you buy me?"

He had been wondering when she would hear of it. "Nay."

"Nay? I heard that Edward demanded a bride price. A big one. Morvan says it is true."

He had been waiting for this. He was ready. "A bride price is not the same as buying someone. Bride prices have an ancient tradition in England. Women were honored thus in the old days. With dowries, the woman is secondary to the property. It is as if a family pays someone to take her off their hands. If you think about it, dowries are much more insulting than bride prices."

"Then it is true?"

He chose his words carefully. If she found out the truth twenty years from now, he wanted to be able to say that he hadn't lied. "Your brother has seen the contract, as you will soon. There is no point in denying that there is a bride price in it."

"And instead of being insulted, you say that I should feel honored."

"Absolutely. Would you prefer if the King had just given you to me?"

"I would prefer if the King had continued to forget that I existed," she snapped.

They rode in silence for a minute. "How big is it? This honorable bride price?" she finally asked.

So Morvan had not told her. She would see the contract soon. David thought of the complicated formula it contained.

"How good are you at ciphering?" he asked casually.

"Excellent."

She would be. "One thousand pounds."

She stopped her horse and gaped at him. "One thousand pounds! An earl's income? Why?"

"Edward would hear of no less. I assure you that I bargained very hard. I personally thought that three hundred would be generous."

Her eyes narrowed suspiciously. "Morvan is right. This marriage never made any sense. Now it makes less."

"Aren't you worth one thousand pounds?"

"You must have been drunk when you made this offer. You will no doubt be relieved when I get you off the hook."

"He has come then?"

She ignored that. "Just as well for your health, too, that I will end this betrothal soon. I have heard about my brother's threat to you."

"Ah. That."

"Wednesday, they say."

"I expect Thursday," he corrected calmly. "Does your brother know that you have heard of this?"

"Of course. I went to him at once and told him that I wouldn't have it."

"Your concern touches me."

"Aye. Well, he wouldn't hear me. But, of course, you won't meet him."

"Of course I will."

She stopped her horse again. Joan and Andrew were far in the distance now. "You cannot be serious."

"What choice do I have?"

"You will not be in town Monday. Can't you extend your trip?"

"Eventually I must come back."

"Oh dear." She frowned fretfully.

He looked at her pretty puckered brow. "He will not kill me."

"Oh, it isn't that," she replied with ruthless honesty. "This just makes a messy situation messier. First a duel, then an abduction, then an annulment . . . well, it will make a terrific scandal."

"Perhaps someone will write a song about it."

"This is not humorous, David. You really should withdraw or leave. Morvan's sword is not a laughing matter. He may not kill you, but he may hurt you very badly."

"Aye. One thousand pounds is one thing. An arm or a leg is another. I certainly hope that you are worth it."

"How can you jest?"

"I am not jesting. But let me worry about Morvan, my lady. Are there any other rumors and gossip that you need to discuss?"

They had approached the city and began circling around its wall to the north. "Aye. Not all of the ladies who know you were so complimentary. Lady Catherine spoke with me. And with Morvan."

David waited. He would not assume what story Lady Catherine had given them.

"She told me that you are a moneylender," Christiana said quietly, as if she didn't want to be overheard by passing riders.

He almost laughed at her circumspection. The girl lived in a world that didn't exist anymore, full of virtuous knights and honored duty and stories of King Arthur's roundtable. King Edward carefully nurtured these illusions at his court with his pageants and festivals and tournaments. A mile away, within the gates of London, time moved on.

"It is true. Most merchants loan money."

"Usury is a sin."

"Perhaps so, but moneylending is a business. It is widely done, Christiana, and none think twice about it anymore. England could not survive without it. One of my sinful loans is to the King at his demand. Two others are to abbeys."

"So you just loan to the King and abbeys?"

"With others I purchase property and resell it back later at an agreed-upon time and price."

"At a profit?"

"Why else would I do it? I have no kinship or friendship with these people. However, often when I sell it back, my management has improved the income, so perhaps the profit is theirs."

"When the time is up, what if they cannot repurchase it?"

He had been trying to put a better face on this for her sake, and he cursed himself now. He had sworn he would not make excuses to this girl for being what he was. "I sell it elsewhere," he said bluntly.

She chewed on that awhile. "Why not keep it?"

It wasn't the argument he had expected. He thought that she would upbraid him for unkindness and chant sentimental pleas for the poor borrowers.

"I don't keep it because of King Edward's damned decrees saying any man with income from land over forty pounds a year has to be knighted. He has almost caught me twice."

"What do you mean, caught you? To be a knight is a wonderful thing. They are more respected than merchants, and of higher degree. You would better yourself if you were knighted."

She said it simply and innocently, stating a basic fact of life. She was oblivious to the insult and so he chose to ignore it. This time.

"Well, I am a merchant, and content as such."

One would have thought that he told her that he would rather be a devil than a saint. "You mean this, don't you?" she asked curiously. "You really don't want to be a knight."

"No one does, Christiana, except those born to it. Even many born to it avoid it. It is why Edward issues those decrees. The realm doesn't have enough knights for his ambitions. The position holds less and less appeal, so Edward plays up the chivalry and elevates the knights higher to compensate." He paused. He would be marrying this girl. He would try to explain. "It is not cowardice or fear of arms. Every London citizen swears to protect the city and realm. We must practice at arms and own what armor we can afford. I have a whole suit of the damn plate. We defend our city and send troops on Edward's wars. Many apprentices are excellent bowmen and Andrew has even mastered the longbow. But if you think about the military life honestly, it has little to recommend it."

"It is a glorious life! Full of honor and strength."

"It is a life of killing, girl. For good causes or personal gain, in honor or in murder, knights live to kill. In the end, for all of the pretty words in the songs, that is what they do. Their wars disrupt trade, ruin agriculture, and burn towns and villages. When they are victorious they rape and they steal all that they can move."

He had lost his patience and this tirade simply poured out. She stared at him as if he had slapped her, and he regretted the outburst. She was young and had lived a sheltered life. It shouldn't surprise him that she had never questioned the small protected world in which she had dwelled.

He had been too hard on her. It was her father and brother whom he described, after all. "I have no doubt that there are still many knights who are true to their honor and their vows," he said by way of a peace offering. "It is said that your brother is such a man."

That seemed to release her from the brutal reality he had thrown at her.

"Did Lady Catherine say anything else that concerns you?"

"Not to me. She said that she told Morvan something important. He said that it was nothing of significance, and then lectured me about not being friends with her."

"Good instruction, Christiana. I do not want you having anything to do with the woman."

"I think that I am old enough to choose my own friends."

"Not this one. When we are married, you are to avoid her."

Her irritation with him was visible, but she held her tongue. She turned her attention to the road as they approached Smithfield.

CHAPTER 6

SMITHFIELD ABUTTED LONDON'S north wall. Around the periphery of the racing area, horse traders had their animals tethered and lively bargaining was underway. Buyers often asked to have the horse run before purchasing, and that was how the informal races had developed. The crowds attracted to this spectacle in turn drew hawkers, food vendors, and entertainers, and so, every Friday, Smithfield, the site of London's livestock markets, was transformed into a festival site.

They found a man with whom to leave the horses and plunged into the crowd. Andrew immediately guided Joan off in a separate direction. Christiana, still thoughtful over their discussion, did not notice. She walked with her hands and arms under her cloak, her pale face flushed from the cold.

"Let us look at the horses," David said. "You will need one once you leave the castle."

"I don't want you to buy me a horse, David."

"You will not be using the royal stables after we are wed. We will find a suitable horse today."

"After I am wed, I will not be riding your suitable horse, since I will not be wed to *you*."

"Then I will sell it. For convenience, we will see if there is one while you are here to choose. Just in case."

She suppressed the urge to get stubborn and fell into step beside him as they went to survey the animals.

As they walked around the field examining and discussing the horses, they found several possibilities. Toward the end of their circuit they came upon a most suitable horse, a beautiful small black palfrey. The owner produced a saddle, and Christiana tried him out. While David came to terms with the man and arranged for delivery to Westminster's stables, she scanned the crowd for signs of the long-absent Joan and Andrew. The field was too big and busy for her to find them. Just like Joan to forget the reason for coming in the first place.

A bear baiter and some dancers arrived to entertain. Christiana had no interest in the bear, but the dancers fascinated her. At court she tried never to miss dancers of any kind. This group was fairly rustic and unschooled compared to others she had seen, but still she followed their movements to the simple music for a long while. A part of her envied these women who were permitted to let the music entrance them, whose bodies swayed and curved and angled like moving pictures.

"I would have liked to be a dancer."

"You dance at banquets and feasts, do you not?" David asked.

She blushed. She hadn't even realized that she had spoken out loud. "Aye. But that is different. That is like a dinner conversation." She gestured to the women. "This is like a meditation, I think. Sometimes I will see one who looks to be in ecstasy, who is not even aware of the world anymore."

She felt his gaze and tore her eyes away from the performance to look at him. His face held that penetrating expression that he directed at her sometimes. There was something invasive about this focused awareness, and it never failed to make her uncomfortable.

It is like I am made of glass, she thought. It wasn't fair that he could do this. He knew how to remain forever opaque to her.

"I think that you would be a beautiful dancer," he said. "If you think that dancing thus will give you pleasure, then you should do it."

Finally the dancers took a break and the crowd that had formed drifted away.

"We should find Joan," she said, peering at the crowd.

"I'm sure that we will cross paths. If not, we will meet at the horses."

She joined him and they examined the wares that the vendors sold. She wondered what Joan was up to with that apprentice, and what Lady Idonia would say if she found out that Christiana had lost track of her.

One of the vendors offered savories of fried bread dipped in honey. The smell coming from the hot oil was delicious, and she glanced over longingly as they walked by. It was messy food and just the sort of thing that Lady Idonia had never let her buy when they went to festivals.

David noticed and went to purchase some.

"It is sure to stain my clothing," she said, echoing the reason Idonia had always given for avoiding such food.

"We will manage."

He took one of the doughy savories, and gestured for her to follow him behind the stall to some trees. The vendors edged the crowd and field, and there was no one back here.

He broke off a piece of the honey-covered bread and held it out. She reached for it but he pulled it away.

"There is no reason for us both to get covered with it," he said, and placed the dough near her lips.

It smelled warm and yeasty and sweet and wonderful. Baring her teeth to avoid the fingers that held it, she stretched her neck forward and took the morsel in her mouth. It tasted heavenly and she rolled her eyes at the pleasure.

He laughed and broke off another small piece. She stretched for it. "I must look like a chicken," she giggled with her mouth full.

Those long fingers fed her again. She felt some honey dripping down her lip and licked to catch it. He gently flicked it away, the pad of his finger grazing the edge of her mouth. Her lower lip quivered at the sensation, and her face and neck tingled.

The last piece was too big and she had to bite into it. Her teeth nipped his fingertips and she blushed, awkwardly conscious of the contact. He still held out the rest of it, and her gaze stayed on that beautiful hand as she chewed quickly and then hesitantly took the last of the savory.

His hand did not move away this time, but followed her head back. His fingertips brushed her lips and rested there. The dough suddenly felt very thick in her mouth.

She looked up at his face and saw the slight hardness around his mouth. His lids lowered as he watched her lips move beneath his hand. An odd stillness descended, and she swallowed the last of the sweet dough with difficulty.

With a deliberate movement and watchful eyes, he ran his finger around the edge of her mouth, collecting the errant honey, and then wiped the sweetness onto her lips.

She had a sudden shocking urge to lick the last of the

honey off those fingers. He looked in her eyes as if he understood. One by one, he wiped his fingers across her mouth like a repeated invitation to her impulse, layering the sticky remains on her lips.

The gesture mesmerized her. The sounds of the field and races receded to a distant roar. In the still silence that engulfed her, she could hear her heart beat harder with the light pressure of each small caress. The exciting intensity that she always sensed in him spread to surround her.

He looked at her a long moment when he finished. Then he abruptly took her hand and pulled her back amongst the trees. She stumbled after him, not really cooperating but not resisting either. Breathless anticipation claimed her as they left the sanctuary of the field. She told herself that she did not want to do this, that she would not go with him, but she went anyway.

He dragged her behind a large oak. With his arm, around her shoulders he pulled her into an embrace. The other arm slid under her cloak and around her waist, pressing her body to his body as he kissed her.

Those new sensations that had snuck up on her so insidiously the last time suddenly exploded all at once. It was if they had been carefully corralled for two weeks but now he had opened the gate and waved them to a frenzy. The intimacy of the embrace felt exhilarating, and a thundering tremor full of sharp sensual spikes shook her from her neck to her thighs.

He gentled his kiss and began biting and licking the honey off her lips in an unhurried way, pulling her yet closer to him. She became very alert but only to him and each touch of warmth on her mouth. Awareness of everything else washed away beneath the stunning waves of slow, tight heat that coursed over and over through her body.

His tongue grazed against her lips, inviting her to open to him. With the one thread of reason still left, she kept her mouth resolutely closed. He smiled before moving his mouth down.

Did she deliberately throw her head back so that he could reach the hollow at the base of her neck? She didn't know for sure, but his mouth was there suddenly and her arms were up and around his shoulders, and both of his hands grasped her beneath her cloak, holding her, bending her up to his kisses.

She grew acutely aware of every touch, every kiss, every wonderful strange reaction that she felt. Her upraised arms brought her body closer to his, and through the stretched fabric of her clothing she could feel his muscles and warmth tingling her breasts. The pressure of his hands around her felt both dangerous and comforting. Her awareness became full of something else, too, something commanding and expectant and connected to the hollow tension that spread through her belly. It was that as much as the exquisite feelings that kept her from stopping him. Vaguely, dully, her mind considered that he was luring her toward something that she did not really understand.

He kissed her mouth again, and his hands moved. Slowly, gently, he caressed down and up her sides beneath her cloak, his fingers splaying around the outer swells of her breasts. Shockingly, insistently, they moved down her back and over her buttocks and up her hips. The tightness in her belly ached and somewhere low inside her a throbbing demand pounded.

One hand stayed on her hips but the other moved up. She knew what he was going to do. She remembered Stephen's crushing grip and tensed, almost finding her senses, almost finding the strength to push him away.

But he did not crush her. His fingers stroked around

the edge of her breast in a gentle, delicate way, tantalizing her to an excruciating anticipation of she knew not what. Her breath quickened to a series of short gasps as her whole body waited.

When he finally caressed her breast, she bit back a moan. The pleasure startled her. She tried to pull away.

He would not let her go. Kissing her beautifully, caressing her softly, he summoned delicious feelings. His fingers touched her as if no cloth lay between them and her skin, finding her nipple and playing with it until that throbbing sensation low by her thighs became almost unbearable. He took the yearning hard bud between his thumb and finger and rubbed gently. This time she could not catch the small cry before it escaped her.

His mouth went to her ear and kissed and probed before his quiet voice flowed into her.

"Come back to my house with me. It is but a few minutes from here through the gate."

"Why?" she muttered, still floating in the sensual stupor that his hand created.

"Why? For one thing you should visit and meet the people who live there," he said, lifting his head to kiss her temple and brow. His hand still caressed her and she found it hard to pay attention to what he said. "For another, I am too old to make love behind trees and hedges."

Naming what they were doing intruded like a loud noise on a dream. The sounds of the races instantly thundered around her. His hand on her body suddenly felt scandalous. Burning with shame, she looked away.

"This is wrong," she said.

"Nay. It is very right."

"You know what I mean."

His hand fell away from her breast, but still he held her.

"Did your lover give you such pleasure?" he asked softly.

She blushed deeper. She could not look at him.

"I thought not."

"It was different," she said accusingly. "We are in love. This is . . . is . . ." What? What was this horrible, wonderful thing?

"Desire," he said.

So this was desire. No wonder the priests always preached against it. Desire seemed a very dangerous thing indeed.

"Well, girl, if I had to have one without the other, I would choose this," he said. "Desire can grow into something more, but if it isn't there at the beginning it never comes, and love dies without it."

He was lecturing her like a child again. She truly resented when he did that. "This is wrong," she repeated firmly, pushing a little, putting some distance between their bodies. "You know it is. You are luring me. It isn't fair."

"Luring you? Why would I do that?"

"Who knows why you do any of this? Why offer for me in the first place? Why pay the bride price?" She studied him. "Maybe you want to bed me so that when he comes, the betrothal cannot be annulled."

"It is a good idea. But that never occurred to me, because I know that he is not coming."

He had said that since the first night. Calmly, relentlessly he had repeated it. "You cannot know that," she snapped. But there had been something in his voice this time that terrified her. As if he did know. Somehow.

"He is not here, Christiana. He has had your message a long time now."

"Perhaps not. Maybe the messenger couldn't find him."

"I have spoken with the messenger whom you hired. He delivered the letter into the hands of the man to whom you sent it ten days after you wrote it."

"You spoke . . . you interfered in this? How dare you!"

"It is well that I did. Your messenger had no intention of leaving at once for your mission. He planned to wait until other business took him north. It could have been weeks. Even then he might have handed it off to any number of other people along the way and spared himself the trip."

"But he went at once for you? And delivered it directly?"

"I paid him a lot of money to do so. And to offer to bring a letter back."

She had been given no return letter. A frightening sadness tried to overwhelm her. She didn't want to hear what David was saying, didn't want to consider the implications. The messenger had been back for a while. If he could return in this time, so could Stephen. He could have at least sent a note. But perhaps the messenger had admitted doing her betrothed's bidding and Stephen did not want to risk it.

Fortunately her anger at David defeated her forebodings, or she might have been undone right there. She glared up at him. "Do you enjoy this? Destroying people's lives?"

He gave her a very hard look, but it quickly softened. His hand left her side and stroked her face. "In truth, it will pain me to see you hurt."

"Then help me," she cried impulsively. "Set me free and help me to go to him."

He looked at her in that way that made her feel transparent. "Nay. Because he does not want you enough to hold on to you, girl, and I find that I do."

For an instant, while he looked at her, she had

thought that she saw wavering, that he might actually do what she asked. His words crushed the small hope. Petulantly she shook off his arms and moved away. "I want to go back to Westminster now."

Wordlessly he led her back to the vendors and over to a woman selling little bits of lace. He spoke a few words to the woman, and then turned to her. "This is Goodwife Mary. Stay with her while I go and find Andrew and Lady Joan. Do not move from here," he ordered before walking away into the crowd.

She got the impression that he wanted to get away from her, and she was glad that he was gone, too. He gave her commands the way that Morvan did, and she resented it. *We will ride north. We will buy a horse. Stand here and do not move.* She was glad that they would not be marrying. Living with him would be like having her brother around all of the time, picking at her behavior. Lady Idonia could always be tricked and subverted. This man would be too shrewd for that.

She was glad that he had left for another reason. She never had any peace with him nearby. She knew now that it had to do with what had just occurred beneath the tree. Something of that excitement, of that anticipation, was there between them even when they just rode down the Strand and talked. Merely thinking about those wonderful feelings could call up her tingling responses again.

Desire, he had called it. She did not much like this desire. She did not like the invisible ties it wove between them. The excitement she had felt with Stephen seemed a thin and childish thing in comparison, and she didn't like that either.

Stephen. He had not come yet, had not sent a letter back. . . . A horrible, vacant ache gripped her chest. She would not think about that, would not doubt him. She especially would not contemplate what it might imply about her and David de Abyndon.

"There you are!" Joan came skipping toward her with Andrew.

Christiana glanced at her friend. Joan looked flush-faced and beautiful. A piece of hay stuck out of her hair.

"Aye, here I am. David has gone looking for you and ordered me to wait here like a child." She eyed the hay and plucked it out. "Where have you been?"

"Oh, everywhere," Joan cried. "This is much more fun if Lady Idonia isn't with us."

"I can only imagine." She held up the hay and raised her eyebrows. Andrew flushed and moved away.

Joan shrugged. "There was a hay wagon beneath a tree and we climbed the tree and jumped in. It was a lot of fun."

"I thought that you were in love with Thomas Holland."

"I am. We just played."

"Joan! He is an apprentice!"

"Oh, you are as bad as Idonia. We only kissed once."

"You kissed . . . for heaven's sake!"

Joan's eyes narrowed. "It was only one kiss. It isn't as if I am going to marry him."

She said it lightly, but the warning was unmistakable. David had been an apprentice like Andrew, and Christiana *was* going to marry *him*. *I love you*, the voice and eyes said, *but you are in no position to criticize me*.

A new, sad emotion surged. Joan pitied her. They all pitied her, didn't they? All of the desire and pleasure in the world could not balance that out, could it?

David emerged from the crowd then. He silently collected them and led the way to the horses.

"He looks angry," Joan whispered. "What did you do?"

It was more a matter of what she didn't do, Christiana suspected. Still, she found herself rather pleased that he was angry. Maybe because this was the first clear emotion that she had ever seen in him. It was the first time that she knew what he was thinking.

They retrieved the horses and headed toward Westminster. Joan and Andrew fell back and began talking again, but David tried to move at a fast pace. At first Christiana kept up with him, but then she simply slowed her horse and let him pull ahead. Shortly he slowed as well and rode beside her. She rather enjoyed making him do that.

His silence became oppressive, and after noting with a sigh that he brooded when angry just like Morvan, she stopped paying him any attention. She occupied herself with speculation about Stephen's home in Northumberland. The worry that David had given her about Stephen quickly disappeared as she found a variety of excuses for his delay in writing or coming back.

"You are thinking about him again, aren't you?" His voice, hard and quiet, intruded on her.

"What makes you say that?" she asked guiltily.

"The look on your face, girl. It is written all over you."

She was very sure that her expression showed nothing when she thought about Stephen. In fact, she worked at it. But then, David always seemed to see and know more than she wanted him to.

"You are a coward, Christiana," he said quietly, but the angry edge was unmistakable. "It would seem that I am too real for you. You refuse to see the truth. Not just about your lover not coming and this marriage really happening, but about us."

"There is no reality to face about us."

"I want you and you want me. That is very real. But it doesn't rhyme with the song that you have composed, does it? You continue to live the lyrics that you wrote in ignorance about this man and yourself."

"I do not live according to some song."

"Of course you do. Duels and abductions are the stuff of songs, not life. Do lutes play when you think of the man who used you? Are your memories colored like the images on painted cloth and tapestries?"

She looked away, trembling at these harsh words that spoke an understanding of her mind that no one should have. She suddenly felt helpless again against the fears those words raised in her. He was horrible to say that Stephen only used her. Cruel. She hated him.

His voice sounded raw and angry when he spoke again. "I should send you to him and let you see how your song ends."

"Why don't you then?" she cried.

He stopped both their horses. His hand came over and took her chin. She resisted its guiding turn.

"Look at me," he ordered.

She deliberately turned away. His hand forced her head around to him. His blue eyes flashed with something dangerous.

"Because he would use you again before he is honest with you. The past is one thing, but you belong to me now. I will let no one else have you so easily. Do not ever forget that."

She suddenly realized that his mood had to do with more than her refusing him. It involved something bigger. It was about her and him and Stephen.

Was he jealous? Of Stephen? It was so unlike him to show his reactions, and this anger flamed hot and alive and visible. Was this emotion one that he was not accustomed to controlling?

Anger unleashed something frightening in this man, and it made her especially unsettled that the fear itself seemed touched with that other tension that always seemed to exist between them.

Westminster looked like a haven from a storm when they finally arrived. She hopped off her horse before anyone could help her and ran inside without so much as glancing back at David de Abyndon.

CHAPTER 7

CHRISTIANA LIFTED HER knees and rested her head on the edge of the large wooden tub. The warm water almost reached the top, and positioned like this, she could float a little in the soothing heat. A circular tent of linen enclosed the tub and held in the steam, creating a humid, sultry environment that loosened her tense muscles.

The castle had been practically empty when she called for the servants to prepare this bath. A rumor spreading through Westminster that Morvan was to meet David on London Bridge had drawn the bored courtiers like flies to a savory. Idonia had stayed behind with her, but Isabele and Joan had attached themselves to a group including young Prince John and Thomas Holland.

Not everyone approved of this duel. Some of the older knights considered it unchivalrous to challenge a mere merchant, but even they understood Morvan's anger. Since the duel was to be so public, everyone assumed that Morvan meant only to humiliate David, and that made it more acceptable, too. After all, these merchants often forgot their place. In overwhelming David, Morvan would be reminding all of London that wealth could never replace breeding and nobility when it really mattered.

She closed her eyes and tried to get the knot in her stomach to untie. She prayed that David had delayed his return to London as she had advised. She had offered a number of such prayers during the last few days as this duel approached. She wouldn't want to see David harmed. He had become a friend of sorts, and she had rather grown to depend on his presence.

She had been thinking about him a lot since that day at Smithfield. Sometimes she listened to the remembered quiet voice in the King's private corridor. The more she thought about it, the more it sounded like David who had been approached by Frans van Horlst that day. Other times her mind drifted to the two of them under the oak tree. Those memories were both compelling and disturbing, and tended to sneak up on her when she least expected them.

Which would be worse? If David had returned from his journey, he would face her brother in front of hundreds of people and be made to look a fool. If he had not returned, the whole world would know him for a coward. Morvan and the court would probably prefer the latter. The lesson would be taught without a sword ever being raised.

Her brother did this out of love for her and concern for the family's honor, but she really wished he had stayed out of things. He was only making a complicated situation worse, and he might well ruin her plans completely. Did Morvan think that the humiliation would make David withdraw? In all likelihood it would only make him more stubborn. He might even refuse to honor his promise to let her go with Stephen.

Of course, Stephen wasn't here and the wedding was only twelve days away. She tried not to think about that, but it was becoming difficult. It was one thing to wait patiently and another to see the sun relentlessly set every day on your unfulfilled dreams. Lately she had found herself listening for horses whenever she went outside. Perhaps he planned some dramatic abduction soon. She imagined him riding down the river road with his boon companions in attendance, maybe on the day before the wedding itself. Would he wait that long? How would he get to her and get her out? There were always so many people about.

She sat up abruptly.

There were hardly any people about right now.

Morvan had been nowhere to be found this morning as the rumor of his duel on London Bridge spread. Who had started those whispers? Morvan himself? Or someone else who wanted Westminster emptied of all but the essential guard?

A heady excitement gripped her. Was Stephen coming for her today? If so, the plan was audacious and brilliant. She couldn't be sure, but it suddenly all made sense. If he had learned of the duel and its location from one of his friends here, he might well make use of it in this way. She hadn't realized that he was that clever.

Smiling happily, she quickly washed herself. She felt the knot of hair piled high on her head and considered whether she had time to wash and dry it.

Her arm froze at the sound of boot steps entering the wardrobe where the tub sat in front of a hearth.

She couldn't believe it! Finally! She eagerly parted the drape to greet her love.

Her gaze fell on beautiful leather boots and a starkly plain blue pourpoint. A sword hung from one belt and two daggers from another. Deep blue eyes regarded her, reading her thoughts like she was made of glass.

"You were expecting someone else?" David asked. He undid the sword belt and placed the weapon on the top of one of the chests that lined that walls of the wardrobe.

She let the drape fall closed and sank into the water.

"Nay. I just wasn't expecting you," she responded through the curtain of cloth.

"I said that I would come. But perhaps you thought that I would be dead."

"Badly wounded at least, if you were fool enough to meet him. Why aren't you?" That didn't come out the way she had planned, and she grimaced. It sounded like she was annoyed that he was whole.

"Edward stopped it as I knew he would. He is counting on that bride price, you see."

She heard him walk over to the wall by the door. He didn't leave.

What if she was right and Stephen came now? He would find David here. Morvan may not have drawn blood, but Stephen just might.

"You have to go, David."

"I think not."

"I must finish my bath. I will attend on you in the hall shortly."

"I will stay here. It is warm and very pleasant."

She splashed the water angrily.

"You are giving him too much credit for drama and intelligence, my girl. Stephen Percy is not in London or Westminster. His is not coming today or any day for a long while."

She sank her shoulders down under the water. *He knows what I am thinking. He knows Stephen's name. Is there anything that he doesn't know?*

"I sent the court to London Bridge, Christiana. I

wanted no one to follow your brother to the place where we really met."

"Why? So that no one would see him best you?"

"Nay. So if he forced me to kill him, I could lie to you and you would never know the truth of it."

The chamber became very still. It was absurd, of course. David could never hurt Morvan. When it came to skill at arms . . . and yet . . .

Footsteps came over to the tub. The drape parted and he handed her a towel through the slit. "Enough of this for now. The water must be cooling. Get out and dry yourself."

She grabbed the towel and jerked the drape closed. She waited as he walked away.

The water was indeed cooling and the steam had disappeared. It was getting chilly in the bath.

"Call the servant, please. She is in the chamber."

"I sent her away."

She looked down at her nakedness. She listened to the silence of the empty castle. She thought of her clothes piled on a stool by the hearth. The bath was losing its warmth quickly, but the chill that shook her had nothing to do with the water.

"Idonia should be returning soon, David. It will embarrass me if she finds you in here."

"Lady Idonia decided to take a ride with Sieg. A very long ride, I should think."

Her annoyance flared at this game he played with her. She grabbed the towel and stood in the water, drying her arms and body with hurried movements.

She would show this merchant what noblewomen were made of.

She draped the large linen towel around her, catching its ends under her arm. She stepped out of the tub and kicked aside the drape. Water from her legs began pooling on the wooden floor.

He sat atop a high chest next to the hearth, his back against the wall and one arm resting on a raised knee. His cool gaze met hers and then drifted down in a lazy way. She fought down the alarm that rose in her chest.

He had placed another log on the fire, and the small wardrobe, crowded with chests that held Isabele's gowns and furs, felt warm enough. She sat on a stool by the tub and patted the ends of the long towel against her legs to dry them.

She did not look at him but she knew that he watched her. She worked hard not to let him see that it unsettled her.

"How did you know his name?" she asked, proud of how casual her voice sounded. Almost as casual and placid as his did all of the time. Except when he was jealous. She groaned inwardly at her stupidity. Perhaps it would be best to avoid talk of Stephen Percy under the circumstances.

"I've known who he was from the beginning. Don't look so surprised. You all but told me his name that first night. I also know that you are not the first innocent girl whom he has seduced, nor will you be the last. Some men have a taste for such things, and he is one of them."

His words probed at forbidden thoughts buried deep in her heart, thoughts that tried to surface late at night as she lay in her bed and counted days passing and days left. She had walled those worries into a dark corner, and she rebelled at this man going near them.

She glared at him. *He sits there so damned calmly*, she thought. *He looks at me like he has a right to be here. Like he owns me.* She braced herself against the feelings of vulnerability and tension which that look summoned.

"I hate you," she muttered.

His lids lowered. "Careful, girl. I may decide to encourage your hatred. I find that I prefer it to your indifference."

He hopped off the chest. The movement made her tense.

"You still wait for him," he said. "After all of this time and when the truth is so clear. It is well that Edward gave you to me. You would have spent your whole life waiting and living in a faded dream."

"Perhaps I still will." She spoke the words like a bold threat.

"Nay. You wake up today."

He stepped toward her. She rose from her stool at once, clutching the towel around her and backing up. He stopped.

She didn't like the way he watched her. Even worse, she didn't like the way that she was reacting to it. For all of her annoyance, that exquisite expectation branched through her. Sharp and vivid memories of the pleasure she had felt at Smithfield forced themselves onto her thoughts and her body.

"I demand that you leave," she said.

He shook his head. "Your brother is out of this now. So is Stephen Percy. There was no duel and there will be no abduction. Finally it is just you and me."

Her heart pounded desperately. "You are frightening me, David."

"At least I have your attention for a change. Besides, I told you before. It is not fear that you feel with me."

"It is now." And it was. A horrible, wonderful combination of fear and anticipation and attraction and denial. Like the lines of a rope twined in on each other, they twisted and twisted together, pulling and stretching her soul. If he didn't leave, she was sure that something would snap.

"If you won't leave, I shall." Somehow she found enough composure to speak calmly.

He gestured to the clothes on the stool to his right and the door to his left. "I will not stop you, Christiana."

She had to pass him to leave. Was it her imagination that his blue eyes dared her to approach? *He is enjoying this*, she thought, and the vexation surged in her again, vanquishing those other feelings for a moment and making her brave.

The daughter of Hugh Fitzwaryn need not be afraid of a tradesman, she thought firmly. A noblewoman could walk naked down the Strand and her status would protect her and clothe her as surely as steel. How many tailors and haberdashers of David's degree had seen her dressed in no more than a shift as they waited upon the princess and her friends? This towel covered her more. Such men did not exist if one chose to have it so.

Aye. It would even be thus with David de Abyndon.

She lowered her eyes and collected herself. She imagined that he was a mercer who had come to show his wares. She let her spirit withdraw from him and from those strange feelings that he summoned so easily, and she wrapped herself in the knowledge of who she was and what he was.

Lifting her gaze, she looked more to the hearth than to him. Holding the towel around her, she calmly walked over to the stool and bent her knees so as to reach the garments.

Fingers stroked firmly into her hair and twisted. The clothes fell from her hand as he yanked her up. Gasping with shock, she found her face inches away from flaming blue eyes.

"Do not do that again," he warned. "Ever."

She was looking into the face of danger and she knew it. She did not move. She barely breathed.

Slowly, as he held her and looked at her, the flames cooled and the hardness left his eyes and mouth. She could see when he regained control and the anger fell from his perfect face.

The expression that replaced it was just as dangerous in its own way, though. His hand did not release her hair. If anything, it gripped a little tighter.

He looked over her face slowly and then down at her bare shoulders and neck. She watched his gaze drift to the damp towel clutched against her body. She had never been so thoroughly looked at in her life. His unhurried possessive inspection left her as breathless and tingling as a caress.

He pulled her toward him. A tremor of fearful anticipation quaked through her. Her legs almost wouldn't support her as her body followed her head. He lowered his mouth to hers.

She fought the emotions. She battled them valiantly with every bit of her strength of will. But her defenses had never been very strong against his kisses, and as this one deepened and his other arm embraced her, she melted against him as those wonderful sensations took control of her.

His mouth moved beautifully over her face and neck and ears and shoulders, kissing and biting gently, drawing softly at the pulse points. He played at the lines of tension stretching through her like they were the strings on a lute, luring her toward acceptance. She knew what was happening, but the pleasure of the heated shocks that spiraled from each kiss made her want more, and the gentle waves flowing through her from his caress on her back promised an ocean of oblivious delight.

He tugged gently at the back of the towel. She fought to the surface of her sensual sea.

"Nay," she whispered.

"Aye," he said.

The towel's edge dislodged from under her arm and fell away from her back. That fear that wasn't fear shrieked and she clutched the edge of the linen tighter to her chest, her arms crossing her breasts.

He did not try to remove it. Untangling his hand from her hair, he embraced her tightly so that her arms were imprisoned between their bodies. He lowered his mouth to the skin just above her hands while his embrace moved down her back.

The feel of his warm hands on her bare skin exhilarated her. Even her awareness of his kisses dimmed as all of her senses focused on those heated caresses. Her whole being waited and felt and savored the progress of that touch. Low and deep in her body that strange pulse began throbbing.

He took her mouth again and his hands went lower, down to her hips and lower back, down finally to her bottom. She started in surprise but he kissed her harder and his hands stayed there, following the swells of her body. That secret pulse grew aching and hot, and she dully realized that it was deep in her belly near her thighs and his hands were very close to it.

The feelings were too exquisite, too delicious to stop him. The voice of her mind grew very quiet and weak. That rational awareness only observed, noticing the scent of the man who held her and the sound of her gasping breaths. The waiting expectation she had first felt at Smithfield obliterated any real thought and grew now into something demanding and impatient and slightly painful.

His hands drifted lower. He cupped her lower buttocks

in a caress of commanding intimacy. She gasped aloud as that throbbing center of pleasure exploded with a white heat.

His fingers rested at the very top of her thighs where they joined. She felt as she had when she waited for him to touch her breast, only the anticipation had a frantic, desperate quality to it and the pulsing expectation possessed a physical reality that stunned her.

Suddenly the fear that had always been there when he kissed and touched her rose from the depths where the pleasure had banished it. The small voice of her mind considered that something was occurring here that had never happened with Stephen.

"David . . ." she whispered, beginning a feeble protest.

He lifted his head and looked at her with a face transformed and more handsome than ever. The glowing warmth in those eyes left her speechless.

He pulled her hips closer to his. Her arms still held the towel to her chest, and she didn't stand of her own will now. The fingers near her thighs shifted as he moved her closer yet.

Her belly pressed against him. She felt warmth and hardness. That hidden place, so full of ache and yearning and so close to his hand, responded forcefully.

Her eyes flew open wide.

He bent to kiss her again. "Aye," he said quietly.

A very peculiar notion teased at her mind and then forced itself on her.

Outrageous, really.

Impossible.

As if reading her thoughts, he slid his hand between the back of her thighs and gently touched her. Effortlessly his fingers found that hungry ache.

She cried out from the shock of the pleasure. Twisting

violently, she jumped out of his arms and just stared at him.

His own reaction was just as strong. She watched breathlessly as surprise gave way to perplexity and then finally to anger. Pulling the towel back around her, she moved away, trying desperately to sort her confused thoughts and emotions.

She didn't want him angry. She wanted to explain. But explain what? That a bizarre, unnatural idea of what he wanted from her had unaccountably lodged in her mind and suddenly seemed . . . logical? She was probably wrong, and if she spoke of this to him, he would think her perverted. All the same, she didn't want him touching her again, especially like that, until she found out for sure that she hadn't grossly misunderstood everything.

He just looked at her, the beautiful warmth dimming from his eyes and the placid expression reclaiming him. She felt like a fool standing there in her towel, but she didn't know what to say.

"Very well, Christiana. If you do not want to give yourself to me now, I will wait," he finally said, walking over to pick up his sword.

Her mind reeled. *Give yourself to me*, Stephen had pleaded that day on the bed. She thought he meant in marriage. But it meant something else, didn't it? Had she gotten absolutely everything wrong?

She needed to talk to someone. Now. Soon. Who? Joan. Would Joan know?

David walked back over to the door. *Today you wake up*, he had said. Dear God, but she felt awake now. Horribly so.

"I will not return here, Christiana. We will do it your way. Today I learned that Edward will attend our wedding. Your brother and the King will deliver you to me two

Tuesdays hence. If you have need of me before that, you know where to find me."

He turned to go. Out of the jumbled confusion of her mind a question that she had pondered leapt forward. Without thinking, she blurted it out. "Who is Frans van Horlst to you?"

Perhaps because it was so unexpected and so irrelevant to what had just occurred, it startled him. He quickly composed himself.

"He is a Flemish merchant. We have business together."

He was lying. She just sensed it. *Dear God, I don't know him at all. Twelve days and I don't know him.*

The shock to her emotions had made her very alert, very awake. Inconsistencies about David suddenly presented themselves. She had never noticed them before. She had never paid attention.

There were a lot, and her suspicions about Frans van Horlst only added to them. What were these trips he took? How did he have access to Edward? Why offer for her and pay a huge bride price? Why did he have a servant who looked like a soldier? How did he know that Stephen was not coming?

He knew that for sure. She just felt it.

Finally she spoke. "Who are you? Really?"

The question startled him anew. For the briefest instant the mask dropped, and in those eyes of lapis lazuli she saw layer upon layer of shadowed emotions. Then his careful expression returned and he smiled at her. It was a faint smile that revealed nothing.

He opened the door. "You know who I am, my lady. I am the merchant who paid a fortune for the right to take you to my bed."

She stood with her arms embracing herself in the

towel and listened to his steps recede through the anteroom.

He had responded to the last question just as she had asked it, in perfect Parisian French.

Christiana waited until the deep of night when the apartment and the castle were silent before slipping out of her bed. At the end of the room, Lady Idonia slept the sleep of the dead. Christiana wasn't surprised. Idonia had returned from her ride with Sieg flush faced and bright eyed, looking very young for her thirty-eight years. Kerchief gone and hair disarrayed, she had only halfheartedly mumbled some criticisms of David's presumptuous servant and of David himself, who had ordered Sieg to carry her off.

She padded the few steps to Joan's bed and slipped between the curtains. She sat on the bed and jostled her shoulder. Total darkness wrapped the bed, and that suited her just fine. She felt like an idiot and didn't need to see Joan's amusement during this conversation.

She sensed Joan jolt wake and heard her sit up.

"It is I," Christiana whispered. "I need to speak with you. It is very important."

Little stretches and yawns filled the tented space. Joan shifted over to make more room. Christiana crossed her legs and pulled part of the coverlet over them.

"Joan, I need you to tell me what happens between a man and a woman when they are married."

"Oh my goodness," Joan said. "You mean . . . no one ever . . . Idonia didn't . . ."

"Idonia did. When I was about ten. But I think that I misunderstood." Christiana remembered well what Idonia had said to her. In its own way it had been quite straightforward, up to a point, and had struck her at the time as very peculiar and not very interesting. She suspected that Idonia had assumed that over the years common sense would fill in the essential gaps, but until this afternoon her imagination had failed her.

"You marry in less than two weeks, Christiana."

"Which is why I need to know now."

"I would say so. The notion usually takes a while to get used to."

"How long?"

"For me, about three years."

Wonderful.

"So tell me."

Joan sighed. "Let's see. Well, haven't you ever seen animals mating?"

"I have lived at court since I was seven. Where in these crowded castles and palaces do animals mate? The stables? The kennels? Not the dinner hall or the garden. I didn't grow up on a country estate like you, Joan."

"Dear saints."

"Tell me bluntly, Joan. Plain language. No gaps."

Joan took a deep breath and then explained quickly. Christiana felt more the fool with each word that she heard. Deep in her heart she had known since David touched her that it was thus, but her mind simply wouldn't accept the appalling logic of it.

Jokes suddenly made sense. Vague lines in songs abruptly became clear. Stephen's hand pushing apart her thighs . . .

He had not done this thing to her, but he had planned to. Only Idonia's arrival had saved her from that brutal shock. She hadn't even known what he was about.

David . . . good heavens.

"Can a man tell if you have done this before?" she asked cautiously.

She could feel Joan's eyes boring through the blackness. "Usually." Joan explained how they could tell. Christiana winced at the description of pain and blood.

"Are you saying that you did this and didn't know it, Christiana? That doesn't make sense."

"Nay. I thought that I had . . . I told David that I had."

Joan barely suppressed a giggle. "Well, that is a switch. Normally girls need to make excuses why there *isn't* evidence of virginity. You, on the other hand . . ."

"Don't laugh at me, Joan. This is serious."

"Aye. He may think that you lied to get out of the marriage, mayn't he?"

Aye, he may, Christiana thought dully.

Joan's hand touched her arm. "Who was it? I didn't realize there was someone. No wonder that you have been so unhappy about this betrothal. I never saw you even speak with a man more than once or twice, except maybe . . ." Her hand gripped tighter. "Is that who it was? Stephen Percy? Oh, Christiana."

She neither agreed nor disagreed. Joan knew she had guessed right, though, and in a way she was glad. It felt good to finally share that agony, even if the pain had been dulling for some time now.

Joan's hand sought hers in the dark. When she spoke, her voice was low and sympathetic. "I must tell you something. You will hear it soon, for it will be all around the court in the next day or so. Stephen's uncle was on the bridge, and Thomas and I spoke with him. He received a messenger today from Northumberland." She squeezed Christiana's hand. "Stephen was betrothed ten days ago. The match had been made when he was just a youth."

A huge, deep fissure opened up inside her, slicing through her soul as if it were carved by hot steel. It reached down to the deepest reaches, releasing at last all of those fears and suspicions and forbidden doubts. They surged and overwhelmed her.

"I am sure that he loves you," Joan said soothingly. "His family no doubt forced him to this. It is common enough when early matches are made."

Aye, common enough. Men married women they did not love or want and amused themselves elsewhere as they pleased. She suddenly and clearly saw Stephen's wooing of her as the insincere, dishonorable thing it had been. A game of seduction to pass the time even while he knew his future wife waited back home. Had Morvan's threats made the siege more interesting, more exciting?

She thought of the letter she had sent him. Had he laughed? Her ignorance about men and women had been making her feel like a fool this evening, but that was nothing compared to the devastating desolation this news of Stephen caused. Her body shook and her heart began burning and shattering. She released Joan's hand and scooted off the bed.

"I'm so sorry, Christiana," Joan said.

Controlling her emotions by a hairbreadth, she pushed through the drapery and rushed to her own bed. She threw herself on her stomach and, biting a pillow to muffle the sound, cried out her humiliation and bitter disappointment.

CHAPTER 8

SHE REMAINED IN bed for two days. During the first one, she wallowed in a bitter pain full of memories suddenly seen anew. Stephen's words and face had not changed in them, but different meanings now became terribly clear. The truth mortified her, and by day's end she was close to hating Stephen Percy for having used and humiliated her.

The next day she lay in a dumb stupor, floating mindlessly through time. The numb daze was soothing and she considered staying forever in it.

On Sunday she rose from her bed and dressed. She managed not to think about Stephen much at all, but on the few occasions that she did, a raw sore of pain and anger reopened before she pushed his memory out of her mind.

By Tuesday she felt much better and more herself again. She even laughed at a little joke that Isabele made while they dressed in the morning. The glances of relief that Idonia and Joan exchanged made her laugh again.

And then, right after dinner, the tailor arrived for the final fitting of her wedding gown, reminding her abruptly that in exactly one week she would marry David de Abyndon.

That reality had been neatly obscured by the violent emotions that had ripped through her upon hearing the news about Stephen. As she stood motionlessly in the silvery pink gown, however, she knew that it was time to face the facts about this marriage.

It was going to happen. In a week Morvan would literally hand her over to him. She would live in the house that she had refused to visit, and be mistress to a household whom she had refused to meet. The center of her life would move from Westminster's court to the merchant community of London. Her life would be tied to and owned by this man forever.

Nothing would be the same. She looked at Joan and Isabele. Would they remain her friends? Perhaps, but they would drift apart because her life would not be here. She thought about the animosity between Morvan and David. Would her husband let her see her brother again? It would be in his power to refuse it.

During her years at court, she had always been a little adrift, but her brother and her few friends had served as anchors for her. After she married, she would have only David for a long while. Without him she would be completely alone in that new life that awaited.

As she turned this way and that while the tailor inspected his work, she contemplated David. She desperately wanted to hate him for being right about Stephen, but she could not. If David had not pointed the way to the truth, would she have ever seen it? How much easier to make excuses for Stephen like Joan had done. How reassuring to avoid the real pain and continue the illusion of a true love thwarted.

She didn't know David very well, but she had come very close to not knowing him at all. In the face of her indifference to him and blind loyalty to Stephen, he had tried to prepare her.

She had left things badly with him. True to his word, he had not come back to Westminster. She had insulted him that day in ways that she didn't fully understand.

The tailor left, and she walked over to a window and gazed down into the courtyard. She pictured David riding in and dismounting, and imagined his steps coming toward the apartment. In her mind he kissed her and her skin awoke with the warmth of his lips. She let the memories fuse and progress, and she felt his firm hand on her breast. She clenched her teeth against the desire that phantom touch awakened. Finally she forced herself to picture the joining that Joan had described.

Her imagination failed her and the image disappeared as if a drape had dropped in front of it. Pain and blood the first time, according to Joan. Lured by pleasure into horror.

He would not come. *You know where to find me*, he had said. An invitation. To what, though? His company or his bed?

It surprised her what these thoughts were doing. Her heart yearned to indeed see him appear in the courtyard below. She missed him, and the knowledge that he waited for her went far to ease the pain of these last days. The fear of what he awaited could not obscure the images of his kind attention to her. Thinking of Stephen still opened hollows in her soul, but David's memory soothed the devastation.

It was whispered that he wanted her so much he had paid that bride price to have her. The idea of the marriage bed filled her with dismay, but at least David had pursued her honorably. He hadn't tried to steal what he wanted in a dusty room in a deserted passageway as Stephen had.

He had a right to know about Stephen. More importantly, she needed to explain the stupid mistake that she had made about that other thing. The world treated virginity as very important, and so she suspected that such things mattered much to men.

It would not be easy to go to him. She steeled her will. They faced a life together. She could not meet him at the wedding with what stood between them unresolved.

Tomorrow she would go and find him. She would ride her black horse and wear her red cloak. She would also deal with one other problem as well.

That evening she went down to the hall well before supper and sought out Morvan. She found him with a young widow who had recently come down from the Midlands to visit Philippa. His black eyes sparkled with their dark fire. The poor girl looked like a stunned animal caught in the light of a torch. Christiana knew well this feminine reaction to him. Now, however, she understood exactly what he was about. Marching over, she interrupted his seduction with a loud greeting and a rude dismissal of the woman.

"Later, Christiana," he snapped.

"Now, brother," she replied. "In the garden, where we can be alone, please."

Fuming silently he took leave of his helpless prey and followed her through the passageways to the garden. The sun had set and twilight dimmed.

He was still annoyed. She didn't care. The stories about her brother were some of those things that made far too much sense all of a sudden. He was little better than Stephen from what she could tell, except that he didn't ruin virgins.

"Tomorrow I want to go and see David in the city," she explained. "I want you to take me to him."

"Send word to him and let him come here."

"He will not come. I left things badly when last we met."

"Then let him wait until the wedding to see you."

"I must speak with him, Morvan. There are things that I need to discuss."

"You will have years to talk, thanks to the King. I will not take you to him." He turned to leave.

She stomped her foot and grabbed his arm. "He thinks that I am not a virgin, Morvan."

That stopped him. He regarded her carefully. "Why?"

She faced him bravely. She understood her brother now, and his overbearing protection. Like David, he knew men well. He protected her from such as himself.

"Because I told him that I was not."

"You lied about such a thing? Even to avoid this marriage, Christiana, such a lie . . ."

"I thought it was the truth."

The implications sank in. "Who?" he asked quietly. Too quietly.

"I will not say. Do not think to bully me, Morvan. It is over and done with and thanks to Idonia I am whole. It is partly your fault, brother. If you had not scared off every boy, I might have had some experience in knowing a man's intentions. As it was, I was helpless against them and, until three days ago, didn't even know what he wanted from me."

He stood silently in the gray light. "Good God," he finally said.

"Aye. Eighteen and as ignorant as a babe. I came close to learning the hard way, didn't I? And almost went to my marriage bed a complete innocent."

"Hell."

"So, I did not lie to David. What had occurred between me and this other man seemed to fit all of the requirements as I stupidly understood them."

"And this merchant, knowing this, still took your hand?"

"Aye. I told him before the betrothal. He said that repudiation would ruin me."

He shook his head thoughtfully. "This marriage never made any sense."

"Nay, but I cannot worry about that now. I must see him before the wedding. I want to explain this."

He brought his arm around her shoulders and began guiding her back toward the castle door. "It is well that you explain. He might hurt you more than he has to if he doesn't know."

The very frank way he said this surprised her. So did this new ambiguous piece of information. Perhaps she should have talked to Morvan instead of Joan. She smiled, picturing her brother's distress as she demanded blunt descriptions with no gaps.

"If you go to him, he will misunderstand why you have come," he said. "It is said that he wants you badly. Perhaps that is the explanation for everything after all."

"Then I wish I had not been so unworldly. I might have traded my body for my freedom that night."

"It doesn't work that way, Christiana."

How does it work? she wanted to ask. "Well, I marry him in less than a week. When he hears what I have to say, he will not misunderstand why I have come. I must go, and I want you to bring me."

A torch by the doorway illuminated his handsome face. "So you go to him before the wedding, and I take you there? Of your own will, prior to the King's command? Having just learned what this man expects from you?"

"I face a life with him, Morvan. I want to see him and start it well. And I want him to know that you accept it, so that perhaps he will not stand between us. Aye, I go of my own will and I want him to see that I do."

He sighed with resignation. "In the morning then. Although it will kill me. Never have I brought such a precious gift to a man I disliked so much."

They stopped their horses at the end of the lane and looked up at David's shop. A large cart stood outside laden with large cylinders wrapped in rough cloth. Sieg pulled strenuously on a rope running up to a round wheel projecting from the beam of the attic. One of the cylinders dangled from the other end of the rope while he hauled it up the side of the building, his large muscles rippling under the strain as he yanked the rope hand over hand.

The cylinder reached the open attic window. Christiana caught a brief glimpse of golden brown hair as a strong arm reached out and grabbed the rope, pulling the load in.

Her courage had been slowly leaking away since yesterday evening and now she debated turning back. If David was busy today . . .

"He will stop his work when you come," Morvan said. He moved his horse forward.

She fell in beside him. "I don't know, Morvan. Perhaps. . . ."

"He wants you and nothing else will matter. Trust me on this, sister. I know of what I speak." He gave her a wink.

Morvan helped her to dismount. Sieg was busy

tying another cylinder to the rope and did not notice her.

"I will come back in a few hours. Early afternoon," Morvan said.

"Maybe tomorrow would be better."

He kissed her brow. "You made your decision with a clear head and an honest heart, Christiana. You were right. This marriage cannot be stopped and it is best that you see him. Courage now."

She nodded and entered the shop.

Two apprentices served patrons inside. The younger, dark-haired one, a youth of perhaps fourteen years, approached her.

"My name is Michael, my lady. How can I serve you?"

"I am Christiana Fitzwaryn. I have come to see your master. He is upstairs?"

Michael nodded, his expression awestruck.

"My horse is in the lane," she said, handing her cloak to him. "Perhaps when you are free you will move him for me."

She marched valiantly down the passageway. She climbed the steep steps to the second level and the sounds of tailors talking and working in the front chamber. Along the wall of this passage rose another set of steps, very steep and open like a ladder. She walked down to their base and, gathering her tattered courage, lifted her skirt to mount them.

She held on to the wall to keep her balance. The treads were narrow and treacherous. Her concentration distracted her and so she was almost at the top before she realized that her way was blocked. A little sound caught her attention.

On the third step from the top perched a small black kitten. It wailed faintly and helplessly as it surveyed its precarious position. Somehow it had gotten itself here, but it knew not how to get back up or down.

She tottered on the stair. She hadn't seen many cats before. Most people were afraid of them. This one, with its puny little sounds, was adorable. And in her way.

She lifted the kitten into her arms. At first it curled against her chest as if grateful for the security. But when she tried to climb the next step, it shrieked in terror and stretched up, clawing into her chest. She gasped as tiny spikes dug into her skin.

Footsteps approached the top of the stairs. Andrew, stripped to the waist, gazed down at her.

"David," he called over his shoulder.

David walked into view. Like Andrew he was naked to the waist, and a slight sheen of sweat glistened on his shoulders from his labors in the warm attic. She noticed with surprise the taut definition of the muscles of his broad shoulders and arms and chest. He looked lean and hard and athletic.

She was unaccustomed to seeing men undressed. In the summer, knights and soldiers stripped thus when they used the practice yards, and some of the girls made it a point to walk by, but Lady Idonia had forbidden it and lectured them about impure thoughts. David's very apparent flesh stunned her. She stared speechlessly up at that handsome face and body.

The kitten decided to move. She cried and tottered as the little paws dug their way up until the furry body straddled her shoulder.

"Steady now," David said. He stepped down and sat on the landing, reaching toward the kitten. He pried its claws out of her skin, removing them carefully so that the fabric of her surcoat and gown would not snag. He lifted the howling animal away.

It curled up contentedly, soft and furry against his chest. He stroked it absently and turned his blue eyes to her. Those beautiful hands holding that black fur against the hard chest struck her as incredibly alluring.

"You are busy. I should have sent word first," she said.

He twisted and placed the kitten on the floor behind him. The action made his muscles stretch with sinuous elegance. "Go find your mother," he told the cat. The little black face closed its eyes and rubbed against his back before scampering off.

He looked at her again and smiled. "I am not so busy. I am glad that you came."

He rose and stepped down toward her. "I will help you back down." He squeezed past and aided her as her feet blindly sought each step. Halfway down he jumped to the floor and plucked her off by her waist, setting her beside him.

"Go downstairs and wait for me."

There had been no greeting. No courtly pleasantries. He had not asked why she had come, and simply acted as if he knew. She scurried down to the invisibility of the lower passageway.

David watched her hurry away. She had surprised him by coming here. He had underestimated her.

Andrew hopped down the steps, carrying both of their shirts. He glanced at Christiana's disappearing skirt. "She's going to bolt," he observed casually.

David took his shirt.

Andrew gestured to the stairs. "By the time you are washed and dressed, she'll be gone."

"Are you giving me advice on women now?"

Andrew laughed. "Women? Hell, no, I wouldn't think of it. But then, she's not a woman, is she? She's just a girl.

I wager I've had more experience with them than you have recently." He pulled his shirt over his head. "One moment they are brave, the next they are shy. First it's aye, then nay. Remember? She used all of her courage to come, and now she is telling herself to leave. Unless, of course, your warm welcome reassured her. Smooth, that."

David looked at the empty stairs. Andrew's sarcasm was justified. He hadn't greeted her well and it *had* taken a lot of courage for her to come.

He went into the counting room and grabbed Andrew's pourpoint and threw it at him. "Then get yourself down there, boy, and stall her until I come," he said. "Block the damn door with a sword if you have to."

Andrew grinned and pulled the garment on. "Aye. And I'll tell Sieg that we'll take a break with the last carpets. He and I can get it done before dinner without you." He sidled to the doorway. "I assume this means that we will forget about that last nightwalking fine."

"Go!"

He followed Andrew down the stairs and watched him head in search of Christiana. He slipped out the back to the well and began washing off the dust in the crisp air.

She had heard about Percy's betrothal, of course. Almost a week ago probably. How bad had it been for her? He didn't like to think of her hurt, but he didn't want her making excuses for the man either. A woman could fill a lifetime with excuses to avoid the truth.

His head had been full of her since he had left her last Thursday. He rarely second-guessed himself, but during the days and long into the nights as he thought about her, he had considered how he had handled this girl and whether he hadn't made some miscalculations. He wasn't used to them so young, of course. He forgot sometimes that there was still something of the child in her. Even his greeting today . . . an Alicia would have welcomed his frank acceptance of her arrival. But Christiana was not like Alicia.

He had visited Westminster on Monday and almost gone to that apartment. He felt pulled there, and only a long inner debate had kept him away. *Let her come to me*, he had decided. *Either on her own or for the wedding.* He had stuck to that resolve until last night, when Oliver had appeared late at the house with some news. And then he had known that he couldn't wait for her to come any longer.

He dried himself as he went back upstairs to dress. But for the early arrival of that ship from Spain and its cargo of carpets, he would have spared her this cost to her pride. He had planned to fetch her from Westminster this morning, and only this work had delayed him. She had come to him first, however. A small gift to him from Lady Fortune. It was better for Christiana this way, too.

He went back downstairs. He could see a bit of red near the entrance of the shoproom. She had already reclaimed her cloak. Andrew's body stretched casually against the threshold, his foot resting across the space on the opposite jamb. He hadn't blocked the way with a sword exactly, but the red cloak could not pass.

He walked toward them and Andrew looked up in a meaningful way. Dropping his leg, he let the cloak ease into the passageway, right into David's arms.

"You are ready to go then?" David asked.

"Go?" she asked, flustered by his sudden presence.

"We will go to the house. John Constantyn is coming

for dinner but first we need to get some salve for the cat scratches. They might make you ill if you aren't careful."

She smiled weakly. "Your house . . . aye, I would like to see it."

There had been the possibility, small but real, that she had come to ask for the annulment. He allowed himself one breath of relief that the request would not come and that he would not have to refuse it.

"How did you get here?"

"My horse is in the alley, I think. Morvan brought me. He comes back in three hours or so."

Interesting. "We will walk. Let me tell the boys to bring the horse."

He went back into the shop and gave the apprentices instructions, then returned to her. He guided her up the lane with his arm about her shoulders, enjoying her warmth beside him and the feel of her arm beneath his hand.

Nothing could hide in this sunlight and he studied her face. She looked as exquisitely beautiful as ever, but subtle changes were apparent. He knew her face well, had memorized its details and nuances, and could read the anguish of the last days in it.

She turned her head and her sparkling eyes regarded him. He saw a change in those dark diamonds as well. Their glitter had dimmed very slightly, as if one facet of trust and innocence had dulled.

I will obliterate your memory of him.

She kept glancing at him and parting her lips as if she planned to speak. Finally the words poured out.

"You were right. About Stephen. He is betrothed as well. An old match. But you knew that, didn't you? You knew on Thursday that I would hear of it soon."

How long before she could read him as clearly as he

did her? She was by nature intelligent and perceptive. The girl often misunderstood what she saw, but the woman would not.

"I knew."

"Why didn't you tell me?"

"It was not for me to do so."

"You knew before the court. Even his uncle only heard that morning."

"Merchants and pilgrims arrive every day from the north. They bring gossip and news."

"You were asking them?"

"Aye."

"I feel like an idiot," she said forcefully. "You must think women are fools and that I am one of the worst."

"I do not think that. And if it makes you feel like an idiot, let us not speak of it."

They turned onto the lane with his house. She stopped and turned to him. Her brow puckered as she looked in his eyes.

"Will you tell me now? Why you marry me?"

He glanced away from her confused curiosity. Sore and wounded, she thought she had nothing to lose from blunt questions and frank answers. How would she react if he told her the truth?

What was the truth?

It had been weeks since he had thought about the bizarre bargain that had given her to him. In his mind, Edward's story had become real, and the license and its payment the deception. He had indeed seen her and wanted her and offered a fortune for her. The money had been for her and the license had become the gift and not the other way around. If the King tomorrow demanded another thousand pounds to let him keep her, he would pay it without a second thought.

He wanted her. Not for one night or a few months. He did not think of her that way and never had. Perhaps the inevitable permanence of marriage had woken this deeper desire in him. He wanted her body and her soul and her loyalty and her joy. He did not question why he wanted her. It just *was*.

"I marry you because I want to," he said.

CHAPTER 9

THE GATE TO the courtyard stood open. She paused in the passageway and then walked bravely into the sunny yard full of laughing women and fluttering cloth. Two large tubs stood side by side, one over a low fire.

Laundry day.

David strolled into the melee. A thin old woman with a kerchief on her hair hustled in their direction. He embraced the crone and kissed her cheek.

"They said you was out for a shipment, and I didn't expect to see you," the woman said, smiling.

"Slow down so you can have dinner with us, Meg," he said. "John is coming." He turned and pulled Christiana forward. "This is Christiana, Meg. My wife."

Meg peered at her with filmy eyes. Her toothless mouth gaped in a grin. "A beauty, David." She winked at Christiana. "Watch yourself. He's been nothing but trouble and mischief since he could walk."

David led Christiana away. "You and the women will stay, Meg. I will tell Vittorio."

Christiana followed him into the hall. "The laundress Meg has known you a long time," she said as she took in the large chamber's furnishings. Nice chairs. A handsome tapestry. Beautiful copper sconces to hold the wall torches.

"My mother worked for her when I was a child."

A middle-aged woman opened a door at the far end, and tumultuous sounds of pots banging and male cursing poured out at them. The plump woman carried a stack of silver plates in her arms. She looked Christiana up and down. David introduced her as Geva, the housekeeper. Geva smiled, but Christiana saw criticism in her sharp gray eyes.

David pushed open the door to the kitchen attached to the side of the hall. "And this is Vittorio." He gestured to a rotund, round-eyed man barking accented orders to a girl and man who assisted him. Worktables laden with knives and chopped food lined the room, and copper pots hung in the immense hearth. Vittorio bent his head to one of the pots, sniffed, and raised his thick black eyebrows in an expression of reluctant approval.

"Vittorio," David called.

The fat man straightened and looked over. "Ah! *La ragazza! La sposa!*" he announced to the assistants. They stopped their chores and smiled greetings.

He clasped his hands effusively. "*Finalmente!* Signorina Christiana, eh? Beautiful name. *Bellissima*, David." He made a comical look of approval.

"Lady Christiana will dine with us, Vittorio. And Meg and her women as well."

Vittorio nodded. "*Si, si.*" He turned back to the kitchen and gestured for the assistants.

David took her into the building across from the gate. She knew from her last visit that the solar was upstairs, but he led her past the steps to a simple bedchamber. "I will have Geva get the salves," he explained before leaving.

She removed her cloak. This chamber held some items of a personal nature. A simple cloak hung on a wall peg. A silver comb lay on a table. She sat on the bed and waited for Geva.

It was David who returned, however, and not the housekeeper. He carried a bowl of water and a rag and a small jar. He placed them on the table.

His long fingers pushed aside the shoulder of her surcoat. She glanced down at that hand and the scratches it uncovered. He moved to her other side and began unlacing the back neckline of the sleeveless outer garment. She glanced up at him in surprise.

"The salve will stain it," he explained, gesturing for her to stand and helping her to step out of it. The intimacy of the simple, practical action unsettled her.

"Is this Geva's chamber?"

The neck of her cotehardie was cut low and broad and exposed the scratches. He dipped a rag in the water and began wiping the little streaks of blood from her skin. "Geva lives in the city with her family and comes by day. This was my mother's chamber. She was David Constantyn's housekeeper for ten years before her death. He met her through Meg. She did laundry here with the others, and when his housekeeper died he gave her the position."

"And later made you his apprentice?"

"Aye."

He carefully cleaned the scratches on the back of her shoulder. She tried to ignore his closeness and the attention he gave his ministrations. She noticed again the objects on the table. They seemed to still hold something of the dead woman's presence.

He picked up the jar. "Don't worry. You are not intruding on a shrine. This chamber is used by visitors."

He soothed some of the salve over the scratches, and she sat very still with the warmth of his fingertips on her skin and the slight sting of the medicine in the sores. She lifted her gaze and saw him looking down at her. She thought that she knew that look.

She had better explain why she had come. Soon. They needed a place to talk alone, but not here in this room.

"Is there a garden?" she asked, rising.

He lifted her cloak to her shoulders. "This way."

The garden stretched behind the building and the kitchen. A high wall enclosed it. It was barren now except for some hedges and ivy, but she could tell that in summer it would be lush. Flower beds, crisscrossed with paths, flowed back to a little orchard of fruit trees. A larger bed near the kitchen would be planted with vegetables.

"There is a smaller garden back here," he said, leading her to a door in the wall.

The tiny second garden charmed her. Ivy grew everywhere, covering the walls and ground and creeping up to form a roof on a small arbor set in one corner. Two tall trees filled the space. In summer this enclosure would be cool and silent. An outer stairway led from the garden to the second level of the building.

She doubted that she would find anyplace more private than this. "Can we sit down? I need to tell you something."

They sat on a stone bench nestled deep inside the ivy covered arbor. Sunlight broke through the dense covering, mottling the shadows with little pools of yellow light.

She bent over and plucked a sprig of ivy from the carpet at her feet. She nervously pulled the little points off the leaves. Probably best to just plunge in.

"When we first met, I told you . . . I indicated that I was not . . . that Stephen and I had . . ."

"That does not matter now."

"It does, though. I must explain something." She tried to remember the exact words that she had rehearsed.

His voice came low and quiet. "Are you saying that there were others?"

"Heavens, nay! I did not lie about that. I am trying to say that there was no one, not even Stephen. It seems that I was wrong. I made a mistake." She thought that she would feel less awkward once it was said. It didn't work that way.

For a long while he didn't move or speak. She concentrated on pulling the ivy leaves off their branch.

"It is a difficult mistake for a girl to make, Christiana. Impossible, I would think," he finally said.

Saints, but she felt like a fool. "Not if she doesn't know what she is talking about, David."

His motionless silence stretched longer this time. She suffered it for a while, and then snuck a glance at him.

"Are you angry?"

"You have it backwards. A man is supposed to get angry when he learns of his new wife's experience, not her innocence."

"You might be angry if you thought that I lied on purpose. To discourage you."

"I don't think that. In fact, what you have told me explains much. When did you realize your mistake?"

She had assumed that she could just blurt this out and be done with it. She hadn't expected a conversation.

"Last Thursday night."

He stayed silent and she knew that he was remembering the two of them in the wardrobe. His body pressed to hers. That intimate caress. Her cry of shock.

"I must have frightened you very badly."

He regarded her with a warm and concerned expression. He could be a very kind man sometimes. Perhaps he even understood how distressing all of this had been. Maybe . . .

"Nay," he said with a small smile.

"Nay what?"

"You are wondering if, under the circumstances, we might put off the wedding or at least that part of it. I think not."

She blushed from her hair to her neck. It really was discomforting to have him read her thoughts like that.

He reached over and lightly touched her hair. "Although, considering this stunning revelation, I probably won't seduce you today as I had planned."

She almost gushed relief and gratitude before she caught herself. Her face burned hotter yet. His fingers on her hair and head felt very nice, though. Comforting.

"Who spoke with you?"

"I asked Joan."

"She is unmarried herself. Are you sure she got it right? That you know what I expect from you?"

"I doubt that Joan gets much wrong where men are concerned."

He laughed. "Aye, I suspect not."

Never in her life had she felt this awkward and embarrassed. She wished that someone would come and announce that John Constantyn had arrived.

"How often were you with him?"

Dear saints. She stared at her lap, covered now with little bits of ivy leaves and branches. She brushed them off.

"Just that once. Do not be too hard on him, David. He had reason to believe that I agreed. My misunderstanding of his intentions and actions was boundless."

"Were you unclothed?"

Her mouth fell open. She continued staring at her lap,

and as she did, his hand appeared and he placed another sprig of ivy there. The gesture and its understanding of her embarrassment touched her. All the same he waited for her answer. It seemed odd that when he thought her experienced, he had requested no information, but now that he knew her not to be, he wanted these details. She had opened a door and he seemed determined to examine the entire chamber behind it.

"Partly. He ripped one of my surcoats." Stephen's carelessness there had assumed a symbolic quality these last few days.

His hand still gently touched her head, brushing a few feathery hairs away from her temple. "Did he touch you?"

"We were on a bed together. He couldn't avoid touching me," she sharply. "I don't want to talk about this. Why do you ask me these things?"

"So I know how careful I must be with you."

She took a deep breath. She realized that there was such a thing as being so embarrassed that it couldn't get any deeper and that she had reached that point. There was a certain freedom in knowing that it wouldn't get any worse.

"Not the way that you did . . . last time. Idonia came in first. Just in time, according to her. He touched my breast, though. He hurt me." It felt good accusing Stephen of that. She had thought at the time that it was the only way.

"I didn't like it," she added, honestly remembering her reaction to that crushing body. "I decided that I was one of those women who . . . who . . ."

"Is cold?"

"Aye. One of those."

"We both know that is not so, Christiana. Besides, I do not think that there are many cold women. There are, however, many men who are ignorant, selfish, or impatient. You will find that I am none of those things."

Deep in her heart, she knew that. It was what kept her from panicking when she thought about this marriage, so inevitable and close now. It was that which had given her the courage to come despite Morvan's warnings of what it might lead to. Still, she was glad that he had decided not to seduce her today.

She waited for his next question as he touched her in that soothing, vaguely exciting way. Her scalp tingled from the light pressure of his fingers. She gazed at her lap and the destruction she had absently wrought on the second sprig of ivy.

There were other things that she needed to say. She wanted to tell him that she accepted the marriage. He deserved to hear it after all of the times she had smugly insisted it would never happen. She needed to promise that she would try to be a good wife to him, whatever that meant. She would like to thank him for being so patient with her. She had expected all of those things to be easier to explain than this first admission, but she found now that they were much harder.

As she groped to phrase these other things and sought the courage to say them, his right hand came into her view and settled on her lap beside her own. He turned it palm up.

She smiled down at that beautiful hand waiting for her. Her gaze locked on its exciting, elegant strength. No kinsman or priest would join them today, but there was an offer and promise in his gesture far more meaningful than the official betrothal.

He understood. He was making it easier for her. Today is the real beginning, that hand said.

Forever. The immensity of it tried to suffocate her for an instant, but she pushed the fear away.

It was why she had come, wasn't it?

She placed her own hand in his. Of her own will.

He pulled gently and lifted her, turning her so that he could set her on his lap. The devastated ivy scattered down her cloak.

She looked into deep blue eyes full of kindness and warmth. It occurred to her that maybe she didn't have to say anything else at all.

Tentatively she placed her arm around his shoulders. A little awkwardly, she reached out and touched his face. It was the first time that she had touched him instead of the other way around. It felt different this way, and she marveled at the sensation of his skin beneath her fingertips.

She let her fingers caress the planes of his handsome face. They came to rest on his lips, and she lightly stroked their warmth.

He did not move. She lifted her gaze to his eyes and collected her bravery. After a little false start she leaned forward and kissed him.

She had never done this before, with him or anyone, and once her lips were on his she really didn't know what to do. It felt very nice though, and she pressed a little harder. His mouth smiled beneath hers.

She pulled away sheepishly. "You are laughing at me because I don't know how to do it."

His hand rose up and cradled her head. "Nay. I am thinking that was the most wonderful kiss I have ever had."

She blushed and kissed him again. He took over this time, responding to her artless start.

She loved the way that he kissed her. She always had. The sensations he awoke in her were always so powerful and sweet and heady. This time she didn't completely lose herself, though, but followed his lead, doing as he did, learning from him. Finally, when he gently bit the corner of her mouth, she parted her lips to him.

He did not choke and gag her as Stephen had, but instead gently stroked the inside of her mouth at first, sending chill upon chill down her spine. The intimacy startled her, and when he deepened the kiss she sensed a change in him and a rising passion that excited her as much as his warmth and touch. She had always been so caught up in her own reactions that she hadn't noticed his. Sharing the pleasure was much richer than just accepting it, and in a way this kiss moved her more than anything they had ever done before.

"Oh my," she gasped when they separated.

"Surely you have kissed like that before."

"It wasn't so nice."

"Ah. Well, perhaps it helps now that you know that it won't get you with child."

She closed her eyes and groaned in mortification. Burying her face into his shoulder, she muttered miserably, "How did you know?"

He began laughing. "You have always kept your lips locked like they were the gate to paradise itself, Christiana. I thought that you simply didn't like it. But it is the only misunderstanding that has any logic."

She laughed too. She lifted her head and wiped the tears brimming at her eyes. "Oh, dear saints. I assure you, it made perfect sense in light of what Idonia had told me when I was younger. You must think that I am the most stupid girl you have ever met."

He shook his head. "I think that you are the most beautiful girl whom I have ever met."

It was sweet of him to say that, but he had no doubt known many beautiful women. Still, it felt nice to be wooed with pretty words. He had never done that before.

"You don't believe me."

"I am pretty enough, David. I know that. But not really beautiful. Not like Joan."

"Lady Joan is like a sunbeam and is a beautiful girl, Christiana. You, however, are the velvet night. Dark sky"—he touched her hair—"Pale light"—his fingers stroked her skin—"Stars"—he kissed the side of her eye.

The sounds of voices intruded from the outer garden. She glanced resentfully in their direction. She wanted to stay in this hidden arbor longer, laughing and talking with David. Maybe kissing again.

"We must go back," he said regretfully. "John will be here by now."

They found John talking loudly with Sieg and peering around the garden for signs of the alerted lovers. He gave David a very male look as the couple emerged through the garden door and greeted him.

CHAPTER 10

CHRISTIANA ASSUMED THAT the dinner was more lavish than the household's usual midday meal. The visit of John Constantyn probably accounted for most of the extra dishes and savories, but she suspected that her own presence had inspired Vittorio to some last minute delicacies.

"He's one of the best cooks in London, I'll wager," John confided. "I wrangle an invitation to eat here whenever I can." He patted his thickening girth. "Better not let him cook for your wedding, David. The King will take him from you."

Vittorio made sure that everything was perfect on the table, and then took a seat with the apprentices and Sieg. Soon that whole table chattered in Italian.

"It is easiest for them to learn it at table," David explained. "They will need it for trade."

Christiana watched the boys. Andrew was older than her and Roger just two years younger. They would not find it odd, though, that a girl their own age married their master. Actually, child brides were more common and she was a bit old for the role.

John helped himself to some salmon. "I heard that you received a shipment today, David."

"Carpets from Castile."

"You have been taking a lot of winter cargo."

"They come when they come."

"Like hell. You expect trade to be disrupted in the spring or summer, don't you?" He lowered his voice. "He's going to do it, isn't he? Another damn campaign. Another army to France and every ship in sight requisitioned for it. I'm glad that I only deal in wool. He'll never interfere with that."

"If Edward keeps borrowing money, there will be no silver in the realm even to buy your wool, John, let alone Spanish carpets."

"You always sell your luxuries, David. You always know what they want." He leaned toward Christiana. "He has golden instincts, my lady. Wouldn't touch the King's monopoly for exporting raw wool a few years back and talked me out of it too. Saved my ass. Most everyone involved lost their shirt."

The meal was long, friendly, and relaxed. David and John chatted about business and politics, and they discussed Edward's policies more bluntly than the courtiers. On occasion certain opinions even sounded faintly disloyal. Barons and knights probably spoke thus amongst themselves, too, she realized, but not in the King's hall.

She surveyed the people sitting at the other three tables. In addition to Sieg, Vittorio, Geva, and the apprentices, four other servants worked here on a regular basis. David's household appeared large, well run, and efficient. He certainly didn't need a wife to manage things. She suspected uncomfortably that her own presence would be superfluous at best and maybe even disruptive.

Throughout the entire meal, David let her know that he had not forgotten her presence. His gestures and glances suggested that despite his attention to his guest, most of his mind dwelled on her. When they had both finished eating, his hand rested permanently over hers atop the table, the long fingers absently caressing the back of her palm while he conversed. In subtle ways he maintained the intimacy they had shared in the ivy garden.

She became very conscious of his touch and looks as the meal drew to a close. As the hall began emptying, the apprentices heading back to the shop and the servants to their duties, she sensed his awareness of her heighten even though nothing changed in his behavior or actions.

John Constantyn did not linger long after the other tables had cleared. They accompanied him into the courtyard.

"I will see you at the wedding, my lady," John said. "Is it true that the King attends, David?"

"So I have been told. Christiana is his ward."

"I hear that the mayor convinced you to move the banquet to the Guildhall."

Christiana tried not to embarrass David by letting it show that she knew nothing of the plans for her own wedding. They had never spoken of it. She had never asked, because she had never expected to be there herself.

She could not blame him if he thoroughly disliked her by now. Maybe he did. He would never let her know. He was trapped as completely as she, but would try to make the best of the situation. Is that all they were? Two people accommodating themselves to the inevitable?

"Aye. And the mayor made clear that if the royal family attended, all of the aldermen should be invited," David said. "We will have the mayor's dull, official banquet, and then another one here for the ward and household. Save your appetite, John. Vittorio cooks for the second one."

John laughed. "And your uncle Gilbert, David? Will he come?"

"I invited him. I borrowed a royal page to send the message, in fact. Gilbert's wife is a good woman and I would not insult her. She will make him attend." His eyes sparkled mischievously. "The decision will drive him mad. Decline and he misses the King. Accept and he honors me."

"Aye," John said, grinning. "His dilemma might be cause enough to get married if the best reason didn't stand by your side now."

She decided not to think about how David came to have use of a royal page.

John left then. The courtyard suddenly seemed very quiet.

David's arm slid around her waist. "Come. I'll show you the house."

They visited the stable first. Her black horse, unsaddled and brushed, stood in a stall beside David's two mounts. The groom was nowhere to be seen. She reached up and petted the black nose. She supposed that she could name him now that she would be keeping him.

In the building facing the street she saw the chambers used by Michael, Roger, and some of the servants. Andrew slept at the shop, she knew. It impressed her that each person had his own small room. The servants of this mercer possessed more privacy than the noble wards of the King.

Silence greeted them as they reentered the hall. Even the kitchen echoed empty. Vittorio was just leaving with a basket on his arm to shop for the evening meal. He smiled indulgently and slipped away.

As David opened the door to the last building, Christiana thought that there should probably be a little more household bustle going on. She realized with a jolt that everyone had left the premises.

She followed David to the storage rooms filled with wooden crates on the first level, beyond his mother's old chamber. The scent of cinnamon and cloves wafted toward her. Carpets and spices and silks. Luxuries. John's observation had been correct. David would always sell these things. They defined status and honor and many people would eat only soup in order to purchase them.

His arm circled her shoulders as he led her back toward the kitchen. The simple gesture suddenly seemed less casual than before. Had he dismissed the whole household, or had natural discretion made them all decide to become scarce so that the master could be alone with his lady?

They were alone, that was certain. The resonating silence had imbued this simple tour with a creeping intimacy. By the time they returned to the stairs leading to the upper level and David's chambers, her caution was fully alerted.

David began guiding her up. She balked on the second step.

His smile of amusement made her feel childish. He took her hand. "Come now, girl. You should see your house."

Her mind chastised her instincts. After all, she had been in the solar before. They would marry soon and, despite Morvan's warnings, he had not misunderstood her reason for coming. She let herself be cajoled upwards.

In the light of day she could see the solar's beauty. The glazed windows on one side looked down on the garden, and in summer the flowers' scents would drift into the square high chamber. David built up the fire and she walked around, admiring the furnishings. Each carved chair, each tapestry, every item down to the silver candleholders, possessed an individual and distinctive beauty.

She fingered the relief of ivy edging the chair on which she had sat that first night. What had this man thought of the child who faced him, her feet dangling as she announced her love for someone else?

Stephen. The thought of him could still open a hollow ache.

She looked up to see David regarding her. "Did these lovely things come to you with the house?" she asked.

"Nay."

She hadn't thought so. Like the severe cut of his clothes, they were, in their own ways, perfect.

"You must spend a lot of time looking for such things."

"Rarely. Something catches my eye and I buy it. It doesn't take long at all."

She gazed at one of the tapestries hanging beside the windows. Superb. She thought about Elizabeth's dependence on his taste. He had a natural eye for beauty. It must give him a tremendous advantage in his trade.

I think that you are the most beautiful girl whom I have ever met.

Her eyes slowly followed the sinuous lead tracery that held the pieces of glass together in the windows. She felt him watching her.

He saw her and wanted her and offered the King a fortune for her.

A small book rested on a low table near the hearth. She knew that if she opened it, she would find richly painted illuminations. Like everything else in this room, it would be exquisite.

Something catches my eye and I buy it. It doesn't take long at all.

Two doors flanked the hearth. She drifted to the one on the right and opened it. She found herself on the threshold to his bedchamber. Ignoring a qualm of misgiving at the way he watched her, she went inside.

The hearth in this chamber backed on the solar's and the windows also overlooked the garden. The chamber was simply furnished, with one chair near the fire and a large bed on a low dais in the center of the room. Heavy blue drapes surrounded the bed and formed a canopy, and one side was tied open to reveal a rich matching coverlet. A fire burned in the hearth.

She walked along the wall overlooking the garden and passed through a door at the far end of the chamber. She entered a wardrobe with chests and pegs for clothes. It included a small hearth and wooden tub just like Isabele's, and a door at its end led to a garderobe and privy. A spout in a wall niche, similar to ones seen elsewhere in the house, provided piped water.

She opened a door cut in the wall and found herself at the top of the stairs leading down to the small ivy garden. Besides the solar, this was the only other way into the apartment.

Back in the bedchamber, she looked around, trying to grow accustomed to this space. David stood at the threshold, his shoulder resting casually against the doorjamb. She smiled weakly at him, feeling like an intruder.

"Where is my chamber?"

"You mean the lady's bower? There is none. Merchants do not live that way. Your place is here with me."

He walked to the hearth. There was no need to build up this fire. It sparked and crackled with new logs. She stared at the hot bright flames and read their flickering significance.

Who had come and prepared this room? Geva? He

would not expose his intentions to a woman. Sieg, then. The big Swede had been the first to leave the hall. She doubted that David had said a word to him. It had simply been done. She managed not to glance at that big bed dominating the room. Of course, Sieg would not know of David's reassurances in the garden.

She could not just stand here forever. She searched for something to look at.

The solar stretched the width of the building and had windows over both the garden and the courtyard. This chamber was not so wide, and its court wall was solid. She spied a door at its end and strode toward it.

As soon as she saw the side chamber she stopped in her tracks. It was a study. She quickly surveyed the objects filling it and knew that now she definitely intruded. She began backing out and bumped into David's chest. His hand came to rest over hers on the door and he pushed it forward.

"This is your home," he said. "There are no doors closed to you here."

Home. She had not had a home since Harclow. Not really. As the royal household moved from one castle or manor to the next, she had never felt at home, not even at Westminster. For eleven years she had been something of a permanent guest.

This small chamber might not be closed to her today, but it obviously was to everyone else. No housekeeper tended this room, and a thin layer of dust covered some of the items on the shelves flanking the high window. Her gaze took in a stack of books and some scrolls of paper. A small painting in the Byzantine style and a beautiful ivory carving were propped at one end beside an ancient hand harp whose frame was inlaid with intricate twining lines of silver.

The only furniture was a large table covered with

parchment papers and documents. A chair angled behind it, and underneath she saw a small locked chest on the floor.

From the corner of her eye she noticed that the wall behind the door also bore shelves. She turned and gasped as a man's face peered back at her.

David laughed and stepped past her to the shelf.

"It is remarkable, isn't it?"

She approached in amazement. The man's face was carved in marble and its realism astonished her. Whichever mason had done this work possessed a god's touch. Subtle shadows modeled the skin so accurately that one believed one could touch flesh and feel bone beneath it.

"I found it in Rome," he explained. "Just lying there in the ancient ruins. I picked up a small section of a column and this was underneath. There are many such statues there. Whole bodies just as real, and stone caskets covered with figures that are used now to hold water at fountains. I saw some statues at the Cathedral of Reims recently that come close, but nothing else similar north of the Alps."

Reims. Near Paris. What was he doing there recently? Stupid question. He was a merchant, after all.

"You carried it all of the way home?"

"Nay. I bribed Sieg to," he said, laughing.

"You seem to like carvings and paintings a lot. Why didn't you become a limner or a mason?"

"Because David Constantyn was a mercer and it was he who gave me an apprenticeship. As a boy I sometimes dawdled around a limner's shop and watched them work, mixing their colors and painting the images in books. The master tolerated me and even showed me how to burn wood to make drawing tools. Fate had other plans for me, however, and I do not regret it."

She stepped behind the table. On its corner were some new parchments folded and closed with a seal showing three entwined serpents. Strewn across it were papers with oddly drawn marks. The top one simply showed jagged lines connected by sweeping numbered curves. Little squares and circles lined up along snaking borders. She glanced away carefully. It was a map. Why did David make maps?

Not today, she reminded herself.

She turned and examined the books on the high shelf. "Can I look at one?"

"Which one do you want?"

"The biggest one."

He lifted the large folio down, placing it on the table, covering the cryptic drawings. Christiana sat in the chair and carefully opened it. She stared in surprise at the lines and dots spread out in front of her.

"It is Saracen, David."

"Aye. The pictures are wonderful. Keep turning."

She flipped the large sheets of parchment. "Can you read this?"

"Some of it. I never learned to write the language well, though."

"Is this forbidden?" she asked skeptically. She knew that the church frowned on certain books.

"Probably."

She came to one of the pictures, and it was indeed wonderful and strange. Little men in turbans and odd clothes moved across a world drawn to look like a carpet.

"Will you teach me to read this?"

"If you wish."

He took down the harp and leaned against the table's edge beside her, looking down at the book while he plucked absently on the strings. The instrument gave a lovely lyrical sound. She continued turning the pages, glancing on occasion at the man resting close to her now and the compelling fingers creating a haunting melody.

Toward the back of the book she found some loose sheets covered with chalk drawings. Spare lines described tents on a desert and a town by the sea. She knew without asking that David had drawn them.

Beneath them, on smaller sheets, lay the faces of two women.

One of them riveted her attention. The face, beautiful and melancholy, appeared vaguely familiar. She realized that she studied an image of his mother. It felt eerie to be facing a dead person thus, but she examined the face closely.

"Will you tell me about her?" she asked quietly.

"Someday."

She turned her attention to the other face. "Who is she?" She gazed at the sloe-eyed exotic beauty captured forever with careful, fine lines. She knew that she pried but she could not ignore the worldly way this woman's face looked at her.

"A woman whom I met in Alexandria."

As with the likeness of his mother, there was much of the artist's feelings in the sensitive way this woman was drawn.

"Did you love her?" she asked, a little shocked by her own boldness but not too much so. He had become much less a stranger since she stepped into this chamber.

"Nay. In fact, she almost got me killed. But I was enchanted by her beauty, as I am by yours."

Something in his quiet tone made her go very still. She lifted her gaze and found him looking at her and not at the book and its drawings. Looking and waiting. He was good at that. Something in his eyes and in the set of his mouth told her that he contemplated waiting no longer.

He saw her and wanted her and paid the King a fortune to have her.

He had stopped playing the harp. Her pulses pounded a little harder in the renewed silence. Total silence. Not a sound in the whole house.

She returned to the book and very carefully turned the page, burying the drawings. Another painting loomed but she didn't really see it.

"Do you know that I have only seen your hair down once, at the betrothal," he said. She sensed his hand reach toward her even before his fingers fell on her head. "Even in the bath it was bound up."

The light pressure of his caress sent a tremor through her. The bath. The wardrobe. His hands and his touch.

"Take down your hair for me, Christiana."

His tone fell somewhere between a request and a command. She leaned back in the chair, away from him.

She would marry this man very soon. She shouldn't be afraid of him. But her quickening blood and unworldly spirit shouted to her that she should get away from him now.

She looked at him, silently asking him to remember their conversation in the garden and to understand and wait a little longer. "Morvan is probably at the shop, David. I should go and meet him."

"I left word that we were coming here."

"Then he most likely waits outside. He will not enter. I should not leave him there."

He gestured to the window. "It looks out on the courtyard. See if he awaits you."

She eased out of the chair and past him, and turned on her tiptoes to glance down at the deserted courtyard.

His quiet voice flowed over her back and shoulders. "He will not come. He accepts that you belong to me now. As you do."

She went down from her toes and looked up at the clear afternoon sky. A part of her wanted desperately to fly out that window. But his touch and words and the expectant silence of this house had awakened those other feelings, and that exquisite anticipation licked through her.

"You frighten me sometimes," she said. "I know that you should not and that you have said that it isn't fear, but a part of it truly is."

He was quiet for a moment. The house seemed to quake with its emptiness. "Aye," he finally said. "For a virgin, part of it truly is."

She sensed him move. She felt his presence behind her. She both awaited and dreaded his touch, her spirit stretched with tension like a string pulled taut.

His hands gently took her waist and she sighed at the feel of each finger. His head bent to her bare shoulder. He kissed the little scratches, and then her neck. She closed her eyes, savoring the delicious closeness of him.

"Take down your hair, Christiana."

She raised her arms and clumsily fumbled for the pins that held her hair. She pulled out the intricate twists and plaits, terribly conscious of how weak and vulnerable she felt, wonderfully aware of those fingers splayed around her.

The heavy waves fell section by section down her neck and back, all the way to his hands. She shook her head to release the last of them, placing the pins on the windowsill.

He nuzzled his face in her unbound hair, and his breath tingled her scalp and neck through the tresses.

His hands turned her to him and took her face, cradling

it gently like something precious and fragile. He kissed her tenderly, beautifully, and fully, and she trembled as his mouth made the low tension and excitement sharpen and rise.

He prolonged the kiss, taking her in an embrace that pulled her to his warmth. She held her arms open at his sides for one worried moment before accepting him.

She sensed a change in him after that. His kiss deepened, commanding her desire. His hand cupped her breast. She gasped and closed her eyes, waiting for the delicious sensations.

They undid her completely. Her limbs went languid as heat poured through her body. His soft hair brushed her face as he lowered his mouth to the skin exposed by her low-cut cotehardie, kissing the top swell of the breasts that his fingers caressed into peaks of yearning.

Fear told her to stop him but the desire would not let her. Rivulets of pleasure merged into a fast-running river, and struggling against its current seemed futile and impossible.

His fingers played at her and the pleasure became a little frantic. *I am drowning in it*, she thought as his mouth claimed hers again.

He lifted his head and looked down at her, watching her responses to his touch. She gazed at the parted lips and deep eyes and knew that there would be no help from him this day.

He began guiding her toward the chamber door.

She thought about where they were going and what he wanted. "I don't . . ." she whispered even as she took another step.

"It is why you came, is it not? For reassurance that this marriage need not be so terrible?"

She resisted at the threshold. His hand returned to her breast and his lips to her neck.

"You said . . . you said that today you wouldn't . . ."

"I said probably," he murmured. "And I lied."

He took her face in his hands again. "His shadow is between us and I would banish that ghost. Today we even the accounts and turn the page. It will be easier for you this way, too."

She read the decision in his eyes.

"Do not be afraid. I will wait until you are ready and until you want me. It will be all right. I will make it so," he promised.

I am helpless against these feelings, she thought. *It is unnecessary to fight them. This is inevitable anyway. I am his forever.*

She turned her face and kissed his hand.

He lifted her in his arms and carried her into the chamber.

CHAPTER 11

HER THIN ARMS encircled his neck and tightened as he approached the bed.

It will be all right. I will make it so. Brave words from a man who hadn't taken a virgin since he was sixteen. Still, he would indeed make it so. Whatever lies he told her today, that would not be one of them.

He should have known. *She's just a girl*, Andrew had said. *One moment they are brave and the next shy. Remember?*

He sat on the side of the bed and settled her into his lap. He kissed her until the arm grasping his neck loosened a bit.

Innocent and ignorant. All during dinner it had been all he could do not to stare in astonishment. While he ate and spoke, his mind had recalculated what this revelation meant. Perhaps it made today unnecessary and he should wait. Perhaps it made it essential. In the end his own desire chose the course. He would not let her leave without claiming her. He wanted her and there was only one way to possess her securely.

She touched his face in that tentative way, and his desire surged. He took her mouth hungrily and fought back the cataclysmic storm that threatened to thunder through him. Slowly and simply, he reminded himself again.

He caressed her breasts and when her arms tightened this time it was not in fear. Her body relaxed into his. She tried to imitate his deep kiss and probed cautiously and delicately. The artless effort almost undid him.

The joy he found in her innocent passion surprised him. He had never sought it in other women. It shouldn't matter with Christiana either, but it did. He felt her body responding to him and listened to her sharpened breathing. He delighted in her awkward embrace and in her startled gasps when his hands raised a new pleasure. He reveled in the knowledge that despite what had occurred with Percy, no man but himself had ever aroused her.

He kissed her again, savoring the soft taste of her and the compliant arch of her back. His hand sought the lacing of her cotehardie, and he began undressing her.

The virgin stiffened for an instant as the garment loosened, but then those glittering eyes watched his hands ease the gown off her arms and down to her waist. Her mouth trembled open and her eyes closed as he touched her breast through the thin batiste of her shift.

A small hand left his shoulders and caressed down his chest, and the thunder tried to erupt again. Her fingers slid under the flap hiding the closures to his pourpoint. He watched her earnest expression as that hand fumbled down his chest. Aye. Having chosen to yield, the sister of Morvan Fitzwaryn would not play the reluctant victim.

He slid the straps of the shift down and uncovered her beautiful breasts. His gaze followed the path of his fingers as he traced their high, round swells. Her breath quickened and she buried her face shyly in his shoulder.

She was beautifully formed, pale and flawless. Her skin was not translucent and white like so many Englishwomen, but rather had the opaque tint of new ivory. It was the color of the bleached beaches along the Inland Sea. He caressed her, whisking and grazing the tight nipples, and her whole body reacted. With a faint moan she arched into his touch. The light brown tips beckoned like an offering. He lowered his head and gently kissed one before taking it into his mouth.

She almost jumped out of his arms.

He held her firmly and looked at the startled shock in her eyes. He kissed her cheek reassuringly.

He lowered his kisses until that sweet breast was in his mouth again. Jesus, the man must have barely touched her. No thought to her at all. If Idonia hadn't found them, he would have brutalized her.

A picture of that formed in his mind, and his spirit reacted with a surge of protective anger followed by a wave of tenderness. He played at her with his tongue and teeth until her bottom pressed against his thigh in her search for relief. He reached back and pulled down the bed coverings. Slowly and simply, but before she left him he would show her the glory of the pleasure. She was all that mattered this time.

He rose with her in his arms and turned and laid her down. Dark eyes, liquid with passion, regarded him cautiously. He gazed down at her lying there, naked to the waist with her clothes falling around her hips, and he considered leaving her thus. She looked sweet and fresh and reminded him of the girls of his youth lying back in hay and grass. He thought of the carpet of ivy in the small garden below. If he lived until summer, the warm starlit nights promised a special ecstasy.

Gently he pulled the cotehardie and shift down her slender curves.

Christiana bit her lower lip as shock and excitement merged at the sight of him undressing her. She watched her naked body emerge. When the gown and shift were gone, he untied the garters at her knees and slid off her hose.

A prickly expectation twisted in her. The fear had not completely disappeared. It acted like a spice in the stew of emotions and sensations that boiled inside her.

He shook off his pourpoint and removed his shirt before lowering down beside her. She watched his hard body come to her, and sighed with relief when he was in her arms again.

She let her hands feel his shoulders and back, and she noted the ridges of scars there. He moved into her caress. The heady warmth and closeness overwhelmed her. That strange pounding need went all through her now, shaking her from shoulders to toes.

He kissed her deeply while his hand followed the tremor, sliding down her stomach and belly, reaching down her thighs and legs. Possessive, hot and confident, his caress took control of every inch of her. Her body arched into his touch and rocked to the rhythm of that hollow hidden pulse. Everything began to spiral into the need now. Her breathing, her blood, her awareness, even the pleasure flowed to and from it.

He cupped her breast in his hand and rubbed the tip with his thumb. "I am going to kiss all of you now," he said. "Do not be shy. Nothing is forbidden if it gives us both pleasure."

And he did kiss all of her, his mouth pressing and biting and drawing down her body, creating new pleasures and surprises and leaving her breathless. Down her stomach and belly, down even to her legs. Several kisses even shockingly landed on the flesh of her thighs and then on the soft mound above them and she cried out as long, hot streaks shot through her.

His lips closed on one breast while he caressed the other and the excitement rose to a frantic level. She grabbed desperately at his back and hair. His muscles felt tense beneath her fingers, and his breath sounded ragged to her ears.

He rose up and loosened the rest of his clothing. She reached down to help and her hand brushed his arousal. She felt a reaction all through him, and she bravely touched him again as he kicked off his clothes.

Fear spiked through the oblivion of desire.

Impossible . . .

He returned her hand to his shoulder and then stroked down her body to her legs. Teasing her thighs apart, he slid his hand up and under to her buttocks. His arm pressed up against her while his tongue and lips aroused her breasts.

The pounding need exploded, obliterating the renewed fear. She pushed down against the pressure of that arm offering relief but only bringing torture. Her whole body wanted to move in abandoned, base ways, and she controlled it with difficulty. Over and over she bit back wanton cries that threatened to fill the room.

The warm water of his voice flowed over her. "Do not fight it, Christiana. The sounds and moves of your desire are beautiful to me."

Gratefully she submitted to the delirium. When his hand came forward, she opened her legs without encouragement. She felt no shyness or shock as he caressed her, only a torturous desire that would surely explode into flames if it was not fulfilled.

The sensations of his magic touch led her into madness. Gentle caresses created streaks of concentrated pleasure. Deliberate touches summoned a wild and desperate excitement.

His quiet voice penetrated the wonderful anguish. "Do you want me now, Christiana?"

He touched her differently and she cried out. She managed to nod.

"Then tell me so. Say my name and tell me so."

In the distance somewhere she heard her voice say it. The frantic need completely took over and her hips rose to meet the body coming over hers.

She reveled in the feel of his long length along her and the total closeness of their bodies. She delighted in the concentrated passion transforming his face as he looked at her.

He took her slowly and carefully and she marveled at the beauty of it. With gentle pressure and measured thrusts he seduced her open. The feared pain was not really pain at all but only a stretching tightness lost in the wonderful relief of him filling that aching need. Without thinking, she rocked up to meet his gentle invasion.

She froze as a burning shock stopped her.

He kissed her softly and pulled back. "It cannot be helped, darling." He thrust and a sharp pain eclipsed the pleasure for a flashing instant.

His body didn't stop and the hurt and its memory quickly disappeared as he withdrew slowly and slid in again. It felt desperately good. Instinctively she embraced him with her legs, holding him closer, taking all of him to herself. She found his rhythm and rocked with it in a soundless chant of acceptance.

Nothing, not the songs or his touch or Joan's lesson, had prepared her for the intimacy that engulfed them. Skin on skin, breath on breath, limbs entwined and bodies joined . . . the physical connections overwhelmed her senses. Each time he withdrew, it was a loss. Each time he filled her, it was a renewed completion. It awed her and she sighed her amazement each time they rocked together.

He paused and she opened her eyes to see him looking at her. The careful mask was gone and those blue eyes showed the depths that he never let people see. She moved her hand and touched the perfect face, then let her caress drift down to his neck and chest.

He moved again and it was less gentle this time. He closed his eyes as if he sought to contain something, but if he fought a battle he lost it. "Aye," she whispered when he moved hard again. It hurt a little but the power of it awoke something in her soul. She wanted to absorb his strength and his need. She wanted to know him thus without his careful defenses.

He looked straight in her eyes and then kissed her as he surrendered. As his passion rose in a series of strong, deep thrusts and peaked in a long, hard release, she felt that she touched his essence and he hers.

She held him to her, her arms splayed across his back and her legs around his waist, and she floated in the emotion-laden silence, feeling his heartbeat against her breast. Her body felt bruised and alive and pulsing where they were still joined.

Slowly the chamber surrounded her again. She felt the reality of his weight and strength above her and his soft hair on her cheek.

Still half a stranger, she thought, wondering at this thing that could connect her in indescribable ways to a man whom she barely knew. Amazing and frightening to touch the soul when you did not know the mind.

Her awareness of the unknown half of him seeped around her. She suddenly felt very shy.

He rose up on his arms and kissed her gently. "You are wonderful," he said.

She didn't know what that meant but she was glad he was pleased. "It is much nicer than I thought it would be," she confided.

"Did I hurt you at the end?"

"Nay. In fact, I'm a little sorry it is over."

He caressed down her leg and removed it from his waist. He shifted off her. "That is because you are not done."

She thought of his almost violent ending. "I would say that we are most done, David."

He shook his head and touched her breast. Her eyes flew open at her immediate forceful response. His hand ventured between her legs. She grabbed onto him in surprise.

"I would have given this to you earlier, darling, but you needed to need me this first time," he said as the frenzy slammed into her again.

He touched and stroked at flesh still sensitive from the fullness of him, and a frantic wildness unhinged her. She called out to him, saying his name over and over as her mind and senses folded in on themselves and she lost hold of everything except the ascending pleasurable oblivion.

And then, when she thought that she couldn't bear it anymore and that she would die or faint, the tension snapped in a marvelous way and she screamed in the ecstasy of release rushing through her body.

She rode the eddies with stunned astonishment until they slowly flowed away.

"Oh my," she sighed as she lay breathless and trembling in his arms.

"Aye. Oh my," he said, laughing and pulling her closer. He reached for the bedclothes and covered them both, molding her against his body. His face rested on her hair, his lips against her temple. They lay together in a lulling peace.

The intimacy of their lovemaking had been stunning and poignant. This quiet closeness felt sweet and full and a little awkward. In the matter of an hour a connection had been forged forever. He had taken possession of her in ways she hadn't expected.

She slept and awoke to a darkened room, the twilight eking through the windows. Distant sounds of voices and activity drifted toward her. She turned and found David up on his arm, looking at her.

He liked looking at her. Like his carvings and books? It was something at least. It could have been a man who cared not for her at all.

"I should be going back," she said.

"You will stay here tonight. I will bring you in the morning."

"Idonia . . ."

"I sent a message that you were with me. She will not worry."

"She will know."

"Perhaps, but no one else will. I will get you back by dawn."

A shout from Vittorio echoed through the garden and into the windows. Everyone here probably knew, or would soon when she didn't leave. She thought of the sidelong glances that she faced from these servants and apprentices, from Idonia and even the whole court if word got out.

"You will stay here with me," he repeated. It wasn't a request.

He rose from the bed and walked to the hearth. His sculpted muscles moved as he stretched for a log and placed it on the fire. In the sudden bright illumination she studied his body, casual and unashamed of its nakedness, and noticed the lines on his back that her fingers had felt. Flogging scars. How had he come by them? His dead master did not sound like a man to do this. He returned to her and she watched him come, surprised by the thrilling pleasure she found in looking at him.

Pulling down the coverlet, he gazed at her body. He caressed her curves languidly. She watched that exciting hand move.

"Are you sore, darling? I would have you again, but not if it would hurt you."

Again? How often did people do this? For all of Joan's bluntness, a lot of information had been left out.

His frank statement of desire sent a tremor through her. She didn't doubt his concern for her, but she knew that his question also offered her a choice. "I am not hurt." She raised her arms to embrace him and the wonder.

Throughout the evening and night he forged an invisible chain of steel tying her to him. She felt it happening and wondered if it was something that he controlled. Links of passion and intimacy joined by pleasure and tenderness encircled her.

Late at night, while they basked in the hearth's warmth, she asked him about the wedding and learned that the ceremony had also been moved. They would wed in the cathedral with the bishop in attendance instead of in David's parish church.

"It is getting very elaborate," she mused.

"It couldn't be helped. Once the mayor found out that Edward was coming, the fat was in the fire. I had hoped no one would know and he could just show up."

He spoke of the King in a casual way. Why did she hesitate to just ask him about that relationship? Why did she feel that the topic was forbidden and that to pursue it would be prying?

She sensed that it would be, though, and tonight she did not want to knock on doors that he might not open. She changed the subject. "David, what else do you expect of me?"

The question surprised him. "What do you mean?"

"Considering how stupid I was about this, it won't surprise you to learn that I know little about marriage. I haven't had a very practical education."

"I expect you to be faithful to me. No other man touches you now."

His firm tone stunned her.

"Do you understand this, Christiana?"

"Of course. I'm not *that* stupid, David. I was referring to household things. Everything here is so organized."

"I hadn't really thought about it."

Then why did you go looking for a wife if you hadn't realized that you needed one.

"Isabele thinks that you expect me to work for you," she said, grinning.

"Does she now? I confess that it hadn't occurred to me, but it is a good idea. I shall have to thank the princess. A wife provides excellent free labor. We will get you a loom."

"I can't weave."

"You can learn."

"How much can you earn off of me after I learn?"

"At least five pounds a year, I would guess."

"That means that in two hundred years I will earn back my bride price."

"Aye. A shrewd bargain for me, isn't it?"

They laughed at that and then he added, "Well, the household is yours. Geva will be glad for it, I think. And the boys need a mother sometimes."

"One of the boys is older than me, David."

"It will not always be so, and Michael and Roger are far from home and could use a woman's understanding sometimes. And you will have your own children, too, in time."

Children. Everything he had mentioned could have been provided by some merchant's daughter who brought a large dowry. Children, too. But her sons would be the grandchildren of Hugh Fitzwaryn.

Morvan suspected that David sought their bloodline for his children with this marriage. Could he be right? She found that she hoped it was true. It would explain much, and mean that she brought something to him that another woman could not.

Late that night she awoke in his sleeping embrace. It seemed normal to be in his arms. She lay motionless, alert to his reality and warmth. How odd to feel so close to someone so quickly.

True to his word, he brought her back to Westminster by dawn. She walked through the corridors of a building that felt slightly foreign to her. She slipped into the hidden privacy of her bed while Joan and Idonia still slept.

A firm hand jostled her awake and she looked up into Joan's beaming face. "Aren't you coming to dinner? You sleep the sleep of the dead," Joan said.

Christiana thought that skipping dinner and just sleeping all day sounded like a wonderful idea, but she pulled herself up and asked Joan to call for a servant.

An hour later, dressed and coiffed, she sat beside Joan on a bench in the large hall, picking at food and watching the familiar scene that now looked slightly strange. Her senses were both alerted and dulled at the same time and she knew that those hours with David had caused this. Joan asked her some questions about David's house, and she answered halfheartedly, not wanting to share any of those memories right now.

Toward the end of the meal, Lady Catherine approached their table, her cat eyes gleaming. She chatted with Joan for a while and then turned a gracious face on Christiana.

"You marry quite soon, don't you, dear?"

Christiana nodded. Joan glanced at Catherine sharply, as if it was rude to mention this marriage.

"I have a small gift for you. I will send it to your chamber," Catherine said before leaving.

She wondered why Lady Catherine would do such a thing. After all, they weren't good friends. Still, the gesture touched her and left her thinking that Morvan, as usual, had overreacted to something in warning her off Catherine.

Thomas Holland spirited Joan away and left Christiana on her own. She returned to Isabele's deserted apartment, glad for the privacy. The court routine seemed intrusive when her thoughts dwelled on yesterday and the future.

She went into Isabele's chamber. *Four days and I leave here forever*, she thought, looking out the window. She no longer feared that. A part of her had already departed.

The sound of a door opening reached her ears. Joan or Idonia returning. She hadn't seen the guardian since her return. She wondered what that little woman would say to her.

The footsteps that advanced through the anteroom were not a woman's, however. Morvan had come. One look at her and he would know. Was she brave enough to say "Aye, you were right and it was magic and I liked it?" His strength had stood for years between her and all men, and now she had given herself to one whom he hated.

The steps came forward. They stopped at the threshold to the bedchamber.

"Darling," a familiar voice said.

Shock screamed through her. She swung around.

There in the doorway stood none other than Stephen Percy.

CHAPTER 12

"STEPHEN," SHE GASPED.

He smiled and advanced toward her, his arms inviting an embrace. She watched him come with an odd combination of astonished dismay, warm delight, and cold objectivity. She noticed the thick muscles beneath his pourpoint. She observed the harsh handsomeness of his features. His blond hair and fair skin struck her as blanched and vague compared to David's golden coloring.

She couldn't move. Confused, horrified, and yearning emotions paralyzed her. *Not now*, her soul shrieked. *A month ago or a month hence, but not now. Especially not today.*

Strong arms surrounded her. A hard mouth crushed hers.

She pushed him off. His green eyes expressed surprise and then, briefly, something else. Annoyance?

"You are angry with me, my love," he said with a sigh. "I cannot blame you."

She turned away, grasping the edge of the window for support. Dear God, was she to have no peace? She had found acceptance and contentment and even the hope of something more, and now this.

"Why are you here?"

"To see you, of course."

"You returned to Westminster to see me?"

"Aye, darling. Why else? I used the excuse of the pre-Lenten tournament."

The tournament was scheduled to begin the day after her wedding. Stephen loved those contests. She suspected that was his true reason for coming, but her broken heart, not yet totally healed, lurched at the notion that he came for her.

The pain was still too raw, the humiliation still too new, for her to completely reject the hope that he indeed loved her. The girl who had been faithful to this man desperately still wanted to believe it. Her heart yearned for that reassurance.

Her mind, however, had learned a thing or two from its agony. "When did you arrive?"

"Two days ago. I did not seek you immediately because I was with my friend Geoffrey. He is in a bad way with a fever. He lies in Lady Catherine's house in London."

"You are friends with Catherine?"

"Not really. Geoffrey is, however." He stepped toward her. "She told me all about your marriage to this merchant," he said sympathetically. "If Edward were not my king, I would challenge him for degrading you thus."

She glanced at the concern in his expression. It struck her as a little exaggerated, like a mask one puts on for a festival.

He reached out and caressed her face. The broken heart, aching for the balm of renewed illusions, sighed.

The spirit and mind, remembering last night's passion and David's rights, made her move away.

"You already knew of my marriage, did you not? I wrote you a letter."

"I knew. I received it, darling. But I never imagined that the King would go through with this. And Catherine has told me of your unhappiness and humiliation."

How kind of Lady Catherine, Christiana thought bitterly. Why did this woman meddle in her affairs? And how had Catherine known about Stephen and her?

Joan. Joan had gossiped. Did everyone know now? Probably. They would all be watching and waiting the next few days, maybe the next few years, to see how this drama unfolded.

"Perhaps I should not have come," Stephen muttered. "Catherine assured me that you would want to see me."

"I am glad to see you, Stephen. At the least I can congratulate you on your own betrothal."

He made a face of resignation. "She was my father and uncle's choice, my sweet. She does not suit me, in truth."

"All the same, she is your wife. As David is my husband."

"Aye, and it tears me apart that there is nought we can do about that, my sweet."

A candle inside her snuffed out then, and she knew that it was the last flame of her illusions and childish dreams. It did not hurt much, but something of her innocence died with it, and she felt that loss bitterly.

Through it all, she had saved a little bit of hope, despite knowing and seeing the truth. If he had not returned, it would have slowly disappeared as she lived her life and spent her passion with David, much as a small pool of water will disappear in the heat of a summer afternoon.

What if Stephen had spoken differently? What if he had come to plead with her to run away together and petition to have both of their betrothals annulled? It was what that reserve of hope had wanted, after all.

A week ago she would have done it, despite the disgrace that would fall on her. Even last weekend, such an offer might have instantly healed her pain and banished her doubts about him.

Now, however, it would have been impossible. Now . . .

A horrible comprehension dawned. Stephen's presence receded as her mind grasped the implications.

Impossible now. David had seen to that, hadn't he?

Last night had consummated their marriage. No annulment would be possible now, unless David himself denied what had occurred. And she knew, she just knew, that he would not, despite his promise that first night.

I expect you to be faithful to me. No other man touches you now.

All of those witnesses . . . even Idonia and her brother.

An eerie chill shook her.

David had known Stephen was coming. He had been asking the pilgrims and merchants. He could not know if Stephen came to claim her, however. Nonetheless, he had still covered that eventuality. Methodically, carefully, he had made sure that she could not leave with Stephen. If she did anyway, despite the invisible chains forged last night, despite the dishonor and disgrace, he possessed the proof necessary to get her back.

The ruthlessness of it stunned her.

She remembered the poignant emotions she had felt last night. Twice a fool. More childish illusions. Her stupid trust of men must be laughable to them.

A warm presence near her shoulder interrupted her thoughts. Stephen hovered closely, his face near hers.

"There is nought that we can do about these marriages, darling, but in life there is duty and then there is love."

"What are you saying, Stephen?"

"You cannot love this man, Christiana. It will never happen. He is base and his very touch will insult you. I would spare you that if I could, but I cannot. But I can soothe your hurt, darling. Our love can do that. Give this merchant your duty, but keep our love in your heart."

She wanted to tell him how wrong he was, how David's touch never insulted. But what words could she use to explain that? Besides, she wasn't at all sure that the magic would return now that she knew why he had seduced her. Perhaps the next time, on their wedding night, she would indeed feel insulted and used.

Well, what had she expected? David was a merchant and she was property. Very expensive property. She doubted that King Edward gave refunds.

Love, she thought sadly. She had thought that there was some love in it. Her ignorance was amazing. David was right. She did live her life like she expected it to be some love song. But life was not like that. Men were not like that.

"I am a married woman, Stephen. What you are suggesting is dishonorable."

He smiled at her much the way one might smile at an innocent child. "Love has nothing to do with honor and dishonor. It has to do with feeling alive instead of dead. You will realize that soon enough."

"I hope that you are not so bold as to ask for the proof of my love now. I wed in several days."

"Nay. I would not give a merchant reason to upbraid or harm you, although the thought of him having you first angers me. Marry your mercer as you must, darling. But know that I am here."

"I am an honest woman, Stephen. And I do not think that you love me at all. I think that this was a game to you, and still is. A game in which you lose nothing but I risk everything. I will not play in the future."

He began protesting and reaching for her. Footsteps in the anteroom stopped him. She turned to the new presence at the threshold.

Good Lord, was there no mercy?

Morvan filled the doorway, gazing at them both. For one horrible moment an acute tension filled the room.

"Percy, it is good to see you," Morvan said, advancing into the chamber. "You have come for the tournament?"

"Aye," Stephen said, easing away from her.

Morvan eyed them both again. "I assume that you are wishing each other happiness in your upcoming marriages."

She nodded numbly. There was no point in trying to explain away Stephen's presence. She saw in her brother's eyes that he had heard the gossip.

"It is a strange thing about my sister's marriage, Stephen," Morvan said as he paced to the hearth. "It is said that the King sold her for money, and I believed that too. But I have lately wondered if this didn't come about for another reason. Perhaps he sought to salvage her reputation and my family's honor, and not disgrace it."

She watched them consider each other. *Not now, Morvan*, she urged silently. *It doesn't matter anymore.*

"I must be going, my lady," Stephen said, turning a

warm smile on her. She gestured helplessly and watched him stride across the chamber.

"Sir Stephen," Morvan called from the hearth. "It would be unwise for you to pursue this."

"Do you threaten me?" Stephen hissed.

"Nay. It is no longer for me to do so. I simply tell you as a friend that it would be a mistake. Her husband is not your typical merchant. And I have reason to think that he knows well how to use the daggers that he wears."

Stephen smirked in a condescending way before leaving the apartment.

She faced her brother's dark scrutiny. He looked her up and down, and searched her eyes with his own.

"It is customary, sister, to wait a decent interval after the wedding before meeting with one's old lovers."

She had no response to that calm scolding.

"And since you spent the night in that man's bed, you are indeed truly wed now."

"David. His name is David. You always call him 'that merchant' or 'that man,' Morvan. He has a name."

He regarded her with lowered lids. "I am right, am I not? You slept with him. With *David*."

It was pointless to lie. She knew he could tell. She nodded, feeling much less secure about that decision now that she understood David's motivations.

"You must not see Percy again for a long while."

"I did not arrange to meet Stephen."

"Still, you should be careful. Such things are taken in stride if the woman is discreet or if the husband does not care, but you have no experience in such deceptions and your merchant does not strike me as a willing cuckold."

"I told Stephen that I am not interested in him anymore."

"He does not believe you."

He was just trying to help her. In this his advice was probably as sound as any man's. He'd certainly bedded his share of married women.

"Do you despise me?" she whispered.

A strained expression covered his face. He strode across the space and gathered her into his arms. "Nay. But I would not have you be this man's wife, and I would not have you be Percy's whore. Can you understand that? And I blame myself because I did not find a way to take you away from here."

She looked into his dark eyes. She read the worry there and thought that she understood part of it.

"I do not think that being David's wife will be so bad, Morvan. He can be very kind."

A small smile teased at his mouth. "Well, that at least is good news. I am glad that he is accomplished at something besides making money."

She giggled. He tightened his embrace and then released her. "Take your meals with me these last days," he said. "I would have this time with you."

She nodded and watched sadly as he walked away.

She never doubted that her brother had requested her attendance at meals because he wanted her company. She would be leaving him soon, and a subtle nostalgia hung between them at those dinners and suppers, even when they conversed merrily with the other young people at their table.

Morvan's presence beside her had other benefits, however, and she suspected that he had thought of them. Stephen did not dare approach her in the hall while Morvan stayed nearby, and the peering, glancing courtiers received no satisfaction to their curiosity about the status of that love affair.

Everyone knew. Stephen had only to rise from his bench and sidelong looks would watch to see if he would speak with her. It became abundantly clear that the court believed an adulterous affair with Stephen was probably inevitable at some point. She got the impression that many of these nobles accepted the notion with relief, as if such an affair would be a form of redemption for her. The marriage to the merchant would just be a formality, then, and much easier to swallow and even ignore.

Aye, Joan had gossiped. When Christiana confronted her, she tearfully admitted it. Just one girl, she insisted. Christiana had no trouble imagining that small leak turning into a river of whispers within hours.

She filled the next days with preparations for the wedding. Philippa came to the apartment to survey her wardrobe on Saturday and immediately ordered more shifts and hose made for her. A new surcoat was fitted as well. Haberdashers descended so that she could choose two new headdresses. Trunks arrived to be filled with linens and household goods for her to bring to her new home.

She spent most of her time in the apartment managing this accumulation, but her mind dwelled on David. They had agreed that he would not come before the wedding because of their time-consuming preparations and because he had his own affairs to put in order. All the same, she expected him to surprise her with a visit. It would be the romantic thing to do, but when he came it would not be for that reason, although he might pretend that it was. She expected him to check that Stephen had not persuaded her to run away or do anything dishonorable. He would want to make sure that his plan had worked.

He did not come. Saturday turned into Sunday and stretched into Monday. She began to get annoyed.

She felt positive that David knew that Stephen had returned. How could he just leave her here to her own devices when another man drifted about who wanted to seduce her? A man, furthermore, with whom she had been in love? Was he that sure of himself? That sure that one night could balance the ledger sheet of a woman's heart? Didn't he worry about what Stephen's presence might be doing to her?

She pondered this sporadically during the days. At night she chewed it over resentfully. But in the dark silence of her curtained bed, her recriminations always managed to flow away as other thoughts of David would flood her like some inexorable incoming tide. Images of his blue eyes and straight shoulders above her. The power of his passion overwhelming his thoughtful restraint. Her breasts would grow sensitive and her thighs moist and the thoughts would merge into wakeful dreams during a fitful sleep.

She awoke each morning feeling as though she had been ravished by a phantom but had found no release.

David did not come, but others did. Singly or in twos or threes, the women of the court approached her.

Aye, Joan had gossiped, and not just about Stephen. It seemed every lady felt obliged to advise the motherless girl who, rumor had it, was unbelievably ignorant about procreation.

Some of the servants joined in. While she bathed on her wedding day, the girl who attended her boldly described how to make a man mad with desire. Christiana blushed from her hairline to her toes. She seriously doubted that noblewomen did most of these things, but she tucked the tamer tidbits away in her mind.

Getting her dressed turned into a merry party with all of her friends there. They gave her presents and chatted as the servants prepared her. Philippa arrived to escort her down to the hall. The Queen examined her closely and reset the red cloak on her shoulders. Then with her daughters beside her, and with Idonia, Joan, and several other women in attendance, Queen Philippa brought her down to the hall.

Morvan awaited them. He wore a formal robe that reached to mid-calf. His knight's belt bound his waist but no sword hung there. "Come now," he said, taking her arm. "The King already awaits."

The doors swung open. She stepped outside.

She froze. "Oh, dear saints," she gasped.

"Quite a sight, isn't it?" Morvan muttered dryly.

The yard was full of horses and people and transport vehicles. She saw Lady Elizabeth entering one of the painted covered wagons, and other feminine arms dangling from its windows. Knights and lords waited on horses decked out for a pageant. King Edward, resplendent in a gold-embroidered red robe, paced his stallion near the doorway. A long line of royal guards stood waiting.

The presence of so many knights and nobles touched her. They came to honor her family and, perhaps, to reassure her. They also came for her brother's sake, and she was grateful.

The extensive royal entourage, and the obvious instructions that everyone should follow the King in parade, were another matter.

The King gestured and three golden chariots drove forward.

"Oh, dear saints," she gasped again, watching this final grandiose touch arrive.

"Aye, one is for you. The Queen herself will ride with you," Morvan explained.

"This retinue will stretch for blocks. All of London will watch this."

"The King honors you, Christiana."

She turned away from Edward's smiling gaze and spoke lowly into her brother's shoulder. "I am not stupid, Morvan. The King does not honor me, he honors London. He does not bring Christiana Fitzwaryn to wed David de Abyndon. He brings a daughter of the nobility to marry a son of the city. He turns me into a gift to London and a symbol of his generosity to her."

He grasped her elbow and eased her forward. "It cannot be undone. You must be our mother's daughter in this and handle it as she would have. I will ride beside you."

She let him guide her to the front chariot and lift her in. She bent and whispered in his ear. "I will think the whole time how I am not the virgin sacrifice they expect."

The parade filed out of the yard, led by the King and his sons. By the time they reached the Strand, thick crowds had formed. Inside the city gates it got worse. The guards used their horses to keep the people back. Slowly, with excruciating visibility, they made their way through to St. Paul's Cathedral.

Morvan lifted her off the chariot. "Well, brother, don't you have anything to say to me?" she asked as they approached the entrance. "No words of advice? No lectures on being a dutiful and obedient wife? There is no father to admonish me, so it falls to you, doesn't it?"

He paused on the porch and glanced through the open portal into the cavernous nave filled with noisy courtiers and curious townspeople.

"Aye, I have words for you, but no lectures." He bent to her ear. "You are a very beautiful girl. There is power for a woman in a man's desire, little sister. Use it well and you will own him and not the other way around."

She laughed. Smiling, he sped her down the nave.

David waited near the altar. Her heart lurched at the sight of him. He looked magnificent, perfect, the equal of any lord in attendance. The narrow cut of his long, belted, blue velvet robe enhanced his height. The fitted sleeves made the exaggerated lengths and widths of the other men's fashions look ridiculous and unmanly. Beautiful gold embroidery decorated the edges and center of the garment. She wondered who had convinced him to agree to that. The heavy gold chain stretched from shoulder to shoulder.

Morvan handed her over. Idonia fluttered by, took her cloak, and disappeared. David gazed down at her while the noise of the crowd echoed off the high stone ceiling.

"You are the most beautiful girl whom I have ever met," he said, repeating the words he had spoken in the ivy garden.

She had a long list of things to upbraid him about, and some deep hurts and misgivings that worried her heart. But the warmth in those blue eyes softened her, and the sound of his beautiful voice soothed her. There would be time enough for worry and hurt. This was her wedding and the whole world watched.

An hour later she emerged from the cathedral with a gold ring around her finger and David de Abyndon's arm around her waist. The chariot awaited but Sieg, looking almost civilized in a handsome gray robe, brought over a horse.

"You will ride with me, darling. With these crowds, those chariots may never make it to the Guildhall."

"You might have warned me about all of this, David," she said as pandemonium spilled into the cathedral yard and surrounding streets. "It was like the prelude to an ancient sacrifice."

"I did not know, but perhaps I should have expected something like this. Edward loves ceremony and pageantry, doesn't he?"

She wasn't convinced. He always seemed to know

everything. She glanced askance at his face as he lifted her onto the saddle and swung up behind. His bland acceptance of Edward's behavior irked her, but then he hadn't been the girl on public display.

"The King must think very highly of you to have brought such an entourage," she remarked dryly.

"I would be a fool to think so. This had nothing to do with you or me."

They joined the flow of mounted knights and lords inching toward the Cheap. David's arm encircled her waist, his hand resting beneath her cloak. She reached up and touched the diamond hanging from a silver chain around her neck. It had been delivered while she dressed. "Thank you for the necklace. It went perfectly with the gown."

"Edmund assured me that it would. I'm pleased that you like it."

"Edmund?"

"The tailor who made your wedding garments, Christiana. And your betrothal gown. And most of your cotehardies and surcoats over the last few years. His name is Edmund. He is one of the leading citizens of the town of Westminster and an important man in his world."

She felt herself blush. She knew the tailor's name. She had simply forgotten it just now. But David was telling her that she should know the people who served her and not think of them as nonentities.

Her chagrin quickly gave way to annoyance. She didn't like it that one of the first things her new husband had said to her had been this oblique scolding.

Other reasons for annoyance marched forward in her mind.

"I thought that you would come to see me," she said.

"We agreed that I would not."

"All the same, I thought that you would come."

She felt him looking at her, but he said nothing.

"He is back at court," she added. "But, of course, you know that, don't you?"

"I know."

That was it. No questions. Nothing else.

"Didn't you wonder what would happen?" she blurted angrily. "Are you that damn sure of yourself?"

"To have come would have insulted you. I assumed that the daughter of Hugh Fitzwaryn had too much pride and honor to leave her marriage bed and go to another man, especially after she had seen the truth about him."

"All the same . . ."

"Christiana," he interrupted quietly, lowering his mouth to her ear and running his lips along its edge, "we will not speak of this now. I did not come because my days were filled making ready for this wedding. In the time I could steal, I settled business affairs so that I could spend the next three days in bed with you. And my nights were spent thinking about what I would do when I had you there."

She would have liked to ignore the shiver of excitement that his lips and words summoned, but her body had been betraying her during the nights too and now it responded against her will.

She forced herself to remember his calculating seduction to claim his property. She resented self-confidence.

"What makes you think that I will choose to spend the next three days that way?" she asked.

"You are my wife now, girl. Surely you know that you only have choices if I give them to you." He pressed his lips to her temple and spoke more gently. "You will find that I am a reasonable master, darling. I have always preferred persuasion to command."

Beneath the full flow of her cloak, he reached up and caressed her breast.

Her body shook with a startling release of pleasure.

She glanced around nervously at the faces turned up to them in smiling curiosity.

He stroked at her nipple and kissed her cheek. She felt the urge to turn and bite his neck. She twisted her head and accepted the deep kiss waiting for her and those wonderful sensations flowed through her like a delicious sigh of relief.

All of London watched.

"David, people . . . they can see . . ." she whispered breathlessly when he lifted his head but did not move his hand. His fingers were driving her mad.

"They cannot. Some might suspect, but none can know for sure," he whispered. "If you are angry with me, you can upbraid me at will after the banquets. I promise to listen very seriously and take all of your criticisms to heart." He kissed her neck again. "Even as I lick your breasts and kiss your thighs, I will be paying close attention to your scolding. We can discuss my bad behavior between your cries of pleasure."

She was already having a very hard time remembering what she wanted to scold or discuss.

At about the point when she felt an unrelenting urge to squirm against the saddle, they arrived at the Guildhall. She worried that she would not be able to stand on her languid legs when he lifted her to the ground.

"That wasn't fair," she hissed.

He took her hand and led her into the Guildhall. "I only play to win, Christiana, and I make my own rules. Haven't you learned that by now?"

CHAPTER 13

DAVID LEANED IN the shadows against the threshold of the hall, watching the dancers whirl around the huge bonfire in the center of the courtyard. Couples romped together in a round dance on the periphery of the circle, but near the center a group of women performed an energetic exhibition alone. Oliver's woman Anne led the group, since she danced professionally on occasion when the opportunity and pay were convenient. Serving girls and women from the ward surrounded her. In the thick of it, her face flushed with delight and her eyes sparkling with pleasure, swung the elegant figure of Christiana Fitzwaryn.

The lights from the bonfire seemed to flame over the women in a rhythm that matched the beating drums. The whole courtyard and house glowed from that huge blaze and from the many torches lining the buildings and the back garden. The fires tinted the night sky orange, and from a distance it probably appeared that the house was burning. No doubt the priests would insist that the scene, with revelers giving themselves over to all of the deadly sins, resembled the inferno of hell itself.

People filled the courtyard, the gardens, and the rooms of the house. Men and woman perched on the roof of the stable. To his left several couples embraced in a dark corner.

A loud laugh caught his attention and he leaned back and glanced into the hall. The milling bodies parted for a moment and he saw the laughing man sitting by the fire with a girl on each knee. The gold embroidery on the red robe was the only proof that this man was a king, for Edward had shed his royal persona as soon as he slipped through the gate with his two guards after sending his wife and family home after the Guildhall banquet. He was well into his cups now, and long ago the party had stopped treating him like the sovereign and simply absorbed him into their merriment.

David returned his attention to his wife. He enjoyed watching her even when she didn't move at all, but her freedom and pleasure in this dance mesmerized him. Like her King, she had quickly succumbed to the unrestrained mood of this second party, and David had delighted in watching her joy as she feasted and drank and traded jests with the neighbors from the ward.

She moved beautifully, languidly, imbuing even this base dance with a noble elegance. Her lips parted in a sensual smile as she twirled around, enjoying at last the ecstasy of movement that she had vicariously felt so often before.

He watched and waited, suppressing the urge to walk to that fire and pick her up and carry her away.

He wanted her. Badly. He had wanted her for weeks, and their night together had only made the wanting more fierce. He had spent the last days in a state of perpetual desire.

Her innocence that day had disarmed him in a dangerous way. Her passion had no defenses, and her total giving and taking had burned down his own. Unlike the experienced women he usually bedded, she knew nothing about protecting herself from the deeper intimacies that could emerge in lovemaking, knew nothing about holding her essence separate from the joining, knew nothing about keeping the act one of simple physical pleasure. She had felt the closeness for what it could be and had simply let the power come and wash over them both. He had seen the wonder of it in her eyes and felt her amazement of it in her grasping embrace and had almost warned her to be careful, for there could be danger and pain in it for her, too. But he had not warned her, for that deep intimacy brought a knowing of her that something inside him craved and in the end he also proved defenseless against the magic that he hadn't felt in so many years.

His gaze followed her, his body responding to the seductive moves of her dance. In his mind's eye she looked up at him and touched his face and his chest and sighed an "aye" that asked for all of himself.

A figure strolled in front of him, mercifully distracting his heated thoughts. Morvan drank some wine as he walked, casually surveying the dancers.

The drums and timbrels beat out a frenzied finale and then the dance ended abruptly. All around the fire, bodies stopped and heaved deep breaths from their exertions. Christiana and Anne embraced with a laugh.

She thought that Anne was Oliver's wife. He would have to tell her the truth, he supposed.

Morvan caught Christiana's eye and gestured for her. She skipped over to him with a broad smile. He bent and said something, and David watched the happiness and pleasure fall from her face and her body like someone had stripped it off.

She threw her arms around him and spoke earnestly, entreating him no doubt to stay longer. Morvan shook his head, caressed her face, and pulled away.

He walked toward the gate. Christiana gazed after him, her straight body suddenly alone and isolated despite the crowd milling around her. David could see her composed expression but he had no trouble reading the sadness in her.

Her whole life, her whole family, her whole past was leaving the house now.

He pushed away from the threshold and went to her. He draped her cloak over her shoulders, and she glanced up with a weak smile before her gaze returned to the retreating tall man.

He smiled and shook his head. He strode after Morvan, calling his name. A part of him couldn't believe that he was going to do this for her.

The young knight stopped and turned. He came back and met David partway. They faced each other in the fire glow.

"You are leaving, Morvan?"

"Aye. It is best if I go now." He glanced at his sister.

"You must come and visit her soon. She will want to see you."

Morvan looked over in surprise.

"Her life will be much changed and it may be hard on her," David continued. "I would not have her unhappy. Come when you will. This house is always open to you."

Morvan looked more surprised yet. He nodded and smiled a little. "I thank you for that, David. For both our sakes."

David walked back to Christiana. The cloak was falling off and he wrapped her in it more warmly, embracing her shoulder.

"What did you say to him?" she asked, her gaze still on her brother.

"I told him that he must visit you whenever he wants."

"Did you, David? Did you really?" She turned to him with a bright smile. Her unaffected surprise and gratitude wrenched something inside him.

"I know that he is all that you have, darling. He only sought to protect you, and I can blame no man for that. I would not stand between you."

She nestled closer to him and looked into his eyes with an almost childish innocence. "Not all that I have, David. Not anymore. There is you now, isn't there? We have each other, don't we?"

He embraced her and she placed her head on his chest, her face turned to the shadows that swallowed her brother's tall body. David laid his face on the silky cloud of her hair.

All that she was, all that she was supposed to be, left through that gate. The life she had led and had been born to live, the position assured her by her blood, returned to Westminster tonight without her. He didn't doubt that she understood that. She knew what this marriage had taken from her.

He kissed her hair and closed his eyes. He could give it back to her. All that she was losing and more. It was in his power to do so. The offer still stood and would be made again, of that he was sure. He had only to play out the game as planned but change the final move. He knew exactly how to do it. He had been considering the possibility for weeks.

As if reading his thoughts, she tilted her head and looked up at him. "You are very good to me, David. I know that you will take care of me and do all that you can for me."

He bent to kiss her and her parted lips rose to meet

his. A tremor shook her and she pressed herself against him as she embraced him tightly. His mind clouded and the restraint of the last hours cracked.

She grasped him as desperately as he did her, her mouth inviting his deep kiss. Perhaps it was the wine and the dance. Maybe it was her gratitude over Morvan. He didn't care. He would accept her passion any way that it came to him.

They stood thus at the edge of the fire glow, two bodies molded together, banishing the separateness, the sounds of revelry echoing around them. He kissed her again and again, wanting to consume her and absorb her into himself.

He found the sanity to pull his mouth away. "Come upstairs with me now," he whispered, his face buried in her neck, her scent driving him mad.

"Aye," she said. "Now."

He turned her under his arm while he kissed her again. Somehow he found his way blindly across the courtyard, into the building, and up the stairs. A group of revelers discreetly poured out of the solar when they arrived, and he kicked the door closed behind them.

In his chamber he threw off their cloaks and fell on the bed with her, covering her with his body, feeling her pliant length bend up into him. His head emptied to everything but the feel and smell of her. He tried to check himself, tried to calm the thundering storm that controlled him, but the deep, probing kiss he gave her turned fierce and needful when she took his head between her hands and pressed him closer.

He managed to remove her surcoat without tearing it, but the cotehardie's lacing defied his practiced fingers. He plucked at the knot as he kissed and bit the tops of her breasts. Finally, in a fury of frustration, he moved aside, turned her on her stomach, and stared at the recalcitrant closure.

"Hold still," he muttered, pulling out his dining dagger and blinking away the obscuring passion. He rose on his knees and slid the blade under the lacings. "It is an old wedding trick. Your servants tied a knot that cannot be undone."

She laughed beautifully, lyrically, and then turned on her back, joyfully helping him push down the gown. When it was gone, she got to her knees and flew to him as if the separation had lasted an eternity.

He lost himself then. In a frantic whirlwind of caresses and kisses, they managed to pull off his clothes. With cries and gasps and little ecstatic laughs, her hands met his on his belt and shirt and finally poured heatedly over his skin. He pushed her shift down from her shoulders, uncovering her breasts, and bent her back so that he could revel in their sweet softness.

Her cries undid him and unraveled his last thread of control. He pushed the shift up her hips and felt for the moisture of her arousal.

"I promise that I will give you slow pleasure later," he said as he laid her down. "All night if you want. But right now I cannot wait, darling."

He spread her legs and knelt between them. She looked up at him, her dark eyes full of stars.

He gazed at her lovely face and her round white breasts. The shift bunched at her waist and the hose were still gartered at her knees. He pushed the bottom of the shift up higher, exposing her hips and stomach. He touched the pulsing, swollen flesh between her thighs and watched the pleasure quake through her.

The fantasies of his desire pressed on him relentlessly. Despite her ignorance and his need, he could not resist them all. He bent her legs so that she was raised and open to him. Her ragged breathing broke through his fog, and he glanced and saw the flicker of wariness and surprise in her eyes.

"Do not be afraid," he said as he lifted her hips. "I want to kiss all of you. That is all."

He knew that he could not indulge himself thus for long. His own body would not let him. Nor, it turned out, would hers. She writhed and cried out from the shock and intensity of this new pleasure, and soon he felt the first flexes of her release.

He left her and came up over her, bringing her legs with him, settling them on his shoulders. She thrashed in frustration that he had brought her to the edge of the precipice but no further.

"Soon, darling. I promise. When we are together," he said soothingly, and he rose up and entered her with one thrust.

His whole body shook from the torturous pleasure of it, but the tremor itself gave him back some of his control. Extending his arms, he stroked into her, his consciousness filling with the exquisite sensation that came from tottering on the edge of his own release.

She watched him as he moved, her hands caressing his shoulders and chest in that open, accepting way of hers, her sparkling eyes and soft sighs telling him that he filled other needs besides those of her body. The emotions seeped out of her and around him and embraced them both as surely as their arms had entwined moments ago.

He felt her tensing, stretching, for her climax. His own control began crumbling. He reached down between their bodies to give her release. As the frenzy possessed her she grabbed fiercely for him, arching her hips up against his thrusts, pulling him with her into the delicious oblivion.

He rarely sought a mutual release. In fact he avoided

them. Now, as their passion peaked and shattered together, he felt her ecstasy even as his own split through him. For an unearthly instant the lightning of the storm melted them into one sharing completeness.

When they were done, he stayed with her, kissing her softly while he moved her legs down, letting himself enjoy the glorious expression on her beautiful face. He rolled over to his back, bringing her with him so that she lay on him. He held her there, her head on his chest and her knees straddling his hips, and watched his hand caress her pale back and hips.

After a long while she lifted her head and cocked it thoughtfully. "I hear lutes," she said.

"You flatter me."

She giggled and thumped his shoulder playfully. "Nay, David. I really do. Listen."

He focused his awareness and heard the lyrical tones amidst the distant noise of the party. He moved her off, got out of bed, and disappeared into the wardrobe.

Christiana waited, still floating in the wonder and magic of their passion. It seemed that the lutes got louder.

He returned and pulled the coverlet off the bed. "They are for you. You should acknowledge them." He draped the warm cover over his shoulders, and she got up and joined him in its cozy cocoon.

The door to the stairs leading to the ivy garden was open, and they went out on the stone landing. David lifted her up and sat her on the low surrounding wall, tucking the coverlet securely around her legs.

Below in the tiny garden she could see four men with lutes. They sang the poetic lines of a love song. She recognized the deep bass of Walter Manny.

"Who are the others?" she whispered.

"They are all from the Pui. It is a tradition when one of them marries."

They began another song. Torches lit the larger garden, but here the singers were only dark forms in the shadows. Above them the clear night sky glittered with a hundred stars. David stood beside her, holding her under their cover, nuzzling her hair. There was something incredibly romantic about being with him in the cold night with the intimacy of their joining still hanging on them while the music played.

Walter sang the next song alone. It possessed a slow, quiet melody that she had heard only once before. It was the song that David had sung that day in the hall, the one she had found so sad at the time. Now she realized that it wasn't sad at all, just soft and beautiful. It had sent her off thinking of Stephen that day, and she hadn't really noticed the words, but this time she listened carefully.

It wasn't really a love song, but more a song that praised a woman and her beauty. The words spoke of elegant limbs and noble bearing. Her hair was described as black as the velvet night, her skin pale as moonlight, and her eyes like the diamonds of the stars. . . .

She grew very still. She listened to the rest of the lovely song that described her. David had written this. He had played it in the hall for her that day, and she hadn't even heard it.

Walter's voice and lute closed the melody. She looked up at the shadow of the man beside her. Her heart glowed warm and proud that he had honored her in this way, so long ago, even as she treated him so badly.

"Thank you," she whispered, stretching up to kiss his face.

They listened to several more songs, and then the four musicians walked forward and bowed to her. "Thank you, Walter," she called quietly.

"My lady," he replied, and the shadows swallowed him.

"What a marvelous tradition," she said to David as they returned to their bed. "Have you done that?"

"Aye, I've spent my share of cold winter nights in gardens singing to new brides. We stay until she acknowledges that she has heard us. On occasion the groom is so enraptured in bed that it takes hours. We give him hell afterwards then."

She laughed and rested her head on his shoulder.

"It was a wonderful wedding, David." A din still leaked through the windows from the continued revelry outside and below. "I had so much fun. Anne says that I dance very well for an amateur. She said that she will teach me more if I want."

"If it pleases you, you should do it."

"I like her. I like Oliver, too. He is an old friend?"

"From when we were boys."

"Have they been married a long time?"

A peculiar expression passed over his face. He looked so handsome now, his golden brown hair falling over his forehead, his deep blue eyes regarding her.

"Christiana, Oliver sells women. Anne lives with him but is not his wife. She is one of his women."

"You mean she is his whore? Anne is a whore? She does this with strangers, for pay? He lets her, and even brings the men to her?"

"Aye."

"How can he? He seemed to care for her, David. How . . ."

"In truth, I do not know."

She pictured Anne, with her pretty brown curls and sweet but worldly face. "It must be horrible for her."

"I suspect that most of her isn't really there with them."

Could people do that? Join like this and not even care about it, not feel anything? Or just take the pleasure and close their eyes to the person giving it? It struck her as a sad and frightening thought.

She turned her head and gazed up at the billowing canopy of blue cloth above them, feeling sorry for Anne and not much liking Oliver for expecting such things of her. They were poor, true, but surely there must be some other way.

And yet, she had to admit that this lovemaking obviously happened in all kinds of ways and for all kinds of reasons. In fact, she suspected that often love had nothing to do with it at all, especially for men. After all, the desire that she and David shared was mostly physical, wasn't it? For him, that was all that it was. And other women had been here, where she was now, experiencing the same thing. He had wanted them and now he wanted her. Whom would he want next?

The magic and wonder suddenly seemed a lot less special.

Did it last long, this desire? Perhaps if a man paid a thousand pounds for a woman, he felt obligated to desire her for a long time. But when the desire faded, what would be left for her? A home and maybe children. Not small things, but she wanted more.

The admission startled her and she didn't understand the feelings that it revealed. She realized, however, that there could be danger in this bed with this man, and the chance of disappointments far worse than she had known with Stephen Percy.

A strange emptiness opened inside her. It felt like a desolate loneliness, despite the man who held her. She had been having a wonderful time these last hours, laughing and dancing and being overwhelmed by their mutual passion. Nestling with him outside while the love songs played had been so romantic. She bleakly realized that she had been foolishly building another illusion, another dream.

She felt him shift and then those blue eyes were above her, studying her.

"What are you thinking about?" he asked.

Don't you know? she wanted to say. *You always know.*

She met his gaze and realized that he did know. At least part of it.

"I am thinking that there is more to all of this than I understand." She made a little gesture that covered the bed. "You must find me very childish and ignorant compared to the other women whom you have known."

Beautiful women. Worldly women. Experienced women. She could never compete with them. She didn't even know how. Why in God's name had he married her?

His hand caressed her cheek and turned her face to his. "I am most pleased with you, Christiana."

She felt a little better then, but not much.

"Alicia was your lover, wasn't she?" she blurted.

"Aye. But it is over."

"There were others, too, others whom I know and who know me," she said blankly.

He just looked at her.

"Elizabeth?" she asked, thinking of that exquisitely lovely woman and feeling a spike of infuriating jealousy. No one could ever compete with Elizabeth.

"Elizabeth is an old friend, but we were never lovers."

Protective indignation instantly replaced the jealousy. "Why not! You are better than most of the men she has been linked with. And that lord she married is old and ugly."

He laughed. "Now you are angry with her because we didn't sleep together? Nay, there was no insult in it. Elizabeth likes her lovers very young."

"You are young."

"Not young enough. She likes them still partly unformed. She wants to influence them."

"Young like Morvan?"

"Aye."

She thought about that, and those months when Morvan had attended on Elizabeth. A long time for him. Worrying about her brother relieved her of the worries about herself.

"Do you know about the two of them, and what happened? Some at court thought that they would marry, but then it just ended. Morvan would never speak to me about it."

He looked down at the pillow for a moment and she could tell that he did know.

"Oh, please, David, tell me," she cajoled. "He is my brother, after all. I am very discreet, you know. I am the only female at court who didn't gossip."

"A rare virtue that I should not corrupt."

"I always *listened*. I just never repeated what I heard," she said.

"Elizabeth didn't marry your brother because he never asked her to. Also, she loved him and he didn't love her. Not the way she wanted. Elizabeth would never bind herself to such an uneven love. Then there is the fact that she is barren. She has known it since girlhood. It is why only old men offer for her. They already have their heirs. One day your brother will be lord of Harclow again and he will want a son."

"Nay, David, I do not think he ever will be. The King swore to see it happen, but he has forgotten."

"Men do not forget the oaths that they swear."

She wondered what else David knew about the people with whom she had spent her life. Perhaps, if she proved very discreet, he would tell her sometime. This felt very pleasant and cozy, talking like this in the warmth of the bed. When he was up and walking about, he still remained a mystery to her, but the intimacy here temporarily banished that.

"I was surprised that the King came here this evening," she said, wondering how far she could push the mood.

"Even kings like to have some fun. Being regal can get tedious, and Edward is still a young man. He isn't much older than I am."

"He seems to know you well."

"We are of similar age, and he is more comfortable with me than with the city officials who are very formal with him. And I have done some favors for him. He sends me on errands. To Flanders mostly. I carried letters to the governor of Ghent on several trips."

"Do you still do this? These errands?"

"Aye. Some of the trips that I take are for Edward."

That was that. She smiled at her foolish hesitation. She should have just asked earlier. It all made perfect and innocent sense. Still . . .

"Are they ever dangerous? These trips?"

"They haven't been."

That wasn't the same as saying that they weren't. She decided to leave it, however.

She snuggled closer, enjoying the feel of his arm around her. She thought about some of the people she had met at the Guildhall banquet. In particular, she remembered the thin-lipped, gray-haired Gilbert de Abyndon, who had tried to ignore David's presence even while David introduced her.

"I liked Margaret, Gilbert's wife. I think that she and I could be friends. Do you think that he would permit that?"

Actually, she wanted to know if David would permit

it. Margaret was not much older than herself, and a friendly blond-haired woman. They had enjoyed their brief meeting and chat, even if their two husbands had stood there like frozen sentinels.

"Most likely. Gilbert is very ambitious. He will overlook your marriage to me because of your nobility and connections at court. Like most of the wealthier merchants, he wants to lift his family into the gentry."

"Still, he may object to her visiting me. It is clear that you and he hate each other very much."

Her comment was met with a long silence. She turned and found him gazing at the blue canopy much as she had done earlier. He glanced at her with a glint in his eyes. Had simply mentioning this uncle angered him? He kissed her hair as if to reassure her.

"I hate him for what he did to my mother, and he hates me because I am alive and use the Abyndon name. He is the worst of our breed, my girl. Judgmental and unbending. He is full of self-righteousness and attends church each morning before he spends his day damning people. If he had been at this house today, he would have seen nothing of the joy and pleasure but only sin and weakness. If you are going to befriend Margaret, you should know this, because that is the man she is tied to. Hopefully, for her sake, her old husband will die soon."

She blinked at his last words. Wishing someone dead was a dreadful thing. The dispassionate way he said it stunned her even more.

"We need to find a servant to help you with your clothes and such," he added. "Geva said that you would want to choose the girl yourself. In a few days, go and visit Margaret and ask for her help in this. See if Gilbert permits it."

He stroked her hair and her shoulder and she stretched against him as the tingling warmth of his caress awoke her skin. She suspected that he wanted to make love again. She waited for him to start, and was surprised when he began speaking, his quiet voice flowing into her ear.

"My uncles Gilbert and Stephen were already in their twenties when my mother was still a girl. Old enough, when she turned fourteen, to know what they had in her. She was beautiful. Perfect. Even when she died, despite everything, she was still beautiful. Her brothers saw her marriage for the opportunity it was. They had it all planned. A nobleman for her. Second choice, a merchant with the Hanseatic League. Third, a husband from the gentry. They settled a fat dowry on her and began pushing her in front of such men. Every banquet, they brought her with them, dressed like a lady."

"And did it work?"

"Aye, it worked. John Constantyn has told me what she did not. The offers poured in. Gilbert and Stephen debated the marriage that would be best for them, of course, and not her. They became too clever and played one man off against the other."

"Did she refuse their choice? Is that why . . ."

"Worse than that, as my body beside you proves. They had not been careful enough with her. Their parents were dead, and the servants who supervised her indulged her. She fell in love. The man was gone by the time she found herself with child."

"Was it one of her suitors?"

"Apparently not. Still, her brothers sought to solve the disaster in the usual ways. They demanded to know his name so they could force a marriage, but she would not give it to them. Gilbert tried to beat it out of her, and still she would not say. And so they found another husband who would accept her under those circumstances and sought to have a quick wedding."

Christiana grimaced inwardly. She remembered that first night in David's solar, and him asking if she was with child. He had thought that it was the same story, and that he was the other man whose quick wedding would cover up a girl's mistake.

"She would not have him," he continued. "She was certain that her lover would return for her. She went to the priest and declared that she was unwilling."

Braver than me, Christiana thought. *My God, what must have been running through David's mind that night as he faced me so impassively in front of the fire?*

"What did they do?"

"They sent her away. There are some relatives in Hastings and she went there. Gilbert told her to give up the child when it was born. If she did not, all of their support of her would cease and she would be as if dead to them. Under no circumstances was she to return to London."

"But she kept you. And she came back."

"She was sure that her lover would come, and she knew that he would not know where to find her if she wasn't here. And so she returned quickly. Somehow she found Meg and began working with the laundresses. Meg served as midwife when I was born. Those early years, we lived in a small chamber behind a stable near the river. Besides Meg and the other workers, I was my mother's only companion. Gilbert and Stephen never saw her, and true to their threat, did not so much as give her a shilling. She could have starved for all they knew or cared."

"And you? Did you know who she was and who they were?"

"Not until I was about seven. And then I would hear

of these men with my mother's name and I began to figure some of it out. Stephen began rising in city politics then. And I knew by then that I was a bastard. The other boys made sure I knew that. Several years later she became David Constantyn's housekeeper and things got better for her, although Gilbert and Stephen never forgave him for helping her. In their minds she deserved all that had happened to her. Her misery was the price of her sin against God and them. Mostly them."

He had told this story simply and evenly, as was his way. But she sensed that many other thoughts were tied to this tale, and that some of them concerned herself.

She remembered the drawing of this woman's face which she had seen, and looking at his perfect bones now, she could see his mother in him. But another face had contributed to these planes and deep eyes. An unknown face.

"What was her name? Your mother's name?"

"Joanna."

"And your father? Do you know him?"

"The only father I ever knew was my master. The first time I saw him, he scolded me for stealing one of his apples. He came out of the ivy garden as I sat beneath the tree eating it while my mother helped with the laundry in the courtyard. I talked fast and hard to get out of a beating, I'll tell you that. He gave me a good wallop anyway and dragged me back to my mother. A few weeks later he showed up while we were here and took me into the city to see a thief hang. On the way back he told me that there were two ways for clever men to get rich. One was through stealing and the other was through trade, but that the thieves lived shorter lives. By age eight I had done my share of stealing, and the lesson was not lost on me."

She pictured the urchins whom she sometimes saw on the city streets sidling up to carts and windows, running off with food and goods. She imagined a little David amongst them. Never getting caught, of course.

"He offered to marry her, I think," he added thoughtfully. "I remember coming upon them one day when I was about twelve. They were sitting in the hall. Something important was being discussed, I could tell. I sensed what it was."

"She refused him, you think?"

"Aye. I assumed then that he offered because he wanted me. We had become close by then, much like father and son. We even shared a name. She had chosen mine from the Bible, but it is an unusual name in England and I knew from the start that it fascinated him that I had it. Even her position here— I thought he had accepted the mother to get the son. But I think now that maybe it was the other way around."

"Did she refuse him because of the other man, your real father?"

"Aye. Her heart waited long after her mind gave up. I despised her for that when I was a youth, but by the time she died I understood a little."

She thought of David's patient understanding during their betrothal, but also of his cruel, relentless prods about Stephen.

You still wait for him, after all of this time and when the truth is so clear. It is well that Edward gave you to me. You would have spent your whole life waiting, living in some faded dream.

In not repudiating her, he had taken a horrible, painful chance.

She pressed herself against the warm comfort of his body, feeling the texture of his skin against her length. It touched her that he had told her about Joanna and his early life. Little by little, in ways like this, perhaps he would cease to be a stranger to her. She also knew that it was not in his nature to make such confidences and that only the intimacy of their marriage and passion had permitted it.

Without thinking, she rubbed her face against his chest and then turned and kissed it. She tasted the skin and kissed again. Her desire to give and take comfort and revel in their new closeness changed to something else as she kissed him, and impulsively she turned her head and gently licked his nipple. He touched her head and held it, encouraging her. A languid sensuality spread through her, and she felt the change in him, too. Only then did she remember that this was one of the things that the servant girl had told her about during her bath this morning.

He let her lips and tongue caress him a while longer, and then gently turned her on her back.

"I think that I promised you slow pleasure," he said. "Let us see how slow we can make it."

Much later, for David could make the pleasure very slow when he chose to, they lay together on the darkened bed, the curtains pulled against the dimming sounds and lights from the wedding party. Christiana began drifting into sleep in his arms.

She felt him move, and sensed him looking at her nearly invisible profile.

"Did you speak with him?" he asked quietly.

She had forgotten about that. Had forgotten about Stephen Percy and her anger and hurt with David. This day and night had obscured her suspicions about his motivations with her, and she really wished now that he hadn't reminded her.

He lives with realities, she thought. *You are the one who constructs dreams and songs.* But he had written that song about her, hadn't he? Not a love song, though. He thought her beautiful and had written about it. Perhaps he composes such melodies about sunsets and forest glens too.

"Aye, I spoke with him."

"What did he want?"

"Nothing honorable."

He was silent awhile.

"I do not want you seeing him," he finally said.

"He is at court often. Are you saying that I cannot go back to Westminster again?"

"I do not mean that. You know what I am saying."

"It is over, David. Like you and Alicia. It is the same."

"It is not. I never loved Alicia."

She turned her head to his. He had opened this door and she felt a compulsion to walk through it now.

"You never planned to let me go with him, did you?"

"I did not lie when I said it, but I was sure it would not come up."

"And if it had?"

His fingers touched her face in the darkness. "I would not have let you go. Early on I knew it."

Why? Your pride? Your investment? To save me from your mother's fate? She could not ask the question. She did not want to know the true answer. A girl should be allowed some illusions and ambiguities if she had to live with a man. There was such a thing as too much reality.

"How did you know that I would come that day?"

"I did not expect it. I planned to go and get you."

"And if I wouldn't come and agree to your seduction?"

"I would not have given you much choice."

She thought about that.

"You were very clever, David, I will grant you that. Very careful. Lots of witnesses. Your whole household. Idonia. How thorough were you? Did you even save the sheets? Did you leave them on the bed until Geva had seen them the next day?" Her tone came out more petulantly than she felt.

He kissed her temple and pulled her into the curve of his body. "The first time I met you and every time after you told me that you loved him, Christiana. Up until last Wednesday itself. Despite what happened between us when I kissed you, despite his misuse of you. Aye, darling, I was thorough. And calculating and clever. I deliberately made this marriage a fact and bound you to me. I took no chances that he might tell the lies that your heart wanted to hear so that he could misuse you again. Would you have had me do otherwise? Should I have stood back from this knight like the merchant I am? Would honoring my promise to let you go have pleased you?"

She trembled a little at the blunt force of his words. It sounded very different when he put it that way, when she saw it through his eyes. It had been so easy to forget how she had been before last Wednesday.

"Nay," she whispered, and it was true. She would not have been pleased at all if he had proven indifferent and had simply let Stephen lure her away. Another reaction that she feared to examine too closely.

The silence descended again, and after a time she relaxed in his embrace. Sleep had almost claimed her when she heard him laugh quietly in her ear.

"Aye, my girl, I was thorough and took no chances. I saved the sheets."

CHAPTER 14

DAVID WAS DROWSILY aware of the curtains being pushed back. He turned his face away from the flooding light.

"Hell," a man's voice said, pulling him awake.

He opened one eye a slit. Unless he was still dreaming, his wife was gone and the King of England stood beside his bed.

"Damnation, David."

Not dreaming.

"My lord?" He rose up on his elbows.

The King stared down with a frown. "Will you be wanting to repudiate her? Philippa assured me the girl was whole, I swear. I told her we should have her examined, but she and Idonia . . ."

David looked to where the King gazed. The coverlet and sheets were bunched over to reveal a bloodless marriage bed.

Hell. The last thing he had expected was someone

looking for evidence of Christiana's virginity. What was Edward doing here, anyway?

"Do not let it concern you, my lord. There will be no repudiation."

Edward's frown relaxed. "Damn chivalrous of you, David."

"I am a merchant and we are apart from chivalry. That is reserved for your knights. I assure you that my wife came to me a virgin, though. If I had thought that some-one would seek the evidence this morning, I would have bled a chicken."

Edward looked at him blankly.

The man was still half besotted. David noted the red robe. The King had been here all night. Where and with whom? David decided that he didn't want to know.

"Do you need to see the original sheets? I have them," he offered with a laugh, but as soon as he said it he real-ized that Edward's mind had moved on.

"I want to speak with you. It will save you a ride to Westminster."

David glanced around the bed. Christiana's and his clothes were still strewn around the posts and floor. "Perhaps in the solar?"

Edward nodded and drifted off.

David grabbed a robe off a peg in the wardrobe, threw it on, and followed. Edward stood by the solar windows with a speculative, hooded expression on his face. David joined him and glanced down at the courtyard. A red-haired serving woman from a nearby house lounged against the well, surrounded by the litter of the night's revelry.

Edward sighed. "I suppose I have to give her some-thing, eh? Hell, I can't even remember." He patted his robe for evidence of a purse or coins.

"She is not a whore," David said. "Wait one moment."

He went back to the wardrobe and returned with a purple silk veil embroidered with gold thread.

Edward examined it. "Awfully nice, David. Don't you have something plainer? I don't even know if I enjoyed myself. This would be good for Philippa, though. Peace offering . . ."

David went to the wardrobe once again and fetched a blue veil with no embroidery.

"What, do you keep a whole box of them to give to your women?" the King teased as he stuffed them in his robe. "Best hide them from your wife. See my wardrobe treasurer about them."

David pictured himself arriving at Westminster without a debenture or tally to claim payment for two veils purchased by the King for his slut and his neglected wife.

"Consider them gifts," he said dryly. "You wanted to speak with me about something?"

"Aye. The council met two days ago. It was decided to embark right after Easter. I'll summon the barons shortly."

David waited patiently for the rest of it.

"We received word that Grossmont engaged with the French and has secured Gascony," the King continued.

David nodded. Gascony, below England's Aquitaine on the west coast of the continent, was territory held by Edward in fief to the French king. Among the many points of contention between the two monarchs had been the degree of control which France wanted to exert there. Henry Grossmont had been sent to stabilize the area.

"Furthermore, he has pushed as far north as Poitiers," Edward said. "The port of Bordeaux is secure now. We will go in that way, join with him, and head northeast. I'll not be needing that last bit of information from you after all."

"Poitiers is a long way from Paris. The spring rains will make movement difficult."

"The council considered all of that. Still, our army and Grossmont's will be a formidable force. And debarking at Bordeaux will be riskless."

Presumably the council of barons knew what they were doing. They were experienced soldiers. But it struck him as a fruitless strategy.

Edward watched him with an amused expression. "You do not approve. Speak your mind."

He knew that a merchant's mind was irrelevant, but he spoke it anyway. "Bordeaux is a seven-day sea voyage. A long way to take an army by boat, and you risk bad winds. The French already await you at Poitiers. Even with a decisive victory you will be a long way from Paris. If the French crown is your goal, you must take that city and the royal demesne, must you not?"

"I will have twenty thousand with me," Edward replied jovially. "We will cut through France like a hot blade through butter."

Like all armies paid with spoils, yours will slog through France like a feather through cream, David silently replied.

"Those weapons you offered me," Edward mused. "Where are they?"

"Nowhere near Poitiers. I have one here, outside the city. If you have room on one of your ships, it is yours. Send me some men and I will train them in its use."

"Ah well, one toy is probably enough. I will need the maps that you have been making of that region. Do you have them ready? We will want to know all of the possible routes and the best roads. Especially where to cross the Loire river during spring floods."

"They are in my study." The King followed him through the door by the hearth into the small chamber.

He took some rolled parchments off the shelf and placed them on the table. "This one is of the north. This other is Brittany, from Brest to the marches of Normandy. The large one shows the routes out from Bordeaux." He unrolled the largest parchment. "Remember that I was there in November, and the marked river crossings are based on conversations that I had with the people in the area, and not on what I saw for myself. The conditions of the roads were obvious even in late autumn, however." He pointed to one line. "This road is fairly direct for your purposes and lies on high ground, so it should be in better condition than the main one. It passes through farmland, and there are few towns along it." Few opportunities for looting. The barons would press for the muddy low road so that they could pay their retinues.

Edward admired the drawing. "You have a knack for this sort of thing. I told the council that you would do the job and none would be the wiser."

"Do you want them all?"

"You can bring the others later. This one I will take now. We are itching to begin our plans." He took the parchment and tucked it under his arm. "A clever idea, to have you map out three possibilities. I know your own mind on this, but it will be Bordeaux."

Aye, David thought. *The army will land and engage. Battles will be fought and towns besieged, and knights and soldiers will grow rich from the looting. And after a summer of fighting, you will come back and nothing will have been resolved. Until you take Paris, this will never end.*

What this decision meant to him and his own plans was another matter, and one that he would consider carefully later.

A sound behind made them both turn. Christiana

stood at the threshold to the bedchamber with a startled expression on her face. She carried a tray with food and ale.

"My lord," she said, stepping in quickly and placing the tray on the table. "My apologies."

They watched her go.

"Do you think that she heard?" Edward asked, frowning.

"If so, she will say nothing." It really didn't matter. One could hardly sail hundreds of ships down the coast of Brittany and France and not be noticed. There would be little surprise when this invasion finally happened.

Was it over? He smiled at his King, but already his mind began recalculating.

On the fourth morning after their wedding, David told Christiana that they would ride north of the city a ways.

"I recently acquired a property in Hampstead," he explained as they headed out the city gate side by side. "We will go there so that you can see it. I have to speak with some workers, and there are other matters to attend."

"Is it a farm?"

"There are farms attached to it, but it is the house that you should see."

"Many farms?"

"Ten, as I remember."

"Aren't you afraid that the income will put you over the forty-pound limit? That Edward will force knighthood on you?" she teased.

"Aye. That is why I put the property in your name."

"My name!"

"Yours. It belongs to you, as do the farms' rents."

She absorbed this startling news. Married women

almost never owned their own property. It went with them to their husbands. The only woman she knew who owned land outright was Lady Elizabeth. Joan had told her that Elizabeth always demanded property in her name as part of her marriage settlements to those old men.

"The dowry manor that Edward settled on you is yours as well, Christiana."

"Why, David?"

"I want you to know that you are secure, and without land you never will feel thus. I am comfortable with wealth based on credits and coin, but you never will be. Also, I take risks in my trade, sometimes big ones. I want to know that should my judgment fail, you will not suffer."

It made a certain sense, but still it astonished her.

"There is something that you should know about this house," he said later as they turned off the road onto a lane. "It came to me through moneylending. You should also know that it was owned by Lady Catherine. If you do not like that, you can sell it and purchase elsewhere. Near London, though. I want you to have someplace to go when the summer illnesses spread in the city."

The twinge of guilt that she felt at this news disappeared as soon as she saw the house. Wide and tall, its base built of stone and its upper level of timber and plaster, it sat beautifully inside a stone wall at the end of the lane, surrounded by outbuildings and gardens. A bank of glazed windows on the second level indicated its recent construction.

Workers were laying tiles on the hall floor when they entered, and David went over to speak with them. She explored the other chambers. Very little furniture had been left, and the building echoed with their footsteps. David explained that he would leave furnishing the house to her.

"We need to ride out onto the property," he said as they reclaimed their horses. "There are some men awaiting me."

The men worked half a mile away on an open field. Three of them stood around a big metal cylinder, narrower at the top than the bottom, propped and angled up on logs. A bulky man with black hair explained something to the others as they approached.

"What is that?" she asked.

"A toy. You will see how it works."

He tied the horses to a tree and walked over to the men. She wrapped her cloak more tightly around her and sat down on the dried grass near a small fire that had been built. David and the others fiddled and fussed with the toy a long time, and the black-haired man kept crouching behind the low end of the cylinder and spying along its length. Her eyes followed the man's line of sight, and in the distance she saw an old wooden building.

David poured some sand in it from a leather bag and stuck a stick down after it. He lifted a large stone from in front of it. A mason had clearly worked it, for the stone was perfectly round. He rolled the stone into the cylinder.

He came over to the fire and lifted a flaming torch.

"Cover your ears," he said. He lit a line of the sand snaking along the lower end of the toy.

A moment later the loudest clap of thunder that she had ever heard cracked the winter silence. Smoke spewed out of the cylinder and it jumped back. Across the deep field, a few seconds after the toy was fired, the farm building's roof burst into pieces.

She jumped up and crossed over to the smoking cylinder. The black-haired man drew the other two aside and began to explain something that sounded a lot like geometry.

"What is this?" she asked, peering into the hot hollow.

"The future. It is called a gonne."

She walked along its length, and noted the stack of round stones nearby. "It is a siege machine, isn't it?"

"Aye, that it is."

She knew more than she wanted about siege machines. As a child she had watched the towers and catapults built outside Harclow. She had seen the horrible damage that they wrought and had lived in fear of those flying missiles and baskets of fire. She looked at the farm building. Only the shells of its side walls remained. It had been old, and built of wood, but this toy possessed more force in hurling its small stones than any of the machines which she had seen at Harclow.

"Do you plan to make and sell these?"

"Nay. But they will be made by others. It is inevitable. I first saw them on my way home on my first trip. There was a demonstration near Pisa. They didn't work well, and never hit their mark then, but already they improve. They fascinate me, that is all. This one is for Edward. Other kings will have them, so he must." He walked toward the horses. "I am going to check the building. You can come if you want to."

She wasn't at all sure that she wanted to, but she went nonetheless.

She gazed at the tatters of the building. No wonder David did not want to be a knight. Of what use were armor and shields against war machines like this?

There were other buildings nearby, all neglected. This had once been a horse farm with many stables.

"I should tell you that this section of the property is not yours," he explained as he dismounted.

She saw no signs of labor here. It appeared that David had kept the poorest portion for himself. "You need a field with old buildings to play with your toys?"

"Aye. And to collect that which makes them work." He led the way into one of the stables.

The roof of this structure was in disrepair, and splotches of sunlight leaked through its holes. David went into one of the stalls and crouched down. He wiped his fingers across the dried dirt and lifted his hand. A sandy substance glittered.

"It is found in stables like this that have been used a long time, and other places where animals live. The powder that makes the machine work requires it. It is said that the secret was brought back overland from Cathay in the Far East. It has no English name, although some translate it to saltpeter."

"Are those men back there from the King?"

"Two are. The other brought the machine from Italy."

"Will Edward use it? Will he take it with him to France? To Bordeaux?"

He did not answer her. They remounted and rode back to the men who had already prepared the machine again. David spoke in Italian to the black-haired one and then led her away.

"I know that you overheard Edward in my study, Christiana," he finally said. "You know, I'm sure, that you cannot repeat such things. Even when everyone else suspects and talks of it, you should pretend ignorance."

It was true, then. She had heard the King mention Bordeaux and had seen the rolled parchment under his arm. It was one of those maps she had noticed that day in David's study. Her husband did not just deliver messages. He did other things for Edward as well. Much more dangerous things. Dangerous enough and important enough that the King told him about Bordeaux.

She prayed that now that Edward had chosen his

course, David would be out of it. He wasn't a knight or noble. It wasn't fair for the King to use him thus when he would see little profit and significant loss from such wars.

They approached the house from the rear. The tilers' wagon had left. A new horse was tethered by the side of the house, however, and a man stood beside it.

David stopped his horse. He gazed hard at the new-comer.

The stranger was a tall man with long white hair and a short beard. A dull brown cloak, no more than a shape-less mantle, hung to the ground. The horse beside him looked bony and old.

David dismounted and lifted her off her horse.

"Wait outside while I speak with this man."

"It is cold."

"I am sorry for it, but do not come in."

They had been out most of the day, and the chill had long ago penetrated her cloak. "I will go up to the solar and you can use the hall," she suggested.

"You are not to come into the house while he is here," he ordered harshly. His gaze had not left the waiting man. "I insist that you obey me on this, my girl."

His tone stunned her. She watched his absorbed atten-tion with the figure by the house. His awareness of her had essentially disappeared. The withdrawal was so complete that she had never felt more separate from him than she did at that moment, not even the night when she first met him as a total stranger in his solar. This sudden indifference, contrasting so vividly with the constant attention that he had shown her since their wedding, sickened her heart.

Giving the stranger a more thorough examination, she strolled toward the garden.

✦　　✦　　✦

David walked slowly toward the house, and with each step the eerie internal silence grew more absorbing. Scattered thoughts scrambled through his mind, and odd emotions welled inside his chest. Emotions that he could not afford to either acknowledge or examine now.

Nor could he afford to indulge himself in the usual fascination with the sound of Fortune's wheel turning yet again. He shook off the silence.

The man waited and watched. He stood too tall and proud to make the worker's cloak an effective disguise, but David doubted that anyone else had paid much attention.

He had expected this man eventually, but not today and not here. Oliver had received no report yet, for one thing. That must mean that he had come by way of a northern port, and not one along the southern or eastern coasts. A long detour, then, to ensure safety. It was the sort of refined and careful strategy that David could appreciate. He had come alone, too. Either he was very brave or very sure of himself. Probably both.

He tied the horses' reins to a post near the stable building and then walked over to the man. The white head rose as high as his own. Deep brown eyes regarded him carefully.

They did not greet each other but David suspected that the odd familiarity which he experienced was felt by the other, too.

"How did you find me?" David asked.

"Frans learned from its previous owner that you had acquired this property. I thought that you might bring your bride here. A beautiful girl, by the way. Worthy of her bloodline. Worthy of you."

He ignored the compliment, except to note that it was

not one which a man like this would normally give a merchant. "Frans has a friendship with Lady Catherine? Is she one of yours? A watcher?"

The man hesitated and David had his answer. No doubt Lady Catherine would do anything for a price.

"You should have waited until my wife was not with me. I do not want her involved in any way."

"I could not wait forever. I am here at great risk to myself. If you had left her side for a few hours . . ."

The man's voice drifted away and a full silence fell. It held for a long time. They faced each other, both knowing that whoever spoke first again would be at the disadvantage.

David calmly let the moments throb past. He had much more experience in waiting than his guest. A lifetime of it, in fact.

"Do you know who I am?" the man finally asked.

"I know who you are. I assume that you seek what Frans sought, and since I told him I would not help, I wonder about the reason for this meeting."

The man reached into the front of his mantle and withdrew a folded piece of parchment. "This is one of yours. It was found amongst the papers of Jacques van Artevelde."

"Your man and I have already discussed my relationship with Jacques. My letters to him were matters of trade, nothing else."

"His relationship with you and others like you got him killed."

Jacques van Artevelde, the leader of Ghent's pro-English burghers, had become a friend. His death last year at the hands of a mob had been more than a political loss for David, and he resented this offhand reference to it.

It went without saying that the Count of Flanders had been behind that mob's murder. Had this other man been involved, too?

"We met for business and nothing more," David said blandly.

"Let us skip the games, Master David. As Frans explained, we know about you. Not everything, I'm sure. But enough. Besides, it was not the content of this letter that made him bring it to me. It was the seal." His long fingers played with the parchment. "An unusual seal. Three entwined serpents. How did you come to use it?"

"It was on a piece of jewelry that my mother owned. It was as useful a device as any other."

"This item of jewelry. Was it a ring? With a gray stone?"

David let the silence pulse as he absorbed this astounding question and its unexpected implications.

"Aye. A ring."

The man sighed audibly. He stepped closer and scrutinized David's face. "Aye, I can see it. The eyes, but not their color. His were brown. The mouth. Even your voice."

David met that piercing gaze with his own. "I, of course, have no way of knowing if you are right or if you lie. You want something from me. It is in your interest to claim a resemblance."

"I do not come here to trick you into treason."

"Merely meeting with you might be construed as treason. Your presence here compromises me. You should have given me a choice."

"It was essential that I see you. I had to know. Surely you understand that."

"I'm not sure that I do."

"Why did you never come to us?"

"I had no need of you, and you none of me."

"We have need of you now."

David examined the man's serious, expectant expression. "You must want this very badly, to appeal to a stranger."

Shrewd eyes met David's own. "Aye, I want it badly. I want it for my country but I want it for myself, too. You are not such a stranger. I have made it my business to learn about you. Your accomplishments in trade will not satisfy you much longer. Already those small victories seem thin and shallow, do they not? Especially compared to the politics of monarchies."

David glanced away, knowing even as he did so that the reflex signaled a certain defeat.

He gestured for the man to follow him into the house.

Christiana huddled in her cloak on the bench under a tree in the garden. She was not at all pleased to be stuck out here while David held this secret meeting. She was even less pleased with the way he had dismissed her, and his tone when he ordered her obedience.

That tall man's presence had obviously surprised him, and that explained some of it. Still, she doubted that this meeting had anything to do with trade or finance. The stranger was no merchant, despite his simple cloak and humble horse. He could no more hide his true status than he could hide his height. She had recognized him for what he was. Any time, any place, nobles knew each other when they met.

They were talking a very long time. Her hands felt a little numb from the raw chill, and she wrapped them in the billows of her cloak.

If David didn't come and get her soon, she was going to disobey him and go inside. It was one thing to be a dutiful wife, and quite another to sit out here and freeze like an idiot who didn't know when to come in from the cold.

She stomped her feet and huddled smaller. She tried to distract herself by thinking about that strange invention David had shown her earlier. For someone who didn't like knights and war, David had a peculiar fascination with siege machines.

Her eyes scanned the house, looking for some sign of movement. They were probably in the solar in front. From her vantage point she could see the rump of the stranger's horse tied by the side of the building.

David had ordered her to stay outside. He hadn't said where.

She got up and walked through the garden, heading to the sorry-looking animal. Not much of a horse for a nobleman. Perhaps it was someone down on his luck seeking a loan.

A bag lay over the animal's hind quarters. Soothing him with her hands and voice, she eyed the loose flap.

She really shouldn't. It was definitely none of her business.

Asking for forgiveness, she lifted the flap and peered inside.

The bag held clothes. Rich clothes. Expensive fabrics. Garments not at all in keeping with this horse and that worn cloak. The man had disguised himself to look poor.

Voices startled her. She let the flap drop and hurried away.

She had just turned the corner of the house when she heard David's voice.

"We must not meet again in England."

That stopped her. She pressed against the stones of the house.

"I leave tomorrow. Do not worry. I know your risk. I have no desire to jeopardize you," the stranger said. He spoke English, but the accent was unmistakable. This man, this nobleman, was French.

"Frans is not to return to England until this is over. The man is careless, and his long stay last time was noticed. His woman friend is a complication that I will not accept. Sever ties with her," David said.

Frans van Horlst. A French noble. Dear saints!

"He will leave with me tomorrow and not return. The lady will be out of it as well."

"There is one final condition. I will want documents from you. Witnessed."

Only the sound of her heart broke the silence that ensued.

"You do not trust me," the stranger finally said. "I suppose I can't blame you. How will I get these documents to you?"

"You will not. I will come to you."

Her mind scrambled to make sense of these cryptic statements. Documents? Why was David meeting in secret with a French noble and discussing such things? Her heart heaved as one horrible possibility sprang to mind. But if that were the case, David would be providing the documents, and not the other way around.

The sounds of a saddle creaking and a horse stomping reached her ears. She began easing away.

"I look forward to knowing you better," the stranger said. "In France, then."

The horse walked away. David would come looking for her now. She plunged away from the house and ran into the garden.

CHAPTER 15

As soon as David returned to his trade, Christiana presented herself at the house of Gilbert de Abyndon. No one seemed surprised at her going alone. She marveled at this and other new freedoms, so in contrast to the close supervision of Westminster. A childish exhilaration gripped her as she walked along the city streets, pausing occasionally to inspect the activities and wares in the tradesmen's windows.

Margaret appeared both delighted and flustered to see her. Hesitation briefly clouded her pale, delicate face before a very mature resolve took its place. "Does your husband know that you are here?" she asked after she sent a servant for some wine.

"He knows. It was his suggestion that I come. I am in need of a servant and he thought that you might be able to help me."

Margaret tilted her head and raised her eyebrows. "You know that they hate each other. Our husbands."

"I know. And it is always deep when kinsmen feel like that with each other. If my visit will cause trouble for you, I will leave."

Margaret sat on a cushioned window seat and patted the space beside her. Christiana joined her. "I will handle Gilbert. I recently learned that I am with child. I will tell him that I was feeling poorly and that your visit healed me." She smiled conspiratorially. "This child has already changed much and will change more. He will be like clay in my hands now."

Christiana blinked at this bald admission of manipulation. Margaret appeared so frail and sweet, it was hard to believe that a steel rod of practicality held her upright in this marriage.

She felt sorry that Margaret had a marriage in which only her breeding potential was valued. Then she reminded herself that was the likely reason for her own match.

Over the next few hours they formed a bond. The next day Margaret sent a girl named Emma to enter service. Although the daughter of a merchant who had fallen on bad times, Emma proved to be a willing and excellent servant. She arrived daily at the house before dawn and helped Vittorio and Geva until Christiana called for her.

Christiana learned about the fall in Emma's fortunes. Her father had been wealthy one day and poor the next because of one shipping disaster. She wondered if David's wealth tottered so precariously. He had suggested as much when he told her about the lands he had put in her name. Her consideration of this and of the household which she now directed led her to a decision. It was time to acquire a practical education, for the day might come when she had no servants. She set about learning how to cook from Vittorio and how to sew from the women. She learned from Geva how to be a housekeeper.

She had visitors, too, those first few weeks. Morvan came several times to take her for rides and to reassure himself that she wasn't miserable. Isabele and Idonia came once so that Isabele could examine Christiana's new home. Margaret visited at least once a week and they formed a fast friendship.

Toward the end of Lent, troops began arriving to muster for the King's French campaign. Most of the men lived in camps on the surrounding fields. During the days, they descended on the crowded city to pass the time while they awaited embarkation. David curtailed her freedom then, and told her not to leave the house alone.

The Tuesday before Easter, she returned from a trip to the market with Vittorio to find Joan waiting for her. The King's purveyors had been busy the last weeks requisitioning food throughout the countryside to feed the army, and the stalls in London had been hawking depleted meats and produce at inflated prices. She began her conversation with Joan by complaining about this.

Joan laughed. "You are sounding like some bootmaker's goodwife, Christiana. It is well that I have come. We will go to your chamber and I will teach your servant a new hairstyle which I learned. You can show me the things that your rich husband has bought you while I tell you the court gossip."

"How is Thomas Holland?" Christiana asked as she led Joan upstairs.

"He has been sent to Southhampton to help with the ships there. Have you ever seen anything like it? There must be two hundred in harbor here alone, and they say it is the same in the Cinque Ports and up the east coast as well. And no one knows where Edward plans to land once he gets to the Continent."

Bordeaux, Christiana almost said. *He goes to relieve Grossmont at Poitiers*. The ships were merchant ships, requisitioned by the King. Overseas trade had stopped. But Joan would not want to hear about the hardships that would cause.

"With Thomas gone, it has been lonely, but fortunately William Montagu has been very attentive, so I do not feel too dour," Joan giggled. "In truth, it would be hard for any girl to feel sad at court right now. Westminster is bursting with knights and barons, all here without their ladies. The few females around are surrounded by men. It is delicious."

"If I were still there, it would not be delicious for me," Christiana said, laughing. "I would die of thirst in that lake of male attention. Morvan would probably stand up at a banquet and issue a general warning and challenge."

"But he has no say now. You have to come and visit," Joan cajoled as she began working Christiana's long hair into thin braids that she then looped around her head. "Before the fleet leaves, while it is still busy and gay."

"I am married, Joan. My place is here now."

"You can come for a few days, can't you? It really isn't as much fun without you. At least come for the Easter banquet. Bring David with you. He can keep the men away."

Christiana thought about the elaborate banquet and tournament held to celebrate Easter at court. It would be nice to attend as an adult rather than a child.

That night she told David about Joan's invitation. They were sitting in the solar while she practiced the Saracen letters that he had taught her.

"You must go if you want to," he said.

She stared down at the shallow box of sand in which she traced the letters with a stick. They had been married five weeks and David had never accompanied her to court, even when she attended a dinner.

"Joan says that she will arrange for us to have a chamber for a few nights if we want," she said. "You don't think the boys will mind if we are gone for Easter?"

"The household can celebrate without us."

"We will go then?"

"As it happens, I must be out of London then."

"And if not, you still would not come, would you?"

"You had and have a life and place there, and I would not deny you that. But it is not my world. I will not be the upstart merchant who enters the King's court by hanging on to the hem of his wife's veil."

His frank admission that he would not share that part of her life saddened her. She missed him when she was at Westminster. A part of her remained removed from the gaiety, thinking about him. Sometimes she would find herself turning to comment on some entertainment or jest and be a little startled not to find him beside her.

She enjoyed those visits to the court, but she always returned to the city eager to see David and relate the gossip and news which she had learned. She realized that there could be no joy in anything unless she could share it with him in some way.

She looked over at the man gazing thoughtfully into the hearth fire as his long body lounged in the wooden chair. She thought about how she filled her days with activities but how, through them all, a part of her was always waiting for something. Waiting for him, for the sound of his horse in the courtyard and his footsteps in the hall. She was always so happy to see him that sometimes, without thinking, she would run to him and he would laugh and sweep her up into a kiss. She thought about how his return to the house for dinner and again each evening filled her with comfort and relief as if, upon his leaving, she had taken a deep breath and only released it when he came back. He was the center of this household, its very heartbeat. His presence brought security and joy and excitement.

"I need to speak with you about this trip, Christiana."

"Will it be a long one?" she asked, returning to her letters. She wondered how she would get through the nights without him.

"It could be. Two weeks, maybe longer."

"Where do you go?"

"West. Towards Salisbury. The King has received reports of corruption among royal purveyors in that shire. He has asked me to find out what I can before he orders an official investigation."

Another favor for Edward? The thing about secret trips for the King was that no one could ever check on them.

"It is the first time that you have left since our marriage."

"That is why we must talk. All journeys have some danger in them. I should explain some things to you before I go."

She glanced up sharply. He faced her impassively, but she had learned much about him these last weeks, and that perfect face could never be a complete mask to her again. Now she noticed the thin veil of concern that diffused the warmth of his eyes. A strange numbness began slipping over her.

"Before I go, I will be giving you a key. It is for the box in my study. There is coin there. I will also show you a trunk in the wardrobe that contains papers regarding properties and banking credits. The mercery accounts are at the shop. Andrew is well familiar with them. Should you ever need help with anything, John Constantyn will aid you." He paused. "He is the executor of my testament."

Somehow she managed to draw another letter despite her shock. "You only ride to Salisbury, David."

"You should know what to do. I have seen too many women who did not."

"I do not want to speak of this."

"Nor do I, but we must nonetheless."

She gritted her teeth and tried to ignore the appalling realization that forced itself into her mind. She knew, she just knew, that David did not go to Salisbury. He was going someplace very dangerous to do something very risky.

For Edward? She wanted to believe that was so, but the memories of Frans van Horlst asking a man for help in the King's secret corridor, and of a French noble meeting David in Hampstead, boiled in her mind.

I have no desire to jeopardize you. In France then.

He watched her with that deep gaze that always saw too much. Could he read these thoughts as he could so many others?

She was surely wrong. The very notion was unworthy of her. But he knew about Bordeaux and he played to win and used his own rules.

He could not do this. He would not. Their gold and silver would not tempt him. He was not ruled by such hungers.

"I expect that with John's help I will be able to manage things," she said. "Do not concern yourself."

"If something ever happens to me, the shop can be either sold or liquidated. Andrew could help with that. The mercers' wardens will see to placing the boys with other masters."

"And me, David? Will they seek to place me with a new master as well?"

"They have no authority over your life. But they will no doubt offer advice and counsel you to remarry and join your property and business with another merchant's."

"Is that the advice that you gave women as a warden?"

"Often. You, of course, need not look to merchants. You will be very wealthy."

He spoke as though that should reassure her. He was telling her that if wealthy, widowed, and noble, she could have the husband she was born to have. It hurt her that he could so blithely talk about her going to another man.

"I assume that the properties in my name are well documented? And there will be money enough to buy more. Perhaps, then, I will not remarry at all."

He reached over and stroked her cheek. "The thought of you living your life alone gives me no pleasure."

"Let us be frank, David. We are speaking of your possible death. Your pleasure afterwards will not matter. Now, are we finished with this morbid topic? When do you leave?"

"Two days."

Holy Thursday. Joan had said that the rumors called for the fleet to embark for France soon after Easter. Two days and then two weeks of empty chambers. She knew that a part of her would simply cease to exist while he was gone. Maybe it would cease to exist forever. She wouldn't believe that, she couldn't accept its possibility, but he had as much as warned her so just now. He would not have spoken thus unless he thought his danger very real.

A ripping ache filled her chest. Wherever he went, he must go for Edward. Surely he would not risk giving her such pain for anything else.

She set aside her box and stared at her lap. She tried not to care. She argued valiantly that if he was involved in something dishonorable, she would not want to see him again anyway. She told herself that if the worst happened and she became a rich widow, that would not be so bad. None of it helped relieve the weight around her heart.

Her throat burned and she fought to hold on to her composure.

Suddenly he stood in front of her. He lifted her up into his arms. Before she buried her face in his chest, she saw surprise in his eyes.

"I did not mean to upset you, my girl."

The warmth of his embrace made the tears flow. "Did you not?" she mumbled. "You speak to me of dying and widowhood as if you speculated about next year's wool shipments."

"That is because I do not expect to be harmed. I am just being practical for your sake. I have survived many worse dangers than I could possibly face on this little adventure."

There was much in this man that remained a mystery to her, but the parts that she knew she had come to know very well. And she knew now that he lied to her. He did not do that too much anymore, mostly because she avoided asking the sorts of questions that led him to it. And his lies had rarely been true lies. Usually they were ambiguous statements like this one.

She nestled her head closer and his embrace tightened. "Can you not stay? Let another do this," she whispered.

"None other can do it," he said quietly. "I have committed myself."

"Then I care not where or why you go," she said. "You are a merchant, and there will be many trips, some of them very long. Go where you have to go, David, as long as you promise to come back."

David and Sieg left Thursday morning. Christiana threw herself into a whirlwind of packing in order to distract herself. She chose and rechose her clothes for court until Emma was frantic. She tried not to think too much about the poignancy that had imbued David's lovemaking the last two nights.

He had hired two men to guard the house in Sieg's absence, and in the afternoon she had one of them escort her to Westminster.

She reclaimed her bed in the anteroom, and tried hard to pretend that it was just like old times. Sometimes it was, but often, as Joan and she lay on Isabele's bed and shared gossip and talk, her mind would suddenly drift away as she wondered where David was and whether he was safe.

Her suspicions about what he might be doing played over in her mind, and more than once she forced herself to analyze the evidence suggesting treason. That's what it was, after all. Treason of the highest kind, that would put people whom she loved in danger. She told herself that there was no proof that David was selling the French information about the fleet's destination and that she had let some overheard phrases work evils in her mind.

At the Easter banquet the King formally announced the embarkation to France, and the cheers in the hall greeted it as joyous news. Word spread that the troops would board the ships on Wednesday.

On Tuesday morning Joan roused her out of bed early. "There is to be a big hunt, and then lots of private parties in the taverns and inns on the Strand before tonight's feast. One last celebration before all the knights leave," she said as she went to Christiana's trunks and began choosing clothes for her. "You must come with William and me and be my chaperon so Idonia won't interfere. It will be a day of play to last everyone through the summer."

Christiana had been enjoying her stay at court, even

if a part of her kept worrying about David. Joan had been right, and Westminster bulged with knights eager to pay any female attention. They practiced their poetic flattery even on unattainable women. It was expected for women at court to accept the milder attentions, and she did so, in part because they helped distract her from her concerns and suspicions about David.

Like most of the women, she merely rode to the hunt and watched the men demonstrate their prowess with arrow and spear. She stayed close to Joan and William Montagu the whole morning. The young earl acted besotted with the Fair Maid of Kent. Joan flirted back enough to give more hope than she ought. Christiana thought about Thomas Holland supervising the loading of ships in Southhampton. First Andrew and now William and who knew how many in between. Joan's constancy hadn't lasted very long.

The hunting parties made their way to the Strand at midday, and Joan's group descended on a large inn close to the city gates. Usually inns did not serve meals, but most had brought in cooks to deal with the large number of visitors to the area. This one's public room became so stuffed with tables and people that one could barely move, and Christiana soon lost track of Joan. She found herself standing against a wall, searching the crowd for friends to join.

"There you are," said a soft voice at her shoulder.

She turned to find Lady Catherine edging up close to her.

The older woman's cat eyes gleamed. "This is horrible, isn't it? I expected as much and took a large chamber upstairs. Come and join my party for dinner, Christiana."

She hesitated, remembering David and her brother telling her to avoid Catherine.

"I expect Morvan to eat with us," Lady Catherine said.

She hadn't seen much of her brother these last days. The King's knights had been managing the troops provided by the city. It seemed odd that Morvan would dine with Catherine, but maybe whatever he held against her had been resolved.

The crowd pressed against her. Catherine touched her arm and gestured with her head. Christiana debated the offer. It would be nice to spend some time with Morvan before he sailed.

"Thank you," she said, deciding quickly. There could be no harm in it, and surely David wouldn't mind if Morvan was there, too.

She followed Catherine through the throng to the stairs leading to the second level. Even up there the bodies were thick, because others had shown Catherine's foresight and taken chambers. Lady Catherine continued up to the inn's quiet third level, led her to a door, and ushered her in.

The chamber had been prepared for a party of fifteen. Two long tables cramped the space between the bed and the hearth. It was a warm April day and the narrow windows overlooking the courtyard had been opened, but the thick walls obscured the sounds from below.

Only one person waited in the chamber. Stephen Percy stood near the farthest window.

"I must go and collect the others," Lady Catherine said brightly, turning to leave. "We will be back shortly."

Christiana stared at Stephen. He smiled and walked to one of the tables and poured wine into two cups.

"A fortuitous coincidence, Christiana," he said as he handed her one of them. "I feared that I would not see you before we left."

She glanced at the tables awaiting the other diners. How long before some of them arrived?

"You will ride with your father?" she asked.

"Aye. The King has collected a huge army. It promises to be a glorious war. Come and sit with me awhile before the others come."

She thought of David's demand that she not see this man. By rights she should leave. But they would only be alone for a few moments and there could be no harm in wishing him well. She took a seat across from him at one of the tables.

"How is your merchant?" Stephen asked.

"David is well."

"He is not with you. He did not accompany you on this visit or on the others." His tone lacked subtlety. He assumed she returned to court to avoid David. That she sought solace amongst her friends.

"He is a busy man, Stephen, and is out of the city now."

"Still, I expected him to welcome the entry to court that you provided."

"He has little interest in such things."

Stephen raised his eyebrows in mock surprise. He leaned forward and his gaze drifted over her face.

His attention evoked an utter lack of feeling. In a strange way she felt as if she were seeing him for the first time. The face which she had once thought ruggedly handsome now appeared a bit coarse. There was something ill defined in the cheeks and jaws, especially compared to the precision of David's features. The blond hair, she felt quite sure, would not feel very soft if she touched it. Those thick eyebrows contrasted so little with the fair skin as to be almost invisible.

"You are so beautiful," he said softly. "I think that you grow more lovely each time that I see you."

She raised the cup of wine to her mouth and watched him over its rim. His hand reached toward her face.

In that instant before he touched her, she suddenly knew several things clearly and absolutely. She knew them as surely as she knew that day would follow night. Although they came as revelations, they did not surprise her at all. Rather she took a step and there they were, new facts of life to be reckoned with.

She knew, first of all, that no other diners would be joining them. No one, least of all Morvan, would arrive at that door. Stephen had arranged this with Lady Catherine's help, or maybe Catherine had done it herself. The tables, the cups, were all a ruse to get and keep her here so that she and Stephen could be alone.

She also knew, as she regarded that suddenly unfamiliar face, that she had never loved this man. Infatuated, giddy, and excited, she had been those things, but those feelings would have passed with time if he had not tried to seduce her and thus disrupted her life. She had decided that she loved him in order to assuage her guilt and humiliation after Idonia found them. She had clung to that illusion in hopes of rescue from the consequences. But she had never really been in love with him, nor he with her, and now she felt only a vacant indifference toward that hand reaching for her.

And finally she knew, with a peaceful acceptance that made her smile, that the daughter of Hugh Fitzwaryn had fallen in love with a common merchant. A glorious burst of tenderness for David flowed through her with the admission.

She leaned back out of reach.

"Nay."

He dropped his hand and sat upright, his green eyes examining her own. She let him search as long as he wanted, for he would not find what he sought. He smiled ruefully and poured some more wine.

"You have grown up quickly. It is a woman's face that I see now."

"I have had little choice. Perhaps I was overlong a child anyway."

"Innocence has its charm," he said, laughing.

"And its convenience."

He glanced at her and shrugged. "Your merchant is a very fortunate man, my sweet."

She felt a vague affection for Stephen. He was a rogue to be sure, but no longer dangerous to her heart. "I know that none at court will ever believe this, Stephen, but I think myself fortunate, too."

It felt good saying that. It felt wonderful standing up for her husband against the pity and sympathy of these people.

Stephen glanced at her sharply and then laughed in an artificial way. "Then my quest is indeed hopeless."

"Aye. Hopeless."

He made an exaggerated sigh. "First your brother's sword and now your husband's love. This story is a tragedy."

Nay, it was always a farce. Written by you and played by me who thought it real life. But she found that she could not hold that against him anymore. It really didn't matter. He didn't matter.

Dinner actually arrived, brought by two servants, and she stayed and ate with Stephen because being alone with him held no betrayal now. Her love for David felt like a suit of armor, and she was sure that Stephen recognized the futility of trying to penetrate it. They spoke casually about many things, and the hour passed pleasantly.

Toward the end of the meal, however, she suspected that he again began weighing her resolve against his skill at seduction. His smiles got warmer and his flattery more florid. His hand accidentally touched hers several times.

She calmly watched the unfolding of his final effort with surprise and amusement. She rose to leave before he could act on his intentions.

He rose more quickly and stepped between her and the door. His slow, insinuating smile filled her with sudden alarm.

"The meal was lovely, and it was good to share this time with an old friend, Stephen. But I must go now."

He shook his head, and his green eyes burned brightly. "The duty that says you must go was not chosen by you. In this world and this chamber, it does not bind you, my love."

She cursed herself for thinking that she could treat this man as a friend. "It is not duty that takes me away, but my love for my husband," she replied, hoping to kill any illusions he might have that she pined for him.

A spring breeze, light and free, blew through her heart with this more blatant admission of her feelings for David. How long had she loved him? Quite a while, she suspected.

How ironic that the first person to whom she admitted her love should be Stephen Percy. Ironic and also fair and just. Now she must tell David when he came back. If he came back. Then again, maybe she would not have to. Maybe he will just look at her and know. Of all her thoughts and emotions that he had read, this would probably be the most obvious.

Stephen had not moved out of her path, and he considered her closely, as if he judged her determination. She looked back firmly. Her response did not evoke the reaction she expected. Instead of backing down, a subtle ferocity entered his eyes and twisted his mouth.

He suddenly reached for her. She tried to duck his grasp, but he caught her shoulder and pulled her toward him. Surprised by his aggressive insistence, she squirmed to get free. He imprisoned her in his arms.

"A woman such as you cannot love such a man. One might as well try to mix oil and water. You have told yourself that you do in order to survive your fall, my love. That is all."

"You are wrong," she hissed, narrowing her eyes at him. "I love David, and I do not love you. Now *unhand me*."

"You may think you do not love me, but you will see the truth of it." His face and lips came toward her.

She leaned back until she could lean no further. She desperately turned her face away, but that bruising mouth found her cheek and neck. He grasped her hair to steady her darting head and forced a crushing kiss on her lips. His other hand slid down to grab her bottom. Her stomach turned. To think that she had cried over this lout! She began using all of her strength to break free.

Stephen laughed. "You are spirited. That will soothe my regret that you are no longer innocent. The memory of the passion that I awoke in you last time has filled my memory ever since, begging for completion."

"Passion? I felt no passion with you, you conceited fool! You hurt and humiliated me that day and you will not do it again! Loose me or I will scream and the whole court will know that you force unwilling women!"

"You are not unwilling, just afraid," he murmured, pressing her against his warmth and forcing a caress down her back. "I will show you the pleasure that love can be when you are with a real man. When you scream, it will be with desire and none will hear you. The walls are thick and the building noisy, so do not be shy."

Good Lord, his arrogance knew no bounds. No wonder Idonia never wanted them to be alone with men.

His hands began wandering freely over her body. She gritted her teeth against the repulsion she felt, and took advantage of his loosening hold. Frantically she groped behind her back on the table, feeling for some weapon. Her hand closed on a crockery pitcher.

Just in time, too. Stephen's breathing had grown ragged and heavy. He began pressing her backward against the table, trying to lay her down. His hand started raising her skirt.

She stopped her fight and leveraged her hips against the table's edge. She smiled at him. Stephen paused, looked at her triumphantly, and readjusted his stance. With a snarl, she lifted her knee with all of her strength up between his legs. Then she crashed the pitcher down on his head.

His face shattered in pain and surprise while he bent over. She roughly pushed him away.

"I am an honest woman who loves her husband," she seethed. "Do not ever touch me again."

She strode to the door. As she left she glanced back at the man in whom she had believed during the last days of her childhood.

As she flew down the stairs she heard his step behind her. On the second level he caught up with her. She shook off the hand with which he tried to restrain her. Pushing her way through the throng of revelers, she hurried to the public room below.

She noticed Lady Catherine in the crowd, and those cat eyes glanced at her smugly. Stephen had said that he was not friends with Catherine, and yet this woman had gone out of her way to help him. She wondered why.

"You might at least bid me farewell, my sweet," Stephen said lowly in her ear. His attempt at lightness could not hide an underlying anger in his tone.

She turned on him, furious at his persistence. Before she could speak, he bent down and kissed her, then smiled and melted into the crowd.

CHAPTER 16

THE FLEET SET sail. Westminster and London, emptied not only of the visiting soldiers but also of many of their workers, grew strangely quiet. Christiana returned home and impatiently counted the days until David returned.

Spring storms arrived and soon the news spread that the fleet was returning. Long before the first masts reappeared on the Thames five days after embarkation, everyone knew that ill winds had forced King Edward to cancel his invasion.

The city filled with soldiers again, this time passing through as they began their return to towns and farms and castles inland. Edward could not hold the troops indefinitely for better sailing and had dispersed them.

Christiana was stunned by the relief that she experienced when the news of the aborted campaign reached her. She thought that she had convinced herself that David indeed had gone to Salisbury, but her reaction spoke the lie of that illusion. Now she just felt gratitude that Edward's plans had changed and made the possibility of David's betrayal irrelevant.

The chance that he had done this thing, or had even tried to, should appall her more than it did. The potential dishonor should disgust her. But all she cared about was his safety and the fact that this turn of events would preserve him from the horrible consequences of discovery.

She longed to see him. Memories of him hung on her every moment of the day and filled the hours of the night. She realized that she had probably loved him for a long while. She had refused to see it because of her obligation of loyalty to Stephen. And, she had to admit, she had long denied her feelings because David was a merchant. Noblewomen were not supposed to love such men. She had been raised to think such a thing contrary to nature.

Did he love her at all? His joy appeared to match her own at his homecomings each day, and he had seemed sad about leaving her for this trip. During their lovemaking she saw more in his eyes than simple pleasure, but in truth she did not know how he really felt. She had no experience in such things, and he remained an enigma in many ways.

It didn't matter. As the days slowly passed she knew that there could be no hope of hiding her feelings. Surely when she gave him a child, some type of love would grow for her. In the meantime she felt confident that he would accept her love kindly. She did not plan when she would tell him. It would simply happen in the warmth of their reunion.

He rode into the courtyard a day early. She heard the sounds of his arrival while she sewed in the solar. She threw aside her needle to run down the stairs. Bursting through the door, she flew to him and jumped into his arms.

He caught her as he always did, and swung her around

as he embraced and kissed her. She clung to him while his scent and touch reawoke her soul.

Her blood raced with joy. "I am so glad that you are back and safe. There is something that I must tell you . . ."

The expression in his eyes brought her up short. He examined her with a haunted scrutiny. No affection reached out to her, despite his embrace. In fact, those arms closed on her in a restrictive way as if he sought to hold her in place while he studied her.

She noticed with misgivings the hard line of his mouth. Something dark and disturbing emanated from him. She had never seen this expression and mood. Indeed, for a horrible instant, she felt as if she had never seen this man before.

"What is it?" Had he been discovered after all? Was he in danger?

He turned her in his arm and guided her toward the hall. The grip holding her shoulder felt hard and commanding. "I have had a bad journey and need a bath and some food, Christiana. We will talk later. Send a servant up to me."

His arm fell away and he walked across the hall toward their chambers. His words and manner made it clear that he did not expect her to follow.

Flustered and hurt, she set about seeing to his needs. She sent Emma and the manservant up to prepare the bath and warned Vittorio to serve dinner as soon as possible. Then she paced the hall, absorbed with concern over this change in him.

Could this be his reaction at having his plans thwarted? If he had gone to France, and risked what he risked, had the turn of events angered him? For there had been anger in those blue eyes, and a cold distance that chilled her.

He joined the household for dinner. He sat beside her

and received reports from Andrew as he ate. Nothing specific conveyed his displeasure, but she could sense it distinctly. At the end of the table, Sieg ate his meal with a methodical silence that suggested he at least recognized David's mood.

She had assumed that they would tumble into bed at the first chance upon his return, but under the circumstances she didn't mind too much when he moved his chair to the hearth after the meal. The others left and she sat across from him and watched him stare into the fire.

A very strange silence descended. She bore it awhile and then tried to fill it with conversation. She described small events in the household while he was gone, and the reaction when the fleet returned. Chattering on anxiously, she told him about her sad leave-taking of Morvan and then her relief upon his unexpected return.

He turned those haunted eyes on her while she spoke. His steady regard made her uncomfortable. She had imagined his homecoming many times, and it had been filled with elation and joy and her newly discovered love. She found all of those emotions retreating from the dark presence sitting near her.

She began telling him about the Easter joust, but he interrupted with an abruptness that suggested that he hadn't been listening to anything.

"You were seen," he said.

She jolted in confusion. The frightening realization struck her that this change in him had something to do with her.

"Seen? What do you mean?" She instinctively felt defensive.

He rose from his chair. Grabbing her arm, he lifted her and began pushing her in front of him through the hall.

"What are you talking about?" She glanced back at the stranger forcing her to scramble up the steps.

He dragged her to the bedchamber and slammed the door behind them. She sensed his anger spike dangerously. Some anger of her own rose in response and mixed with her worry and fear. She shook off his grip and backed up to the windows.

He faced her with tense hands on his hips. "You were seen, girl. With your lover."

"There were men at court who paid me attention, David, but it was harmless. No doubt many saw me, but not with any lover."

Her light response only made it worse. His anger surged. "Men paying you attention are inevitable. Stephen Percy, it seems, was inevitable, too, despite your vows and your assurances to me. It did not take you long to find your way back to that knight's bed."

His crisp words stunned her. She had actually forgotten about that dinner with Stephen these last few days. Stephen Percy had ceased to exist for her as she reveled in her love for David. She stared at him speechlessly and knew that the truth, that she had met with Stephen, was written on her face.

"That was harmless, too," she said, knowing that her denial would not matter. The meeting itself was the betrayal and he would assume the worst.

"You have no talent for adultery, darling. You don't even know when to lie and how to do it. Harmless? Lady Catherine was seen taking you up to a chamber in that inn and then returning without you. An hour later you emerged with Percy. I am told that your kiss of farewell was chaste enough, but he could afford restraint and discretion by then."

"What you were told is true, but I did nothing wrong in that chamber," she explained with a calm she did not feel at all. She could offer only her word against the damning evidence. "Who told you of this, David? Many saw, I am sure, and I am sorry that I did not think how it would appear to them and what it might cost your pride. But who felt the need to tell you? Was it Catherine? She helped Stephen in the ruse that brought me to him unknowingly."

"No doubt Lady Catherine eagerly awaits letting me know," he said bitterly.

"Then who?" but even as she asked it she knew the answer. He had just arrived back in London. Whoever had told him this was someone he trusted. Her indignation at the implications helped beat back the desperation.

"Oliver," she gasped. "You were having me followed. Dear saints! All of the time? When I walked about the city, was he always there? Did he hide in the shadows of Westminster and follow us into the forest for the hunt? Did you trust me so little . . ."

"He followed you for your protection, and not to catch you thus. In this one thing I surely trusted you, or I would not have let you go back to court where he could not follow."

"He was there? At the inn?"

He advanced toward her, dangerous and tense, and she backed up until she bumped against the window.

"He tried to hide the truth from me, but I can read him as I read you, and I forced it out." He reached out and laid his hand against her face. There was nothing soothing in his quiet voice or reassuring in that touch. "So you have finally had your knight, my lady. Was it all that you expected? Like the songs and poetry of chivalry on which you were raised? Did that knight's hands give you comfort that you are still who you were born to be? That you had not been debased beyond redemption in the bed of a merchant?"

Nay, she wanted to say, *it was the other way around*. But admitting that Stephen had touched her would only throw oil on this fire.

He neither crowded her nor restrained her, but she suddenly felt extremely helpless. A sensual edge in his soft tone made her wary.

"I did nothing wrong . . ." She repeated, searching his eyes for belief and understanding. She saw only shadows and fire and something else that alarmed her.

When he lowered his head, she tried to turn away. His hand twisted into her hair and held her as his mouth claimed hers.

She loved him and missed him and wanted him, and at first her body and spirit accepted him gratefully. But as she felt his passion rise and his kiss deepen, she knew that it was neither love nor affection driving him but rather pride and anger, and this reminded her too much of Stephen's assault. She jerked her head away and struggled as he pulled her into his arms.

"Nay. Do not . . ."

"Aye, my girl. I have been two weeks without a woman. That is the best thing about marriage. One need not waste time wooing and seducing when it waits for you at home." He imprisoned her with his embrace and cradled her head steady with a forceful grip. "This is the problem with adultery, and you might as well learn it today. The man can avoid his wife if he chooses, but the woman must return to a husband who still has his rights."

He held her firmly and kissed her again. She desperately squirmed against those strong arms. Her shock eclipsed every other emotion. He might have been a stranger handling her.

"I feared that you might repulse me, knowing where you had been and what you had been doing the first time I left the city," he said as his hands moved over her body.

He smiled faintly but she could tell that his anger hadn't abated at all. "It would be ironic, wouldn't it? To have paid all of that silver for property and then found that I no longer wanted the use of it."

Her mind clouded with horror at hearing him speak so coldly of their marriage. There had certainly been evidence that he thought of her thus and had even seduced her to lay claim to what was his, but to hear the words bluntly spoken and to have the confirmation thrown into the face of her love sickened her.

"Property . . ." she gasped.

"Aye. Bought and paid for."

Her eyes blurred and she thought that her heart would shatter. But his words also insulted her pride and her fury flared.

"I don't choose to be property to be used at your convenience," she cried, twisting and kicking to break free. "You will not do this in anger and punishment."

Her struggle only infuriated him. With two rough moves he pinned and immobilized her against the window.

"You are my wife. You have no choices."

She screamed as he lifted her and carried her to the bed as if she were a carpet. When he threw her down, she rolled away and tried to scramble free. He caught her and pulled her to him, pressing his chest into her back and throwing a leg over hers.

He held her until her thrashing stopped. She emerged from her delirium of rebellion. He softly stroked her hair and back as if she were a skittish animal.

Devastation flooded her. She bit her lower lip and fought back tears. She thought of the stupid and trusting joy which she had carried down to him just a few hours before. Love, alive but battered, searched for shelter somewhere inside her.

He shifted off of her and ran his hand down her back. His fingers pried at the knot of her cotehardie's lacing.

"I'm sorry if I frightened you, but I share you with no man, least of all that one." His voice came quietly and gently, but anger still radiated from him, mixing with the passion of his body. "You must never go to him again. If you do, I will kill him."

He said it simply and evenly, in the voice of the David she knew. The hands that she relished stroked her back through the loosened garment, their warmth flowing through the thin fabric of her shift. Her foolish love glowed in response. Her bludgeoned pride pushed it back into a corner.

She turned onto her back. His mood had not improved much although he tried to hide it now. She gazed at that handsome face that could so easily make her heart sigh. His expression softened, and he caressed her stomach and breast. A pleasurable yearning fluttered through her and it horrified her that she could respond under these conditions. Her love started stringing through her, offering to weave an illusion for escape.

His blunt words repeated themselves in her head. She grabbed his wrist and stayed his hand. Love or not, she could not delude herself about what was about to happen and why he did it and what it meant to him.

"So, we are down to base reality at last," she said, narrowing her eyes. "How tedious it must have been to have to pretend otherwise with the child whom you married."

He stared at her. His lack of response and denial turned her anguish to hateful spite. "The merchant has need of his property, much as he rides his horse when it suits him? Well, go ahead, husband. Reclaim your rights. Show that you are equal to any baron by using one of their daughters against her will. Will you hurt me, too? To make sure that the lesson of your ownership is well learned?"

Still he did not react. Her heart broke with a suffocating pain and she threw out whatever she could to hurt him, in turn. "Do not bother with seduction and pleasure, mercer. Soil feels nothing when it is tilled, nor wool when it is cut. I will think about who I am and what you are and feel nothing, too. But be quick about it so that I can go cleanse myself." And then she looked at him and through him the way she had that day after her bath.

She thought that he was going to hit her. In that brief moment of his renewed anger, as he drew up and his eyes darkened, she rolled frantically off the bed and half ran, half crawled to the door of the wardrobe.

She slammed and barred it just as he reached her. A vicious kick jarred the door and bolt. She pushed a heavy trunk over against them and stood back fearfully as he kicked again.

Then came only silence. She ran to the door leading to the exterior stairs and barred it too. She waited tensely a long time but the quiet held and he made no more attempts to enter.

Heaving breaths of relief, she sank down on a stool and finally let the tears flow. She cried long and hard, awash in misery and shock, his cruel words echoing in her ears. Her pathetic love fluttered out of hiding and added to the agony.

Eventually a numb stupor claimed her. Only one thought came clearly, over and over again. She had to get away and leave this house and this man. She would not, could not, live with the reality he had forced on her this day. Not now. Not for a long while. Maybe not ever.

✦   ✦   ✦

The rain pounded relentlessly, its blowing spray stinging David's face. He stood on the short dock and watched the patterns that the drops made in the muddy Thames. Beautiful, rhythmic splashes, full of faint highlights of purity, existed for split instants before the dirty flow absorbed them.

He let the rain wash over him. It soaked his clothes and plastered his hair to his head. After a long while it cleansed the black anger from his mind.

And then, with the madness gone, he faced the memory of what had occurred. That would never wash away and he lived it all again. His spiteful words. Her harsh insults. His vicious debasement of her.

Thank God she had gotten away.

They knew each other well enough to point the daggers expertly and draw blood from each other's weaknesses. He would never forget what she had said, but he couldn't blame her for admitting those feelings and thoughts. Since the day she had come to him, she had tried valiantly to ignore what this marriage meant to her life.

He had never been as cruel and hard to a woman as he had been with Christiana this day. Oliver and Sieg had been right. He should never have returned home and confronted her while the knowledge of her infidelity still flared like a fresh log tossed on a fire. He had known that they were right even as he ignored their advice and entreaties.

He pictured Oliver sitting across the tavern table from him and Sieg, listening with studied absorption to their tale of waiting on the Normandy coast for signs of the fleet passing. David described how the days had turned dark with storms and how he had realized that this month at least he would be spared the decision awaiting him in France.

And all the time that Oliver carefully listened and prolonged the tale with questions, he had watched the signs of ill ease on his old friend's face. They betrayed him worse when David asked after Christiana. Poor Oliver. He had tried to lie and then to equivocate when he probed for details. David knew that his own expression had turned dangerous when he felt Sieg's hand on his shoulder and that lilting voice urging him to stay away from the house for a few more days.

Impossible, of course. He had to see her at once and look into those diamonds knowing what he knew. He wanted and expected to feel dead to her, to be free of the love that was complicating his life and making him suddenly indecisive.

For when he had stepped off Albin's boat this morning after two treacherous days at sea, he had known that he loved her. He had recognized the feelings for a long time, but in Normandy he had put the name to them. He had sought out Oliver before returning home, because he knew that when he entered that house he would not want to leave again for a long while.

In his mind he saw her running to him, face flushed and eyes bright. He had watched her exuberant greeting with dark fascination. He had not expected her to be so good at deception. And mixed with that initial reaction had been the appalling realization that he still wanted her.

A dangerous mix, he thought now as he raised his face to the rain. Anger and desire and jealousy. Why had he let her play the game out? Why had he permitted those hours to pass as she pretended that nothing had changed and his own rancor grew? He grimaced and wiped the water from his face. He had been watching and waiting and, aye, hoping. Waiting for a confession and hoping it included the admission that her infidelity had been disillusioning.

Waiting for her to beg forgiveness and say that she now knew that she no longer loved Percy.

Fool. Unfaithful wives never did such things. Even when cornered with the evidence, the prudent course was to lie. Honesty was too dangerous. Men reacted too violently. He had certainly proven that today, hadn't he? He had forced her into lies born of her fear.

He closed his mind to the memory of her shock and terror.

She had denied it, but he didn't believe her. She loved Sir Stephen and her knight had been leaving for war. Her own testimony suggested that Stephen had no skill as a lover, but that did not reassure him in the least. A woman in love sought more than pleasure in bed and would forgive any clumsiness.

He contemplated that denial as he walked back to his horse. One part rang true. *Lady Catherine brought me to Stephen unknowingly*, she had said. He believed that, and it was something at least. Christiana had not arranged that meeting on her own, but had been lured there. Considering how she felt about Stephen, perhaps the rest had been so inevitable as to make her practically innocent.

As for Lady Catherine and her role in this . . . Well, when he settled this new account, he would permit himself the pleasure of revenge and not just justice.

He couldn't stay away from the house forever, and so he rode back, not knowing what he would say to Christiana when he got there. The temptation presented itself to pretend that the whole day had never happened, that he had never confronted her in his rage.

Would she accept their behaviors as an effective trade? One infidelity and betrayal for one attempted rape? If it had just been that, the accounts might be cleared, but his words and manner had insulted her more than any bodily assault could. To hurt her, he had told her that she was only a noble whore whom he had bought. She would not quickly forgive him that.

He rode into the wet courtyard and handed his reins to the groom. As soon as he entered the hall, a corner of his soul suspected.

The house felt as it had before their wedding. It had been his home for years and he had found contentment in it and so he had never noticed the voids that it held after his mother and master died. Only after Christiana filled those spaces with her smiles and joy had he realized their previous vacancy. Now he heard his footsteps echo in the large chamber as if all of the furniture had been removed. He paced to the hearth, avoiding the confirmation of his suspicion.

Geva entered from the kitchen with crockery plates in her arms. She glanced at him and shook her head.

"You be soaking wet, David. Best get out of those garments," she scolded.

He turned his back to the fire. Geva hummed as she set out the plates for supper. She acted as if nothing was amiss, and his foreboding retreated. With one final glance at him, she disappeared back into the kitchen.

He looked at the tables. He counted the plates. One short. The foreboding rushed back.

He slowly walked across the hall and up to his chambers, knowing what he would find.

In the wardrobe, hanging on their pegs and folded in trunks, were all of the garments that he had given her, including the red cloak. He flipped through them, noting that her other things, her old things, were mostly gone. Not all of them, however. One trunk still held some winter wools. He lifted them to his face and savored her scent, and an invisible hand squeezed his heart.

He left the wardrobe and passed quickly through the

bedchamber, not wanting to look at that space that still held the vivid images of the wounds they had inflicted on each other.

Sieg squatted in the solar, building the fire. He raised his eyebrows at the soaked garments.

"Did you throw yourself in the river then?"

David ignored him.

"Did you harm her?"

He shook his head.

Sieg finished with the fire and then rose. "I told you to wait, David. Your mood was blacker than night. I've not seen you like that, even when the Mamluks first threw you into that hell with me after that slut sold you out to them. Not even during our escape when you killed the one who had flogged us."

"I should have listened."

"*Ja*, well you never have where this girl goes, so this is no different."

David hesitated. With any other man he would not have asked, but Sieg had seen him weak before.

"Where is she?"

Sieg's eyes flashed and his posture straightened. "Hell! You don't know? I swear she told me that you'd agreed to it or I'd not have taken her . . ."

"Where?"

"Back to Westminster." He turned toward the door. "I go and get her now. Hell."

"Do not. Leave her stay awhile."

"Do you mean to say that you will stand down to this fool of a knight who steals your wife? You will permit this?"

"If it comes to that, I have driven her to it," he said. "Do you think that she plans to remain at court? Did you sense that she intended to continue on else-where?"

"She promised to remain there, which I found odd, since she owes me no explanation."

"Sir Stephen left for Northumberland several days ago. Oliver told me. She knows that I will know, or find out. Her promise was to assure me that she does not go to him." He smiled thinly. "I said that I would kill him if she did. My behavior gave her reason to believe me."

Sieg threw up his hands. "It makes no sense, David. If this man is up north, why does she just go to Westminster? If she doesn't go to him, why run away at all?"

David didn't reply, although the answer was obvious. *She does not run to Percy*, he thought. *She runs from me.*

Christiana sat in a garden redolent with the scent of late May flowers. She gazed at the pastel buds and smiled. Being a woman instead of a child wasn't all bad. Last year she would have taken the flowers' beauty for granted. Today she carefully admired their fresh purity.

David had taught her this. To pay attention to the fleeting beauties in the world. Not a small gift.

She sighed into the silence. The garden was empty despite the warm weather because the court attended dinner in the hall right now. She had avoided those crowded meals and all other events where she would be required to chat and make merry. She had escaped to Westminster for sanctuary and to heal her heart and soul.

She had found welcome and sympathy when she arrived. Lady Idonia had taken one look at her and known the reason for the visit. That little woman asked no questions and settled her in as if they had been expecting her. Joan and Isabele, warned by Idonia no doubt, sought no explanations either.

They were the only family she had known for years, and they surrounded her and protected her in her pain. Even Philippa, on hearing of her extended stay, had come to see her. Alone together in the ante-room, the Queen had tried to be a mother to her for once as she explained the difficulties of marriage. Upon leaving, she had offered to write to David and say that she requested his wife's continued attendance. He would not dare come for her then, and Christiana would have more time.

More time. For what? To reconcile herself to living her life with a man who at most wanted her available to satisfy his needs? Who had purchased a well-bred and well-formed bedmate, much as he carefully chose his horses? A man who did not believe her now after she had always been honest with him to the point of cruelty? A man who barely cared for her at all, but whom she loved despite everything?

There lay the real problem, of course. The rest she could manage and accept if she didn't love him. It was the lot of most women, and she had even ridden to her wedding assuming that it would be hers. Mutual indifference would make it bearable. Wasn't Margaret surviving?

Aye, she needed time. Time to stop loving him.

She had been working hard at that these last few weeks. She kept the memory of his harsh indifference and his attempted rape sharp in her brain. She reexamined the evidence implicating him in some treasonous game. It hadn't worked and she was in a quandary. The love wouldn't die and he had robbed her of the chance to build illusions out of ambiguities.

She looked up from the flowers. More time. How much would it take? How long before she could return to that house and that bed as indifferent to him as he was to her? How long before he could touch her and she would feel no more than simple pleasure or, if not that, remove herself from the experience? Hadn't David said that Anne handled her whoring that way? What was she but some incredibly expensive whore?

Surely just being away from him should kill these feelings eventually.

A palace door opened. Morvan paused in the threshold. He looked at her a moment before walking over. He sat down and stayed there in silence with his arm around her back. She let her head rest on his shoulder.

She hadn't spoken with him all of this time and had actually avoided him. When they briefly saw each other, she turned away from the questions in his eyes. Now he had deliberately sought her out and she felt grateful. He possessed so much strength that there always seemed to be extra to spare for her.

She turned and looked at his profile and saw his concern. She also saw something else and suspected with a numb resignation that her time was up.

"Why are you here, Christiana?" he finally asked, demanding the information that no one else had required.

"I could not stay there."

"Why not?"

Because my husband does not love me at all. She could not say it. It sounded too childish. Like most nobles, Morvan probably thought the issue of love irrelevant in marriages.

"Did he hurt you? Abuse you?"

"Nay." Not the way that Morvan meant. If he had, she would have lied. She did not want her brother killing David.

"Does he use you too hard?" he asked softly.

"Nay," she whispered.

"Has he gone to other women? If it is that, Christiana, I must tell you that with men . . ."

"To my knowledge he has not, Morvan. He thinks that I went to another man. To Stephen. He does not believe me when I deny it. He was mad with anger and jealousy. We argued and said things . . . ugly things."

"All couples argue. Our parents had terrible fights."

"This was different."

"Perhaps not."

"Did our father love our mother?"

The question surprised him. "It was a love match. I think they still loved each other at the end."

"Then it was different."

"That is a rare thing, Christiana. What they had. I do not think that it is given to most. Not really."

"Not you?"

"Nay. Not me. Like most men, I settle for brief simulacrums of it."

She thought that sad. She remembered David saying that Elizabeth would not marry Morvan because of their uneven love. She understood Elizabeth now and knew why Elizabeth had chosen instead that old baron for whom she felt nothing. Marriage to Morvan would have torn her heart daily.

"You cannot stay here," Morvan said gently. "Philippa spoke with me. Edward has become aware of your presence and questioned her about it. She does not think that David said anything, but the King has some affection for your husband, it seems, and interfered on his own."

"I cannot go back there."

"There is no place else to go."

She closed her eyes.

"God willing, Christiana, the day will come when I will have a home. If you still need to leave, I will take you in forever and keep him from getting you back. But for now, there is no choice." He paused and added carefully,

"Unless you want to go north to Percy. Did Stephen offer to keep you?"

She uttered a short laugh. "Nothing so formal or permanent, brother. Even if he had, I would not go, because I do not care for him now and would not dishonor you thus even if I did. Also I would not go because David has said that he will kill Stephen if I do, and I believe him." She smiled mischievously. "Would you have let me go?"

"Probably not."

"I did not think so."

He smiled kindly at her. "I have asked Idonia to pack your things. Horses await. I am taking you home now."

Her stomach twisted. "So soon?"

"Whatever is between you and David will only be a day worse tomorrow."

He rose and held out his hand.

"I do not know if I can bear this, Morvan. The last time I saw him . . ."

The last time she saw him, he was about to hit her because she had spoken to him noble to commoner and implied that his touch would debase and dirty her. The last sound she had heard him make was that kick trying to break down the wardrobe door.

"He will probably be happy and relieved to see you," Morvan said as he raised her to her feet. "It occurs to me that this is the third time that I have brought you to him. The man should have great affection for me by now."

She forced a laugh at her brother's attempt at levity, but she didn't think for one moment that David would be relieved to see her.

David heard the horses enter the courtyard just as dinner ended. Andrew was leaving the hall and he glanced over meaningfully, confirming the riders' identities.

Michael, crowding in behind Andrew at the door, announced happily to the servants that their mistress had returned.

David gestured for everyone to go about their business. He went to the door and stepped outside. The apprentices greeted Christiana as they passed her on their way to the gate. She rode forward slowly beside her brother.

She had been gone for almost three weeks. No messages or notes had passed between them, and his option of fetching her back had been cut off by the Queen's interference. Three weeks and before that two more. He'd only had that horrible afternoon with her in all of that time.

They stopped their horses right in front of him. Christiana looked down impassively. Morvan tried to appear casual and amiable. He swung off his saddle and walked around to lift his sister down.

"Christiana asked me to escort her home," he said as he began untying the small trunks on the saddle. "She was finding Westminster tedious."

David waited. Christiana walked a few steps and faced him.

"He is lying," she said quietly. "He made me come."

"All the same, it is good to have you back."

She glanced at him skeptically. "Did you keep Emma?"

"She is inside."

"I will go and rest now," she announced. "I find that I have a headache and am a bit dizzy."

He let her pass, nodding acknowledgment of her old excuse for avoiding him.

Morvan set the trunks down near the door.

"I thank you, Morvan."

Morvan's face hardened. "Do not thank me. She is pained about something, although I know not what. If there had been anywhere else to take her, I would have done so."

He mounted his horse. "I will come in a few days to see her," he said pointedly.

"I will not hurt her over this."

He turned his horse. "All the same, I will come."

David crossed the courtyard and entered the side building. As he approached the stairs he saw Emma emerge from his mother's old chamber. She softly closed the door and eased over to him.

"She is most poorly, I think. She said that she could not make the steps."

He glanced at the door behind which his young wife hid from him. Would she ever open it again of her own will, or would he eventually have to tear it down? He would wait and see. He was good at waiting.

"She will use that chamber until she feels better, then. Make her as comfortable as you can, Emma."

CHAPTER 17

THE BED FELT a little strange. Christiana snuggled under the covers even though the June night was warm enough to leave the windows open. She gazed up at the pleated blue drapery.

She did not have to be here, she reminded herself, and she still had time to change her mind. He would not be back for several nights. No one knew that their sick mistress had stolen up these stairs and entered this chamber while the household slept. She could return to Joanna's room before morning and continue her deception.

She doubted that anyone continued to be fooled by her illness, except maybe trusting Emma. The concern with which she had been treated those first days had long ago dissolved into silent curiosity.

Her arm stretched out and slid over the cool sheets where normally David slept. Perhaps it had been a mistake to come here tonight. Even if she left now and never returned, he would undoubtedly sense that she had been here. It had probably been foolish to steal up to this bed and try to imagine whether she could return to him without being devastated.

He had supported her claim of illness. For three weeks he had treated her with concern in front of the others. He greeted her warmly upon returning to the house and placed his hand over hers while the conversations continued after the meals.

When they were alone, she had seen other things in those blue eyes, however. The knowledge that she deliberately avoided him. A forbearing but not eternal patience. Sometimes, perhaps, an intelligent male mind calculating his options with her.

Since she ostensibly could not climb the stairs, she had taken to sewing in the hall after the evening meals. After the first few days, he began joining her there. A subtle tension underlaid the stilted conversations which they held across the hearth, but recently its tremoring pulse had gotten worse during the long silences. She would look up from her sewing and find him watching her and the look in his eyes would summon that old fear that wasn't fear. She would curse herself and pray that he would leave her alone in peace and not remind her with his presence and his gaze how much she still loved and wanted him.

It had been deliberate. Every touch, every gentle kiss good night when she left the hearth to return to Joanna's room, had been intended to remind her of the pleasure she felt with him. He had been playing a slow, methodical melody on the strings of her desire.

It had succeeded. The last week as she lay in her lonely bed, she had begun considering that maybe she could live this life in which she had been imprisoned. She could take the pleasure for what it was. Why deny herself? It had become clear that this special hunger, once awakened, did not sleep easily ever again.

Since the day she had returned, she had lain in that

bed every night, unable to sleep quickly, listening for the step outside her door that warned that he finally came to demand his rights and her duty.

Last night she had barely slept at all. He had intended to leave in the morning to attend one of the trade fairs inland. She did not doubt the truth of his destination this time, because John Constantyn was going with him. It would not be a long journey, but their silent evening by the hearth had been heavy with the knowledge of his impending departure. Did his memories turn as hers did to his last emotional leave-taking and what had occurred upon his return?

His kiss when she finally left him had been long and less chaste, and his hands had caressed her while he embraced her. Hungry, aching feelings long denied had flooded her before he drew away. If he had lifted her up and carried her back to his bed then, she could not have stopped him.

He did not, though. He let her leave him as he always had these last weeks. She went to the small chamber that had become her home. She waited, praying this time that he would indeed come and end this even as she dreaded that he would. Her need for his closeness overpowered her. Her insulted pride and her hurt at his indifference ceased to matter. That her desire was totally entwined with her love did not frighten her so much anymore. She would manage those feelings somehow.

He had come, but not during the night. At first light her door had opened and she had turned to find him standing there, looking down at her. She rose up against the headboard and pulled the sheet around her naked shoulders.

He sat down beside her and she saw signs of weariness in his face that suggested he had not slept much either.

"You are leaving now?" she asked.

"Aye. John awaits outside. Sieg will stay here. There are rumors that Edward has summoned the army again, Christiana. If men start arriving in the city, do not leave the house without Sieg or Vittorio."

She hadn't known that Edward had renewed his plans about France, but then she hadn't left this house in weeks because of her illness. Margaret had visited her several times, but Margaret had no interest in court gossip or politics and so had told her nothing. Nor had David until now.

Perhaps there were no rumors yet. Perhaps David only knew because the King had told him.

He only travels to a trade fair, she told herself firmly. *John Constantyn goes with him, not Sieg.*

He placed his hand on her knee. She looked down at it, so exciting in its elegant strength, so warm despite the sheet between their flesh. That quivering intensity that always emanated from him seemed especially apparent this morning.

"This cannot go on," he said. "You cannot stay here."

They had never spoken of that day nor of why she feigned this illness. A part of her had hoped that they never would.

"That is what Morvan said. He came to me at Westminster and said I could not stay there. Now you say it about this house."

"Nay. I say it about this chamber. I'll not see another woman buried alive in it."

"Then give me some money to pay servants and I will go live in Hampstead. I will repay you from the farm rents."

A glint of anger glowed in those blue eyes before he suppressed it. He slowly shook his head.

His hand still rested on her knee, beckoning her with its warmth, offering her its pleasures. Better if he had just carried her upstairs last night. Better to have never put words to what was happening.

"What are you saying, David? Are you ordering me to my duty?"

"I am asking you to return to our marriage and our bed."

"What about Stephen Percy?"

"We will put that behind us."

"You still do not believe me, do you? But you kindly forgive me. That is most generous of you, but I neither want nor need your forgiveness."

"Perhaps I want and need yours."

"I do not know if I can give it," she whispered, as memories of that day drifted into the space between them. "Even now, as you ask me to come back to you, I know that you just find that you have need of your property and resent being denied it. It may be the way these things always are, but I do not think many women have to hear it so frankly stated and then live with the truth in such a naked way. Perhaps that is the reason for dowries. To give women some other value in marriages so that their dignity is preserved."

That exciting hand rose from her knee and stroked her cheek above the bunched sheet with which she shielded herself. It rested there, and its warmth flowed into her and down her neck. "We both spoke harsh things to each other. I think of no person as property, Christiana. Least of all you."

He leaned toward her. She knew that it would not be a simple kiss of parting and that she should turn away, but she could not even though the connection would bring her anguish. The warm touch, the quiet voice, the intense blue eyes had made her defenseless. Sensual memories during the night had left her tired body half aroused. His kiss lingered and deepened and she could not fight it because something inside her, apart from her reason and her hurt, hungered for him.

He kissed her as if the world had ceased to exist. Gently, almost lazily, he bit along her lips. The nips and warmth stunned her. He slowly pried his tongue into her and she parted her mouth stiffly, accepting him with a hesitation her trembling, anxious body didn't feel at all. The heady intimacy of this small joining washed over her and submerged her resentment and hurt.

A small internal voice cried a warning, but her appalling, forceful longing ignored it. She released one hand's hold on the sheet and awkwardly embraced the shoulders leaning toward her.

They kissed again tentatively, like first-time lovers finding their way. Then slowly, carefully, as if each touch revealed something precious, he pressed his lips to her neck and shoulders. Her whole body tremored with grateful relief at the repeated warm contact of that mouth.

She opened her eyes and found him looking at her, and she guessed that he could, as always, see everything and knew that her traitorous body had vanquished her resolve. She silently begged him to stay and also prayed that he would not.

"Come here," he said, reaching for her. He lifted and turned her and set her on his lap, resting her head and shoulders on the support of one arm while his other one embraced her to him. She still clutched the sheet and it followed her, trailing over her body as it twisted from the bed. Despite the sheet and his clothing, she felt his warmth and strength and sighed at the closeness. Her buttocks pressed against the hard muscles of his thighs and her hip felt the hot ridge of his arousal. It had been months since he had held her, and she lost herself in a mindless fog of connected warmth.

Cradling her in his arms, he lifted her to a hungry,

probing kiss. She felt his passion overwhelm his restraint of the last weeks. Her barely controlled desire also broke loose of her tenuous hold. Her last clear thought was an indifferent awareness that she would pay for this pleasure with pain.

With her free hand she encircled his neck and pressed him closer, asking for more, encouraging him. Her long abstinence had made her shameless, and she would not let him end the deep, frantic kiss. His embracing arm loosened and she moaned into him as his wonderful hand caressed her bare back and hip.

He broke the kiss and looked down into her eyes. His gaze lowered and his fingers traced down to where she still grabbed the top of the sheet.

"It did not help you much that day in the wardrobe, darling," he said quietly. "Let go now."

He spoke of the sheet, but he also meant much more. He softly stroked her clutching hand until her fingers relaxed beneath his seductive touch. She turned her face into his shoulder as he eased the sheet from her grip and slid it away. Cool air alerted the skin of her entire body.

She knew that he looked at her as he so often had done, only now she felt suddenly shy and stunned by a furious anticipation. She gritted her teeth and buried her face harder in his shoulder.

He kissed her neck and his quiet voice flowed with his breath into her ear. "Do not hide your face from me, Christiana. The desire that we feel for each other is a wonderful thing. I want you to watch me as I give you pleasure."

Gently he turned her face to his and forced her to meet his gaze. He had not even touched her yet, but that aching need already tensed her belly and a hot insistence throbbed between her legs.

She watched as he demanded. Watched as he cradled

her and kissed her breasts and moistened their hard tips with his tongue. Watched as his fingers slowly traced along her breastbone and teased in a circle. Her breasts swelled beneath that wandering touch, anxious, begging, and her consciousness focused on nothing besides her silent, breathless urging. His fingers slid to one moist nipple. She saw her body arch toward that devastating touch, and then she saw little else. Incredible sensations and single-minded desire obliterated all thought.

He aroused her as if time didn't matter, as if no one awaited him in the courtyard and no journey beckoned. Her breasts had never been so sensitive, and his deliberate caresses raised excruciating pleasures. When his strong arm lifted her shoulders and his mouth replaced his hand, the delicious need he created with his lips and teeth became consuming and painful.

He lifted his head and looked down her body. Her own dazed eyes followed. His hand splayed over her belly, his light golden skin contrasting in a compelling way with her creamy whiteness. He pressed down, stilling the rock of her hips. He caressed her thighs and they both watched that hand's progress. Her breath shortened to a series of low sighs.

"I am thinking that it is in my interests to leave you ill contented," he said softly as his hand trailed over her body. "Abstinence is a powerful enhancement to passion. I do not think that you would remain ill too long after my return."

She barely heard this frank assessment of her condition and resolve. She watched and felt his hand follow the crevice where her legs joined. Stabs of heat distracted her.

"But I find that I cannot do it," he said, "I have missed your passion and would at least have that from you this day."

His gaze claimed her attention, and his words penetrated her stupor. He kissed her beautifully. "Open to me, darling," he said while his fingers touched the soft mound of hair.

She had been waiting for him to rise and turn and lay her down. She had been waiting for the intimacy of his body along hers and the obliteration of her choices. She realized that he had never intended to use her desire against her like that today.

She hesitated, and almost said, as he made her say that first time, that she wanted him.

"Open," he commanded gently. His fingers caressed so close to her need that her breathing stopped and that hidden flesh pulsed. "There is no defeat in taking pleasure from me thus."

She had no resistance. She closed her eyes and parted her legs and accepted the relief he offered. It did not take long. He touched her slowly and gently as if to prolong the ecstasy, but her body already cried for release and each touch sent lines of frantic sensations through her until soon she felt the incredible tension wind inside and she thrashed and stiffened and exhaled sounds of mounting desire. He pulled her shoulders to him and held her firmly, kissing her ferociously while he pushed her over the edge into fulfillment, taking her cries into himself when the violent climax finally crashed through her.

He held her in a tight embrace for a long while, his face buried in the angle of her neck and shoulder. She awoke from the delirium to find her hands clawing the garments at his chest. She doubted that he had found satisfaction in this.

He loosened his hold and looked down at her. She noticed a little blood on his lip where she must have bitten him.

Silently he rose and laid her down on the bed. He caressed her face and looked into her eyes. "I must go."

He had contented her, but her deeper desire still burned. She almost urged him to stay longer and to finish what had begun. The choice would not really be hers then.

He left. Left her with the proof that he possessed the power to seduce her back. Forcing would have never been necessary, this parting visit had said, because this gentler persuasion had always been available to him and would be in the future. For a while longer the choice would be squarely hers, though. He had left her to decide if she could live this marriage and come to him, once again, of her own will.

She gazed at the blue pleats billowing above the bed. Aye, maybe she could. During that brief submersion into pleasure she hadn't thought about anything else, not even what she meant to him. Only later, when he left, had the pain and doubts closed in. In time perhaps they would cease to torment her. In a few years maybe her love would only exist as an amusing memory.

She should leave this bed now, before she fell asleep. If Emma found her upstairs in the morning, the whole household would assume that her illness had ended and Joanna's room would cease to be an option. No choice then. She smiled at how greedily her soul grasped at the possibility for self-deception. *Stay here, fall asleep, and it is done. An accident rather than a decision.*

The bed had lost its strangeness and a delicious relaxation claimed her. Even as she admonished herself to leave, her lids lowered. She surrendered to the prideless love that would accept any pain to be close to him and would gratefully accept the small part of himself that he chose to give her.

She did not know how long she slept, but suddenly

her eyes flew open. A sound had penetrated her dream, prodding her out of her peace. She raised herself on an elbow.

A large dark shadow moved past the window nearest the wardrobe door.

"David?" she mumbled, wiping her eyes.

A strange presence filled the chamber. She heard soft, scuffling footsteps. The shadow moved, and two others joined it.

Suddenly alert with shock, she started to scream. The large shadow lunged toward her. Strong arms pinned her down while rough hands pried and shoved a cloth into her mouth.

She thrashed violently against the suffocating gag. More hands pressed on her until she became immobile. She stared up into strange faces barely visible in the moonlight while her heart pounded wildly in the renewed silence.

"Now you be calm, my lady, and no harm will come to you," a man's voice said softly, just inches from her ear. Not an English voice, she considered as she jerked motionlessly against the restraining hands. Scottish.

One hand released her and a glint of steel appeared in it and waved in front of her eyes. "Listen carefully. We will let you up, but there be three of us here and armed at that, so do as I say. You will go into the wardrobe and dress and pack some things for yourself."

Pack? These men planned to take her someplace. Where and for what possible purpose?

Her mind frantically assessed her danger. How had they gotten into this house with its surrounding wall? Where was Sieg?

"Do you understand? Don't raise your hands to the gag."

She dumbly nodded. The hands fell off her one by

one and the talking man eased away. Shaking with terror, she slid out of the bed, grateful that she had not lit a candle and that these men could not see her naked body very well in the moonlight.

She staggered on wobbly legs to the wardrobe, trying to control the panic that threatened to cloud her mind of all reason and sense. Despite their warnings, she wanted to run and run and let the terror consume her as she did. She rashly decided that in the blackness of the wardrobe she would remove the gag and scream for help.

Upon entering, she saw the door to the garden open. Enough light seeped through to make the lines of her shadow visible and her actions obvious.

They watched as she fumbled for a loose gown and pulled it on. One of the men found a small traveling trunk, and she stuffed clothing into it, not knowing what she grabbed.

Thrusting her feet into shoes, she turned to them. She tried to remain calm although the deathly panic still wanted to unhinge her. Her only hope was to keep her wits about her. If Sieg still lived, he would save her when they tried to leave. She would make as much noise as possible on the courtyard stones in hopes of awakening him and the others.

"Now we will walk down those steps out there and go to the back of the garden," the man said.

Her heart sank. They had come in over the wall, not through the gate. Sieg slept unknowingly in the front building. He and the others would never hear.

They surrounded her like a prisoner being moved and guided her down the stairs and out the gate to the main garden. At the back wall two of them disappeared up a crude ladder.

"Now you. There's another on the other side. Take care, my lady. The drop could hurt you," the Scot said.

She tottered up, turned her body blindly, and felt for the wooden slats on the other side. Hands plucked her off halfway down and set her on the ground. They walked up the alley to where horses waited. Someone tied her hands before lifting her onto a saddle. Being bound made her feel even more helpless. They trailed out through the city lanes, towing her along.

She watched the streets anxiously, hoping to see the flames of torches that indicated other night travelers or the ward constable. If they were stopped, would the constable notice her gag? Would these men use their steel if they were challenged?

No challenge came. Her fear grew as she noted their approach to the city's gate. To her anguished dismay, the gate guard let them pass.

The lead man continued straight ahead after they passed through the wall. She straightened in shock. They headed for the northern road.

North. Northumberland. *Stephen?*

The Percy family held lands in Scotland and on England's border in Northumberland. Was this Scot one of their retainers?

Stephen abducting her? Now? It would be madness. Nay, not Stephen. Unless his pride had been wounded because he had lost his game to a mercer. During tournaments, Stephen had never been especially gracious in defeat. And if not Stephen, then who? She could think of no other possibility.

As they rode silently through the night, she told herself that Stephen would never do something so absurd, but a part of her worried that in fact he might. He might even consider it chivalrous and romantic and a grand gesture of salvation.

Duels and abductions are the stuff of songs, not life. Unless you were dealing with some childish girl and a foolish knight. Stephen, she suspected, could be very foolish.

He had seemed in the end to accept her refusal at that dinner. Had he later reconsidered her resolve? Had his conceit led him to conclude that she fought him against her heart's true desire?

Dear saints. David would kill them both.

Her misgivings flared when, some miles north of London, she spied shadows on the road ahead. Her small group approached two other figures on horses and stopped.

"You made quick work of it," a woman's voice said.

Christiana's eyes widened and she peered in the dark toward the hooded cloak. She knew this voice. This *was* Stephen's doing. And once again he had enlisted Lady Catherine's help.

Catherine's arm stretched out. "Here is the coin you will need. Do it exactly as I told you, and do not delay. The man will pay you your fee. And remember, she is not to be harmed."

Christiana made a loud sound from behind her gag. Lady Catherine turned toward her. "You want to speak, child? Remove her gag."

Dirty fingers pried the wadded cloth out of her mouth. She gasped deep breaths of air before speaking.

"Where do you take me?" she demanded.

"You will find out soon enough."

"If you abduct me for ransom, tell me now. Name your price and return me home. I will pay it."

"A generous offer, but there will be no ransom," Catherine said.

"Then why? Who bids you do this? Stephen Percy?"

Catherine laughed lightly. "All will be explained in good time, my dear. In the end you will thank me for this."

Did Catherine assume, like so many others at court, that she must welcome redemption in Stephen's arms?

"My husband will kill you for this," she hissed toward the men who waited. She realized that it was the first time she had claimed David's protection instead of Morvan's. But David *would* kill them. The thing about property was that one didn't like it stolen.

"By the time he finds you, it may not matter so much to him," Catherine said. "He will have bigger concerns. Take her now, and remember that she is not to be molested or handled. Do not try to run away, Christiana, for they have their orders to deliver you and will tie you to the horse if they have to."

"This is madness—" she began to protest, but the gag suddenly filled her mouth again and she choked on the words.

Lady Catherine and her silent companion turned south while her captors tugged the reins and started north. Christiana held the front of the saddle with bound hands and swayed into the animal's quicker walk.

North. Of all of the times for Stephen Percy to finally decide to live out some chanson!

Didn't he remember that violent deaths and jealous murders often ended those long love songs?

CHAPTER 18

DAVID LET HIS father's blood flow. He unblocked it from the recesses and fissures in which he kept it dammed and controlled. He permitted all of its dark strength to wash through him.

Sieg walked beside him as he rode across the court-yard. He looked down on the Swede's furrowed brow. Sieg blamed his own negligence for Christiana's disappearance and would not rest contented until he had helped bring her back. David would welcome his friend's help in the end, but not right now.

"The swords, Sieg. Don't forget to pack them," he said. Sieg nodded and David passed to the gate. It was possible that he wouldn't need the preparations that he was leaving Sieg to make. Possibly he would find her elsewhere. He doubted it, however. Still, he would have to check.

He paused and looked back at the buildings where he had lived his youth and manhood. If things turned out as he expected, he would never see this home again.

His father's blood didn't give a damn. He smiled thinly. Nay, no sentiment there. Not when faced with a quest or a goal. Or revenge.

He had known for years that it was in him and what it could do. As a youth he had examined his face and soul to know what came from the Abyndons and what came from the other side. He had tried to reconstruct the image of his absent father from the disconnected pieces that bore no Abyndon legacy. The love of beauty. The emotional restraint. The dark calculations. The ability to kill. Even Gilbert's self-righteous cruelty could not match his own inclinations to cold ruthlessness. That in particular had always been in him, a strength to be used and a weakness to be feared, and it went far beyond the shrewd analysis taught as part of a mercer's trade. His mother's blood had tempered it some, but the real lessons in controlling it had been David Constantyn's greatest gift to him.

It had been his father's half that had hurt Christiana.

He would check London and Westminster first, just to be sure.

A short while later he rode into the courtyard of Gilbert de Abyndon's house for the first time in his life. A groom approached for his horse but he ignored the man and tied the reins to a post.

The household sat to dinner when he entered the hall. He had planned it this way. He did not want Margaret to have to confront her husband's wrath if he came when Gilbert wasn't home, and he wanted plenty of people around so that maybe he wouldn't smash his fist into Gilbert's face when his uncle insulted him, as the man was sure to do.

Gilbert looked up from his conversation as David approached his table, and one would have thought that the man had seen an apparition, so complete was his shock. Margaret visibly paled.

David simply nodded acknowledgment of his uncle and turned his attention to Margaret.

"I am seeking Christiana, Margaret."

She frowned. "Seeking?"

"She has left the house."

"She is better then?"

So Christiana had not confided in her new friend. "Aye. But she is two days gone, Margaret. Did she come to you?"

Realization took hold, but Margaret hid it from her expression. Gilbert proved less discreet.

"So your noble wife has left you so soon?" he jeered softly.

"Is she here, Margaret?"

She shook her head.

"You have never known your place, boy," Gilbert snarled. "The conceit of marrying such a woman! Of course she is gone. It is a wonder she stayed this long."

David managed to ignore him. "Do you know where she is, Margaret?"

Poor Margaret shook her head again. Distressed eyes flickered up to his. Her hand rested protectively on her slightly swelled belly.

Gilbert laughed. "It is a pleasure to see great pride humbled. Such are the wages of that sin. Look you to the beds in the castles of the realm for her, nephew. Those women have no morals."

His hand shot out and he grabbed his uncle by the neck. Gilbert cried out and fell back in his chair. David let his arm and hand follow until he had the man pinned against the wooden back. The hall fell silent and a dozen pairs of eyes watched.

"You will say no more, Uncle, or I will release your young wife from the misery of this marriage," he said. "Now, you will permit Margaret to accompany me to the door and you will not follow. Do you agree to this?"

Gilbert glared at him. David squeezed. Gilbert nodded.

Margaret eased off her bench and came around the table. David dropped his hand.

"I am sorry," he said as they walked across the hall. "There was nothing for it but to come here."

"I understand. Do not worry. He will sputter for a few days and speak ill of you to all he meets, but that is nothing new, is it?"

David paused at the door. "Did she ever speak of Sir Stephen Percy to you?"

Margaret's surprise and shock were genuine. "Nay, David. She spoke of no man to me except you and her brother. Even when she described a humorous event at court, the players had no significance."

He nodded and turned to go. "Be well, Margaret."

She stopped him, and stepped out into the courtyard so that she could speak privately. "Why do you ask me about this man, David? Do you think Christiana has run away?"

"It is possible."

"With this man?" She looked at him incredulously. "I always thought that you were the exception to the rule that men were fools, David. If she held another in her heart, then I did not know her at all. She spoke only of you, and with warmth and affection and respect. If she is gone, it is not of her will, I am sure." She frowned with distress. "She is in danger, isn't she? Oh dear God . . ."

"I do not think that she is in danger," he said soothingly. "Go back to your husband now. Tell him that I would not let you leave me until you answered my questions."

"You must find her . . ."

"I will find her."

David stood against the wall of the practice yard and watched Morvan Fitzwaryn swing his battle-ax and land it against his opponent's shield. A bright sheen of sweat glistened on Morvan's naked chest and shoulders.

David sensed a movement behind him and turned to see two women peering over the wall as they strolled past. They eyed the tall knight appreciatively and giggled some comments to each other behind raised hands before they moved on.

He waited. Morvan had noticed him already. Eventually this practice must end.

Soon it did. Morvan's opponent gestured a finish. The two knights walked over to a water trough and sluiced themselves. Morvan came over as he shook the water from his head.

"You want me?" he asked, his voice still a little breathless from his exertions.

"Aye. Three nights ago Christiana left the house. None saw her and she told no one where she was going."

Morvan had been in the process of wiping his brow. His hand froze there.

"Did she come here, Morvan?"

"Nay."

"You said that you would have taken her elsewhere if possible. Have you done so now?"

Morvan glared at him. "If I had taken her from you, I would have let you see me do it."

David began walking away.

"She has not gone to him," Morvan called after him. He pivoted. "How do you know?"

"Because she told me she would not."

"Then you received more assurances than I did."

"Why give assurances to a man who does not believe them?" Morvan asked tightly as he walked up to him.

"I will know the truth of it soon enough, I suppose."

Morvan stared thoughtfully at the ground. "The last time she left and came here, she let you know where she was."

"Aye."

"But not this time. And she told me that she no longer cares for him. If she is with Percy, David, I do not think that it is her choice."

"I thought of that. You know the man better than me. Is it in his nature to do this? To abduct her?"

Morvan glanced blindly around the practice yard. "Hell if I know. He is vain and conceited and, I always thought, a little dull in the wits. The women say that he does not take rejection well. The men know that he is quick with a challenge if he thinks himself slighted."

David absorbed this. He should have met Sir Stephen or at least learned more about him. Pride had prevented it, but that had been a mistake. One should always know one's competitors' strengths and weaknesses. Even a green apprentice knew that.

"I will let you know when I find her."

"Do you ride north, then?" Morvan asked cautiously.

"Aye."

"I will come with you."

"I will go alone. For one thing, the King will need you here as the army musters. For another, I do not plan to do this in a knight's way."

He turned to leave, but Morvan gripped his arm. He looked into sparkling, troubled eyes so like those others.

"You must promise me, if you find her there, that you will give her a chance to speak. If there is an explanation, you must hear it," Morvan said.

David glanced down on the hand restraining him, and then at the intense bright eyes studying his face. Did he look as dangerous as Morvan's worry suggested?

"I will hear her out, brother."

He left then, to meet Sieg and Oliver and begin the journey to Northumberland. First, however, he made his way to the stone stairs that led to Edward's private chambers.

David and Oliver eased along the gutter of the inn, their backs pressed against the steep roof. Below them the lane that led to this hostelry appeared deserted except for the large shadow of a man resting casually against a fence rail. The shadow's head looked up to check their progress.

It went without saying that Sieg could not join them up here. He weight would have broken the tiles. He would wait below and then enter the normal way, dispatching in his wake any inconvenient squires or companions who might try to interfere.

"This reminds me of the old days," Oliver whispered cheerfully as they carefully set their steps into the gutter tiles. "Remember that time we boys got into the grocer's loft through the roof? Filled our pockets with salt."

"Nothing so practical, Oliver. It was cinnamon, and worth more than gold. They'd have hung us if they caught us, children or not."

"A great adventure, though."

"At least your mother used what you took. Mine knew it was stolen, gave it away, and dragged me to the priest."

"Her sensitivities on such things are no doubt why your life took a turn for the worse when you got older," Oliver said. "School and all."

"No doubt."

Oliver's foot slipped and a tile crashed to the ground. Both men froze and waited for the sounds that indicated someone had heard.

"I've a good mind to slit this knight's throat just to express my annoyance that he was so hard to find," Oliver muttered in the silence.

David smiled thinly. Percy had certainly been hard to find, and the length of their search had not improved David's own humor much. The man seemed to be hiding. Not a good sign.

They had ridden first to his father's estate, then his uncle's, and finally to the properties which Stephen himself managed. There had been no need to approach the castles and manor houses. A few hours in the nearest town or village gave them the information they sought. Young Sir Stephen had not been seen for at least a week. Finally, on the road south, a chance conversation with a passing jongleur had revealed that Percy had been resting at length at this public inn several miles north of Newcastle.

David surveyed the ground below him, dimly lit by one torch. Sieg glanced up and nodded. They were just above the window to Stephen's chamber on the top level of the inn. The warm June night had caused the window to be left open.

It was the dead of night and no sounds came from the inn or the chamber below. David turned to the roof, crouched, and grasped the eaves. He lowered his body down, slowly unbending his arms. His feet found the opening and he angled in, dropping with the slightest thud on the floor of the chamber.

He peered around at the flickering shadows cast by one night candle. Curtains surrounded the beds in this expensive inn, but here they had been left open. He saw a man's naked back and blond hair, and a strong arm slung over another body. Long dark tresses poured over the sheet.

His stomach clenched. A bloody fury obscured his sight. He unsheathed the dagger on his hip.

Oliver swung in the window and landed beside him. He gestured for David to be still, and then eased over to the door. Sieg waited on the other side.

With Sieg's arrival there could be little hope of keeping their presence a secret. The Swede stomped in, unsheathing his sword. Stephen Percy's head jerked up.

Sieg reached him before he had fully turned over. He placed a silencing finger to Percy's lips and the sword to his throat. Stephen froze. The woman still slept.

David found a taper near the hearth and bent it to the guttering night candle. He walked over and inspected the man who had caused him so much trouble.

Bright green eyes stared back warily over the shining blade. Stephen had rugged features and his skin appeared very pale, especially with all of the blood gone out of it now. David grudgingly admitted that women might find this man attractive.

"Who are you?" Stephen asked hoarsely in a voice that tried to sound indignant.

David leaned into better view. "I am Christiana's husband. The merchant."

Stephen's gaze slid over David, then angled up at Sieg and over to Oliver. "Thank God," he sighed with relief.

Sieg frowned at David. David gestured to Oliver. The wiry man moved to the other side of the bed.

Oliver pushed back the raven tresses spilling over a thin back. The girl jolted awake and turned. She managed one low shriek before Oliver's hand clamped down over her mouth.

Oliver stared. "Hell, David, it isn't her!"

"Nay. I never really thought it would be. She would not come on her own, and he never cared enough to abduct her. But I had to be sure."

The girl had noticed the sword at Percy's throat, its point not far from her own neck. She huddled herself into a ball and stared around wild-eyed.

David smiled down at Sir Stephen. "You thought we might be her kinsmen?"

Stephen gave a little shrug.

"Another virgin sacrifice to your vanity, Sir Stephen?"

Stephen's eyes narrowed. "Have you lost something, merchant? You can see she is not here, so be gone."

"Do you have her elsewhere?"

Stephen laughed. "She was sweet, but not worth that much trouble."

Dangerous anger seeped into David's mind. "Sweet, was she?"

A sneer played on Stephen's face. Sieg lifted the blade a bit, forcing Percy's chin to rise with it. Stephen glowered down at the sword and hesitated, but conceit won out.

"Aye," he smirked. "Very sweet. Well worth the wait."

"I kill him now, David," Sieg said matter-of-factly.

"Nay. If he dies, he is mine."

The girl had begun crying into her knees. Oliver sat beside her and patted her shoulder. She muttered something between her sobs.

"Considering your position, you are either very brave or very stupid to taunt me thus," David said.

Stephen laughed. "You are no threat to me, mercer.

Harm a hair on my head and you had best leave the realm. If the law doesn't hang you, my family will."

"A good point. Except that I had already planned to leave the realm, and so it appears that I have nothing to lose."

The smug smile fell from Stephen's face.

"David," Oliver said, "this girl is little more than a child. Look at how small she is. How old are you, girl?"

"Just fourteen this summer," she sobbed miserably. She glared at Stephen. "He was going to take me to London, wasn't he?"

Stephen rolled his eyes. "We will go, my sweet. After it is safe . . ."

"Nay, you won't," Oliver said to her. "He will leave you to the wrath of your kinsmen, and you'll be lucky to end up in a convent. What are you? Gentry? Aye, well, they won't press case against a Percy, will they? Nay, girl, it's a convent or whoring for you, I'm afraid."

The girl wailed. Percy cursed.

"So do we kill him now?" Sieg asked.

Quick. Easy. So tempting. David gazed impassively at the rugged face trying to remain brave and cool.

"I think not," he finally said.

Stephen's eyes closed in relief as Sieg cursed and sheathed his sword.

"Give me your dagger, David," Sieg said, holding out his hand. "The Mamluk one."

"What for?"

Sieg sniffed. "In honor of the love I feel for this country and in protection of the few virgins left in it, I'm going to fix this man."

Stephen frowned in perplexity.

"Remember that physician in prison, David? The one who had once worked at the palace? Well, he told me how they made eunuchs. It is a simple thing, really. Just a quick cut . . ."

Stephen's eyes widened in horror.

"Sieg . . ." David began.

"The dagger, David. You always keep it sharp. We'll be out of here as quick as a nick."

David looked at Sir Stephen's sweating brow. He looked at the crying girl and Oliver's gentle comfort. He thought about Christiana's pain over this man.

"If you insist," he said blandly.

"Aye. Oliver, help hold him down for me."

The girl saw the dagger approach and began a series of low, hoarse screams. Sir Stephen practically jumped out of his skin. He inched back on the bed, staring at the looming, implacable Sieg. He turned to David. "Good God, man, you can't be serious!"

"As I said, I have nothing to lose."

Stephen laughed nervously and held up a hand as if to ward off the dagger. "Listen. Seriously. What I said before about Christiana . . . I was lying. I never had her. In truth I never did."

"It is more likely that you are lying now."

"I swear to you, I never . . . I barely touched her! I tried, I'll admit, but, hell, we all try, don't we?" He turned wildly to Sieg and Oliver, seeking confirmation.

"Let's see. Kneel on his legs, David. Oliver, climb over and put your weight on his chest," Sieg said as he reached for the sheet.

"*Jesus!*" Stephen yelled. "I swear it on my soul, she wouldn't have me."

David smiled. "I already knew that."

Sieg took another step forward. Stephen looked ready to faint.

"How?" Stephen croaked while he stared at the ugly length of steel.

"She told me." He placed a hand on Sieg's shoulder. "Let us go, Sieg. Leave this man."

"Hell, David, he is disgusting . . ."

"Let us go."

Oliver got up from the bed and fetched some garments from a stool. "You wait outside, we will be down soon."

"*We?*"

"We can't leave her here, can we? He's ruined her if she's found. I told her that we'd take her to Newcastle and leave her at an abbey. She'll say that she got knocked on the head and lost her memory and wandered for days until some kind soul brought her to the city."

"Ah. The knocked-on-the-head-and-wandered-for-days explanation. A bit overused, don't you think?"

"Her family will believe it because they will want to. On the way, I'll tell her how to fake the evidence when she gets married."

"Oliver . . ."

"She's just a child, David. Too trusting, that is all."

"You are a whoremonger, Oliver. You are supposed to recruit girls who have fallen, not save them." He looked at the girl not much younger than Joanna had been. He sighed and went to the door with Sieg.

Hell. At this rate, he'd never get out of England.

But, then, that had been the whole point of forcing him to make this search in the first place.

CHAPTER 19

CHRISTIANA PULLED THE knotted sheets and towels tautly to be sure they held together. She slid her arm through the center of the coiled rope of cloth and draped her light cloak over all of it.

It will work, she decided. It has to.

Leaving the chamber and building, she walked across the courtyard to the hall. She sought out Heloise sewing with her servants and three daughters. Beautiful, blond Heloise looked up kindly as she approached.

"The evening is fair," Christiana said in the distant tone she had maintained since her arrival. "I will sit in the garden for a while, I think."

"The breeze is cooling," Heloise said.

"I have brought my cloak if I need it."

The woman nodded and returned to her conversation.

Christiana forced her steps to slow indifferently. Outside she nipped into the walled garden behind the hall. She meandered through the plantings so that her progress would appear accidental. Slowly, deliberately, she worked her way toward the tall tree in the back corner of the garden.

Five days. Five days she had been a prisoner, and she still did not know why they had brought her here. She doubted that Heloise knew either. Perhaps her husband, the mayor of Caen, in whose palatial home she now found herself, had the answer, but he had explained nothing. Since the day she had stumbled into that hall, filthy and disheveled from her journey on horse and sea, furiously indignant and ready to kill or be killed, no one had told her anything. They had welcomed her as a guest, however, and shown her every honor and hospitality.

Except one. She could not leave.

Well, she would leave now. Yesterday she had found this tree. It grew higher than the wall, and she had eagerly climbed it, praying that some structure to which she could jump abutted the wall on the other side. Hovering amongst the obscuring branches and leaves, she had looked down at the sheer twenty-foot drop awaiting her. Even as disappointment flooded her, however, she had laid her plans.

She glanced around cautiously while she backed up into the shadow of the tree. At least two hours before nightfall. Enough time to get away from this city and find shelter somewhere.

Hoisting the line of sheets up her arm, she climbed the tree. She found a strong branch overhanging the wall's crest and settled herself on it. Easing off the sheets, she tied one end to the branch and threw the rest over the wall.

She shimmied out over the precipice and looked down. The dangling white line reached within ten feet of the ground. If she hung near the end and dropped, she should be safe enough.

She eyed the sheets and their knots. If they failed to support her weight, this could maim her. She prayed that the mayor of Caen bought top-quality linen for his bedding.

Lowering her feet to the top of the wall, she grabbed the first knot. She stepped back.

She had hoped that she could basically walk down the wall, but it didn't work that way. She found herself dangling against it, her hands clawing at the white line that supported her. The muscles in her arms and shoulders immediately rebelled.

Only one way to go now. Grasping with all of her strength, she began to jerk her way down, hand over hand. Halfway to the ground, she began to hear a distant commotion. It grew and moved toward her.

Noises and voices resonated through the stone wall. A lot of people were in the garden, thrashing around. She continued her painful progress and stared up at the tree limb fearfully, waiting for the face that would discover her. The leaves must have hidden her rope's end, because the noises retreated.

She had tied some towels at the end to lengthen the rope, and she reached them now. The knot stretched against her weight. Just as her hands were about to give out anyway, she heard the rip that sent her crashing to the ground.

It had only been a drop of eight feet, but it still stunned her. She cautiously rose to her feet and glanced around.

Another wall, of another house, stretched in front of her. Between the two ran a very narrow alley where she now stood. At one end she saw a jumble of roofs that suggested it gave out on a city lane. The other way looked clearer.

Staying in the wall's shadow, she quickly walked

up the alley with a triumphant elation pounding through her. Whatever the mayor of Caen had planned for her, he could find another Englishwoman for the role.

She would cross the river and and stay off the roads and make her way to the coast and a port town. Maybe she would find an English fisherman or merchant there who would help her.

She stopped near the end of the wall and strained her ears for the sounds of the searchers. All was silent. She started forward again.

Suddenly a man stepped from behind the wall's end. He stood twenty yards in front of her with his arms crossed over his chest. She paused and stared at him in the evening light.

Definitely not the portly, short mayor. Too tall and lean, although the long hair was just as white and the clothing just as rich. Not one of his retainers either. She carefully walked forward, hoping that this man's presence had nothing to do with her, despite the concentrated way that he watched her approach.

She had just decided to smile sweetly and pretend that she belonged in this alley and neighborhood when she drew near enough to see his face.

She recognized him and, she knew, he recognized her. Her heart sank as her feet continued bringing her closer to the French noble who had disguised himself to meet with David at Hampstead.

She had not met him up close that day, but she stopped only a few paces away and faced him squarely now. She remembered more about his appearance than she had thought, for he looked very familiar to her in unspecified ways. Hooded brown eyes gazed down examining her. Between the white mustache and short beard, a slow smile formed.

"You have spirit," he said. "A good sign." He looked

down the alley to the swaying white line of sheets and towels. "You might have hurt yourself."

"Does it matter?"

"It matters a great deal."

"Well, that at least is good news."

He stepped aside. With a flourishing gesture, he pointed her back toward her prison.

Christiana plied her needle in the twilight eking through the open window. A low fire burned in the hearth, but the early July evening was very warm and the fire would not be built up when the daylight faded.

She glanced at the women and girls sitting around her, speaking lowly to each other as they bent to their own needlework. Occasionally one would look at her curiously. They still did not know why she had been foisted on them to befriend and entertain, and nothing beyond the previous polite courtesy had developed over the seven days since her attempted escape.

She looked down the hall to the other hearth and the four men gathered around it. Two of them were local barons from the region who had arrived during the last few days with their retinues at the French king's command. Others had come before them. The city was filling with knights and soldiers. Some camped across the river that served as a natural defense to this Norman city. A few had entered the castle, but most came here, to the mayor's house, and consulted with the tall white-haired man sitting by the other hearth.

She knew his name now. Theobald, the Comte of Senlis. Not just a noble, as she had surmised that day in Hampstead, but an important baron equal in rank to an English earl, and an advisor to the French king.

He had only spoken to her enough to ascertain that she had not been harmed or molested. He had ignored her demanding questions. She suspected, however, that she had been brought here at his initiative and command, and not the mayor's.

A prisoner still. *His prisoner*. To what end and what purpose? The women did not know. The Comte would not say. She sat in this house day after day, keeping to herself, refusing all but the barest hospitality, and watched the lords' arrivals and the daily consultations at the other end of the hall.

The light had faded. She rose and went to a bench below a window on the long wall of the hall. She would sit alone for a while and give the ladies time to gossip and speculate about her. Her unnatural and strained social situation did nothing to alleviate the chilling fear that she had carried inside her ever since those men had pulled her from her home. She admitted that the chill had gotten colder since she had faced the Comte at the end of the alley.

She had imagined during her first days here that David would come to rescue her. Perhaps he would bring Morvan and Walter Manny and some of the other knights to help. They would ride up to the river and across the bridge and into the city and demand her release. Like something out of a chanson.

She grimaced at her foolishness. If David were coming, he would have been here by now. In fact, he could have arrived before her. Returning home and finding her gone, he could have sailed from London and reached France before her own boat. Her captors had dragged her all the way north, almost to Scotland, before securing passage at a seaside port. A waste of time that made no sense, but then none of this did.

She had closed her eyes as she contemplated her situation, and the hall had receded from her awareness. A slight commotion intruded on her reverie now.

At the far hearth the Comte had risen from his chair and bent his ear to a gesturing man-at-arms. A broad smile broke over his face. He turned and said something to the mayor. One of the barons clapped his hand merrily on the other's shoulder.

The entrance to the hall swung open and she had a view of the anteroom beyond. Through the threshold to the courtyard she saw a man approach. Torchlight reflected off armor before the darkness of the anteroom swallowed him.

Another baron. They came to prepare for King Edward's invasion, of course. No doubt similar councils and musterings were taking place all over France.

One of the Comte's squires entered first, carrying a helmet and shield. She glanced at the newly painted and unscarred blue and gold coat of arms on it. Five gold disks over three entwined serpents, and the bar sinister of a bastard son.

Three entwined serpents . . . shocked alertness shook her. She sat upright and stared.

The knight entered the chamber. Tall and lean, he looked around placidly as he removed his gauntlets. His body moved fluidly in the clumsy armor as if he wore a second skin. He stood proudly with a touch of arrogance. Mussed brown hair hung around his perfect, weather-bronzed face. Blue eyes met hers intently.

She watched speechlessly. To her right, the women turned to regard the strong and handsome new man. To her left, the Comte strode forward, smiling, his hands outstretched.

"Welcome to France, nephew."

David de Abyndon, her David, her merchant, turned to the Comte de Senlis.

Nephew! Stunned, she looked from him to the Comte and then back again. She suddenly understood the odd familiarity she had felt when she looked in that older man's face.

She glared at David, standing there so casually and naturally in his damn armor, looking for all the world like a knight, accepting a kinsman's welcome from this French baron.

Of course. Of course. Why hadn't she seen it before? The height. The strength. The lack of deference. He hadn't told her. He had never even hinted. The urge to strangle her husband assaulted her.

The Comte spoke quietly and gestured David toward the hearth.

"I will see to my wife first," David said, and dismissing his uncle's interest, he crossed the space to her.

She glanced up the molded metal plates and looked him accusingly straight in the eyes. He looked straight back. Placid. Inscrutable. Cool.

"You are well and unharmed?"

"Aside from feeling like an ignorant and stupid fool who is married to a lying stranger, I am well."

He bent to kiss her. "I will explain all when we are alone," he said quietly. "Come now, and sit with me. Do not take to heart what I say to him, darling. I would have the Comte think that we are not content together."

"I should be able to help you with that."

The Comte wanted to speak with David alone. He had dismissed the barons and mayor, and frowned in annoyance when David led Christiana to the hearth.

"Thanks to you, I gamble with her life now as well as my own," David said. "She has a right to know my situation."

She sat in a chair. David stood near the hearth and she

watched him with confusion and shock and anger. In a strange way, however, a small part of her nodded with understanding. Something seemed appallingly *right* about seeing him like this, as if a shadow that had always floated behind him had suddenly taken substance and form. *Who are you really?*

She glanced at the Comte and could tell from that old man's approving gaze that he saw what she saw.

David turned to his uncle and let his annoyance flare. "I told you that she was not to be involved."

The Comte raised his hands. "You did not come in April. I sought to encourage you."

"I did not come because the storms rose as soon as I reached Normandy. Why deliver news that would have no value? The fleet barely made it back to England."

So he had come to France at Easter. But then, she had known that as soon as she saw him enter the hall.

"I had men waiting for you at Calais and St. Malo. You did not come."

"Do you think that I am so stupid as to put in at a major trading port where I might be recognized? Would you be so careless?"

The Comte considered this and made a face of tentative acceptance. "Still, you are late. I expected you weeks ago. The army is ready to move."

"I am late because my wife disappeared and I sought to find her."

"You knew where she was."

"I did not. I could hardly leave England without knowing her fate."

The Comte flushed. "They were to leave—"

"No note or word was left." David stared hard at the Comte. "You sent Frans to do this, didn't you? Against our agreement."

"He knew the people. He knows your habits."

"Aye. But he relied on Lady Catherine, who holds no love for me. Also against our agreement. And she had her own plans for me. I was lucky to get out of England alive."

The Comte reddened. "She endangered you?"

"You probably assumed that I would know, note or not, that you had taken Christiana. What other explanation could there be? What you did not know is that my wife has a lover who lives in the north country."

The Comte glanced in scathing disappointment at her. She faced him down. David had better have a damn good reason for telling his uncle that.

"Lady Catherine knew this, however," David continued. "And so she had the men whom she and Frans hired leave no note or sign, so I would wonder if Christiana had gone to this man. They even took her out of the country by way of a northern port, so that I could follow her trail toward her lover. All the while, time is passing and I am still in England." He paused and smiled unpleasantly. "And during that time, Catherine went to King Edward and told him about me. She had a lot to tell, because Frans had let her know of my relationship to you."

A very hard expression masked the Comte's face. Christiana drew back in alarm. She had seen that expression before, but not on this Frenchman's face.

"I will deal with them both. The woman and Frans."

"I have already done so."

"If the woman betrayed you to Edward, what you know may be useless. He may change the port."

She had been correct in her suspicions then. David planned to give the port's location to the Comte and the French. But not in exchange for silver and gold. And, as a son of Senlis, not even in treason. Every noble knew and respected the loyalties of blood ties. An oath of fealty bound one just as strongly, but a wise king or lord never asked his liegemen to make a choice between the two obligations.

"I thought of that," David said. "And it may happen. But before I slipped out, I learned that, even two weeks after hearing Catherine's tale, he had not changed his mind. He had already sent word to the English forces on the Continent, and there was no time to undo that. But he may hope that you expect him to, so that you resist committing all of your forces to the one place. I wonder if he did not let me escape with the news of Lady Catherine's betrayal in order to cast doubt on the value of this information in the event that I had managed to send it to you earlier."

All of David's attention was concentrated on his uncle, and those blue eyes never wavered in their scrutiny of the older man's face. The Comte's own eyes, brown rather than blue but so similar nonetheless, appeared just as piercing whenever he studied David.

Who are you really? Well, now she knew. She was too numb and confused to decipher how she felt about this startling revelation. She should be relieved. Her husband was not common. His father's blood, the important blood, had been noble.

So why did this anger unaccountably want to unhinge her?

The Comte paced and nodded to himself. "I think that you are right. The summer is passing quickly. If he comes at all, he must do so now. His army has been mustered. It is too late to change course." He pivoted toward David. "Do you have it, then?"

"I have it. More than he knows that I have. The roads he will take and the direction he will head. The size of his force. I have it all."

The Comte waited expectantly.

David smiled faintly. "Do you have the documents?"

The Comte gave an exasperated sigh. "Mine is here and witnessed. The constable brings that from the King when he arrives. But we waste time . . ."

"You have already broken most of our spoken agreement. And because of that, I have been left no choice but to do this. I cannot return to England, and although Edward may one day acknowledge Christiana's innocence and welcome her back, she is forced now to a future that she did not choose either. I do not plan to start life over with the little gold I brought with me. I go no further without the documents."

A very ugly tension seemed to paralyze the two men, and something threatening and dark flowed out of the Comte. Christiana sucked in her breath. She had felt this dangerous presence before, too. She wondered what the Comte contemplated. He was as unreadable as David.

Except to David.

"I was tortured once in Egypt," David said calmly. "The French mind cannot compete with Saracen invention on that. You will buy no time that way, and will have an heir who waits to see you dead."

Beneath hooded lids, brown eyes slid subtly in her direction. A horrible chill prickled her neck.

David's eyes narrowed. "Do not shame your name and your blood by even considering it. She knows absolutely nothing, as your wife would not under the circumstances."

But I do know, she thought frantically. She suspected that this uncle could read people as well as David. She lowered her eyes from his inspection and prayed that he saw only her palpable fear in her face.

The Comte considered her a moment and then laughed lightly.

"When do you expect the constable?" David asked.

"By early morning."

"You are too impatient then, and too quickly consider

dishonor. Is it any wonder that I demand written assurances?"

A dangerous scolding for a merchant to give a baron, kinsman or not. Laden with distrust and insult. But the Comte seemed more impressed than angry.

"All men consider things that they would never do, nephew. Recognizing one's options is not the same as choosing them."

David frowned thoughtfully and then nodded, as if he completely understood the Comte's explanation and had reason to accept it as sound.

The tension slowly unwound.

"I promise that there will be time enough to move your forces. The ships were not even half ready to sail when I left," David said.

That seemed to lighten the mood even more. The Comte smiled pleasantly, even warmly.

David walked over and took her hand. "Show me our chamber, Christiana. I want to get out of this steel that has broiled my body under the hot sun all day."

"I will send my squires to help you," the Comte said. "And tell the mistress to have servants prepare a bath for you."

Christiana wordlessly led David out of the hall and toward the tall side building that held the chambers.

"The man drains me," David muttered as they walked through the warm night. "It is like negotiating with the image I see in a mirror."

CHAPTER 20

THE TWO SQUIRES removed David's armor. They kept calling him "my lord." Christiana glanced with annoyance at her husband's tall body standing spread legged while the plate came off. One would think he had done this a thousand times.

Near the low-burning hearth fire, servants prepared the water in a deep wooden hip bath. One girl kept looking at David and smiling sweetly whenever she caught his eye. Christiana grabbed her by the scruff of the neck when the last pail had been poured.

"Out. I will attend my husband."

The servants scurried away. The squires finished their long chore and, calling merry farewells, drifted off. David stripped off his inner garments and settled into the tub.

The sight of his body stirred her more than she cared to admit. She cursed silently at her weakness and at her traitorous heart's independence from her will and mind. *Our life together has been one long illusion*, she fumed. *It was a mistake to think that I could find contentment in pleasure alone. He will always be a stranger. I will always be the play-thing who shares his bed but not his life. I will have it out with him once and for all and then demand another chamber.*

She pulled over a stool, sat down, and faced him.

"Aren't you going to attend me?" he asked.

"Wash," she ordered dangerously, throwing him a chunk of soap. "And talk."

"Ah," he said thoughtfully.

"And no 'ahs,' David. One more 'ah' and I will drown you."

"I understand that you are angry, darling. Believe me, I went through great trouble not to involve you. I intended you to know nothing. Edward would never have blamed you for my sins. The Comte surprised me with this abduction. Frankly, I am disappointed in him."

"Are you indeed?"

"Aye. I expected more chivalry of him. To abduct and endanger an innocent woman . . . It is really very churlish."

"He wants the name of the port, David. He would probably kill me if he thought it would make you give it to him a minute sooner."

"Which is why I want him to think that we are not content together. I do not want him debating whether he can use you against me. Once the Constable d'Eu arrives, I will get his assurance of your safety before I speak with them. The constable is reputed to be honorable to the point of stupidity."

She rolled her eyes. "Let us start at the beginning. Is the Comte in fact your kinsman?"

"It would seem so."

"How long have you known?

"Almost my whole life. My mother told me of my father when I was a child. So I would know that I was not an ordinary, gutter variety bastard."

"Why didn't you tell me?"

"It is a claim easily made but hard to prove, Christiana. And unless a bastard is recognized, it has no value." He watched himself lather an arm. "Would it have helped, darling?"

She sorely wished that she could say not. "It might have. At the beginning."

"Then I am sorry that I didn't tell you."

"Nay, you are not. Your pride wanted me to accept you as the merchant, not the son of Senlis. You can be very strange, David. Not many men would think noble blood makes them less than they are instead of more."

He glanced at her sharply. She let him see her anger.

"You lied to me," she said. "Over and over."

"Only to protect you. This began long before we met. I sought to keep you out of it, ignorant of it, so that you would be spared if something went wrong."

"I am your wife. No one would believe my ignorance."

"You are the daughter of Hugh Fitzwaryn and were a ward of the King. All would believe it. Neither Edward nor his barons would have blamed you for the actions of your merchant husband."

His bland excuses infuriated her. She raised her fists and slammed them down on her lap. "I am your *wife*! If something went wrong, I would have had to watch them tear your body apart even if I was spared. I still may have to, for all that I know. But worse, you hid yourself from me, hid your true nature, who you are."

That hardness played around his mouth and eyes. "You have not been my wife for months now. Should I have trusted the girl who lived in my home like a guest or a cousin?"

"Better a guest than some precious artwork. Better a

cousin than a piece of noble property purchased to salve the forgotten son's wounded pride."

His eyes flashed. "If you truly believe that, then there is no point in explaining anything to you. No matter what I said that day, you should know better of me."

"Know better of you? Right now I don't think that I know you at all, damn you. And do not insinuate that our separation led you to maintain your deception. You had no intention of telling me anything until this was over, no matter how dutiful I might have been. What then? Would you have stayed in France and sent for me? Written a letter that bid me to attend on you here?"

"It always was and still is my intention to give you a choice."

"Indeed? Well, your uncle has closed that door!"

"That remains to be seen."

She looked away until she regained control. She smoothed the skirt of her gown. "I want you to tell me all of it. Now. I would know my situation and my choices. From the beginning."

He told his tale while he washed. "It began simply enough. Edward had asked me to make the maps. It occurred to me that when the time came, I might learn the port that he chose from the questions that he asked me about them. I have never really forgiven my father for what he did to Joanna. He destroyed her and left her to the mercy of the world. Perhaps I also resented his ignorance and neglect of me. Anyway, not really expecting it to work, I began making enough mistakes in France so that anyone paying attention might suspect what I did there. And I began using the three serpents as the device on my seal. They were carved into a ring my father left with my mother. She thought it like a wedding ring, but I suspect he had intended it as payment for her favors."

He paused and lathered the soap between his hands. The gesture distracted him. Christiana watched him examine the white foam and then the cake itself. She had to smile. The merchant's wife had been similarly distracted during her first bath here.

"It comes from a town on the Loire," she said.

David smelled the foam. "Superior, isn't it? I wonder . . ."

"Twenty large cakes for a mark."

He raised his eyebrows. She watched him silently begin calculating the cost of importation and the potential profit.

"David," she said, calling him back.

"Aye. Well, my plan was to let the Comte know of me, realize our connection, and then approach me for the port. I would resist and let him cajole me by playing on the bonds of kinship. I would relent, accepting no payment so he thought that I did it for my blood and so trusted me. But I would give him the wrong port. The French army would go in one direction, Edward would come from the other, and the way would be clear for an English victory."

She looked at his expression. Matter-of-fact. Blasé. As if men calculated such elaborate schemes all of the time and spent years manipulating the pieces.

He enjoys this, she realized. He traveled to the Dark Continent and he crosses the Alps every other year. He needs the adventure, the planning, the challenge.

"And you would have punished that family for your mother's fate," she added.

"That too. I doubt that the Comte de Senlis would remain on the King's council after giving such bad advice. A loss of status and honor, but no real harm. Unlike Joanna's fall. Still, some justice."

"So what went wrong?"

"Nothing. It unfolded as planned. Except for a few surprises. Early on, Honoré, the last Comte, died, and his brother Theobald took his place. A more dangerous man, Theobald."

She stood up and paced slowly around the chamber. She waited for the rest. David waited longer.

"What did you mean when you said that about his heir wanting him dead?" she blurted.

"The other surprise. A very big one. He did not offer me silver. He offered me recognition and Senlis itself. Honoré's and Theobald's other sons are dead. He offered to swear that his brother had made secret vows with my mother. It would be a lie, but it would secure my right to inherit."

She stared at him.

David. Her merchant. The Comte de Senlis.

"Men have been tempted to treason by much less, my girl."

"You said that you had no interest in being a knight."

He laughed. "Darling, a knight is one thing. A leading baron and councilor to the King of France is quite another."

"You are going to do it then?"

"I have not yet decided. What would you have me do?"

"Nay, David. You began this long ago. You do not foist the choice on me now."

She began pacing again, thinking out loud. "There are many men who owe fealty to two kings or lords. Many English barons also have lands in France. Everyone understands that loyalties conflict sometimes."

He reached out and caught her arm as she passed. His grasp held her firmly and he looked up at her, shaking his head. "Let us not pretend that I face other than I do.

What you say is true, but there are rules that decide which way a man goes in those cases. This is different. If I help the Comte and France, if I do this, I betray a trust and a friendship and my country. For the prize that is offered, I am not above doing it, but I will not pretend it is prettier than it is."

Damn him. *Damn him*. There were enough ambiguities here for a bishop to rationalize his actions. He could at least let her find some comfort in them.

"France is your country, David," she pointed out. "Your father was French."

"In truth, I find that it is not England that concerns me. Or even Edward. He has had barons do worse by him, and he possesses a large capacity for understanding and even forgiving such things. Nay, it is London that has been on my mind. If not for my city, I do not think that I would hesitate."

He held up the soap. "Since you sent the servants away, you could at least wash my back."

She knelt behind him and smoothed the lather over his muscles. Despite her inner turmoil, she couldn't help but notice that it was the first time that she had touched his body in months. A slight tensing beneath her palm told her of his awareness of it, too.

"You lied to me in April. You came to France and did not go to Salisbury."

"I could hardly implicate you with the truth." He glanced over his shoulder. "That day in the wardrobe. Your questions. How much did you suspect?"

"Most of it eventually, but not about your father. I heard Frans's first approach to you. I was hiding in the passageway. But I wasn't sure that it had been you there. I learned that he was an agent for the French cause. I saw you meet with him again at Westminster. When the

Comte came to Hampstead, I heard his voice before he left.
I knew that he was French and a noble."

"You thought that I might be selling Edward's plans
for silver?"

"It was one explanation for these things. Actually, it
was the silver that didn't make sense. You enjoy your
wealth, but are too generous to be a man who would do
anything out of greed."

He twisted around and looked down at her. "If you
knew so much, I am surprised that you did not leave sooner,
while I was gone, for your own safety and the honor of your
family. You might have gone to Edward with your suspicions. Why didn't you?"

She looked away from his knowing eyes. She did not
want the vulnerability that answering would expose.
Besides, it was her turn for questions.

"You had said that you would come back in April and
I believed you. Did you lie about that, too?"

He shook his head. "I had not decided what I
would do once I got here, but I expected to come back
in either case. If I had given the Comte the port of Bordeaux, and he had gone there, Edward would never have
suspected me or anyone else even if the whole of France
waited for him. Half of their army is already in the south
dealing with Grossmont. The rest might have received
reports of the ships sailing down the coast, or have gone
to reinforce the siege at Angiullon down there. I fully
expected to return, assuming that Theobald would permit it."

His steady gaze and quiet voice, his face so close to
hers, disconcerted her. Her resolve began loosening. She
pushed his shoulder so that she could rinse off the soap,
and he turned away.

"But now Lady Catherine has told Edward about you,

and so you cannot go back. Why would she do this? Is she angry about the property in Hampstead?"

He didn't respond for several moments. She suspected that he debated his answer. She braced herself for more lies.

"Lady Catherine and I have a long history. The property is a small and recent part of it. She did me an injury when I was a youth. The evidence is beneath your fingers now. Some months ago I responded in kind."

She rocked back on her heels in shock. She looked down at the strong back and the diagonal scars on it. Despite her determination to treat him with the same indifference he felt for her, her heart tore.

She didn't need to hear the story, because she could imagine it. Her fingertips traced the thin, permanent welts. She pictured him being flogged as a boy. She saw Lady Catherine, secure in the immunity that her nobility gave her, ordering it for some perceived slight or crime. Not in London, of course. Even as an apprentice, he would have been protected there.

He had responded in kind. Did that mean Catherine's own skin bore scars now? She hoped so.

She felt a wave of tenderness for the youth who had been so harshly abused. She barely resisted the urge to kiss those welts.

This is madness, she admonished herself. *He wants no sympathy or tenderness from me. I am no part of his history or his revenge. I have no role in the pageant unfolding now, either. At best I am an inconvenience with which the Comte has complicated his plans.*

"You say that you have not decided what to do, David. What will happen if you will not give the port tomorrow?"

She was glad that she couldn't see his face. If he lied to her, she didn't want to know.

"The Comte has done everything possible to ensure that that isn't much of a choice anymore. Catherine did go to Edward as I said, but the Comte's surprise at the news was false. He sent her to betray me, to force my hand in this. Her plan to keep me in England so that Edward could capture me was all her own, however. Still, he sought to force me out of England, and he took you so that I would have to come here. With my life endangered in England, he knows that his offer becomes very attractive." He paused. "However, kin or not, I do not think that he will allow me to leave here alive if I refuse him."

She wished that he had indeed lied. "Then you have no choice."

"Of course I do."

She felt sick. On the one hand, status and wealth awaited. More than he had ever expected in life. Senlis was his right and his due and he should take it. But, dear God, men whom she knew and loved would ride those ships to France. Her brother, her King, Thomas and others . . . and now he had all but said that Theobald would kill him if he did not cooperate.

It should not matter to her. He should not matter.

She almost embraced him and begged him to find a way to take both choices and thus none at all.

She returned to the stool. "Were you truly almost captured?"

"No one challenged or questioned me. The armor proved a good disguise, since there are knights moving everywhere in England. Even here, it helped me travel without suspicion."

"The coat of arms on your shield?"

"Do you like it? I could hardly pass myself off as a knight with a blank shield. Fortunately, I met no heralds who would know it was new and unofficial."

"You followed me north, then?"

"Aye." He shot her a piercing look. "Do not worry. He was not harmed. Although when Sieg threatened to make him a eunuch, I thought he might die of fright. Since I saved him from that, he will probably be glad to lay down his life for me now."

She glanced to the hearth, not much caring if Sieg had made Stephen a eunuch, whatever that was.

"We were further delayed when Oliver insisted on taking the girl with Stephen under his wing and trying to save her from her family's wrath."

She barely heard him. She went over to the hearth. A bucket of water warmed there and she picked it up and carried it the few steps to the tub.

She noticed David looking at her.

"What?" she asked.

"Didn't you hear me? Aren't you jealous? I said he had a girl with him."

She narrowed her eyes. "For a clever man, you can be an idiot!" she shrieked, pouring the water over his head. She upturned the bucket, slammed it down to his ears, and stomped away.

She stared at the wall, blind with fury. She heard him leave the tub and dry himself. A few moments later he came up behind her.

He touched her shoulder lightly.

"You still do not believe me," she spat, shrugging off his hand. "You have told me lie after lie, while I gave you nothing but the truth from the beginning. Do you assume that everyone lives the kind of deceptions that you do?"

"I believe you. But I wonder if you still love him. You never said that you had stopped."

"I told you it was over."

"That is not the same thing."

"You should have just asked me, then, if you wondered."

He stepped closer and spoke quietly. "I did not ask you about this, just as you did not ask me about France, and for the same reasons. We have not spoken to each other about the things which might pain us. I never asked you, because I feared the answer. I hoped that time would deal with it. But we have run out of time and I am asking you now. Do you still love him?"

She closed her eyes and savored the sound of his beautiful voice and wished that its quiet tones were not asking questions which led down this path. She feared where it might lead.

Still, he was right. Finally, today, he had given her honesty. She should not start her own deceptions now. But honesty about them, the two of them, could well leave her bereft of everything even as it destroyed the fragile resolve with which her anger had conquered her passion and love.

"I no longer care for him at all and doubt that I ever loved him."

"Why do you doubt it?"

Because I know what love feels like now, she almost said.

The silence pulsed as he awaited her answer. She suddenly felt terribly vulnerable. This was the second question that if answered honestly would demand an admission of love from her.

Why not just tell him? Admit the truth, and then walk out the door. She grimaced. A grand gesture totally lacking the hoped-for drama and impact. He would simply let her go, and then proceed to live the life he chose for himself. He did not care enough to be touched by either the admission or the rejection.

"Why do you believe me now about that meeting, David? Did Stephen tell you the truth? Did you believe that fool when you hadn't believed me?"

"He told me, but he would have sworn to being chaste from birth under the circumstances. It did not matter because I already believed you. Whenever I thought about that day, I kept seeing a beautiful girl running into my arms. Full of joy, not guilt or fear." His hands gently took her shoulders. "What was it you wanted to tell me then?"

Again a probing question.

He suspects, she realized with shock. *His mind's reflection has seen what his anger did not.*

She became acutely conscious of his warmth and scent behind her. The silence tightened as something else flowed from him. Something expectant and impatient.

She ached to say it, but she thought about the things she had thrown at him that afternoon in their chamber. She remembered how she had avoided him and his affections during their betrothal. She imagined the apprentice being tortured at the will of the noble Lady Catherine.

She certainly could not tell him now. Even if he put some small value on her feelings for him, he would think that his change in fortune from merchant to baronial heir had made her find sudden love.

"I do not remember," she muttered.

He stayed silent, softly stroking her arms. She closed her eyes and absorbed his touch and closeness. His exciting intensity surrounded her in a luring, seductive way. Despite the knot into which the day's revelations had tied her emotions, despite her decision to leave this stranger, she drew amazing comfort from his slow caress.

"I need to know some things from you now," he finally said.

"No story I can tell will be nearly as interesting as yours."

"Were you harmed at all?"

"Nay. Not really. We rode for days and my rump

got sore from the saddle and my skin red from the summer sun, but that is all. At nights we stayed in rude inns and all shared one hot chamber, but the men did not bother me, although one looked at me too boldly for comfort. The food was horrible and the sea trip frightening, and I arrived looking like the worst peasant, and smelling too ripe for decent company, but I was not harmed."

He turned her around. He had thrown on a loose, long robe, like something a Saracen might wear. She looked up into his face and saw things hiding beneath his calm expression that she had never witnessed in him before. Worry. Indecision. Doubt. He looked much less contained than he had in the bath.

He touched her face. "If I do this thing, you need not stay. Very soon Edward will accept that you were no part of it. You can return home."

She gazed at him, her love twisting her heart. This small contact of skin on skin was enough to awaken all of her senses to him. "That is why you put the properties in my name, isn't it? So they could not be confiscated."

"Aye. There was always the chance that Edward would learn enough to suspect me, no matter what my intentions. I did not want you left dependent if this dangerous game went wrong."

"Why didn't you wait? To marry? You said that this began long before we met. Long before you offered for me. Why complicate things thus for yourself?"

Even as she said it, an eerie sensation swept through her. A knowledge that she did not want to face stretched and stood tall and presented itself squarely. An explanation for one of the first and most enduring questions she had ever had about this man stared at her.

Dear God. *Dear God.* Even that had been a lie, an illusion! It hadn't been much, but at least, as her love sought a compromise with her life, it had been something to hold on to.

His fingers still rested on her face. She looked desperately into his blue eyes and sought all the awareness she had ever had of him during their closest intimacy. She gazed through the veils and intensity, trying to see his soul.

"You never offered for me, did you?" she said. "It was Edward's idea. He proposed this marriage, for my sake perhaps, but also to get money out of you. You could not refuse him."

He took her face in his hands and bent closer. He looked straight back at her. The control and restraint fell away and he permitted her to see what she sought. He let her look through the shadows and layers, down to his depths. Naked of all defenses and armor he met her inspection. Her breath caught at the emotions suddenly exposed to her.

"Nay," he said quietly. "I saw you and wanted you and paid Edward a fortune to have you. And I did not wait because I could not. It was selfish of me." His thumbs stroked her cheekbones. "I am out of time, Christiana. I need to know my true choices, and what I gain and what I lose. If I do this thing, are you going to stay with me?"

She barely heard his words because the stunning truth written inside him made the events which had created this marriage suddenly irrelevant. She could not turn from his warm, binding gaze. She did not want to lose this soulful connection, this total knowing that he offered her. She doubted that he had ever before let anyone, even his mother, see him thus.

Everything was reflected in those deep eyes. Everything. His guilt at endangering her. His fear of himself. His hard hungers and conflicting needs and dark inclinations. But illuminating all of those shadows, warming their chilly depths, flowed a sparkling emotion that she recognized for its beauty and joy and salvation. Her own love spread and reached out to meet it gratefully. His lips parted and a glorious warmth suffused his gaze. An exquisite, anguished relief poured out of him.

"Will you stay?" he repeated, his face inches from hers.

"I will not leave," she whispered, for there could be no other answer after what she had just seen. "Noble or merchant, I will stay with you."

He pulled her into an embracing kiss. She grasped his shoulders and lost herself in a warm rush of poignant intimacy. For a breathless, eternal moment, their bodies seemed to dissolve within the dazzling brilliance flowing between them.

The connection and knowing was so complete that she felt no need to speak of it. But David did.

"What did you want to say to me that day, Christiana?"

"Couldn't you tell? I was sure that you would see it at once."

"My anger and pain blinded me to everything else. I stepped off that boat with a head and heart full of love for you, and Oliver's tale cut me like a dagger and made me a madman."

She lifted her eyes to his, rendered speechless by this calm articulation of what she had just seen and felt in him. In speaking first, he made it easier for her. He had always done that, every step of the way. Out of sympathy and understanding at first maybe, but later because of his love.

She touched his face. She let her fingers drift over the tanned ridges of his cheekbones and jaw, and caress his lips. "I wanted to tell you that day that I was in love with you. I realized it when Catherine delivered me to Stephen. The love was just there, very obvious and completely real. I knew that I have loved you a long while."

He kissed her again, so gently and sweetly that her awareness of his love filled her to the point of weightlessness.

His lips moved to her ear. "They took you from my chamber. Upstairs. Geva had touched nothing when I returned."

His quiet, beautiful voice warmed her as much as his breath and touch. A delicious peace flowed through her like a breeze. She was grateful that he knew that she had loved David the mercer long before she learned the whole truth about him. Glad that he knew that she had returned to him of her own will.

"Do you want me, Christiana? Will you come to bed with me now?"

"You know that I do. You know that I will."

He held her and let her innocent love and joy overwhelm him. Ever since he had returned to the house and seen that disheveled bed, his physical desire for her had beat a low, constant rhythm in his soul and body. Now, however, he resisted the movements that would take her to bed. Her loving embrace soothed him as no passion would.

Noble or merchant, I will stay with you. More than he had asked for or expected. Far more than he deserved.

She broke his long kiss and smiled up at him. "Has it been so long that you have forgotten how to do it?"

He laughed. "Aye. Perhaps I should have kept in practice."

Her brows rose in surprise and he laughed again. "There has been no one else. I found sitting near you at the hearth more compelling than seducing my way into some strange bed."

She frowned. "It is strange, David. I sat there loving you and you sat loving me and we didn't see it. Why not? You see everything. Can thoughtless, cruel words build such walls?"

"It is over. We do not have to—"

"I want to. I spoke to hurt you, and you did the same. We threw the other's fears and illusions at each other and we each believed the words even though the truth stared us in the face." She gazed intently at him. "If I had thought clearly then, as I have since, I would have known that you never thought of me as property. In fact, you behaved just the opposite. If you had bought yourself a noble whore, you certainly did not make much use of her, did you? Why?"

She surprised him. She was growing up fast, and her sharp intelligence, freed of its isolating shelter, had already learned to see to the heart of things.

He loved the girl. He suspected that he would worship the woman.

"You were very innocent, darling."

"Not so innocent. Women speak to girls before they marry. I knew that men usually expected more than you ever asked of me. I knew there could be more to lovemaking than you ever sought."

"We were not together very long, Christiana."

She bit her lower lip thoughtfully. "I do not think it was that. You knew your blood, but I did not. I think that you worried that I would indeed feel debased and used. For all of your pride, David, you did not meet me as an equal in our bed."

She astonished him. He had been very careful with her. He had never gone beyond the impulsive acts of their wedding night. The restraint had come naturally to him and he had never thought about it, but now he had to admit some truth in what she said.

A very worldly and determined expression flickered in those diamonds. "I have been jealous, you know. I do not like knowing that you did things with Alicia and others that we never did. Noble or merchant, I will stay with you, David, but not as some precious vessel that you fear to break."

Playfully, she pushed him back, up against the post of the bed. She leaned up into him, pressed her body along his, lowered his head with her hand, and kissed him. He accepted her erotic little assault. Lightning flashed through him and the tightness grew and spread.

She glanced up, very pleased with herself. He grasped her hips and pulled her closer and she deliberately rubbed against him. Weeks of need and waiting responded forcefully and he lifted her into a devouring, obscuring kiss. She gave herself over to it and their passion melted them together. But then her hands smoothed over his shoulders and down to his chest and she subtly pushed away.

"On my wedding a day, a servant gave me some very explicit lessons," she said, looking more to his chest than his face. "She said that men like to watch women undress. Would it please my merchant husband if I undressed now?"

She looked up at him and blushed. He thought his heart would tear his chest open. She turned and walked away, her hands plucking at the knot on her gown's laces. The simple gesture almost undid him. He leaned against the bedpost and crossed his arms over his chest.

He had seen her undress many times, of course, but not like this. She moved so beautifully, so elegantly, that her sudden awkwardness at finding herself watched thus almost wasn't apparent. But he could tell that she immediately found it harder than she had thought. He managed not to smile at the slight flush on her face and the hot look in her eyes as she turned to him and let the gown slide to the floor. She bent to her hose.

"Nay," he said. "The shift first."

She straightened. Crossing her arms over her chest, and appearing very much the shy virgin she had so recently been, she slid the shift off her shoulders. Her hands and arms followed its descent, unfolding to reveal first her breasts and then her hips and thighs.

The thin garment fluttered to her feet and she stepped out of it. She looked at the floor a moment before raising her eyes to his. The glint in those diamonds told him that she had discovered that this could arouse the woman as much as the man.

Her beauty mesmerized him as always. Her frank desire to give him pleasure transformed the pleasure itself. His storm of need subdued itself into a threatening but controllable gale. He knew that he could ride its wind indefinitely.

"Now the hose."

She bent and her graceful arms reached for the garter of one forward-stepping leg. He glimpsed the taper of her shoulder to her waist and the gentle flair of hips beyond. Her breasts, tight with need, hung for a moment like two perfect half globes as she rolled the hose off her leg.

"Turn for the other."

She glanced over in surprise, but then did as he asked.

The graceful curves of her hips and buttocks fell into erotic swells as she bent to untie the garter. She must have sensed her vulnerability, because her bravery deserted her and she made quick work with the hose.

She straightened and faced him with eyes like liquid stars. He let his memory be branded with her image. Not short and not even small, but beautifully formed in her slender fullness.

"Your hair, Christiana. Take down your hair for me."

Her arms rose as she sought the pins. The movement brought her breasts high and their hard tips angled upward. She unplaited her raven locks and they began spilling around her. He made no effort to hide what he felt from her gaze.

"Come here, my girl, and kiss me the way a bride in love should."

She walked slowly toward him, her expression a heart-stopping combination of passion and love and joy and invitation.

More than he ever expected. Far more than he deserved.

The morning was a lifetime away.

She stepped up to him and placed her hands on his chest. She stretched up toward him. He lowered his head and took her kiss with more restraint than he felt. He let her lead, biting gently around his mouth. Delicately, but not so artlessly, her tongue grazed his lips and then flickered more intimately.

He embraced her with one arm, reveling in the sensation of her skin beneath his hand. A slight sheen of sweat covered her and the warmth and moisture sent a flare through his whole body.

He caressed her face, and broke their kiss so he could watch his hand and her body as it traced down. His embrace arched her back, and her breasts rose to him. Her tremor when he touched her taut nipple flowed right into his hips and thighs.

Neither one of them succumbed to the waiting frenzy. They both sought to prolong the exquisite anticipation she had begun.

Her hands still lay on his chest and now they caressed at the loose lacing down the front of the long robe.

"It looks very exotic. Very handsome."

"Saracens know how to dress for hot weather."

She stroked his chest lazily. "The servant said that men like to be undressed by women, too."

He didn't answer, but watched as she carefully untied and pulled out the laces down to his waist.

She caressed him through the gap. He closed his eyes to the heat of that small hand. It had been too long since he had even this small connection and affection from her.

She pushed the garment open, almost off his shoulders, and laid her face against him. Languidly, deliciously, with a slow care that only increased the tension between them, she rubbed her cheek against his chest and watched her hand follow his muscles.

"You were right," she said as she turned to kiss him. "Abstinence is a powerful enhancement to passion. A part of me cannot wait and already screams for you, but another part wants to prolong this forever."

"You know how it will end. I have never failed you there. Let us enjoy the journey. We will never take quite the same path again."

She smiled sensually and nodded. Running both hands up his chest, she slid the robe off his shoulders and guided it down his back.

His control threatened to dissolve when she extended her caresses to his hips and thighs.

"What else did the servant tell you?" he asked, touching her as she did him, feeling tremors quake subtly through her.

"That men like to be kissed and touched, but I have already learned that is true." She proved it by mouthing at his chest. Rumbling shocks rocked through him with each kiss and nip. "Other things. I thought them shocking at the time. I do not find them so now."

The robe still hung from his hips. She gently shook

off his embrace. She caressed and kissed down his body as she lowered herself.

He watched and waited, his breath barely coming to him. An obscuring haze of passion clouded his mind and he saw both nothing and everything. Saw her hands push the robe to his feet. Felt her fluttering caress on his thighs and legs. Saw her fingers stroke his hard phallus while her lips pressed to his belly and hip. Her boldness both touched and stunned him. He wondered at the deceptive calm his body maintained, because desire began splitting him apart.

She caressed the back of his thighs and moved her head away. Questioning eyes glanced up at him. He bent and reached down for her and drew her up to his embrace. "Only if you want to, darling. And never on your knees."

She nestled into his arms. "Then take me to bed, merchant, so I can show you my love and honor."

He lifted her into a kiss that removed her feet from the floor. He turned and laid her down and lowered himself next to her.

The warm night air flowing through the window felt cool against the heat of their entwined bodies. He lost himself in the intimacy of her scent and swells and slick sweat.

He would show her such a journey as she had never imagined.

Slowly, deliberately, using all of his knowledge of her, he obliterated her shaky control. Never touching her below her hips, he drew her toward completion. Caresses on her inner arm, biting teeth on her nipples, consuming mouth on her neck—her passion rose with each knowing demand. She tried, despite her growing mindlessness, to give him pleasure in return, but he would not let her. He listened to her low sounds of abandon and felt her body climbing, shaking, toward its peak of sensation.

She grasped his shoulders. "David, I . . . please . . ."

He stilled his hands and mouth and held her. She twisted against him in rebellious frustration. Her eyes flew open.

"David!" she cried accusingly.

"Hush, darling. I said that I have never failed you."

"You mean to torture me to death first?" She pummeled his shoulder none too playfully.

He laughed lightly. "It is only torture if you think only about the release. Take the pleasure of the climbs for themselves, knowing that eventually you will fly."

Her passion had receded and the frenzy had passed. Her arms surrounded his shoulders and he turned his head to kiss the bend of her arm while his hand stroked down her body. "Again, then," he said.

She clung to him and opened her legs and accepted his touch. Her folds and passage already throbbed with her arousal, and he deliberately caressed her in ways that would bring pleasure but not fulfillment. She rebelled at first, and tried to move toward more productive touches, but then she relaxed and took the streaks of pleasure with joyful gasps and low moans.

He saw the glorious ecstasy on her face and nearly lost control himself. He touched her differently and watched her climb again, higher this time, as it would be every time. He took her to the peak and kept her there, tottering on its exquisite contracting edge, and let her taste the first tremor before he withdrew his hand.

Her nails had dug into his arm and shoulder. He kissed her and soothed her with soft caresses.

"That was wonderful," she whispered. "Does it keep getting better each time?"

"Up to a point."

"Do you plan to do this all night?"

He laughed. "I seriously doubt it. Love has made me very noble and chivalrous, but I have my limits."

She regarded him. "I think that two can play this game of yours, David. Would that please you?"

"Very much, if you desire it."

She rose up and pushed his shoulders down on the bed. She gave him a smug little smile full of unwarranted self-confidence. She kissed him fully before moving her hands and her mouth down his chest. He closed his eyes and stroked her back.

"Nay, David. You did not let me touch you, so you cannot touch me."

The luxurious spots of heat she created moved lower. He sensed her pause to consider the situation. Then he felt her turn and draw up her legs and lean against his stomach.

He had taught her to please him with her hands, and her caresses drove him close to delirium. When she paused again he opened his eyes just as she lowered her head.

He knew no thought after that. He looked through a cloud of engulfing sensation and pleasure at the erotic lines of her back and buttocks and the two delicate feet tucked beneath her.

He knew his limits but she did not. As he neared them he reached down and slid his fingers along the cleft of her bottom.

She groaned and shifted and accepted his touch. He rearranged their bodies so that his mouth could reach her. Bracing himself for control, he let them share the ecstatic pleasure a while longer as he brought her as far as she had him, to the very edge. Finally it was too much for them both and she sensed it. She released him and turned toward him and as she did he lifted her body and brought her down straddling his hips.

For an instant she seemed surprised to find herself there. Then wordlessly, instinctively, she rose up and took him into herself.

His sigh met hers in the space between them. She closed her eyes at the sensation, then slowly rose and lowered again.

Passion veiled her eyes when she opened them. She moved again and sighed. "This is incredible, David."

He reached up and caressed her breasts so she could see just how incredible it could be. He rubbed the taut nipples between his fingers. Her head fell back and she lolled sensually into a wonderful rhythm as she repeatedly drew him into her tight warmth and released him. Enhanced by abstinence and love, the pleasure moved him in ways he had never known.

He pulled her down toward him.

"Come up to me. Move forward a bit," he instructed.

She slid up but halted. "I will lose—"

"You will not. Come up to me."

She lowered and he eased her forward until he could take her breast in his mouth. She hovered above him breathlessly, her body barely still joined to his. He felt her grasping to absorb more of him, driving him mad with the mutual caress they created.

"David," she gasped, her body shaking from the combination of tantalizing pleasures at her breast and between her legs. He stroked her back down to its lowest curve and continued to arouse her breasts. He felt the first deep tremor and knew what it meant even if she did not.

"David," she cried again, frantically this time.

He released her and she slammed down on him with a needful cry. Burying her face in his chest, she moved hard again.

"Aye, it can happen thus, too," he reassured her, and

he held her hips firmly and took over and helped her find that different, more elusive fulfillment.

He had never seen a woman reach such a violent and complete release. Wonder, desire, and love echoed through her cries. She kissed him ferociously and gazed into his eyes as her passion peaked and her open acceptance of the magic made the intimacy fuse their souls as it always had. Her whole being seemed to fold in on itself, taking his own essence to its burning center, before flying out in all directions. At the end she rose up in a magnificent display of sensual ecstasy as she cried her abandon. Their mutual fulfillment momentarily obliterated time and space and consciousness.

She collapsed on him and he floated with her in their unity. Her love awed him and filled him with its innocent peace and grace. The hungry and needful response of his own soul astonished him.

Her face lay buried near his neck.

"Do you think anyone heard us?"

"Us?"

She giggled and playfully swatted his chest. "All right. *Me*?"

He thought about the open window and the silent city night. The whole household and half of Caen had probably heard her. So much for pretending that they were not content together.

It would not matter now. If the Comte thought to use her in that way, he would have already come for them both.

"I am sure that no one heard, darling."

She moved and settled down next to him. He had never known such peace and contentment, and he let himself savor it, knowing it would not last long and might never come again.

He probably should have told her everything.

Eventually he would have to. This love would not permit long deceptions, even for her sake.

"Have you ever been there?" she asked. "To Senlis?"

"Twice. The first time some years ago, and then again recently."

"Did you go inside?"

"Aye. The Comte was not there, and I entered as a traveling merchant with luxuries to sell. No one will remember. The vanities absorbed the women, not me."

"Do you want it? Senlis?"

"Who would not?"

She rose up and looked in his eyes. "*You* might not."

All the same, a choice awaited. "It is your fate that I decide as well as my own. I would know your will in this."

"I would have you with me forever, alive and whole. That is all that really matters to me, but I know that you will not make your choice for your own safety, and I will not ask it of you. As to the rest, there is no clear right and wrong here, is there? Both hold some pain and betrayal. England and France both have a claim on you. Both men, Edward and Theobald, deserve your loyalty." She paused, considering the dilemma. "I think that you should choose the life that you were born to live, whichever you think it was."

To the heart of things. Life with her would be fascinating.

"And what about you, Christiana? What about the life that you were born to live?"

She smiled and rested her face against his chest. "I was born to marry a nobleman, David. And you have always been one of the noblest men I have ever known."

CHAPTER 21

CHRISTIANA AWOKE TO an empty bed and the early morning light streaming in the chamber's window. The mellow memories of the night vanished at once. She rose and quickly dressed.

He was meeting with them now. It was being done. She could not pray for one outcome or another, even though she knew which she would prefer. He could give them the port, become the heir to Senlis, and live the life that few men had. Or he could refuse, be deprived of his old life but not given a new one, and maybe be killed. Not much of a choice to her mind, nor, she hoped, to his either. All the same, despite the status of Senlis and all that it entailed, she did not look forward with any enthusiasm to living in that strange place so far from home.

She paced the room but the confined space only increased her worry. She left the chamber and sought the stairs that led to the flat roof of this tall building with its many chambers for sleeping and storage.

Tubs of summer flowers and vines dotted the roof. As

she stepped out onto it she heard the sounds of activity floating up from the city below. The usual drone of commerce and movement had been replaced by a din of wagons and horses and men shouting orders.

David stood by the low wall surrounding the roof, looking down into the city streets to the west. Another man of middle years with a thick build and long brown hair watched beside him.

David turned and noticed her. He held out his hand. "My lord, this is my wife, Christiana Fitzwaryn. This is the Constable d'Eu, darling."

Christiana met the inspecting gaze of the chief military leader of France.

"I am Theobald's cousin, my lady, and so a kin of your husband's." He glanced at David. "The daughter of Hugh Fitzwaryn, no less. You did well for Senlis. Theobald is pleased that your wife brings such blood to the family."

Christiana stepped to the wall beside David. In the streets beyond, she could see the feverish activities of an army preparing to move.

It was done, then. She glanced at David's impassive face.

"My lady, your husband will be staying here in Caen," the constable said.

She looked from one man to the other. Something was wrong. She could feel it.

"Are you saying that I am still a prisoner?" she asked.

"You are free to go. I will arrange an escort to take you to Senlis."

"Then my husband is now a prisoner?"

"A guest. Until the English land. He can join you then. He is not trained in warfare, and this battle is not his."

"I would prefer to stay with my husband."

The constable looked at David. David didn't react at all. The older man smiled. "As you wish," he said, and he turned away and walked across the roof to the stairs.

She waited until he had gone.

"Why must you stay here, David?"

"He does not trust me. He fears that I have lied to them. But your choice to stay with me has reassured him a little."

"But why keep you here if the army moves?"

"Theobald will take the army. He has already left the house. But the constable has decided to remain in Caen with a small force, to be available in case Edward comes a different way. The King's chamberlain is here, too. He agreed that this would be wise."

"And your uncle agreed to this?"

"Even the Comte de Senlis does not stand against the constable and chamberlain of France. Theobald wanted me with him, so that I could see the glorious French victory that I have helped bring about. The constable insisted that I stay with him here, however, so that he would have me at his disposal if I betrayed them in some way. He thinks that I might steal away from the army during its march, or that, if it came to it, Theobald would not take vengeance on his heir." He smiled. "The constable does not know his cousin very well."

He embraced her and placed his cheek against her hair. He still looked down into the city. She felt conflicting emotions in him and wished that she could say something to comfort him. This decision had not been an easy one, no matter what prize it brought.

"Why doesn't the constable trust you? Surely the logic of your choice should be clear to him. It is the decision any man would have made, and there will even be English knights and lords who recognize the fairness of it."

"He explained it to me just now. Almost apologized. It seems that if I were a knight, he would have no doubts about me. It is the fact that I am a merchant, and a London merchant at that, which gives him pause."

"That is outrageous. Does he think merchants less honorable?"

"Undoubtedly, as all do. Still, in a way, he credits me with more rather than less honor. He told me that he knows burghers, and has met many from London. He knows that we owe our first loyalty to the city itself. He does not claim to understand men who give their fealty to a place rather than a man, but he knows it is so with us and he has seen its power. He could accept that I would betray Edward, or even the realm, but not London. And so, while he and the chamberlain agreed with Theobald that the army should move with speed, the constable will stay here to organize a defense if I lied to them."

A steady stream of knights and mounted soldiers streamed across the gate bridge from the other side of the river. They moved through the city toward its southern edges. Foot soldiers, carts, and workers plodded with them. The streets looked like colorful, moving rivers.

David's gaze followed the lines. "I should have insisted that you go to Senlis, but I feared never getting you out later. Theobald can be ruthless when angered, I suspect. Still, it would have been safer for you. The constable assured your safety, but there are limits to his protection."

"What are you saying, David? Do you think that Edward has indeed changed his plans and that the constable will blame you in some way?"

He pushed away from the wall and walked across to the southern view with his arm around her shoulders. In the distance, past the lower rooftops, they could see the field on which the army gathered. At the front, with gold and blue banners, no more than dots to their eyes, sat three men on horseback.

"Theobald?" she asked.

He nodded. "There are five thousand here with him. Others will join the army as they pass south."

"They go to Bordeaux, then?" she asked, even though the answer was obvious. She needed to hear it said, however, so that she could begin reconciling herself to the future he had chosen for them.

She wished that she felt some joy, but her stomach churned in an odd way. She thought about his question last night before they slept, and of her response.

He had misunderstood. She had sought to assure him that she loved him no matter what his degree, and had found him noble even before she learned about his father.

He has done this in large part for me, she realized. *To give me back the life which this marriage took from me.*

The Comte and Duke began to ride. The thick, undisciplined mass of the army oozed after them.

"Aye, they go to Bordeaux," he confirmed.

He wore a peculiar expression on his face. His eyes narrowed on the disappearing blue banners. "Edward, however, does not."

She gaped at him. His gaze never left the southern field.

"I went to Edward before Catherine did. I told him everything, and offered to finish the game as I had started it. I would give them one port, and our army would arrive at another one. I pressed for him to consider Normandy, since half the French army was already in the south and if I failed he would still only face an inferior host. His experience trying to sail to Bordeaux had already inclined him to change plans, and a Norman knight has been at court these last months, also telling him about Normandy's unwalled towns and clear roads."

She glanced in the direction of his gaze. She could still see reflections off the Comte's armor.

"Edward will debark in Normandy? Here on the northern coast?" Tremendous relief swept her, but with it came a sickening fear for David and what he now faced.

"Assuming that he doesn't get clever at the last moment, which is entirely possible. Or that he doesn't grow to doubt me. Catherine probably told lurid tales of my duplicity, but I am counting on Edward knowing what he has in her. Godefrey, the Norman knight, and I were able to give him three possible ports, small and out of the way. He will use the one which the winds favor."

"Does the King know about Senlis and what you were offered? If he does, he may well doubt you. He will not understand your choice."

"I told him everything. I could not be sure that Lady Catherine was involved in your disappearance, or that she planned to betray me, but I suspected it. I could not be sure that she remained ignorant of my relationship with the Comte. It was well that I spoke frankly with Edward. When I finally got a hold of Frans, I had my suspicions confirmed."

"So you were never in danger in England? And you can return?" *Assuming that he could get out of Caen alive.*

"Aye."

"Still, having convinced Edward on Normandy, you might have betrayed him. When did you decide what to do?"

He still looked to the flow of the army. "Early this morning. Knight or merchant, you said. I took you at your word."

"And if I had spoken differently? If I had said that I wanted to be the wife of a comte?"

"I would have given it to you, and learned to live with my conscience." He looked down and smiled. "I suspect that I could have rationalized it. The power and luxury of Senlis can probably obscure any guilt. Such a life has its appeal. I will not pretend that I was not tempted."

She embraced him tightly. "You have sacrificed much for your city and your King, David. Edward owes you much."

"He owes me nothing, Christiana. He gave you to me. The debt is all mine."

His gaze had returned to the distant field. The Comte was barely visible now. She saw that peculiar expression on his face again, and a flicker of yearning pass through those eyes.

He had executed a brilliant victory, a daring strategy, a magnificent game, but no triumph showed in him. She doubted his subdued reaction had anything to do with the danger he now faced. She snuggled closer under his arm and tried to comfort him.

"In time he will understand, David. He knows about honor and the hard choices it gives a man. He may not forgive you, but he will understand."

He tensed at this mention of the Comte and the blood ties which he had betrayed.

She tried again. "David, I know there is pain here. He is your uncle . . ."

His fingers came to rest on her lips, silencing her. "I should have told you last night," he said. "I feared your reaction to the truth, and also did not know if he would try to learn what you knew. I have spent the last hour wondering if I would ever tell you."

She frowned in confusion. She searched his face for some explanation.

"Theobald is not my uncle, Christiana."

His words stunned her. It took a few moments for the full implication to penetrate her dazed mind.

"Are you that clever, David?" That audacious? You found a man whom you resembled in some way and plotted this elaborate scheme? You fed me this story so that I could convincingly support you if I was questioned?"

That peculiar, yearning expression passed over him again.

He shook his head. "It is much worse than that, my girl." He glanced to the speck of a man being swallowed by sunlight and haze. "Theobald is not my uncle. He is my father."

Christiana did not know how long they stood there with his words hanging in the air, but when he spoke again the straggling ends of the army were passing out of the city.

"He did not even remember her name."

They still stood near the roof wall. He rested his arms against it and he looked south, but at nothing in particular now.

"He seduced her, took her love, left her with child, and destroyed her life. I use her name, but it meant nothing to him. Both he and Honoré had been to London several times as young men, and he assumed that I was the product of one of his brother's sins. It was the final mockery of Joanna's timeless trust."

She spoke to comfort him more than defend Theobald. "It was thirty years ago. When you are fifty-five, do you think that you will remember the name of every woman you bedded?"

"Aye. Every one."

"Perhaps only because he did not."

He appeared not to hear. "There had been two rings, one gray and one pink. He assumed that I had Honoré's, the gray one, and never asked to see it. At Hampstead, he looked at me and saw only his brother."

"He knew his brother's face better than his own. How often do we see clear reflections of ourselves in glass and metal?"

"She meant nothing to him. She was merely a beautiful girl with whom he amused himself for a short while. A merchant's daughter who counted for nothing in the life of a son of Senlis."

She didn't know what else to say. He had watched Joanna's misery and patience. He had lived in the shadow of her disillusionment. He had watched the master whom he admired love her in vain. She doubted that his anger at Theobald could be assuaged by words.

"Why didn't you tell him the truth? Why let him think you are his nephew?"

"At Hampstead, when I realized his mistake, it stunned me. Otherwise, my plan had unfolded perfectly. I told myself at the time that correcting him might complicate things. For all I knew, he might resent the sudden appearance of a bastard son, or even suspect that I sought revenge against him. But in truth, it was my own resolve that I questioned. Meeting him was much harder than I thought it would be. I had fully intended to despise him. And then, there he was, and suddenly a hundred unspoken questions that I had carried in my soul all of my life were answered. The answers were mainly unpleasant, but at least I had them." He smiled ruefully. "The connection, the familiarity, was immediate. Unexpected and astounding. If he had known me for his own, and appealed to me father to son, I do not know what I would have done. So, I let him think otherwise."

He did not have to tell her this. She ~~would have~~ never known or suspected.

"So, Christiana. You are married to a man who lured his own father into disrepute and betrayed him. It is a serious crime in any family, especially noble ones."

He searched her eyes for disapproval or disappointment. She knew that he found only understanding and love.

She thought about the yearning she had seen in him, and her heart swelled with sympathy. "Do you regret it? As you watch him ride off, would you change things?"

"Only for you would I have done it differently and changed course. Never for him. I wish that I could say that I regret having started this, but I do not. I am what I am, my girl, and a part of me, the Senlis part, is glad that I have revenged Joanna a little."

"Do you hate your father, David?"

He smiled and shook his head. "It would be like hating myself. But I hold no love for him either. Theobald may have given me life, but the only father I ever knew and loved was David Constantyn."

He took her hand and eased away from the wall.

"What now, David?"

He glanced around the roof, as if inspecting it. "Now I see to your safety." He grinned down at her. "The danger that I face from the Comte de Senlis and the Constable d'Eu is nothing compared to what Morvan Fitzwaryn will do if I let anything happen to you. I think that you should ask the lovely Heloise to show me her house. All of it. Tell her that I am curious to see how Caen's wealthiest burghers live."

David and Christiana had their tour. David peered around without subtlety and effused compliments, and Heloise beamed with pride at the appreciation of this handsome London merchant. Christiana thought that he overdid it somewhat, but his praise dragged the afternoon out and gave him the opportunity to examine every chamber and storage room, every window and stable. He seemed especially fascinated with an attic at the top of the main building. Loaded with cloth and mercery, it could only be reached by a narrow flight of steps angling along the inner wall.

They finally left Heloise at the hall and strolled into the garden.

"There does not appear to be any way out except the front gate, short of getting a ladder to the wall," David said.

"Is that what you looked for? I could have told you that. There is one way, but you will need rope." She began angling him in the direction of the tree. She smiled at this simple solution. David would escape, she would join him, and then . . . what? A run to safety, to Edward and his army. How long was the Comte's reach if he sought revenge? Perhaps they would leave both England and France behind and go to Genoa.

As they neared the garden's corner, her heart fell. Where the tall strong oak had stood, they found only its stump.

"I went out this way a week before you came," she explained. "Theobald caught me. He must have ordered it cut after that."

"It doesn't matter. I doubt that we would have made it through the bridge gate."

She sought the comfort of his arms.

"How long?" she asked, bravely broaching the subject that she had avoided. "When does Edward land?"

"I calculate five days, maybe six."

"You must get away. You cannot be here when they

find out. Tonight, I will distract the guards at the front gate and you—"

"I do not leave without you."

"Then we must find a way," she cried desperately.

"If there is one, I will find it. But I think that it is out of our hands. Who knows? When the English army begins ravaging Normandy, the constable and chamberlain may be so busy organizing the defense that they will forget about me."

He said it so lightly that she had to smile. But she didn't believe that would happen, and she knew that he didn't either.

When she awoke to an empty bed the Wednesday morning after the army departed, she threw on a robe and went in search of him. She found him on the roof, gazing toward the west. Dawn's light had just broken, and the city still appeared as gray forms below them. Despite the stillness, the air seemed laden with a strange fullness, as if a storm brewed somewhere beyond the clear horizon.

She drifted up beside him. His blue eyes glanced at her, then returned to their examination of the field beyond the river.

"Look there," he said. "Approaching the bridge."

She strained to see. The light was growing and a large shadow on the field moved down the far bank of the river. She watched and the shadow broke into pieces and then the pieces became people. Hundreds of them.

They moved quickly, carrying sacks and leading animals. The sun began to rise and she saw that the crowd included women and children. They poured through the buildings across the river, past the abbeys built by William the Conqueror and his wife Matilda, and then began massing at the far end of the bridge, shouting for entry to the city.

"Who are they?"

"Peasants. Burghers. Priests. They are refugees, fleeing Edward's army."

Additional guards ran to reinforce the watch at the bridge gate. The mob of refugees coalesced and their shouts rose. On the near side of the river, two men mounted horses and began riding through the deserted streets toward the mayor's house.

"Is the army nearby?" she asked.

"I would guess only hours away."

"It comes here? To Caen? You might have told me, David. I would not have worried so much."

"I could not be sure. In April, by accident, I found a port on the Cotentin peninsula just to the west. Sieg and I waited there for the English ships to pass before I met with Theobald here in Caen. During the storm, a merchant ship was pushed inland toward the coastal town where we waited. It came within one hundred yards of the coast and did not run aground. The sea must have shifted the coast over the years and the port gotten deeper. Perfect for the army's debarking. Still, the winds may have taken Edward further east to one of the other ports I had found earlier."

"You did not want to give me false hopes," she said.

"I did not want to give you more worry, darling."

"Worry? This is good news! Edward will obtain your release. The flower of English chivalry comes to save you," she said, smiling.

"If the city surrenders, it may happen that way."

"Of course the city will surrender. There is no choice."

"London would not surrender."

"*London has walls.*"

"I hope that you are right."

"What is it, David? What worries you?"

But before he could reply, the answer appeared on the roof in the persons of two knights from the constable's retinue.

CHAPTER 22

DAVID PACED AROUND the small storage chamber. The space reeked of herring from the barrels stacked against one wall. A small candle lit the windowless cell, and he tried to judge the time passing by its slowly diminishing length.

He was fortunate to still be alive. Upon confronting him in the hall about his betrayal, the constable had barely resisted cutting him down with his sword. The panic and confusion brought on by the English army's approach had saved his life. The hall had been in an uproar as the constable and chamberlain tried to organize a defense of the city while their squires strapped on their armor. Word had been sent east and south, calling back Theobald's army and rousing the general population to gather and fight this invasion. David had been imprisoned in this chamber to await hanging after the more pressing threat had been defeated.

Before being led away, he had tried to reason with the constable and chamberlain and convince them not to resist Edward. He had told them that the English army numbered at least twenty thousand, while the constable had at best three hundred men still in Caen. He had reminded them that surrender would spare the people of the city and only mean the loss of property. Only the mayor had listened, but the decision had not been his. The French king had told the Constable d'Eu to stop Edward, and the constable intended to fight for the honor of France despite the odds. Caen would not surrender or ask for terms.

He strained to hear the sounds leaking through the thick cellar wall. The house had quieted and the more distant activity only came to him as a dull rumble. The real battle would be fought at the gate bridge. If the city could retain control of that single access, the river would prove more formidable than any wall.

For Christiana's sake, he hoped that the gate bridge held. If the city fell, she would not be safe from those English soldiers as they pillaged this rich town. He doubted that they would listen to her claims of being English, just as they would not listen to him when they broke into this storage room to loot the goods that it contained. He grimaced at the irony. He would undoubtedly die today, but if he lived long enough to hang, if Edward failed to take this city, at least Christiana would be safe.

He pounded his fist into the wall in furious frustration that he could not help her. She had been sent to Heloise and the other women immediately upon his arrest. She had fought the knights who pulled her away. Those knights had not returned, and he prayed that they guarded the chamber in which the women waited. It would be some protection, at least.

He lifted the candle and reexamined his tiny prison. He wished it contained other than dried herring, and not just because of the smell. Whoever went to the trouble to break down this door would probably kill him out of resentment at finding nothing of value for their time and labor.

As if echoing his thoughts, a sound at the door claimed his attention. Not the crash of an ax or battering ram, though. The more subtle tone of metal on metal.

Perhaps Edward had decided to move on. Maybe it would be hanging after all. He moved to the far wall and watched the door ease open.

At the threshold, her face pale like a ghost's, appeared a haggard Heloise. Christiana stood behind her holding his long steel dagger at the blond woman's throat.

"She knew it was the only sensible thing to do, David, but she is one of those women who only obeys her husband, so I had to encourage her," Christiana said. She replaced the dagger into the sheath hanging from her waist.

Heloise looked ready to faint. She leaned against the wall for support.

"What has happened?" he asked.

"The bridge has been taken," Christiana explained. Her own face was drawn with fear that she tried bravely to hide. "The knights protecting us left long ago, and I have been watching from the roof. Our army is all over the town, like a mob. It is as you said. In victory they are taking all that they can move. The people are throwing benches and rocks down on them from the roofs, and that is slowing their progress, but not by much."

"No one is here," Heloise cried. "The gate is guarded only by some grooms and servants. When the bridge fell, the soldiers all left, some to fight in the streets, others to run."

Christiana moved up close to him and spoke lowly. "She wanted to take her daughters and run, too, but I convinced her that she was better behind these walls than in the city. They are not castle walls, and will not stop the army long, but the soldiers are killing all they meet. Even from the roof I could see many bodies fall."

He looked in her eyes and read her deep realization of the danger which she faced. He turned to Heloise.

"It is well that you released me, madame," he said soothingly. "Fortune has always smiled on me. Perhaps she will be kind today as well." He eased the woman away from the wall. "Let us go and assess our situation."

Bad news awaited in the courtyard. The servants guarding the gate had fled, and the entry stood open to the street. In the distance they could hear the screams of a city being sacked.

He ran over to close and bar the gate. A group of six women surged in just as he arrived. They looked to be burghers's wives and they threw themselves at Heloise.

"That devil of an English king has ordered everyone put to the sword," one of them cried. "They are stripping the bodies of their garments and cutting off fingers to get the rings. They are raping the women before slitting their throats."

The other women joined in with hysterical descriptions of the horrors they had seen. David barred the gate and looked around the courtyard. Christiana was right. These were not castle walls and they marked the house as that of a wealthy merchant. Eventually some soldiers would decide to batter down the gate or scale their heights. But they were better off here than outside in the city.

Christiana stood to the side, listening to the tales of mutilation and destruction with an ashen face. The sounds of the pillaging army gradually moved closer.

He walked over and embraced her. "Do you remember the attic storage above the bedchambers? The one reached by the narrow stairs? Take them there."

"And you?"

"I will join you shortly. It appears that I will need that armor after all. I never thought to wear it against Englishmen. It appears that my father will have his way in the end. It is an ironic justice that my betrayal of him has put you in such danger."

"Do not blame yourself for this. You did not bring me here," she said, instinctively knowing the guilt that wanted to overwhelm him.

"All the same, you are here." He hesitated, not wanting to speak of the horror that threatened. "If they come, let them know who you are. Speak only English. Claim the protection of your brother and the King."

"It will not matter," she said, turning to the knot of women nearby. "I have seen it before. At Harclow. It had begun before we left. My brother accepted defeat and possible death to save my mother from what we face today."

She approached the women and spoke to them. Grateful to have some instruction that at least offered hope, they fell in around her as she led the way to the tall building and the attic chamber.

David followed, but detoured to the room he and Christiana had shared. He slipped the breastplate of his armor over his shoulders and then lifted the pieces for his arms. He considered whether, with weapons and armor, he would be able to get Christiana alone out through the city streets. He shook his head. He had no jerkin that identified him as part of an English baron's retinue, and his shield bore no arms that these soldiers would recognize. They would think him French. In any case, he did not have it in him to abandon those other women and girls, nor would Christiana want him to. In death at least he could be the husband she deserved. Hoisting his sword with the other hand, he made his way to the stairway and the hiding women.

Christiana had already set the women to work. Lengths of cloth stretched on the floor, and they used his dagger to slice off sections of it.

"What are you doing?" he asked, setting down the armor.

"Banners," she said. "The white and green of Harclow. Thomas Holland's colors, and those of Chandros and Beauchamp. We will hang them from the windows. Who knows, it may attract someone who can help us."

She looked at the armor and stepped close. "I will do it." Her fingers began working the straps and buckles.

It took a long while to fit all of the armor, and he didn't even have the leg pieces. When they were done, she unstrapped the sheath from her waist and handed it to him, then retrieved the dagger from the women.

He looked a moment at the long length of sharp steel. Their eyes met.

"It will do me no good against armed men," she said, slipping it into its sheath on his hip. "And I am not brave enough to use it on the others and myself."

The women opened the windows and slid out the banners. The summer breeze carried the sounds of screaming death. As they closed the windows to secure the cloth, a crash against the gate thundered into the attic space. The noise jolted everyone into utter silence.

The air in the chamber smelled sour from the fear pouring out of its occupants. David glanced at the eight women and three girls. Their faces were barely visible in the room darkened now by the cloth at the windows. He drew Christiana aside and turned his back on the others.

He held her face with his hands and closed his eyes to savor the delicate softness of her lips. An aching tenderness flooded him, and her palpable fear tore his heart. "When I go to Genoa this fall, you will come with me," he said. "After this, crossing the Alps will seem a minor thing.

We will spend the cold months in Italy and travel down to Florence and Rome."

"I would like that," she whispered. "Perhaps we can even cross the sea to a Saracen land, and make love in a desert tent."

He kissed her closed eyes and tasted the salty tears welling in them.

Unmistakable sounds of the gate giving way pounded into the chamber.

"Look at me, Christiana," he said. Her lids lifted slowly and he gazed into those liquid diamonds and let her see his soul's love for her. She smiled bravely and sorrowfully and stretched up to kiss him.

The shouts and clamoring of men pouring into the courtyard bounced around them. Christiana lifted his sword and handed it to him. Behind him the attic chamber held complete silence. The women were beyond hysteria. Heloise's young daughters stared at him with wide-eyed solemnity.

With one last long look at his beautiful wife, he opened the door and took a position at the top of the narrow stairs.

The primitive noise of rampage and looting filled the building. David stood tensely at his post, his sword resting against the wall beside him, and waited for the soldiers to eventually find the passage that led to these steps and this attic.

The door behind him had been closed, but it could not be barred from the inside. Once he fell, there would be no protection for Christiana and the others.

The bedchambers and hall and lower storage rooms had kept them occupied for at least an hour now. It would not be long.

If he was fortunate, the men who had broken in might have closed the gate to others in order to keep the rich booty of the mayor's house for themselves and there might not be too many. If he was really fortunate, there would be no archers among them. If Fortune truly favored him, someone in authority might eventually arrive to secure the mayor's house for the King's pleasure and disposal.

He wondered if there were knights amongst them, and if appeals to chivalry would do any good.

He could not see the bottom of the stairs, for they rose up the side of the building to a landing before angling along the back wall to him. But he heard the scurrying below, and a man's shout to his friends when he discovered them.

They mounted the steps quickly, full of good cheer while they traded descriptions of the garments and jewelry and silver which they had already procured. He could tell that they were not knights from their speech. He waited.

Six men turned the corner of the landing. They began filing up. The first had reached the seventh step from the top when they finally noticed him. Six heads peered up in surprise.

"Who the hell are you?" the lead man barked.

"An Englishman like yourselves. A Londoner. A merchant."

"You don't look like a merchant."

"None of us looks or acts like ourself today. War does that."

They stretched and craned to see around each other.

"What is behind that door, merchant?" one of them yelled.

"Cloth. Ordinary and not of much value."

"He's lying," the leader said. "These stairs are hidden. This is the chamber with the spices and gold."

"I swear that neither spices nor gold are in this room."

"Step aside and let us see."

"Nay."

More footfalls on the steps. More faces joining the others. The line turned the corner and out of sight. David eyed the long daggers and swords while the word was passed that gold and spices awaited above.

The closest men eyed him hard, measuring him, trying to decide if the armor indicated superior skill. The narrow steps meant that they could not rush him all at once and the first to come might well die.

The long row began jostling around. A red head moved through them, pushing upward. "Stand aside!" a young voice commanded.

The others squeezed over and let the young man pass. He eased up next to the front man. A squire, David guessed from his youth and livery. Maybe twenty years old. Separated from his lord and enjoying his power and status in the hell that Caen had become.

The squire glanced to David's sword and unsheathed his own.

"We opened this gate. The spoils are ours," he said.

"Since I stand on the top step, it is clear that I arrived before you," David replied.

Agitated complaints and curses rumbled up the stairs. The men in the rear began calling for David to be dispatched so they could get to the gold.

David stared at the squire and the man beside him. The shouts rose and filled the stairway. Both men grew hard faced as their comrades urged them to action. He watched and waited, reading their resolve, bracing himself for the attack.

It will be the young one, he thought regretfully.

The red head suddenly surged upward. The long sword rose. David's hand went to his hip. Before the youth had climbed two steps he jerked upright. His shocked eyes glanced down at the steel dagger embedded in his throat. Then the body crumbled, blocking the stairs.

The mob of soldiers took a collective pause, and then the shouts and curses resumed at a louder, more insistent level. David reached for his sword.

He noticed an inexorable crowding forward, as if more men had joined the others and all pressed upward. The pressure on those in front became physical as well as vocal. Hands reached out and pushed the squire out of the way. The acrid smell of unleashed bloodlust permeated the closed space. He let the ruthless blood of Senlis flow to give him its cold strength.

And then, suddenly, silence began rolling up from the rear. The men on the landing looked behind them and then at each other. Bodies crushed against the walls, out of the way.

The tall, dark-haired figure of a knight wearing the King's livery stepped up into view.

Dark fiery eyes looked at David and flashed amusement and surprise. Sir Morvan waited calmly and silently for the soldiers above him to realize he wanted to pass. They jostled each other and pointed and cleared a path for him. He slowly mounted the steps until he came to the fallen squire. Glancing at David, he casually reached down and withdrew the dagger and blood began pouring from the wound. He wiped the weapon on his jerkin and joined David in front of the door.

"That is the problem with a dagger," he said lightly as he handed it over. "Once you have thrown it, you don't have a weapon anymore." His gaze raked over David's armor. "Nice steel. German?"

"Flemish."

"Aren't you supposed to be in England? Northumberland, wasn't it?"

"Other business led me here."

"And my sister?"

"I found her. Not with Percy."

Several of the men began muttering loudly about knights always taking the best portions for themselves. Morvan all but yawned as he unsheathed his sword. The grumbling stopped.

"You are in a bad position here," he observed.

"Aye. It is well that you arrived."

Morvan shrugged. "Once the bridge fell, the fun was over. Rape and looting don't appeal to me, so I decided to see about this house that flew the colors of Harclow." He glanced back at the door. "Whatever you guard, it is not worth it. Step aside and let these men have it. They cannot be controlled once they have smelled spoils and tasted blood. Thomas Holland and I have spent the last hours trying to keep women and children from being murdered or defiled."

"I cannot step aside."

"It is just a matter of time before they find an archer. Is it truly gold as they said below?"

David shook his head and gestured to the door. Morvan opened it a crack, peered inside, and stiffened. He frowned and peered in again. Hot eyes turned on David as he closed the door. "Tell me that wasn't my sister who I just saw among those women."

"If you insist. It wasn't your sister."

Morvan snarled, opened the door once more, then slammed it shut. "Hell's teeth. What is she doing here?"

"Visiting friends of mine in this city. Whoever expected our army to come and sack it?"

"Once I get her out of here, I am going to kill you."

"If you can get her out of here, you may do so." He gestured to the men. Impatient complaints and mumbling had resumed, and he suspected that plans were being laid. "How many are there?"

Morvan shrugged. "Twenty. Thirty."

"Which is it? I would say it makes a difference."

Morvan smiled wryly. "Hardly. Twenty against two or thirty against two is equally hopeless. I am damn good, David, but not that good, and my King's livery will only deter them for a while longer." All the same, he turned to the stairs and took a battle stance. With an exasperated sigh he reached over to David's sword hand and jerked it so the weapon pointed up rather than down. "Considering how you handle a sword, it is more like twenty or thirty against one and a half. You'd best stay on my right side. That is where we put the young squires."

Just then a quake shook the stairway. It repeated over and over. A series of grunts accompanied it, and the men on the lower landing looked behind themselves wide-eyed and then tried to melt into the wall. A massive body stepped up and a craggy face grinned at David.

"I correct myself," Morvan said dryly. "Thirty against ten."

"*Ja*, but it was hell finding you, David," Sieg said as he climbed toward them. Two men made the mistake of not peeling away quickly enough. Sieg calmly lifted them by their necks, crashed their heads together, and let them drop. "First I went to that castle across the river, but that bishop holding it has it sealed as tight as a coffin. I tried the Guildhall where the King has set up, then figured, hell, maybe they had her here at the mayor's house."

Indignation at Sieg's handling had made several men brave. Glinting knives were brandished behind him. Without missing a step, he reached back with his huge hand, grabbed the nearest fool, and smashed the man's head into the stone wall.

"Is Oliver with you?" David asked as Sieg joined them.

The Swede laughed and drew his sword to menace the threats forming below. His face positively glowed at the prospect of fighting all of these men. "I lost him in the streets. All these houses open and all these goods for the taking got the better of him. Said how it was a pity you weren't with him. Like old times, he said."

Morvan raised an eyebrow at this conversation. David smiled and shrugged.

"We still need some help to move these women out," Morvan said. "Now that your man is here, I will go and fetch some. Thomas should be nearby, and some others. You might cover my back with that dagger, David."

He wore a more dangerous expression leaving than he had when he came. No one challenged him.

"Did any messengers get through to warn the Comte?" David asked when Morvan had gone.

"Nay. Oliver and I stayed a few miles out on the road south as you said. They came right to us. When the King sent some men to block the news from following the French army, we finally left and gave the messengers to them. The Comte won't hear of Edward's landing for many days now." He gestured with his sword. "I clear these men out now."

"Try not to kill them all. They are supposed to be on our side."

Sieg descended two steps so that he could stretch to his fullest height. He raised his dagger in his left hand and his sword in his right, glared at the men facing him, and let loose a primitive Viking war cry.

The realization that a King's knight went to get more help had already subdued the soldiers. Sieg's display of strength thoroughly discouraged most of them. Heads began bobbing and shifting as men turned and tried to squeeze down the stairs.

By the time Morvan returned with Thomas Holland and two other friends, most of the soldiers had melted away. Their arrival took care of the rest.

David opened the door and led the way into the attic.

A hysteria of relief swept the women when they saw rescue walk through the door. Several began wailing with delayed shock. Christiana ran into David's arms.

"Thank God you are whole! You saved us all, David!"

"It was your banner that did it, darling. It seems that sacking cities bores your brother, and he came to investigate your colors."

She turned with surprise to the four knights. "Morvan!" she cried. "Thomas!"

Morvan sidled over and accepted his sister's embrace. He glanced over her shoulder dangerously at David. Christiana pulled back in time to see the look.

"Don't you dare, Morvan. He saved me, and all of the others here. The French knights and soldiers abandoned us and he put his own life between us and danger. You could not have done better."

Morvan's expression softened as he looked at his sister. "If that is how you say it was, then I will not kill him this time."

Thomas Holland walked over. "There is nothing for it but to take them all to Edward. Nowhere else will be safe. But it is some ways, and the city . . ."

David read his expression and concern. "We will keep them between us. Christiana, gather the women and tell them what we will be doing. Tell them to look to the ground as we move."

She nodded and went over to Heloise and her daughters first. David gestured for Sieg. "You will carry the youngest one," he said. "Do not let her see the bodies."

While his wife explained to the other women, David

approached Heloise. She hadn't moved since they entered, and she sat on a stack of cloth looking spent and numb. Her hands clasped something. A faint glitter dangled down her skirt.

She looked up at him. Her hands opened to reveal a gold and emerald necklace. "I thought maybe, if it came to it, I could buy my daughters' safety."

"They will be secure now, madame. I am sure that your husband is safe as well. He will probably be taken to England to await ransom like the rest of the wealthy burghers, but there is no profit in killing such men."

She looked down on the necklace. "Please accept it. To repay you for my husband's role in taking your wife, and for your help here today."

He had no trouble calculating the value of the gold and emeralds. But his role in the day's events was not nearly so chivalrous as the woman assumed, and he would not profit from them. "It was the arrival of my wife's brother that saved you. If you wish to express gratitude, show it to him." He lifted her to her feet. "We must go now. Follow the instructions my wife gave you."

The men led the ladies down the steep steps. In the courtyard they all drew their swords. Sieg had convinced the youngest girl to let him bind her eyes, and he lifted her up while she clung to him. David placed his left arm around Christiana. Then they began walking the women through the hell of death and destruction that had once been the great city of Caen.

Edward sat in the Guildhall, surrounded by clerks who carefully listed ownership of the spoils to be sent back to England. The arriving pageant of knights and women silenced the chamber. Along the way, other desperate women had attached themselves to the group, and

Thomas Holland had even broken away to rescue several. Twenty women marched in on the King, flanked by sword-bearing knights.

Whatever inclinations Edward might have had regarding the disposal of these females became irrelevant. In the face of his young knights, he had no choice but to display the chivalry which he had always celebrated in his court. He formally extended his protection to them and had them sent to another chamber for safety.

David turned to go with Christiana, but the King gestured for him to stay. He dismissed the men around him and faced David over a table strewn with maps, grinning broadly.

"A splendid plan, David! God, what a victory!"

David thought of the hundreds of bodies they had just passed. People of all ages and degrees, butchered and stripped naked. The streets were covered with blood.

"Is it true that you ordered everyone put to the sword?"

Edward scowled. "It was my right when they did not surrender, and they knew it. Hundreds of our men died from their resistance. Not just at the bridge, but in the streets. Those damn stones and benches . . . I have rescinded the order, however. Hell, they should have yielded."

When faced with twenty thousand, they should have. But London would not have yielded, David thought. *Nor would you have wanted her to.*

Edward waved off the destruction of Caen like so much flotsam of war. He beamed with delight and pointed to the map on the table. "We will be clear all the way to Paris. Their army cannot return in time and none will stop us now. No sieges will delay us once word of Caen spreads." He frowned a little. "Do you know the river

Somme, David? It worries me. We could find ourselves trapped between it and the Seine, and there appear to be no crossings except a few bridges. Damn, I should have had you make this map as well. Yours are far better."

David walked over to procure a quill from a clerk. He returned and bent to the map, and drew two lines across the river. "Here. You can ford the river, but the water moves like a tide, so you must cross when it is low."

Edward rubbed his hands together. "Splendid. We have the constable and chamberlain, you know. Rich ransoms there. I am sending them and the other hostages downriver in the morning, along with the spoils. Shipfuls of it. By the way, where are those weapons?"

"Nearby in the town of Bayeaux."

"Excellent. We will be going there next."

"My man will come and show you their location."

"Not you? You must join us. This will be a glorious campaign."

"My role is over. I would like to return to London with my wife."

Edward regarded him, and a different expression replaced his glee. "You sacrificed much to remain loyal to me, David. I do not forget such things. During the last two days I have been knighting men whom I never met before. Let us do it now. Take the place assured by your blood and earned by your loyalty."

"I am honored by the offer, but I prefer that you did not."

Edward looked a little annoyed. David smiled amiably. "I do request some other favors from you, however, if you feel moved to grant them."

The King's eyebrows rose.

"When I return to London, I will bring your treasurer one third of the price of the license which you granted me.

The next third will come in two years, and the rest four years hence, as I first suggested."

"You have already paid . . ."

"Nay. That was the bride price for Christiana. I wish to turn that story into the truth, and I ask that you never reveal our original bargain. She is never to know."

Edward laughed. "The girl has won your heart, has she? Well, I would be fool to turn down another thousand pounds. It will be as you request. And the other favors?"

"I ask that you remember your oath to help reclaim Harclow, and aid her brother as you can when the time comes."

Edward looked down thoughtfully before nodding.

"Lady Catherine must be removed from London," David added. "She knows too much, and my continued value to you, should you require me, will be compromised by her."

Edward grinned. "I wish you could have been there when she came to tell her tale. I let her spin on and on. A clever woman, I suspect. I've never much cared for clever women. I have already sent her to Castle Rising to attend on my mother. She will be held in close confinement with her there. Those two can drive each other mad with their schemes. The merchant, Frans, is enjoying less comfortable accommodations until I return and he is ransomed. The disadvantages of being a commoner."

"I would like Christiana and myself to go downriver with your people in the morning."

"Of course. I will give you some documents to bring back. We found written plans for the invasion of Southampton. I will have the priests read it from the pulpits so the people know how close England came to seeing French troops on her soil."

The Earl of Warwick entered then, and Edward turned to greet him with a new spurt of excitement. David took his leave and made his way to the chamber which held the women. Sieg waited outside its door.

"You will go to Bayeaux with the King before heading south," David explained.

"*Ja*. You want me to show him where the gonnes are?"

David nodded. He reached into his pourpoint and withdrew some folded parchments. "Here is Theobald's recognition and the French king's permission for my succession at Senlis. You already have the ring and the drawing. Wait until he has already learned of my betrayal. You will not be safe if you bring that news. You may not be safe in any case once he sees that the ring's stone is pink, and is his and not his brother's."

"I know what to do."

"Will you come back to London afterward? Today you more than repaid that debt you always claim you owe."

"Hardly repaid, David. Those Mamluks were set to kill me. If you hadn't planned that escape . . ."

"Morvan and I could not have held them off today."

"*Ja*, well, I may join this war for a while. When the French finally catch this army, the battle should be wonderful. I will send word to you if I don't return by fall."

David looked to the documents held in the massive hand. "Be careful, my friend. In this one thing, I cannot guess how he will react."

CHAPTER 23

MEN CROWDED THE docks, carrying looted goods to the waiting boats. The spoils had been listed and assessed, and now it all headed back to England.

David stood amidst the fruits of war stacked on one of the piers. A river breeze offered some refreshment from the stench of death hanging over the city. An open box of silver plates glittered ten paces away in the summer heat.

He watched as Christiana walked down the dock to meet her brother. He could tell that this leave-taking weighed heavily on her. She had seen far too much of war's ruthlessness last night, and knew that Morvan might not survive this campaign.

David could not avoid contemplating the implications of that. He did not even try to. The son of Senlis was incapable of ignoring the fact that it was in his interest to have Morvan Fitzwaryn never return to England.

For with Morvan gone, Christiana became the heir of Harclow, and one day Edward would indeed reclaim the lands in the name of his dead friend Hugh Fitzwaryn.

With Morvan gone, David de Abyndon, bastard son of the noble Theobald of Senlis, would become the lord of Harclow as Christiana's husband.

Being an English knight was one thing, being an English baron was quite another.

But in truth, the land and status were the least of it. The merchant in him knew the real value of Harclow. He had been there, just as he had been to most of the estates along the Scottish border. He alone knew that in the hills of Harclow and other Cumbrian lands there were many caves, ancient caves, in which animals had lived since time began. And in the caves of Harclow alone there lay an earl's ransom of the rare stuff called saltpeter that was essential to make powder for gonnes.

And he had paid King Edward one thousand pounds for the right to be the crown's exclusive agent for the purchase and sale of saltpeter, and had taken Christiana Fitzwaryn to wife in order to hide the arrangement.

He watched brother and sister meet and embrace. His mind began involuntarily calculating the tremendous loss of profit when he actually paid Morvan for the contents of those caves.

Aye, it was very much against his interests to have Morvan return. In fact, having Sieg guarantee that Morvan fell during battle . . .

Christiana looked up at her brother with glistening eyes. Even at a distance, her worry was palpable.

Her sadness twisted his heart. His mind emptied of everything but the desire to comfort her.

Theobald had been right. Recognizing one's options was not the same as choosing them. He would turn his back on these golden opportunities which Lady Fortune had capriciously offered him.

He would do it for Christiana, because he loved her.

✦ ✦ ✦

Christiana and Morvan stood arm in arm while men burdened with booty jostled past.

This was what war was really all about. Profit, of the most primitive sort. All of the talk of chivalry and honor appeared very false to her today.

"Every farmhouse in England will have new cookware and cloth," Morvan said, surveying the boats riding low in the water.

"Is any of it yours?"

"Nay. My prize is your safety. It is enough for me." He glanced to where David waited fifty paces away. "And for your merchant, I think. This time, at least."

"David. His name is David."

"Aye. David."

"I know that you still do not favor him, Morvan, but he is a good man. You can not deny that he proved that."

"He has goodness in him, but much more too. Things that I do not understand. But he has proven that he can protect you. I can part from you today with an easy mind, if not an easy heart."

"It will not be such a long parting. This war cannot last once winter threatens."

He turned his attention from the boats to her. "However long it lasts, I do not think that we will see each other for many months. Knowing that you are safe and have a home frees me to leave the court. I may not return with the army. I think that I will seek some adventure when this campaign ends."

Her spirits had been battered by the destruction of Caen, and now a new sadness spread through her.

She embraced him. "I pray that you change your mind. My place with him does not dim my love for you. If you must seek adventure, let it be for a short while only. And my home is yours too. Please believe that."

"It will not be so long. But you have found your future, Christiana, and now it is time for me to find mine." He set her away, and smiled down at her. "I must leave you now. Edward has duties for me. No tears, sister. This is not forever. Go to your husband."

He walked away, and soon the sight of him became lost in the bustling crowd. She kept watching, hoping to see his dark hair one more time, praying that his words were true, and not the last that she would ever hear him speak.

David came up behind her. She felt his presence, and then the comfort of his arms surrounding her, holding her closely.

"I love you," he said.

How like him to know that she needed that right now. But then those blue eyes had always seen into her heart. She turned to him, and to the sanctuary that his declaration offered.

"I worry about him," she said.

"He is skilled and strong, Christiana. And in battles, they do not try to kill knights, but take them for ransom."

"Aye. But I know the value of a knight's ransom and there is no father to pay it. He could live his life in the hole of some French keep if Edward fails."

"If he is captured, I will get him out."

She looked in his eyes and knew that was true. Whether it took coin or a dagger, he would do it for her.

The horrible images of the last day receded. The brilliance of his love and care burned away the fog of melancholy that had thickened with Morvan's departure.

"Where is Sieg? Isn't he returning with us?"

"He decided to join this war. It is his nature to enjoy such things."

"But he has gone to your father first, hasn't he? You sent him to return the documents, didn't you? Your mother's picture was missing from the book in your study. You sent that too. So he would know who you really are and why you did it."

That surprised him. His smile showed amazement. And admiration. "You are becoming dangerously clever, darling."

"So how long do you think that we have?"

"I will be in England. He cannot harm me there."

"Of course he can, but that is not what I meant. How long do you think the Comte will live? How long before Senlis is yours?"

Not just surprise this time. Astonishment. That in turn astonished her. He had not considered this possibility. He truly had not foreseen how this would end.

"He is a nobleman, David, and the last of an ancient line. In this one thing I know him better than you. He does not want the line to die out and the lands returned to the crown. Such men will do anything to assure they have an heir. Despite what you did, he will not forget that you are all he has left once he learns the truth."

He stood very still while he absorbed that.

"So how long do you think we have?"

"He is about fifty-five. If you are right, and I think that you misjudge him, it should be a long while before I face that choice again."

He said it lightly, but she felt a change in him. She sensed his mind and emotions begin to churn. She knew him very well now, and easily recognized the quiet drama that his soul controlled and contained.

He had seen that she was right, and that Senlis could one day be his after all. He had begun waiting again. He was good at waiting.

She reached up to caress his face. "I love our life, and I am not sorry that it will probably be a long while. And I love you. I thank God for our love, David. There is beauty and goodness in it, and in you, always waiting for me."

"Whatever goodness you see in me is merely a reflection of yourself, my girl. You make me better than I was ever born to be."

"That is not true. For a man who sees so clearly, there are parts of yourself that you do not know very well."

"Parts I would have never known if you had not touched them."

She began to object. The intensity in his expression stopped her. Maybe he was right. Hadn't his love taught her things about herself that she might have never learned without him?

Two men carting a bed jostled by. The din on the docks intruded.

"Maybe love is all that stands against what we have seen here in Caen," she said. "That is sad."

He shook his head. "I understand the darkness in men like your innocence never will, Christiana, and the acts of war are the least of it. Trust me when I say that love is a formidable foe. Perhaps the only foe."

For a moment his gaze revealed his soul like it had the night of their reunion, and it was all there. The shadows that he spoke of, and the power of love to contain them. Aye, Morvan had been right. There was goodness in him, but other things too.

"Then let us love each other as well as we can, David. Let us build a life full of hope and light that never dims, no matter what the world brings us. I want our love to be the hearth at the center of our home, wherever it is, burning hotly forever. I never want to look back on what we shared here and wonder if it was an illusion that we embraced in our desperation."

"It was no illusion. You owned my heart long before I found you here, and it is yours forever. Our love is as real as the arms embracing you, and always will be. I am not a man who loses hold on something precious once it is in his possession."

He kissed her, his mouth lingering and claiming, a welcome reminder of the passion they had found. He held her so closely that they molded as one and made an image of love amidst the greed swarming the docks.

He turned her under his arm. "Let us leave this place now. Let us go home."

A few men had paused their hauling to watch the lovers. She met their eyes frankly, and hoped that the display had reminded them about the true value of things.

"Aye, David, let us go home. Take me back to our garden and our bed."

They walked down the pier side by side, with no prize in their arms except each other.

ABOUT THE
AUTHOR

MADELINE HUNTER's first novel was published in 2000. Since then she has seen twelve historical romances and one novella published, and her books have been translated into five languages. She is a four-time RITA finalist and won the long historical RITA in 2003. Nine of her books have been on the *USA Today* bestseller list, and she has also had titles on the *New York Times* extended list. Madeline has a Ph.D. in art history, which she teaches at an Eastern university. She currently lives in Pennsylvania with her husband and two sons.

Don't miss

Madeline Hunter's

upcoming tale of intrigue and passion

THE
RULES OF
SEDUCTION

Coming in Fall 2006

Read on for a sneak peek. . . .

MADELINE HUNTER

Enemy. Protector. Lover.
He is the seducer every woman
dreams of....

The
RULES
of
SEDUCTION

THE RULES OF SEDUCTION

On sale fall 2006

Mr. Rothwell waited in the reception hall, surrounded by walls that had already been stripped of paintings. As Alexia entered he was bent, examining a marquetry table in the corner, no doubt calculating its worth.

She did not wait for his attention or greeting. "Mr. Rothwell, my cousin Timothy is not on the premises. I believe he is selling the horses. My cousin Miss Longworth is indisposed and her sister is too young to assist you. Will I do for whatever your purpose in coming might be?

He straightened and swung his gaze to her. She grudgingly admitted that he appeared quite magnificent today, dressed for riding as he was in blue coat and gray patterned silk waistcoat. She suspected he dominated large ballrooms as thoroughly as he did this small chamber. His presence, bearing and garments announced to the world that he knew he was handsome and intelligent and rich as sin. It was rude to look like that in a house being deprived of its possessions and dignity.

"I expected a servant to—"

"There are no servants. The family cannot afford them now. Falkner only remains until he finds another position, but he no longer serves. I fear you are stuck with me."

She heard her own voice sound crisp and barely civil. His lids lowered just enough to indicate he did not miss the lack of respect.

"If I am stuck with you, and you with me, so be it, Miss Welbourne. My purpose in intruding is very simple. I have an aunt who has an interest in this house. She asked that I determine if it would be suitable for her and her daughter this season."

"You want a tour of the property so you can describe it to potential occupants?"

"If Miss Longworth would be so kind, yes."

"I doubt Miss Longworth would be so kind, although kindness is in her heart in most situations. She is also far too busy. Being ruined and made destitute is very time-consuming."

His jaw tightened enough to give her a small satisfaction. The victory was brief. He set down his hat on the marquetry table. "Then I will find my own way. When I said my aunt had an interest I did not mean a casual curiosity but rather that of ownership. This property is already my aunt's, Miss Welbourne. Timothy Longworth signed the papers yesterday. I presented my requirements as a request out of courtesy to his family, not out of any obligation."

The news stunned her. The house had already been sold. So fast! Alexia quickly calculated what that might mean to her plans, and to Roselyn and Irene.

She swallowed her pride. Its taste was growing increasingly bitter. "My apologies, Mr. Rothwell. The new ownership of the house had not been communicated to either Miss Longworth or myself. I will show you the house, if that will do."

He nodded agreement and she began the ordeal. She led him into the dining room, where his sharp gaze did not miss a thing. She heard him mentally counting chairs and measuring space.

The rest of the first level went quickly. He did not open drawers and cabinets in the butler's pantry. Alexia guessed he knew they were already empty.

"The breakfast room is through that door," she said as they returned to the corridor. "My cousin Roselyn is there, and I must beg you to accept my description instead of entering yourself. I fear seeing you will greatly distress her."

"Why would my presence be so distressing?"

"Timothy told us everything. Roselyn knows that you brought the bank to the brink of failure and forced this ruin on the family."

He absorbed that. A hard smile played at the corners of his mouth. Really, the man's cruelty was not to be borne.

He noticed her glaring at him. He did not seem at all embarrassed that she had seen that cynical smile.

"Miss Welbourne, I do not need to see the breakfast room. I am sorry for your cousin's distress, but matters of high finance exist on a different plane from everyday experiences. Timothy Longworth's explanations were somewhat simplified, no doubt because he was giving them to ladies."

"They may have been simple, but they were clear, as were the consequences. A week ago my cousins lived in style in London and soon they will live in poverty in the country. Timothy is ruined, the partnership is sold, and he will have debts despite his fall. Is any of that incorrect, sir?"

He shook his head, nonplussed. "It is all correct."

She could not believe his indifference. He could at least appear a little chagrined, a bit embarrassed. Instead he acted as if this were normal. Perhaps he ruined families frequently.

"Shall we go above?" he asked.

She showed him up the stairs and into the library. He took his time browsing the volumes on the shelves while she waited, silently tapping her foot. She hoped he did not plan to open every book and memorize every title.

"Will you be going to Oxfordshire?" he asked.

"I would not allow myself to be a burden on this family now."

Most of his attention remained on the books. "What will you do?"

"I have my future well in hand. I have drawn up a plan and listed my expectations and opportunities."

He replaced a book on its shelf, quickly surveyed the rug and desk and sofas, then walked toward her.

"What opportunities do you see?" It sounded as if he knew the expectations were nonexistent.

She led him through the other rooms on the floor. "My first choice is to be a governess in town. My second is to be a governess anywhere else."

"Most sensible."

"Well, when facing starvation it behooves one to be so, don't you think?"

The third level was not as spaciously arranged as the public rooms. He cramped her in the corridor. She became too aware of the large, masculine presence by her side as she showed the bedrooms. It seemed very wrong for this stranger to be intruding up here.

"And if you do not find a position as a governess?" The casual query came some time after their last exchange. His curiosity raised her pique to a reckless pitch. It was unseemly for the man who caused this grief to want the details.

"My next choice is to become a milliner."

"A hat maker?"

"I am very talented at it. Years hence, if you

should see an impoverished woman wearing a magnificent hat artfully devised of nothing more than an old basket, sparrow feathers and withered apples, that will be me." She threw open the door of Irene's bedroom. "My fourth choice is to become a soiled dove. There are those who say a woman should starve to death first, but I have never held with that. One must be practical, and I am very much so."

She received a long, sharp glance for that. One that managed to take her in thoroughly. Beneath his annoyance at how she mocked his lack of guilt, she also saw bold, masculine consideration, as if he calculated her value at the occupation fourth on her list.

Her face warmed. That stupid liveliness woke her skin and sank right through to churn in her core, affecting her in a shocking way, creating an insidious, uncontrollable awareness of her body's many details. The sensation appalled her mind even as she acknowledged its lush stimulation.

She had to step back, out of the chamber and out of his sight, to escape the way his proximity caused a rapid drumbeat in her pulse. In the few seconds before he joined her she called up her anger to defeat the shocking burst of sensuality.

She continued her goads so he would know she did not care what he thought. She wanted this man to appreciate how his whims had created misery.

"My fifth choice is to become a thief. I debated which should come first, soiled dove or thief, and decided that while the former was harder work, it was a form of honest trade while being a thief is just plain evil." She did not resist adding, "No matter how it is done, or even how legal it may be."

He stopped walking and turned into her path, forcing her to stop walking too. "You speak very frankly."

He hovered over her in the narrow corridor. His gaze demanded her total attention. A power flowed, one masculine and dominating and challenging. An intuitive caution shouted retreat. The liveliness purred low and deep. She ignored both reactions and stood her ground.

"You are the one who asked the question about my future, sir, even though it does not matter at all to you what becomes of any of us." She peered up at him severely. "I hope that you are proud of yourself. These are decent, good people and you have destroyed their lives. You did not have to remove all your business from Timothy's bank. It is as if you deliberately ruined him, and I do not know how you can bear to live with yourself."

He gazed down at her, his dark blue eyes almost black in the dim hall's lights and his jaw as set as it had been in the drawing room the other day. He was angry. Well, good. So was she.

"I live with myself very well, thank you. Until you have more experience in business and finance, Miss Welbourne, you can only view these developments from a position of ignorance. I am sincerely sorry for Miss Longworth and her sister, and for you, but I will not apologize for doing my duty as I saw fit."

His tone startled her. Quiet but firm, it commanded that no further argument be given. She retreated, but not because of that. She was wasting her breath. This man did not care about other people. If he did, they would not be taking this tour.

She guided him toward the stairs rising to the higher chambers, but he stopped outside a door near the landing. "What is this room?"

"It is a small bedroom, undistinguished. I believe it was once the dressing room to the chamber next door. Now, up above—"

He turned the latch and pushed the door open. She pursed her lips and waited for him to take his quick, mental inventory.

Instead he paced into the small space and noted every detail. The two books beside the bed, the small, sparsely populated wardrobe, the neat stack of letters on the writing table—all of it garnered his attention. He lifted a hat from a chair by the window.

"This is your room," he said.

It was, and his presence in it, his perusal of her private belongings, created an intimacy that made her uncomfortable. His touching her hat felt too much like his touching her. It created a physical connection that made the simmering liveliness more shocking and embarrassing.

"*For now* it is my room."

He ignored the barb. He examined the hat,

turning it this way and that. It was the one she had begun remaking in the garden two days ago. No one would recognize it now. "You do have a talent at it." He glanced at her sharply, then back to the hat, as if mentally putting the two together and picturing the hat on a head.

"Yes, well, but as I said, being a milliner is only choice number three. If a lady works in such a shop, she can no longer pretend she is a lady at all, can she?"

He set the hat down carefully. "No, she cannot. However, it is more respectable than being a soiled dove or thief, although far less lucrative. Your list is in the correct order if respectability is your goal."

That was an odd thing for him to say. It almost sounded as if he thought she should have different goals and a differently ordered list.

She still hated him by the time they were finished with the tour. She could not deny he was less a stranger, however. Entering the private rooms together, seeing the artifacts of the family's everyday lives, being so close, *too* close, on the upper levels, had created an unwelcome familiarity.

Her susceptibility to his overbearing presence had placed her at a disadvantage. She wanted to believe she was above such reactions, especially with this man who probably thought it his due from all women. She resented the entire, irritating hour with him.

They returned to the reception hall and he retrieved his hat.

She broached the reason she had agreed to receive him at all. "Mr. Rothwell, Timothy is distracted. He is not conveying the details to his sisters, if indeed he even knows them himself. If I may be so bold—"

"You have been plenty bold without asking permission, Miss Welbourne. There is no need to stand on ceremony now."

She grimaced. She *had* been bold and outspoken. She had allowed her vexation to get the better of her good sense. In truth, she had not been very practical in a situation where she badly needed that virtue.

"What is your question?"

"When have you told Timothy that the Longworths must vacate the house?"

"I have not said yet." He levelled a disconcertingly frank gaze at her. "When do you think is reasonable?"

"Never."

He smiled. "That is not reasonable."

"A week. Please give them a week more."

"A week it is. The Longworths may remain until then." He narrowed his eyes on her. "You, however..."

Oh, dear heavens. She had raised the devil with her free tongue. He was going to throw her out at once.

"My aunt has a passion for hats."

She blinked. "Hats? Your aunt?"

"She loves them. She buys far too many, at exorbitant prices. As her trustee I pay the bills, so I know."

It was an odd topic to start on the way out the door. In truth he sounded a little stupid.

"I see. Well, they often are very expensive."

"The ones she buys are also very ugly."

She smiled and nodded and wished he would leave. She wanted to tell Roselyn about the week's reprieve.

Once more she received one of his piercing examinations. "A governess, you said. Your first choice. Do you have the education to be a finishing governess?"

"I have been helping prepare my young cousin for her season. I have the requisite skills and abilities."

"Music? Do you play?"

"Yes. I am well suited to be a governess for any age, and especially young ladies. My own education was superior. I was not always as you see me now."

He looked right into her eyes. "That is clear. If you had always been as you are now, you would have never dared be as rude and outspoken with me as you have been today."

Her face warmed furiously. Not because she had been rude and he knew it, but because his invasive gaze was causing that annoying stimulation again.

"Miss Welbourne, my aunt will be taking possession of this house because she is launching her daughter in society this season. My cousin Caroline will require a governess and my aunt a companion. Aunt Henrietta is . . . well, a sobering influence in the household is advisable."

"One that would keep her from buying too many ugly hats."

"Exactly. Since the position matches your first choice in opportunities, and would ensure you need not contemplate choices four or five, would you be interested in taking it? If you are so honest with me in sharing your thoughts, I think that you would also tell my aunt when a hat is ridiculous."

A variety of reactions barraged her mind. At first she thought he was teasing her about her list of choices, but she realized that he was serious.

He was asking her to stay in this house where she had lived as a family member, only now she would continue as a servant.

He was asking her to serve the man who had ruined the Longworths and reduced her yet further, pushing her down the path of diminishment begun when her father died and his heir refused the support he had promised.

Of course Mr. Rothwell did not see any of that. She was merely a convenient solution to staffing his aunt's household. She provided a unique combination of skills that were perfect for the position. Even if he saw the insult, this man would not care.

She wanted to refuse outright. She itched to say something far more outspoken and rude than she had ventured thus far.

She bit her tongue and checked her anger. She could not afford insulted pride these days.

"I will consider your generous offer, Mr. Rothwell."

MEXICAN SANGRIA,
COCK 'N' BULLSHOT, APPLE DAIQUIRI,
COFFEE COOLER, GIN MILK PUNCH, CREOLE MARTINI,
SAMOVAR SLING, SPICED ORANGE BLOSSOM,
DUBONNET MANHATTAN, RASPBERRY MA TAZZ,
CHERRY RUM FIX . . .

You'll find recipes for these and thousands of other exotic and delicious-sounding concoctions in this comprehensive bartender's guide. You'll also find out how the Bloody Mary got its name, how much is in a "tot" of liquor, as well as the difference between a *Shooter* and a *Shrub*, or between a *Fizz* and a *Flip*, and the meaning of such mixologist's terms as *Smash*, *Puff* or *Bang!* With this remarkable guide you'll be talking and serving and mixing drinks like a pro!

THE
NEW
AMERICAN

BARTENDER'S GUIDE

JOHN J. POISTER has written four books on food and wine; writes a regular column, THE FLAVOR CHASE, for *Wine & Spirits* magazine; and is Executive Editor of Editorial Marketing Network, Ltd., creators of magazine and newspaper supplements on travel and lifestyle subjects. He is also President of General Strategics, Inc., a communications consulting firm with one of the world's largest collections of drink recipes.

THE
NEW
AMERICAN
BARTENDER'S
GUIDE

JOHN J. POISTER

A SIGNET BOOK

SIGNET
Published by the Penguin Group
Penguin Books USA Inc., 375 Hudson Street,
New York, New York 10014, U.S.A.
Penguin Books Ltd, 27 Wrights Lane,
London W8 5TZ, England
Penguin Books Australia Ltd, Ringwood,
Victoria, Australia
Penguin Books Canada Ltd, 10 Alcorn Avenue,
Toronto, Ontario, Canada M4V 3B2
Penguin Books (N.Z.) Ltd, 182–190 Wairau Road,
Auckland 10, New Zealand

Penguin Books Ltd, Registered Offices:
Harmondsworth, Middlesex, England

Published by Signet, an imprint of Dutton Signet,
a division of Penguin Books USA Inc.

First Printing, May, 1989
11

 REGISTERED TRADEMARK—MARCA REGISTRADA

Printed in the United States of America

BOOKS ARE AVAILABLE AT QUANTITY DISCOUNTS WHEN USED TO PROMOTE PROD-
UCTS OR SERVICES. FOR INFORMATION PLEASE WRITE TO PREMIUM MARKETING DIVI-
SION, PENGUIN BOOKS USA INC., 375 HUDSON STREET, NEW YORK, NEW YORK 10014.

PUBLISHER'S NOTE

This book provides a wonderful variety of drink recipes to please every palate. At the same time, the reader is asked to exercise moderation on all occasions. We all know that drunken driving is the number one cause of automobile fatalities. If you are a host, keep an eye on your guests and try to provide safe conveyance home for those who overindulge. If a guest who brings along this book for others' enjoyment, remember to choose a safe driver beforehand. That said, let us welcome you to the world of the expert mixologist, where every request becomes a perfect drink every time.

CONTENTS

Meaning of Symbols
Adjacent to Drink Names

C = CLASSIC

Classic or standard drink recipes
that have retained their popularity
over the years are designated by a **C**

N = NEW

New recipes that have been recently
introduced and which are not likely to be
found in older drink books are marked with an

O = ORIGINAL

Original recipes or innovations
on standard recipes created by
the author are indicated by an **O**

HOW TO MAKE A GOOD DRINK EVERY TIME

> "If good work came easy
> everybody would be doin' it."
> —Louis Armstrong

During the golden age of the cocktail in the 1930s and '40s, contrary to what many may think, people did not actually drink a great deal more—they drank *better*. Great bars and famous restaurants prided themselves on their very attractive, delicious, innovative drinks, and hosts delighted their guests by offering them delectable cocktail creations; they took the time to turn out a New Orleans Gin Fizz, Sidecar, Rum Collins, Bacardi Cocktail, or Whiskey Sour that was well-made and satisfying.

Today's bartenders, responding to their clientele, spend much of their time pouring wine, pouring whiskey on the rocks and making about a dozen drinks such as a Bloody Mary, Daiquiri, Screwdriver, or Pina Colada because there is little incentive to try to make new and exciting libations. In fact, one beverage manager at a big hotel said that his barmen had gotten so lazy, he doubted if they could make a first-class Cooler or Sling because they had gotten out of practice. Happily, there are exceptions.

Some top restaurants and bars are beginning to feature new mixed drinks or are creating their own house specialties. And consumers, tiring of off-the-shelf refreshments as a steady diet, are showing interest in new drinks and new kinds of drinks which are, as this is written, cream-type mixed drinks, new tropical fruit coolers, wine-based mixed drinks, and schnapps concoctions. This will change, of course. Tastes always do, but they go in cycles and old fads and fashions have a way of coming back in new garb. This explains why some of the old drink recipes are being rediscovered by a whole new generation of drinkers. A visit to a bar that serves a young college crowd will reaffirm the essential truth in the song "Everything Old Is New Again."

This book—and particularly this chapter—was written for the professional bartender as well as the home drink maker. It, and most of the recipes you will find between these covers, is aimed at improving the variety and quality of what you serve.

Some bartenders lack self-esteem and are of the opinion that the mixing of drinks does not require much talent or skill. Unfortunately for their customers, they can make the drinks to prove it. It is only when you have seen a master mixologist at work does the old copy book slogan become obvious: If you will make the effort to achieve good results, *you will achieve them.*

The first step is to find out what "good" is, what really constitutes a good drink, how to produce them and how to do it consistently.

THE LANGUAGE OF MIXOLOGY

Just as there are many recipes for beef stew and it is called different names in different places, so too with beverage terminology. Names go in and out of style, and their meanings are changed by usage and the passage of time. The first name on our list is a good example. Originally an *apéritif* was a fortified, aromatized wine such as vermouth, which was and is popular throughout Europe as an appetizing beverage to be taken before a meal. Now it embraces a wide range of wines and spirits.

Apéritif. Originally a reference to an apéritif wine, fortified and aromatized by the addition of various herbs and spices, it was traditionally drunk before meals as a stimulant to the appetite. The term was also applied to various other wine concoctions of a proprietary nature such as Dubonnet, Byrrh, St. Raphael, and bitter-based liqueurs like Campari, Amer Picon, and even to bitters themselves such as Fernet Branca. Now the term encompasses pre-prandial spirits such as ouzo, Calisay, Pernod, Ricard, anesone; all kinds of cocktails and even white table wine, which has become popular as a before-dinner drink in the U.S. Today, what constitutes an apéritif is of less importance than *when* it is imbibed. In other words, an apéritif is anything alcoholic taken prior to dining.

Bang! A term of our own invention used to identify double- or triple-flavor reinforced drinks such as Orange Bang! or Cherry Bang!—i.e., cherry juice, cherry liqueur, and cherry brandy.

Cobbler. A tall drink traditionally served in a highball or Collins glass filled with finely crushed ice and decorated with fresh fruit and mint sprigs. It may use any type of wine or spirit with or without a sweetener. The classic Cobbler from the gaslight era was made of sherry and pineapple syrup and various fresh fruit garnishes.

Chaser. A mixer that is tossed down the gullet after one has drunk a straight shot of whiskey or other spirit instead of being combined with a spirit in a glass. (See *Shooter.*) The Boilermaker originally was "a shot-and-a-beer," meaning a shot glass of whiskey followed by a beer chaser.

Cocktail. A combination of spirits (including wines) and flavorings, sweeteners, and garnishes of various kinds intended to be consumed before dining. Today the term "cocktail" is used interchangeably with apéritif. The usual cocktail recipe consists of a *base*, such as gin, whiskey, rum, brandy, vodka, or even a wine such as sherry, champagne, or in some cases a table wine; to which is added an *accent* spirit, e.g., triple sec, or a wine, e.g., Madeira; and often a *sweetener* (sugar syrup) or *flavoring* (orange juice) with or without garnishes (maraschino cherry). The *base, accent, sweetener* (if required), and *flavoring* is the basic formula for almost all cocktails. The exceptions are usually cococtions called cocktails that are not.

Collins. Basically a sour in a tall glass with club soda or seltzer water. The famous Tom Collins made with gin has been extended to include everything from applejack (a Jack Collins) to Irish whiskey (Mike Collins). The John Collins is one you can win a bet on. If asked to describe it, many will say it is made with whiskey. Wrong! It is made with Hollands or jenever gin.

Cooler. There are many recipes for coolers, which all have these things in common: true coolers are made with ginger ale, club soda, or other types of carbonated beverage, and the rind of a lemon or orange, cut in a continuous spiral, with one end hooked over the rim of the glass. All coolers are served in tall glasses such as a Collins glass, which is sometimes called a cooler glass.

Crusta. A short drink of the sour type served in a glass that is completely lined with an orange or lemon peel cut in a continuous strip. Any spirit may be used as the base for this drink, but the Brandy Crusta was the prototype.

Cup. A punch-type drink that is made by the cup or glass instead of in a punch bowl.

Daisy. An oversize, sour-type drink sweetened with a fruit syrup such as raspberry and usually served in a large goblet with crushed ice and straws. (See *Fix.*)

Eggnog. A traditional Christmas holiday bowl containing a delectable combination of eggs, sugar, cream or milk, and brandy, rum, or bourbon served cold in individual cups in all its rich, creamy goodness. There are many old and famous recipes, including the Tom and Jerry, which is a hot Eggnog.

Fix. A sour-type drink similar to the Daisy and traditionally made with pineapple syrup and served with crushed ice in a large goblet with straws, if you wish.

Fizz. There are many fine old recipes for Fizzes, which are, as the name suggests, products of the old siphon bottle that "fizzed" the drink with a stream of bubbles as it was being made. The Gin Fizz is typical and similar to the Tom Collins. Other famous Fizzes such as the Ramos Gin Fizz, the Silver Fizz, and the Sloe Gin Fizz are not at all like a Tom Collins and are worth trying even without a siphon.

Flip. A creamy, cold drink made of eggs, sugar, and your favorite wine or spirit. The Brandy Flip and the Sherry Flip are perhaps best known. The Flip began in Colonial times as a hot drink made of spirits, beer, eggs, cream, and spices, mulled with a red-hot flip iron or flip dog that was plunged into the drink; hence the name, Flip.

Frappé. Anything served with finely crushed ice.

Grog. Originally a mixture of rum and water that was issued to sailors in the Royal Navy and later improved with the addition of lime juice and sugar. Now a Grog is any kind of drink, usually made with a rum base, fruit, and various sweeteners, and served either hot or cold in a large mug or glass. Reputedly named after Admiral Edward Vernon, who was called "Old Grog" because of the grogram cape he wore.

Highball. Any spirit served with ice and club soda in a medium to tall glass. Other carbonated beverages may be used, but if other ingredients are added, it is no longer a Highball.

Julep. A venerable drink made of Kentucky bourbon, sugar, mint leaves, and plenty of crushed ice. An American classic.

Lowball. A short drink consisting of spirits served with ice alone, or with water or soda in a short glass. Also called *On-the-Rocks*.

Mist. A glass packed with crushed ice to which spirits are added, usually straight.

Mulls. Wine or wine drinks that are heated and served as hot punches. Also called mulled wine from the time when drinks were heated with a red-hot poker, loggerhead, or flip iron.

Neat. A straight shot of any spirit taken in a single gulp without any accompaniment. Also called a *Shooter*.

Negus. A hot, sweet wine drink, with or without spices. Port or sherry is traditional. Named after Colonel Francis Negus, an eighteenth-century English luminary.

Nightcap. Any drink that is taken immediately before retiring. Milk punches, toddies, and short drinks such as liqueurs or fortified wines are favored.

On-the-Rocks. Any wine or spirit poured over ice cubes, usually in an Old Fashioned glass. Also called a *Lowball.*

Pick-Me-Up. Any concoction designed to allay the effects of overindulgence in alcoholic beverages.

Posset. An old English invention consisting of a mixture of hot wine, milk, and spices. Eggs were often used, with or without milk, and ale was sometimes used in combination with wine or used in place of it.

Puff. A combination of spirits and milk mixed in equal parts and topped with club soda. Usually served in an Old Fashioned glass.

Punch. A combination of spirits, wine, sweeteners, flavorings, fruit garnishes, and sometimes various carbonated beverages mixed in and served from a large bowl to a number of people. Individually made punches are called Cups.

Rickey. A drink made with gin or other spirit, lime juice, and club soda, usually served with ice in a small highball or Rickey glass, with or without sweetening. Named for Colonel Joe Rickey, an old-time Washington lobbyist.

Sangaree. A tall drink containing chilled spirits, wine, or beer, sometimes sweetened and given a good dusting with grated nutmeg. There are also recipes for hot Sangarees.

Shooter. A straight shot of whiskey or other kind of spirit taken neat. Also called a *Neat.*

Shrub. Spirits, fruit juices, and sugar, aged in a sealed container such as a cask or crock, then usually bottled.

Sling. A tall drink made with lemon juice, sugar, and spirits, usually served cold with club soda. The most famous Sling is the Singapore Gin Sling. There are also recipes for hot slings.

Smash. A short Julep made of spirits, sugar, and mint, usually served in an Old Fashioned glass.

Sour. A short drink made of lemon or lime juice, sugar, and spirits. The Whiskey Sour is the classic Sour, but it may be made with vodka, gin, rum, brandy, or various liqueurs, especially fruit-flavored cordials such as apricot, peach, etc.

Swizzle. Originally a tall rum cooler filled with cracked ice that was swizzled with a long twig or stirring rod or spoon rotated rapidly between the palms of the hands to produce frost on the glass. The Swizzle, a Caribbean invention, is made with any kind of spirit today and is traditionally served in a tall highball or Collins glass.

Syllabub. An old English recipe consisting of milk, cream, sugar, and spices, blended with sherry, port, or Madeira to produce a very sweet, creamy mixture that is often served in a sherbet glass as a dessert. In a more liquid form it may be drunk like a Posset. There are many variations of the Syllabub.

Toddy. Originally a hot drink made with spirits, sugar, spices such as cinnamon, cloves, etc., and a lemon peel mixed with hot water and served in a tall glass. Now a Toddy may be served cold with ice with any combination of spices and spirits.

Tot. A small amount of any beverage, a "short shot," "a wee dram," "a touch."

HOW TO TASTE A DRINK

Professional blenders depend to a great degree on their olfactory senses rather than their sense of taste. There are many reasons for this, but one important factor is that the sense of smell seems to hold up to extended sampling better than the sense of taste. The sense of smell, in fact, is essential to taste. Most people do not realize the significance of smell until they have severe nasal congestion and discover they have lost their sense of taste. Remembering flavors and aromas is another factor that is essential to tasting, since it is important to be able to recall specific sensory experiences when confronted with a similar scent or taste at another time and in another place. Since most people enjoy the taste of a beverage more than the aroma, the following checklist may be helpful for the nonprofessional in sampling and comparing spirits in their pristine state from the bottle, or in combination with other ingredients.

The author uses the following procedures in evaluating and ranking mixed-drink recipes as well as new distilled products. In the case of *unmixed* spirits, they are tested in sherry glasses, or *copitas*, which have been steam-cleaned without soap or detergents. Samples from freshly opened bottles are mixed with an equal portion of demineralized, distilled water at room temperature. No ice is used. Evaluations are made on color, aroma, flavor, body, aftertaste, and other perceptions relating to longevity of aroma, flavor intensity, smoothness or finish, and off-tastes suggesting chemical additives or woodiness from the barrel, sweetness, acidity, astringency, mustiness, corkiness, bitterness, or any other taste that is perceived as being unpleasant. Flavor accents, or "high notes," that give a beverage distinctively pleasant characteristics are noted in the most specific terms possible. For example, if a straight bourbon has overtones of spice, an effort should be made by the taster to define it. Is it similar to cinnamon, cloves, nutmeg, or is it herbal? If it is perceived as a nutty flavor (a popular descriptive term for certain brandies and fortified wines such as sherry and Madeira), what kind of a nutty flavor? Peanuts, hazelnuts, walnuts, and pecans are all nuts, but have very different flavors. A professional taster must fix a precise, definitive flavor or aromatic experience in his memory so that he can recall this sensory encounter at a future time when a similar (but not necessarily identical) situation arises. This ability to discriminate between subtleties of aroma and taste is one of the essential skills every professional taster or blender must have. Some say that it is a talent one is born with; others believe that much of this ability is acquired through experience.

The tasting/rating of mixed-drink concoctions is not nearly as demanding, and, for most, is more pleasant because the flavor differences are more obvious and require less concentration than that needed by a blender when comparing whiskey samples from different barrels of various ages from the same distillery. But whatever is being sampled, whether it be food or beverages, even the nonprofessional can learn to use his or her senses more effectively. The sense of smell is underused by most people. The proof of this can be demonstrated by asking a friend or associate to sample something to eat or drink. Most people immediately take a taste instead of first giving it a good sniffing. If you want to develop your sense of smell, start sniffing things like a dog. This is a good way to broaden your olfactory horizons and, along the way, you are certain to come across new sensory experiences that may surprise you.

Mixed drinks can be rated on these important factors:

1. Appearance	Appetite appeal is the main thing.
2. Aroma	Try to describe it to someone else.
3. Flavor	Describe first and subsequent impressions.
4. Refreshment Factor	Does it refresh? Is it zesty and satisfying? Does it perk you up?
5. Aftertaste	Does it leave a different taste in your mouth? Is it pleasant or out of keeping with the flavor experience?
6. Longevity Factor	Does it taste as good after a few more sips? After many sips?

When you try a new drink anywhere, even in an elegant restaurant, don't hesitate to take the time to evaluate it to your satisfaction:

Look at it. Does it look appealing, appetizing, tasty? Does it look refreshing? Does the color make you want to taste it?

Smell it. Really use your nose, not once but several times with a rest in between. Is your nose telling you about the ingredients that are in the drink? Is your nose filled with a heady, pleasant bouquet or just an odor that is flat and uninteresting?

Taste it. Take a small sip. Roll it around your mouth. Concentrate on your initial reaction. Now swallow it and remember the sensation. Take another sip and concentrate on the different taste experiences from different parts of your mouth. Try it again and suck in a little air with the liquid. Does it taste differently the second and third time? How? In what way? Is it flavorful? In what way? Is it generally pleasant and satisfying? Is the residual aftertaste good? Does it leave you with a pleasant memory, a good impression? After you have had a whole drink, do you want another? Not right away? Maybe someday? Maybe never?

The same procedures are used in the tasting of wines with certain differences having to do with nomenclature and a profusion of descriptive terms that confuse even some professional vintners.

The key here is concentration. Many people never really know how to taste because from childhood they learn to eat without thinking, seldom use their noses in the eating process, become addicted to certain kinds of food and beverages (e.g., snack foods, ice cream, candy, cheeseburgers, and soft drinks) and are not motivated to try new gustatory experiences. The oft repeated phrase, "I *know* what I like," typifies an attitude that effectively blocks the objective investigation of new flavor experiences. For this reason, travel is a means of broadening one's culinary horizons. When in a foreign land we are often reluctantly forced to try new kinds of things to eat and drink, and frequently with rewarding results. The rapid growth of the popularity of table wines in America was a direct result of increasing travel abroad by Americans, both in the military and civilian life.

WHEN AND HOW TO POUR,
STIR, SHAKE, AND WHIRL

Mastering the techniques of mixology is important to the amateur bartender as well as the professional, for in food and beverage preparation whether in the home or a five-star restaurant, *presentation* is a vital factor in the proper enjoyment of food and drink. Imagine dining in a fine restaurant and being subjected to an embarrassing display of ineptitude by a clumsy captain who in attempting to bone a beautifully prepared Dover sole turns it into a mangled mound of mush. Who could possibly relax at a bar littered with used cocktail napkins, puddles of melted ice, drippings from sloppily poured drinks, and unemptied ashtrays. This says something about the man or woman behind the bar. It says the person in charge doesn't give a damn, and the drinks that are dispensed will undoubtedly reflect this attitude.

Pouring properly requires practice. The experienced pro turns a jigger into a highball glass, pitcher, or shaker with a quick, smooth turn of the wrist that allows no spillage on the bar. The seasoned wine waiter, or sommelier, pours wine at the table with nary a drop to spot the fresh, white linen tablecloth, rotating the bottle ever so slightly each time to avoid drips and filling champagne glasses in stages so the foam never overflows on the table.

Then, of course, there are those who simply do not know how to serve properly. When a young, inexperienced bus boy in a restaurant splatters you with water drops while filling glasses at your table, it is annoying but forgivable. Not so with a professional bartender who is unable to pour a drink into your glass without spilling a portion of it on the bar, or who fills the glass so full that you inevitably dribble some of your cocktail on your clothes. There is also a new breed of bartender: always in a hurry. You order a Martini and he quickly fills a glass to the brim with cracked ice or mini-ice cubes (which pack together so tightly there is very little room for anything else), throws in a dash of vermouth, and then fills it to the rim with gin. No time to stir, or even to ask if you wanted the lemon twist he added gratuitously instead of the olive you prefer. Before you have a chance to ask for your olive, he's off to another part of the bar to hurriedly make another unmixed drink for another potentially dissatisfied customer. Contrast this performance with that of a famous Chicago bar where the barmen take pride in the fact that their Martinis are stirred at least a hundred times before they are served. Perhaps Martinis need not be stirred this much, but drinks do not mix themselves, and at least the customer gets the feeling that someone cares enough to take the time to do what is necessary, in his opinion, to produce an exemplary drink. After all, they say, every really good bartender has to be a little "stir crazy."

Drink recipes requiring the least amount of blending are stirred. Martinis and Manhattans are good examples of simple recipes that are stirred, not shaken. James Bond enjoys his Martinis shaken, not stirred, and there is nothing really wrong about this, since the aeration from the shaking, no doubt, improves the taste of the drink. Why not shake everything, if this is true? The reason is purely cosmetic. Mixing by electric blender or shaker using clear ingredients such as gin and vermouth results in a cloudy drink due to the dispersion of fine air bubbles. Even though the drink eventually clears up, it just isn't as attractive to many people as a sparkling, crystal-clear Martini shimmering in a cocktail glass. On the other hand, a drink recipe containing fruit juices is seldom as good-tasting when stirred as when well shaken or whipped in a blender.

The cocktail shaker was invented long ago for hard-to-mix drinks. This includes fruit-based drinks, recipes using dairy products such as cream and milk, and ingredients that must be mixed thoroughly, such as an egg or a thick sweetener such as coconut syrup or honey. Old-time master bartenders like the legendary Harry Craddock of London's Savoy Hotel took great pride in their skill with the shaker, and some stoutly maintain that many drinks are better made by shaker than by blender. Craddock was fond of helping young bartenders with good advice: "Shake the shaker as hard as you can," he was quoted as saying. "Don't just rock it, you're trying to wake it up, not send it to sleep!"

However affectionately a bartender regards his shaker, there can be no doubt that the electric blender does a superb job in mixing certain exotic, so-called Polynesian drinks that call for a number of different ingredients. Moreover, the blender makes frappéed or "frozen" drinks such as the Margarita in much less time than a hand shaker. A strong case also can be made for the flavor enhancement of the blender through the process of aeration. Take a simple test: Open a carton container of orange juice and pour half into a cocktail shaker and half into an electric blender. Shake and mix the orange juice, with a little cracked ice if you wish, for exactly one minute and pour into glasses. Let your taste be the judge. From that day forward, let your motto be:

> If the flavor has abated,
> It snaps back when aerated.

Much good bartending is simply common sense and attention to detail. Many hallmarks of a good bar operation are just matters of good manners and good judgment. For example, serving a drink in a chilled glass, especially in warm weather, is far more appealing than in a glass that will warm the drink quickly. After all, stemmed glasses were invented so that one could hold a glass of chilled wine or an ice-cold cocktail without having it warmed by the heat of your hand.

When making any kind of mixed drink, do not ruin it by allowing it to drown as a result of too much ice meltage. Use plenty of ice—for most drinks, the more, the better—but mix them briskly and quickly and serve them *immediately*. By the same token, the recipient is well advised to drink his libation while it is crackling cold.

Common courtesy dictates that when a customer or guest drinks his drink and is ready for another, that a fresh start be made. Begin with a *new glass*, properly chilled, and it will look good and taste even better. Nothing is drearier than to refill a used glass. It is something that most of the better commercial bars would never do, but unfortunately, many home bartenders will commit this breach of good bar etiquette during the rush of the party.

MEASURES AND MEASURING

Cheat me on the price,
but don't cheat me on the goods.
—Old New York garment-
district saying

Everyone is entitled to fair measure. In the marketplace it is important because one buys—and sells—according to measures of various kinds. In the home, fair measure has nothing to do with getting value received for your money, but it has everything to do with making or getting a good drink.

Some bartenders, both professional and amateur, do not believe that accurate measuring of drinks is important. There are also good cooks who don't feel that measuring is important. Their argument seems convincing: "You've eaten my food and enjoyed it. Isn't that proof that measuring isn't really necessary?" The problem with the "pinch of this and a dab of that" school of cooking—and with the bartender who pours everything from shoulder height and never uses a measuring cup—is that they not only have difficulty in precisely duplicating their results, but, of much greater consequence, in producing accurate recipes that others can use with any degree of confidence. Many of us have had the experience of trying to get Grandmother's cake recipe without success until someone took the time to stand beside Grandmother, taking notes, checking and measuring every ingredient, and carefully describing the methods used from the flour sifting right through to the final icing and decoration. Even great chefs work from recipes in planning and preparing menus, and, of paramount importance, the others who work in the kitchen must know precisely how to prepare certain dishes. Drink recipes are without question much simpler than food recipes, but the difference between a good drink and a poor one is usually not the ingredients or the recipe, but the person behind the bar, wielding bottle, jigger, shaker, and spoon.

Experienced professional bartenders use the jigger-and-a-splash, the timed speed-pourer, or the "finger method" with a highball glass or mixing glass. But, remember, they have a lot of experience, and it is relegated to probably a dozen drinks that are ordered most of the time by most of the patrons—not counting *unmixed,* mixed drinks such as scotch and soda, Canadian on-the-rocks, bourbon and water, glass of white wine, etc. Many good bars make it a policy to pour generous drinks, especially for the regular customers. The jigger-and-a-splash usually ends up being a two-ounce drink. At the other end of the spectrum, the gyp-bar dispensing by the very same method delivers a wee bit more than an ounce. Then, there is the great middle ground—the big hotels and restaurants as well as bars that do a big business—where strict portion control dictates a measured drink. The ounce-and-a-half jigger is considered standard. The finger method is all right for home use but it is not accurate. Place two fingers around the bottom of the glass and fill the glass to the top of the uppermost finger. Now change glasses. A small glass gives you less and a fat glass gives you more. Slim fingers give you less and plump fingers give you more. That's not portion control. The speed-pourer timed by the bartender's count (usually a four-count) is fast and accurate in practiced hands, but is not recommended for home use because the amateur mixer does not have the volume to require either the speed-pourer or that particular mixing method. The home bartender is better off with a standard, double-ended metal jigger, as is the professional bartender who is using an unfamiliar recipe or a recipe calling for a number of ingredients and fractional measurements.

The mixologist is called upon to use other measures in addition to the jigger, especially when concocting a quantity of party-drink makings in advance or in the making of punches and other beverages for a multitude. This chart shows the relationship between various measures.

MIXOLOGIST'S MEASUREMENT CROSS-CHECK CHART

	Dashes	Barspoons	Teaspoons	Tablespoons	Ounces	Ponies	Milliliters	Jiggers	Wine Glasses	Cups
Dash	1	1/3	1/6	1/18	1/36	1/36	0.81	1/54	1/144	1/288
Barspoon	3	1	1/2	1/6	1/12	1/12	2.43	1/18	1/48	1/144
Teaspoon	6	2	1	1/3	1/6	1/6	4.91	1/9	1/24	1/48
Tablespoon	18	6	3	1	1/2	1/2	14.75	1/3	1/8	1/16
Ounce	36	12	6	2	1	1	29.5	2/3	1/4	1/8
Pony	36	12	6	2	1	1	29.5	2/3	1/4	1/8
Milliliter	0.81	1/3	1/5	1/15	1/29	1/29	1	1/44	1/118	1/236
Jigger	54	18	9	3	1 1/2	1 1/2	44.25	1	3/8	1/5
Wine Glass	144	48	24	8	4	4	118	2 2/3	1	1/2
Cup	288	96	48	16	8	8	236	5 1/3	2	1

This chart is designed to be read across or vertically. The horizontal reading is for the equivalency of various measures. For example, by reading across you can find the equivalent of an ounce or a teaspoon. Reading down will tell you how many ounces are in a wineglass, etc. The relationship of common measures to one another underscores the importance of accurate measuring to produce predictable results.

MEASUREMENT RELATIONSHIPS—U.S. UNITS

These are useful measurements from a cup to a hogshead in case you are planning a lavish party.

$$1 \text{ cup} = \frac{1}{2} \text{ pint} = 8 \text{ fluid ounces} = 2 \text{ gills}$$
$$2 \text{ cups} = 1 \text{ pint} = 16 \text{ fluid ounces} = 4 \text{ gills}$$
$$4 \text{ cups} = 2 \text{ pints} = 1 \text{ quart} = \frac{1}{4} \text{ gallon}$$
$$8 \text{ cups} = 4 \text{ pints} = 2 \text{ quarts} = \frac{1}{2} \text{ gallon}$$
$$16 \text{ cups} = 8 \text{ pints} = 4 \text{ quarts} = 1 \text{ gallon}$$
$$31\frac{1}{2} \text{ gallons} = 1 \text{ barrel}$$
$$2 \text{ barrels} = 1 \text{ hogshead}$$

NEW METRIC SYSTEM MEASURES
FOR DISTILLED SPIRITS

Old Bottle Size	U.S. Measure	New Metric Measure	U.S. Measure	Servings (1½ oz.) Per Bottle
Miniature	1.6 oz.	50 ml.	1.7 oz.	1
Half pint	8 oz.	200 ml.	6.8 oz.	4½
Pint	16 oz.	500 ml.	16.9 oz.	11¼
Fifth	25.6 oz.	750 ml.	25.4 oz.	17
Quart	32 oz.	Liter	33.8 oz.	22
Half gallon	64 oz.	1.76 l.	59.2 oz.	39½

WINE BOTTLE MEASURES

Name	Metric Measure	U.S. Measure	Servings (4¼ oz.) Per Bottle
Split	187 ml.	6.3 oz.	1½
Tenth	375 ml.	12.7 oz.	3
Fifth	750 ml.	25.4 oz.	6
Quart	Liter—1000 ml.	33.8 oz.	8
Magnum	1.5 l.	50.7 oz.	12
Double Magnum	3 l.	101.4 oz.	24

Note: Serving sizes may be adjusted for large groups, but six servings per 750 ml. bottle of still wine is considered standard. In some cases, more servings are indicated for sparkling wines because it was in vogue at one time to serve champagne in a shallow saucer with a capacity of four ounces. But times change and the larger tulip glass, which is considered proper for sparkling wines, holds between six and eight ounces, so the six-per-bottle rule still holds. As has been pointed out in the section on gyp bars and dull drinks, serving a skimpy drink is a false economy. Take the magnum and instead of a 4¼ ounce serving, you economize with a 3½ ounce serving. You will get two more glasses from the bottle, and your guests may wonder if you could afford to give a party. Or, if patrons are buying wine by the glass in a restaurant, the fact that they are getting a small serving will *not* go unnoticed. It's a fact: People would rather pay more for a substantial drink than to be served a miserly drink at any price.

MEASURES FOR FOOD ITEMS
FREQUENTLY USED IN DRINK PREPARATION

(The following measures are approximate.)

1 cup of *heavy cream*, when whipped, yields 2 cups.

A *pinch* of ground pepper or other powdered ingredient is that which can be held between the thumb and forefinger.

A *splash* is an imprecise measure left to the discretion of the cook or mixologist. It is more than a dash and generally conceded to be less than ½ ounce.

Depending on size, 4 to 6 *whole eggs* yield 1 cup; 8 to 11 *egg whites* yield 1 cup; and 12 to 14 *egg yolks* yield 1 cup.

1 *medium lemon* yields 3 tablespoons of juice.

1 *medium lemon* yields 1 tablespoon of grated rind.

1 *medium orange* yields ⅓ cup of juice.

1 *medium orange* yields 2 tablespoons of grated rind.

1 pound *granulated sugar* yields 2½ cups.

1 pound unsifted *confectioner's sugar* yields 4½ cups.

1 pound *brown sugar* yields 2½ cups.

GLASSWARE

Why is it that a drink always seems to taste better when served in a beautiful glass?

The answer, as every astute bartender, perceptive hostess, and experienced restaurateur knows, is presentation. As every caring chef knows, if something looks good, it will probably taste better. At the bar it is not only lovely crystal that counts, but the presentation of a drink, in the right kind of glass, clean, chilled, and properly garnished. In England, whiskey is often served in a stemmed glass similar to a wine goblet. Many Americans find it is an appealing way to serve a Highball. The drink seems to have more importance than when served in a tumbler or ordinary highball glass. It also stays cold longer when held in the hand by the stem.

There are reasons why many drinks are served in special glasses. They usually look better, are made to hold just the right amount of liquid, and often stay cold longer. A Whiskey Sour will probably taste just as good in an Old Fashioned glass as it does in a Whiskey Sour glass, but somehow it wouldn't seem the same to a Whiskey Sour devotee. What about an Old Fashioned in a Whiskey Sour glass? Not likely. The heavy bottom of the Old Fashioned glass serves a purpose. A strong glass is needed to withstand the force that bartenders exert muddling sugar and bitters as well as fruit, which is the traditional method of preparing this drink.

Also, as every professional blender and wine connoisseur knows, certain glasses are designed to present maximum aroma from the glass to the taster. The brandy snifter is perhaps the best known among traditional glasses that enhance the bouquet of spirits. By the same token the large, globular burgundy wine glass is perfectly suited to the business of allowing a fine wine "room to breathe" and give off its rich, complex bouquet. Many experts are of the opinion that the Spanish *copa* or *copita*, the classic sherry wine glass that one finds everywhere in Spain, is the best glass ever made for "nosing," or scrutinizing the olfactory properties of a wine or spirit. For this reason you will find that master blenders in whiskey distilleries invariably are surrounded by an array of *copas* at the blending table.

Glasses that are not designed to potentiate the aroma of their contents still fulfill a special function. A tall Collins glass is made for coolers. Long drinks with ice cubes are not to be bolted down, but savored leisurely on a hot summer evening. Here, the cooling effect and refreshment is the thing, while aroma is a minor consideration. Other glasses like the stately Hurricane or chimney glass and the graceful, willowy stemmed liqueur glass are designed to glorify the drink that is being served. Such appetite-appealing presentation is an important part of going out for cocktails and dinner—and of the mystique or atmosphere that characterizes many outstanding restaurants. In fact, proper presentation is so important that some hotels and grand luxe restaurants have their own custom-designed glassware. Some shapes and designs have become popular enough to be adopted for general usage. The Delmonico glass, also known as the Whiskey Sour glass (or a version thereof) is named after a famous restaurant that flourished in New York at the turn of the century. The very tall Collins glass was devised and popularized by Don the Beachcomber for the Zombie and other tall specialty drinks, just as the original Tom Collins glass is an elongation of the traditional highball glass, which wasn't thought to be glamorous enough for a new generation of specialty, exotic drink creations.

There is nothing more complimentary to a finely made mixed drink or a rare wine than to have it presented to your guest in a lustrous, full-lead, cut crystal glass fashioned by Baccarat, Waterford, Orrefors, or Steuben. The feel, glint, clarity, and design of the crystal all combine to make the cocktail hour or dinner an important occasion. Unfortunately, expensive cut crystal is just not practical for even a five-star hotel or restaurant because of the amount of breakage in any commercial food service operation. However, there are sturdy, attractive makes of good-quality glassware that are suitable for bar and restaurant use. Of equal importance is having a variety of sizes and styles so that wine and mixed drinks may be properly and professionally dispensed. The principal kinds of glasses are:

Shot glass. The original bar measure seen littering saloon bars in a hundred Western movies. Designed to hold one drink ranging from a fraction of an ounce to two ounces or more. Some cleverly designed shot glasses appear to be enormous, but hold less than an ounce.

Pony glass. A stemmed glass holding one to two ounces for liqueurs and brandies.

Cocktail glass. A stemmed glass ranging in size from three to six ounces and with variously shaped bowls.

Highball glass. The familiar, straight-sided glass that usually has a capacity of eight to ten ounces. The present trend is to serve highballs in larger glasses.

Collins or chimney glass. An elongation of the highball glass that holds from ten to fourteen ounces.

Tall Collins or chimney glass. With a capacity of as much as sixteen ounces, this glass is usually used for exotic specialty drinks such as the Zombie or Singapore Sling.

Old Fashioned glass. Sometimes called a "rocks" glass because it is just the right size for a cocktail on-the-rocks or a and a splash of soda or water. Holds from eight to ten ounces.

Double Old Fashioned glass. With its fourteen- to sixteen-ounce capacity, this glass is becoming increasingly popular for all types of drinks.

Whiskey Sour glass. Sometimes called a Delmonico glass, this is the traditional glass for all kinds of sours. Holds from five to six ounces.

All-purpose balloon glass. Originally designed for wine drinking, this big—ten- to fourteen-ounce—glass is being used to serve everything from whiskey to beer and many kinds of cocktails and coolers. May be used when a large wine goblet is specified.

Sherry glasses. The American flared sherry glass holding about three ounces may be used for cordials and liqueurs, but the Spanish *copita,* the traditional flower-shaped sherry glass, is being used more frequently because it enables the drinker to enjoy the full aroma of whatever is in the glass. Capacity is slightly less than four ounces.

Brandy snifter. The classic blown-glass globular shape is designed to funnel all of the bouquet of a fine cognac, armagnac, or Spanish brandy to the brandy connoisseur's educated nose. It comes in many sizes ranging from four ounces to twenty-four ounces, and if you look diligently, you'll even come across some forty-eight-ounce snifters.

Champagne glasses. The champagne saucer, a stemmed glass, has been in use in the U.S. for a long time. It is relatively flat and shallow, disperses the bubbles in the wine rather quickly, and is also subject to spills at a crowded reception or party. It holds from four to six ounces (the larger size sometimes has a hollow stem), but can carry as little as two-and-a-half ounces in glasses used at glitzy tourist bars. The hollow stem is attractive but difficult to clean, so it isn't in general use except in private bars. The tulip glass, with a capacity of from six to nine ounces or more, is artfully designed to conserve the natural carbonation of champagne. It has been popular in Europe for many years and is coming into more common use in this country as *the* correct glass for sparkling wines.

Wine glasses. Wine may be drunk and enjoyed from almost any size or shape of glass. Red wine glasses are usually much larger than white wine glasses so that the bouquet of a full-bodied, robust Burgundy can be enjoyed to the fullest. White wines, with a few exceptions, are not strong on aroma or bouquet, thus the smaller glass, which is easier to chill, and since its contents are consumed more quickly, the wine stays properly cool. In recent years the "all-purpose" wine glass has been promoted aggressively. It is a good compromise for most people who are not in the habit of serving two or three table wines in the appropriate glass during dinner. Red wine fanciers lean toward a large glass with a capacity of sixteen ounces or more, but for many red wine lovers, the ten- to fourteen-ounce all-purpose glass will do nicely.

Beer glasses. Steins and schooners holding as much as a liter of suds were once looked upon as a mark of depravity by non-beer drinkers. But with a strong resurgence of draft beer underway, pint mugs and other large glasses are back in style again. It's the perfect way to drink fresh, foamy beer from the tap. For bottled-beer drinkers, the classic Pilsener glass, footed and shaped like an elongated V, is preferred. Pilsener glasses usually hold ten or twelve ounces of beer.

Specialty glasses. There are many special-purpose glasses that were designed or adapted for a new drink creation. The Irish coffee cup is an adaptation of the hot drink mug used for hot buttered rum and other winter warmers. There are flip glasses, fizz glasses, parfait glasses, water goblets, rickey glasses, compotes, ten-pin glasses, pousse cafe glasses, lamp chimney glasses, and punch cups. It is doubtful that even the largest bar will have all of these containers, but they all have their place in enhancing one's enjoyment of a favorite wine, beer, or mixed drink.

When shopping for glasses, bear in mind that the trend over the years has been to serve drinks in larger glasses. It not only looks better, but for the home bartender it *is* better since large glasses can accommodate many different types of drinks such as a Highball and a tall cooler and one needs less different shapes and sizes. It is interesting to look at old Art Deco cocktail glasses from the 1920s. Many of them held only about three ounces compared with today's four-to-six-ounce glasses. The same is true of wine glasses. Generally among wine lovers who have learned the importance of being able to savor the fragrance of the wine, the attitude seems to be: the bigger, the better.

TOOLS OF THE TRADE

Good tools are essential to good results, so it is important to obtain good basic equipment for the bar before stocking up on the many different kinds of gadgets and novelties that are available in every department store, housewares store, and gift shop.

BASICS

Professional bartender's shaker set. Consisting of a sixteen-ounce mixing glass and metal top, this is a must. Get a fancy cocktail shaker if you like, but for the money the shaker set can't be beat.

Double-ended jigger. The standard metal jigger measures one-and-a-half fluid ounces in the large end and one fluid ounce in the small end. Check capacity with a chemist's graduate or have it checked by your pharmacist as home mixing cups are not precise enough.

Strainers. They come in all sizes and shapes. Get the regular professional bar strainer that fits the mixing glass in your shaker set.

Electric blenders. These high-speed mixers are essential for making many of today's popular mixed drinks. A good blender with a strong motor and variable speeds aerates most drinks in a way that no amount of shaking can accomplish. Some models have blades strong enough to frappe ice cubes (an ordinary blender needs ice cubes that are already cracked).

Corkscrews. Cork extractors come in many styles, but the secret to getting one that can really pull corks is to look for a *coil* and not a screw. The conventional screw-type cork-puller is not wide enough to get a good grip on a bad cork. The coil-type (it looks like a metal worm) does a better job because it is distributed through the cork in a wider area. There are four devices that are better than the old-fashioned corkscrew with a wooden handle, which requires the bottle opener to place the bottle between his legs and pull carefully in order to extract the cork without spilling the wine all over the floor. The **sommelier's corkscrew** (usually a coil) looks like a Swiss Army knife and holds a corkscrew, bottle opener, and a small knife for removing sealing materials from around the cork. It is small, portable, and does the job. The **gourmet** or **wing-type corkscrew** has two arms that rise when it is inserted into the cork. Press down on the arms or wings and the cork comes out. It is reliable in the hands of the inexperienced. The **double-action corkscrew** is ingenious in that once the screw is in the cork, the crossbar that doubles as a handle locks so that you continue turning and the cork is gradually extracted. The pulling—like the wing-type cork—is done by the device and not the bottle opener. Another excellent cork puller is the **Twistup** or cork-fork, which does not employ a screw or coil, but instead two prongs or tines attached to a sturdy handle that are inserted down into the neck of the bottle on each side of the cork. A gentle rocking motion will loosen the cork so that it may easily be extracted. Works well on spongy or crumbling corks that are too soft for a screw-type cork extractor.

Mixing spoons or barspoons. A long-handled spoon is indispensable for stirring mixed drinks, especially in a tall glass. The ten-inch stainless spoon is popular, but some prefer a twelve- or fourteen-inch length.

Measuring spoons. Buy the common kitchen-variety set of four nesting spoons. They are a necessity.

Ice bucket and ice tongs. Keeping a supply of ice by the bar for home entertaining eliminates the need to run back and forth to the refrigerator to get cubes. Ice tongs are a genteel way of serving ice in a drink, and sanitary too. Professional bartenders use an ice scoop, or *should,* since handling ice cubes and handling money is not a desirable combination.

Cutting board and knife. This is basic equipment for any bar and useful for all kinds of drink preparations. Buy a heavy, laminated board no more than eight inches in diameter, for easy storage.

Pitchers. Indispensable for home entertaining, pitchers are necessary for serving water and fruit juices and making stirred drinks such as the Martini and the Manhattan. Highballs for guests made with water from a pitcher rather than from the tap says something about the host.

Juice squeezers. Hand-held and electric juice squeezers are an important bar item. The new generation of compact electric juice squeezers is a real boon to drink making.

Muddler. A good muddler is made of an extremely hard wood such as lignum vitae. It is used to crush condiments and muddle sugar, fruit, and mint for Juleps, Smashes, and Old Fashioneds.

Can and bottle openers. These housekeeping items seem unimportant until they are needed. Keep a sturdy bottle opener, a piercing can opener for soda, and an anchor opener for jars in the bar and another set in the kitchen. A snubber for stubborn jar lids and a conventional, key-operated can opener should be available if needed.

OPTIONAL EQUIPMENT

Electric ice crushers. These labor-saving devices are worth the price if you are going to make drinks like Mint Juleps or frappéed coolers for many guests because crushing ice by hand is tedious and a blender should not be used for extensive ice-crushing.

Wine cork retrievers. These gadgets are the only sure way to salvage corks that have been accidentally pushed down into the bottle. One simple, inexpensive French extractor consists of a wooden handle attached to three long wire rods with little prongs, turned inward, at the end. When the rods are thrust into the bottle they open and surround the cork. When the rods are pulled up, they close tightly around the cork, which is then pulled out.

Stirrers, coasters, and cocktail napkins. These basic hostess items are called for when guests come over for cocktails and add a nice touch. Coasters fulfill a valuable function in keeping rings from wet glasses from marring your furniture.

Champagne buckets and wine coolers. These are more than elegant accouterments for entertaining; they fulfill an important function, since sparkling wines and still white wines lose their chill quickly in a warm dining room unless kept in a bucket or cooler. There are iceless wine chillers on the market and inexpensive wine coolers of conventional design using ice. The classic silver champagne bucket with handles, which looks much like a Grecian urn, is a compliment to anyone's dinner table. There are also sleek modern buckets with stands, which save table space.

Electric juice extractor. This valuable piece of equipment is not to be confused with the electric juicer for oranges, lemons, and limes. It is designed to extract liquid from fruits and vegetables (even nuts), that one normally could not squeeze using home kitchen equipment. Excellent for providing juices for unusual mixed drinks and a wide range of nonalcoholic mixed drinks.

Tap-Icer. Here is a wonderful little invention consisting of a convex steel weight attached to a nine-inch, flexible plastic handle. With a little wrist action it's a snap to crack ice cubes when making individual drinks. The springiness of the handle is the secret, and it has saved many a sore hand.

Gadgets, novelties, and heavy-duty equipment. All of these inventions and refinements have their place. Some are amusing, such as the vermouth atomizer for making Martinis, silver swizzle sticks for hurrying the bubbles out of your champagne and CO_2, corkscrews that push wine corks out of bottles by injecting gas into the bottle. The elegant brass decanting cradles for decanting old vintage wines, giant cork pullers that can disgorge a wine cork with one pull of the handle, temperature- and humidity-controlled wine vaults for the home holding several hundred bottles, and nitrogen-gas wine-preservation units represent the state of the art for serious wine connoisseurs. And for the mixologist, home bars are being custom-built with such conveniences as dual sinks with running water, miniature refrigerators, and special racks to store glasses out of the way yet instantly accessible. The proliferation of ingenious gadgetry, the adaptation of professional heavy-duty equipment to home use, and the increasing popularity of electrically operated labor-saving devices reflect the broadening interest in the world of wines and spirits on the part of people everywhere.

THE SECRET OF EVERY WELL-MADE MIXED DRINK (AND THE MOST OFTEN IGNORED)

Ice. Ice that is pure, fresh, and really ice-cold is the least expensive, yet one of the most important, ingredients in any mixed beverage—and it is the most frequently overlooked even by experienced bartenders. After all, ice is ice. Right?

Wrong. It is true that all ice is frozen water, but there are other important factors to consider even with respect to the temperature of the ice being used.

The first consideration is generosity. Some bartenders, mistakenly believing they are doing a great service for their employers, make stingy drinks. But even a parsimonious barkeep can be lavish with ice. Every drink benefits from generous amounts of ice *properly used.* This does not mean lots of ice to make the weak, watery, pusilanimous cocktails that one is subjected to at gyp-bars and some big commercial hotel and restaurant beverage operations where everything is done by the numbers—to the customer's sorrow. A professional mixologist knows the importance of using ice in generous quantities to chill beverages thoroughly and quickly, while avoiding excessive ice meltage and drink dilution, which is a better way to lose customers than serving a cockroach in a cocktail. Patrons recognize that a bug can find its way into a glass, but a watery drink results from ineptness or the work of a niggardly bartender trying to save a few pennies.

The next factor is quality. All ice is not the same. Ice cubes made from tap water may impart an off taste to drinks due to chlorination and other chemical treatments to safeguard the municipal water supply. Ice stored in the proximity of other refrigerated or frozen food can quickly absorb odors that will definitely affect the quality of mixed drinks. Ice should be made from water that does not have a high mineral content and is not chemically treated—not an easy task for many city dwellers. The answer, of course, is a good grade of bottled water, preferably spring water rather than water that is simply filtered. Drinks made with ice that is pure and unadulterated really sparkle in both taste and appearance. And be sure to store "clean ice" in a freezer compartment that is not used to store other aromatic or strongly flavored foods.

Next to ice-cold drinks come ice-cold glasses and various ingredients for drink mixing. Glasses should always be chilled, especially in warm weather. As one savant said regarding drink temperatures, "A lukewarm drink makes a lukewarm guest." The methods of chilling glasses and ingredients are fairly obvious; it is simply a matter of taking the time to make this extra step a part of your drink-mixing routine.

Big bars and restaurants have cold cases under the bar where glasses, wines, fermented beverages, soft drinks, and fruit juices as well as other ingredients can be stored. This is the most convenient arrangement. Other methods involve plunging glasses upside down into a mound of crushed ice in the proximity of the bar, or filling glasses with cracked ice on the bar as the drink is being made. Punch makings should always be chilled in advance, since warm fruit juices and spirits poured into a punch bowl will melt the ice cake much too rapidly. There is nothing more insipid than a warm punch on a hot summer day. Other popular drinks that are served frequently such as Daiquiris, Martinis, Collinses, and Gimlets may be made with spirits from the freezer, where they are kept at 0°F. There is practically no ice meltage when these supercold rums, gins, and vodkas are used—which is not to everyone's taste. A little ice meltage may be good in that the libations are not quite so strong and the cocktail hour is prolonged for a civilized period of time. But the aficionado who savors the ultra-dry Martini finds zero-degree gin and vodka to his or her liking, all of which brings us to the question: How cold should cold be with respect to drink making?

Ice cubes in a big commercial bar are usually brought in from an ice maker (not situated in the bar) in a large container, and poured into an ice compartment in the bar's well, where they remain until the supply is exhausted or melts away. This ice is not the same as that the home drink mixer uses when he reaches into his freezer for ice cubes from the ice tray. His ice cubes are usually large and quite cold. The commercial bar's ice cubes are almost always half-cubes or small discs that have been sitting in the well at room temperature. The cooling capacity of these different types of ice cubes and the meltage factor is far apart. For this reason the professional bartender needs to use a maximum amount of ice in his shaker and to make the drink with dispatch, whereas the home bartender (working under more leisurely conditions) needs to extend the mixing time so his drinks will not be too strong.

All ice is not equal. It is not alike in appearance, taste, or cooling ability, and the mixologist must take this into consideration, especially when making refreshments for the multitude. The home bartender is admonished to lay in a large supply of ice when entertaining. A safe rule is to arrange to buy commercially made ice. How much should you order? About twice as much as you think you will need. And if you are giving a lawn party or a barbecue in the backyard in mid-August, better make that three times as much.

A WORD ABOUT MIXERS

Besides ice, mixers—carbonated beverages such as club soda, ginger ale, lemon-lime, tonic, cola, and various fruit flavors—are the cheapest ingredients you will use to make an alcoholic mixed drink. When entertaining, buy top-quality mixers because they play an important part in the results you achieve when making highballs, Collinses, coolers, and other party drinks such as a punch. Even when capped with a good sealer or securely fastened by their own screw crown, mixers that have been opened lose their zip after a day or so. Don't use them for guests. Use freshly opened bottles that are well chilled in advance. As we all have experienced, opening a warm bottle of soda on a hot day showers the bartender and others nearby, but the worst thing is that a lot of the fizz that should be in the drink is on the floor.

GYP-BARS AND DULL DRINKS

He was so busy learning the tricks of the trade, he never learned the trade.

—Anonymous

Sooner or later every person who drinks will get caught in a gyp-bar. Contrary to popular belief, gyp-bars are found in some of the best places, not just in sleazy singles-bar mob scenes, tourist-trap nightclubs, and skid-row gin mills. In fact, the gyp-bar is more likely to be the product of greed than poverty, vice, or social degradation. And the root of this evil is often not the bartender, but a stingy restaurant owner, an ambitious, big-hotel beverage manager who wants to look good at the cash register, or a crooked tavern owner who is chiseling and skimming everything in sight to make a few extra bucks. And, yes, sometimes a misguided barkeep may be trying to ingratiate himself with the boss by cutting corners on his customers.

Whatever the reasons, it is the consumer who pays the price. Not only is he defrauded by paying more than he should for what he receives, but he must suffer through weak, watery, poorly made drinks, and in some cases, cheap, substandard liquor. The most common sign of a gyp-bar is a lousy drink. It could be a mistake, but usually it's someone behind the bar hoarding nickels and dimes at your expense. Considering the tremendous profitability of selling liquor by the drink: The difference between a good scotch and soda (usually standardized at a 1½-ounce serving, but frequently closer to 2 ounces in top drinking establishments) and a skimpy 1-ounce drink amounts to only pennies. A 750-ml. bottle of spirits will yield about 17 1½-ounce drinks or about 25 1-ounce drinks. If a bottle of ordinary bar vodka costs $6.00 (remember, he is *not* paying retail prices), 17 1½-ounce drinks will cost him $.35 a drink, and 25 1-ounce drinks will cost him $.24 a drink—a difference of $.11 per drink. But those pennies mount up, you say. They do indeed, but considering the long-term negative effect of customer reaction to poorly made drinks, the proprietor might be far better off if he poured a good drink and charged accordingly. Unfortunately, this logic is lost on the professional chiseler. He will invariably charge the higher price and dispense the smaller drink.

Here are a few of the ways the gyp-bar operates to bilk its clientele:

Dice-ice. Many hotels and restaurants use ice cubes that are smaller than those you make at home in your refrigerator because they chill fast and are easier to handle. But the gyp-bar uses a tiny ice cube known as dice-ice, since they are about the same size as dice or sugar cubes. Their function is to pack a highball or Old Fashioned glass so full there is very little space left for your drink. At a recent visit to a big air-terminal bar we were served whiskey on-the-rocks in a small glass filled with dice-ice. When the contents were poured into another glass there was barely an ounce of liquid, including ice meltage. When this was called to the attention of one of the busy bartenders, he said offhandedly, "That's the regular drink. If you have a complaint, see the boss."

The cheap-shot. The standard glass measure, or shot glass, as it is often called, holds from one and a half to two ounces. Then there is the trick shot glass beloved by the gyp-bar. It is a masterpiece of illusion and surely must have been invented by a magician. It is a shot glass with a heavy bottom and actually appears to be larger than a standard shot glass. It has a white fill-line running around its circumference about a quarter of an inch from the rim. When the bartender serves you a highball, he usually fills it above the fill line so you feel you are receiving not only full measure but a little extra dividend as well. Some dividend! If you examine this cheap-shot glass from the top, you will see that it is conical in shape—wide at the top and ending up as a small point at the bottom of the glass. If you fill this glass to the top and pour the liquid into a standard measuring glass, you find you have been served the total of one ounce of liquid. The amount of liquid you get if your drink is poured to the fill-line is a generous five-eighths of an ounce, yet from the drinker's perspective it appears to be a big belt.

The frigger-jigger. The standard double-ended, or hourglass, jigger, usually made of metal—stainless steel, chrome-plated steel, or silver—has a capacity of one-and-a-half ounces at the large end and one ounce in the small end. From time to time you may come across some old-fashioned jiggers that are one-ounce/one-half-ounce combinations, but these are not in general use at most commercial bars. There are many different ways of measuring in the business of drink making, but the one-and-a-half-ounce serving is now pretty much the rule—except at the gyp-bar. There are many ways of cheating on the portion served, and gyp-bars know them all. One method, unlike the "gyp-flip" and the "pygmy-pourer," takes no skill at all and involves the use of the frigger-jigger, sometimes just called the frigger. It looks like the standard double-ended jigger, but it has a false bottom so that the large end delivers only one ounce and the small end, one-half ounce. The frigger is so skillfully made that the only way to tell the frigger from the standard jigger is to actually measure the contents. However, since most bar patrons do not reach behind the bar to check the house measuring cup, only one's sense of taste can tell them that they are only receiving one ounce of spirits instead of one and a half ounces.

The gyp-flip. More sophisticated cheaters do not need phony jiggers or dice-ice, they can swindle you right before your very eyes by employing the technique known as the gyp-flip. You have, no doubt, often seen busy bartenders pour from the bottle into a jigger, quickly flip it into a glass, and then follow up with a quick pour directly into the glass. In an honest bar you are getting an ounce and a half *plus* by this method. In the dishonest bar you are getting less than the standard measure, since the bartender only fills the jigger a little more than half full on the first pour and just a tiny amount directly from the bottle. You are convinced you are getting a standard drink and a dividend. Actually, the gyp-flip only delivers a scanty one ounce and a wee bit more—quite a difference from the two-ounce drink you thought you were getting.

The pygmy-pourer. Most big bars today have their bottles equipped with "speed-pourers," actually corks that fit into the bottle with a curved metal spout that enables the bartender to quickly, and without spillage, pour from the bottle. Experienced bartenders can time the pouring with extreme accuracy so that exactly the right amount of liquid is delivered to shaker, blender, or glass. The "four count," with bottle inverted, will yield exactly one and a half ounces. With practice, the mixologist learns to count to four at exactly the right speed and pour the correct amount. It is all so simple. How can a gyp-bar find a way around this dispensing technique when the bartender, standing only a few feet away, is pouring drinks in plain view of everyone? Gypsters can always find a gimmick to give them an edge, so the pygmy-pourer was born. The pygmy-pourer looks exactly like the regular speed-pourer, except upon close inspection you will find that the opening at the top of the spout is the same length as the standard pourer, but only half the width. When the pygmy is poured to the count of four, it delivers half the amount delivered by the regular pourer. When viewed from the side, the stream from the pygmy-pourer looks the same as that dispensed by the speed-pourer; only your taste buds can tell you that you've received, and will pay for, a pygmy-sized drink.

The service-bar shuffle. Experienced drinkers imbibe at the bar. They know that the drinks are generally better when made out in the open and you can tell the bartender exactly how you want your drink prepared. Also, there is the incentive of the gratuity, the reward for good drinks and good service. Experienced drinkers also know that drinks made at the service-bar are usually less than generous and many times poorly made. Why? For very sound reasons. In a big bar or restaurant, where many people are served at tables in the dining room or cocktail lounge, the service-bar is often out of sight back in the kitchen area. You won't find the best bartenders stuck back in the service-bar, usually only the juniors, the apprentices. These mixers work alone, their only contacts are the cocktail servers, and if they pour light drinks and run a sloppy bar, no one will know or care unless the boss happens by. A service-bar in a gyp-joint is a license to steal, and nearly everyone at some time has been the victim of the service-bar shuffle. The signs of the gyp service-bar are well known: dice-ice, the "slyball," the "floater," cheap, off-brand liquor, "no-show" drinks, and dull, insipid cocktails.

(For the uninitiated, the slyball is an undersized highball glass with a capacity of six ounces instead of the standard eight to twelve ounces. The reason for this disparity is disarmingly simple: A weak, one-ounce measure would be unacceptable in a twelve-ounce highball glass unless it was packed with dice-ice, which would be a bit conspicuous. So the slyball is used in which the small measure of spirits is tolerable, at least to the unsophisticated drinker.)

If the service-bar is part of a gyp-bar operation, there may be a "midnight bottler" at work, so named since he plys his nefarious trade after the bar is closed. His job is to fill premium "call-brand" bottles (prestigious, well-known brand names that are advertised and promoted) with off-brand spirits such as a cheap, bulk scotch that is shipped in tanks to the U.S. to be rectified and bottled locally. So you order Chivas Regal, and the bottle may have been refilled in the dead of night with Loch Nowhere or Old MacSwigger. One evening an out-of-town friend hosted us for cocktails at a big, bustling hotel bar. He ordered his favorite drink, an Old Forester Old Fashioned. He got Old Overshoe. It was ghastly. He sent it back and got another drink with an Old Forester taste and aroma that didn't last beyond the second sip—a floater, an old routine in the repertoire of the service-bar shuffle. Our curiosity aroused, we returned the following evening, and our friend again ordered his favorite drink with the same disappointing results. Before he sent it back, we placed a small glass button in the Old Fashioned to see if the service bartender would mend his mischievous ways and send us the real premium bourbon that had been ordered instead of a spurious imitation. The "new" drink was back in a trice. My friend sniffed it and sampled it. Again it had a first blush of the real thing that did not last through the second tasting. Another floater? Sure enough, when we held up the glass to the light, our little button was resting on the bottom. Same old glass. Same old hooch. The same old service-bar shuffle. My friend might have received better treatment if he had been sitting at the bar, but if the bottles had been doctored by a midnight bottler, who knows?

There is no defense against the gyp-bar except to question anything that doesn't look, smell, or taste good to you. Speak up! If a drink is poorly made, warm, or watery, send it back. If a drink tastes weak, send it back. If you're paying for a premium gin in your martini, make sure you get it and not Tinker Bell or some other off-brand. If you want a call-brand vodka in your Bloody Mary, you should get it, not Ivan The Terrible or some other obscure name. Some bars don't use any vodka in their Bloody Marys, as some investigative reporters learned when researching a story for a New York magazine. They discovered no-show Bloody Marys in one of the city's more elegant watering places through the simple expedient of taking samples of the drinks that were served at the bar and having them analyzed by a chemist. When confronted by the evidence, the owner, who charges top prices for his restaurant's drinks, said it was all a mistake, an oversight, and that it would never happen again. It *did* happen again. Some weeks later other samples were analyzed in a chemical laboratory, and again, nary a drop of alcohol could be found.

The only way gyp-bars and dull drinks can be eliminated is through vigilance on the part of consumers; perceptiveness (know what you're paying for); and a determined effort by everyone who patronizes a bar or restaurant to, as one old Scot put it, "get the worth of your money."

Awareness of what constitutes a good drink is a first step, whether one is drinking in a public place or in the privacy of one's home.

A COLLECTION OF FINE FLAVORINGS AND EXOTIC SWEETENERS

When drinks need sweetening, we immediately think of white sugar—granulated, superfine, or powdered (confectioners')—or brown varieties or sugar syrup—sometimes referred to in bartender's guides as simple syrup or, in very old drink recipe books, as gomme syrup. Since sugar crystals do not readily dissolve in alcohol, sugar syrup, which is easily made (mix 1 cup of water with 3 cups of sugar and boil for 5 minutes, bottle, and refrigerate), is essential for well-made mixed drinks with a minimum of shaking or blending.

Other commonly used sweeteners include honey, maple syrup, and fruit syrups such as grenadine. All have advantages and disadvantages. Honey is fine for flavor, but difficult to mix in a cold drink unless diluted with warm water in advance. Maple syrup is excellent, but has a very strong flavor, which limits its use as a drink sweetener. Grenadine is better for coloring than sweetening unless it is made from pomegranate juice in a high proportion to the syrup it is mixed with. Cheap grenadines are simply sugar syrups artificially colored and flavored, with a sickish-sweet, cloying taste that is all too evident if used in large amounts in a mixed-drink recipe.

Here are some sweeteners of various kinds that you may want to experiment with. Many are outstanding and contribute to the making of flavorful drinks:

Sirop de citron. A favorite with French cooks and bartenders. Its mild, lemony zestiness makes this acceptable in those recipes in which sweetened fresh lemon juice would be too acidic.

Almond syrup. This is a versatile sweetener for all kinds of tropical-style drinks. Also known as **orgeat syrup** or **sirop d'amandes,** this delightful flavoring may be used in recipes calling for almond extract.

Blackcurrant syrup. Once unknown in bars in the U.S., **sirop de cassis** and its slightly alcoholic cousin, **crème de cassis,** is used in Kir and other vinous and spiritous mixed drinks.

Coffee syrup. This sweetener is used mainly in hot and cold drinks as a flavoring and sweetening agent. It may be used in any recipe in which a coffee flavor is desired.

Fruit syrups. Cherry, raspberry, strawberry, blueberry, gooseberry, and mulberry syrups are used for cooking and may be used in flavoring punches, coolers, and other exotic drinks. To prepare, filter fruit juice through cheesecloth and mix *thoroughly* with sugar (approximately 1 cup sugar to 2 cups juice, depending upon the sweetness of the fruit) and bring to a boil in a saucepan, filter again, and bottle. Most fruit syrups are also commercially available. All fruit syrups should be refrigerated after opening. The addition of vodka or grain neutral spirits (100 proof) will act as a preservative. One ounce of spirits to 10 ounces of syrup should suffice.

Falernum. This spicy, limey, somewhat fruity sweetener with overtones of ginger and almonds originated on the island of Barbados in the West Indies. It was originally concocted, no doubt, for rum drinks, and remains a superb flavoring for drinks made of various fruit juices and rum, gin, or vodka.

Orange syrup. This old-time flavoring dates from pre-refrigeration days when fresh oranges were not always available. It has been supplanted by the real thing, fresh or frozen, and orange liqueurs such as curaçao and triple sec, which are frequently used in mixed-drink recipes as sweeteners. It is still available commercially, although not always easy to find.

Redcurrant syrup. Along with its sister fruit syrup, cassis, *sirop de groseilles* is widely used in France as a flavoring in the kitchen. It also has many uses as a sweetener for beverages.

Coconut syrup. Coconut flavor has become increasingly popular in the U.S. in both food and beverage applications. Coconut syrup has many uses in the making of coolers, punches, and exotic, tropical-style drinks.

Artificial sweeteners. A teaspoon of cane sugar contains about 18 calories. Considering the high caloric content of most fruit-based mixed drinks, the use of synthetic sweeteners, unless one's carbohydrate intake is severely restricted, seems hardly worth the effort; but then, you shouldn't be drinking those sweet concoctions to begin with.

Molasses. Molasses is the product of cane juice reduced by boiling. Unsulfured molasses is considered the most desirable for ordinary kitchen uses. It has a role in the sweetening and flavoring of beverages because it is not as sweet as sugar and imparts a distinctive flavor to foods and mixed drinks. Blackstrap molasses is a product of the third boiling (the first boiling of cane juice is the best) and is as unpalatable and harsh as its name. Sorghum, the juice of sorgo, a cereal grass, is a thinner, slightly sour version of molasses and is used as a molasses substitute. Golden syrup is a processed residual molasses with a light, very agreeable flavor that makes it quite usable in a variety of food and drink recipes. Although treacle is synonymous for molasses in Great Britain, it is usually a mixture of molasses and corn syrup in the U.S. It is not considered a satisfactory substitute for molasses in most food recipes.

Corn syrup. This versatile sweetener has about half the sweetening power of cane sugar, but possesses excellent cooking and food-processing qualities. It is not commonly used in the making of mixed drinks, but has the advantage of smoothing out other ingredients in a mixture and has a more subtle sweetening effect than sugar. It is available in light and dark versions.

Jams, jellies, and preserves. While it might seem improbable that grape jelly, strawberry jam, or pineapple preserves would ever be used in the making of mixed drinks, these popular staples provide a vast, readily available, inexpensive source of delicious and flavorful sweeteners for punches, cocktails, and party drinks. Of course, jams, jellies, and preserves have been around forever—so long, in fact, that their rich source of flavor has lain untapped by America's mixologists. The electric blender has opened up all kinds of new possibilities, and now, once impossible tasks, such as making frappés quickly to order, are easily accomplished. So too are mixed drinks calling for a dab of orange marmalade, a spoonful of damson plum preserves, or a dollop of black raspberry jelly.

In the creation of new mixed drinks, both alcoholic and nonalcoholic, the imaginative use of new kinds of flavorful sweeteners opens up new vistas for the innovative bartender.

A BATTERY OF BITTERS

Bitters live up to their name. They are aromatic mixtures of a variety of botanicals, such as seeds, roots, leaves, fruits, bark, and stems of various flora in an alcoholic base. Once prized for their medicinal qualities, bitters generally are used today as flavor catalysts and enhancers in the preparation of food recipes and a great variety of mixed drinks. Most are proprietary formulas made from closely guarded recipes. A few of these bitter concoctions have become famous as apéritifs rather than miniscule ingredients in mixed drinks to provide a flavor accent. Campari and Amer Picon are well-known examples. Other types of bitters are not intended for beverage use and should not be used for this purpose.

Master bartenders in the nineteenth century prided themselves on the imaginative and skillful use of various bitters to make a mixed drink more flavorful, unique, and perhaps even memorable enough to bring favored customers back for more. Legend has it that the first cocktail was made by a New Orleans apothecary, Antoine Peychaud, who mixed his family's secret bitters formula with brandy and regularly dispensed this mixture at his store located at 437 Royal Street.

Today the mixologist has a battery of bitters available to add subtle nuances of flavor to drinks of all kinds. Some of the famous old names, such as Boker's and Abbott's, as well as a fine imported orange bitters, may not be easy to find, but are surely worth the effort, since they have a valuable place in the world of creative drink making.

Abbott's Bitters. This is a popular general-purpose preparation for food and beverage recipes made by the C.W. Abbott Co. of Baltimore, Maryland.

Amer Picon. A bitter formulation of cinchona bark, oranges, and gentian, which has become popular as an apéritif taken neat or mixed with vermouth, a dash of grenadine, or a soft drink. Made in France by Picon & Co. at Levallois Perret.

Angostura Aromatic Bitters. Introduced in 1824 from a recipe developed by a surgeon, Dr. Johann Gottlieb Benjamin Siegert, who served in the Prussian army under Marshal Blücher at the battle of Waterloo, Angostura Bitters have become indispensable, in the opinion of many, for the making of a proper Pink Gin, Old Fashioned, or Manhattan cocktail. The name comes from the town of Angostura (Ciudad Bolivar), Venezuela, and not angostura bark, which is not used in its manufacture.

Bokers Bitters. This is a famous old name in aromatic bitters. Although it is not in wide distribution, correspondents report that they come across a bottle occasionally and eagerly snap it up.

Boonekamp Bitters. A Dutch product dating back to 1743, this bitters has a largely European following.

Calisay. This is a popular Catalonian specialty made in Barcelona from cinchona and other ingredients. It is more commonly served as an apéritif and as a *digestif* than used as an ingredient in mixed drinks, although it is called for in recipes that appear in old bar books.

Campari. This bitter apéritif with its distinctive brilliant red color and pungent quinine flavor has seemingly become the national drink of Italy. It is frequently drunk with soda or tonic water and is an essential ingredient for several cocktails such as the Negroni and the Americano.

China-Martini. This is another popular Italian bitter liqueur made by Martini and Rossi, and characterized by a quinine flavor and a syrupy consistency. It is not used generally as a cocktail ingredient, but is served rather as an apéritif and an after-dinner drink.

Fernet Branca. Originally compounded for use as a stomachic, Fernet Branca is popular with some drinkers as a hangover remedy. It is a complex, assertive combination of a variety of ingredients including cinchona bark, gentian, rhubarb, calamus, angelica, myrrh, chamomile, and peppermint. It is used as an apéritif to stimulate flagging appetites and as an ingredient in mixed drinks requiring a strong, bitter additive.

Jaegermeister. This complex, aromatic concoction containing some 56 herbs, roots, and fruits has been popular in Germany since its introduction in 1878. It may be used as a cocktail bitters, but is traditionally consumed as an apéritif or an after-dinner drink.

Orange Bitters. Specified in many mixed-drink recipes, orange bitters was very popular during the heyday of the cocktail in the World War I era and the Roaring Twenties that followed. The best orange bitters reputedly come from England, where famous old names such as Field, Son & Co. and Holloway's orange bitters were considered first quality products.

Peychaud's Bitters. Purportedly derived from an ancient and closely guarded family recipe that Antoine Amedée Peychaud, a young French Creole, brought to New Orleans around the latter part of the eighteenth century. Peychaud, an apothecary, made his bitters famous in Louisiana by dispensing it from his pharmacy mixed with French brandy. It was later sold commercially by the L.E. Jung & Wulff Co. of New Orleans and became a staple for many mixed drinks because of its pungent bitter anise flavor. It is essential for making the Sazerac, a classic New Orleans libation.

Stonsdorfer. This is a German proprietary bitters popular as a *digestif*.

Underberg. Well-known in Germany where it is made, Underberg is reputed to work wonders in ameliorating hangovers and calming the morning-after "clangs."

Unicum. Here is a fine old name in bitters, made since 1840 by the venerable Viennese firm of Zwack, originally from Hungary and renowned for their outstanding clear fruit brandies.

Peach Bitters. Popular when Granddad rode home from his favorite saloon in a hansom cab, peach bitters, like many another ingredient that has gone out of style in the making of mixed drinks, will no doubt be rediscovered some day and become all the rage. In the meantime you may have difficulty in finding a bottle of these bitters at your neighborhood store.

WHAT'S IN A NAME?

Bright with names that men remember.
Loud with names that men forget.
                                        —Swinburne

Many drink names are, sad to say, frivolous, overly cute, and inconsequential. Some are precious and contrived either to attract attention, arouse curiosity, or to appear trendy. Worst of all, many drinks that are basically similar except for minor differences have been given different names. You will find some in this book. It is not because of sloppy research or inattention to detail, but because in different parts of the world these concoctions are known by a particular name just as a strip sirloin steak is called a "strip steak" or a "shell steak" or a "New York cut," all names for the same thing in different parts of the country. Or the use of the term "rye" in the Northeast when it is not really rye whiskey that is being ordered, but blended whiskey. But if you order rye in Maryland or some parts of Delaware and Pennsylvania, you get rye—straight rye whiskey.

Although most mixer's manuals are silent on the origin or significance of drink names, there are nevertheless, for the historically inclined, many meaningful names that were given to specific recipes in honor of a person, place, or event. You will find many drinks named after restaurants, bars, hotels, clubs, and resorts. Some of these names live on as the only vestiges of their birthplaces, which long ago succumbed to economic misfortune, natural calamities, or the juggernaut of urban renewal. Many drinks were named in honor of a distinguished or steady customer or a novel, stageplay, musical comedy, or a motion picture; some forgotten, but many well remembered. Stars of opera, ballet, stage, and screen have often been recipients of this special kind of liquid tribute. The list also includes kings and queens, presidents, political candidates who didn't make it; wars, battles, and peace treaties; athletic victories, civic events, and all manner of anniversaries in recognition of everything from the invention of the electric light to the one hundredth birthday of the Statue of Liberty.

Place names have always been popular, and in perusing this book you will find many, including a number of Indian names as well as drinks that have been named after cities and towns. There is scarcely a major city in the world that has not been lionized by its own specially created drink. And then, of course, there are many drink mixtures that have been named after family, friends, and business associates. If you feel like naming a cocktail after someone, invent a drink or take one you like and customize it to your own tastes. Who knows, you may like it so much, you'll do as so many others have done: Name it for yourself.

GIN: THE JOYS OF JUNIPER

Get me out of this wet coat
and into a dry martini.
—Robert Benchley

A well-made gin is a work of art. It is a product of the blender's talent and skill. Juniper, and the many botanicals (extracts from roots, leaves, bark, seeds, etc., of plants) of which gin is composed, make up its essential quality and character. It is unaged and, except for dilution with water, is bottled just as it comes from the still. The first distillation results in a grain neutral spirit. After dilution with distilled water the neutral spirit is distilled once more in a gin still with all of the flavoring agents either mixed into the spirits or placed in racks and percolated by the spirit vapors during the redistillation process. Some American gins are compounded, which simply means that spirits are mixed with the essential oils of various botanicals without redistillation. Sometimes botanicals are added to the grain mash before it has been distilled the first time, and the entire process is carried out in a single distilling cycle. Every distiller has slightly different methods of achieving their desired result. The important thing to remember is that gin is a flavored spirit. Without flavorings it would not be gin. It would be vodka.

Every gin distiller has a treasured, secret recipe that is usually known to but a few and guarded like the crown jewels. What does gin contain? A broad spectrum of botanicals chosen from around the world for their particular flavor and aromatic qualities. Here is a typical sampling of ingredients with the omission of a secret ingredient or two: juniper berries (a primary ingredient), coriander seeds, angelica root, orris (iris) root, licorice, lemon peel, orange peel, almonds, cassia bark, cardamom seeds, anise, caraway seeds, fennel, cinnamon bark, bergamot, and cocoa.

As with so many spiritous inventions, gin began life as a

possible therapeutic specific for certain tropical diseases that sailors on Dutch East India Company ships were bringing back to the Netherlands in the seventeenth century. In the year 1650 Franciscus de la Boe, also known as Dr. Sylvius, a professor of medicine at the University of Leiden, was diligently searching for ways to cope with these exotic maladies from faraway places. It is recorded that he was unsuccessful in his research, but he did discover something else that had demonstrable medicinal qualities when taken in moderation: a spirituous infusion of juniper berries. Juniper had been used by physicians to help reduce fever with some success. Although this juniper infusion did not cure tropical afflictions, it had other benefits as a sedative, a mild diuretic, a vasodilator that can be beneficial for many types of cardiac conditions; as well as a stimulant to the appetite and a tonic for the elderly.

Dr. Sylvius called his discovery "aqua vitae," which gives some hint as to the high esteem he held for his invention. His countrymen called it jenever, the Dutch name for juniper. The French named it genièvre, which, so the story goes, the English interpreted as having something to do with Geneva (which they later contracted to gin). Jenever (genièvre or genever) pertains to juniper the fruit, not Geneva the city. Jenever was also called Schiedam gin or Hollands gin, referring to the city and country of origin. Whatever the etymology, one thing seems to be well documented: English soldiers fighting in the Netherlands in the late seventeenth century tried the spirit, liked its pungent, assertive flavor, and piquant aroma. Because of its restorative powers, they christened it "Dutch courage," and took ample supplies of jenever back to England in the same manner that the armies of Henry II in 1170 brought whisky home from their forays in Ireland. In both instances it was much appreciated by the populace, since the English have never been diffident in matters of libationary pursuits.

In the later part of the seventeenth century, distilleries began to proliferate in England and the Netherlands, but the flavor characteristics of the spirits produced became quite different. In the Netherlands the center of the distilling industry was in Schiedam near the great port of Rotterdam, a strategic location (the grain poured in from as far away as Russia, and the spirits poured out). The popularity of jenever was accelerated by the war in progress with the French because imports of French brandy were shut off. The Dutch, who were great lovers of brandy, turned to jenever, and the distilleries of Schiedam covered the city with a pall of black smoke so dense it became known as the Black City, or Black Nazareth.

About the same time in England (1690) the Parliament under William of Orange passed "An Act for the Encouraging of the Distillation of Brandy and Spirits from Corn." This not only was a great boon to British distillers, but the increased use of corn instead of barley malt made a difference in the flavor of English gin, which became more pronounced with the passing of time. English gin tended to be lighter in body and taste and eventually became famous as London dry gin with a characteristic crisp, clean juniper flavor. Jenever, on the other hand, retained its original full-bodied quality with a definite malty aroma and taste that reflects a high proportion of barley malt that is used in the mash.

Today, jenever is widely consumed in the Netherlands and is not used for cocktails because of its pronounced flavor, but rather drunk like Scandinavian *snaps*, or aquavit, neat or with quantities of wonderful Dutch beer. Jenever is aged, unlike London dry gin, and there is an old (*oude*) and a young (*jonge*) type of jenever, the latter being the most popular in the Netherlands, due, no doubt, to the fact that it is lighter and has less of a malt flavor than the old type.

London dry gin is made in the United States, and some of the American formulas have gained popularity on their own merits. The term "dry" has become outmoded, since almost all gin is dry today. An exception is Old Tom gin, which can be best described as a sweetened gin. It has become a rare commodity because the trend of popular tastes, as gauged by the relentless pursuit of the driest possible gin for the driest possible Martini, may be approaching absolute alcohol with barely a wisp of flavor. All of which means that Old Tom has become old hat. But don't count it out. Old things have a way of being recycled in the most improbable ways and at the most unexpected times.

Another distinguished gin is called Plymouth, not a brand but a type of English gin that is strongly flavored and quite aromatic. Tradition has it that the Royal Navy used Plymouth gin and Angostura bitters to concoct the first Pink Gin, a stomachic and a tonic that was used to guard against the ravages of loathsome and insidious tropical diseases. It didn't work any better than gin and quinine water for preventing malaria in India, Burma, and Malaysia for Her Majesty's forces during the days of the British Raj.

Aside from its apparent lack of efficacy in combating tropical diseases, gin is quite remarkable as a beverage. It is, aside from vodka, the most mixable of all those spirits having distinct flavors of their own, and for this reason mixed-drink recipes using gin as a base occupy large portions of every mixer's manual and bartender's guide.

ABBEY No. 1

1½ oz. gin
¾ oz. Lillet blanc
¾ oz. orange juice
Maraschino cherry or orange
   peel

Mix all ingredients, except
cherry, with cracked ice and strain
into a chilled cocktail glass.
Garnish with cherry or orange
peel.

ACACIA

2 oz. gin
½ oz. Benedictine
Dash kirsch
½ oz. lemon juice

Mix with cracked ice in a shaker
or blender and strain into a
chilled cocktail glass.

ADMIRAL BENBOW

2 oz. gin
1 oz. dry vermouth
½ oz. lime juice
Maraschino cherry

Pour all ingredients, except
maraschino cherry, into a mixing
glass with several ice cubes.
Stir well and strain into a chilled
Old Fashioned glass

ADMIRAL COCKTAIL

2 oz. gin
¾ oz. lime juice
½ oz. Peter Heering or Cherry
   Marnier

Mix with cracked ice in a
shaker or blender and strain into
a chilled cocktail glass.

ADMIRALTY COCKTAIL

1 oz. gin
½ oz. dry vermouth
½ oz. apricot brandy
1 tsp. lemon juice

Mix all ingredients with cracked
ice in a shaker or blender. Pour
into a chilled Old Fashioned
glass.

ALASKA

1½ oz. gin
¾ oz. yellow Chartreuse
Several dashes orange bitters

Mix all ingredients with cracked
ice in a shaker or blender. Strain
into a chilled cocktail glass.

ALBEMARLE FIZZ

1½ oz. gin
½ oz. lemon juice
1 tsp. raspberry syrup
Several dashes framboise or
   raspberry schnapps
Club soda

Mix all ingredients with cracked
ice in a shaker or blender and
pour into a chilled highball
glass. Add ice cubes if necessary
and fill with club soda.

ALEXANDER'S BROTHER

1 oz. gin
1 oz. crème de cacao
1 oz. heavy cream

Mix all ingredients with cracked ice
in a shaker or blender and strain
into a chilled cocktail glass.

ALEXANDER'S SISTER

1½ oz. gin
½ oz. white or green crème
   de menthe
¾ oz. heavy cream

Mix all ingredients with cracked
ice in a shaker or blender and
strain into a chilled cocktail
glass.

ALFREDO

1½ oz. gin
1½ oz. Campari
Orange peel

Mix all ingredients, except orange
peel, with cracked ice in a shaker
or blender. Pour into a chilled
Old Fashioned glass. Twist orange
peel over drink and drop in.

ALMOND COCKTAIL

2 oz. gin
1 oz. dry vermouth
6 slivered almonds
Peach kernel, crushed
½ tsp. sugar syrup
1 tsp. kirsch
½ oz. peach brandy

Warm gin. Add almonds, peach
kernel, and sugar syrup. Chill
and pour mixture into a chilled
Old-Fashioned glass along with
several ice cubes. Add remaining ingredients and stir.

BARTENDER'S SECRET NO. 1

Beware the "soda gun" and how you use it. This invention is
popular in big, busy bars, enabling bartenders (and others at

the service end of the bar) to fill glasses with carbonated mixers at a machine-gun pace. The device consists of a battery of buttons and a pouring spout attached to a long hose that leads to storage tanks under the bar. At the press of a button the soda gun—also known as the "arm" or the "snake"—will dispense cola, lemon-lime soda, ginger ale, club soda, or water. It's a handy, time-saving gadget, good for busy bartenders, not so good for unbusy customers. Some people complain that frequently the carbonation is not what it should be, meaning that their drinks are flat, not bubbly. The more serious problem is the mixing of flavors from the small amount of residue left from the last filling. Super-premium spirits selling at super-premium prices deserve the best mixer money can buy, which explains why top bars use bottled mixers.

AMAGANSETT

1½ oz. gin
½ oz. dry vermouth
½ oz. Pernod
1 tsp. white crème de menthe

Mix all ingredients with cracked ice in a shaker or blender and strain into a chilled cocktail glass.

AMER PICON COOLER

1 oz. gin
1½ oz. Amer Picon
½ oz. Peter Heering
1 tsp. sugar syrup or to taste
1 tsp. lemon juice
Club soda

Mix all ingredients, except club soda, with cracked ice in a shaker or blender and pour into a chilled highball glass. Fill with club soda.

 ANITA'S SATISFACTION

1½ oz. dry gin
Several dashes grenadine
Several dashes Angostura
  bitters
Several dashes orange bitters

Mix all ingredients with cracked ice in a shaker or blender and strain into a chilled cocktail glass.

ANTIBES

1½ oz. dry gin
½ oz. Benedictine
2 oz. grapefruit juice
Orange slice

Mix all ingredients, except orange slice, with cracked ice in a shaker or blender and pour into a chilled Old-Fashioned glass. Garnish with orange slice.

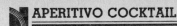 **APERITIVO COCKTAIL**

1½ oz. dry gin
1 oz. Sambuca Romana
   liqueur
Several dashes orange bitters

Blend all ingredients in a mixing glass with plenty of cracked ice and strain into a chilled cocktail glass.

APPIAN WAY

1½ oz. gin
½ oz. Strega
½ oz. amaretto
Orange slice

Mix all ingredients, except orange slice, with cracked ice in a shaker or blender and strain into a chilled cocktail glass. Decorate with orange slice.

ARUBA

1½ oz. gin
½ oz. curaçao
1 oz. lemon juice
1 egg white (for two drinks)
1 tsp. orgeat or Falernum
   syrup

Mix all ingredients with cracked ice in a shaker or blender and strain into a chilled cocktail glass.

ASCOT

1 oz. gin
½ oz. dry vermouth
½ oz. sweet vermouth
1 tsp. anisette
Generous dash Angostura
   bitters
Lemon peel

Mix all ingredients, except lemon peel, with cracked ice in a shaker or blender and strain into a chilled cocktail glass. Twist lemon peel over drink and drop into glass.

 AVIATION

1½ oz. gin
½ oz. lemon juice
½ tsp. maraschino liqueur
½ tsp. apricot brandy

Mix all ingredients with cracked ice in a shaker or blender and strain into a chilled cocktail glass.

BACK BAY BALM

1½ oz. gin
3 oz. cranberry juice
½ oz. lemon juice
Several dashes orange bitters
Club soda

Pour all ingredients, except club soda, into a chilled highball glass with several ice cubes and stir gently. Fill with club soda.

BALI HAI

1 oz. gin
1 oz. light rum
1 oz. okolehao
1 oz. lemon juice
3 oz. lime juice
1 tsp. orgeat or sugar syrup to taste

Brut champagne

Mix all ingredients, except champagne, with cracked ice in a shaker or blender. Pour into a chilled Collins glass and fill with cold champagne.

BARBARY COAST

¾ oz. gin
¾ oz. light rum
¾ oz. scotch
¾ oz. white crème de cacao
¾ oz. cream

Mix all ingredients with cracked ice in a shaker or blender and pour into a chilled Old-Fashioned glass.

BARNEGAT BAY COOLER

2 oz. gin
3 oz. pineapple juice
½ oz. lime juice
1 tsp. maraschino liqueur
Club soda or lemon-lime soda or ginger ale

Mix all ingredients with cracked ice in a shaker or blender. Pour into a chilled double Old-Fashioned glass.

BARNUM

1½ oz. gin
½ oz. apricot brandy
Several dashes Angostura bitters
Several dashes lemon juice

Mix all ingredients with cracked ice in a shaker or blender and strain into a chilled cocktail glass.

BAYARD FIZZ

2 oz. gin
½ oz. maraschino liqueur
1 oz. lemon juice
1 tsp. raspberry syrup
Club soda
2 raspberries

Mix all ingredients, except club soda and raspberries, with cracked ice in a shaker or blender and strain into chilled highball glass. Fill with club soda, stir gently, and garnish with raspberries.

BEAULIEU BUCK

2 oz. gin
½ oz. Cointreau
Several dashes dry vermouth
Ginger ale
Lime wedge

Mix all ingredients, except ginger ale and lime wedge, with cracked ice in a shaker or blender and pour into a chilled highball glass. Fill with ginger ale and squeeze lime over drink and drop into glass.

BEEKMAN PLACE COOLER

1½ oz. gin
1 oz. sloe gin
3 oz. grapefruit juice
½ oz. sugar syrup
Club soda

Mix all ingredients, except soda, with cracked ice in a shaker or blender and pour into a chilled Collins glass. Fill with cold club soda and stir gently.

BEE'S KNEES

1½ oz. gin
1 tsp. honey
Several dashes lemon juice
    or to taste

Mix all ingredients with cracked ice in a shaker or blender. Strain into a chilled cocktail glass.

BELGRAVIA

1 oz. gin
½ oz. Dubonnet blanc
1 tsp. maraschino liqueur
3 oz. champagne or dry
    sparkling wine
Orange peel

Mix all ingredients, except wine and orange peel, in a mixing glass with ice and strain into a chilled wine goblet. Fill with champagne. Twist orange peel over drink and drop into glass.

BERLINER

1½ oz. gin
½ oz. kummel
½ oz. dry vermouth
½ oz. lemon juice

Mix all ingredients with cracked ice in a shaker or blender and strain into a chilled cocktail glass.

BERMUDA COCKTAIL

1½ oz. dry gin
1 oz. apricot brandy
½ oz. lime juice
1 tsp. Falernum or sugar
   syrup
Dash grenadine
Orange peel
½ tsp. curaçao

Mix all ingredients, except orange peel and curaçao, with cracked ice in a shaker or blender and pour into a chilled Old-Fashioned glass. Twist orange peel over drink and drop into glass and top with curaçao.

BERMUDA HIGHBALL

oz. gin
1 oz. brandy
1 oz. dry vermouth
Club soda or ginger ale

Pour all ingredients, except club soda, into a chilled highball glass with several ice cubes. Fill with club soda or ginger ale.

BETWEEN THE SHEETS No. 2

1 oz. gin
1 oz. brandy
1 oz. Cointreau

Mix all ingredients with cracked ice in a shaker or blender and strain into a chilled cocktail glass.

BIG JOHN'S SPECIAL

3 oz. grapefruit juice
1½ oz. gin
1 oz. vodka
1 oz. orange juice
Several dashes orange flower
   water
4 maraschino cherries

Several dashes maraschino
   cherry juice
Wedge preserved cocktail
   orange

Mix all ingredients with crushed ice in a blender or shaker until frapéed. Serve in double Old Fashioned glass.

BISCAYNE

1 oz. gin
½ oz. light rum
½ oz. Forbidden Fruit
½ oz. lime juice
Lime slice

Mix all ingredients, except lime slice, with cracked ice in a shaker or blender and strain into a chilled cocktail glass. Garnish with lime slice.

BISCAYNE BREAKFAST JOY

2 oz. gin
½ oz. frozen grapefruit concentrate
1 oz. frozen orange juice concentrate
1 tsp. orgeat syrup

Several dashes grenadine
Several dashes kirsch

Mix all ingredients with cracked ice in a shaker or blender. Pour into a chilled Old Fashioned glass.

BISHOP'S COCKTAIL

2 oz. gin
2 oz. ginger wine

Mix all ingredients with cracked ice in a shaker or blender and strain into a chilled cocktail glass.

BITER

1½ oz. gin
¾ oz. green Chartreuse
¾ oz. lemon juice
Dash Pernod

Mix with cracked ice in a shaker or blender and strain into a chilled cocktail glass.

BLOODHOUND

1½ oz. gin
½ oz. sweet vermouth
½ oz. dry vermouth
1 tsp. strawberry liqueur

Several whole strawberries

Mix all ingredients with cracked ice in a blender and pour into a chilled cocktail glass.

BLOOMSBURY BLAST

1½ oz. gin
1½ oz. medium sherry
½ tsp. sweet vermouth
½ tsp. dry vermouth
¼ oz. curaçao
¼ oz. cherry brandy

¼ oz. crème de cacao
1 oz. lemon or lime juice

Mix all ingredients with plenty of cracked ice in a shaker or blender and pour into a large, chilled wine goblet.

BODEGA BOLT

1 oz. gin
1 oz. fino or amontillado
  sherry
Club soda
Lime peel

Pour gin and sherry into chilled
highball glass with several ice
cubes and fill with club soda.
Stir gently and twist lime peel
over drink and drop into glass.

BONNIE PRINCE

1½ oz. gin
½ oz. Lillet blanc
¼ oz. Drambuie
Orange peel

Mix all ingredients, except orange
peel, with cracked ice in a shaker
or blender and strain into a chilled
cocktail glass. Twist orange peel
over drink and drop into glass.

BORDEAUX COCKTAIL

1 oz. gin
¾ oz. Cordial Medoc
½ oz. dry vermouth
½ oz. lemon juice

Mix all ingredients with cracked
ice in a shaker or blender and
strain into a chilled cocktail
glass.

BOOMERANG No. 2

1½ oz. gin
¾ oz. dry vermouth
Several dashes Angostura
  bitters
Several dashes maraschino
  liqueur

Lemon peel

Mix all ingredients, except
lemon peel, with cracked ice in a
shaker or blender and strain
into a chilled cocktail glass. Twist
lemon peel over drink and drop
into glass.

BOTANY BAY

2 oz. gin
4 oz. orange juice
4 oz. grapefruit juice
1 oz. boysenberry syrup

Mix with cracked ice in a
shaker or blender and pour into a
chilled double Old Fashioned
glass.

BRAVE COW

1½ oz. gin
1½ oz. Kahlua
Lemon peel

Pour gin and coffee liqueur into a
chilled Old Fashioned glass with
several ice cubes. Twist lemon
peel over drink and drop into
glass and stir.

BRISTOL COCKTAIL

1½ oz. gin
½ oz. ruby port
Several dashes Pernod

Mix all ingredients with cracked
ice in a shaker or blender and
pour into a chilled cocktail glass.

BRITTANY

1½ oz. gin
½ oz. Amer Picon
½ oz. orange juice
½ oz. lemon juice
1 tsp. sugar syrup
Orange peel

Mix all ingredients, except orange
peel, with cracked ice in a shaker
or blender and strain into a chilled
cocktail glass. Twist orange peel
over drink and drop into glass.

BRITTANY FIZZ

1 oz. gin
1 oz. brandy
1 oz. dry vermouth
Club soda
Lemon peel

Mix all ingredients, except club

soda and lemon peel, with cracked
ice in a shaker or blender and
pour into a chilled highball
glass. Fill with club soda and
twist lemon peel over drink
and drop into glass.

BROKEN SPUR

1 oz. gin
1½ oz. white port
1 oz. sweet vermouth
1 tsp. anisette
1 egg yolk

Mix all ingredients with cracked
ice in a shaker or blender. Pour
into a chilled Old Fashioned
glass.

BRONX COCKTAIL, The Original

1½ oz. gin
½ oz. orange juice
Dash dry vermouth
Dash sweet vermouth

Mix all ingredients with cracked
ice in a shaker and strain into a

chilled cocktail glass.
Note: Johnnie Solon, a famous
bartender at the old Waldorf-
Astoria Hotel in New York, is
credited with inventing this
drink.

BRONX COCKTAIL

1½ oz. gin
½ oz. dry vermouth
½ oz. sweet vermouth
1 oz. orange juice

Mix all ingredients with cracked
ice in a shaker or blender and
strain into chilled cocktail glass.
Note: For a dry Bronx cocktail,
omit sweet vermouth.

BRONX GOLDEN

1½ oz. gin
½ oz. dry vermouth
½ oz. sweet vermouth
1 oz. orange juice
1 egg yolk

Mix all ingredients with cracked ice in a shaker or blender and strain into a chilled cocktail glass.

BRONX SILVER

1½ oz. gin
½ oz. dry vermouth
½ oz. sweet vermouth
1 oz. orange juice
1 egg white

Mix all ingredients with cracked ice in a shaker or blender and strain into a chilled cocktail glass.

BRYN MAWR COCKTAIL

1½ oz. gin
½ oz. apricot liqueur
½ oz. lime juice
1 tsp. grenadine

Mix all ingredients with cracked ice in a shaker or blender and pour into a chilled cocktail glass.

THE BULLDOG CAFE

½ oz. gin
½ oz. rye
½ oz. sweet vermouth
½ oz. brandy

Several dashes triple sec or orange bitters

Mix all ingredients with cracked ice in a shaker or blender and strain into a chilled glass.

B.V.D.

¾ oz. gin
¾ oz. light rum
¾ oz. dry vermouth

Mix all ingredients with cracked ice in a shaker or blender and strain into a chilled cocktail glass.

CABARET No. 1

1½ oz. gin
1½ oz. Dubonnet rouge
Several dashes Angostura
  bitters
Several dashes Pernod
Maraschino cherry

Mix all ingredients, except maraschino cherry, with cracked ice in a shaker or blender and strain into a chilled cocktail glass. Garnish with cherry.

CABARET No. 2

1½ oz. gin
½ oz. dry vermouth
½ oz. Benedictine
Several dashes Angostura
  bitters
Maraschino cherry

Stir all ingredients, except
cherry, in a mixing glass with
cracked ice and strain into a
chilled cocktail glass. Garnish
with cherry.

CAFÉ DE PARIS

2 oz. gin
½ oz. heavy cream
1 tsp. Pernod
1 egg white (for two drinks)

Mix all ingredients with cracked
ice in a shaker or blender and
strain into a chilled cocktail
glass.

CAGNES-SUR-MER

1½ oz. gin
½ oz. Forbidden Fruit
½ oz. curaçao
2 oz. orange juice
½ tsp. lemon juice
Several dashes orange bitters
Club soda
Orange slice

Mix all ingredients, except club
soda and orange slice, with
cracked ice in a shaker or
blender and pour into chilled
Collins glass. Fill with club
soda and garnish with orange
slice.

CANNES CHAMPAGNE CUP

1 oz. gin
Several dashes Angostura
  bitters
Several dashes prunelle or
  framboise
Several dashes crème de
  cassis
Orange peel

Pour gin, bitters, prunelle, and
cassis into a chilled highball
glass with several ice cubes.
Fill with champagne. Stir gently
and twist orange peel over
drink and drop into glass.

CARMEN CAVALLERO

1 oz. gin
¾ oz. dry vermouth
¾ oz. dry sherry
Dash curaçao

Pour all ingredients into a mixing glass with several ice cubes.
Stir and strain into a chilled
cocktail glass.

CHANTICLEER

2 oz. gin
1 oz. lemon juice
½ oz. raspberry syrup or to
  taste
1 egg white (for two drinks)

Mix all ingredients with cracked ice in a shaker or blender and pour into a chilled Old Fashioned glass.

CHATHAM

1½ oz. gin
½ oz. ginger-flavored brandy
½ oz. lemon juice
1 tsp. sugar syrup
Small section of preserved
  ginger

Mix all ingredients, except ginger, with cracked ice in a shaker or blender and strain into a chilled cocktail glass. Garnish with ginger.

CHERRY BANG!

1½ oz. gin
½ oz. Cherry Marnier
¼ oz. maraschino liqueur
½ oz. lemon juice
Several dashes kirsch
Maraschino cherry

Mix all ingredients, except kirsch and cherry, with cracked ice in a shaker or blender and strain into chilled cocktail glass. Garnish with cherry and top with kirsch.

CHERRY COBBLER

1½ oz. gin
½ oz. Peter Heering
½ oz. crème de cassis
½ oz. lemon juice
½ oz. sugar syrup
Lemon slice
Maraschino cherry

Mix all ingredients, except lemon slice and cherry, with cracked ice in a shaker or blender and pour into chilled Old Fashioned glass. Garnish with lemon slice and maraschino cherry.

CHOCOLATE SOLDIER

1½ oz. gin
1 oz. Dubonnet rouge
½ oz. lime juice

Mix all ingredients with cracked ice in a shaker or blender and pour into a chilled Old Fashioned glass.

CLARIDGE COCKTAIL

1½ oz. gin
1 oz. dry vermouth
½ oz. apricot brandy
½ oz. triple sec

Mix all ingredients with cracked ice in a shaker or blender and strain into a chilled cocktail glass.

CLOISTER

1½ oz. gin
½ oz. yellow Chartreuse
½ oz. grapefruit juice
1 tsp. lemon juice
1 tsp. sugar syrup or to taste

Mix all ingredients with cracked ice in a shaker or blender and strain into a chilled cocktail glass.

CLOVER CLUB

1½ oz. gin
1 oz. lime juice
½ oz. grenadine
1 egg white (for two drinks)

Mix all ingredients with cracked ice in a shaker or blender and strain into a chilled cocktail glass.

COCO CHANEL

1 oz. gin
1 oz. Kahlua or Tia Maria
1 oz. heavy cream

Mix all ingredients with cracked ice in a shaker or blender and strain into a chilled cocktail glass.

COCONUT GIN

1½ oz. gin
¼ oz. cream of coconut
¾ oz. lemon juice
¼ oz. maraschino cherry juice
   or 1 tsp. maraschino
   cherry liqueur

Mix all ingredients with cracked ice in a shaker or blender and strain into a chilled cocktail glass.

COLONY CLUB

1½ oz. gin
1 tsp. anisette
Several dashes orange bitters

Mix all ingredients with cracked ice in a shaker or blender and strain into a chilled cocktail glass.

CONNECTICUT BULLFROG

2 oz. gin
½ oz. light or gold rum
½ oz. lemon juice
½ oz. maple syrup or to taste

Mix all ingredients with cracked ice in a shaker or blender and strain into a chilled cocktail glass.

COPENHAGEN DREAM

1½ oz. gin
½ oz. aquavit
½ oz. lemon juice
1 tsp. sugar syrup or to taste
1 tsp. heavy cream
1 egg white (for two drinks)

Mix all ingredients with cracked ice in a shaker or blender and pour into a chilled Old Fashioned glass.

CORDIAL MÉDOC SOUR

1½ oz. gin
¾ oz. Cordial Médoc
½ oz. lemon juice
Orange slice

Mix all ingredients, except orange slice, with cracked ice in a shaker or blender and strain into a chilled Whiskey Sour glass. Garnish with orange slice.

CORNELL COCKTAIL

2 oz. gin
½ oz. maraschino liqueur or to taste
1 egg white (for two drinks)

Mix with cracked ice in a shaker or blender and strain into a chilled cocktail glass.

CORONADO

1½ oz. gin
½ oz. curaçao
2 oz. pineapple juice
Several dashes kirsch
Maraschino cherry

Mix all ingredients, except maraschino cherry, with cracked ice in a shaker or blender and pour into a chilled Old Fashioned glass. Garnish with cherry.

COSTA DEL SOL

1½ oz. gin
1 oz. apricot brandy
1 oz. Cointreau or curaçao

Mix all ingredients with cracked ice in a shaker or blender and pour into a chilled Old Fashioned glass.

CRIMSON

2 oz. gin
½ oz. lemon juice
1 tsp. grenadine
1 oz. port

Mix all ingredients, except port, with cracked ice in a shaker or blender. Pour into a chilled highball glass and top with port float.

CRISTIFORO COLUMBO

1½ oz. gin
½ oz. Campari
4 oz. orange juice
Dash grenadine
Club soda
Dash curaçao

Mix all ingredients, except club soda and curaçao, with cracked ice in a shaker or blender and pour into a chilled highball glass. Fill with club soda and top with dash of curaçao.

DAMN THE WEATHER

1 oz. gin
½ oz. sweet vermouth
1 oz. orange juice
1 tsp. curaçao

Mix all ingredients with cracked ice in a shaker or blender and pour into a chilled Old Fashioned glass.

DANISH GIN FIZZ

1½ oz. gin
¾ oz. Peter Heering
¼ oz. kirsch
½ oz. lime juice
½ oz. sugar syrup
Club soda
Lime slice

Mix all ingredients, except club soda and lime slice, with cracked ice in a shaker or blender and strain into a chilled Collins glass. Fill with club soda and garnish with lime slice.

DARB

1 oz. gin
1 oz. dry vermouth
1 oz. apricot brandy
½ oz. lemon juice
1 tsp. sugar syrup or to taste

Mix all ingredients with cracked ice in a shaker or blender and strain into a chilled cocktail glass.

DARBY

1½ oz. gin
½ oz. lime juice
½ oz. grapefruit juice
1 tsp. sugar syrup

Mix all ingredients with cracked ice in a shaker or blender and strain into a chilled cocktail glass.

DEMPSEY

1 oz. gin
1 oz. applejack or calvados
1 tsp. sugar syrup or to taste
2 dashes Pernod
2 dashes grenadine

Mix all ingredients with cracked ice in a shaker or blender and pour into a chilled Old Fashioned glass.

DERBY No. 1

1½ oz. gin
Several dashes peach bitters
Mint sprigs

Mix all ingredients, except mint sprigs, with cracked ice in a shaker or blender. Pour into a chilled Old Fashioned glass and garnish with mint sprigs.

 ## DEVIL'S SMILE

1 oz. gin
1 oz. brandy
1 oz. triple sec
1 oz. lemon juice
Dash amaretto

Mix all ingredients with cracked ice in a shaker or blender and strain into a chilled cocktail glass.

 ## DIAMOND HEAD

1½ oz. gin
½ oz. curaçao
2 oz. pineapple juice
1 tsp. sweet vermouth

Mix all ingredients with cracked ice in a shaker or blender. Strain into chilled cocktail glass.

DIXIE

1 oz. gin
½ oz. Pernod
½ oz. dry vermouth
1–2 oz. orange juice
Several dashes grenadine

Mix all ingredients with cracked ice in a shaker or blender and strain into a chilled Old Fashioned glass.

DIXIE DELIGHT

1 oz. gin
1 oz. Southern Comfort
1 oz. dry vermouth
½ tsp. sugar syrup
Several dashes Pernod

Mix all ingredients with cracked ice in a shaker or blender and strain into a chilled cocktail glass.

DOCTOR'S ORDERS

1 oz. gin
1 oz. cognac
1 oz. Forbidden Fruit
Several dashes lemon juice

Mix all ingredients with cracked ice in a shaker or blender. Strain into a chilled champagne saucer glass.

DOCTOR YES

1½ oz. gin
½ oz. crème de cacao
½ oz. amaretto

Mix all ingredients with cracked ice in a shaker or blender and strain into a chilled cocktail glass.

DOUGLAS FAIRBANKS

2 oz. gin
¾ oz. apricot brandy
1 oz. lemon juice
1 tsp. sugar syrup or to taste

1 egg white (for two drinks)

Mix with cracked ice in a shaker or blender and strain into a chilled cocktail glass.

DRAKE GIN SOUR

2 oz. gin
1 tsp. lemon juice
1 tsp. orgeat syrup or sugar syrup
1 egg white (for two drinks)

Mix all ingredients with cracked ice in a shaker or blender and strain into a chilled Whiskey Sour glass.

DUBONNET COCKTAIL

1½ oz. gin
1½ oz. Dubonnet rouge
Lemon peel

Mix all ingredients, except lemon peel, with cracked ice in a shaker or blender and pour into a chilled Old Fashioned glass. Twist lemon peel over drink and drop into glass.

DUNDEE

1 oz. gin
¾ oz. scotch
½ oz. Drambuie
½ oz. lemon juice
Lemon peel

Mix all ingredients, except lemon peel, with cracked ice in a shaker or blender and pour into a chilled Old Fashioned glass. Twist lemon peel over drink and drop into glass.

DUQUESNE CLUB

1½ oz. gin
½ oz. amaretto
½ oz. lime juice
Dash grenadine

Mix all ingredients with cracked ice in a shaker or blender and strain into a chilled cocktail glass.

ELK

1 oz. gin
1 oz. prunelle
Several dashes dry vermouth

Mix all ingredients with cracked ice in a shaker or blender and pour into a chilled Old Fashioned glass.

FERNET BRANCA COCKTAIL

2 oz. gin
½ oz. Fernet Branca
½ oz. sweet vermouth

Mix all ingredients with cracked ice in a shaker or blender and strain into a chilled cocktail glass.

FILBY

2 oz. gin
¾ oz. amaretto
½ oz. dry vermouth
½ oz. Campari
Orange peel

Stir all ingredients, except orange peel, with cracked ice in a mixing glass and pour into a chilled cocktail glass. Garnish with orange peel.

FINE AND DANDY

1½ oz. gin
¾ oz. triple sec
¾ oz. lemon juice
Dash Angostura or orange
  bitters

Mix all ingredients with cracked
ice in a shaker or blender and
strain into a chilled cocktail
glass.

FOGHORN

2 oz. gin
Ginger beer
Lemon slice

Pour gin into a chilled highball glass with several ice cubes.
Fill with ginger beer and garnish
with lemon slice.

FRANKENJACK COCKTAIL

1 oz. gin
½ oz. dry vermouth
½ oz. apricot brandy
½ oz. Cointreau
Maraschino cherry

Mix all ingredients, except
maraschino cherry, with cracked
ice in a shaker or blender and
pour into a chilled Old Fashioned
glass. Decorate with cherry.

FROTH BLOWER COCKTAIL

2 oz. gin
1 tsp. grenadine
1 egg white (for two drinks)

Mix all ingredients with cracked
ice in a shaker or blender and
pour into a chilled Old Fashioned glass.

GALE FORCE

1½ oz. gin
¾ oz. gold rum
3 oz. orange juice
½ oz. lemon juice
Several dashes of 151-proof
  Demerara rum or Jamaica
  rum

Mix all ingredients with cracked
ice in a shaker or blender and
pour into a chilled Old Fashioned glass.

THE GATE OF HORN

2 oz. gin
½ oz. curaçao
2 oz. orange juice
1 oz. grapefruit juice
Dash orgeat syrup or to taste

Several dashes orange flower water

Mix with cracked ice in a shaker or blender and pour into a chilled wine goblet.

GEISHA CUP

1½ oz. gin
1 oz. apricot brandy
2 oz. orange juice
2 oz. grapefruit juice
Maraschino cherry

Mix all ingredients, except maraschino cherry, with cracked ice in a shaker or blender and serve in a chilled Collins glass. Garnish with cherry.

GENOA

¾ oz. gin
¾ oz. grappa
½ oz. Sambuca Romana
½ oz. dry vermouth
Green olive

Mix all ingredients, except green olive, with cracked ice in a shaker or blender and strain into a chilled cocktail glass. Garnish with olive.

GEORGE V COCKTAIL

1½ oz. gin
1 oz. Lillet blanc
1 tsp. Cointreau
Several dashes orange bitters

Mix all ingredients with cracked ice in a shaker or blender and strain into a chilled cocktail glass.

THE GILDED ORANGE No. 1

2 oz. gin
½ oz. dark Jamaica rum
2 oz. orange juice
1 oz. orgeat syrup or to taste
Several dashes orange bitters
Dash lemon juice
Orange peel

Mix all ingredients, except orange peel, with cracked ice in a shaker or blender and pour into a chilled Old Fashioned glass. Twist orange peel over drink and drop into glass.

GILROY

1 oz. gin
1 oz. cherry brandy
½ oz. dry vermouth
½ oz. lemon juice
Several dashes orange bitters

Mix all ingredients with cracked ice in a shaker or blender and pour into a chilled Old Fashioned glass.

 ## GIMLET No. 1

2 oz. gin
¼ oz. Rose's lime juice
Lime slice

Mix all ingredients with cracked ice in a shaker or blender and pour into a chilled Old Fashioned glass. Garnish with lime slice.

 ## GIMLET No. 2

2 oz. gin
½ oz. fresh lime juice
Lime peel

Mix all ingredients, except lime

peel, vigorously with cracked ice in a mixing glass and pour into a chilled Old Fashioned glass. Twist lime peel over drink and drop into glass.

 ## GIN AND BITTERS Pink Gin

2–3 oz. gin
½ tsp. Angostura bitters

Mix gin and bitters in a glass

with ice cubes until chilled. Strain into a chilled Old Fashioned glass without ice, since this drink is traditionally served neat.

GIN & GINGER

1½ oz. gin
Ginger ale
Lemon peel

Pour gin into chilled highball glass with several ice cubes. Twist lemon peel over drink and drop in. Fill with ginger ale. Stir gently.

 ## GIN AND TONIC

2 oz. gin
Tonic water
Lime wedge

Pour gin into chilled Collins glass with several ice cubes. Fill with tonic water and squeeze lime wedge over drink and drop into glass.

GIN BOLOGNESE

1 oz. gin
½ oz. Fernet Branca
½ oz. orange bitters
Lemon peel

Mix all ingredients, except lemon peel, with cracked ice in a shaker or blender. Strain into a chilled cocktail glass. Twist lemon peel over drink and drop into glass.

GIN CASSIS

1½ oz. gin
½ oz. lemon juice
½ oz. crème de cassis

Mix all ingredients with cracked ice in a shaker or blender and pour into a chilled Old Fashioned glass.

GIN COBBLER

2 oz. gin
1 tsp. sugar syrup or orgeat syrup
Club soda
Orange slice

Mix gin and syrup with cracked ice in a double Old Fashioned glass and fill with cold club soda. Stir gently and garnish with orange slice.

GIN DAISY

2–3 oz. gin
1 oz. lemon juice
¼ oz. raspberry syrup or grenadine
½ tsp. sugar syrup or to taste
Club soda
Orange slice or mint sprigs

Mix all ingredients, except club soda and orange slice, with cracked ice in a shaker or blender and pour into a chilled highball glass. Fill with cold club soda and garnish with orange slice.

GIN FIZZ

2–3 oz. gin
½ oz. sugar syrup
Juice of ½ lemon
Juice of ½ lime
Club soda
Maraschino cherry

Mix all ingredients, except cherry and club soda, in a shaker or blender and pour into a chilled highball glass and fill with cold club soda. Garnish with cherry.

GINGERINE

2 oz. gin
4 oz. tangerine juice
4 oz. grapefruit juice
Dash sugar syrup or to taste
Dash grenadine or raspberry
    syrup

Mix with cracked ice in a
shaker or blender and pour into a
chilled double Old Fashioned
glass.

 # THE GIN-GER MAN

2 oz. gin
4 oz. orange-grapefruit juice
2 oz. cranberry juice
1 tablespoon ginger
    marmalade
Orange slice

Mix all ingredients, except orange
slice, with cracked ice in a
shaker or blender and pour into a
chilled double Old Fashioned
glass. Garnish with orange slice.

 # GIN-GER MAN No. 2

2 oz. gin
4 oz. orange juice
2 oz. grapefruit juice
½ oz. orgeat syrup or to taste
1 tablespoon ginger
    marmalade

Mix with cracked ice in a
shaker or blender and pour into a
chilled Collins glass.

 # GIN MILK PUNCH

1½ oz. gin
5 oz. milk
1 tsp. sugar syrup
Pinch of ground nutmeg

Mix all ingredients, except nutmeg, with cracked ice in a shaker
or blender and pour into a
chilled highball glass. Sprinkle
with ground nutmeg.

GIN RAY

2 oz. gin
1 oz. light rum
3 oz. orange juice
1 oz. lemon juice
1 tsp. orgeat syrup or sugar
    syrup

*Several dashes maraschino
    liqueur*

Mix all ingredients with cracked
ice in a shaker or blender and
pour into a chilled double Old
Fashioned glass.

GIN RICKEY

1½ oz. gin
Club soda
Juice of ½ lime

Pour gin into a chilled highball glass with several ice cubes.
Fill with club soda, add lime
juice, and stir gently.

GIN SIDECAR

1½ oz. gin
¾ oz. triple sec
1 oz. lemon juice

Mix all ingredients with cracked
ice in a shaker or blender and
pour into a chilled Old Fashioned glass.

 GIN SLING

2–3 oz. gin
1 oz. lemon juice
½ oz. orgeat or sugar syrup
   or to taste
Club soda or water

Mix gin, lemon juice, and syrup
with cracked ice in a double Old
Fashioned glass and fill with
cold club soda or water. Stir
well.

GIN SMASH No. 1

6 mint leaves
1½ oz. gin
½ oz. peppermint schnapps
½ oz. lemon juice
½ oz. sugar syrup
Lemon slice
Mint sprig

Muddle mint leaves, gin, schnapps,
lemon, and sugar syrup in a
double Old Fashioned glass
with a little water. Add cracked
ice, stir well, and garnish with
lemon slice and mint sprig.

GIN SMASH No. 2

Mint leaves
2 oz. gin
½ oz. curaçao
½ oz. lime juice
Dash orange bitters
Lemon slice
Several mint sprigs
Club soda

Muddle mint leaves, gin,
curaçao, lime juice, and orange
bitters in a chilled Old Fashioned glass until well mixed.
Add crushed ice and garnish
with lemon slice and mint sprigs.
Add a splash of club soda and
stir well.

 GIN SOUR

2–3 oz. gin
1 oz. lemon juice
1 tsp. sugar syrup or to taste
Orange slice
Maraschino cherry

Mix all ingredients, except orange slice and maraschino cherry, with cracked ice in a shaker or blender and strain into a chilled Whiskey Sour glass. Decorate with fruit.

GOLDEN FIZZ

2–3 oz. gin
1 oz. lemon or lime juice
1 tsp. sugar syrup or to taste
1 egg yolk
Club soda
Lemon or lime slice

Mix all ingredients, except fruit slice, with cracked ice in a shaker or blender and pour into a chilled Collins glass. Fill with cold club soda, stir gently, and garnish with fruit slice.

GOLDEN DAWN

2 oz. gin
¾ oz. apricot liqueur
2 oz. orange juice
Juice of ½ lime
Dash grenadine or raspberry
    syrup

Mix with cracked ice in a shaker or blender and strain into a chilled cocktail glass.

GOODBYE DOLLY

1½ oz. gin.
½ oz. maraschino liqueur
1 tsp. grenadine
1 egg white (for two drinks)
1 tsp. parfait amour or
    anisette

Mix all ingredients but the last with cracked ice in a shaker or blender. Strain into a chilled cocktail glass. Add a float of parfait amour or anisette.

 GRADEAL SPECIAL

1½ oz. gin
¾ oz. light rum
¾ oz. apricot brandy or
    apricot liqueur
1 tsp. sugar syrup

Mix with cracked ice in a shaker or blender and strain into a chilled cocktail glass.
Note: If apricot liqueur is used, omit sugar syrup.

GRAND MOMENT

1½ oz. gin
¾ oz. Grand Marnier
½ oz. lime juice
1 egg white (for two drinks)

Mix all ingredients with cracked ice in a shaker or blender. Pour into a chilled brandy snifter.

GRAND PASSION

2 oz. gin
1 oz. La Grande Passion
Several dashes Angostura
    bitters

Mix all ingredients with cracked ice in a shaker or blender and pour into a chilled cocktail glass.

GRANVILLE

1½ oz. gin
¼ oz. Grand Marnier
¼ oz. calvados
¼ oz. lemon juice

Mix all ingredients with cracked ice in a shaker or blender and strain into a chilled cocktail glass.

GRAPEFRUIT COCKTAIL

1½ oz. gin
1 oz. grapefruit juice
1 tsp. maraschino liqueur
Maraschino cherry

Mix all ingredients, except maraschino cherry, with cracked ice in a shaker or blender and strain into a chilled cocktail glass. Garnish with cherry.

GRAPE VINE

1½ oz. gin
2 oz. grape juice
1 oz. lemon juice
½ oz. sugar syrup
Dash grenadine

Pour all ingredients into a chilled Old Fashioned glass with several ice cubes and stir well.

BARTENDER'S SECRET NO. 2

Clean, sparkling glassware adds to the appeal of any drink. But don't rely on either home or institutional dishwashers to give you spotless glasses every time. As every bartender knows, water spots (not dirt) are the problem, and, occasionally, grease smears from lipstick. Always check glasses that come from the dishwasher against the light to see if the detergent is doing its job. If glasses are hand-washed, use two towels: one for drying and one for polishing. Change towels frequently. From a hygienic standpoint, air-drying after washing is best. If washing glasses in a home dishwasher, do not remove glasses after the final rinse cycle. Give them time to dry in the heat before removing.

GREAT DANE

1 oz. gin
½ oz. dry vermouth
½ oz. Peter Heering
1 tsp. kirsch
Lemon peel

Mix all ingredients, except lemon peel, with cracked ice in a shaker or blender and strain into a chilled cocktail glass. Twist lemon peel over drink and drop into glass.

GREAT SECRET

1½ oz. gin
¾ oz. Lillet blanc
Several dashes Angostura
  bitters
Orange peel

Mix all ingredients, except orange peel, with cracked ice in a shaker or blender and strain into a chilled cocktail glass. Twist orange peel over drink and drop into glass.

GREENBRIER COLLINS

2 oz. gin
½ oz. lemon juice
1 tsp. white crème de menthe
1 tsp. sugar syrup
Club soda
Mint sprigs

Mix all ingredients, except club soda and mint leaves, with cracked ice in a shaker or blender and pour into a chilled Collins glass. Fill with cold club soda, stir gently, and garnish with mint sprigs.

GREEN DRAGON

1½ oz. gin
1 oz. green crème de menthe
½ oz. kummel
½ oz. lemon juice
Several dashes peach or orange bitters

Mix all ingredients with cracked ice in a shaker or blender and strain into a chilled cocktail glass.

GREEN LAGOON

1 oz. gin
1 oz. green crème de menthe
2–3 oz. pineapple juice

Mix all ingredients with cracked ice in a shaker or blender and strain into a chilled cocktail glass.

GUARDS COCKTAIL

1½ oz. gin
½ oz. sweet vermouth
½ oz. curaçao

Pour all ingredients into a chilled Old Fashioned glass with several ice cubes and stir until well mixed.

HABIT ROUGE

1½ oz. gin
1½ oz. grapefruit juice
1½ oz. cranberry juice
1 tsp. maple syrup or honey

Mix all ingredients with cracked ice in a shaker or blender and pour into a chilled wine goblet or cocktail glass.

HARLEM COCKTAIL

1½ oz. gin
1 oz. pineapple juice
1 tsp. maraschino liqueur
1 tbsp. diced canned pineapple

Mix all ingredients in a blender with cracked ice and pour into a chilled Old Fashioned glass.

HASTY COCKTAIL

1½ oz. gin
½ oz. dry vermouth
½ tsp. grenadine
Several dashes Pernod

Mix all ingredients with cracked ice in a shaker or blender and strain into a chilled cocktail glass.

HAWAIIAN

1½ oz. gin
1 oz. pineapple juice
1 egg white (for two drinks)
Several dashes orange bitters

Mix all ingredients with cracked ice in a shaker or blender and strain into a chilled cocktail glass.

HAWAIIAN COOLER

1½ oz. gin
4 oz. pineapple juice
½ oz. orgeat syrup
Club soda
Maraschino cherry

Mix all ingredients, except club soda and cherry, with cracked ice in a shaker or blender and pour into a double Old Fashioned glass. Fill with cold club soda and stir gently. Garnish with a cherry.

HAWAIIAN ORANGE BLOSSOM

1½ oz. gin
1 oz. curaçao
2 oz. orange juice
1 oz. pineapple juice

Mix all ingredients with cracked ice in a shaker or blender and strain into a chilled Whiskey Sour glass

HOFFMAN DOLAN FIZZ

1½ oz. gin
¾ oz. apricot brandy
1 tsp. anisette or Pernod
1 tsp. lemon juice
Club soda
Lemon peel
½ apricot

Mix all ingredients, except club soda, lemon peel, and apricot, with cracked ice in a shaker or blender and pour into a chilled Collins glass. Fill with club soda, twist lemon peel over drink and drop in glass. Garnish with apricot.

THE HOMESTEAD SPECIAL

1½ oz. gin
½ oz. blackberry liqueur
½ oz. lime juice

Mix all ingredients with cracked ice in a shaker or blender and strain into a chilled cocktail glass.

HYANNIS HIATUS

1½ oz. gin
Cranberry juice
Orange slice

Pour gin into chilled double Old Fashioned glass with several ice cubes. Fill with cranberry juice and garnish with orange slice.

ISTRIAN SMILING

1½ oz. gin
1 oz. crème de cassis
1 tsp. Mandarine Napoleon
Tonic water

Stir gin, cassis, and Mandarine liqueur with ice in a mixing glass and pour into a tall highball glass. Add ice cubes and fill with cold tonic water.

JAMAICA GLOW

1½ oz. gin
½ oz. dry red wine
¼ oz. dark Jamaica rum
½ oz. orange juice
Lime slice

Mix all ingredients, except lime slice, with cracked ice in a shaker or blender and strain into a chilled cocktail glass. Decorate with lime slice.

 ## THE JAY BIRD

2 oz. gin
1 oz. sloe gin
2 oz. pineapple juice
Dash orgeat syrup
Pineapple stick

Mix all ingredients, except pineapple, with cracked ice in a shaker or blender and serve in a chilled Collins glass. Garnish with pineapple stick.

JEWEL

1 oz. gin
1 oz. sweet vermouth
1 oz. green Chartreuse
Several dashes orange bitters
Lemon peel

Mix all ingredients, except lemon peel, with cracked ice in a shaker or blender and strain into a chilled Old Fashioned glass. Twist lemon peel over drink and drop into glass.

 ## JOAN COLEMAN'S COCKTAIL

1½ oz. gin
½ oz. maraschino liqueur
1 egg white (for two drinks)
Dash orange flower water

Mix all ingredients with cracked ice in a shaker or blender and strain into a chilled cocktail glass.

JOCKEY CLUB

2 oz. gin.
½ tsp. crème de noyeaux
½ tsp. lemon juice
Several dashes Angostura
   bitters
Several dashes orange bitters

Mix all ingredients with cracked ice in a shaker or blender and strain into a chilled Old Fashioned glass.

JOHN'S IDEA

1½ oz. Seagram's Extra Dry
   Gin
¾ cup orange juice
1–2 tsp. Pina Colada mix or
   to taste

Mix all ingredients with cracked ice in a shaker or blender and strain into a chilled Collins glass.

Note: Created for the Seagrams Distillers Co. by the author

JOULOUVILLE

1 oz. gin
½ oz. apple brandy
½ oz. sweet vermouth
½ oz. lemon juice
Several dashes grenadine

Mix all ingredients with cracked ice in a shaker or blender and strain into a chilled cocktail glass.

JUDGE, JR.

1 oz. gin
1 oz. light rum
½ oz. lemon juice
1 tsp. grenadine

Mix all ingredients with cracked ice in a shaker or blender and strain into a chilled cocktail glass.

JUAN-LES-PINS COCKTAIL

1 oz. gin
¾ oz. Dubonnet blanc
½ oz. apricot brandy
Dash lemon juice
Maraschino cherry

Mix all ingredients, except maraschino cherry, with cracked ice in a shaker or blender and strain into chilled cocktail glass. Garnish with cherry.

JUPITER COCKTAIL

1½ oz. gin
¾ oz. French vermouth
1 tsp. parfait amour or crème
  de violette
1 tsp. orange juice

Mix all ingredients with cracked ice in a shaker or blender and strain into a chilled cocktail glass.
Note: As with any gin-vermouth combination, feel free to change the proportions to suit individual tastes.

KCB

1½ oz. gin
¼ oz. kirsch
Several dashes apricot brandy
Several dashes lemon juice
Lemon peel

Mix all ingredients, except lemon peel, with cracked ice in a shaker or blender and strain into a chilled cocktail glass. Twist lemon peel over drink and drop into glass.

KENSINGTON CHEER

1½ oz. gin
3 oz. green ginger wine
2 oz. orange juice
Club soda
Slice of candied ginger

Mix all ingredients, except club soda and ginger, with cracked ice in a shaker or blender and pour into a chilled highball glass. Fill with club soda, stir gently, and garnish with candied ginger.

KEY CLUB COCKTAIL

1½ oz. gin
½ oz. dark Jamaica rum
½ oz. Falernum
½ oz. lime juice
Pineapple stick

Mix all ingredients, except pineapple stick, with cracked ice in a shaker or blender and strain into a chilled cocktail glass. Decorate with pineapple.

KNOCKOUT

1 oz. gin
1 oz. dry vermouth
1 oz. Pernod
Dash lemon juice
Maraschino cherry

Mix all ingredients, except maraschino cherry, with cracked ice in a shaker or blender and strain into a chilled cocktail glass. Decorate with cherry.

KYOTO COCKTAIL

1½ oz. gin
½ oz. dry vermouth
½ oz. melon liqueur
Dash lemon juice

Mix all ingredients with cracked ice in a shaker or blender and strain into a chilled cocktail glass.

 LA CÔTE BASQUE COCKTAIL

1½ oz. gin
½ oz. Forbidden Fruit
½ oz. triple sec
Several dashes orange bitters

Mix all ingredients with cracked ice in a shaker or blender and strain into chilled cocktail glass.

LADBROKE ROAD COCKTAIL

1½ oz. gin
1 oz. strawberry liqueur
½ oz. lemon juice
Dash triple sec
Club soda
Lemon peel
1 whole strawberry

Mix all ingredients, except club soda, lemon peel, and strawberry, with cracked ice in a shaker or blender and strain into a chilled Collins glass. Fill with club soda and twist lemon peel over drink and drop in. Garnish with strawberry.

LADYFINGER

1 oz. gin
½ oz. Peter Heering or
    Cherry Marnier
½ oz. kirsch

Mix all ingredients with cracked ice in a shaker or blender and pour into a chilled Old Fashioned glass.

LEAP FROG

1½ oz. gin
½ oz. lemon juice
Ginger ale

Mix gin and lemon juice with cracked ice in a tall highball or Collins glass and fill with cold ginger ale.

LE COQ D'OR

1 oz. gin
½ oz. dry vermouth
½ oz. triple sec
½ oz. apricot brandy
Maraschino cherry

Mix all ingredients, except maraschino cherry, with cracked ice in a shaker or blender and pour into a chilled Old Fashioned glass. Decorate with cherry.

LE TOUQUET COCKTAIL

1½ oz. gin
½ oz. calvados
½ oz. light rum
¼ oz. Grand Marnier
Club soda
Orange peel

Mix all ingredients, except club soda and orange peel, with cracked ice in a shaker or blender and pour into a chilled highball glass. Fill with club soda and twist orange peel over drink and drop into glass.

LILLET NOYAUX

½ oz. gin
1½ oz. Lillet blanc
1 tsp. crème de noyaux
Orange peel

Mix all ingredients, except orange peel, with cracked ice in a shaker or blender and strain into a chilled cocktail glass. Twist orange peel over drink and drop into glass.

 ## LILLIAN LANGELL

2 oz. gin
Several dashes crème yvette
Several dashes orange flower
    water
1 egg white (for two drinks)

Mix all ingredients with cracked ice in a shaker or blender and strain into a chilled cocktail glass.

 ## LITTLE DEVIL

1 oz. gin
1 oz. gold rum
½ oz. triple sec
½ oz. lemon juice

Mix all ingredients with cracked ice and strain into a chilled cocktail glass.

LONDON COCKTAIL No. 1

1½ oz. gin
¾ oz. triple sec
½ oz. lemon juice

Mix all ingredients with cracked ice in a shaker or blender and pour into a chilled cocktail glass.

LONDON COCKTAIL No. 2

1½ oz. gin
*Several dashes maraschino
   liqueur*
Several dashes orange bitters
*Several dashes sugar syrup
   or to taste*

Mix all ingredients with cracked
ice in a shaker or blender and
strain into a chilled cocktail
glass.

LONDON FRENCH "75"

1½ oz. gin
Juice of ½ lemon
1 tsp. sugar syrup
Brut champagne

Mix gin, lemon juice, and sugar
syrup with cracked ice in a shaker
or blender and pour into a
chilled Collins glass. Add ice
cubes and fill with cold champagne.

LONE TREE

¾ oz. gin
¾ oz. dry vermouth
¾ oz. sweet vermouth
Several dashes orange bitters
Olive

Mix all ingredients, except olive,
with cracked ice in a shaker or
blender and strain into a chilled
cocktail glass. Garnish with olive.

LORELEI

1½ oz. gin
½ oz. green crème de menthe
¼ oz. kummel
¼ oz. lemon juice

Mix all ingredients with cracked
ice in a shaker or blender and
strain into a chilled cocktail
glass.

LUMBERJACK

1 oz. gin
½ oz. applejack
½ oz. Southern Comfort
½ oz. maple syrup

Mix all ingredients with cracked
ice in a shaker or blender and
strain into a chilled cocktail
glass.

MAIDEN'S BLUSH No. 1

1½ oz. gin
1 tsp. curaçao
½ tsp. lemon juice
½ tsp. grenadine

Mix all ingredients with cracked ice in a shaker or blender and strain into a chilled Whiskey Sour glass.

MAIDEN'S BLUSH No. 2

2½ oz. gin
¾ oz. Pernod
½ tsp. grenadine

Mix all ingredients with cracked ice in a shaker or blender and strain into a chilled cocktail glass.

MAIDEN'S PRAYER No. 1

1½ oz. gin
¾ oz. Cointreau
¼ oz. orange juice
¼ oz. lemon juice

Mix all ingredients with cracked ice in a shaker or blender and strain into a chilled cocktail glass.

MAIDEN'S PRAYER No. 2

1½ oz. gin
½ oz. Lillet blanc
¼ oz. lemon juice
¼ oz. orange juice

Mix all ingredients with cracked ice in a shaker or blender. Strain into a chilled cocktail glass. *Note:* Some recipes specify ¼ oz. calvados and ¼ oz. apricot brandy in place of lemon and orange juices.

MAINBRACE No. 1

1½ oz. gin
¾ oz. triple sec or curaçao
1 oz. grape juice

Mix all ingredients with cracked ice in a shaker or blender and strain into a cocktail glass.

MAINBRACE No. 2

1 oz. gin
1 oz. curaçao
1 oz. grapefruit juice

Mix all ingredients with cracked ice in a shaker or blender. Strain into a chilled cocktail glass.

MANDARINE FIZZ

1 oz. gin
1 oz. Mandarine Napoleon
2 oz. orange or tangerine
    juice
½ oz. sugar syrup
Club soda
Tangerine wedge

Mix all ingredients, except club soda and tangerine wedge, with cracked ice in a shaker or blender and strain into a chilled highball glass. Fill with club soda and garnish with tangerine wedge.

MARIEMONT SPECIAL

1 oz. gin
1 oz. dry vermouth
1 oz. orange juice
1 tsp. grenadine
Dash triple sec

Mix all ingredients with cracked ice in a shaker or blender and pour into a chilled Old Fashioned glass.

MARMALADE COCKTAIL

2 oz. gin
1 oz. lemon juice
1 tbsp. orange marmalade

Mix all ingredients with cracked ice in a blender and pour into a chilled cocktail glass.

MATINEE

1½ oz. gin
½ oz. sambuca
½ oz. lime juice
1 tsp. heavy cream
1 egg white (for two drinks)
Pinch of ground nutmeg or
    cinnamon

Mix all ingredients, except spice, with cracked ice in a shaker or blender and strain into a chilled cocktail glass. Sprinkle with ground nutmeg or cinnamon.

MARTINI Note: Basic recipe. See page 98 for Martini Variations

2 oz. gin
½ tsp. dry vermouth or to
    taste
Olive or lemon twist

Stir gin and vermouth in a mixing glass with plenty of ice and strain into a chilled cocktail glass. Garnish with olive or lemon twist.

MAYFAIR

1½ oz. gin
½ oz. apricot-flavored brandy
3 oz. orange juice
Dash grenadine

Mix all ingredients with cracked ice in a shaker or blender and strain into a chilled cocktail glass.

MELON COCKTAIL No. 1

1½ oz. gin
½ oz. maraschino liqueur
½ oz. lemon juice
Maraschino cherry

Mix all ingredients, except cherry, with cracked ice in a shaker or blender and strain into a chilled cocktail glass.

MELON COCKTAIL No. 2

1½ oz. gin
¾ oz. melon liqueur
½ oz. triple sec
½ oz. lemon juice

Mix all ingredients with cracked ice in a shaker or blender and strain into a chilled cocktail glass.

MERRY WIDOW

1 oz. gin
1 oz. dry vermouth
Several dashes Pernod
Several dashes Benedictine
Several dashes Peychaud's
  bitters or Angostura bitters
Lemon peel

Mix all ingredients, except lemon peel, with cracked ice in a shaker or blender and strain into a chilled cocktail glass. Twist lemon peel over drink and drop into glass.

BARTENDER'S SECRET NO. 3

The conventional Martini employs traditional garnishes: the lemon peel and the green olive. The Gibson, an extra-dry Martini using tiny bottled pearl onions, was, when it became popular, considered to be a rather daring innovation. Nowadays, Martini makers and drinkers are experimenting with a wide range of garnishes with rewarding results. Here are some variations that are used individually, not in combination: chili pepper, lime or orange twist, dill-pickle slice, capers, anchovies, avocado slice, artichoke heart, radish slice, water-chestnut sliver, pickled green bean, button mushrooms marinated in vermouth, baby eggplants steeped in white wine vinegar, olives stuffed with anchovies or onion or almonds, olives marinated in port, sherry, or Madeira, and even garlic slices or sliver of Bermuda onion. There is no end to creative garnishes. The classic Martini seems to be strong enough to stand up to anything in the way of additives. As every bartender knows, there is no accounting for individual taste.

MICHEL'S PASSION

2 oz. gin
1 oz. dry vermouth
1 oz. La Grande Passion
Orange peel

Mix all ingredients, except orange peel, with cracked ice in a shaker or blender and strain into a chilled cocktail glass. Twist orange peel over drink and drop into glass.

MILLION DOLLAR COCKTAIL

1½ oz. gin
¾ oz. sweet vermouth
½ oz. pineapple juice
1 tsp. grenadine
1 egg white (for two drinks)

Mix all ingredients with cracked ice in a shaker or blender and strain into a chilled cocktail glass.

MILLIONAIRE COCKTAIL No. 1

1½ oz. gin
¾ oz. Pernod
1 egg white (for two drinks)
Dash anisette

Mix all ingredients with cracked ice in a shaker or blender and pour into a chilled cocktail glass.

MISSISSIPPI MULE

1½ oz. gin
¼ oz. crème de cassis
¼ oz. lemon juice

Mix all ingredients with cracked ice in a shaker or blender and pour into a chilled Old Fashioned glass.

MOLDAU

1½ oz. gin
½ oz. plum brandy
½ oz. orange juice
½ oz. lemon juice
Brandied cherry

Mix all ingredients, except brandied cherry, with cracked ice in a shaker or blender and pour into a chilled cocktail glass. Garnish with cherry.

MOLL COCKTAIL

1 oz. gin
1 oz. sloe gin
1 oz. dry vermouth
Dash orange bitters

Mix with cracked ice in a shaker or blender and strain into a chilled cocktail glass.

MONKEY GLAND

1½ oz. gin
¾ oz. orange juice
Several dashes Benedictine
Several dashes grenadine

Mix all ingredients with cracked ice in a shaker or blender and strain into a chilled cocktail glass.

MONTREAL COCKTAIL

1 oz. gin
1 oz. Cherry Marnier
1 oz. orange juice
1 oz. lime juice
½ oz. sugar syrup or to taste

Mix all ingredients with cracked ice in a shaker or blender and strain into a chilled cocktail glass.

MOONSHOT

1½ oz. gin
3 oz. clam juice
Dash red pepper sauce

Combine all ingredients in a mixing glass with several ice cubes. Strain into a chilled Whiskey Sour glass.

MORNING JOY

1 oz. gin
1 oz. crème de banane
2 oz. orange juice

Mix all ingredients with cracked ice in a shaker or blender and strain into a chilled Whiskey Sour glass.

MORNING KISS

¾ oz. gin
¾ oz. apricot brandy
1 oz. orange juice
Brut champagne

Mix all ingredients, except champagne, with cracked ice in a shaker or blender and strain into a large, chilled wine goblet. Fill with cold champagne and stir gently.

MORNING SUN

2 oz. gin
2 oz. grapefruit juice
2 oz. orange juice
½ tsp. maraschino cherry
   juice
Dash Angostura bitters
Maraschino cherry

Mix all ingredients, except maraschino cherry, with cracked ice in a blender. Pour into a chilled double Old Fashioned glass and garnish with maraschino cherry.

MOULIN BLEU

1½ oz. gin
1½ oz. Pernod
Orange slice

Pour all ingredients into a chilled Old Fashioned glass with several ice cubes and stir and garnish with orange.

MULE'S HIND LEG

¾ oz. gin
¾ oz. apple brandy
¾ oz. Benedictine
¾ oz. apricot brandy
¾ oz. maple syrup or to taste

Mix all ingredients with cracked ice in a shaker or blender and pour into a chilled cocktail glass.
Note: This is the original recipe. Modern versions sometimes utilize more gin and apple brandy in proportion to other ingredients.

NEGRONI

2 oz. gin
½ oz. sweet vermouth
¾ oz. Campari
Orange peel

Blend all ingredients, except orange peel, with cracked ice in a mixing glass and strain into a chilled cocktail glass. Twist orange peel over drink and drop into glass.

NEWPORT COOLER

1½ oz. gin
½ oz. brandy
½ oz. peach liqueur
Several dashes lime juice
Ginger ale or lemon-lime
   soda

Mix all ingredients, except soda, in a chilled Collins glass with ice cubes. Fill with ginger ale or lemon-lime soda.

NIGHT TRAIN

2 oz. gin
1 oz. Cointreau
½ oz. lemon juice
Dash kirsch

Mix all ingredients with cracked ice in a shaker or blender and strain into a chilled cocktail glass.

THE NOON BALLOON

2 oz. gin
3 oz. orange juice
1 oz. grapefruit juice
1 oz. cranberry juice
½ oz. Falernum or sugar
  syrup to taste

Maraschino cherry

Mix all ingredients, except cherry, with cracked ice and in a shaker or blender and serve in a chilled double Old Fashioned glass.

NORMANDY COCKTAIL No. 2

1½ oz. gin
¾ oz. calvados or applejack
½ oz. apricot brandy
Several dashes lemon juice

Mix all ingredients with cracked ice in a shaker or blender and pour into a chilled cocktail glass.

NORMANDY NIP

1½ oz. gin
¾ oz. calvados
½ oz. lemon juice
½ oz. sugar syrup

Mix all ingredients with cracked ice in a shaker or blender and strain into a chilled cocktail glass.

NYACK COCKTAIL

1 oz. gin
¾ oz. cherry brandy
½ oz. dry vermouth

Mix all ingredients with cracked ice in a shaker or blender and strain into a chilled cocktail glass.

OPERA

1½ oz. gin
¾ oz. Dubonnet rouge
½ oz. maraschino liqueur
Orange peel

Mix all ingredients, except orange peel, with cracked ice in a shaker or blender and strain into a chilled cocktail glass. Twist orange peel over drink and drop into glass.

ORANGE BANG! No. 2

1½ oz. gin
1 oz. orange juice
½ oz. triple sec or curaçao
Several dashes orange bitters
1 large orange wedge

Mix gin, orange juice, triple sec, and orange bitters with cracked ice in a shaker or blender and strain into a chilled cocktail glass. Garnish with orange wedge.

ORANGE BLOSSOM

1½ oz. gin
1 oz. orange juice
Orange slice

Mix all ingredients, except orange slice, with cracked ice in a shaker or blender. Strain into a chilled cocktail glass. Decorate with orange slice.

ORGEAT COCKTAIL

2 oz. gin
1 oz. lemon juice
¾ oz. orgeat syrup or to taste
1 egg white (for two drinks)

Mix with cracked ice in a shaker or blender and strain into a chilled cocktail glass.

OUR HOME

1 oz. gin
1 oz. peach brandy
½ oz. dry vermouth
Dash lemon juice
1 egg white (for two drinks)

Mix all ingredients with cracked ice in a shaker or blender and strain into a chilled cocktail glass.

PALL MALL

1 oz. gin
1 oz. sweet vermouth
1 oz. dry vermouth
1 tsp. white crème de menthe
Several dashes orange bitters

Pour all ingredients into a mixing glass with several ice cubes and strain into a chilled cocktail glass.

THE PANDA

1 oz. gin
1 oz. calvados or applejack
1 oz. slivovitz
1 oz. orange juice

Dash sugar syrup or to taste

Mix with cracked ice in a shaker or blender and strain into a chilled cocktail glass.

PARISIAN

1 oz. gin
1 oz. dry vermouth
1 oz. crème de cassis

Pour all ingredients into a mixing glass with several ice cubes. Stir and strain into a chilled cocktail glass.

PARK AVENUE COCKTAIL

1½ oz. gin
½ oz. cherry brandy
½ oz. lime juice
¼ oz. maraschino liqueur

Mix all ingredients with cracked ice in a shaker or blender and strain into a chilled cocktail glass.

 ## PASSION CUP No. 1

2 oz. gin
2 oz. orange juice
1 oz. passion fruit juice
1 oz. Pina Colada mix or
   equal parts of pineapple
   juice and coconut milk
Maraschino cherry

Mix all ingredients, except cherry, with cracked ice in a shaker or blender and pour into a chilled wine goblet. Garnish with maraschino cherry.

 ## PEACH BLOW FIZZ

2–3 oz. gin
1 oz. lemon juice
1 oz. heavy cream
1 tsp. sugar syrup or to taste
4 mashed strawberries
Club soda

Mix all ingredients, except club soda, with cracked ice in a shaker or blender and pour into a chilled highball glass. Fill with club soda and stir gently.

BARTENDER'S SECRET NO. 4

Many mixed drinks are enhanced by garnishes such as lemon, lime, and orange peel as well as olives, cherries, and onions. Many bartenders will twist a lemon peel (to release the essential oils) and rub it around the rim of a cocktail glass when making a Martini, for example. The lemony aroma and taste enhance the drink. Why not try it with lime, orange, and even an olive or maraschino cherry? The suggestion of flavor on the rim of the glass gives a hint of the enjoyment of a well-made cocktail that awaits the drinker.

PEGU CLUB COCKTAIL

1½ oz. gin
¾ oz. orange curaçao
1 tsp. lime juice
Dash Angostura bitters
Dash orange bitters

Mix all ingredients with cracked
ice in a shaker or blender and
strain into a chilled cocktail glass.

 ## PENDENNIS CLUB COCKTAIL

1½ oz. gin
¾ oz. apricot brandy
½ oz. lime juice
1 tsp. sugar syrup
Several dashes Peychaud's
    bitters

Mix all ingredients with cracked
ice in a shaker or blender and
strain into a chilled cocktail
glass.

PIMLICO COOLER

1½ oz. gin
3 oz. orange juice
Ginger ale

Pour gin and orange juice into
a chilled highball glass with ice
cubes and fill with cold ginger
ale. Stir gently.

PINEAPPLE MINT COOLER

2 oz. gin
½ oz. peppermint schnapps
1 oz. lemon juice
3 oz. pineapple juice
½ oz. sugar syrup
Club soda
Pineapple stick
Green cherry (optional)

Mix all ingredients, except club
soda, pineapple stick, and green
cherry, with cracked ice in a
shaker or blender and pour into a
chilled highball glass. Fill with
club soda and garnish with fruit.

 ## PINK GIN

2–3 oz. gin
Angostura bitters to taste

Mix gin and bitters with plenty
of ice in a mixing glass and
strain into a chilled cocktail or
Old Fashioned glass.

 **PINK LADY**

1½ oz. gin
1½ oz. applejack or calvados
1 oz. lemon juice
1 tsp. sugar syrup or to taste
1 tsp. grenadine
1 egg white (for two drinks)

Mix all ingredients with cracked ice in a shaker or blender and strain into a chilled cocktail glass.

PINK PANTHER

1½ oz. gin
¾ oz. dry vermouth
½ oz. crème de cassis
1 oz. orange juice
1 egg white (for two drinks)

Mix all ingredients with cracked ice in a shaker or blender and strain into a chilled cocktail glass.

PINK ROSE

1½ oz. gin
1 tsp. lemon juice
1 tsp. heavy cream
1 egg white
Several dashes grenadine

Mix all ingredients with cracked ice in a shaker or blender and strain into a chilled cocktail glass.

 POLISH SIDECAR

1 oz. gin
¾ oz. blackberry liqueur or
   blackberry brandy
¾ oz. lemon juice
4 fresh blackberries (optional)

Mix all ingredients, except fresh blackberries, with cracked ice in a shaker or blender and pour into a chilled glass. Garnish with blackberries.
Note: If blackberry brandy is used, it may be necessary to sweeten drink with sugar syrup.

 PRÉ CATELAN COCKTAIL

1½ oz. gin
1 oz. parfait amour
Several dashes lemon juice

Mix all ingredients with cracked ice in a shaker or blender and strain into a chilled cocktail glass.

PRINCETON

1½ oz. gin
¾ oz. port
Several dashes orange bitters
Lemon peel

Mix all ingredients, except
lemon peel, with cracked ice in a
shaker or blender and strain
into a chilled cocktail glass. Twist
lemon peel over drink and drop
into drink.

PRUNELLE ALEXANDER

1½ oz. gin
1 oz. prunelle
1 oz. heavy cream
Pinch ground cinnamon

Mix all ingredients, except
cinnamon, with cracked ice in a
shaker or blender and strain
into a chilled cocktail glass.
Sprinkle with cinnamon.

 ## PUERTO BANUS COCKTAIL

1½ oz. gin
1 oz. Cherry Marnier
1 tsp. fino sherry or dry
  vermouth

Mix all ingredients with cracked
ice in a shaker or blender and
strain into a chilled cocktail
glass.

 ## PUNT E MES NEGRONI

½ oz. gin or vodka
½ oz. Punt e Mes
½ oz. sweet vermouth
Orange peel

Mix all ingredients, except orange
peel, with cracked ice in a shaker
or blender and strain into a
chilled cocktail glass. Twist
orange peel over drink and drop
into glass.

 ## PUNXATAWNY PHIL

1 oz. gin
1 oz. light rum
1 tsp. lemon juice
Dash grenadine
Ginger ale

Mix all ingredients, except ginger
ale, with cracked ice in a shaker
or blender. Pour into a chilled
highball glass and fill with cold
ginger ale.

RADNOR COCKTAIL

1 oz. gin
1 oz. apricot brandy
1 tsp. lemon juice
½ tsp. sugar syrup

½ tsp. grenadine

Mix all ingredients with cracked
ice in a shaker or blender. Strain
into a chilled cocktail glass.

RAMOS GIN FIZZ

2 oz. gin
½ oz. lime juice
½ oz. lemon juice
1 tsp. sugar syrup
1 tsp. heavy cream
Several dashes orange flower
    water

1 egg white (for two drinks)
Club soda

Mix all ingredients, except club
soda, with cracked ice in a shaker
or blender and pour into a tall
Collins glass. Fill with cold club
soda and stir gently.

RED CLOUD

1½ oz. gin
¾ oz. apricot liqueur
½ oz. lemon juice
1 tsp. grenadine
Dash Angostura bitters

Mix all ingredients with cracked
ice in a shaker or blender and
strain into a chilled cocktail
glass.

RED LIGHT

1 oz. gin
2 oz. sloe gin
1 oz. lemon juice
Maraschino cherry

Mix all ingredients, except
cherry, with cracked ice in a
shaker or blender and strain
into a chilled cocktail glass.
Garnish with cherry.

 ## THE RED LION COCKTAIL

1 oz. gin
1 oz. Grand Marnier
½ oz. orange juice
½ oz. lemon juice

Mix all ingredients with cracked
ice in a shaker or blender and
strain into a chilled cocktail
glass.

RENDEZVOUS

1½ oz. gin
½ oz. kirsch
½ oz. Campari or to taste
Lemon peel

Mix all ingredients, except
lemon peel, with cracked ice in a
shaker or blender and strain
into a chilled cocktail glass. Twist
lemon peel over drink and drop
into glass.

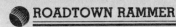 **ROADTOWN RAMMER**

1½ oz. gin
½ oz. curaçao
½ oz. dry vermouth
½ oz. pineapple juice

Mix all ingredients with cracked ice in a shaker or blender and strain into a chilled cocktail glass.

ROCKY GREEN DRAGON

1 oz. gin
¾ oz. green Chartreuse
½ oz. cognac

Mix all ingredients with cracked ice in a shaker or blender and pour into a chilled cocktail glass.

ROMAN COOLER

1½ oz. gin
¾ oz. Punt e Mes
½ oz. lemon juice
½ oz. sugar syrup
Dash sweet vermouth
Club soda
Orange peel

Mix all ingredients, except club soda and orange peel, with cracked ice in a shaker or blender and pour into a chilled highball glass. Fill with club soda, stir, and twist orange peel over drink and drop into glass.

 ROYAL GIN FIZZ

1½ oz. gin
½ oz. Grand Marnier
1 oz. lemon juice
½ oz. sugar syrup
1 egg
Club soda
Maraschino cherry

Mix all ingredients, except soda and cherry, with cracked ice in a shaker or blender and pour into a chilled Collins glass. Fill with cold club soda and garnish with a cherry.

ROYAL ORANGE BLOSSOM

1½ oz. gin
¾ oz. Grand Marnier
3 oz. orange juice
1 tsp. orgeat syrup or honey

Mix all ingredients with cracked ice in a shaker or blender and strain into a chilled cocktail glass.

RUSSIAN COCKTAIL No. 2

1 oz. gin
1 oz. vodka
½ oz. white crème de cacao
½ oz. crème de noyaux

Mix all ingredients with cracked ice in a shaker or blender and pour into a chilled cocktail glass.

SAN REMO COCKTAIL

2 oz. gin
½ oz. dry vermouth
1 oz. Strega

Mix all ingredients with cracked ice in a shaker or blender and strain into a chilled cocktail glass.

SECRET FLOWER

2 oz. gin
2 oz. orange juice
2 oz. grapefruit juice
½ tsp. maraschino liqueur or
   to taste
¼ tsp. orange flower water

Mix with cracked ice in a shaker or blender and strain into a chilled wine goblet. Float a drop or two of orange flower water on top of drink.

SELF-STARTER

1 oz. gin
½ oz. Lillet blanc
1 tsp. apricot brandy
Several dashes Pernod

Mix all ingredients with cracked ice in a shaker or blender and strain into a chilled cocktail glass.

SEVILLE

1½ oz. gin
½ oz. fino sherry
½ oz. orange juice
½ oz. lemon juice
½ oz. sugar syrup or to taste

Mix all ingredients with cracked ice in a shaker or blender and pour into a chilled Old Fashioned glass.

BARTENDER'S SECRET NO.5

Having a big party at home? A convenient place to store all of the ice you'll need, as well as bottled mixers and fruit juices that must be chilled, is your automatic washing machine. It will hold enough to serve an army. When the party's over, just turn on the machine and wash the remaining ice away.

 ## SHEAPARD'S SUFFERING BASTARD

Angostura bitters
1½ oz. gin
1½ oz. brandy
1 tsp. Rose's lime juice
Ginger beer
Mint sprig
Cucumber slice
Orange or lemon slice

Swirl bitters around a chilled 14-oz. double Old Fashioned glass so it is thoroughly coated and discard excess bitters. Add several ice cubes to glass along with gin, brandy, and lime juice, mix well, and fill glass with cold ginger beer. Stir gently and garnish with mint, cucumber, and orange or lemon slice.

SILVER BULLET

2 oz. gin
1 oz. kummel
1 oz. lemon juice

Mix all ingredients with cracked ice in a shaker or blender. Strain into a chilled cocktail glass.

SILVER STALLION

2 oz. gin
1 oz. lemon juice
1 oz. lime juice
1 scoop vanilla ice cream
Club soda

Mix all ingredients except club soda with cracked ice in a shaker

or blender and pour into a chilled double Old Fashioned glass. Fill with club soda and stir gently.
Note: Shake or blend only for a few seconds until smooth.

 ## SINGAPORE SLING

2 oz. gin
1 oz. cherry brandy or Peter Heering
Juice of ½ lemon
Dash Benedictine
Club soda
Lemon slice
Mint sprig (optional)

Mix gin, brandy, lemon juice, and Benedictine with a splash of soda or water in a shaker with

cracked ice and strain into a 12-oz. Collins glass that has been well chilled. Add ice cubes, fill with cold club soda, stir gently, and garnish with lemon slice and mint sprig.
Note: If you use a red, fruity cherry brandy or a cherry liqueur then no additional sweetening is required. If you use a kirsch, then you may want to add some sugar syrup.

SLOE BOAT TO CHINA

2 oz. gin
1 oz. sloe gin
4 oz. orange juice
4 oz. grapefruit juice

Mix with cracked ice in a shaker or blender and serve in a double Old Fashioned glass. Add additional ice if needed.

SNOWBALL

1 oz. gin
¼ oz. white crème de menthe
¼ oz. anisette or Pernod
¼ oz. crème de violette
¼ oz. heavy cream.

Mix all ingredients with cracked ice in a shaker or blender and strain into a chilled champagne saucer glass.

THE SPICED ORANGE BLOSSOM

2 oz. gin (or vodka)
4 oz. orange juice (suggest freshly squeezed)
Dash maraschino cherry juice
Dash Angostura bitters

2 maraschino cherries
Pinch of cinnamon

Mix all ingredients with cracked ice in a blender and pour into a chilled double Old Fashioned glass.

STAR DAISY

1 oz. gin
1 oz. apple brandy
1 oz. lemon juice
1 tsp. sugar syrup
¼ tsp. curaçao

Mix all ingredients with cracked ice in a shaker or blender and strain into a chilled wine goblet.

STEAMBOAT GIN

1½ oz. gin
¾ oz. Southern Comfort
½ oz. grapefruit juice
½ oz. lemon juice

Mix all ingredients with cracked ice in a shaker or blender and strain into a chilled cocktail glass.

BARTENDER'S SECRET NO. 6

A legendary Martini maker in a bar on Chicago's Michigan Boulevard famous for its generous, well-made Martinis delights in using an atomizer connected to a vermouth bottle to make very, very, very dry Martinis for the regulars. It not only works efficiently, but Martini devotees are tantalized by the aroma of vermouth from the clouds of mist that are generated as each Martini is made at the bar. The atomizer may also be used effectively to "top" certain cocktails with aromatic spirits such as Pernod, crème de menthe, kirsch, Cointreau, and even Angostura bitters. Apparently spraying certain highly scented liqueurs and brandies into the atmosphere increases the intensity of the aroma. It is also quite economical, for a little squirt of crème de violette or Drambuie seems to go a long way.

STRAWBERRY BLOW FIZZ

1½ oz. gin
½ oz. strawberry liqueur or strawberry schnapps
1 oz. cream
½ oz. lemon juice
¼ cup frozen strawberries, thawed (including syrup)
1 tsp. Falernum or sugar syrup
Club soda

Mix all ingredients, except club soda, with cracked ice in a shaker or blender, and pour into a chilled Old Fashioned glass. Add more ice, if you wish, and fill with club soda.

STREGA SOUR

1½ oz. gin
½ oz. Strega
½ oz. lemon juice
Lemon slice

Mix all ingredients, except lemon slice, with cracked ice in a shaker or blender and strain into a chilled cocktail glass. Garnish with lemon slice.

SUTTON HOUSE SPECIAL

1½ oz. gin
½ oz. peppermint schnapps
½ oz. sugar syrup
½ oz. lemon juice
6 mint leaves

Mix all ingredients, except mint leaves, with cracked ice in a shaker or blender. Pour into a chilled double Old Fashioned glass and bruise mint leaves with a bar spoon and add additional cracked ice. Stir vigorously.

TANGIER

1 oz. gin
1 oz. triple sec
1 oz. Napoleon Mandarine
Orange peel

Mix all ingredients, except orange peel, with cracked ice in a shaker or blender and strain into a chilled cocktail glass. Garnish with orange peel.

TANGO

1½ oz. gin
¼ oz. sweet vermouth
¼ oz. dry vermouth
1 oz. orange juice
Several dashes curaçao or
   triple sec

Mix all ingredients with cracked
ice in a shaker or blender and
pour into a chilled Old Fashioned glass.

 ## THE TANQUERAY EMERALD No. 1

1½ oz. Tanqueray gin
¾ oz. green Chartreuse
¾ oz. lime juice
1 egg white (for two drinks)
Minted green cherry (optional)

Mix all ingredients, except
green cherry, with cracked ice in
a shaker or blender and strain
into a chilled cocktail glass.
Note: Created for Tanqueray by
the author.

 ## THE TANQUERAY EMERALD No. 2

1½ oz. Tanqueray gin
½ oz. Rose's lime juice
Dash blue curaçao
Lime slice

Mix all ingredients, except lime
slice, in a shaker or blender and
strain into a chilled cocktail
glass.
Note: Created for Tanqueray by
the author.

 ## THE TANQUERAY EMERALD No. 3

1½ oz. Tanqueray gin
½ oz. green crème de menthe
1 oz. cream or half-and-half

Mix all ingredients with cracked
ice in a shaker or blender and
strain into a chilled cocktail
glass.
Note: Created for Tanqueray by
the author.

 ## TOM COLLINS

2–3 oz. gin
1½ oz. lemon juice
½ oz. sugar syrup or to taste
Club soda
Maraschino cherry

Mix all ingredients, except soda
and cherry, in a tall Collins glass
with ice, fill with club soda,
and garnish with cherry.

TRAVELER'S JOY

1 oz. gin
1 oz. cherry liqueur
1 oz. lemon juice

Mix with cracked ice in a shaker or blender and strain into a chilled cocktail glass.

TROPICAL COCKTAIL

2 oz. gin
1 oz. frozen pineapple juice concentrate
1 oz. guava nectar
½ oz. La Grande Passion
Orange peel

Mix all ingredients, except orange peel, with cracked ice in a shaker or blender and pour into a chilled Old Fashioned glass. Twist orange peel over drink and drop into glass.

 ## TUTTI-FRUTTI

3 oz. gin
1 oz. maraschino liqueur
1 oz. amaretto
2 oz. diced apples
2 oz. diced pears

2 oz. diced peaches

Mix all ingredients with cracked ice in a blender until smooth. Pour into a chilled highball glass.

 ## ULANDA

1½ oz. gin
¾ oz. Cointreau
Several dashes Pernod

Mix all ingredients with cracked ice in a shaker or blender and pour into a chilled cocktail glass.

UNION LEAGUE CLUB

1½ oz. gin
1 oz. ruby port
Several dashes orange bitters
Orange peel

Mix all ingredients, except orange peel, with cracked ice in a shaker or blender and pour into a chilled cocktail glass. Garnish with orange peel.

 ## VALENCIA COCKTAIL No. 2

1½ oz. gin
1 oz. dry sherry
Lemon peel

Pour gin and sherry into a

mixing glass with several ice cubes. Stir well and strain into a chilled cocktail glass. Twist lemon peel over drink and drop into glass.

VELVET KISS

1 oz. gin
½ oz. crème de banane
½ oz. pineapple juice
1 oz. heavy cream
Dash grenadine

Mix all ingredients with cracked ice in a shaker or blender and strain into a chilled cocktail glass.

VERA'S THEME

2 oz. gin
Several dashes crème yvette
1 egg white (for two drinks)

Mix all ingredients with cracked ice in a shaker or blender and pour into a chilled Old Fashioned glass.

 ## VERMONT VIGOR

1½ oz. gin
1 oz. lemon juice
½ oz. maple syrup or to taste

Mix all ingredients with cracked ice in a shaker or blender and pour into a chilled Old Fashioned glass.

 ## VERNE'S LAWYER

1½ oz. gin
½ oz. apple brandy or
   calvados
¼ oz. lime juice

Several dashes grenadine

Mix all ingredients with cracked ice in a shaker or blender. Pour into a chilled cocktail glass.

 ## VERONA COCKTAIL

1 oz. gin
½ oz. sweet vermouth
1 oz. amaretto
Dash or two of lemon juice
Orange slice

Mix all ingredients, except orange slice, with cracked ice in a shaker or blender and pour into a chilled Old Fashioned glass. Garnish with orange slice.

 ## VIVIAN'S JURY

1½ oz. gin
½ oz. dry vermouth
½ oz. blue curaçao
Several dashes Pernod

Mix all ingredients with cracked ice in a shaker or blender. Strain into a chilled cocktail glass.

WARDAY'S COCKTAIL

1 oz. gin
1 oz. sweet vermouth
1 oz. calvados or applejack
1 tsp. yellow Chartreuse

Mix all ingredients with cracked ice in a shaker or blender and strain into a chilled cocktail glass.

 ## WEDDING BELLE

1 oz. gin
1 oz. Dubonnet rouge
½ oz. cherry brandy
1 oz. orange juice

Mix all ingredients with cracked ice in a shaker or blender and pour into a chilled cocktail glass.

WENDY FOULD

¾ oz. gin
¾ oz. Cointreau
¾ oz. apricot brandy
Orange slice

Mix all ingredients, except orange slice, with cracked ice in a shaker or blender and strain into chilled cocktail glass. Garnish with orange slice.

 ## WHITE BABY No. 2

1 oz. gin
1 oz. Cointreau or triple sec
1 oz. heavy cream

Mix all ingredients with cracked ice in a shaker or blender and strain into a chilled cocktail glass.

 ## WHITE CARGO No. 1

2½ oz. gin
½ oz. maraschino liqueur
Dash dry white wine
1 scoop vanilla ice cream

Mix in a blender until smooth, adding a little extra white wine if necessary. Serve in a chilled wine goblet.

 ## WHITE CARGO No. 2

2 oz. gin
Several dashes cream sherry
¼ cup vanilla ice cream
Maraschino cherry

Mix all ingredients, except maraschino cherry, for a few seconds in a blender until smooth. Pour into chilled parfait or sherbet glass and garnish with cherry.

WHITE LILY

1 oz. gin
1 oz. Cointreau
1 oz. light rum
Dash of Pernod

Mix all ingredients with cracked ice in a blender or shaker and strain into a chilled cocktail glass.

WHITE ROSE

1½ oz. gin
¾ oz. maraschino liqueur
2 oz. orange juice
½ oz. lime juice
1 tsp. sugar syrup
Egg white (for two drinks)

Mix all ingredients with cracked ice in a shaker or blender and strain into a chilled cocktail glass.

WHITEOUT

1½ oz. gin
1 oz. white crème de cacao
1 oz. heavy cream

Mix all ingredients with cracked ice in a shaker or blender and strain into a chilled cocktail glass.

XANTHIA

1 oz. gin
1 oz. cherry brandy
1 oz. yellow Chartreuse

Mix all ingredients with cracked ice in a shaker or blender and pour into a chilled cocktail glass.

MARTINI VARIATIONS

The Martini in all of its many versions, proportions, and formulations is unquestionably the emperor of cocktails. A gin Martini is the classic cocktail, and although the vodka-based Martini (see page 136) has become enormously popular, purists still consider the gin Martini the only real version of this redoubtable—and controversial—drink.

An apocryphal story illustrates the strong and divergent opinions that surround the ceremonial protocol involved in concocting a proper Martini. It seems a U.S. Air Force pilot was in the habit of carrying a small bottle of gin and vermouth, a jar of olives, a mixing spoon and large metal cup in his survival kit. Upon seeing the kit for the first time, his copilot said, "How on earth will those Martini makings ever help you if you're lost in the jungle?" The pilot replied, "If I'm lost out in the middle of nowhere, all I have to do is start making a Martini and sure enough, somebody will appear out of the bushes and say, 'That's no way to make a Martini!' "

Every Martini drinker has a special preference for the kind of gin and vermouth that is used, the garnish that is added, and even the number of ice cubes that are put into the mixing glass. As to mixing techniques, some say it should be stirred briefly so as "not to bruise the gin." A head bartender at a distinguished Chicago club famous for their great Martinis insists that Martinis must be stirred "at least a hundred times." Some devotees, including James Bond, prefer their Martinis "shaken, not stirred." Shaking aerates the mixture, so perhaps the flavor is improved slightly, but most people do not find the cloudy drink that results very appealing. There are even strong feelings about whether everything, including all the ingredients, should be chilled in advance. Some keep their gin stored in the freezing compartment of their refrigerator. Others stoutly maintain that the resulting drink is too strong because there is insufficient ice meltage. And when it comes to meltage, almost everyone agrees that a watery Martini is *totally unacceptable*.

A stormy debate can be generated instantly if one broaches the subject of proportions of gin vis-à-vis vermouth. Bernard DeVoto wrote a classic essay in *Harper's* magazine way back in 1949 in which he set forth an iron-bound principle which stated that the ideal ratio was precisely 3.7 parts of gin to one part of vermouth. Times have changed, and although DeVoto's formula makes a very pleasant drink, it would never suit those Martini lovers, who, like Winston Churchill, maintained that the world's finest Martini involved nothing more than glancing at the vermouth bottle (unopened) while pouring gin into the mixing glass.

Aside from serious experimentation with regard to the right ratio between gin and vermouth, there is considerable division of opinion as to additives. Purists are convinced that even a drop of lemon essence squeezed from a lemon peel is a violation of the integrity of this hallowed potation. The more audacious mixologist will use accents such as a minum or two of scotch, Pernod, curaçao, various bitters, crème de menthe, or whatever seems to add zest to the palate of the brash, restless, or jaded drinker. Obviously, if a dry cocktail sherry or a white wine vinegar in place of vermouth makes an exemplary cocktail in the opinion of the imbiber, then who can say that these things are adulterants rather than flavor enhancers?

Much is made of the dryness quotient of Martinis. Once a 12-to-1 Martini was considered potent, then came the 20-to-1 version. Of course we all know where this kind of one-upmanship leads: to straight gin chilled with ice. This is what some bars, including New York's famed "21" Club serves, when a valued customer asks for a *very* dry Martini. As one of their bartenders put it, "It is the only way you can convince some people that you have made the driest Martini possible in accordance with their request." Straight gin on the rocks is not a Martini or even a cocktail. It is a straight shot, a shooter, a rammer, a belt, or whatever you wish to call it, but not a mixed drink by any standard.

The cocktail that is believed to be the progenitor of the Martini is the Martinez, invented in the middle of the nineteenth century in San Francisco by a legendary bartender of the day, Jerry Thomas. The original recipe was 4-to-1—not 4 parts gin to one of vermouth, but the other way around, including a dash of bitters and two dashes of maraschino liqueur. In the Roaring Twenties a proper Martini was made with a large proportion of vermouth by today's tastes. Now, after hearing tales of the thousand-to-one Martini, it seems that a new generation of drinkers have discovered the Martini and are drinking them very much the way Bernard DeVoto did in the late Forties.

The Martini controversy is bound to continue and will never be resolved, but there are a few basics that almost everyone seems to subscribe to: Use the best ingredients, gin, vermouth, olives, etc., or at least what you consider to be the best. Use plenty of ice and make your drink with dispatch so it is crisp and crackling cold, and serve immediately in a chilled glass. By the same token, Martinis should be consumed while bright and fresh. They do not improve if left to warm to room temperature or to dilute if served on the rocks. As to additives or garnishes, this is purely a matter of personal taste. No matter what seems trendy or in, a good rule to follow is, if you don't like your Martini a certain way, don't drink it that way. This elegant concoction is meant to be enjoyed, to each his or her own. After all, that's why it was invented in the first place.

The following recipes are for various Martinis and the many Martini variations that have proliferated through the years.

ALLIES

1 oz. gin 1 oz. dry vermouth *Several dashes kummel*	Mix all ingredients with cracked ice in a shaker or blender. Pour into a chilled Old Fashioned glass.

ATTA BOY

2 oz. gin
1 oz. dry vermouth
½ tsp. grenadine
Lemon peel

Mix all ingredients, except lemon peel, with cracked ice in a shaker or blender and strain into a chilled cocktail glass. Twist lemon peel over drink and drop into drink.

DUTCH MARTINI

2 oz. Dutch genever gin
½ tsp. dry vermouth
Lemon peel

Pour gin and dry vermouth into mixing glass with plenty of ice cubes. Stir briskly and strain into a chilled cocktail glass. Twist lemon peel over drink and drop into glass.

FINO MARTINI

2 oz. gin
¼ oz. fino sherry
Lemon twist or olive

Pour gin and fino sherry into mixing glass with several ice cubes. Stir well and strain into a chilled cocktail glass. Twist lemon peel over drink and drop into glass or garnish with olive.

 ## GIBSON

2½ oz. gin
Several dashes dry vermouth
Cocktail onions

Pour gin and dry vermouth into mixing glass with ice cubes. Stir briskly and strain into a chilled cocktail glass. Garnish with cocktail onions.

GIN AND IT

1 oz. gin
1 oz. sweet vermouth

Combine in a chilled cocktail glass without ice.
Note: This is the original recipe. It may also be made with dry vermouth. Modern tastes opt for more gin, less vermouth, and ice.

GOLF MARTINI

1½ oz. gin
1 tsp. dry vermouth or to
    taste
Several dashes Angostura
    bitters
Green olive

Pour gin, dry vermouth, and
Angostura bitters in mixing glass
and stir vigorously with ice
cubes for one minute. Strain into
a chilled cocktail glass and
garnish with an olive.

HAWAIIAN MARTINI

1½ oz. gin
½ tsp. dry vermouth
½ tsp. sweet vermouth
½ tsp. pineapple juice

Mix all ingredients with cracked
ice in a shaker or blender and
strain into a chilled cocktail
glass.

HOFFMAN HOUSE

1½ oz. gin
½ oz. dry vermouth
Dash orange bitters
Olive

Stir gin, vermouth, and bitters
with ice and strain into a chilled
cocktail glass. Garnish with
olive.

IMPERIAL

1½ oz. gin
1½ oz. dry vermouth
Several dashes maraschino
    liqueur
Several dashes Angostura
    bitters

Olive

Mix all ingredients, except
green olive, with cracked ice in a
shaker or blender and strain
into a chilled cocktail glass.
Garnish with olive.

MARINER'S MARTINI

2–3 oz. gin
White wine vinegar with
    anchovies
Lemon twist or olive

In a mixing glass add plenty
of ice, gin, and several drops of
white wine vinegar in which
fillets of anchovies have been
steeped. Stir briskly and strain
into a chilled brandy snifter. Add

one or two anchovies and twist
lemon peel over drink and drop
into glass, or garnish with olive.
Note: To prepare anchovies and
vinegar, open a 2 oz. can of
anchovies and drain on paper
towels to *remove all oil* and steep
in white vinegar for several
days in refrigerator. When vinegar has a slight anchovy flavor,
it is ready to use.

THE MARTINEZ Forerunner of the Martini

Dash of bitters
2 dashes maraschino liqueur
1 pony Old Tom gin
1 wine glass vermouth
¼ slice lemon

Mix all ingredients, except lemon, in a shaker with cracked ice and strain into a chilled cocktail glass.
Note: Original recipe advised adding two dashes of "gum (sugar) syrup, if the guest prefers it very sweet."

MARTINI MELONZONA A LA MEDICI

2–3 oz. gin
White wine vinegar (in which baby eggplant have been steeped)
Lemon twist

Drain a jar of preserved baby eggplant and replace liquid with white wine vinegar and let steep in the refrigerator for several days. Pour gin into a mixing glass with ice cubes and add a few drops of vinegar from jar. Stir briskly and strain into a chilled brandy snifter. Garnish with one or two baby eggplant that have been drained on paper towels and decorate with lemon twist.

MARTINI ROMANA

1½ oz. gin
½ tsp. dry vermouth
Several dashes Campari

Pour all ingredients into a mixing glass with plenty of ice and stir briskly. Strain into a chilled cocktail glass.

MÉDOC MARTINI

2 oz. gin
½ tsp. dry vermouth
½ oz. Cordial Médoc

Mix all ingredients with cracked ice in a mixing glass and strain into a chilled cocktail glass.

NEWBURY

1½ oz. gin
1½ oz. sweet vermouth
Several dashes curaçao
Lemon peel
Orange peel

Mix all ingredients, except fruit peels, with cracked ice in a shaker or blender and strain into a chilled cocktail glass. Twist lemon and orange peels over drink and drop into glass.

PAISLEY MARTINI

2 oz. gin
½ tsp. dry vermouth
½ tsp. scotch

Mix all ingredients with plenty of cracked ice in a shaker or blender and strain into a chilled cocktail glass.

PALM ISLAND MARTINI

1½ oz. gin
½ oz. dry vermouth
¼ oz. white crème de cacao

Mix all ingredients with cracked ice in a shaker or blender and pour into a chilled Old Fashioned glass.
Note: Vermouth and crème de cacao should be adjusted to individual tastes.

PEGGY COCKTAIL

1½ oz. gin
½ oz. vermouth
Generous dash Dubonnet
Generous dash Pernod

Stir all ingredients with ice in a mixing glass and strain into a chilled cocktail glass.

PERFECT MARTINI

1½ oz. gin
½ tsp. dry vermouth
½ tsp. sweet vermouth
Green olive

Mix all ingredients, except green olive, with cracked ice in a mixing glass and strain into a chilled cocktail glass. Garnish with olive.

RACQUET CLUB

1½ oz. gin
½ oz. dry vermouth
Dash orange bitters

Stir all ingredients with ice in a mixing glass and strain into a chilled cocktail glass.

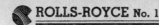 ROLLS-ROYCE No. 1

1½ oz. gin
½ oz. dry vermouth
½ oz. sweet vermouth
Several dashes Benedictine

Stir all ingredients in a mixing glass with ice and strain into a chilled cocktail glass.

SAKETINI

2 oz. gin
¼ oz. sake
Green olive or lemon twist

Mix all ingredients, except olive or lemon twist, with cracked ice in a shaker or blender and strain into a chilled cocktail glass. Garnish with olive or lemon twist.

SICILIAN MARTINI

1½ oz. gin
¼ oz. dry vermouth
½ oz. dry Marsala
Lemon peel

Pour gin, dry vermouth, and dry Marsala into mixing glass with ice cubes. Stir briskly and strain into a chilled cocktail glass. Twist lemon peel over drink and drop into glass.

SWEET MARTINI

2 oz. gin
½ oz. sweet vermouth
Dash orange bitters
Orange peel

Pour gin, vermouth, and bitters into a mixing glass with ice cubes. Mix well and strain into a chilled cocktail glass. Twist orange peel over drink and drop into glass.

THIRD DEGREE

1½ oz. gin
½ oz. dry vermouth
½ tsp. Pernod

Stir all ingredients with ice in a mixing glass and strain into a chilled cocktail glass.

WEMBLEY No. 1

1½ oz. gin
½ oz. vermouth
¼ oz. calvados or applejack

Stir all ingredients with ice in
a mixing glass and strain into a
chilled cocktail glass.

YALE COCKTAIL

1½ oz. gin
½ oz. dry vermouth
Several dashes orange bitters
Several dashes maraschino
* liqueur*

Stir in a mixing glass with
cracked ice and strain into a
chilled cocktail glass.

VODKA: THE GREAT WHITE SPIRIT

Drinking is the joy of the Rus!
—Grand Prince Vladimir,
First Czar of all
the Russias

Vodka, now the largest-selling category of spirits in the United States, is a highly refined liquor that, after processing, has no discernible taste, color, or odor. Unlike whiskey, vodka is distilled at a high proof (190 proof or about 95% pure alcohol) and thus is free of congeners, esters, botanicals, and those elements that give other kinds of spirits their distinctive flavor, aroma, and color. Contrary to popular belief, vodka is rarely made from potatoes today. Most of the better imported vodkas—and all vodkas distilled in the U.S.—are made from grain.

America's love affair with vodka began late in life—in 1946, to be exact, a period of severe war-caused shortages that had stripped liquor dealers' shelves of nearly all the old favorite brands. In those days vodka was known only vaguely as a beverage that people drink in Chekhov plays, Tolstoy novels, and in films about dashing cossacks and the brothers Karamazov roistering to strains of gypsy violins amid shouts of "Nazdorovye."

In their frantic search for something resembling potable spirits, it seems that some enterprising hedonists stumbled upon bottles of Smirnoff vodka, an obscure product that had been distilled in this country since the mid-1930s. The discovery was, as its ultimate impact upon the populace indicates, a noteworthy event, the magnitude of which was unsuspected at the time. The Smirnoff label, emblazoned with czarist crowns and royal regalia, represented not only a fine-quality distilled beverage, but, of even greater significance, had the unique characteristics of being tasteless, colorless, and odorless. As the Smirnoff folks were wont to say in their advertising, "It leaves you breathless"—a selling proposition of some consequence to a generation of Americans spending millions of dollars annually on mouthwash, chewing gum, and assorted breath purifiers.

The turning point came in the late 1940s when Smirnoff used an alien mule to propel its product to new popularity throughout the land. The Moscow Mule, in case you don't remember, was a refreshing combination of Smirnoff vodka, half a lime, and ginger beer served in a copper mug. It still is regarded in the spirits industry as one of the greatest promotions of its kind, and if you come across any of the old copper mugs inscribed with the picture of a mule, snap them up, since they are collector's items.

In the years that followed, many other distinguished brands have emerged; some like Smirnoff with authentic Russian antecedents and others Russian only in name, as well as a host of imports such as Stolichnaya (Russia), Wyborowa (Poland), Absolut (Sweden), Finlandia (Finland), and vodkas from such improbable places as Turkey, Israel, England, Ireland, and China.

In the United States, vodka by law is defined as "neutral spirits so distilled, or so treated after distillation with charcoal or other materials, as to be without distinctive character, aroma, taste, or color." The only differences among the various brands are the types of grain used, the distillation methods, the filtration techniques, and the water used to control the alcoholic strength. These strictures do not necessarily apply to vodkas made in foreign countries. A case in point is Stolichnaya, a vodka distilled in Russia. If you sip a little Stolichnaya on the rocks, you will detect a subtle flavor, a quite distinctive nuance for which some people with highly educated palates are willing to pay a premium price.

The Russians have contributed importantly to the art of distilling vodka. The techniques of filtering vodka through charcoal, which gives the finished product its "clean" taste, was discovered in 1810 by a Russian pharmaceutical chemist, Andrey Albanov. This process is used by nearly all distillers today.

The improvement in the smoothness, quality, and taste resulting from Albanov's charcoal filtration techniques brought vodka to new heights of popularity in Russia. At one point it is estimated that there were more than four thousand vodka brands being sold in the country. It has traditionally been tossed off neat with *zakuski* or appetizers such as smoked salmon, sturgeon, and eel, and, of course, freshly salted caviar, herring, smoked tongue, and exotic comestibles such as fish pie made from the head and cheeks of large sturgeon. It is reported that the Russian nobility, apparently in an attempt to emulate the lavish culinary bacchanalia of ancient Rome, enjoyed such delicacies as pate of songbirds and jellied wild boar's head, while downing large amounts of vodka before, during, and after the various courses. This practice, although somewhat attenuated, persists today in Russia and especially the Scandinavian countries, where the Swedish *smörgåsbord* and the Danish *kolde bord* are enjoyed to the accompaniment of cold akvavit and beer.

The practice of flavoring vodka is an ancient one, dating to the earliest mentions of vodka in Poland during the reign of Boleslaus I (992–1025), and in Russia, where twelfth-century records make numerous allusions to *zhiznennia voda* (water of life). Flavoring of vodka with various fruits and herbs is said to have originated with housewives who did not enjoy the raw taste of the early, crude distillates. Besides vodkas that are flavored by the distiller, even today the stuffing of citrus fruit peel, anise, basil, or black currants into a bottle of vodka to produce subtleties of flavor through the venerable process of infusion is common practice in Russian households.

As to the often raised question as to who was the first to invent vodka, the Russians or the Poles, historical writings provide clues, but no definitive answers. The Poles had their Boleslaus I, who made vodka drinking a royal custom during the tenth century. The Russians are quick to point out that also in the tenth century, Grand Prince Vladimir, the first Czar of a completely unified Russia, is supposed to have exclaimed upon being told that the use of vodka was contrary to the religious law of his Moslem subjects, "But drinking is the joy of the Rus!"

In spite of vodka's strong Russian image, the Poles, quietly but with firm conviction, claim to be the true originators of vodka. In addition to massive historical documentation that indicates that vodka was in common use in Poland in the fourteenth century, they point out that vodka (or *wodka* as it is spelled in Polish) is a diminutive term for water, springing originally from the Latin *aqua vitae* or "water of life." The Poles also contend that when their country was partitioned in 1795 (between Austria, Prussia, and Russia), Russia annexed the major part of their vodka distilling industry. In spite of this, they say, even today more Polish vodka is exported to Russia than to any other country.

The most telling argument of all, perhaps, is Wodka Wyborowa, a superb product made by Agros, a Polish state-operated trade organization. Like Stolichnaya, it is a clean-tasting vodka with an ephemeral bouquet and a subtle flavor. If your taste buds are alert, you might detect a whisper of rye or some fleeting mineral taste from the type of water used. In any event, Wodka Wyborowa is an experience worth repeating.

The popularity of vodka spread from Russia and Poland throughout northern Europe, where its restorative properties in helping combat the ravages of long, freezing winter nights were especially appreciated. The Scandinavians flavored their vodkas with caraway, dill, and other herbs and spices—and called the end result *akvavit* (or *aquavit* from *aqua vitae*). Elsewhere in this chapter we shall explore some of the delightful ways of using this bracing spirit.

For many years in Sweden, an unflavored akvavit called *renat brännvin* has been popular. As the consumption of vodka increased in America, the Scandinavians began to export their high-quality neutral spirits with considerable success. Finlandia, noted for its striking ice-sculptured packaging, has built up a loyal following in this country. *Renat brännvin* was introduced to the U.S. market as Absolut Vodka in a starkly modern bottle that immediately attracted the attention of quality-import vodka enthusiasts. Its bright, clean, zesty qualities combined with aggressive marketing has made it the top-selling imported vodka in the country.

The best way to sample vodka is to take it neat, as old-world vodka drinkers do, in one gulp, or to pour an ounce over ice, savor the bouquet, if any, swirl a few drops around the mouth, and swallow. Some purists are adamant that you should not swallow any spirit you are taste-testing—but if you don't, you will never be able to really judge the aftertaste. More important is the water your ice is made from, since this can affect the taste. This detail is often overlooked not only by tasters, but wary tourists who eschew the tap water in a foreign country, and then proceed to guzzle drinks cooled with ice made from tap water.

The great white spirit is an international affair that will titillate your taste buds, and at times puzzle your palate, but you should always find it refreshing and satisfying, as the "water of life" was meant to be.

Vodka's universal and growing popularity has produced important sub-classifications within the category, some of which have reached the level of cult subjects. The Bloody Mary and the Vodka Martini in all of their many forms and variations are good examples. Flavored vodkas and the practice of flavoring them in the home are also subjects worthy of special attention.

Following the main body of vodka drink recipes in this chapter are special sections on the Bloody Mary, page 138, Vodka Martini, page 146; flavored vodka (including do-it-yourself recipes and distilled specialties such as aquavit), page 148; and a collection of light, low-alcoholic concoctions called "Splash Drinks" for those who desire to drink moderately, page 156.

ALEXANDER NEVSKY

1 oz. vodka
1 oz. apricot liqueur
½ oz. lemon juice
4 oz. orange juice
Orange slice

Mix all ingredients, except orange slice, in a shaker or blender with cracked ice and pour into a chilled wine goblet. Garnish with orange slice.

ANNA'S BANANA

1½ oz. vodka
1 oz. lime juice
½ small ripe banana, peeled and sliced
1 tsp. orgeat syrup or honey
Lime slice

Mix all ingredients, except lime slice, with cracked ice in a blender until smooth. Strain into a chilled wine glass and garnish with lime slice.

BANANA BALM

1½ oz. vodka
½ oz. banana liqueur
1 tsp. lime juice
Club soda
Mint sprigs

Mix vodka and banana liqueur with cracked ice in a shaker or blender. Pour into a chilled highball glass. Fill with club soda. Stir gently. Garnish with mint sprigs.

BEAU RIVAGE

1½ oz. vodka
1 tsp. sugar syrup
1 tsp. Pernod
1 cucumber slice (lengthwise)

Mix all ingredients, except cucumber, with cracked ice in a shaker or blender and pour into an Old Fashioned glass. Decorate with cucumber slice.

BARTENDER'S SECRET NO. 7

Don't overchill beer. It makes the beer look cloudy, suppresses the head, and interferes with the flavor. The 45 degree (F) range is just about right, give or take a few degrees. Ale and stout are best when served around 55 degrees because of their more complex flavors. Bottled beer should be stored in a cool place and away from sunlight. If a bottle or can of beer has no fizz when poured into a glass, discard it. It may be spoiled. And never wash beer mugs or glasses in soap and water. It destroys the head. Instead, wash in a solution of salt or soda and air dry.

BEER BUSTER

2 oz. 100-proof vodka, ice
   cold
Several dashes Tabasco sauce
Beer or ale, ice cold

Pour all ingredients into chilled
beer mug and stir gently.

BELMONT STAKES

1½ oz. vodka
½ oz. gold rum
½ oz. strawberry liqueur
½ oz. lime juice
½ tsp. grenadine
Orange slice

Mix all ingredients, except orange
slice, with cracked ice in a
shaker or blender. Strain into a
chilled cocktail glass. Garnish
with orange slice.

BLACKHAWK

1½ oz. vodka
½ oz. blackberry brandy
½ oz. lime juice
Lime slice

Mix all ingredients, except lime
slice, with cracked ice in a shaker
or blender. Strain into a chilled
cocktail glass and garnish with
lime slice.

BLACK RUSSIAN

1½ oz. vodka
¾ oz. Kahlua

Mix both ingredients with cracked
ice in a shaker or blender. Pour
into a chilled Old Fashioned
glass.
Note: To make a Black Magic,
add several dashes lemon
juice.

BARTENDER'S SECRETS NO. 8

When making Bloody Marys or other drinks requiring pepper,
perceptive bartenders, mindful that a pinch of black pepper on
the surface of a drink is about as appetizing as a used cigar,
follow the custom of French chefs, who for many years have
used ground *white* pepper in cream soups, salad dressings,
and light sauces. It is not only invisible to the casual observer,
but blends better than ground black pepper. The flavoring
imparted is about the same.

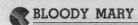 **BLOODY MARY**

Note: Basic recipe. See page 138 for Bloody Mary variations

2 oz. vodka
4–6 oz. tomato juice
1 tsp. lemon juice
¼ tsp. Worcestershire sauce
Several dashes Tabasco sauce
Pinch white pepper
Several pinches celery salt
   or to taste

½ tsp. chopped dill (fresh or
   dried)

Mix all ingredients well with cracked ice and serve in a chilled Collins glass with additional ice cubes if needed.

BLUE LAGOON

1½ oz. vodka
½ oz. blue curaçao
1½ oz. pineapple juice
Several dashes green
   Chartreuse
Pineapple slice

Mix all ingredients, except pineapple slice, with cracked ice in a shaker or blender. Strain into a chilled cocktail glass. Decorate with pineapple slice.

BLUE LOU

2 oz. vodka
1 oz. blue curaçao
Several dashes kirsch

Mix all ingredients with cracked ice in a shaker or blender. Strain into a chilled cocktail glass.

BLUE SHARK

1 oz. vodka
1 oz. tequila
Several dashes blue curaçao

Mix all ingredients with cracked ice in a blender or shaker and pour into a chilled Old Fashioned glass.

BORODINO

1 oz. vodka
1 oz. gin
1 oz. triple sec

Mix all ingredients with cracked ice in a shaker or blender. Strain into a chilled cocktail glass.

THE BOTTOM LINE

1½ oz. vodka
½ oz. Rose's lime juice
Tonic water
Lime slice

Mix vodka and lime juice with ice cubes in a highball glass and fill with tonic. Garnish with lime slice.

BOYAR

2 oz. vodka
½ oz. dry vermouth
¼ oz. kummel

Mix all ingredients with cracked ice in a shaker or blender and strain into a chilled cocktail glass.

BRIDGETOWN GIMLET

2½ oz. vodka
½ oz. Rose's lime juice
½ oz. fresh lime juice
½ oz. Falernum or to taste

Mix all ingredients with cracked ice in a shaker or blender and pour into an Old Fashioned glass.

BULLFROG

1½ oz. vodka
4 oz. limeade
1 tsp. triple sec
Lime slices

Mix all ingredients, except lime slices, with cracked ice in a shaker or blender and pour into a chilled double Old Fashioned glass. Garnish with lime slices.

BULL ROAR

2 oz. vodka
4 oz. beef bouillon, beef consommé, or beef broth
½ oz. lemon juice
½ tsp. Bovril beef extract
Dash Tabasco sauce
Dash A-1 sauce

Dash Worcestershire sauce
Pinch freshly ground white pepper

Mix all ingredients with cracked ice in a mixing glass and pour into a chilled Old Fashioned glass.

BULL SHOT

1½–2 oz. vodka
4 oz. beef consommé or beef bouillion
1 tsp. lemon juice
Several dashes Worcestershire sauce
Several dashes Tabasco sauce (optional)

½ tsp. horseradish (optional)
Pinch celery salt or celery seed (optional)

Mix all ingredients with ice cubes in a chilled double Old Fashioned glass.

BUTTER CREAM

1 oz. vodka
1½ oz. butterscotch schnapps
3 oz. Irish cream

Mix all ingredients with ice in a chilled double Old Fashioned glass.

 ## THE CAMP FIRE CLUB COOLER

4 oz. vodka
2 oz. Pina Colada mix
4 oz. grapefruit juice
4 oz. orange juice

Mix all ingredients with cracked ice in shaker or blender and pour into chilled Collins glasses. Makes 2 drinks.
Note: Created for the Camp Fire Club of America, Chappaqua, N.Y.

 ## CAPE CODDER

1½ oz. vodka
Dash lime juice
4 oz. cranberry juice
1 tsp. sugar syrup or to taste

Mix all ingredients with cracked ice in a shaker or blender and strain into a chilled double Old Fashioned glass.

 ## CAROL'S DELIGHT

1½ oz. vodka
4 oz. orange juice
½ oz. cherry-flavored brandy
1 tsp. Falernum or to taste

Mix all ingredients with cracked ice in a shaker or blender and serve in a chilled double Old Fashioned glass.

 ## CAYMAN CUP

1½ oz. vodka
½ oz. triple sec
2 oz. mango nectar
2 oz. orange juice
½ oz. lemon juice
Mango or peach slices

Mix all ingredients, except mango slices, with cracked ice in a shaker or blender. Pour into a chilled Collins glass. Decorate with fruit slices.

 ## CHERRY ORCHARD

1½ oz. vodka
1 oz. kirsch
1 oz. cherry liqueur
Dash lemon juice

Mix all ingredients with cracked ice in a shaker or blender and pour into a chilled cocktail glass.

CHERRY RUM FIX

1 tsp. confectioner's sugar
Water
1 oz. vodka
1 oz. light rum
½ oz. Peter Heering or Cherry Marnier
½ oz. lemon juice
Brandied cherry
Lemon slice

Muddle sugar and water in a chilled double Old Fashioned glass until sugar is dissolved and add all other ingredients, except cherry and lemon slice. Mix well with ice cubes or cracked ice and garnish with cherry and lemon slice.

CHIQUITA

1½ oz. vodka
½ oz. banana liqueur
¼ cup bananas, sliced
½ oz. lime juice
1 tsp. orgeat syrup or sugar syrup

Mix all ingredients with cracked ice in a shaker until smooth. Pour into chilled deep-saucer champagne glass.

CIRCASSIAN CREAM

1 oz. vodka
½ oz. sweet vermouth
1 oz. heavy cream
½ oz. curaçao
½ oz. white crème de cacao

Mix all ingredients with cracked ice in a shaker or blender. Pour into a chilled Old Fashioned glass.

COFFEE COOLER

1½ oz. vodka
1 oz. Kahlua
1 oz. heavy cream
4 oz. iced coffee
1 scoop coffee ice cream

Mix all ingredients, except ice cream, with cracked ice in a shaker or blender. Pour into a chilled double Old Fashioned glass and top with coffee ice cream.

COLD COFFEE CHANTILLY

1 oz. vodka
1 oz. coffee schnapps
3 oz. heavy cream
½ oz. triple sec

Mix all ingredients with cracked ice in a shaker or blender and pour into a chilled wine glass or brandy snifter.

COPACABANA BANANA

1 oz. vodka
1 oz. gold rum
1 oz. lime juice
1 tsp. orgeat syrup
½ banana, peeled and sliced
1 tsp. banana liqueur

Mix all ingredients, except banana liqueur, with cracked ice in a blender and pour into a chilled wine goblet and top with banana liqueur.

 ## CORAL REEF

1½ oz. vodka
2 oz. Malibu or CocoRibe
6 fresh strawberries or tbsp. strawberry preserves

Mix all ingredients with cracked ice in a blender and pour into a chilled wine goblet.

CORTINA COCKTAIL

1½ oz. vodka
1½ oz. white port
1 tsp. Campari
Dash grenadine

Stir all ingredients in a mixing glass with ice and pour into a chilled cocktail glass.

 ## CORTINA CUP

1 oz. vodka
½ oz. white crème de cacao
½ oz. sambuca
½ oz. heavy cream

Mix all ingredients with cracked ice in a blender until smooth. Strain into chilled cocktail glass.

 ## COSSACK CHARGE

1½ oz. vodka
½ oz. cognac
½ oz. cherry brandy

Mix all ingredients with cracked ice in a shaker or blender and pour into a chilled cocktail glass.

 ## COSSACK COFFEE GROG

1½ oz. vodka
1 oz. Kahlua, Tia Maria, or crème de cacao
½ cup black coffee, chilled
¼ tsp. vanilla extract
¼ tsp. ground cinnamon
1 scoop chocolate ice cream

Mix all ingredients with a small amount of crushed ice in a blender and serve in a chilled double Old Fashioned glass.

THE COUNTESS COCKTAIL

1 oz. vodka
1 oz. Peter Heering
½ oz. triple sec
1½ oz. orange juice
1½ oz. grapefruit juice

Mix all ingredients with cracked ice in a shaker or blender and pour into a chilled Old Fashioned glass.

COUNT OF PARIS

1 oz. vodka
1 oz. cognac
½ oz. anisette
½ oz. triple sec

Mix all ingredients with cracked ice in a shaker or blender. Strain into a chilled cocktail glass.

 ## COUNT STROGANOFF

1½ oz. vodka
¾ oz. white crème de cacao
½ oz. lemon juice

Mix all ingredients with cracked ice in a shaker or blender. Strain into a chilled cocktail glass.

 ## COW-COW COOLER

1½ oz. vodka
¾ oz. root beer schnapps
Root beer
Large scoop vanilla ice cream

Combine vodka and root beer schnapps in a chilled Collins glass with ice cubes and fill with cold root beer. Drop in ice cream scoop.

 ## CRIMEA COOLER

1½ oz. vodka
3 oz. grapefruit juice
½ oz. crème de cassis
Ginger ale
Mint sprig (optional)
Orange slice

Mix vodka, grapefruit juice, and cassis with cracked ice in a shaker or blender and pour into a chilled Collins glass. Fill with cold ginger ale and garnish with mint sprig and orange slice.

 ## THE DRAKE COOLER

1½ oz. vodka
1 oz. sloe gin
4 oz. pineapple juice
4 oz. grapefruit juice
Dash Falernum or simple
  syrup to taste

Mix all ingredients with cracked ice in a shaker or blender and pour into a tall chilled Collins glass.
Note: Created for Drake University, Des Moines, Iowa.

DUBROVNIK

1½ oz. vodka
¾ oz. slivovitz
½ oz. lemon juice
½ tsp. sugar syrup

Mix all ingredients with cracked ice in a shaker or blender and pour into a chilled cocktail glass.

 ## DUBONNET FIZZ No. 1

1 oz. vodka
3 oz. Dubonnet rouge
Club soda
Lemon peel

Mix vodka and Dubonnet with several ice cubes in a highball glass and fill with club soda. Twist lemon peel over drink and drop in.

EGGHEAD

1½ oz. vodka
4 oz. orange juice
1 egg

Mix all ingredients with cracked ice in a blender until smooth and pour into a chilled Old Fashioned glass.

FLYING GRASSHOPPER

1½ oz. vodka
½ oz. green crème de menthe
½ oz. white crème de menthe

Mix all ingredients with cracked ice in a shaker or blender and pour into a chilled Old Fashioned glass.

 ## FUZZY NAVEL No. 2

1 oz. vodka
½ oz. peach schnapps
6 oz. orange juice
Orange slice

Mix all ingredients, except orange slice, with cracked ice in a shaker or blender and pour into a chilled Collins glass.

 ## GAZPACHO MACHO

1½ oz. vodka or tequila
2 oz. gazpacho soup
2 oz. beef bouillon
½ oz. lemon juice
Dash Tabasco sauce
Dash Worcestershire sauce
Pinch freshly ground white
   pepper

Pinch celery salt
1 tsp. dry sherry

Mix all ingredients, except sherry, with cracked ice in a mixing glass and pour into a chilled Old Fashioned glass. Float sherry on top.

GENOA

1½ oz. vodka
2 oz. orange juice
¾ oz. Campari

Mix all ingredients with cracked ice in a blender or shaker and pour into a chilld Old Fashioned glass.

GEORGIA PEACH

1½ oz. vodka
¾ oz. peach-flavored brandy
1 tsp. peach preserves
1 tsp. lemon juice
1 slice canned or fresh peach, peeled and chopped

Mix all ingredients with cracked ice in a blender until smooth and pour into a chilled double Old Fashioned glass.

GINGERSNAP

3 oz. vodka
1 oz. Stone's ginger wine
Club soda

Combine vodka and ginger wine with several ice cubes in a double Old Fashioned glass. Fill with soda and stir gently.

GINZA MARY

1½ oz. vodka
1½ oz. V-8 or tomato juice cocktail
1½ oz. sake
½ oz. lemon juice
Several dashes Tabasco sauce

Dash soy sauce or to taste
Pinch freshly ground white pepper

Mix all ingredients with cracked ice in a mixing glass and pour into a chilled Old Fashioned glass.

THE GODMOTHER

1½ oz. vodka
¾ oz. Amaretto di Saronno

Mix with ice cubes in a chilled Old Fashioned glass.

GOLDEN FROG

½ oz. vodka
½ oz. Galliano
½ oz. Strega
½ oz. lemon juice

Mix all ingredients with cracked ice in a blender until smooth. Pour into a chilled cocktail glass.

GREEN DRAGON

2 oz. Stolichnaya vodka
1 oz. green Chartreuse

Mix with cracked ice in a shaker or blender and strain into a chilled cocktail glass.

GREEN ISLAND

1½ oz. vodka
3 oz. pineapple juice
Juice of 1 lime
½ tsp. sugar syrup
½ oz. green crème de menthe
Pineapple spear

Mix all ingredients, except crème de menthe and pineapple spear, with cracked ice in a shaker or blender and pour into a chilled Hurricane glass. Top with float of green crème de menthe and garnish with pineapple spear.

GYPSY

2 oz. vodka
½ oz. Benedictine
1 tsp. lemon juice
1 tsp. orange juice
Orange slice

Mix all ingredients, except orange slice, with cracked ice in a shaker or blender and strain into a chilled cocktail glass. Garnish with orange slice.

GYPSY SPELL

1½ oz. vodka
½ oz. Benedictine
½ oz. brandy
Several dashes curaçao

Mix all ingredients with cracked ice in a shaker or blender and strain into a chilled cocktail glass.

HANLEY SPECIAL

2 oz. vodka
1 oz. gin
⅔ cup tangerine juice
Falernum to taste (sugar
   syrup may also be used)

Mix with cracked ice in a shaker or blender and pour into a chilled double Old Fashioned glass.

HARVEY WALLBANGER

1½ oz. vodka
4 oz. orange juice
½ oz. Galliano

Pour vodka and orange juice into a chilled Collins glass with several ice cubes and stir well. Top with Galliano float.

HAVERFORD HOOKER

4 oz. vodka or gin
1 oz. orgeat syrup or to taste
½ pint vanilla ice cream
Club soda
Mint sprigs (Optional)

Mix all ingredients, except soda and mint, with cracked ice in a shaker or blender and pour into a chilled double Old Fashioned glass. If mixture is too thick, add a little soda and stir gently. Garnish with mint sprigs. *Note:* Created for the Haverford School, Haverford, Pa.

THE ICE PICK

1½ oz. vodka
Iced tea
Lemon wedge

Fill a highball or Collins glass with several ice cubes and vodka and fill with iced tea. Squeeze lemon over drink and drop into glass.

 ## INEZ COCKTAIL

1 oz. vodka
1 oz. brandy
1 oz. cream sherry
2 oz. dry red wine
½ oz. Swedish Punsch
2 oz. orange juice
Dash sugar syrup or to taste

Mix all ingredients with cracked ice in a shaker or blender and pour into chilled cocktail glasses. Makes 2 drinks.

JAEGERMEISTER

1½ oz. vodka
½ oz. kummel
½ oz. lime juice
Lime peel

Mix all ingredients, except lime peel, with cracked ice in a shaker or blender. Strain into a chilled cocktail glass. Twist lime peel over drink and drop in.

 ## JUNGLE JIM

1 oz. vodka
1 oz. crème de banane
1 oz. milk.

Mix with cracked ice in a shaker or blender and pour into a chilled Old Fashioned glass.

KEMPINSKY FIZZ

1½ oz. vodka
½ oz. crème de cassis
1 tsp. lemon juice
Ginger ale, bitter lemon soda,
   or club soda

Pour all ingredients, except soda, into chilled highball glass with ice. Fill with soda and stir gently.

KIEV CUP

1½ oz. 100-proof vodka
½ oz. Peter Heering
½ oz. lime juice
Dash cherry brandy

Mix all ingredients, except brandy, with cracked ice in a shaker or blender and strain into a chilled cocktail glass. Top with cherry brandy.

KRETCHMA

1 oz. vodka
1 oz. crème de cacao
½ oz. lemon juice
½ tsp. grenadine

Mix all ingredients with cracked ice in a shaker or blender. Strain into a chilled cocktail glass.

LE DOYEN

1 oz. vodka
1 oz. crème de banane
1 oz. cream

Mix all ingredients with cracked ice in a shaker or blender. Strain into a chilled cocktail glass.

LIEUTENANT KIJE

1 oz. vodka
1 oz. apricot liqueur
1 oz. orange juice

Mix all ingredients with cracked ice in a shaker or blender and strain into a chilled cocktail glass.

MADAME DE MONTESPAN

1 oz. vodka
½ oz. white crème de cacao
½ oz. curaçao
1 oz. heavy cream

Mix all ingredients with cracked ice in a shaker or blender. Pour into a chilled cocktail glass.

MOSCOW MILK TODDY

1½ oz. vodka
½ oz. grenadine
4 oz. milk
Powdered cinnamon

Mix all ingredients, except cinnamon, with cracked ice in a shaker or blender and pour into a chilled Old Fashioned glass. Top with powdered cinnamon.

MOSCOW MULE

2–3 oz. vodka
1 tsp. lime juice
Ginger beer
Lime slice or wedge

Pour vodka and lime juice in a chilled coffee mug or a high-ball glass with several ice cubes. Stir and fill with ginger beer. Garnish with lime.

This is the original Moscow Mule from the Cock n' Bull Restaurant, Los Angeles.

MOTHER'S WHISTLER

1½ oz. vodka
4 oz. pineapple juice
½ oz. orgeat syrup
Dash kirsch
Pineapple stick

Mix all ingredients, except pineapple stick, with cracked ice in a shaker or blender and pour into a chilled Old Fashioned glass. Decorate with pineapple.

MOSCVATINI

1½ oz. Stolichnaya vodka
1 oz. kummel
Black olive

Mix with cracked ice in a mixing glass and strain into a chilled cocktail glass. Garnish with black olive.

NEVSKY PROSPECT

1½ oz. vodka
½ oz. light rum
½ oz. curaçao
¼ oz. lime juice

1 tsp. sugar syrup or to taste

Mix all ingredients with cracked ice in a shaker or blender, and strain into a chilled cocktail glass.

NINOTCHKA'S NIGHT CAP

1 oz. vodka
½ oz. gold rum
½ oz. coffee liqueur

4 oz. milk

Mix all ingredients with ice in a chilled Old Fashioned glass.

OMSK PEACH

1½ oz. vodka
½ oz. peach brandy
½ oz. orgeat syrup or to taste
1 tsp. lemon juice
1 ripe peach peeled and diced
  or canned peach, diced.

Mix all ingredients with cracked
ice in a blender until smooth
and serve in a chilled wine goblet.

 ORANGE BANG! No. 1

2 oz. vodka
4 oz. fresh orange juice
½ oz. curaçao
½ cup orange sections, fresh
  or canned

Mix all ingredients with cracked
ice in a shaker or blender and
pour into a chilled double Old
Fashioned glass.

ORANGE DELIGHT

1 oz. vodka
1 oz. curaçao
½ oz. lime juice
½ oz. lemon juice
4 oz. orange juice
Orange slice

Mix all ingredients, except orange
slice, with cracked ice in a shaker
or blender. Pour into a chilled
double Old Fashioned glass. Garnish with orange slice.

PASSION CUP No. 2

1 oz. vodka
1 oz. Jamaica rum
½ oz. La Grande Passion
½ oz. lemon juice
Lemon peel

Mix all ingredients, except lemon
peel, with cracked ice in a shaker
or blender. Pour into a chilled
Old Fashioned glass. Twist lemon
peel over drink and drop in.

PAVLOVA COCKTAIL

1½ oz. vodka
¾ oz. light rum
½ oz. strawberry liqueur
1 fresh strawberry (optional)

Mix all ingredients, except strawberry, with cracked ice in a
shaker or blender and strain into
a chilled cocktail glass. Garnish
with strawberry.

PEACH BUCK

1½ oz. vodka
½ oz. peach brandy
½ oz. lemon juice
Ginger ale
Peach slice

Mix all ingredients, except ginger ale and peach slice, with cracked ice in a shaker or blender and pour into chilled highball glass. Fill with ginger ale and garnish with peach slice.

PEACH TREE STREET

1½ oz. vodka
¾ oz. peach schnapps
3 oz. cranberry juice
3 oz. orange juice
Peach slice

Mix all ingredients, except peach slice, with cracked ice in a shaker or blender and pour into a chilled wine goblet. Garnish with peach slice.

PETER'S CHEER

1 oz. vodka
1 oz. Peter Heering
½ oz. dry vermouth
2 oz. orange juice

Mix all ingredients with cracked ice in a shaker or blender. Strain into a chilled cocktail glass.

PETROGRAD PUNCH

1½ oz. vodka
3 oz. grapefruit juice
2 oz. concord grape wine

Mix vodka and grapefruit juice with cracked ice in a shaker or blender and pour into a chilled wine goblet. Top with wine float.

PETROUCHKA

1 oz. vodka
½ oz. light rum
½ oz. strawberry liqueur
1 tsp. lime juice
Dash grenadine
Brut champagne
1 fresh strawberry

Mix vodka, rum, strawberry liqueur, lime juice, and grenadine with cracked ice in a shaker or blender and pour into a large, chilled wine goblet. Fill with cold champagne and garnish with strawberry.

PILE DRIVER

2 oz. vodka
3 oz. prune juice
½ tsp. lemon juice

Stir well with ice in a double Old Fashioned glass.

PINE VALLEY No. 2

1½ oz. vodka
½ oz. peppermint schnapps
Limeade or lemon-lime soda
Lime slice

Pour vodka and schnapps into a chilled Collins glass with ice cubes. Add limeade or soda and stir gently. Garnish with lime slice.

PINK PEARL

2½ oz. vodka
4 oz. grapefruit juice
1 oz. maraschino cherry juice
1½ oz. Rose's lime juice
Maraschino cherry

Mix all ingredients, except cherry, with cracked ice in a shaker or blender. Strain into a chilled double Old Fashioned glass. Garnish with maraschino cherry.

THE PINK PUSSYCAT

2 oz. vodka
4 oz. orange juice
2 oz. cranberry juice
¼ oz. maple syrup or to taste

Mix all ingredients with cracked ice in a shaker or blender and pour into a chilled double Old Fashioned glass.

BARTENDER'S SECRET NO. 9

To freeze a bottle of vodka or akvavit in a block of ice is not only a very fashionable way to serve these spirits crackling cold in pony glasses to be quaffed neat with caviar or whatever else is being offered as an hors d'oeuvre, but it is a practical way of ensuring your spirits will be properly iced. One method is to cut the top off a half-gallon milk carton and fill with water and place a bottle of spirits in the center of the carton, place in freezing compartment standing vertically and fill with additional water until the carton is filled to the rim. After ice is frozen solid, remove carton and save for use in replacing ice meltage when the cake of ice is served at room temperature. Bottle may be stored in the carton in the freezer and additional water added for refreezing ice block as needed.

PLUM BOB

2 oz. vodka or gin
Juice of 2 ripe red plums
2 tbsp. plum jelly
Juice of ½ lemon
Sugar syrup to taste
Lemon-lime soda

Mix all ingredients, except lemon-lime soda, with cracked ice in a shaker or blender and pour into a chilled double Old Fashioned glass. Fill with soda and stir gently.

POLYNESIAN PEPPER POT

1½ oz. vodka
¾ oz. gold rum
4 oz. pineapple juice
½ oz. orgeat syrup or sugar syrup
½ tsp. lemon juice
1 tbsp. cream
Several dashes Tabasco sauce
¼ tsp. cayenne pepper
Curry powder

Mix all ingredients, except curry powder, with cracked ice in a shaker or blender. Pour into a chilled double Old Fashioned glass and sprinkle with curry powder.
Note: This was intended to be a hot, spicy drink. Seasonings should be adjusted to personal tastes.

PRINCE IGOR

1½ oz. vodka
¾ oz. Grand Marnier
4 oz. orange juice
1 tsp. grenadine

Mix all ingredients, except grenadine, with cracked ice in a shaker or blender. Pour into a chilled double Old Fashioned glass and top with grenadine.

PROVINCETOWN PLAYHOUSE

1 oz. vodka
1 oz. gold rum
3 oz. cranberry juice
½ oz. sugar syrup or to taste

Dash lime juice

Mix all ingredients in a chilled Old Fashioned glass with several ice cubes.

PRUSSIAN SALUTE

1½ oz. vodka
½ oz. blackberry brandy
½ oz. slivovitz
½ oz. triple sec

Mix all ingredients with cracked ice in a shaker or blender. Strain into a chilled cocktail glass.

PUERTO PLATA

1½ oz. vodka
½ oz. banana liqueur
2 oz. pineapple juice
½ oz. orgeat syrup
1 tsp. lemon juice

Mix all ingredients with cracked ice in a shaker or blender. Strain into a chilled Old Fashioned glass.

PURPLE PASSION

1½ oz. vodka
2–3 oz. grape juice
Ginger ale or club soda

Mix vodka and grape juice with ice cubes in a Collins glass and fill with ginger ale or soda. Stir gently.

PUSHKIN'S PUNCH

1 oz. vodka
1 oz. Grand Marnier
Dash lime juice
Dash orange bitters
Champagne or dry sparkling
    wine

Mix all ingredients, except wine, with cracked ice in a blender or shaker. Strain into a large chilled wine goblet and fill with chilled champagne. Stir gently.

QUAKER CITY COOLER

1 oz. vodka
3 oz. chablis
½ oz. sugar syrup
½ oz. lemon juice
Several dashes vanilla extract
1 tsp. grenadine

Mix all ingredients, except grenadine, in a shaker or blender with cracked ice and pour into a chilled wine goblet. Top with grenadine.

RACING DRIVER

2 oz. vodka
1 oz. sloe gin
3 tbsp. frozen orange juice
    concentrate
3 maraschino cherries
Dash kirsch

In blender with cracked ice combine vodka, sloe gin, orange juice, and cherries. Add ice, continuing to blend until mixture is very thick and smooth. Pour into sherbet glasses and top with kirsch. Serves two.

RAINY SUNDAY

2 oz. vodka
2 oz. gin
3 oz. orange juice
3 oz. grapefruit juice
Generous tbsp. orange sections
Generous tbsp. grapefruit sections

Dash simple syrup or to taste
Several dashes orange flower water

Mix all ingredients with plenty of cracked ice in a shaker or blender and pour into double Old Fashioned glasses. Makes 2 drinks.

RASPUTIN'S REVENGE

1½ oz. 100-proof vodka
1 oz. cognac
1 oz. Grand Marnier
1 oz. lime juice
Several dashes orange bitters or Angostura bitters
Orange slice

Mix all ingredients, except orange slice, with cracked ice in a shaker or blender and strain into a cocktail glass or a Whiskey Sour glass and garnish with orange slice.

 THE RED BIRD

2 oz. vodka
1 oz. sloe gin
3 oz. cranberry juice
3 oz. orange juice

Mix all ingredients with cracked ice in a shaker or blender and pour into a chilled double Old Fashioned glass.

RED LIGHT

1½ oz. vodka
1 oz. cranberry liqueur
Dash lime juice

Pour all ingredients into a chilled cocktail glass with several ice cubes. Stir gently.

 THE ROMANOFF APPLE

1½ oz. vodka
¼ oz. calvados or applejack
½ oz. lime juice
1 tsp. sugar syrup
¼ cup chopped apples, cored and pared

Mix all ingredients with cracked ice in blender until smooth and pour into a chilled champagne saucer.

ROSE COLLINS

3 oz. vodka
1½ oz. sloe gin
2 packages of dry Tom Collins mix or 2 oz. lemon
   or lime concentrate
1 egg white

Mix all ingredients with plenty of
cracked ice in a blender and
pour into chilled double Old Fashioned glasses. Makes 2 drinks.

 ## RUSSIAN BEAR

1 oz. vodka
1 oz. dark crème de cacao
1 oz. heavy cream

Mix all ingredients with cracked
ice in a shaker or blender and
strain into a chilled cocktail glass.

 ## RUSSIAN COCKTAIL

1 oz. vodka
1 oz. gin
1 oz. white crème de cacao

Mix all ingredients with cracked
ice in a shaker or blender and
strain into a chilled cocktail glass.

 ## RUSSIAN COFFEE

½ oz. vodka
1½ oz. coffee liqueur
1 oz. heavy cream

Mix all ingredients with cracked
ice in a blender and pour into
a chilled brandy snifter.

RUSSIAN PORT

1 oz. vodka
1 oz. white port wine
Dash Angostura bitters

Mix all ingredients in a mixing
glass with cracked ice and
strain into a chilled cocktail glass.

RUSSIAN ROB ROY

1½ oz. vodka
½ oz. dry vermouth
½ oz. scotch
Lemon twist

Stir all ingredients, except lemon
twist, in a mixing glass and
pour into a chilled cocktail glass.
Garnish with lemon twist.

RUSSIAN ROSE

2 oz. vodka
½ oz. grenadine
Dash orange bitters

Mix all ingredients with cracked ice in a mixing glass and strain into a chilled cocktail glass.

 RUSSIAN WOLFHOUND

Pinch salt
1½ oz. vodka
2 oz. bitter lemon soda
2 oz. grapefruit juice

Moisten rim of a chilled wine goblet with several dashes bitter lemon soda, and roll rim in salt. Pour vodka, grapefruit juice and remaining bitter lemon soda into glass with several ice cubes. Stir gently.

 SALTY DOG

Pinch salt
Pinch granulated sugar
Lime wedge
2 oz. vodka
Grapefruit juice

Mix salt and sugar and spread out on a sheet of aluminum foil or wax paper. Wipe the rim of an Old Fashioned glass with lime wedge and roll glass in salt-sugar mixture until rim is evenly coated. Fill chilled glass with several ice cubes, vodka, and grapefruit juice and stir.

 SAMOVAR SLING

2 oz. vodka
½ oz. Benedictine
½ oz. cherry brandy
½ oz. lemon juice
Several dashes Angostura
  bitters
Several dashes orange bitters
Club soda

Mix all ingredients, except club soda, with cracked ice in a shaker or blender. Pour into a chilled Collins glass, fill with cold club soda, and stir gently.

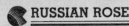 **SCREWDRIVER**

1½ oz. vodka
4 oz. orange juice
Orange slice

Pour vodka and orange juice into a chilled double Old Fashioned glass with several ice cubes. Stir and decorate with orange slice.

SEA BREEZE No. 1

2 oz. vodka
3 oz. grapefruit juice
3 oz. cranberry juice

Mix all ingredients with cracked
ice in a shaker or blender and
pour into a chilled highball glass.

SEA BREEZE No. 2

1½ oz. vodka
4 oz. grapefruit juice
1 oz. cranberry liqueur
Orange slice

Mix all ingredients, except orange
slice, with cracked ice and pour
into a chilled highball glass.
Garnish with orange slice.

 ## SEA GARDEN COCKTAIL

2 oz. vodka
2 oz. tomato juice
2 oz. V-8 juice
2 oz. clam juice
½ tsp. lemon juice
½ tsp. finely chopped dill

2–3 dashes Worcestershire
  sauce
2–3 dashes Tabasco sauce

Mix all ingredients with cracked
ice in a shaker or blender and
pour into a chilled Collins glass.

SERGE'S SUNSHINE

1½ oz. vodka
4 oz. grapefruit juice
½ oz. triple sec

Mix all ingredients with cracked
ice in a shaker or blender and
pour into a highball glass.

 ## SEWICKLEY HUNT STIRRUP CUP

1½ oz. vodka
½ oz. sloe gin
4 oz. orange-grapefruit juice

Mix with cracked ice in a blender
or shaker and pour into a silver stirrup cup or a double Old
Fashioned glass.

SIBERIAN SUNSET

2 oz. vodka
1 oz. raspberry or cherry or
  strawberry liqueur
½ oz. lime juice

Mix all ingredients with cracked
ice in a shaker or blender and
strain into a chilled cocktail glass.

SILENT GEORGE

1½ oz. vodka
½ oz. peppermint schnapps
4 oz. pineapple juice
Fresh pineapple slice

Mix all ingredients, except pineapple slice, with cracked ice in a shaker or blender and pour into a double Old Fashioned glass. Garnish with pineapple.

SOVIET COCKTAIL

1½ oz. vodka
½ oz. dry vermouth
½ oz. amontillado sherry
Lemon peel

Mix all ingredients, except lemon peel, with cracked ice in a shaker or blender and strain into a chilled cocktail glass. Twist lemon peel over drink and drop into glass.

ST. PETERSBURG

2 oz. vodka
¼ tsp. orange bitters
1 orange wedge

Pour vodka and bitters into mixing glass with several ice cubes. Stir until very cold and pour into a chilled Old Fashioned glass. Score peel of orange wedge with tines of fork and drop into drink.

THE STEVERINO

1 oz. vodka
2 oz. dry red wine
1 oz. pineapple juice
Several dashes triple sec

Mix all ingredients with cracked ice in a shaker or blender and strain into a chilled wine glass.

Created for Steve Allen, composer, writer, and motion picture and TV star.

STOLI FREEZE

1 oz. Stolichnaya vodka
Several grindings of black or
    white pepper

Place bottle of vodka in freezer for several hours (or store there permanently) and chill a small pony or sherry glass. Fill chilled glass with ice cold vodka and grind pepper on top.

STRAW HAT

1 oz. vodka
2 oz. Malibu or CocoRibe
¼ cup fresh strawberries
Several whole strawberries

Mix all ingredients, except for strawberries to be used for garnish, with cracked ice in a shaker or blender until smooth and pour into a chilled wine goblet and garnish with strawberries.

 ## SURFER'S COLA

1½ oz. vodka
½ oz. cola schnapps
Canada Dry Half-and-Half
Lemon slice

Combine vodka and cola schnapps in a Collins glass with ice cubes. Fill with Half and Half and garnish with lemon slice.

 ## SURREY RUFF

1½ oz. vodka
3 oz. tonic water
3 oz. bitter lemon soda
Lemon or lime wedge

Mix all ingredients, except lemon or lime wedge, in a chilled Collins glass with cracked ice and squeeze lemon or lime over drink and drop wedge into glass.

 ## TIMOCHENKO'S TOT

2 oz. vodka
½ oz. gin or light rum
½ oz. amaretto
4 oz. orange juice or equal parts orange and grape-fruit juice

Mix all ingredients with cracked ice in a shaker or blender and pour into a chilled wine goblet.

TORTOLA GOLD

1 oz. vodka
1 oz. gold rum
½ oz. La Grande Passion
2 oz. pineapple juice
½ oz. lemon juice
Mint sprigs

Mix all ingredients, except mint sprigs, with cracked ice in a blender until smooth. Strain into a chilled Collins glass. Garnish with mint sprigs.

VODKA COOLER

1½ oz. vodka
½ oz. sweet vermouth
½ oz. lemon juice
½ oz. sugar syrup
Club soda

Mix all ingredients, except club soda, with cracked ice in a shaker or blender. Pour into a chilled Collins glass and fill with club soda.

 ## VODKA GIMLET No.1

2 oz. vodka
½ oz. Rose's lime juice

Combine all ingredients in a mix-

ing glass with several ice cubes, stir, and strain into a chilled cocktail glass.

 ## VODKA GIMLET No. 2

1½ oz. vodka
1 oz. fresh lime juice
½ oz. sugar syrup

Mix all ingredients with cracked ice in a shaker or blender and strain into a chilled cocktail glass.

 ## VODKA GRAND MARNIER

1½ oz. vodka
½ oz. Grand Marnier
½ oz. lime juice
Orange slice

Mix all ingredients, except orange slice, with cracked ice in a shaker or blender and pour into a chilled cocktail glass. Garnish with orange slice.

 ## VODKA GRASSHOPPER

½ oz. vodka
¾ oz. green crème de menthe
¾ oz. white crème de cacao

Mix all ingredients with cracked ice in a shaker or blender and strain into a chilled cocktail glass.

 ## VODKA MARTINI

Basic recipe. See page 146 for Vodka Martini variations

2–3 oz. vodka
Dash dry vermouth or to taste
Lemon peel or olive

Combine vodka and vermouth in a mixing glass with a generous amount of ice cubes. Stir quickly but thoroughly and strain into a chilled cocktail glass. Garnish with lemon peel or olive.

Note: The secret of a good vodka Martini is thorough mixing with a great deal of ice in a matter of seconds to minimize ice melt-age. Vermouth proportions are critical since this provides the flavor of the drink. It must be adjusted for individual tastes.

VODKA SOUR

1½–2 oz. vodka
¾ oz. lemon juice
1 tsp. sugar syrup
Lemon slice
Maraschino cherry

Mix all ingredients, except lemon slice and maraschino cherry, with cracked ice in a shaker or blender. Strain into a chilled Whiskey Sour glass and garnish with lemon slice and cherry.

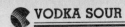 VODKA STINGER

1½ oz. vodka
1 oz. white crème de menthe

Mix vodka and crème de menthe with cracked ice in a mixing glass and strain into a chilled cocktail glass.

VOLGA BOATMAN

1½ oz. vodka
1 oz. cherry-flavored brandy
1 oz. orange juice
Maraschino cherry

Mix all ingredients, except maraschino cherry, with cracked ice in a shaker or blender and strain into a chilled cocktail glass. Garnish with cherry.

THE VULGAR BOATMAN

1½ oz. vodka
¾ oz. cherry liqueur
¼ oz. dry vermouth
½ oz. lemon juice
¼ tsp. kirsch

Dash orange bitters

Mix all ingredients with cracked ice in a shaker or blender and strain into a chilled cocktail glass.

WAIKIKI COMBER

1½ oz. vodka
6 oz. guava juice
½ oz. fresh lime juice
½ oz. black raspberry liqueur

Mix all ingredients, except raspberry liqueur, with cracked ice in a shaker or blender and pour into a chilled Collins glass. Over the back of a spoon, pour in raspberry liqueur.

WARSAW

1½ oz. vodka
½ oz. blackberry liqueur
½ oz. dry vermouth
1 tsp. lemon juice
Lemon peel

Mix all ingredients, except lemon peel, with cracked ice in a shaker or blender and strain into chilled cocktail glass. Twist lemon peel over drink and drop into glass.

WHITE CARNATION

1½ oz. vodka
1½ oz. lemon juice
1 oz. pineapple juice
Club soda

Mix all ingredients, except for club soda, in a shaker or blender and pour into a Collins glass. Fill with club soda and stir gently.

WHITE RUSSIAN

1½ oz. vodka
1 oz. white crème de cacao
¾ oz. heavy cream

Mix all ingredients with cracked ice in a shaker or blender and strain into a chilled cocktail glass.

WHITE WITCH

1 oz. vodka
1 oz. white crème de cacao
½ cup vanilla ice cream

Mix all ingredients in a blender at low speed for 10 seconds. Spoon into a chilled sherbet glass or wine goblet.

YORSH

1½ oz. vodka
12 oz. mug of beer

You may quaff the vodka neat and follow it with a mug of beer, or you may pour the vodka into the beer and drink them together.

BLOODY MARY LORE AND VARIATIONS

If the Moscow Mule helped make vodka famous in America, then the Bloody Mary surely helped make it profitable. In a very short time, perhaps ten years, vodka came from out of nowhere and was propelled to the heights, becoming the best-selling spirit in the land. And the Bloody Mary, far and away the most popular vodka drink in America, has won its place in the pantheon of classic mixed drinks alongside the Martini, Daiquiri, Manhattan, and that other redoubtable vodka creation, the Screwdriver.

What is the origin of this famous drink? There are many fanciful stories regarding the birth of the Bloody Mary and some misconceptions about the drink itself. This much we do know: The Bloody Mary was (a) invented a long time ago; (b) originally was a simple concoction made up of nothing more than vodka and tomato juice with perhaps a pinch of salt and pepper, and, just maybe, a dash of lemon juice; (c) was formulated as a cocktail, not a tall drink; and (d) that it originated not in America—where many good things happen—but in France, where many good things also happen.

Harry's New York Bar in Paris is generally credited as being the birthplace of the Bloody Mary. Located at 5 Rue Daunou between the Rue de la Paix and the Avenue de l'Opera, not far from another world-famous bar, the Ritz, Harry's is a font of new drink creations and lays claim to such classics as the Sidecar. In the early 1920s Harry's Bar was a gathering place for American expatriates living in Paris, such as Ernest Hemingway and F. Scott Fitzgerald. Legend has it that George Gershwin plinked out themes for "An American in Paris" on the downstairs piano while Gertrude Stein scribbled poetic fragments on the dining room's tablecloths. Among the regulars were the Dolly Sisters and the Prince of Wales, who would stop by now and again for a nightcap.

Perhaps the glamorous and gifted clientele that frequented Harry's inspired the staff to be creative and innovative. One who rose to the challenge was Fernand Petiot, a bartender born in America of French parents. One day in 1924 he concocted the first Bloody Mary. The authentic, original recipe for this drink, according to Andy MacElhone, son of Harry MacElhone (the Harry of Harry's New York Bar) is as follows:

> **"In a cocktail shaker, place plenty of ice,**
> **a pinch of salt, some black pepper,**
> **two ounces of vodka, and some tomato juice.**
> **All of these should be well shaken and**
> **poured into a tumbler."**

"This caught the fancy of the morning trade," Mr. MacElhone said in a 1977 interview. "Although some of the clients insisted that it should be more spiced up, whereupon Pete added red pepper, lemon juice, and Worcestershire sauce, and four or five drops of Tabasco to his recipe."

Other accounts insist that the original recipe was simply vodka and tomato juice mixed with ice. Then came the salt, pepper and lemon juice. Worcestershire sauce came even later, and Tabasco entered the picture long after that, although the McIlhenny Company, makers of Tabasco sauce, insists it was used early on and that a proper Bloody Mary cannot be made without it.

As the popularity of the Bloody Mary grew, so did speculation as to the origin and significance of such a vivid, unappetizing name. Here are some of the theories that have been proposed:

The Bloody Mary was a house specialty of the Bucket of Blood Club in Chicago, a long-vanished hangout for newspapermen in the 1920s, where the membership met regularly for the purpose of drinking themselves under the table.

Bloody Mary was coined by a bartender at Harry's New York Bar whose girlfriend, Mary, was always late for dates and to whom he referred in a fit of pique as "that bloody Mary!"

Bloody Mary was a legendary character in the South Seas who became famous as a result of the musical *South Pacific*, based upon James Michener's *Tales of the South Pacific*.

Bloody Mary alluded to a Scottish queen known for her vengeful ways, which earned her the name Bloody Mary. The name was supposedly coined by Harry MacElhone, one of the owners of Harry's Bar and a Scot.

Joseph Scaialom, a legendary barman from Cairo's Sheapard's Hotel and later maître d' at the Four Seasons and Windows on the World in New York, claims that the real Bloody Mary was invented in Manhattan at Vladimir's Bar long before Petiot's concoction. He maintains the name Vladimir was corrupted to Bloody Meyer, which later became Bloody Mary.

Take your choice. The Scottish connection makes more sense to me than the other explanations. In any event, I believe most people would rather drink a Bloody Mary than speculate as to the origin of the name, the inventor, or the original formula.

As with every significant innovation, a host of challengers crawl out from behind the back of the bar to vie for a place of honor as the originator. One thing we do know with some certainty is that Fernand Petiot returned to his native land in 1934 and brought his invention with him, and in his capacity as a bartender at New York's distinguished St. Regis Hotel introduced the Bloody Mary to a thirsty and appreciative generation of Americans.

A thorough perusal of the St. Regis Hotel bar, kitchen, and banquet department files, through the courtesy of Mr. August Ceradini, general manager of this venerable U.S. birthplace of the Bloody Mary, failed to reveal any startlingly new information on the subject, nor did that legendary paper napkin with the original recipe written on it in pencil by the inventor come to light. But Petiot's St. Regis version of the Bloody Mary—then called the "Red Snapper" for reasons of propriety (the hotel did not feel the name "Bloody Mary" was proper for a genteel clientele)—*is* a matter of record.

RED SNAPPER

1½ oz. vodka
2 oz. tomato juice
1 dash lemon juice
2 dashes salt
2 dashes black pepper
2 dashes cayenne pepper
3 dashes Worcestershire sauce

Add the salt, pepper, Worcestershire sauce, and lemon juice to a shaker glass. Then add ice, vodka, and tomato juice. Shake, pour into a highball glass, garnish, and serve.

There have been changes over the years, some good, some not so good. The most radical, in the opinion of purists, is the switch from a short drink, a cocktail, to a tall drink on-the-rocks. They also decry the substitution of lime juice for lemon juice. When drinks became classics, the ingredient variations, mixing techniques, and opinions proliferate like mushrooms after a summer shower. Craig Claiborne, the food editor of *The New York Times*, for one, has definite ideas as to what constitutes "the best Bloody Mary in town." He stoutly maintains that the best Bloody Marys are made by "our favorite barman, Jimmy Fox, who presides over the Blue Bar in the Algonquin Hotel on the edge of New York's theater district." And here is Jimmy's recipe:

ALGONQUIN BLOODY MARY

1½ oz. vodka
4 oz. tomato juice
Salt and freshly ground black
 pepper to taste
Juice of half a lime
1 tsp. Worcestershire sauce
4-6 dashes Tabasco sauce
1 lime wedge

Ideally, a Bloody Mary should be shaken, using a bartender's standard glass and metal cocktail shaker set. Add the vodka, tomato juice, and so on to the metal container. Fill the glass container with ice, the smaller the cubes the better. Invert the glass into the metal container and shake quickly nine times. If the drink is shaken excessively, the tomato juice may separate. Immediately strain the Bloody Mary into a glass and serve with a lime wedge dropped in. Yield: one cocktail.

As the Bloody Mary's popularity soared, it was only natural that many variations would appear, using a variety of spirits and seasonings. People may be intrigued momentarily by the prospect of trying a Bloody Mary made with tequila, aquavit, or even rum and whiskey, but they quickly return to vodka because it is a perfect foil for tomato juice and other seasonings that are used. But when it comes to spices, sauces, and other flavoring agents, everyone, it seems, has a favorite additive. Some like to use V-8 juice in place of tomato juice, or a more or less equal mixture of beef consommé or bouillon or straight beef consommé and no tomato juice. Clam juice added to tomato juice in a ratio of one part clam juice to two parts tomato juice appeals to the seafood set, and health buffs have been known to lace their Bloody Marys with sauerkraut juice.

In the realm of condiments, there are many options to be explored. Celery salt imparts a crisp accent flavor to a Bloody Mary, although some prefer celery seed instead so as not to add to the saltiness imparted by the Worcestershire sauce. And speaking of sauces, try A-1 in place of, or in addition to, Worcestershire sauce in your next Bloody Mary. It adds quite a different flavor tone and makes a zesty, spicy drink. Herbs have been used with great success. Try some chopped fresh dill in your next Bloody Mary, or you may prefer oregano or tarragon or sweet basil. Onion lovers enjoy chopped chives or scallions in their drink, and some even have used a few drops of garlic from a garlic press. Tex-Mex food fans have used chopped jalapena peppers with some success, but it results in a libation that is just too hot for most palates. A nominal amount of fresh horseradish is a much vaunted "secret ingredient" used by some bartenders, and it does add extra zip to a Bloody Mary. Flavoring variations are limited only by your own imagination. Texans toss in hot barbecue sauce, San Franciscans are said to savor a good dollop of soy sauce, Spanish go for anchovy paste, and Bostonians delight in crushed capers.

There are many Bloody Mary variations, ranging from the Virgin Mary (also called the Contrary Mary because of the absence of alcohol) to the O Sole Maria, made with Galliano or grappa. Others with humorous as well as flavorful qualities are: the Shamrock Mary (Irish whisky), Sake Mary (sake), Bonnie Mary (scotch), Bloody Maria (also called Tequila Maria and Mexicali Mary), Danish Mary (akvavit), Red Marija (slivovitz), Bloody Bull (equal parts beef consommé and tomato juice), Hot Beefy Mary (beef bouillon), Nautical Mary (clam juice and tomato juice), and La Bonne Maria (cognac). There are undoubtedly others and perhaps a few that haven't even been thought of yet.

BLOODHOUND

1½ oz. vodka
½ oz. dry sherry
4 oz. tomato juice
Dash lemon juice
Pinch salt

Pinch white pepper
Lime slice

Mix all ingredients, except lime slice, in a Collins glass with ice and garnish with lime slice.

BLOODY BLOSSOM

1½ oz. vodka
3 oz. orange juice
3 oz. tomato juice
Mint sprig (optional)

Mix vodka and juices in a shaker or blender with cracked ice and pour into a Collins glass. Garnish with mint.

BLOODY BREW

1½ oz. vodka
3 oz. beer
4 oz. tomato juice
Pinch salt
Dill pickle spear

Mix all ingredients, except pickle spear, gently in a highball or Collins glass with ice. Garnish with pickle.
Note: Proportions of beer to tomato juice should be adjusted to individual tastes. Condiments may be added as in a basic Bloody Mary.

BLOODY BULL

2 oz. vodka
3 oz. V-8
3 oz. beef bouillon, beef broth, or beef consommé
½ oz. lemon juice
Dash Tabasco sauce

Dash Worcestershire sauce
Pinch freshly ground white pepper

Mix all ingredients with cracked ice in mixing glass and pour into a chilled Old Fashioned glass.

BLOODY MARIE

1½–2 oz. vodka
4 oz. tomato juice
¼ oz. lemon juice
½ tsp. Pernod
Several dashes Worcestershire sauce
Several dashes Tabasco sauce
Salt to taste
Freshly ground white pepper to taste

Mix all ingredients, except salt and pepper, with cracked ice in a mixing glass and strain into a chilled double Old Fashioned glass.

BOMBAY MARY

1½ oz. vodka
4 oz. tomato juice
½ tsp. curry powder or to
   taste
Pinch ground coriander
Pinch celery seed or celery
   salt
Dash soy sauce or to taste

Dash Worcestershire sauce
Dash Tabasco sauce
Dash lemon juice

Mix all ingredients with cracked
ice in a 14-oz. double Old Fashioned glass.
Note: Seasonings should be
adjusted for individual tastes.

BORSCHT BELT

2 oz. vodka
4 oz. beet borscht
Several dashes Worcester-
   shire sauce or to taste
Several dashes lime juice
Several dashes Tabasco sauce
Sour cream or yogurt

Mix all ingredients, except sour
cream or yogurt, in a Collins
glass or a double Old Fashioned
glass with cracked ice. Top with
a dollop of sour cream or yogurt.

BROODY MALY

2 oz. vodka
4 oz. tomato juice
½ oz. lemon juice
Pinch white pepper
Pinch celery salt
1 egg white (for two drinks)

Several dashes oyster sauce
Several fresh celery tops or
   leaves (optional)

Mix all ingredients with cracked
ice in a blender until smooth and
pour into a chilled highball
glass.

CLAM DIGGER

2 oz. vodka
4 oz. V-8
2 oz. clam juice
2 tsp. lemon juice
Several dashes Tabasco sauce
Dash Worcestershire sauce
Pinch freshly ground white
   pepper

Mix all ingredients with cracked
ice in a mixing glass and pour
into a chilled highball glass.

CLAM UP

2 oz. vodka
2 oz. clam juice
3 oz. tomato juice
Several dashes lemon juice
Several dashes Worcester-
    shire sauce

Several dashes Tabasco sauce
Pinch white pepper
Pinch chopped dill

Mix all ingredients with cracked
ice in a shaker or blender. Pour
into a chilled highball glass.

COCK 'N' BULL SHOT

1½ oz. vodka
2 oz. chicken consommé
2 oz. beef bouillon, beef
    consommé, or beef broth
½ oz. lemon juice
Dash Tabasco sauce
Dash Worcestershire sauce

Pinch freshly ground white
    pepper
Pinch celery salt

Mix all ingredients with cracked
ice in a mixing glass and pour
into a chilled Old Fashioned
glass.

THE HAPPY MARY

2 oz. vodka
4–6 oz. V-8 juice
1 tsp. lime juice
Several dashes Tabasco sauce
Several dashes Worcester-
    shire sauce
Generous pinch white pepper

Generous pinch celery salt
Generous pinch oregano or
    dill or tarragon

Mix all ingredients with cracked
ice in a mixing glass and pour
into a double Old Fashioned
glass.

MEL TORMÉ'S BLOODY MARY

1½ oz. vodka
4 oz. tomato juice
4 slices cucumber, peeled
4–6 slices of celery
1 slice Bermuda onion, diced
Pinch white pepper
Dash Tabasco sauce
Dash Worcestershire sauce
Celery stalk

Mix all ingredients, except celery
stalk, with cracked ice in a
blender and pour into a chilled
highball glass. Garnish with
celery stalk. Add additional
tomato juice, if necessary.

SMOKY MARY

1½ oz. vodka
Tomato juice
½ oz. lemon juice
½ oz. barbecue sauce
Dash Tabasco
Dash Worcestershire sauce
Lemon slice

Mix all ingredients with cracked ice in a double Old Fashioned glass. Garnish with lemon slice.

SWEDISH CLAM DIGGER

2 oz. aquavit
6-oz. can Clamato
Dash Worcestershire sauce
Dash lemon juice
Dash Tabasco sauce
Several pinches of chopped dill

Mix all ingredients, except dill, in a large Collins glass or a double Old Fashioned glass with cracked ice and sprinkle with chopped dill.

VELVET MARY

1½ oz. vodka
4 oz. tomato juice
½ oz. lemon juice
½–1 tbsp. grated horseradish
1 egg white (for two drinks)

Several dashes Worcestershire sauce
Several dashes Tabasco sauce

Mix all ingredients with cracked ice in a shaker or blender. Pour into a chilled Collins glass.

VODKA: MARTINI VARIATIONS

The vodka Martini is rapidly overtaking its sibling, the gin Martini, which for many years occupied the number-one position as America's favorite mixed drink. Times change, and the growth of vodka, which can only be described as meteoric, reflects the tastes of the nation. The vodka Martini has a clean, uncomplicated flavor and the perception of lightness and dryness that makes it a winner.

There are many ways to make a vodka Martini, ranging from a goodly portion of vermouth to just a whisper or none at all. And there are a variety of garnishes that provide zest and variety. At the moment, the Cajun Martini (made with either gin or vodka) is the rage, and every bar that features them has its own special recipe.

No matter how you like your Martinis, there is one rule that should always be followed—and is, invariably, by master bartenders. Use plenty of ice, mix the drink thoroughly and quickly so there is a minimum amount of ice meltage, but a great deal of chill. The glasses, as we remind you in every recipe in this book, must be *crackling cold*. The Martini should be consumed with dispatch while it is still crisply cold.

 ## CAJUN MARTINI No. 1

1½-2 oz. vodka *Dash dry vermouth or to taste* *Large jalapena pepper*	Mix vodka and vermouth with plenty of ice, rapidly and briskly, and strain into a chilled cocktail glass. Garnish with pepper.

CAJUN MARTINI No. 2

1½-3 oz. vodka *Dash dry vermouth* *1 thin slice garlic* *Several slices of pickled jalapena pepper* *Several pickled cocktail onions, blotted to remove vinegar taste*	An hour or so before you mix Martinis, let vodka steep with garlic, pepper, and onions in a sealed container in the refrigerator or freezer. Mix in a mixing glass with plenty of ice and strain into a chilled cocktail glass. Garnish with a pepper slice or onions.

 ## THE DILLATINI

1½-2½ oz. vodka *Dash of dry vermouth or to taste* *Kosher dill pickle stick*	Mix vodka and vermouth in a mixing glass with plenty of ice and strain into a chilled cocktail glass. Garnish with dill pickle.

OCHI CHERNYA

2 oz. vodka *¼ oz. dry vermouth* *¼ oz. sweet vermouth* *1 large black olive*	Mix rapidly with plenty of ice in a mixing glass and strain into a chilled cocktail glass. Garnish with a black olive. *Note:* From the Russian Tea Room, New York City.

# THE ROLATINI

2 oz. vodka
Dash dry vermouth
1 Rolaid tablet

Mix vodka and vermouth in a
mixing glass with plenty of ice
and strain into a chilled cocktail glass. Garnish with a Rolaid

tablet instead of an olive or
lemon peel.
Note: For harried advertising
people. The Rolaid tablet will
perhaps soften the impact of the
dry Martini after a full day
with a difficult client.

SPANISH VODKA MARTINI

2½ oz. vodka
½ oz. dry sherry
Lemon peel

Mix vodka and sherry with
cracked ice in a mixing glass
and strain into a chilled cocktail glass. Twist lemon peel over
drink and drop into glass.

VODKA GIBSON

2–3 oz. vodka
½–1 tsp. dry vermouth or to
    taste
Pearl onions, pickled

Mix vodka and vermouth in a
mixing glass with plenty of ice,

very rapidly so as to limit ice
meltage and strain into a chilled
cocktail glass. Garnish with
several pickled pearl onions after
blotting them on paper towels
to prevent residual vinegar flavor
from affecting the drink.

FLAVORED VODKAS

Distilled spirits take on the flavor and character of the mash
used in the distilling process. In the case of spirits made at
very high proof from low flavor-intensive grains such as corn,
wheat, rice, or barley—and spirits that have been processed
into grain neutral spirits—flavors must be added to the spirits
by rectifying (redistilling), infusion, maceration, or percolation.

The addition of such things as pepper, buffalo grass, or
orange peel to vodka is flavoring by means of infusion or
maceration, a common practice in eastern European households, dating from the fifteenth century and probably much
earlier. London dry gin and akvavit are, in a real sense, flavored "vodkas." Gin is made by distilling a fermented grain
mash, which yields alcohol as high as 190 proof. At this point
it is, practically speaking, a "vodka." It is then reduced in

proof by the addition of distilled water and redistilled with assorted botanicals that provide the flavor and aroma. It is reduced in proof and bottled immediately. There is no aging. Akvavit is made in the same way. This process of flavoring could be done by infusion (similar to making a cup of tea) except for the fact that distillation yields an end product with more intense flavor and aroma than is possible by infusion.

A wide variety of liqueurs and cordials through the years have been made by the infusion method, and, in fact, all homemade liqueurs are traditionally produced in this manner since stills are either impractical or illegal for home use. Since the base, except when brandy is used, is grain neutral spirits, the end product is in reality *a flavored vodka*. In Sweden, little flavoring kits are sold so that unflavored vodka (*renat brännvinn*) may be flavored at home. These flavors approximate popular liqueur flavors as well as herbs, fruits, and spices. These are reminiscent of the gin-making kits that were sold in drugstores during prohibition to make what became known as "bathtub gin."

From the earliest times there was a need to flavor these spirits not because they were bland, but rather because they were harsh and raw and laced with noxious impurities. The custom parallels that of the ancient Greeks and Romans, who doused their wine with all manner of herbs, fruits, flower blossoms, and other botanicals to preserve the vintage and make the wine palatable.

The Russians and the Poles have a long tradition of flavoring vodkas. Some of the more popular, traditional homemade vodka flavors are: *pertsovka* (vodka infused with black-and-white peppercorns, reputedly a great favorite with Peter the Great); *zubrovka* (vodka flavored with buffalo grass); *starka* (vodka aged in old wine casks for as much as ten years and steeped in apple and pear leaves); *okhotnitchya* (known as "hunter's vodka" and flavored with herbs and berries); *chesnochnaya* (an infusion of pepper, garlic, and dill); and *limonovka* (lemon- or orange-flavored vodka). For special occasions, a "jubilee vodka," *yubileyneya osobaya*, laced with brandy and honey was much in vogue.

The neutral state of vodka cries out for experimentation. The imaginative cook and the innovative mixologist will delight, as in times past, in trying new flavorings. Here are some that have been used in the past, and, it is quite obvious when scanning this list, only the bounds of individual tastes limit the inventive pursuit of new flavor experiences.

Fruits of all kinds have been used with success, including cherries and cherry pits, tangerines, lemons, oranges, grapefruit, cranberries, raspberries, black currants, blueberries, apricots and apricot pits, apples, plums, peaches, and pineapple.

Coffee beans, tea, fennel, vanilla beans, saffron, coriander, absinthe (or absinthe substitutes), almonds, cumin, mint, bitter orange, hazelnuts, red peppers, anise, violets, caraway, cardamom, cocoa, lingonberries, cedar, dill, juniper, cornflowers, sage, cinnamon, and rose petals compose a partial listing of ingredients that have been utilized as flavoring agents. Actually, anything that is not toxic may be steeped in vodka and the essential flavor extracted by the time-honored infusion process.

Some flavored vodkas are now bottled by distillers, such as Stolichnaya Pertsovka and Absolut Peppar, and are readily available in the U.S. If the present trend continues, it is likely other flavors will be introduced into the market. Meanwhile, there is nothing to prevent you from trying out some of your favorite flavors on your own. Here are some tips on vodka flavoring:

Select a good-grade vodka that will make it all worthwhile. Use the original bottle for flavoring or, if you decide to use a decanter or other container, make sure it is clean and odor-free. If using fruits and herbs, buy them fresh rather than using canned fruit or dried herbs. If using spices, pass over any old caraway seeds or cinnamon sticks and buy them fresh. The flavor difference is worth it. Seal container tightly after adding ingredients and steep for 24 to 48 hours, turning the bottle several times daily. Do not leave strong-flavored ingredients to steep too long because the flavor can become harsh. Garlic, lemon peel, anise, cumin, coriander, and peppers can become overpowering if infused for extended periods. After vodka has been infused, store in the refrigerator or freezer. Small amounts of flavoring substances may be left in the bottle for decoration, such as a sprig of dill or mint or a thin spiral of orange peel.

Here are some representative recipes:

ANISE VODKA

1 liter vodka
1 tbsp. anise seeds or to
   taste
Sprig of fresh tarragon or
   fennel (optional)

Put anise seeds into vodka and steep for 24 hours, turning bottle from time to time to circulate anise. Check flavor, strain vodka into a new container, decorate with a sprig of tarragon or fennel, and store in refrigerator or freezer.

APRICOT VODKA

1 liter vodka
1 dozen dried apricots, diced
6 apricot kernels (optional)

Put diced apricot into vodka
and infuse for 24 hours, turning
bottle from time to time to
circulate apricots. Apricot kernels
may be used for a more intense,
bitter flavor. Check flavor and
strain into a new container. Store
in refrigerator or freezer.

BASIL VODKA

1 liter vodka
1 dozen fresh basil leaves

Wash leaves and put into bottle
for about 24 hours at room
temperature. Turn bottle several
times to circulate leaves. Check
for flavor. Remove vodka from
leaves and store in refrigerator or
freezer. A sprig of basil may
be added for decorative purposes.

CUCUMBER VODKA

1 liter vodka
1 medium cucumber

Scrub cucumber and peel. Cut
into thin, lengthwise strips and
put into vodka. Steep at room
temperature for 48 hours, turning
bottle occasionally to circulate
cucumber. Check flavor and steep
for a longer period if stronger
flavor is desired. Strain into new
container and store in refrigerator
or freezer.

GARLIC AND DILL VODKA

1 liter vodka
1 or 2 garlic cloves
Several sprigs of fresh dill
Half dozen peppercorns
   (optional)

Bruise garlic to release flavor
and put into vodka with dill sprigs
and a few peppercorns, if you
wish. Steep for about 24 hours at
room temperature, turning the
bottle every so often to circulate
ingredients. Check flavor and
strain into a new bottle. Store in
refrigerator or freezer. A sprig
of dill may be kept in the bottle
for decorative purposes.

GINGER VODKA

1 liter vodka
Fresh ginger root

Peel a section of ginger root
long enough so that a dozen
slices ⅛-inch thick can be cut.
Quarter slices and put into bottle
and steep for about 48 hours at
room temperature, turning bottle
occasionally to circulate ginger.
Check flavor and steep longer for
more intensive flavor. Strain into a
new container and store in freezer.

LEMON-PEPPER VODKA

1 liter vodka
4 dozen black-and-white
  peppercorns, mixed
Peel of 1 lemon

Put peppercorns into vodka
and peel lemon so that only the
yellow, outer peel (zest) is used
and put into bottle. Steep for 24
to 48 hours, turning bottle
occasionally. Check flavor and
strain into a new container.
Store in refrigerator or freezer.

RASPBERRY VODKA

1 liter vodka
2 cups sugar
1 lb. fresh red raspberries
Large container with tightly
  fitting lid

Add vodka, sugar, and raspberries to large container, cover,
and store in a cool, dark place.

Every week open container and
stir well. After about two months,
strain liquid through a fine sieve
into a bottle and store in refrigerator or freezer.
Note: This is a traditional and
widely used method of flavoring vodka, and works well with
any fresh fruit.

Recently Carillon Importers, Ltd. of Teaneck, N.J., who are
responsible for the successful marketing of Absolut vodka in
the U.S., introduced Absolut Peppar vodka. It is a fine product
designed for those vodka drinkers who enjoy a crisp, snappy,
flavorful, pepper taste.

The following five original recipes were developed especially for Absolut Peppar vodka by the author.

CLAM SHOT

1½ oz. Absolut Peppar vodka
3 oz. fresh or bottled clam
  juice
Several dashes Worcester-
  shire sauce

Dash lemon juice
Dash Tabasco sauce
½ tsp. horseradish

Mix all ingredients with cracked
ice in a double Old Fashioned
glass.

CREOLE MARTINI

1½-2 oz. Absolut Peppar
  vodka
Dash dry vermouth or to taste
Large pepperoncini (pickled
  medium-hot pepper)

Rapidly mix vodka and vermouth
with plenty of ice in a mixing
glass and strain into a chilled
cocktail glass and garnish with
pepperoncini (which may be
eaten as drink is consumed).

NAUTICAL MARY

1½ oz. Absolut Peppar vodka
3 oz. tomato juice or V-8 juice
3 oz. clam juice
½ tsp. horseradish
Several dashes Worcester-
    shire sauce
Several dashes Tabasco
    sauce

½ tsp. lemon juice or to taste
Several pinches of chopped
    dill

Mix all ingredients with cracked
ice in a mixing glass and pour
into a double Old Fashioned
glass.

 PEPPER BULL

1½ oz. Absolut Peppar vodka
5 oz. beef consommé
Generous dashes Worcester-
    shire sauce

1 tsp. lemon juice
Pinch of celery salt or celery
    seed (optional)

Mix all ingredients with ice in
a double Old Fashioned glass.

 SURF AND TURF

1½–2 oz. Absolut Peppar
    vodka
3 oz. beef consommé
3 oz. clam juice
½ tsp. lemon juice
Several dashes Tabasco
    sauce
Several dashes Worcester-
    shire sauce

Mix all ingredients with ice in
a 14-oz. double Old Fashioned
glass.
Note: Proportions of clam juice
to consommé may be adjusted.
Some prefer 2 parts consommé to
1 part clam juice.

Aquavit or Akvavit (depending on whether you are drinking it
in Denmark, Sweden, or Norway) is, with respect to social
custom, tradition, and culinary habit, what vodka is to Russia,
cognac is to France, scotch is to Great Britain, tequila is to
Mexico, and ouzo is to Greece, to use just a few rather obvious
analogies. Actually, aquavit occupies a special place in the
Scandinavian dining protocol since it is consumed *with* food,
and not drunk as a cocktail or an apéritif. In the U.S. there is
no spirit that is comparable, since generally we consume only
wine or beer with food.

As a matter of historical record, the first license to sell
aquavit in Sweden was granted in 1498, just six years after the

discovery of America. The practice of flavoring aquavit with herbs has gone on for generations, dating back to the days when every housewife had a small herb garden for growing various botanicals that were used in cooking and for medicinal purposes. Sweden produces many excellent aquavits, the best known of which is Absolut. O.P. Anderson is another popular brand, and it is deliciously flavored with a combination of anise, caraway, and fennel. Herrgard's Aquavit is flavored with caraway and whisky and aged in old cherry casks, which gives it a very smooth, intriguing taste. Skåne (pronounced "skona") is a mild aquavit produced in southern Sweden and is a big seller in Scandinavia. Linie Aquavit is made in Oslo, Norway, and the label usually carries the name of the ship on which it was stored during its aging, the theory being that spirits aged this way benefited greatly from the rocking of the ship on the high seas. Probably the best-known aquavit in America is the Danish Akvavit, produced in the city of Aalborg, which is an excellent product with a clean, crisp, refreshing caraway flavor.

The custom in Scandinavian countries is to drink *snaps*, or aquavit, crackling cold in little pony glasses accompanied by glasses of cool beer. The aquavit is quaffed in one gulp, with or without a beer chaser, to lusty shouts of *skål!* And all the while, you are enjoying a vast array of delicacies from the smorgasbord table, which in Denmark is called the *kolde bord*, as aquavit and beer are traditionally taken together with food at the table.

As good as aquavit is neat, it also provides an unusual flavor dimension to a number of mixed drinks. Here are some selected, original recipes that were developed for the U.S. importers of Aalborg Akvavit by the author.

AALBORG SOUR

2 oz. Aalborg Akvavit
Juice of ½ lemon
1 tsp. sugar syrup or to taste

Mix all ingredients with cracked ice in a shaker or blender and strain into a chilled cocktail glass.

AKVATINI

2–3 oz. Aalborg Akvavit
Dash dry vermouth or to taste
Anchovy olive or lemon twist

Mix akvavit and vermouth with plenty of ice in a mixing glass

and strain into a chilled cocktail glass. Garnish with an anchovy olive or secure a rolled anchovy and a green olive together with a toothpick or drop in lemon twist.

COPENHAGEN COCKTAIL

1 oz. Aalborg Akvavit
1 oz. gin
Dash dry vermouth or to taste
Large stuffed olive

Stir all ingredients, except olive, in a mixing glass with ice and strain into a chilled cocktail glass. Garnish with olive.

 # DANISH BORSCHT

1–2 oz. Aalborg Akvavit
4 oz. cold beet borscht
Dash Tabasco sauce
Dash lemon juice
Yogurt or sour cream

Mix all ingredients, except yogurt or sour cream, in a shaker or blender and pour into a double Old Fashioned glass. Top with a generous dollop of yogurt or sour cream.

 # THE DANISH BULL

2 oz. Aalborg Akvavit
4 oz. beef consommé or beef bouillon
1 tsp. lemon juice
½ tsp. Worcestershire sauce or to taste

Several pinches celery salt or celery seed.

Mix all ingredients with cracked ice in a double Old Fashioned glass.

 # MIDNIGHT SUN

1½ oz. Aalborg Akvavit
1 oz. grapefruit juice
½ oz. lemon juice
1 tsp. sugar syrup or to taste
Dash grenadine
Orange slice

Mix all ingredients, except orange slice, with cracked ice in a shaker or a blender and pour into a chilled cocktail glass. Garnish with orange slice.

 # THE ÖRESUND

2 oz. Aalborg Akvavit
2 oz. V-8 juice
2 oz. tomato juice
2 oz. clam juice
½ tsp. lemon juice
½ tsp. Worcestershire sauce
Pinch finely chopped dill

Pinch finely chopped parsley
Sprig of fresh dill

Mix all ingredients, except dill sprig, with cracked ice in a shaker or a blender and pour into a large Collins glass. Decorate with dill sprig.

1½ oz. Aalborg Akvavit
¼ oz. kirsch
1 oz. lime juice
1 tsp. sugar syrup or to taste
1 oz. cream

Mix all ingredients with cracked ice in a shaker or a blender and strain into a chilled wine goblet.

THE LIGHT DRINK CONCEPT—
A "SPLASH" OF SPIRITS

The powerhouse potations of the Roaring Twenties were in vogue because the quality of bootleg spirits in this country was atrocious, so, as a consequence, men and women of the Jazz Age drank for effect rather than flavor. Partly in an attempt to mask the taste of crudely made gin and whiskey, some truly abominable concoctions were foisted upon unsophisticated, gullible drinkers. Some of these mixtures survive today, as do some of the old bar guides where they may still be found, but drinking habits and tastes have changed. Now it is no longer fashionable to swig brutally strong mixtures nor is it considered smart to drink to excess. Drinking in moderation is now very much the order of the day, not only for reasons of health and fitness, but perhaps more important: the realization that people must drink responsibly. And there is a growing grassroots opinion that maintains that if driving an automobile is required, people should not drink at all—meaning not even a sip of anything alcoholic.

Moderation is a growing trend, and somewhere between the never-never land of the jumbo 20-to-1 Martini on the one hand and the club soda on the rocks with a wedge of lime on the other is a middle ground of moderate drink recipes that are imaginative and satisfying and that fulfill the primary objective of the cocktail hour: to induce fleet conversation, to give a lift to the spirit without obliterating the evening that follows, to quicken the appetite, and to provide a happy opportunity to enjoy friends, relax, and banish the cares of the day. Recognizing the need for a new generation of truly moderate mixed drinks, we were asked by Heublein, Inc., to develop some appetizing concoctions using the "splash" concept involving a very modest amount of spirits. In the case of the 27 recipes that follow in this section, the amount of vodka specified is only a half ounce instead of the traditional one-and-one-half ounces. This concept and the recipes that resulted became known as the "Smirnoff Splash." The recipes are simple, easy to make, and, according to consumer-tasting panels, flavorful and satisfying. No, these drinks are not drunk-proof any more than beer and wine or anything alcoholic is. If you drink too much alcohol in any form, you will become intoxicated. But if you are in the habit of taking two cocktails before dinner, try one of these Smirnoff Splash drinks. If you stick to two, you'll automatically be taking in less alcohol and calories than if you imbibed standard mixed drinks.

The following recipes were created especially for Heublein, Inc., and Smirnoff Vodka by the author.

 ## BEACHCOMBER

3 oz. dry red wine *3 oz. cranberry juice* *Splash of vodka (½ oz.)* *Lemon twist*	Stir with ice and serve in a chilled highball glass with ice. Add lemon

 ## BEAULIEU

4 oz. champagne *2 oz. orange juice* *2 oz. grapefruit juice* *Splash of vodka (½ oz.)* *Dash grenadine*	Mix all ingredients, except champagne, in a blender with ice and pour into a chilled Collins glass. Add champagne and stir gently.

 ## CADIZ

3 oz. Harvey's Bristol Cream *Splash of vodka (½ oz.)* *2–3 dashes Angostura bitters*	Stir all ingredients with ice in a chilled Old Fashioned glass.

 ## COBLENZ COOLER

3 oz. Rhine wine *Splash of vodka (½ oz.)* *Club soda* *Orange slice*	Serve chilled wine in a chilled highball glass with ice. Add vodka and fill with soda. Garnish with orange slice.

COLOMBE d'OR

4 oz. champagne
2 dashes orange curaçao
Splash of vodka (½ oz.)
Dash Angostura bitters

Gently stir chilled ingredients which have been stored in refrigerator for a day and serve in a chilled stem glass.

 ## GAMIN

3 oz. white wine
Splash of vodka (½ oz.)
Dash or two of cherry brandy

Club soda

Stir all spirits in a chilled Collins glass with ice. Fill with soda.

 ## GILDED LILY

3 oz. Lillet blanc
Splash of vodka (½ oz.)
Orange slice

Stir with ice, strain, and pour into a chilled stem glass. Add orange slice.

 ## GOLDEN ROOSTER

1 oz. dry vermouth
1 oz. medium sherry
Splash of vodka (½ oz.)
Lemon twist

Stir with ice, strain, and pour into a chilled stem glass. Add lemon twist.

 ## HARVEY'S CIDER

4 oz. apple cider
Splash of vodka (½ oz.)
2–3 dashes Harvey's Bristol
  Cream

Stir with ice and serve in a chilled stem glass.

 ## KIRNOFF FIZZ

4 oz. champagne
½ oz. crème de cassis
Splash of vodka (½ oz.)

Chill ingredients in refrigerator and stir gently in a chilled stem glass.

LÀ CAMELIA

3 oz. dry white wine
Splash of vodka (½ oz.)
2 dashes apricot brandy

Stir all ingredients with ice in
a mixing glass, strain and serve
in a chilled stem glass.

 ## LA NAPOULE

3½ oz. dry white wine
Splash of vodka (½ oz.)
½ oz. crème de cassis

Chill ingredients in refrigerator and stir in a chilled stem
glass.

 ## LE CHEVAL BLANC

3 oz. chablis
Splash of vodka (½ oz.)
2–3 dashes maraschino liqueur

Stir all ingredients with ice.
Strain and serve in a chilled
stem glass.

 ## LEFT BANK

3 oz. St. Raphael
Splash of vodka (½ oz.)
Dash triple sec
Lime
Club soda

Stir spirits with ice in a chilled
10-oz. Collins glass. Add ice,
dash of lime, and fill with club
soda.

 ## MERRY DU BARRY

3 oz. rosé wine
Splash of vodka (½ oz.)
1 tsp. crème de cassis

Stir all ingredients with ice
in a chilled goblet.

 ## PAPARAZZI

2 oz. Campari
Splash of vodka (½ oz.)
Quinine water
Lime

Stir Campari and vodka with
ice and pour into a chilled Collins
glass. Fill with quinine water
and add a squeeze of lime.

 PORT OF CALL

3 oz. tawny port
Splash of vodka (½ oz.)
Dash orange curaçao

Stir port and vodka with ice, add orange curaçao, and serve in a chilled stem glass.

QUAI d'ORSAY

2 oz. Byrrh
2 oz. dry vermouth
Splash of vodka (½ oz.)
Orange slice

Stir spirits with ice in a chilled stem glass. Garnish with orange slice.

REGATTA

4 oz. champagne
Splash of vodka (½ oz.)
1–2 dashes mirabelle or pear brandy

Chill ingredients in refrigerator and stir gently in a chilled stem glass.

RIGHT BANK

3 oz. dry vermouth
Splash of vodka (½ oz.)
Club soda
Orange slice

Stir spirits in a chilled Collins glass. Add ice and club soda.

RIVIERA TONIC

3 oz. soave
3 oz. quinine water
Splash of vodka (½ oz.)
Orange slice

Chill ingredients in refrigerator and add to a chilled Collins glass. Add ice and stir. Garnish with orange slice.

ROSTANG

3 oz. dry red wine
Splash of vodka (½ oz.)
2 dashes orange curacao

Stir all ingredients with ice in a chilled stem glass.

RUE ROYALE

4 oz. champagne
Splash of vodka (½ oz.)
Dash of framboise or kirsch

Chill ingredients in refrigerator, serve in a chilled stem glass and stir gently.

 SMIRNOFF MIMOSA

3 oz. champagne
3 oz. orange juice
Splash of vodka (½ oz.)

Chill ingredients in refrigerator, serve in a chilled stem glass and stir gently.

 TOVARICH

1 oz. sweet vermouth
1 oz. Campari
Splash of vodka (½ oz.)
Club soda
Orange peel

Stir spirits well in a chilled highball glass with ice. Fill with soda. Add orange peel.

 TROIKA

1 oz. sloe gin
Splash of vodka (½ oz.)
4 oz. orange juice

Mix all ingredients with cracked ice in a blender and serve in a large chilled goblet.

TROIS MARCHES

3 oz. Dubonnet rouge
Splash of vodka (½ oz.)
2–3 dashes orange curaçao
Club soda
Orange slice

Stir spirits with ice in a chilled Collins glass. Fill with soda, add orange slice.

RUM: A TASTE OF THE TROPICS

Boy, bring a bowl of china here
Fill it with water cool and clear;
Decanter with Jamaica ripe,
A spoon of silver, clean and bright,
Sugar twice fin'd in pieces cut,
Knife, sieve and glass in order out,
Bring forth the fragrant fruit, and then
We're happy till the clock strikes ten.

—Benjamin Franklin
Poor Richard's Almanac

One of the great pleasures of traveling in the Caribbean is the opportunity to become intimately acquainted with a wide variety of different rums found throughout the islands. No other spirit category offers rum's infinite variety of flavor and taste experiences. The availability of an array of fresh, exotic tropical fruits and spices helps explain why rum drinks made in the U.S. with less than fresh tropical fruits "don't taste the same." It is the rums themselves, however, that really make the difference. Almost every island of consequence makes its own rum, only a few of which are exported to foreign shores.

Exploring different rum types is an exciting and challenging culinary adventure. One may begin with something as basic as a Martini, which can be made dusty dry with the light white rums of Puerto Rico; or try a sturdy, flavorful Rum Sour made with the gold rums of Barbados and the Dominican Republic. A festive punch has seldom been put to lips that could not be improved by the addition of the rich, dark, full-bodied rums of Jamaica or Demerara. Tall, frosty coolers develop tantalizing overtones with the addition of a Haitian rum while the dry, pungent rums of the French West Indies bring elegant accents to even mundane cocktails; when sipped from a snifter like fine cognac, a Martinique rum reportedly made Ernest Hemingway exclaim that it was "the perfect antidote for a rainy day."

Rums appear even in unlikely places (countries not thought of as rum-producing areas) such as Colombia, which produces the mellow, amber Ron Medellin, distilled in the city of the same name. And neighboring Venezuela makes an outstanding gold rum, Cacique Ron Añejo, which, like Ron Medellin, occasionally appears on dealers' shelves in the U.S. Nearby Trinidad is a treasure trove of excellent but little known rums such as Old Oak, Ferdi's 10-Years Old, and Siegert's Bouquet rum. Those powerhouse, spicy, dark, pungent rums from the Demerara River area of Guyana, which run as high as 151-proof, were no doubt the self-same spirits described by a Colonial writer as being "strong enough to make a rabbit bite a bulldog." These rums are produced by two respected firms: Hudson's Bay and Lemon Hart & Sons.

The rums of Barbados have happily been discovered by American rum drinkers. Although Mount Gay is the best known in the U.S. there are other excellent brands with the typical smoothness, flavor, and finesse of Bajan gold rums such as Cockspur, Cockade, and Alleyne Arthur's. Other jewels of the islands worthy of special mention are Bermudez rum, a velvety smooth product made in the Dominican Republic; Rhum Barbancourt, a classic rum of exceptional quality made in Haiti; the wonderful, pungent Rhums of Martinique such as Rhum La Mauny, Rhum Clément, Rhum Saint-James, and Rhum Negrita; robust British Navy Pusser's Rum from the British Virgin Islands (used as the Royal Navy's rum ration for nearly three hundred years) and, of course, the great company of aromatic, full-bodied rums from Jamaica carrying such famous names as Myers's, Appleton, and Captain Morgan.

Credit for the bourgeoning popularity of rums of all kinds in the U.S. must go to the highly respected firm of Bacardi & Company, Ltd., which began corporate life in the year 1862 in Santiago de Cuba. The first plant consisted of a shed housing an ancient, cast-iron pot still, a few fermenting tanks, and some aging barrels. The tin-roofed shed also housed a colony of fruit bats; hence, the bat trademark that appears on every bottle of Bacardi rum. From these meager beginnings Bacardi has grown into the producer of the world's largest-selling brand of spirits, with distribution in 175 different countries. The firm's dedication to quality has been the driving force behind the success of this famous brand.

Rum is the product of sugarcane. Unlike spirits made from grain, such as whiskey, the juice from the cane can be fermented directly into alcohol instead of having to be converted first from starch to sugar. After the juice is pressed from the sugarcane, it is boiled, reduced, and clarified. The heavy sugar syrup that results is processed into sugar and molasses. To start the fermentation process, a little molasses is removed from the batch, diluted, and taken to the laboratory, where a tiny portion of yeast is added. The yeast is a vital part of the entire process. Every rum distiller has its own special strain of yeast, which is a closely guarded trade secret. In the case of Bacardi, their yeast strain was developed more than a century ago.

After the yeast has grown sufficiently—a week or ten days—this fermentation culture is added to molasses in the fermenting tanks. The fermentation process usually takes about seventy-two hours. Then the fermented batch is distilled in continuous-column stills more than four stories high. These modern stills differ from the old-fashioned pot still in that live steam is used to draw off the distillate at very high proofs, which eliminates certain impurities that can produce harshness in the end product. The process is continuous, whereas in the pot still, spirits can only be made in batches. After distillation is completed, the rums are aged in barrels (American white oak is preferred) until they have matured. At the proper time the blender proceeds to "marry" rums of various ages and from different batches until the precise blend is achieved with the proper color, bouquet, flavor, smoothness, and balance.

Rum and rum drinks are very much a part of the American heritage. By the end of the seventeenth century rum was the most quaffed spirit in the American colonies. And by all accounts, the Colonials were a hard-drinking lot, and, considering some of the concoctions that were in vogue, "hard" is used advisedly. Some of the popular libations of the day were Kill-Divil, Stonewall and Bogus, Coo-Woo, Whistle-Belly Vengeance, and Rattle-Skull. The latter consisted of a large peg of rum mixed with brandy, wine, and porter (a dark, full-bodied malt brew similar to stout), and seasoned with lime peel and nutmeg.

The Flip also was all the rage with our founding fathers and no doubt gave them both sustenance and comfort during the trying times of the American Revolution. It is the only mixed drink recipe that has survived to the present, and with the omission of one ingredient, the Flip is made today with the same basic recipe that was used over two hundred years ago.

Flips were made as both hot and cold drinks, but the hot version was extremely popular, as were all mulled potations during those days without central heating. The hot Flip was made by mixing rum and beer with beaten eggs, cream, and spices, then mulled with a red-hot poker known as a "flip-iron," "flip-dog," or "loggerhead." During heated discussions over hot drinks, so the story goes, loggerheads sometimes were used to drive home a point. This is believed to be the origin of the phrase "being at loggerheads."

During the eighteenth century the Caribbean was known as the Spanish Main, an appellation that was not recognized by the British navy, American privateers, or the motley assortment of pirates, freebooters, and rogues who sailed the high seas. One thing all could agree to, however, was that Grog was the most popular drink to be had, whether in port or at sea. This forerunner of the highball was simply rum mixed with water. The Grog was standard issue to sailors in the Royal Navy and is named for Admiral Edward Vernon, who was nicknamed "Old Grog" for his habit of wearing a grogram cape and for cutting the rum ration with generous amounts of water to prevent drunkenness aboard ship.

Legend has it that Henry Morgan, the notorious British buccaneer, improved the grog ration by adding lime juice to prevent scurvy among his crew. If he added a little sugar, he might well have been remembered and revered as the inventor of the Daiquiri (which came later and originated in, and was named for, a small village of the same name not far from the original Bacardi distillery in Cuba).

For those who would like to expand their spiritous horizons, a Caribbean Rum Baedeker has been provided for the adventurous who would consider a trip to exciting and exotic places, and the opportunity to experience new and different rum drinks a smashing way to have a holiday.

A CARIBBEAN RUM BAEDEKER

Country	Indigenous Rum Brands
Antigua	Cavalier Antigua Rum
Barbados	Alleyne Arthur's Special Old Barbados Rum Cockade Fine Rum Cockspur 5 Star Gosling's Choicest Barbados Rum Lamb's Navy Rum (rums from Barbados, Guayana, Jamaica, and Trinidad blended and bottled in London) Lightbourn's Selected Barbados Rum Old Brigand Rum (Alleyne Arthur) Mount Gay "Eclipse" Rum Mount Gay Sugar Cane Brandy (ten years old)
Bermuda	Gosling's Black Seal
Cuba	Casa Merino 1889 Havana Club Ron Matusalem (*Note:* Santiago de Cuba was the site of the original Bacardi distillery.)

Country	Indigenous Rum Brands
Colombia	Ron Caldas Ron Medellin Tres Esquinas
Costa Rica	Ron Viejo Especial
Dominican Republic	Barceló Bermudez Brugal Macorix Siboney
Guyana	Lemon Hart & Sons Finest Demerara Rum Hudson's Bay Demerara Rum (Both of these rums are bottled in the U.K.)
Haiti	Rhum Barbancourt Barbancourt Rum Liqueurs
Jamaica	Appleton Coruba Daniel Finzi Fine Old Rum Gilbey's Governor General Jamaica Rum Hudson's Bay Jamaica Rum (bottled in the U.K.) Kelly's Jamaica Rum Captain Morgan Myers's Rum Rumona Jamaica Rum Liqueur Skol Wray & Nephew
French West Indies	Rhum Saint-James Rhum Clément Liqueur Créole Clément Rhum Bally Rhum La Mauny Rhum Negrita (bottled in Bordeux)
Panama	Abuelo Carta Vieja Cortez

Country	Indigenous Rum Brands
Puerto Rico	Bacardi
	Carioca
	Castillo
	Boca Chica
	Don Q
	Grenado
	Llave
	Myers's Rum
	Ron Merito
	Palo Viejo
	Ronrico
	Ron del Barrilito
	Ron Matusalem
	Trigo
St. Lucia	Jos. Jn. Baptiste Crystal
	Clear White Rum
St. Vincent	Sunset St. Vincent Rum
Virgin Islands (British)	British Navy Pusser's Rum
Virgin Islands (U.S.)	Cruzan Rum
	Old St. Croix
	Poland Spring
	Pott Rum
	Ron Chico
	Ron Popular
Trinidad	Fernandes "Vat 19"
	Ferdi's 10 Year
	Old Oak Rum
	Siegert's Bouquet Rum
Venezuela	Cacique Ron Añejo

Note: This partial listing of Caribbean rums does not include private label brands.

ACAPULCO

1½ oz. light rum
½ oz. triple sec
½ oz. lime juice
1 tsp. sugar syrup or to taste
1 egg white (for two drinks)
Mint leaves, slightly torn

Mix all ingredients, except mint leaves, with cracked ice in a shaker or blender, strain into a chilled cocktail glass, and garnish with mint.

ADMIRAL NELSON

1 oz. light rum
1 oz. gin
1 tsp. triple sec
½ oz. lime juice
Orange slice

Mix all ingredients, except orange slice, with cracked ice in a shaker or blender and pour into a chilled Old Fashioned glass. Garnish with orange slice.

ADMIRAL VERNON

1½ oz. light rum
½ oz. Grand Marnier
½ oz. lime juice
1 tsp. orgeat syrup

Mix all ingredients with cracked ice in a shaker or blender and strain into a chilled cocktail glass.

ADOLPH'S ALM

1½ oz. light rum
½ oz. amaretto
½ oz. lime juice
1 tsp. maraschino liqueur or
    sugar syrup
Dash orange bitters

Mix all ingredients with cracked ice in a shaker or blender and strain into a chilled cocktail glass.

AMERICAN FLYER

1½ oz. light rum
¼ oz. lime juice
½ tsp. sugar syrup or to taste
Champagne or sparkling wine

Mix all ingredients, except champagne, with cracked ice in a shaker or blender and strain into a chilled wine goblet. Fill with chilled champagne.

ANDALUSIA

¾ oz. light rum
¾ oz. brandy
¾ oz. dry sherry
Several dashes Angostura
  bitters

Combine all ingredients in a
mixing glass with several ice
cubes, stir well, and strain
into a chilled cocktail glass.

ANKLE BREAKER

1½ oz. 151-proof Demerara
  rum
1 oz. cherry brandy
1 oz. lemon or lime juice
1 tsp. sugar syrup or to taste

Mix all ingredients with cracked
ice in a shaker or blender and
pour into a chilled Old Fashioned glass.

APPLE DAIQUIRI

1½ oz. light Puerto Rican
  rum
½ oz. calvados or applejack
½ oz. lemon juice
1 tsp. sugar syrup or to taste
Dash apple juice

Apple wedge

Mix all ingredients, except apple
wedge, in a shaker or blender
with cracked ice and strain
into a chilled cocktail glass.
Garnish with apple wedge.

APPLE PIE

1½ oz. light rum
¾ oz. sweet vermouth
½ oz. calvados
1 tsp. lemon juice
Dash grenadine

Dash apricot brandy

Mix all ingredients with cracked
ice in a shaker or blender and
strain into a chilled cocktail
glass.

APRICOT LADY

1½ oz. light rum
1 oz. apricot-flavored brandy
  or apricot liqueur
½ oz. curaçao
½ oz. lime juice
1 egg white (for two drinks)
Orange slice

Mix all ingredients, except orange
slice, with cracked ice in a shaker
or blender at low speed for
fifteen seconds, pour into a
chilled Old Fashioned glass,
and garnish with fruit slice.

APRICOT PIE

1½ oz. light Puerto Rican
   rum
½ oz. sweet vermouth
1 oz. apricot brandy
1 tsp. lemon juice
Dash grenadine

Mix all ingredients with cracked
ice in a shaker or blender and
pour into a chilled cocktail
glass.

ARAWAK PUNCH

1½ oz. gold Jamaica rum
½ oz. passion fruit juice or
   pineapple juice
½ oz. lime juice
1 tsp. orgeat syrup

Mix all ingredients with cracked
ice in a shaker or blender, and
pour into a chilled Old Fashioned glass.

AZTECA Aztec Cocktail

1½ oz. light rum or tequila
1 oz. Kahlua
1 oz. crème de cacao
Dash curaçao

Mix all ingredients with cracked
ice in a shaker or blender and
strain into a chilled cocktail
glass.

BACARDI

1½ oz. light or gold Bacardi
   rum
½ oz. lime juice
½ tsp. grenadine

Mix all ingredients with cracked
ice in a shaker or blender and
pour into a chilled cocktail
glass.

BACARDI SPECIAL

1½ oz. light Bacardi rum
¾ oz. gin
1 oz. lime juice
1 tsp. grenadine

Mix with cracked ice in a
shaker or blender and strain into
a chilled cocktail glass.

BAHIA DE BOQUERON

1½ oz. light Puerto Rican
   rum
½ oz. triple sec
1 oz. orange juice
½ oz. lime juice
Lemon-lime soda
Lemon and lime slices

Mix all ingredients, except soda
and lemon and lime slices, with
cracked ice in a shaker or
blender and pour into a chilled
Collins glass. Fill with soda,
stir gently, and garnish with
lemon and lime slices.

BANANA DAIQUIRI

1½ oz. light rum
½ oz. lime juice
1 tsp. sugar syrup or crème
   de banane
⅓ ripe banana, sliced

Mix all ingredients with cracked
ice in a blender until smooth and
pour into a chilled cocktail
glass.

BANANA RUM

½ oz. white rum
½ oz. banana liqueur
½ oz. orange juice

Mix all ingredients with cracked
ice in a shaker or blender, and
strain into a chilled cocktail
glass.

BANYAN COCKTAIL

1½ oz. gold rum
¾ oz. apricot brandy
½ oz. lime juice
½ oz. orgeat syrup or sugar
   syrup to taste

Dash grenadine

Mix with cracked ice in a
shaker or blender and strain into
a chilled cocktail glass.

BARBADOS PLANTER'S PUNCH

3 oz. Barbados gold rum
Juice of 1 lime
1 tsp. sugar syrup or to taste
Dash Angostura bitters
Water or club soda
Ripe banana slice
Orange slices
Maraschino cherry
Pinch ground nutmeg

Mix all ingredients except
banana, orange slices, cherry,
and nutmeg, with cracked ice in
a shaker or blender and pour into
a large, chilled Collins glass.
Garnish with banana, orange
slices, and maraschino cherry.
Sprinkle ground nutmeg on top.

BARRANQUILLA BUCK

1½ oz. light Colombian rum
   (Medellin or Tres Esquinas)
½ oz. Falernum
1 oz. lemon juice
Club soda
Orange slice

Mix all ingredients, except club soda and orange slice, with cracked ice in a shaker or blender and pour into a chilled Old Fashioned glass. Fill with club soda and garnish with orange slice.

BATIDA DE PIÑA

2–3 oz. light rum
⅔ cup crushed pineapple
1 tsp. sugar syrup
Mint sprig (optional)

Mix all ingredients, except mint sprig, with cracked ice in a blender until smooth, and pour into a chilled double Old Fashioned glass. Garnish with mint sprig.

BEACHCOMBER

1½ oz. light rum
½ oz. Cointreau
½ oz. lime juice
Several dashes maraschino
   liqueur

Mix all ingredients with cracked ice in a shaker or blender and strain into a chilled cocktail glass.

BEACHCOMBER'S GOLD

1½ oz. light rum
½ oz. dry vermouth
½ oz. sweet vermouth

Combine all ingredients with several ice cubes in a mixing glass, stir well, and strain into a chilled cocktail glass.

BEEKMAN PLACE COFFEE

1 cup hot black coffee
2 cinnamon sticks
1 oz. Tia Maria
1½ oz. dark Jamaica rum
Dash amaretto
1 scoop chocolate ice cream
Whipped cream
Pinch ground nutmeg

Prepare coffee and let steep with cinnamon sticks until it is

cool. Chill in refrigerator (remove cinnamon sticks) along with other ingredients. Chill blender bowl. Add chilled coffee, Tia Maria, rum, and amaretto to blender and mix well. Add scoop of ice cream and blend for no more than 3 seconds. Pour into a chilled highball glass, top with a generous helping of whipped cream, and sprinkle with nutmeg.

BEE'S KISS No. 1

1½ oz. light Puerto Rican
   rum
1 tsp. honey
1 tsp. heavy cream

Mix all ingredients with cracked
ice in a shaker or blender and
strain into a chilled cocktail
glass.

BEE'S KNEES No. 2

1½ oz. gold rum
½ oz. orange juice
½ oz. lime juice
1 tsp. sugar syrup or to taste
Several dashes curaçao
Orange peel

Mix all ingredients, except orange
peel, with cracked ice in a shaker
or blender and strain into a
chilled cocktail glass. Twist
orange peel over drink and drop
into glass.

BETWEEN THE SHEETS

¾ oz. light rum
¾ oz. brandy
¾ oz. Cointreau
½ oz. lemon juice

Mix all ingredients with cracked
ice in a shaker or blender and
strain into a chilled cocktail
glass.

BITCH'S ITCH

2 oz. 86-proof Demerara
   rum
½ oz. white crème de cacao
½ oz. triple sec
1 oz. lime juice
½ oz. Falernum or sugar
   syrup to taste
1 tsp. 151-proof Demerara rum

Pinch ground cinnamon
Pinch ground nutmeg

Mix all ingredients, except
151-proof rum, cinnamon, and
nutmeg, with cracked ice in a
shaker or blender and pour into
a large Collins glass. Top with a
float of 151-proof rum and sprinkle
with cinnamon and nutmeg.

BLACK STRIPE No. 2 Cold

2 oz. dark Jamaica rum
½ oz. golden molasses
½ oz. lemon juice

Mix with cracked ice in a
blender and pour into a chilled
cocktail glass.

BLACK WITCH

1½ oz. gold rum
½ oz. pineapple juice
1 tsp. dark Jamaica rum
1 tsp. apricot brandy

Mix all ingredients with cracked ice in a shaker or blender and strain into a chilled cocktail glass.

BLUE MOUNTAIN

1½ oz. Jamaica rum
¾ oz. vodka
¾ oz. Tia Maria
2 oz. orange juice

Mix all ingredients with cracked ice in a shaker or blender. Pour into a chilled Old Fashioned glass.

BLUE MOUNTAIN COOLER

2 oz. light rum
½ oz. triple sec or curaçao
½ oz. lemon juice
1 tsp. blueberry syrup
Club soda
Fresh blueberries (optional)
Lemon slice

Mix all ingredients, except club soda, blueberries, and lemon slice, with cracked ice in a shaker or blender and pour into a chilled Collins glass. Fill with club soda and garnish with a few blueberries and lemon slice.

BOCA CHICA COFFEE

2 oz. dark or gold Jamaica rum
1 scoop vanilla or mocha ice cream
Cold black coffee

Mix rum and ice cream in a chilled highball or double Old Fashioned glass until smooth but not too melted. Fill with cold black coffee and stir once or twice only.

BOLERO

1½ oz. light rum
¾ oz. apple brandy or applejack
Several dashes sweet vermouth
Lemon peel

Mix all ingredients, except lemon peel, with ice in a mixing glass, stir briskly, and strain into a chilled cocktail glass. Twist lemon peel over drink and drop into glass.

 **BONAIRE BOOTY**

½ oz. gold rum
½ oz. amaretto
1 oz. chocolate almond liqueur
1 oz. cream

Mix with cracked ice in a blender and pour into a chilled cocktail glass.

 BONGO COLA

1½ oz. gold Barbados,
   Haitian, and Jamaica rum
1 oz. Tia Maria
2 oz. pineapple juice
Dash kirsch
Dash lemon juice
Cola
Maraschino cherry

Mix rum, Tia Maria, pineapple juice, kirsch, and lemon juice with cracked ice in a shaker or blender and pour into a tall, chilled Collins glass. Add several ice cubes, fill with cold cola, stir gently, and garnish with a cherry.

BON TON COCKTAIL

1 oz. gold Barbados rum
1 oz. Southern Comfort
½ oz. Grand Marnier
½ tsp. lemon juice
Several dashes orange bitters

Mix all ingredients with cracked ice in a shaker or blender and strain into a chilled cocktail glass.

 BURMA BRIDGE BUSTER

1 oz. light rum
½ oz. brandy
¼ oz. Peter Heering
½ oz. lemon juice
1 tsp. sugar syrup or to taste

Mix all ingredients with cracked ice in a shaker or blender and pour into a chilled cocktail glass.
Note: Created for the 490th Bombardment Squadron of the 10th and 14th Air Forces.

BUSHRANGER

1 oz. light rum
1 oz. Dubonnet rouge
Several dashes Angostura
   bitters
Lemon peel

Mix all ingredients, except lemon peel, with cracked ice in a shaker or blender and strain into a chilled cocktail glass. Twist lemon peel over drink and drop in.

CALICO JACK

1 oz. dark Jamaica rum
1 oz. rye or bourbon
½ oz. lemon juice
½ oz. sugar syrup or to taste

Mix all ingredients with cracked ice in a shaker or blender and strain into a chilled cocktail glass.

CALYPSO COCKTAIL

1½ oz. gold Trinidad rum
1 oz. pineapple juice
½ oz. lemon juice
1 tsp. Falernum or sugar
    syrup to taste
Dash Angostura bitters
Pinch grated nutmeg

Mix all ingredients except nutmeg with cracked ice in a shaker or blender and strain into a chilled cocktail glass. Sprinkle with nutmeg.

CANEEL BAY CREAM

1½ oz. light rum
½ oz. white crème de cacao
½ oz. coffee liqueur
1 oz. light cream

Mix all ingredients with cracked ice in a shaker or blender and strain into a chilled cocktail glass.

CANNES-CANNES

1½ oz. light rum
1½ oz. gin
½ oz. Cointreau
3 oz. grapefruit juice
Orange slice

Mix all ingredients, except orange slice, with cracked ice in a shaker or blender, pour into a chilled Old Fashioned glass, and garnish with orange slice.

CANTALOUPE CUP

1½ oz. light Puerto Rican
    rum
⅓ cup ripe cantaloupe, diced
½ oz. lime juice
½ oz. orange juice
½ tsp. sugar syrup or to taste
Cantaloupe slice, cut long
    and slim

Mix all ingredients, except cantaloupe slice, with cracked ice in a blender until smooth and pour into a chilled Old Fashioned glass. Garnish with cantaloupe slice.

CARDINAL COCKTAIL No. 1

2 oz. light rum
½ oz. amaretto or crème de
   noyaux
½ oz. triple sec
1 oz. lime juice
½ tsp. grenadine
Lime slice

Mix all ingredients, except lime
slice, with cracked ice in a shaker
or blender and pour into a
chilled Old Fashioned glass. Garnish with lime slice.

CASA BLANCA

2 oz. gold Jamaica rum
¼ tsp. curaçao
¼ tsp. maraschino liqueur
1 tsp. lime juice
Dash Angostura bitters

Mix all ingredients with cracked
ice in a shaker or blender and
strain into a chilled cocktail
glass.

CAT CAY COCKTAIL

1½ oz. Haitian rum or Martinique rum
½ oz. Grand Marnier
½ oz. lime juice
Lemon peel

Mix all ingredients, except
lemon peel, with cracked ice in a
shaker or blender. Strain into
a chilled cocktail glass, twist
lemon peel over drink, and
drop into glass.

CHALULA CREAM

1½ oz. gold Jamaica rum
½ oz. maraschino liqueur
½ oz. lime juice
1 tsp. heavy cream
1 egg white (for 2 drinks)

Mix all ingredients with cracked
ice in a shaker or blender and
strain into a chilled cocktail
glass.

CHAPULTEPEC

1 oz. light rum
¾ oz. brandy
¼ oz. sweet vermouth
¼ oz. tequila
1 tsp. sugar syrup or to taste

Mix all ingredients with plenty
of cracked ice in a shaker or
blender and pour into a chilled
Whiskey Sour glass.

CHARLOTTE AMALIE CELEBRATION CUP

1½ oz. light Virgin Islands
  rum
1 oz. Peter Heering
1 oz. lemon juice
1 tsp. sugar syrup or to taste
2 oz. lemon-lime soda
Lemon slice

Mix all ingredients, except soda
and lemon slice, with cracked ice
in a shaker or blender and
pour into a chilled double Old
Fashioned glass. Fill with cold
lemon-lime soda and garnish with
lemon slice.

 ## CHEERY COKE

2 oz. Jamaica rum
Several dashes cherry brandy
  or cherry cordial
Cola
Lemon peel

Combine rum, brandy, and a
little cola in a chilled double Old
Fashioned glass and stir well.
Fill with cold cola and stir gently.
Twist lemon peel over drink
and drop into glass.

CHERRY DAIQUIRI

1½ oz. light rum
½ oz. Peter Heering
½ oz. lime juice
Several dashes kirsch
Lime peel

Mix all ingredients, except lime
peel, with cracked ice in a shaker
or blender and strain into a
chilled cocktail glass. Twist lime
peel over drink and drop into
glass.

CHICAGO FIZZ

1 oz. gold rum
1 oz. port
½ oz. lemon juice
1 tsp. sugar syrup or to taste
1 egg white (for two drinks)
Club soda

Mix all ingredients, except club
soda, with cracked ice in a shaker
or blender. Strain into a chilled
Collins glass and fill with cold
club soda.

CHICKASAW COCKTAIL

1 oz. gold rum
1 oz. Southern Comfort
½ oz. curaçao
1 tsp. lemon juice
Several dashes orange bitters

Mix all ingredients with cracked
ice in a shaker or blender and
strain into a chilled cocktail
glass.

CHI-CHI

2 oz. light rum
5 oz. pineapple juice
½ oz. blackberry brandy

Mix rum and pineapple juice with cracked ice in a shaker or blender and pour into a chilled highball glass. Top off with blackberry brandy.

CHINA

2 oz. gold Barbados rum
1 tsp. curaçao
½ oz. passion fruit juice
Several dashes grenadine
Several dashes Angostura
    bitters

Mix all ingredients with cracked ice in a shaker or blender and strain into a chilled cocktail glass.

 COCONUT BANG! No. 1

1 oz. light rum
1 oz. coconut rum
½ oz. coconut juice
½ oz. coconut cream (canned)
1 oz. orange juice
2 oz. fresh coconut, cut in
    small pieces
½ oz. lemon juice

Drain the water or juice from a coconut by puncturing the "eyes" at one end and drain into a tumbler. There should be sufficient liquid in the average coconut to make 3 or 4 drinks. Crack coconut with a hammer and remove meat by using a

table knife. Coconut meat may be frozen for future use. Mix all ingredients in a blender with cracked ice until smooth and pour into a chilled Hurricane or chimney glass.
Note: Many coconut recipes call for using the coconut shell as a drinking glass. This looks great in photos taken in exotic tropical settings, but almost never works well due to the fact that the coconut was never designed to be used as a drinking vessel. Use a big glass. It eliminates a lot of spilled drinks.

 COCONUT BANG! No. 2

1½ oz. coconut rum
2 oz. pineapple juice
1 oz. lime juice
½ oz. coconut syrup
1 tsp. CocoRibe or Malibu
Fresh coconut, grated

Mix all ingredients, except grated coconut, with cracked ice in a shaker or blender. Pour into a chilled double Old Fashioned glass and sprinkle with grated coconut.

COLUMBIA

1½ oz. light rum
½ oz. raspberry syrup or raspberry or cherry liqueur
½ oz. lemon juice
1 tsp. kirschwasser

Mix all ingredients with cracked ice in a shaker or blender and strain into a chilled cocktail glass.

CONTINENTAL

1½ oz. light rum
½ oz. green crème de menthe
½ oz. lime juice
1 tsp. sugar syrup or to taste

Mix all ingredients with cracked ice in a shaker or blender and strain into a chilled cocktail glass.

CORKSCREW

1½ oz. light rum
½ oz. dry vermouth
½ oz. peach liqueur
Lime slice

Mix all ingredients, except lime slice, with cracked ice in a shaker or blender, strain into a chilled cocktail glass, and garnish with lime slice.

CORONADO GOLD

1½ oz. gold rum
1 oz. brandy
½ oz. lemon juice
½ oz. sugar syrup or to taste
1 egg yolk

Mix all ingredients with cracked ice in a blender and pour into a chilled Whiskey Sour glass.

COZUMEL COFFEE COCKTAIL

1 oz. Barbados or Mexican gold rum
1 oz. coffee liqueur
1 oz. triple sec

Mix all ingredients with cracked ice in a shaker or blender and strain into a chilled cocktail glass.

BARTENDER'S SECRET NO. 10

Exotic rum drinks deserve exotic presentation in some novel or unusual glass. So reasoned Trader Vic when he was introducing his elegant liquid inventions in an atmosphere of a romantic, tropical island hideaway. No container, if attractive, was too bizarre for his Polynesian potations. Trader Vic used flower vases, pottery bowls, ceramic mugs shaped like skulls, and even ceramic pineapples and coconuts. China rum kegs and footed tiki bowls (decorated with South Seas religious figures) were used for communal drinks. All kinds of glassware were utilized to make drinks look appealing, important, and romantic. A big beer schooner or a king-size brandy snifter properly garnished with fruits and flowers has a certain allure that one does not feel when the same drink is served in a highball glass. It is not usually necessary to shop around for rare and unusual glassware to achieve an exotic effect when serving party drinks to your guests. Instead of serving a Rum Collins in a Collins glass, try using a tall pilsener beer glass (if it has a small stem, so much the better) or a big wine goblet. Those oversize brandy snifters that are used only occasionally will give an aura of importance to any tall drink. Footed iced-tea glasses, parfait, and sherbet glasses, even tall water goblets, can add just the right touch to cocktails and coolers. Search the back of the cupboard. Those heavy coffee mugs you thought you'd never use again might be just the thing for your next party.

CREOLE CUP

1½ oz. light rum
Beef bouillon or consommé
1 tsp. lemon juice
Several dashes Tabasco sauce
Several dashes Worcestershire sauce
Pinch celery salt
Pinch white pepper

Put several ice cubes into a chilled double Old Fashioned glass. Add rum, bouillon, lemon juice, and seasonings and stir well.

CUBA LIBRE

2 oz. light, gold, or dark rum
Cola, ice cold
Wedge of lemon or lime

Half fill a chilled highball or Collins glass with ice cubes, add rum, and fill with cold cola. Stir gently and squeeze lemon or lime wedge over drink and drop into glass.

CUBANO ESPECIAL

1½ oz. light Cuban or Puerto
  Rican rum
½ oz. curaçao
½ oz. lime juice
½ oz. pineapple juice
Pineapple slice

Mix all ingredients, except
pineapple slice, with cracked ice
in a shaker or blender, pour
into a chilled cocktail glass, and
garnish with pineapple slice.

CULROSS

1 oz. gold rum
½ oz. Lillet blanc
½ oz. apricot brandy
½ oz. lemon juice

Mix all ingredients with cracked
ice in a shaker or blender and
pour into a chilled cocktail
glass.

CURAÇAO COOLER

1 oz. dark Jamaica rum
1 oz. curaçao
1 oz. lime juice
Club soda
Orange slice

Mix all ingredients, except club
soda and orange slice, with
cracked ice in a shaker or
blender. Pour into a chilled highball glass, fill with cold club
soda, and garnish with orange
slice.

DAIQUIRI

2 oz. light rum
Juice of ½ lime
½ tsp. sugar syrup or to taste

Mix all ingredients with cracked
ice in a shaker or blender and
strain into a chilled cocktail
glass.

DAIQUIRI DARK

2 oz. Jamaica rum
½ oz. lime juice
1 tsp. Falernum or sugar
  syrup to taste

Mix all ingredients with cracked
ice in a shaker or blender and
strain into a chilled cocktail
glass.

DEMERARA DROP-SHOT

2 oz. 90-proof Demerara
  rum
½ oz. coconut cream
½ oz. lemon juice

Mix all ingredients with cracked
ice in a blender and pour into a
chilled Old Fashioned glass.

DERBY SPECIAL

1½ oz. light rum
½ oz. Cointreau
1 oz. orange juice
½ oz. lime juice

Mix all ingredients with cracked ice in a blender and pour into a chilled cocktail glass.

DEVIL'S TAIL

1½ oz. gold rum
½ oz. vodka
½ oz. apricot liqueur
½ oz. lime juice
½ tsp. grenadine
Lime peel

Mix all ingredients, except lime peel, with cracked ice in a blender and pour into a chilled cocktail glass. Twist lime peel over drink and drop into glass.

DOCTOR FUNK

½ lime
½ lemon juice
1 tsp. sugar syrup
Dash grenadine
2–3 oz. dark Jamaica, Haitian, or Martinique rum
Club soda
½ tsp. Pernod or Herbsaint

Fill a mixing glass with ice cubes and squeeze lime into glass (reserve shell). Add all other ingredients, except soda and Pernod, and stir briskly. Strain into a chilled, tall Collins glass, add additional ice cubes, fill with cold club soda, and top off with Pernod and lime shell.

DOUBLOON

1 oz. Jamaica rum
1 oz. light rum
1 oz. 151-proof rum
1 oz. grapefruit juice
1 oz. orange juice
Several dashes orange
  curaçao
Several dashes Pernod

Orange slice
Maraschino cherry

Mix all ingredients, except orange slice and maraschino cherry, with cracked ice in a shaker or blender. Pour into a chilled double Old Fashioned glass and garnish with fruit.

THE DRINKING MAN'S FRUIT CUP

2 oz. gold Barbados rum
1 oz. dark Jamaica rum
1 oz. cranberry juice
1 oz. orange juice
1 heaping tbsp. orange and
  grapefruit sections

Lemon-lime soda

Mix all ingredients, except soda, with cracked ice in a blender and pour into a chilled Collins glass. Fill with cold lemon-lime soda and stir gently.

EL SALVADOR

1½ oz. light rum
¾ oz. Frangelico
½ oz. lime juice
1 tsp. grenadine

Mix all ingredients with cracked ice in a shaker or blender and strain into a chilled cocktail glass.

AN ENHANCED PLANTER'S PUNCH

2½ oz. dark Jamaica rum
1 oz. curaçao
2 oz. orange juice
1 oz. pineapple juice
1 oz. lime or lemon juice
Falernum, orgeat, or sugar
  syrup to taste
Dash grenadine
Club soda
Pineapple slice

Orange slice
Maraschino cherry

Mix all ingredients, except soda, pineapple and orange slices, and cherry, with cracked ice in a shaker or blender and pour into a large, chilled Collins glass. Fill with cold club soda and stir gently. Garnish with pineapple and orange slices and cherry.

EYE OPENER No. 1

1½ oz. light rum
1 tsp. triple sec
1 tsp. white crème de cacao
1 tsp. sugar syrup
½ tsp. Pernod

1 egg yolk

Mix all ingredients with cracked ice in a shaker or blender and strain into a chilled cocktail glass.

EYE OPENER No. 2

2 oz. dark Jamaica rum
2 oz. Barbados rum
½ oz. curaçao
2 oz. orange juice
1 oz. grapefruit juice

1 oz. sweetened lemon juice
  or liquid Whiskey Sour mix

Mix all ingredients with cracked ice in a shaker or blender and pour into a chilled double Old Fashioned glass.

FER DE LANCE

2 oz. Jamaica rum
1 oz. lime juice
1 oz. orange juice
½ oz. sugar syrup
1 tsp. 151-proof Demerara rum

Mix all ingredients, except Demerara rum, with cracked ice in a shaker or blender and pour into a chilled cocktail glass. Float Demerara rum on top.

FERN GULLY

1 oz. dark Jamaica rum
1 oz. light rum
½ oz. coconut cream
1 oz. orange juice
½ oz. lime juice
½ oz. amaretto or crème de noyaux

Mix all ingredients with cracked ice in a shaker or blender and serve in a chilled cocktail glass or wine goblet.

52ND STREET

1½ oz. dark Jamaica rum
1 oz. lemon juice
½ oz. cognac
½ oz. Cointreau
1 tsp. grenadine

Mix with plenty of ice in a blender until frappéed and serve in a chilled champagne glass.

FIG LEAF

1 oz. light rum
1 oz. sweet vermouth
½ oz. lime juice
Several dashes Angostura bitters
Lemon peel

Mix all ingredients, except lemon peel, with cracked ice in a shaker or blender and strain into a chilled cocktail glass. Twist lemon peel over drink and drop into glass.

FIJI FIZZ

1½ oz. dark Jamaica rum
½ oz. bourbon
1 tsp. Cherry Marnier
Several dashes orange bitters
4 oz. cola
Lime peel

Mix all ingredients, except cola and lime peel, with cracked ice in a shaker or blender, pour into a chilled Collins glass, fill with cold cola, and garnish with lime peel.

FORT DE FRANCE

1½ oz. gold rum
½ oz. brandy
½ oz. pineapple juice
1 oz. lime juice
1 tsp. Cointreau
Lime slice

Mix all ingredients, except lime slice, with cracked ice in a shaker or blender and pour into a chilled Collins glass. Garnish with lime slice.

 FROGDON

1 oz. gold rum
½ oz. dark Jamaica rum
½ oz. cranberry liqueur
1 oz. lime juice
½ oz. sugar syrup or to taste
1 egg white (for 2 drinks)

Mix all ingredients with cracked ice in a shaker or blender and pour into a chilled Old Fashioned glass.

FROZEN DAIQUIRI

2 oz. light rum
½ oz. lime juice
1 tsp. sugar

Mix all ingredients with plenty of crushed ice in a blender at low speed for a few seconds until snowy and pour into a chilled deep-saucer champagne glass.

FROZEN GUAVA DAIQUIRI

1½ oz. light rum
1 oz. guava nectar
½ oz. lime juice
1 tsp. crème de banane
(optional)

Mix all ingredients with plenty of crushed ice in a blender for a few seconds until snowy and pour into a chilled deep-saucer champagne glass.

FROZEN PASSION

1½ oz. light Puerto Rican rum
½ oz. La Grande Passion
½ oz. lime juice
½ oz. orange juice
1 tsp. lemon juice

Mix all ingredients with plenty of crushed ice in a blender for a few seconds until snowy and pour into a chilled deep-saucer champagne glass.

FROZEN PEACH DAIQUIRI

1½ oz. light Puerto Rican rum
½ oz. lime juice
1 heaping tbsp. fresh, canned, or frozen peaches, diced
½ oz. syrup from canned or frozen peaches or sugar syrup

Mix all ingredients with plenty of crushed ice in a blender for a few seconds until snowy and pour into a chilled deep-saucer champagne glass.

FROZEN PINEAPPLE DAIQUIRI

1½ oz. light Puerto Rican
  rum
½ oz. lime juice
½ tsp. pineapple syrup or
  crème de banane
2 oz. canned pineapple, finely
  chopped

Mix all ingredients with plenty
of crushed ice in a blender for a
few seconds until snowy and
pour into a chilled deep-saucer
champagne glass.

FT. LAUDERDALE

1½ oz. gold rum
½ oz. sweet vermouth
½ oz. orange juice
½ oz. lime juice
Preserved cocktail orange
  section

Mix all ingredients, except orange
section, with cracked ice in a
shaker or blender and pour
into a chilled Whiskey Sour glass.
Garnish with orange section.

GEORGIA RUM COOLER

2–3 oz. light rum
½ oz. lemon juice
1 tsp. Falernum
Dash grenadine
1 tsp. salted peanuts
Club soda
Pinch of ground cinnamon

Mix all ingredients, except club
soda and cinnamon, with cracked
ice in a blender at high speed
for 30 seconds, pour into a chilled
Collins glass, and fill with
cold club soda. Stir gently and
sprinkle with ground cinnamon.

GOLDEN GATE

1 oz. light rum
½ oz. gin
½ oz. white crème de cacao
1 oz. lemon juice
1 tsp. 151-proof Demerara rum
1 tsp. Falernum or orgeat
  syrup to taste

Orange slice

Mix all ingredients, except orange
slice, with cracked ice in a shaker
or blender, pour into a chilled
Old Fashioned glass, and garnish
with orange slice.

GRAND OCCASION COCKTAIL

1½ oz. light rum
½ oz. Grand Marnier
½ oz. white crème de cacao
½ oz. lemon juice

Mix with cracked ice and pour
into a chilled cocktail glass.

GUANABANA

1½ oz. light rum
1 oz. guanabana (soursop)
   nectar
1 tsp. lime juice

Mix all ingredients with cracked ice in a shaker or blender and strain into a chilled cocktail glass.

GUANABARA GUAVA

2 oz. gold rum
½ oz. maraschino liqueur
1½ oz. guava nectar
Juice of ½ lemon
½ oz. pineapple juice
1 tsp. coconut syrup or to
   taste
Lemon-lime soda
Lemon slice

Mix all ingredients, except soda and lemon slice, with cracked ice in a shaker or blender, pour into a chilled Collins glass, and top with cold club soda. Stir gently and garnish with lemon slice.

HAPPY APPLE

1½ oz. gold Barbados rum
3 oz. sweet apple cider
½ oz. lemon juice
Lime peel

Mix all ingredients, except lime peel, with cracked ice in a shaker or blender and pour into a chilled Old Fashioned glass. Twist lime peel over drink and drop into glass.

HAMMERHEAD

1 oz. gold rum
1 oz. amaretto
1 oz. curaçao
Dash Southern Comfort

Mix all ingredients with cracked ice in a shaker or blender and strain into a chilled cocktail glass.

HAMMERTOE

1½ oz. light rum
½ oz. curaçao
½ oz. lime juice
1 tsp. amaretto

Mix all ingredients with cracked ice in a shaker or blender and pour into a chilled Old Fashioned glass.

HAVANA BANANA FIZZ

1½ oz. light rum
2 oz. pineapple juice
1 oz. lime juice
⅓ ripe banana, sliced
Several dashes Peychaud's
  bitters
Bitter lemon soda

Mix all ingredients, except soda, with cracked ice in a blender until smooth. Pour into a chilled highball glass and fill with cold bitter lemon soda.

HAVANA BANDANA

2 oz. light Cuban or Puerto
  Rican rum
½ oz. lime juice
1 very ripe banana, sliced
Dash banana liqueur

Mix all ingredients, except banana liqueur, with cracked ice in a blender until smooth and pour into a chilled double Old Fashioned glass. Float dash of banana liqueur on top.

HAVANA CLUB

1½ oz. light rum
½ oz. dry vermouth

Mix all ingredients with cracked ice in a shaker or blender and strain into a chilled cocktail glass.

HONEY BEE

2 oz. light Puerto Rican
  rum
½ oz. honey
½ oz. lemon juice

Mix all ingredients with cracked ice in a shaker or blender and strain into a chilled cocktail glass.

HOP TOAD

1 oz. light rum
1 oz. apricot brandy
1 oz. lime juice

Mix all ingredients with cracked ice in a shaker or blender and strain into a chilled cocktail glass.

HURRICANE

1 oz. light rum
1 oz. gold rum
½ oz. passion fruit syrup
½ oz. lime juice

Mix all ingredients with cracked ice in a shaker or blender and strain into a chilled cocktail glass.

IBO LELE

2 oz. gold Haitian or Barbados rum
½ oz. 151-proof Demerara rum
½ oz. orgeat syrup or to taste
1 tsp. cream
1 egg (for 2 drinks)

Pinch of ground nutmeg

Mix all ingredients, except nutmeg, with cracked ice in a shaker or blender and strain into a chilled wine glass. Sprinkle with ground nutmeg.

INDEPENDENCE SWIZZLE

2 oz. Trinadad rum (Ferdi's, Old Oak, or Siegert's)
Juice of ½ lime
1 tsp. honey or to taste
Several dashes Angostura bitters
Lime slice

Mix all ingredients, except lime slice, with crushed ice in a tall, chilled Collins glass with a swizzle stick. Sometimes it is better to dissolve honey with a little water before trying to mix it in a cold drink. Garnish with lime slice.
Note: A swizzle stick may be made from a small twig with many little branches or you may substitute a long spoon.

IPSWICH SWITCHELL

2 oz. light rum
1 oz. cranberry juice
1 tsp. sugar syrup or to taste
Dash lime juice

Mix all ingredients with cracked ice in a shaker or blender and strain into a chilled double Old Fashioned glass filled with crushed ice.

 ISLAND ICED TEA

1 oz. light rum
½ oz. dark Jamaica rum
1 cup iced tea, cold
1 tsp. Falernum or sugar syrup to taste
Dash lemon juice
Dash 151-proof Demerara rum

Lemon slice
Mint sprig (optional)

Mix light rum, Jamaica rum, tea, syrup, and lemon juice in a tall, chilled highball or Collins glass, add ice, and top with 151-proof rum. Garnish with lemon slice and mint sprig.

BARTENDER'S SECRET NO. 11

Time was that tropical fruits in most of the U.S. were limited to oranges, lemons, grapefruits, limes, bananas, pineapples, and coconuts (the latter, not really a fruit but a seed, is included here because it is a popular mixed-drink ingredient). Thanks to jet transportation, increased demand for exotic tropical fruits, and important technological improvements in food processing, new kinds of tropical fruits are becoming available. Sweet, syrupy papaya, mango, and guava nectars are being replaced with appetizing juice drinks that are a boon to the professional bartender and the home drink maker. These are now becoming available in supermarkets. Rare tropical fruits like the soursop, sweetsop, custard apple, mammee apple, akee, and Malay apple will no doubt find their way to grocery-store shelves. It wasn't long ago that the kiwi, passion fruit, and the papaya were just curiosities. When more exotic fruits become readily available, mixologists will have a field day and the rum drinker will be the beneficiary.

ISLAND SCHOONER FLOAT

1 oz. Bacardi Premium
   Black rum
4 oz. chilled cola
2 scoops vanilla ice cream
Maraschino cherry

In a chilled fountain glass combine rum, cola, and ice cream with an iced-tea spoon. Do not overmix. Garnish with a cherry. Serve with an iced-tea spoon.
Note: Created by the author for Bacardi Imports, Inc., Miami.

ISLAND SUNRISE

2 oz. Bacardi Premium
   Black rum
6 oz. orange juice
1½ oz. heavy cream
2 tbsp. superfine sugar or to
   taste
Orange slice

Mix all ingredients, except orange slice, with cracked ice in a shaker or blender and strain into a chilled wine goblet. Garnish with orange slice.
Note: Created by the author for Bacardi Imports, Inc., Miami.

ISLE OF THE BLESSED COCONUT

1½ oz. light rum
½ oz. lime juice
½ oz. lemon juice
½ oz. orange juice
1 tsp. cream of coconut
1 tsp. orgeat syrup or to taste

Mix all ingredients with cracked ice in a blender until smooth and pour into a chilled deep-saucer champagne glass.

ISLE OF PINES

1½ oz. light Puerto Rican
   rum
½ oz. lime juice
1 tsp. peppermint schnapps
6 mint leaves

Mix all ingredients with plenty
of crushed ice in a blender for a
few seconds until snowy and
pour into a chilled cocktail glass.
Serve with a straw.

JADE

1½ oz. gold Barbados rum
½ tsp. green crème de menthe
½ oz. lime juice
½ tsp. curaçao
1 tsp. sugar syrup or to taste
Lime slice

Mix all ingredients, except lime
slice, with cracked ice in a shaker
or blender, strain into a chilled
cocktail glass, and garnish with
lime slice.

JAMAICA EGG CREAM

1½ oz. dark Jamaica rum
1 oz. gin
1 oz. light cream
1 tsp. lemon juice
1 tsp. sugar syrup or to taste
Club soda

Mix all ingredients, except club
soda, with cracked ice in a shaker
or blender, pour into a chilled
highball glass, and fill with cold
club soda.
Note: Inspired by the New York
City Egg Cream drink, which
contains no egg or cream.

JAMAICA MULE

1½ oz. light Jamaica rum
½ oz. dark Jamaica rum
½ oz. 151-proof rum
½ oz. Falernum or sugar
   syrup
½ oz. lime juice
Ginger beer
Pineapple stick
1 section preserved ginger
   (optional)

Mix all ingredients, except ginger
beer, pineapple, and ginger, with
cracked ice in a shaker or
blender and pour into a chilled
Collins glass. Fill with cold
ginger beer and stir gently.
Garnish with pineapple stick and
ginger.

 ## JAMAICA PEACH

1½ oz. dark Jamaica rum
1½ oz. peach brandy
2 oz. orange juice
2 oz. pineapple juice
1 oz. grapefruit juice
1 oz. guava juice
Several dashes Falernum
Pineapple stick
Orange slice

Mix all ingredients, except
pineapple stick and orange slice,
in a shaker or blender with
cracked ice and pour into a chilled
double Old Fashioned glass.
Garnish with pineapple stick and
orange slice.

JAMAICA STONE FENCE

2 oz. dark Jamaica rum
6 oz. apple cider, chilled
Cinnamon stick
Pinch grated nutmeg

Stir rum and cider with ice in
a mixing glass and pour into a
double Old Fashioned glass.
Garnish with cinnamon and
nutmeg.

JAMBO JACK

2 oz. dark Jamaica rum
½ oz. curaçao
½ oz. apricot brandy
1 oz. lime juice
½ oz. orgeat syrup or Falernum
Pineapple stick

Mix all ingredients, except
pineapple stick, with cracked ice
in a shaker or blender and
pour into chilled highball glass.
Garnish with pineapple stick.

 ## JAVIER SAAVEDRA

1 oz. dark Jamaica rum
1 oz. white tequila
2 oz. pineapple juice
1 oz. grapefruit juice
Orange slice

Mix all ingredients, except orange
slice, with cracked ice in a shaker
or blender, strain into a chilled
cocktail glass, and garnish with
orange slice.

JOLLY ROGER

1 oz. light rum
1 oz. Drambuie
½ oz. lime juice
Several dashes scotch
Club soda

Mix all ingredients, except club
soda, with cracked ice in a shaker
or blender. Pour into a chilled
highball glass and fill with club
soda.

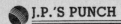 ## J.P.'S PUNCH

1½ oz. light Puerto Rican
   rum
1 oz. dark Jamaica rum
2 oz. orange juice
1 oz. pineapple juice
½ oz. lime juice

½ sliced ripe banana
Maraschino cherry

Mix all ingredients, except
cherry, with cracked ice in a
shaker or blender and serve in
a double Old Fashioned glass.
Garnish with a cherry.

 ## JU-JU

1 oz. Haitian or Martinique
   rum
1 oz. Southern Comfort
1 oz. orange juice
½ oz. lime juice

1 tsp. Falernum or orgeat
   syrup
½ ripe banana, sliced

Mix with cracked ice in a
blender until smooth and pour
into a chilled Collins glass.

 ## THE JUMBY JOLT

½ oz. gold Jamaica rum
½ oz. gin
½ oz. scotch
½ oz. lime juice
1 tsp. sweet vermouth
1 tsp. cherry brandy

Maraschino cherry

Mix all ingredients, except
maraschino cherry, with cracked
ice in a shaker or blender and
pour into a chilled Collins glass.
Garnish with cherry.

 ## KAMEHAMEHA RUM PUNCH

1 oz. light rum
1 oz. blackberry brandy
2 oz. pineapple juice
½ oz. lemon juice
½ oz. sugar syrup or to taste
1 tsp. blackberry brandy

Pineapple stick

Mix all ingredients, except
pineapple stick, with cracked ice
in a shaker or blender. Pour
into chilled highball glass, top
with float of Jamaica rum, and
garnish with pineapple stick.

BARTENDER'S SECRET NO. 12

Fresh ripe coconuts are troublesome to prepare, but worth it in
terms of flavor dividends for both food and drink preparation.
When buying a coconut, select one that is heavy in the hand
and full of liquid which can be plainly heard when coconut is

shaken. First puncture the "eyes" at one end of the shell with an ice pick and drain out liquid and save. It may be frozen or kept in the refrigerator for a day or two. If you wish to use the shell as a container, saw it in half and remove coconut meat by inserting a long, thin, flexible kitchen knife in between shell and meat and pry out. Remove brown skin with a vegetable parer and shred with a grater or chop in a blender by adding just a few pieces at a time. Some cooks find it easier to open the shell and extract the meat by baking the whole coconut in an oven for about 15 minutes at 325°. Then the shell is easily cracked open. If you wish to make coconut milk, chop meat in blender with about ¼ cup of water for a small coconut. Use milk in place of water for coconut cream. Add the liquid you drained from the coconut for more intense flavor. Strain mixture and use for drink-making. If more liquid is needed, return coconut meat to blender and repeat the process.

KE-KALI-NEI-AU

1½ oz. light rum
½ oz. kirsch
1½ oz. passion fruit juice
1 oz. lemon juice
½ oz. orgeat or sugar syrup
  to taste
1 oz. dark Jamaica rum
1 coconut shell, halved
Red hibiscus and assorted
  tropical fruits (optional)

Mix all ingredients, except Jamaica rum, coconut, hibiscus, and assorted fruits, with cracked ice in a shaker or blender. Pour into coconut shell, top with float of Jamaica rum, and garnish with red hibiscus and assorted fruits. Serve with straws.
Note: To prepare coconut, puncture "eyes" and drain out water.* Saw coconut in half and place open end up in a cup, small dish, or ashtray so that it will not fall over when filled with liquid. If coconuts are not available, use any large decorative glass.

*Save water for punches and other tropical rum drinks.

KENT CORNERS COMFORT

1½ oz. dark Jamaica rum
½ oz. lime juice
1 tsp. maple syrup
Lime slice

Mix all ingredients, except lime slice, with cracked ice in a shaker or blender, pour into a chilled Old Fashioned glass, and garnish with lime slice.

KILAUEA KUP

1½ oz. gold rum
½ oz. crème de banane
4 oz. pineapple juice
1 oz. Rose's lime juice
1 tsp. coconut rum
Orange slice
Maraschino cherry

Mix all ingredients, except coconut rum, orange slice, and maraschino cherry, with cracked ice in a shaker or blender and pour into a chilled Collins glass. Top with coconut rum and garnish with fruit.

KILL DIVIL

2 oz. light or gold rum
1 oz. brandy
½ oz. honey or to taste
Several pinches of freshly
   grated ginger

Stir all ingredients with a little water until honey is dissolved, add cracked ice, and stir again until cold. Pour into a chilled Old Fashioned glass and add additional ice if necessary.

KINGSTON No. 1

1½ oz. dark Jamaica rum
¾ oz. kummel
¾ oz. orange juice
Dash Pimiento Dram

Mix with cracked ice in a shaker or blender and strain into a chilled cocktail glass.

KINGSTON No. 2

1½ oz. dark Jamaica rum
¾ oz. gin
Juice of ½ lime
1 tsp. grenadine or to taste

Mix with cracked ice in a shaker or blender and strain into a chilled cocktail glass.

KINGSTON COCKTAIL

1½ oz. dark Jamaica rum
1 oz. Tia Maria
1 tsp. lime juice

Mix all ingredients with cracked ice in a shaker or blender and strain into a chilled cocktail glass.

KINGSTON COFFEE GROG

1½ oz. gold Jamaica rum
1½ oz. Tia Maria
½ tsp. powdered instant coffee
½ tsp. sugar syrup or to taste

Mix all ingredients in a mixing glass with ice until coffee powder is dissolved and strain into a chilled Delmonico glass.

KOKO HEAD

2 oz. light rum
½ oz. triple sec
½ oz. pineapple liqueur or
   apricot liqueur
1 oz. lime juice
Lime slice

Mix all ingredients, except lime slice, with cracked ice in a shaker or blender, pour into a chilled Old Fashioned glass, and garnish with lime slice.

KUAI KUP

3 oz. light rum
4 oz. pineapple juice
2 oz. orange juice
½ oz. passion fruit juice
Pineapple slice

Mix all ingredients, except pineapple slice, with cracked ice in a shaker or blender and pour into a chilled double Old Fashioned glass. Garnish with pineapple slice.

LALLAH ROOKH

1½ oz. light rum
¾ oz. cognac
½ oz. crème de vanille or
   vanilla extract
1 tsp. sugar syrup or to taste
1 generous tbsp. whipped
   cream

Mix all ingredients, except whipped cream, with cracked ice in a shaker or blender and serve in a chilled wine goblet and top with whipped cream.

LEMON RUM ICE

2 oz. light rum
4 oz. lemon ice, sorbet, or
   sherbet

Chill blender bowl, rum and lemon ice in freezer before making this drink. Spoon out a generous ½ cup of lemon ice and add to blender bowl with chilled rum. Turn blender on for 3 seconds. Spoon mixture into a chilled wine goblet. Serve with spoon and straw.
Note: The secret to this drink is to mix quickly so ice does not get mushy. Thus everything must be well chilled in advance.

LIMBO COCKTAIL

2 oz. light rum
½ oz. crème de banane
1 oz. orange juice

Mix all ingredients with cracked ice in a shaker or blender and strain into a chilled cocktail glass.

◥ LITTLE DIX MIX

1½ oz. dark Jamaica rum
½ oz. crème de banane
½ oz. lime juice
1 tsp. curaçao

Mix all ingredients with cracked ice in a shaker or blender and pour into a chilled Old Fashioned glass.

LOCO COCO

1½ oz. light rum
½ oz. crème de cacao
1 oz. cream of coconut
1 oz. lemon juice
1 tsp. coconut rum
Club soda
Lemon slice
Maraschino cherry

Mix all ingredients, except club soda, lemon slice, and cherry, with cracked ice in a shaker or blender and pour into a chilled Collins glass. Fill with cold club soda, stir gently, and garnish with fruit.

◥ LOMA LOMA LULLABY

1½ oz. light rum
1 oz. passion fruit syrup or
　La Grande Passion
1 oz. lime juice
1 egg white (for two drinks)
1 tsp. 151-proof Demerara rum

Mix all ingredients, except Demerara rum, with cracked ice in a blender and pour into a chilled Whiskey Sour glass. Top with Demerara rum.

LONDON DOCK COOLER

1½ oz. Jamaica or gold rum
3 oz. claret
½ oz. kirsch
½ oz. Falernum or to taste
Orange peel

Mix all ingredients, except orange peel, into a chilled high-ball glass with several ice cubes and stir well. Twist orange peel over drink and then drop into glass.

BARTENDER'S SECRET NO. 13

Spills happen under the best of circumstances. Fast action can often prevent permanent damage to a dress or suit. Red wine stains are particularly stubborn. The affected area should be bathed with club soda or cold water immediately, followed by liquid detergent or mild bar soap (Ivory), which is rubbed into stain. The same treatment should be used on coffee stains. Club soda is a handy, inexpensive grease-cutter that some bartenders use to clean wood and stainless-steel surfaces as well as spots from their customer's jackets and ties.

LOUISIANA PLANTER'S PUNCH

1½ oz. gold rum
¾ oz. bourbon
¾ oz. cognac
½ oz. sugar syrup or orgeat
   syrup
1 oz. lemon juice
Several dashes Peychaud's
   bitters
Several dashes Herbsaint or
   Pernod

Lemon slice
Orange slice
Club soda (optional)

Mix all ingredients, except lemon and orange slices and club soda, with cracked ice in a shaker or blender and pour into a chilled highball glass. Garnish with fruit slices. Fill with cold soda if you wish.

MAGENS BAY

1½ oz. light rum
½ oz. apricot brandy
1 oz. orange juice
1 oz. lime juice
½ oz. sugar syrup or to taste
Orange slice
Maraschino cherry

Mix all ingredients, except orange slice and maraschino cherry, with cracked ice in a shaker or blender and strain into a chilled cocktail glass. Garnish with orange slice and maraschino cherry.

MAHUKONA

1½ oz. light rum
½ oz. triple sec
½ oz. lemon juice
Several dashes rock-candy
   syrup or orgeat syrup
Several dashes Angostura
   bitters
Pineapple slice
Mint sprigs (optional)

Mix all ingredients, except pineapple slice and mint sprigs, with cracked ice in a shaker or blender. Pour into a chilled Collins glass and garnish with pineapple slice and mint.

 **MAI KAI NO**

1 oz. light rum
1 oz. dark Jamaica rum
½ oz. 151-proof Demerara rum
1 oz. lime juice
½ oz. orgeat syrup
½ oz. passion fruit juice or
    La Grande Passion
Club soda

Pineapple or orange slice
Mint sprig (optional)

Mix all ingredients, except fruit
slice and mint, with cracked ice
in a shaker or blender and
pour into a tall, chilled Collins
glass. Fill with club soda and
garnish with fruit slice and mint
sprig.

 MAI TAI

1 oz. Jamaica rum
1 oz. Martinique rum
½ oz. curaçao
¼ oz. rock-candy syrup
¼ oz. orgeat syrup
Lime peel
Mint sprig
Pineapple stick

Mix all ingredients, except lime
peel, mint, and pineapple, with
cracked ice in a shaker or
blender and pour into a chilled
double Old Fashioned glass.
Garnish with lime peel, mint
sprig, and pineapple stick.
Note: This is Trader Vic's original
recipe.

MALLARD'S REEF

1½ oz. gold Jamaica rum
½ oz. Galliano
2 oz. orange juice
Dash grenadine
Orange slice
Maraschino cherry

Mix all ingredients, except orange
slice and cherry, with cracked
ice in a shaker or blender and
serve in a chilled wine goblet.
Garnish with orange slice and
cherry.

 MAMBO PUNCH

2 oz. Haitian rum
½ oz. curaçao
2 oz. orange juice
1 oz. pineapple juice
¾ oz. lime juice

½ oz. tamarind syrup,
    Falernum, or sugar syrup
    or to taste
½ ripe banana, sliced

Mix all ingredients with cracked
ice in a blender and pour into a
chilled double Old Fashioned
glass.

MANDINGO GRINGO

1½ oz. Jamaica dark rum
½ oz. crème de banane
2 oz. pineapple juice
1 oz. orange juice
½ oz. lime juice

Mix all ingredients with cracked ice in a blender at low speed for 15 seconds and pour into a chilled Old Fashioned glass.

MANGO DAIQUIRI

2 oz. light rum
1 oz. curaçao
2 oz. mango juice or nectar
½ oz. lime juice
½ oz. sugar syrup or to taste

Mix with plenty of cracked ice in a blender until frappéed and pour into a chilled wine glass. Serve with straws.

MARACAS BEACH BOLT

2 oz. Demerara rum
½ oz. curaçao or triple sec
1 oz. lime juice
Mint leaves (optional)

Mix all ingredients, except mint leaves, with cracked ice in a shaker or blender. Pour into a chilled Old Fashioned glass and garnish with mint.

MARTINIQUE COOLER

1½ oz. rum
½ oz. Mandarine Napoleon
1 oz. lime juice
½ oz. orgeat or sugar syrup
   to taste
Lime slice

Mix all ingredients, except lime slice, with cracked ice in a blender, pour into a chilled highball glass, and garnish with lime slice.

MARY PICKFORD

1½ oz. light Martinique rum
¼ oz. maraschino liqueur
¼ oz. grenadine
1½ oz. pineapple juice

Mix all ingredients with cracked ice in a shaker or blender and pour into a chilled cocktail glass.

MAUNA LANI FIZZ

2 oz. gold rum
½ oz. 151-proof rum
3 oz. pineapple, finely chopped
½ oz. lemon juice
½ oz. pineapple juice
½ oz. orgeat syrup or sugar
  syrup to taste

1 egg white (for two drinks)
Club soda
Lime slice

Mix all ingredients, except club soda and lime slice, with cracked ice in a blender until smooth and pour into a chilled highball glass. Fill with club soda and garnish with lime slice.

 ## MARIE GALANTE

1 oz. light rum
½ oz. triple sec
1 oz. grapefruit juice
½ oz. La Grande Passion

Mix all ingredients with cracked ice in a shaker or blender and strain into a chilled cocktail glass.

MAYAGUEZ WATERMELON COOLER

2 oz. light Puerto Rican rum
1 oz. melon liqueur
½ oz. lime juice
½ oz. sugar syrup or to taste
1 cup watermelon, seeded
  and diced
Lime slice

Mix all ingredients, except lime slice, with cracked ice in a blender at low speed for 15 seconds and pour into a chilled double Old Fashioned glass. Garnish with lime slice.

MERENGUE COFFEE

1 oz. light rum
1 tsp. Kahlua
1 tsp. crème de cacao
Scoop coffee ice cream
5 oz. cold black coffee

Mix all ingredients in blender until smooth and pour into a large, chilled coffee mug. Do not overmix.

MESA VERDE

1½ oz. light rum
½ oz. lemon juice
4 oz. pineapple juice
1 tsp. green crème de menthe

Mix all ingredients, except crème de menthe with cracked ice in a shaker or blender, pour into a chilled highball glass, and top with crème de menthe.

MEXICANO

2 oz. light rum
½ oz. kummel
1 oz. orange juice
Several dashes Angostura
  bitters

Mix all ingredients with cracked
ice in a shaker or blender and
pour into a chilled cocktail
glass.

MIKE DEVCICH'S BAHAMA MAMA

1 oz. light rum
1 oz. coconut rum
2 oz. orange juice
2 oz. pineapple juice
½ oz. grapefruit juice
Dash grenadine

Mix with cracked ice in a
shaker or blender and strain into
a chilled double Old Fashioned glass.

 ## MINT CONDITION

1½ oz. light rum
½ oz. peppermint schnapps
1 oz. guava, mango, or papaya juice (nectar)
Several dashes grenadine

Mix all ingredients, except
grenadine, with cracked ice in a
shaker or blender. Pour into a
chilled Delmonico glass and float
grenadine on top.

 ## MIXED BLESSING

1½ oz. Puerto Rican rum
½ oz. 151-proof Demerara rum
2 tbsp. crushed pineapple
4 oz. pineapple juice
½ oz. Falernum or to taste
Several dashes lime juice

Mix all ingredients with cracked
ice in a blender until smooth and
pour into a chilled double Old
Fashioned glass.

MOBAY COCKTAIL

1½ oz. dark Jamaica rum
½ oz. Dubonnet rouge
Several dashes Grand Marnier
Lemon peel

Mix all ingredients, except
lemon peel, with cracked ice in a
shaker or blender, and strain
into a chilled cocktail glass. Twist
lemon peel over drink and drop
in.

🌀 MOJITO

½ lime
1 tsp. sugar
Several mint sprigs
2 oz. light rum
Club soda (optional)

Squeeze lime juice into a chilled double Old Fashioned glass, add sugar and mint, and muddle until sugar is dissolved. Fill glass with crushed ice and pour in rum. Swizzle until glass frosts, adding additional crushed ice and rum as needed. Garnish with mint sprig and serve with straws. You may top off drink with cold club soda if you wish, or some prefer a dash of dark Jamaica rum.

MORNE FORTUNE

1½ oz. light rum
½ oz. brandy
2 oz. orange juice
½ oz. lemon juice
1 tsp. orgeat syrup
Dash orange flower water or
    orange bitters

Mix all ingredients, except orange flower water, with cracked ice in a shaker or blender, strain into a chilled cocktail glass, and top with orange flower water or bitters.

MORNING DIP

1½ oz. gold Puerto Rican
    rum
1 tsp. maraschino liqueur
1 oz. orange juice

1 tsp. Falernum or sugar
    syrup to taste

Mix with cracked ice in a shaker or blender and strain into a chilled cocktail glass.

MORNING JOY

1½ oz. gold rum
Grapefruit juice
1 tsp. sloe gin

Pour rum into chilled highball glass with several ice cubes, fill with grapefruit juice, and stir well. Top with sloe gin.

THE MORRO CASTLE COOLER El Castillo Morro Frio

1 oz. light Puerto Rican rum
¾ oz. triple sec
3 oz. orange juice
3 oz. brut champagne

Mix all ingredients, except champagne, with cracked ice in a shaker or blender and pour into a chilled Collins glass. Add cold champagne and stir gently. *Note:* Created by the author for Rums of Puerto Rico, New York City.

MYRTLE BANK PUNCH

1½ oz. 151-proof Demerara
    rum
Juice of ½ lime
1 tsp. grenadine
1 tsp. sugar syrup or to taste
½ oz. maraschino liqueur

Mix all ingredients, except
maraschino liqueur, with cracked
ice in a shaker or blender and
pour into a chilled highball glass.
Top off with a maraschino float.

NANCY FRIEDMAN'S BLUE MEANIE

3 oz. light Bermudez rum
1 oz. Parfait Amour
1 oz. lemon juice
Dash triple sec
Maraschino cherry

Mix all ingredients, except triple
sec and cherry, with cracked
ice in a shaker or blender and
serve in a chilled cocktail glass.
Garnish with cherry and top
off with a dash of triple sec.

NAVY GROG

1 oz. light or gold Puerto
    Rican rum
1 oz. dark Jamaica rum
1 oz. 86-proof Demerara rum
½ oz. orange juice
½ oz. guava juice
½ oz. lime juice
½ oz. pineapple juice

½ oz. orgeat syrup or to taste
Lime slice
Mint sprig (optional)

Mix all ingredients, except lime
slice and mint sprig, with cracked
ice in a shaker or blender and
pour into a chilled double Old
Fashioned glass. Garnish with
lime slice and mint sprig.

NEW ORLEANS BUCK

1½ oz. light Haitian rum
1 oz. orange juice
½ oz. lime juice
Several dashes Peychaud's
    bitters (optional)
Ginger ale
Lime slice

Mix all ingredients, except
ginger ale and lime slice, with
cracked ice in a shaker or
blender, pour into a chilled
Collins glass, and fill with cold
ginger ale. Garnish with lime
slice.

NOEL'S NOONER

1 oz. dark Jamaica rum
1 oz. gin
1 oz. dry red wine
1 oz. orange juice
Lime slice

Mix all ingredients, except lime
slice, with cracked ice in a shaker
or blender, pour into a chilled
Old Fashioned glass, and garnish
with lime slice.

OCHO RIOS

1½ oz. dark Jamaica rum
1 oz. guava nectar
½ oz. heavy cream
½ oz. lime juice
1 tsp. Falernum or sugar
  syrup to taste

Mix all ingredients with cracked ice in a blender and pour into a chilled cocktail glass.

ORCABESSA FIZZ

1 oz. Jamaica rum
1 oz. coconut rum or coconut
  liqueur
2 oz. pineapple juice
½ oz. lime juice
Club soda
Pineapple slice

Mix all ingredients, except club soda and pineapple slice, with cracked ice in a shaker or blender. pour into a chilled highball glass, fill cold club soda, and garnish with pineapple slice.

OUTRIGGER No. 2

1 oz. gold rum
1 oz. brandy
1 oz. triple sec
½ oz. lime juice

Mix all ingredients with cracked ice in a shaker or blender and strain into a chilled cocktail glass.

PAGO PAGO

2 oz. gold Barbados rum
½ tsp. white crème de cacao
½ tsp. green Chartreuse
½ oz. pineapple juice
½ oz. lime juice

Mix all ingredients with cracked ice in a shaker or blender and pour into a chilled Old Fashioned glass.

PALM BAY SPECIAL

1½ oz. light rum
½ oz. lemon juice
1 tsp. honey or to taste
Champagne
Pineapple slice

Mix all ingredients, except pineapple slice and champagne, in a shaker or blender. Strain into chilled goblet and fill with cold champagne. Garnish with pineapple slice.

PALM ISLAND

1½ oz. gold rum
1½ oz. Grand Marnier

Pour rum and Grand Marnier into a chilled Old Fashioned glass with several ice cubes and stir well.

PANCHO VILLA No. 2

1 oz. light rum
1 oz. gin
1 oz. apricot liqueur or apricot brandy
1 tsp. cherry brandy
1 tsp. pineapple juice

Mix all ingredients with cracked ice in a shaker or blender and strain into a chilled cocktail glass.

PARISIAN BLONDE

1 oz. dark Jamaica rum
1 oz. triple sec
1 oz. heavy cream

Mix with cracked ice in a shaker or blender and strain into a chilled cocktail glass.

A PASSIONATE DAIQUIRI

1½ oz. light rum
½ oz. lime juice
½ oz. sugar syrup or to taste
½ oz. passion fruit juice

Mix all ingredients with cracked ice in a shaker or blender and strain into a chilled cocktail glass.

PEACH DAIQUIRI

2 oz. light rum
½ oz. lime juice
1 tsp. sugar syrup or to taste
½ ripe peach, fresh, canned, or frozen, diced

Mix all ingredients with cracked ice in a blender until smooth and pour into a chilled wine glass.

PELICAN BAY

1 oz. gold Puerto Rican rum
¾ oz. crème de banane
¼ oz. Pernod

Mix all ingredients with cracked ice in a shaker or blender and strain into a chilled cocktail glass.

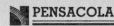 **PENSACOLA**

1½ oz. light Barbados rum
½ oz. guava nectar
½ oz. orange juice
½ oz. lemon juice
1 tsp. La Grande Passion
   (optional)

Mix all ingredients with cracked ice in a blender until smooth and pour into a chilled deep-saucer champagne glass.

 PENSACOLA COLA

1½ oz. gold rum
½ oz. Cherry Marnier
Cola
Lemon peel

Mix rum, Cherry Marnier, and cold cola in a tall, chilled Collins glass with ice cubes. Stir gently and twist lemon peel over drink and drop into glass.

 PEPPER TREE PUNCH

2 oz. light Jamaica rum
1 oz. dark Jamaica rum
1 oz. lime juice
1 tsp. sugar syrup or orgeat
   syrup
Several dashes Angostura
   bitters

Pinch of ground cinnamon
Pinch of cayenne pepper

Mix all ingredients in blender with cracked ice and serve in chilled double Old Fashioned glass.

PILOT BOAT

1½ oz. dark Jamaica rum
1 oz. crème de banane
2 oz. lemon or lime juice

Mix all ingredients with cracked ice and strain into a chilled cocktail glass.

 PINA COLADA

2 oz. gold rum
2 oz. cream of coconut
4 oz. pineapple juice
Pineapple stick
Maraschino cherry

Mix all ingredients, except pineapple stick and maraschino cherry, with cracked ice in a shaker or blender and pour into a chilled Collins glass. Garnish with fruit.

PINEAPPLE BANG!

2 oz. light Hawaiian rum
1 oz. crème d'anana or pine-
    apple schnapps
½ oz. lime juice
½ cup pineapple sherbet
1 heaping tbsp. diced fresh
    or canned pineapple
Pineapple stick

Mix all ingredients, except
pineapple stick, with cracked ice
in a blender until smooth and
pour into a chilled chimney glass
or a double Old Fashioned
glass. Garnish with pineapple
stick.

 ## PINEAPPLE BLUSH

2 oz. light rum
½ oz. crème de noyaux
3 oz. crushed pineapple
Maraschino cherry

Mix all ingredients, except
cherry, with plenty of cracked ice
in a blender until frappéed
and pour into a chilled double
Old Fashioned glass. Garnish
with cherry.

PINEAPPLE DAIQUIRI

2 oz. light rum
½ oz. Cointreau
3 oz. pineapple juice
¼ oz. lime juice

Mix all ingredients with plenty
of cracked ice in a blender until
frappéed and pour into a chilled
wine glass.

PINK MERMAID

1½ oz. light rum
½ oz. lime juice
1 tsp. heavy cream
1 tsp. grenadine
1 egg white (for two drinks)

Mix with cracked ice in a shaker
or blender and strain into a
chilled cocktail glass.

PINK RUM AND TONIC

2 oz. light rum
½ oz. lime juice
1 tsp. grenadine
Tonic water
Lime slice

Mix all ingredients, except tonic
water and lime slice, with cracked
ice in a shaker or blender and
pour into a chilled Collins glass.
Fill with cold tonic water and
garnish with lime slice.

PINK VERANDA

1 oz. gold Puerto Rican
   rum
½ oz. dark Jamaica rum
1½ oz. cranberry juice
½ oz. lime juice
1 tsp. sugar
1 egg white (for two drinks)

Mix all ingredients with cracked ice in a shaker or blender and pour into a chilled Old Fashioned glass.

PINO FRIO

1½ oz. light rum
2 oz. pineapple juice
½ oz. lemon juice
2 pineapple slices, cubed
Dash Falernum
Mint sprigs (optional)

Mix all ingredients, except mint sprigs, with cracked ice in a blender at high speed for a few seconds, pour into a chilled Collins glass, and garnish with mint sprigs.

PIRATE'S JULEP

6 mint leaves
1 tsp. orgeat syrup or sugar
   syrup
Several dashes Peychaud's
   bitters or Pernod
2–3 oz. gold Jamaica rum
1 tsp. Mandarine Napoleon
   or curaçao
Mint sprig
Powdered sugar

Muddle mint leaves in a chilled double Old Fashioned glass with syrup. Add bitters and fill glass with crushed ice and pour in rum. Swizzle until glass frosts, adding more ice if necessary. Top with liqueur and garnish with a mint sprig dusted with powdered sugar.

PISCADERA BAY

1½ oz. Jamaica rum
½ oz. curaçao
½ oz. Falernum or sugar
   syrup
½ oz. lime juice
1 tsp. cherry brandy
Dash Angostura bitters

Maraschino cherry
Orange slice

Mix all ingredients, except maraschino cherry and orange slice, with cracked ice in a shaker or blender. Pour into a chilled double Old Fashioned glass and garnish with fruit.

● PLANTER'S PUNCH The Original

1½–2 oz. Myers's dark rum
3 oz. orange juice
Juice of ½ lemon or lime
1 tsp. superfine sugar
Dash grenadine
Orange slice
Maraschino cherry

Mix all ingredients, except orange slice and cherry, with cracked ice in a shaker or blender and pour into a tall, chilled Collins glass. Garnish with orange slice and cherry.
Note: The Myers's rum people lay claim to the origination and popularization of the Planter's Punch, and this is the original recipe that appears on the back label of Myers's rum.

PLANTER'S PUNCH No. 2

2 oz. Puerto Rican rum
1 oz. dark Jamaica rum
½ oz. sugar syrup or Falernum to taste
1 oz. lime juice
Several dashes Angostura bitters
Club soda
Orange slice
Lemon slice

Mix all ingredients, except club soda, orange, and lemon slices, with cracked ice in a shaker or blender. Pour into a chilled Collins glass, fill with cold club soda, and garnish with orange and lime slices.

PLANTATION PUNCH

1½ oz. dark Jamaica rum
¾ oz. Southern Comfort
1 tsp. brown sugar or to taste
1 oz. lemon juice
Club soda
Orange slice
Lemon slice
1 tsp. port

Mix all ingredients, except soda, fruit slices, and port, with cracked ice in a shaker or blender and pour into a tall Collins glass. Fill with cold club soda, garnish with fruit, and top with port.

PLAYBOY COOLER

1½ oz. gold rum
1½ oz. Kahlua
3 oz. pineapple juice
½ oz. lemon juice or lime juice
Cola
Maraschino cherry

Mix all ingredients, except cola and maraschino cherry, with cracked ice in a shaker or blender and pour into chilled highball glass. Fill with cola and garnish with cherry.

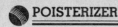 POISTERIZER

2½ oz. Barbados rum
1 oz. orange juice
1 oz. pineapple juice
1 oz. coconut cream
Lemon-lime soda
½ oz. 151-proof Demerara rum

Mix all ingredients, except soda and Demerara rum, with ice in a shaker or blender and pour into a tall, chilled Collins glass. Fill with lemon-lime soda and top with Demerara rum.

POKER COCKTAIL

1½ oz. light rum
¾ oz. sweet vermouth
Orange peel

Mix rum and vermouth with cracked ice in a shaker or blender and strain into a chilled cocktail glass. Twist orange peel over drink and drop into glass.

POLYNESIAN SOUR

1½ oz. light rum
½ oz. La Grande Passion
1 oz. orange juice
½ oz. lemon juice
1 oz. pineapple juice
½ tsp. rock candy syrup or
   sugar syrup or to taste

Pineapple slice

Mix all ingredients, except pineapple, with cracked ice in a shaker or blender, strain into a chilled Whiskey Sour glass, and garnish with pineapple slice.

POMME DE ANTILLAIS Antilles Apple

1½ oz. gold Martinique rum
½ oz. calvados
½ oz. sweet vermouth
Lemon peel

Mix all ingredients, except lemon peel, with cracked ice in a shaker or blender and pour into a chilled cocktail glass. Twist lemon peel over drink and drop into glass.

POOLABANGA SLING

1½ oz. gold rum
2 oz. orange juice
½ oz. lime juice
½ oz. Falernum
1 tsp. cherry brandy
Club soda
Mint sprigs (optional)

Mix all ingredients, except mint, with cracked ice in a shaker or blender and pour into a chilled highball glass and fill with cold club soda. Garnish with mint.

PORT ANTONIO

1 oz. gold rum
½ oz. dark Jamaica rum
½ oz. Tia Maria
½ oz. lime juice
1 tsp. Falernum
Lime slice

Mix all ingredients, except lime slice, with cracked ice in a shaker or blender, pour into a chilled Old Fashioned glass, and garnish with lime slice.

POTTED PARROT

1½ oz. gold rum
½ oz. orange curaçao
3 oz. orange juice
1 oz. lemon juice
1 tsp. orgeat syrup
1 tsp. rock-candy syrup
Mint sprigs (optional)
1 tsp. 151-proof Demerara rum

Mix all ingredients, except mint sprigs and 151-proof rum, with cracked ice in a shaker or blender, strain into a chilled double Old Fashioned glass, and garnish with mint. Float Demerara rum on top.

PRESIDENTE COCKTAIL No. 1

1½ oz. light rum
½ oz. dry vermouth
½ oz. curaçao
Dash grenadine
Lemon peel

Mix all ingredients, except lemon peel, with cracked ice in a shaker or blender and pour into a chilled cocktail glass. Twist peel over drink and drop into glass.

PRESIDENTE COCKTAIL No. 2

1½ oz. light rum
1 oz. orange juice
Several dashes grenadine

Mix all ingredients with cracked ice in a shaker or blender and pour into a chilled cocktail glass.

PUNTA DEL ESTE

1½ oz. light rum
½ oz. white crème de cacao
½ oz. light coconut rum
   (CocoRibe or Malibu)
2 oz. pineapple juice

1 oz. cranberry juice
1 oz. cream

Mix all ingredients with cracked ice in a blender and pour into a chilled Collins glass. Add additional ice if needed.

PUSHKIN'S PUNCH

2 oz. dark Jamaica rum
1 oz. triple sec
Juice of 1 lemon
Juice of 1 lime
2 oz. orange juice

Orgeat syrup to taste
Dash Angostura bitters

Mix with cracked ice in a
shaker or blender and serve in a
tall, chilled Collins glass.

 ## PUSSER'S PAIN KILLER

4 oz. British Navy Pusser's
  Rum
4 oz. pineapple juice
1 oz. orange juice
1 oz. coconut cream or syrup
Orange slice

Mix all ingredients, except orange
slice, with cracked ice in a shaker
or blender and pour into a
chilled Collins glass. Garnish
with Union Jack flag.

QUARTER DECK

1½ oz. dark Jamaica rum
¾ oz. cream sherry
1 tsp. lime juice

Mix all ingredients with cracked
ice in a shaker or blender and
strain into a chilled cocktail
glass.

 ## RAMPART STREET PARADE

1 oz. light rum
¾ oz. crème de banane
½ oz. Southern Comfort
1 oz. lime juice

Mix all ingredients with cracked
ice in a shaker or blender and
strain into a chilled cocktail
glass.

 ## RANGIRORA MADNESS

2 oz. dark Jamaica rum
2 oz. pineapple juice
2 oz. orange juice
Bitter lemon soda
1 tsp. 151-proof Demerara rum
Maraschino cherry
Pineapple slice

Mix all ingredients, except
lemon soda, 151-proof rum, pineapple, and maraschino cherry,
with cracked ice in a shaker or
blender and pour into a large,
chilled highball glass. Fill with
bitter lemon soda, top with float
of 151-proof rum, and garnish
with pineapple and cherry.

ROADTOWN SPECIAL

2 oz. light Virgin Islands
    rum
½ lime
Ginger beer

Pour rum into a chilled highball glass with several ice cubes.
Squeeze lime over drink and
drop into glass. Fill with cold
ginger beer and stir gently.

ROSE HALL

1 oz. dark Jamaica rum
½ oz. crème de banane
1 oz. orange juice
1 tsp. lime juice
Lime slice

Mix all ingredients, except lime
slice, with cracked ice in a shaker
or blender, pour into a chilled
cocktail glass, and garnish with
lime slice.

RUM AND BITTER LEMON

1½ oz. light, gold, or dark
    rum
Bitter lemon soda
Lemon slice

Pour rum and bitter lemon soda
into a chilled highball glass with
several ice cubes and stir
gently. Garnish with lemon slice.

RUM BEGUINE

1½ oz. Martinique rum or
    Haitian rum
2 oz. sauterne, chilled
2 oz. pineapple juice
1 oz. lemon juice
½ oz. sugar syrup or Falernum
    to taste

Several dashes Peychaud's
    bitters or Angostura bitters
Pineapple slice

Mix all ingredients, except
pineapple slice, with cracked ice
in a shaker or blender and
pour into a chilled Collins glass.
Garnish with pineapple.

RUM BLOODY MARY

1½ oz. light Puerto Rican
    rum
4 oz. tomato juice
½ oz. lime juice or lemon
    juice
Several dashes Worcester-
    shire sauce
Several dashes Tabasco
    sauce

Pinch of freshly ground
    pepper
Pinch of celery salt

Stir all ingredients well with
cracked ice in a mixing glass
and pour into a chilled highball glass.

RUM BUCK

1½ oz. light rum
½ oz. lime juice
Ginger ale, chilled
Lime slice
Toasted almonds, grated
  (optional)

Mix rum and lime juice with cracked ice in a shaker, pour into a chilled Collins glass, and fill with cold ginger ale. Stir gently and garnish with lime slice and sprinkle top with grated almonds.

RUM COLLINS

2 oz. light or gold rum
1 tsp. sugar syrup
½ lime
Club soda

Combine rum and sugar syrup in chilled Collins glass and stir. Squeeze in juice of lime, drop in peel, fill with club soda, add several ice cubes, and stir gently.

RUM DUBONNET

1 oz. light rum
1 oz. Dubonnet rouge
1 tsp. lime juice
Lime peel

Mix all ingredients, except lime peel, with cracked ice in a shaker or blender and strain into a chilled cocktail glass. Twist lime peel over drink and drop into glass.

RUM OLD FASHIONED

1 tsp. sugar syrup
Splash water
Several dashes Angostura
  bitters
2–3 oz. gold Barbados,
  Haitian, or Martinique rum,
  or gold or dark Jamaica
  rum

Lemon peel
Orange peel

Stir syrup and water in a chilled Old Fashioned glass, add bitters and rum. Mix well and add ice. Garnish with lemon and orange peel. Add additional water if you wish.

RUM MARTINI

2 oz. light Puerto Rican
  rum
Dash dry vermouth or to taste
Olive stuffed with almond or
  lemon peel

Combine rum and dry vermouth in mixing glass with several ice cubes, stir well, and strain into a chilled cocktail glass. Garnish with stuffed olive or twist lemon peel over drink and drop into glass.

RUM ROYALE

1½ oz. Bacardi Premium
    Black rum
1½ oz. cold black coffee
½ cup vanilla ice cream
Cinnamon stick
Pinch ground cinnamon

Mix rum, coffee, and ice cream
in a chilled wine goblet until
slightly slushy. Garnish with
cinnamon stick and sprinkle with
ground cinnamon.
Note: Created by the author for
Bacardi Imports, Inc., Miami.

 RUM ROSE

1 oz. dark Jamaica rum
1 oz. light Jamaica rum
1 oz. Rhum Negrita
2 oz. orange juice
Falernum or simple syrup to
    taste
Dash grenadine
Lemon-lime soda

Mix all ingredients, except
soda, with cracked ice in a shaker
or blender and pour into a
chilled double Old Fashioned
glass. Fill with lemon-lime soda
and stir gently.

RUM SCREWDRIVER

2 oz. light Puerto Rican
    rum
4–6 oz. orange juice
Orange slice

Mix rum and orange juice in a
blender with cracked ice and
pour into a chilled Collins
glass. Garnish with orange slice.

RUM AND SHERRY

1½ oz. light rum
¾ oz. amontillado sherry
Maraschino cherry

Combine rum and sherry in a
mixing glass with several ice
cubes and stir well. Strain into
a chilled cocktail glass and
garnish with maraschino cherry.

 RUM SOUR

2 oz. light or dark rum
Juice of ½ lime
1 tsp. sugar syrup or to taste
1 tsp. orange juice (optional)
Orange slice
Maraschino cherry

Mix all ingredients, except orange
slice and cherry, with cracked
ice in a shaker or blender and
strain into a chilled Whiskey
Sour glass. Garnish with orange
slice and cherry.

RUMBO

2 oz. gold Haitian or Barbados rum
1 oz. dark Jamaica rum
2 oz. orange juice
2 oz. guava juice
Dash lime juice

Mix with cracked ice in a
shaker or blender and pour into a
chilled double Old Fashioned
glass.

SAN JUAN No. 1

1½ oz. light rum
¾ oz. brandy
1 tsp. grenadine
½ oz. lime juice

Mix all ingredients with cracked
ice in a shaker or blender and
strain into a chilled cocktail
glass.

SAN JUAN No. 2

1½ oz. light or gold Puerto
  Rican rum
1 oz. grapefruit juice
1 oz. lime juice
½ oz. cream of coconut or to
  taste
1 tsp. 151-proof Demerara rum

Mix all ingredients, except
151-proof rum, with cracked ice
in a blender until smooth. Pour
into a chilled wine goblet and
top with a float of 151-proof
rum.

SAN JUAN SUNDOWNER

1½ oz. Bacardi Premium
  Black rum
2 oz. orange juice
2 oz. pineapple juice
Bitter lemon or lemon-lime
  soda
Orange slice

Mix rum, orange juice, and
pineapple juice with cracked ice
in a shaker or blender and
pour into a tall, chilled Collins
glass. Add several ice cubes
and fill with bitter lemon soda.
Stir gently and garnish with
orange slice.
Note: Created by the author for
Bacardi Imports, Inc., Miami.

BARTENDER'S SECRET NO. 14

The flavor enhancement of rum-based fruit drinks, as well as
those made with other spirits such as gin and vodka, can be
effectively accomplished by the use of fruit-flavored liqueurs.
Triple sec, curaçao, peach liqueur, maraschino, apricot li-

queur, crème de noyaux, anisette, sloe gin, crème de menthe, crème de cacao, kummel, amaretto, and crème de cassis are all well-known and readily available. In addition to these generic flavors, there are many distinguished proprietary liqueurs, which when used with good judgment contribute new and unusual flavor dimensions to various mixed drinks.

Here are some especially good flavor catalysts: Benedictine, Chartreuse (green for intense flavor, yellow for fragrance), Grand Marnier, Peter Heering, Cointreau, Galliano, Kahlua, Tia Maria, Drambuie, Frangelico, La Grande Passion, and Irish Mist. There are many others, of course. Accomplished mixologists use these complex and comparatively expensive formulations as elegant sweeteners (most liqueurs have a high sugar level), as aromatic floats on top of drinks, as a foil or flavor accent to balance or modify another dominant taste, or to create a more interesting flavor in a conventional, "cliché" drink recipe.

The new, flavor-intensive schnapps products such as peach, pear, apple, and other fruit, spice, candy, and soft drink flavors are excellent for giving old drink recipes a new zest.

SANTA MARTA SLING

2 oz. light Colombian or
  Puerto Rican rum
½ oz. lime juice
1 tsp. coconut syrup
Club soda
1 tsp. amaretto

Mix all ingredients, except club soda and amaretto, with cracked ice in a shaker or blender and pour into a chilled Old Fashioned glass. Fill with club soda, stir gently, and top with amaretto float.

SAVANE

1½ oz. light rum
½ oz. banana liqueur
1 oz. lemon juice
1 tsp. Falernum

Mix all ingredients with cracked ice in a shaker or blender and strain into a chilled cocktail glass.

SEA HAWK

1 oz. dark Jamaica rum
½ oz. Barbados rum
½ oz. Bermuda Gold liqueur
Dash Cointreau
Dash grenadine
Juice of 1 lime
Juice of ½ orange

Mix with cracked ice in a shaker or blender and strain into a silver mug filled with shaved ice.
Note: Originated by Bru Mysak of New York's "21" Club.

SEPTEMBER MORN

2–3 oz. light rum
½ oz. lime juice
1 tsp. grenadine
1 egg white

Mix all ingredients with cracked ice in a shaker or blender and strain into a chilled cocktail glass.

SEVILLA No. 1

1 oz. dark Jamaica rum
1 oz. sweet vermouth
Orange peel

Mix rum and vermouth with cracked ice in a shaker or blender and strain into a chilled cocktail glass. Twist orange peel over drink and drop into glass.

SEVILLA No. 2

1½ oz. light rum
1½ oz. port
1 egg
½ tsp. sugar syrup or to taste
Freshly grated nutmeg

Mix rum, port, egg, and sugar syrup with cracked ice in a blender and pour into a chilled cocktail glass. Sprinkle with grated nutmeg.

 ## SEWICKLEY HEIGHTS GUN CLUB PUNCH

1½ oz. dark Jamaica rum
¾ oz. light Puerto Rican rum
1½ oz. pineapple juice
1½ oz. grapefruit juice
1½ oz. orange juice
1 oz. lemon juice

Pinch ground cinnamon
3–4 maraschino cherries

Mix all ingredients with cracked ice in a blender and pour into a tall, chilled Collins glass.
Note: Otherwise known as the Skeet Shooters Special.

 ## SCORPION

2 oz. light Puerto Rican rum
1 oz. brandy
2 oz. orange juice
1½ oz. lemon juice
½ oz. orgeat syrup
Gardenia

Mix all ingredients, except flower, with shaved ice in a blender and pour into a chilled wine goblet. Garnish with a gardenia.
Note: This is an original Trader Vic's recipe.

SHARK'S TOOTH No. 1

1 oz. 151-proof Puerto Rican
   rum
Juice of ½ lime (save shell)
½ oz. lemon juice
Dash grenadine
Dash rock-candy syrup
Club soda

Mix all ingredients, except club
soda, in a shaker or blender with
ice and pour into a large pilsener
glass. Fill with cold club soda
and add lime shell for garnish.
Stir gently.
Note: This is an original Trader
Vic's recipe.

SHARK'S TOOTH No. 2

1 oz. dark Jamaica rum
1 oz. Haitian, Martinique, or
   Barbados gold rum
¼ oz. sloe gin
1 oz. lemon juice
Several dashes passion fruit
   syrup or nectar
Club soda

Mix all ingredients, except club
soda, with cracked ice in a shaker
or blender and pour into a
chilled double Old Fashioned
glass. Fill glass with cold club
soda and stir gently.

SHANGHAI

1½ oz. dark Jamaica rum
½ oz. anisette
1 oz. lemon juice
Several dashes grenadine

Mix all ingredients with cracked
ice in a shaker or blender and
pour into a chilled cocktail glass.

SHANGO

2 oz. Haitian rum
1 tsp. 151-proof Demerara rum
2 oz. pineapple juice
½ oz. lemon juice
½ oz. Falernum or sugar
   syrup
Bitter lemon soda
Lemon slice

Mix all ingredients, except soda
and lemon slice, with cracked ice
in a shaker or blender and
pour into a chilled Collins glass.
Fill with bitter lemon soda,
stir gently, and garnish with fruit
slice.

BARTENDER'S SECRET NO. 15

Toppings for exotic, tall coolers and party drinks have been
the hallmarks of this kind of refreshment since the practice
was begun by establishments such as Trader Vic's and Don

the Beachcomber when they wanted to popularize their so-called Polynesian-type rum drinks in the 1930s. The fact that nobody in Polynesia had ever seen one of these elegant, show-case libations is unimportant. The ingredients (fruits, spices, and flavorings from faraway places combined with rare rums), the toppings (aromatic liqueurs), and the decorations (hibiscus, orchids, and gardenias) proclaimed to adoring patrons: "This is what is drunk in a tropical paradise." Toppings will add luster and enjoyment to almost any drink, tropical or not. Sometimes a dash, splash, or a teaspoon of spirits such as brandy or a high-proof rum is used as a float on top of a drink, but more often the choice is a liqueur.

SKULL CRACKER

4 oz. light rum
1 oz. white crème de cacao
1 oz. pineapple juice
1 oz. lemon juice
Lime slice

Mix with cracked ice in a shaker or blender and serve in a chilled wine goblet. Makes a pirate-sized portion for one, or it may be shared with a piratess.

SLEDGEHAMMER

¾ oz. gold rum
¾ oz. brandy
¾ oz. calvados or applejack
Dash Pernod

Mix all ingredients with cracked ice in a shaker or blender and strain into a chilled cocktail glass.

SLOPPY JOE'S No. 1

1 oz. light rum
1 oz. dry vermouth
½ tsp. triple sec
½ tsp. grenadine

Juice of 1 lime

Mix with cracked ice in a shaker or blender and strain into a chilled cocktail glass.

SPEIGHTSTOWN SWIZZLE

1½ oz. Barbados rum
1 oz. calvados or applejack
1 tsp. lime juice
1 tsp. orgeat syrup or Falernum
Several dashes Angostura
    bitters

Mix all ingredients with cracked ice in a shaker or blender and pour into a chilled Old Fashioned glass.

SPICE ISLAND

2 oz. gold rum
½ oz. CocoRibe
½ oz. Captain Morgan Spiced
  Rum
3 oz. orange juice

2 oz. red grape juice
2 oz. cranberry juice

Mix with cracked ice in a
shaker or blender and pour into a
chilled 16-oz. Zombie glass.

STRAWBERRY COLADA

2–3 oz. gold Puerto Rican
  or Virgin Islands rum
4 oz. Pina Colada mix
1 oz. fresh or frozen
  strawberries
1 tsp. strawberry schnapps
  or liqueur

Mix all ingredients, except
strawberry schnapps and whole
strawberry, with cracked ice in
a blender until smooth, pour into
a chilled pilsener glass, and
top with strawberry schnapps or
liqueur and a whole strawberry.

STRAWBERRY DAIQUIRI

1½ oz. light rum
½ oz. lime juice
1 tsp. sugar syrup or to taste
6 large fresh or frozen
  strawberries

Mix with cracked ice in a
blender until smooth and pour
into a chilled cocktail glass.

ST. VINCENT SURPRISE

1½ oz. gold rum
½ oz. triple sec
1 tsp. Pernod
1 oz. lime juice
½ ripe banana, sliced

Mix all ingredients with cracked
ice in a blender and pour into a
chilled wine goblet.

 SUFFERIN' SWEDE

2½ oz. Haitian or Barbados
  gold rum
1 heaping tbsp. lingonberries
4 oz. orange juice
2 oz. grapefruit juice
½ oz. Falernum or to taste

Mix with cracked ice in a
blender until lingonberries are
well whipped into other ingredients. Pour into a chilled double
Old Fashioned glass. Add more
ice if necessary.

SUGAR MILL TOT

1½ oz. gold rum
Juice of 1 lime
Light molasses to taste

Mix all ingredients with cracked ice in a shaker or blender and serve in an Old Fashioned glass.

SUNDOWNER No. 2

2 oz. light rum
½ oz. lime juice
Tonic water
Dash triple sec
Dash grenadine

Mix all ingredients, except tonic water, with cracked ice in a shaker or blender and pour into a chilled highball glass. Fill with cold tonic water and stir gently.

SURINAM SUNDOWNER

1½ oz. 86-proof Demerara rum
   or dark Jamaica rum
½ oz. sweet vermouth
½ oz. gin
Several dashes Angostura
   bitters

Combine all ingredients in a mixing glass with several ice cubes, stir well, and strain into a chilled cocktail glass.

SUTTON PLACE SLING

2 oz. dark Jamaica rum
2 oz. orange juice
Several dashes Angostura
   bitters
Several dashes lime juice
Several dashes maraschino
   cherry juice

Bitter lemon soda
1 tsp. 151-proof rum

Mix all ingredients, except lemon soda and 151-proof rum, with cracked ice in a shaker or blender and pour into a chilled Collins glass. Fill with bitter lemon soda, stir gently, and top with float of 151-proof rum.

SWEET N' SILKY

1 oz. light rum
1 oz. triple sec
1 oz. heavy cream

Mix all ingredients with cracked ice in a shaker or blender and strain into a chilled cocktail glass.

TAHITI CLUB

2 oz. light or gold rum
½ oz. pineapple juice
½ oz. lime juice
½ oz. lemon juice
½ tsp. maraschino liqueur
Orange slice

Mix all ingredients, except orange slice, with cracked ice in a shaker or blender and pour into a chilled Old Fashioned glass. Garnish with orange slice.

 ## TE HONGI

3 oz. Jamaica, Barbados,
  or Haitian gold rum
3 oz. orange juice
3 oz. pineapple juice
2 oz. apricot nectar
1 oz. lemon juice
Falernum or simple syrup to
  taste
Dash grenadine
Ginger ale
Orange slice
Maraschino cherry

Mix all ingredients, except ginger ale, orange slice, and maraschino cherry, with cracked ice in a shaker or blender and pour into a 16-oz. Hurricane or Chimney glass. Add more ice if necessary and fill with cold ginger ale. Stir and garnish with orange and cherry.

 ## TIGER'S MILK No. 1

1½ oz. Bacardi Anejo gold
  rum
1½ oz. cognac
4–6 oz. half-and-half
Sugar syrup to taste
Grated nutmeg or cinnamon

Mix all ingredients, except ground spice, with cracked ice in a shaker or blender and pour into a chilled wine goblet. Dust with grated nutmeg or cinnamon.

TOBAGO CAYS

1½ oz. gold rum
½ oz. lime juice
½ oz. sugar syrup
½ tsp. maraschino liqueur
½ tsp. Pernod

Mix all ingredients, except Pernod, with cracked ice in a blender until smooth. Pour into a chilled wine goblet and top with Pernod.

TOM TOM A Real Head Pounder

1 oz. Haitian rum
1 oz. coconut rum
1 oz. brandy
½ oz. La Grande Passion
1 oz. lemon juice
1 oz. pineapple juice
1 oz. orange juice

Orange slice
Mint sprig

Mix all ingredients, except mint sprig and orange slice, with cracked ice in a blender and strain into a chilled Hurricane glass. Garnish with mint sprig and orange slice.

TORRIDO

2 oz. Haitian or Martinique rum
½ tsp. Benedictine
½ oz. lime juice
1 tsp. grenadine
Dash Pernod

Mix all ingredients, except Pernod, with cracked ice in a shaker or blender and pour into a chilled cocktail glass. Top with Pernod float.

TORRIDORA COCKTAIL

1½ oz. light rum
½ oz. Tia Maria
¼ oz. heavy cream
1 tsp. 151-proof Demerara rum

Mix all ingredients, except 151-proof rum, with cracked ice in a shaker or blender and strain into a chilled cocktail glass. Top with float of 151-proof rum.

TORTOLA MILK PUNCH

2–3 oz. British Navy Pusser's Rum
1 tsp. coconut cream or orgeat syrup or Falernum to taste
6 oz. milk

Pinch powdered cinnamon
Pinch powdered nutmeg

Mix rum, sweetener, and milk with cracked ice in a blender or shaker and pour into a chilled Collins glass. Sprinkle with spices.

TRADE WINDS

2 oz. gold Barbados rum
½ oz. slivovitz
½ oz. lime juice
½ oz. Falernum or orgeat syrup

Mix with plenty of cracked ice and frappé in a blender. Serve in a chilled cocktail glass.

TROPICAL BIRD

1 oz. gold rum
½ oz. dark Jamaica rum
½ oz. dry vermouth
½ oz. lemon juice
1 tsp. raspberry syrup
Lemon peel

Mix all ingredients, except lemon peel, with cracked ice in a shaker or blender and strain into a chilled cocktail glass. Twist lemon peel over drink and drop into glass.

TWELVE GAUGE GROG

1½ oz. dark Jamaica rum
¾ oz. 151-proof Demerara rum
2 oz. orange juice
1 oz. lemon juice
1 tsp. sugar syrup or to taste
Several dashes Angostura
    bitters
Grapefruit soda
Orange slice

Maraschino cherry

Mix all ingredients, except grapefruit soda, orange slice, and maraschino cherry, with cracked ice in a shaker or blender and pour into a tall, chilled Collins glass. Fill with cold grapefruit soda, stir gently, and garnish with fruit.

UNDERTOW

1 oz. gold Jamaica rum
1 oz. gin
½ oz. crème de noyaux
1 oz. lime juice
1 tsp. guava syrup or pas-
    sion fruit syrup

Lime peel

Mix all ingredients, except lime peel, with cracked ice in a blender and pour into a chilled double Old Fashioned glass. Garnish with lime peel.

VERACRUZ COCKTAIL

1½ oz. gold Mexican rum
½ oz. dry vermouth
2 oz. lime juice
1 oz. sugar syrup or to taste
1 oz. pineapple juice

Mix all ingredients with cracked ice in a shaker or blender and pour into a chilled Old Fashioned glass.

VICTORIA PARADE

1½ oz. gold Jamaica rum
1 oz. Southern Comfort
4 oz. iced tea
½ oz. lemon juice
1 tsp. orgeat or sugar syrup
Club soda

Combine all ingredients, except club soda, with several ice cubes in a chilled Collins glass, stir well, and top off with a splash of cold club soda.

VILLA HERMOSA

1½ oz. dark Jamaica rum
½ oz. Kahlua
1 oz. heavy cream

Mix all ingredients with cracked ice in a shaker or blender and strain into a chilled cocktail glass.

VIÑA DEL MAR COOLER

1½ oz. light rum
¼ oz. kirsch
4 oz. orange juice
Ginger ale, chilled
Lime peel

Mix all ingredients, except ginger ale and lime peel, with cracked ice in a shaker or blender, pour into a chilled Old Fashioned glass, and fill with ginger ale. Twist lime peel over drink and drop into glass.

WAIKOLOA FIZZ

1½ oz. Barbados rum
½ oz. Jamaica rum
3 oz. pineapple juice
½ oz. passion fruit juice
1 tsp. coconut syrup
Lemon-lime soda
Lime slice

Mix all ingredients, except lemon-lime soda and lime slice, with cracked ice in shaker or blender and pour into a chilled Collins glass. Fill with lemon-lime soda, stir gently, and garnish with lime slice.

WHITE LION

1½ oz. dark Jamaica rum
1 oz. lemon juice
½ oz. Falernum or orgeat
   syrup or to taste
Several dashes raspberry
   syrup

*Several dashes Angostura
   bitters*

Mix all ingredients with cracked ice in a shaker or blender and pour into a chilled cocktail glass.

WHITE PIGEON

1½ oz. light rum
¾ oz. anisette

Mix all ingredients with cracked ice in a shaker or blender and pour into a chilled cocktail glass.

WHITE WITCH

1 oz. light Jamaica rum
½ oz. white crème de cacao
½ oz. Cointreau
½ lime
Club soda
Mint sprigs coated with
  powdered sugar

Mix all ingredients, except
lime, club soda, and mint sprigs,
with cracked ice in a shaker or
blender and pour into a chilled
Collins glass. Squeeze in lime
juice, fill with cold club soda,
and stir gently. Garnish with
sugar-dusted mint sprigs.
Note: This is an original Trader
Vic's recipe.

WINDWARD PASSAGE

1½ oz. light rum
3 oz. pineapple juice
1 tsp. crème de cassis
1 tsp. kirsch

Mix all ingredients with cracked
ice in a shaker or blender and
strain into a chilled cocktail
glass.

XANGO

1½ oz. light rum
½ oz. Cointreau
1 oz. grapefruit juice
Lemon peel

Mix all ingredients, except
lemon peel, with cracked ice in a
shaker or blender and strain
into a chilled cocktail glass. Twist
lemon peel over drink and drop
into glass.

XYZ COCKTAIL

2 oz. dark Jamaica rum
1 oz. Cointreau
1 oz. lemon juice

Mix all ingredients with cracked
ice in a shaker or blender and
pour into a chilled cocktail
glass.

YAKA-HULA-HICKY-DULA

1½ oz. dark rum
1½ oz. dry vermouth
1½ oz. pineapple juice

Mix all ingredients with cracked
ice in a shaker or blender and
strain into a chilled cocktail
glass.

ZAMBOANGA

1½ oz. gold Philippines rum
    (Tanduay)
½ oz. sweet vermouth
½ oz. triple sec
1 oz. lime juice

1 tsp. maple syrup or light
    molasses to taste

Mix all ingredients with cracked
ice in a blender until smooth and
pour into a chilled wine goblet.

 ## THE ZOMBIE

2 oz. light Puerto Rican
    rum
1 oz. dark Jamaica rum
½ oz. 151-proof Demerara rum
1 oz. curaçao
1 tsp. Pernod or Herbsaint
1 oz. lemon juice
1 oz. orange juice
1 oz. pineapple juice
½ oz. papaya or guava juice
    (optional)
¼ oz. grenadine

½ oz. orgeat syrup or sugar
    syrup to taste
Mint sprig (optional)
Pineapple stick

Mix all ingredients, except mint
and pineapple stick, with cracked
ice in a blender and pour into
a tall, chilled Collins glass.
Garnish with mint sprig and
pineapple stick.
Note: This is a re-creation of
the original Zombie recipe by
Don the Beachcomber.

BRANDY: THE REGAL SPIRIT

> Claret is the liquor for boys;
> port for men; but he who aspires
> to be a hero must drink brandy.
> —Dr. Samuel Johnson

Brandy, the most universal, venerable, and perhaps the most readily available of all spirits in the world, was, according to some historians, probably the first product resulting from the invention of the still. It has not been called *"eau-de-vie"*—the water of life—frivolously. In Europe during the Middle Ages, pure water was unknown in the cities and waterborne diseases were rampant; a condition that prevailed through the nineteenth century and wreaks havoc in parts of Europe even today. This explains why frail Tiny Tim, along with many of his peers, swigged down a pint of ale with his breakfast. It explains the popularity of tea and coffee, not to mention wine, and spirits made from wine, fruits, and grains.

In medieval times eau-de-vies of various kinds were endowed with great medicinal properties. In 1250 Arnaud de Villeneuve wrote of the almost magical properties of spirits to alleviate sickness and prolong life. And the spirit at hand came from the Charentes region, which borders the Atlantic midway between the Pyrenees and Brittany, the capital of which is Cognac. The very name summons forth images of oaken casks, cob-webbed bottles, and crystal brandy snifters yielding the incomparable bouquet of a fifty-year-old cognac being sipped and savored by candlelight at the end of a memorable evening of haute cuisine.

Cognac, the royal family of the brandy world, is made by a distinguished group of distillers located in the strictly delimited Cognac region. The area has been subdivided, by French government decree, into seven parts: *Grande Champagne, Petite Champagne, Borderies, Fin Bois, Bons Bois, Bois Ordinaires,* and *Bois Communs.* The two Champagne districts are considered the premier producing sections by many connoisseurs, but the entire area regularly makes an exemplary brandy by any standard. The "Champagne" designation has no connection with the bubbly wine made far to the north, but refers to a geologic division of the area which separates the Champagne districts from the Bois subdivisions.

Cognac is distilled in large alembics that resemble the distilling apparatus used by the alchemists of the Middle Ages. The distilling process, which is carried out in two stages, is a delicate procedure requiring constant attention. After distillation the cognac is put into oak casks made of wood from the forests of Limousin or Troncais and ages for as long as sixty or seventy years. This is considered maximum, since cognac aged too long loses much of its character. During the aging period, which is carried out above ground in *chais*, or storehouses, a great deal of the brandy is lost by evaporation through the porous oak. This is a necessary part of the maturation process. It is called, philosophically perhaps, *"la part des anges"*— the angel's share. After blending, the cognac is bottled and, unlike wine, the aging stops. Thus, a bottle of cognac aged for ten years and bottled in 1890 is still only a ten-year-old brandy.

There is much confusion in the minds of many cognac lovers about the meaning of all the stars and letters that have traditionally adorned cognac labels. In recent years terms have been regulated by the French government if the designation refers to age, i.e., V.O. "Very Old," which signifies that it is *not very* old, but at least four-and-a-half years old, and V.S.O.P., "Very Superior Old Pale," another popular designation, signifies that the brandy has been aged as long as ten years. Every distiller has premium cognacs with appellations such as "Napoleon," "Extra," etc., which can be quite old, but certainly not aged in oak since the Battle of Waterloo. Apart from minimum age requirements by law, the actual age is left to the integrity and honesty of the individual cognac producer.

Some of the leading cognac brands are Curvoisier, Hennessy, Martell, and Remy Martin. Many lesser-known brands are also outstanding, including names such as Hine, Camus, Otard, Monnet, Bisquit-Dubouche, Delamain, and L. de Salignac.

Armagnac is France's other great brandy. It is distilled in the Armagnac region of southwestern France in Gascony, home of d'Artagnan, who was immortalized by Alexander Dumas in *The Three Musketeers*. Armagnac is made like cognac in great pot stills, aged in oak, and carefully blended to achieve its distinctive flavor, which has been described as earthy, full-bodied, and nutty, with floral overtones of violets and a hint of fruit such as plums, prunes, peaches, or grapes. Each armagnac lover finds a distinguishing flavor, scent, or aftertaste that is described subjectively. Some important brands include Cles de Ducs, De Montal, Lapostolle, Larressingle, Loubere, Sempe, Caussade, and Montesquiou.

Normandy in northwestern France produces many good things to eat and drink, such as Camembert cheese and calvados apple brandy, which has become famous for its crisp, clean, apple flavor. It is similar to American applejack but with more finesse—the result of aging as long as ten to fifteen years. Calvados may be enjoyed before, after, and even during meals. The custom of drinking a tot of calvados as a *digestif* in the middle of a meal is known as "Trou Normand." It is supposed to enhance one's appetite for the courses to come and many people maintain that it performs this task admirably. The best calvados comes from a small section of Normandy designated by the French government as *Pays d'Auge* and is so stated on the label, i.e. *Calvados du Pays d'Auge.* This certifies that this calvados was made in pot stills (as opposed to continuous stills) and is double-distilled in the same way cognac is produced.

French distillers also make a wide range of fruit brandies. These are clear eau-de-vie called *alcools blanc.* Pear brandy made from the Williams or Bartlett pear is particularly well-known and frequently is bottled with a whole pear inside. Framboise from raspberries, fraise from strawberries, mirabelle from plums, and kirsch from cherries are all popular. These and other fruit brandies also are made by distillers in Switzerland, Germany, Hungary, Yugoslavia, and the United States. A brandy distilled from grape pomace (skins and pulp remaining after the juice or wine has been removed from the grape press or fermenting vat) is popular in Burgundy. It is called *marc,* and like *grappa,* the Italian pomace brandy, when unaged can be quite strong and assertive, although these pomace brandies, including those made by California distillers, have their devotees.

California brandies are on the rise and at this writing account for three out of every four bottles of brandy sold in the U.S. Most of the brandy produced is made from a large proportion of Thompson Seedless and Flame Tokay grapes and a sprinkling of other grape varieties using continuous stills. By law California brandy must be aged for two years in oak barrels, but it is usually held longer, which makes for a smoother product. The end result is a brandy that is light, clean, and fruity with a definite grape flavor that may vary from slightly dry to sweet. In addition to traditional, postprandial brandy-snifter sipping, California brandies also lend themselves to the making of mixed drinks, which has, no doubt, been an important factor in their increasing popularity. Good representative brands include Christian Brothers, Cresta

Blanca, Petri, Italian Swiss Colony, Lejon, Coronet VSQ, E & J Brandy, A.R. Morrow, Aristocrat, Paul Masson Conti Royal, Royal Host, as well as many winery labels such as Korbel, Almaden, and Bealieu, who market brandies under their respective names.

Having spent much time in Spain, I have developed a taste for Spanish brandies shipped from Jerez de la Frontera in the "Sherry Triangle" of southern Spain by Pedro Domecq, Duff Gordan, Sandeman, and others among the great sherry producers. Most Spanish brandies are not made from sherry wines, as many suppose, but from wines that are produced in La Mancha, an area south of Madrid made famous as the home base of Don Quixote. Spanish brandies have a distinctive character that carries overtones of sherry, perhaps from aging in casks that were used for sherry wine. The flavor and bouquet are pronounced, sometimes pungent, with a slightly sweet aftertaste and a nutty quality. Some of the most distinguished Spanish brandies are Carlos I and Fundador made by Pedro Domecq; Capa Negra from Sandeman; and Cardinal Mendoza produced by Sanchez Romate.

Many countries produce excellent brandies with unique qualities that are not found anywhere else. Metaxa from Greece (almost a liqueur due to the addition of sugar); Asbach-Uralt from Germany; and Pisco brandy from Peru (produced in Ica, an oasis in the coastal desert, a four-hour drive along the sea south of Lima, where logically nothing should grow) are prime examples of good spirits made in countries not generally thought of as brandy producers. Other examples are Mexico, the source of the popular Presidente brandy and South Africa, which produces K.W.V. brandy in the beautiful wine-growing area near Capetown.

Brandy has an historic and universal appeal. Its restorative qualities are well-known, and its function as a digestive at the end of a meal is appreciated by gourmet and gourmand alike. And the mixability and versatility of brandy in various cocktails and other libations will, it is hoped, be amply demonstrated in the recipes that follow.

A.J.

1½ oz. calvados or
   applejack
1½ oz. grapefruit juice
Several dashes grenadine

Mix all ingredients with cracked ice in a shaker or blender and pour into a chilled cocktail glass.

ADRIENNE'S DREAM

2 oz. brandy
½ oz. peppermint schnapps
½ oz. white crème de cacao
½ oz. lemon juice
½ tsp. sugar syrup or to taste
Club soda
Mint sprig

Mix all ingredients, except soda and mint, with cracked ice in a shaker or blender and pour into a chilled Collins glass. Fill with cold club soda and garnish with mint sprig.

ALABAMA

1 oz. brandy
1 oz. curaçao
½ oz. lime juice
½ tsp. sugar syrup or to taste
Orange peel

Mix all ingredients, except orange peel, with cracked ice in a shaker or blender and strain into a chilled cocktail glass. Twist orange peel over drink and drop into glass.

ALABAMA SLAMMA

1 oz. cognac
½ oz. blackberry brandy
1 oz. coffee brandy
½ oz. dry vermouth
½ oz. amaretto
1 oz. lemon juice

Mix all ingredients with cracked ice in a shaker or blender and pour into a chilled brandy snifter.

ALABAMMY BOUND

1 oz. brandy
1 oz. Southern Comfort
1 oz. lemon juice
½ tsp. sugar syrup or to taste
Mint sprig

Mix all ingredients, except mint sprig, with cracked ice in a shaker or blender, strain into a chilled cocktail glass, and garnish with mint.

ALEXANDER'S SISTER

1½ oz. brandy
1 oz. white crème de menthe
1 oz. heavy cream

Mix all ingredients with cracked ice in a shaker or blender and pour into a chilled cocktail glass.

Note: This cocktail may also be made with gin in place of brandy.

ALHAMBRA

1½ oz. brandy
½ oz. fino sherry
½ oz. Drambuie
Orange slice
Lemon peel

Mix all ingredients, except orange slice and lemon peel, with cracked ice in a shaker or blender and pour into a chilled Old Fashioned glass. Garnish with orange slice, then twist lemon peel over drink, and drop into glass.

AMBASSADOR WEST

1½ oz. brandy
1 oz. gin
1 tsp. dry vermouth
Green olive

Combine brandy, gin, and dry vermouth in a mixing glass with several ice cubes, stir well, and strain into a chilled cocktail glass. Twist lemon peel over drink and drop in, or garnish with cocktail olive.

AMBROSIA FOR TWO

3 oz. brandy
3 oz. apple brandy
Several dashes raspberry
   syrup or raspberry liqueur
Champagne

Mix all ingredients, except champagne, with cracked ice in a shaker or blender and pour equally into two chilled wine glasses. Fill each glass with cold champagne.

AMBULANCE CHASER

2 oz. cognac
¼ oz. port
1 egg yolk
Several dashes
   Worcestershire sauce

Several grindings white
   pepper
Mix with cracked ice in a blender and pour into a chilled cocktail glass.

AMERICAN ROSE

1½ oz. brandy
1 tsp. grenadine
½ fresh peach, peeled and
   mashed
Several dashes Pernod
Champagne

Mix all ingredients, except champagne, with cracked ice in a shaker or blender and pour into a chilled wine goblet. Fill with champagne and stir gently.

APPLE BANG!

2 oz. calvados or applejack
3 oz. apple cider
Several dashes lemon juice
1 egg white (for two drinks)
Club soda (optional)
1 tsp. apple schnapps

Mix all ingredients, except soda and apple schnapps, with cracked ice in a shaker or blender and pour into a chilled, large wine goblet. Fill with cold club soda and add additional ice if needed. Top with apple schnapps.

APPLE BLOSSOM No. 1

1½ oz. brandy
1 oz. apple juice
1 tsp. lemon juice
Lemon slice

Mix all ingredients, except lemon slice, with cracked ice in a shaker or blender, strain into a chilled cocktail glass, and garnish with lemon slice.

APPLE BLOSSOM No. 2

1½ oz. applejack
1 oz. apple juice
½ oz. lemon juice
1 tsp. maple syrup
Lemon slice

Mix all ingredients, except lemon slice, with cracked ice in a blender at low speed for 15 seconds, pour into a chilled deep-saucer champagne glass, and garnish with lemon slice.

APPLE BLOW FIZZ

2–3 oz. applejack or calvados
¼ tsp. lemon juice
1 tsp. sugar syrup or to taste
1 egg white (for two drinks)
Club soda

Mix all ingredients, except soda, with cracked ice in a shaker or blender and pour into a chilled highball glass. Add ice cubes if necessary and fill with cold club soda. Stir gently.

APPLE BRANDY COCKTAIL

2 oz. applejack or calvados
½ tsp. lemon juice
½ tsp. grenadine

Mix all ingredients with cracked ice in a shaker or blender and strain into a chilled cocktail glass.

APPLE BRANDY FRAPPÉ

1½ oz. applejack or calvados
½ oz. lime juice
1 tsp. sugar syrup or to taste
1 egg white (for two drinks)

Mix with plenty of cracked ice in a blender for a few seconds until slushy and pour into a chilled wine glass.

APPLE BRANDY COOLER

2 oz. brandy
1 oz. light rum
4 oz. apple juice
½ oz. lime juice
1 tsp. Falernum or sugar
  syrup to taste
1 tsp. dark Jamaica rum
Lime slice

Mix all ingredients, except dark rum and lime slice, with cracked ice in a shaker or blender and pour into a chilled Collins glass. Top with float of dark rum and garnish with lime slice.

APPLE BUCK

1½ oz. applejack
½ oz. lemon juice
1 tsp. ginger-flavored brandy
Ginger ale
Preserved ginger

Mix all ingredients, except ginger ale and preserved ginger, with cracked ice in a shaker or blender and pour into a chilled highball glass. Fill with cold ginger ale, stir gently, and garnish with ginger.

APPLE BYRRH

1½ oz. calvados
½ oz. dry vermouth
½ oz. Byrrh
½ tsp. lemon juice
Lemon peel

Mix all ingredients, except lemon peel, with cracked ice in a shaker or blender and pour into a chilled Old Fashioned glass. Twist lemon peel over drink and drop into glass.

APPLE CART

1 oz. applejack
¾ oz. Cointreau or curaçao
½ oz. lemon juice

Mix all ingredients with cracked ice in a shaker or blender and strain into a chilled cocktail glass.

APPLE DUBONNET

1½ oz. calvados or applejack
1½ oz. Dubonnet rouge
Lemon slice

Mix all ingredients, except lemon slice, with cracked ice in a shaker or blender, pour into a chilled Old Fashioned glass, and garnish with lemon slice.

APPLE FIZZ

2 oz. apple brandy
4 oz. apple juice
Dash lime juice
Club soda
Lime slice

Combine all ingredients, except lime slice, in a chilled Collins glass with several ice cubes, stir gently, and garnish with lime slice.

APPLE GINGER SANGAREE

1½ oz. apple brandy
¾ oz. green-ginger wine
1 tsp. sugar syrup
Ground nutmeg

Mix all ingredients, except nutmeg, with cracked ice in a shaker or blender, pour into a chilled goblet, and sprinkle with nutmeg.

APPLE KNOCKER

3 oz. apple brandy
½ oz. sweet vermouth
4 oz. orange juice
½ oz. sugar syrup or to taste
1 tsp. lemon juice

Mix all ingredients with cracked ice in a shaker or blender and pour into a chilled Collins glass. Add additional ice if necessary.

APPLE RUM-DUM

1 oz. applejack
1 oz. light rum
½ oz. lime juice
½ oz. orgeat syrup or sugar syrup to taste
Club soda
Orange peel
Lemon peel

Mix all ingredients, except soda, orange and lemon peels, with cracked ice in a shaker or blender and pour into a chilled Collins glass. Add additional ice and fill with cold club soda. Twist orange and lemon peels over drink and drop into glass.

APPLE SIDECAR

1½ oz. apple brandy
½ oz. triple sec
½ oz. lime juice

Mix all ingredients with cracked
ice in a shaker or blender and
pour into a chilled cocktail
glass.

APPLE SWIZZLE

1½ oz. applejack
1 oz. light rum
½ oz. lime juice
1 tsp. sugar syrup or to taste
Dash Angostura bitters

Mix with cracked ice in a
shaker or blender and pour into a
chilled Old Fashioned glass.
Add more ice if necessary.

APPLEJACK COLLINS

2 oz. applejack
1 oz. lemon juice
1 tsp. sugar syrup
Several dashes orange bitters
Club soda, chilled
Lemon slice

Mix all ingredients, except club
soda and lemon slice, with cracked
ice in a shaker or blender and
pour into a chilled Collins
glass. Fill with club soda, stir
gently, and garnish with lemon
slice.

APPLEJACK DAISY

1½ oz. applejack
½ oz. lime juice
1 tsp. raspberry syrup
Club soda, chilled
1 tsp. ginger brandy
Lime slice

Mix all ingredients, except club
soda, ginger brandy, and lime
slice, with cracked ice in a
shaker or blender and pour into a
chilled highball glass. Fill with
club soda, stir gently, and top
with float of ginger brandy.
Garnish with lime slice.

APPLEJACK MANHATTAN

1¾ oz. applejack
¾ oz. sweet vermouth
Dash orange bitters
Maraschino cherry

Combine all ingredients, except
maraschino cherry, in a mixing
glass with several ice cubes,
stir well, and strain into a chilled
cocktail glass. Garnish with
cherry.

APPLEJACK SOUR

2 oz. applejack
1 oz. lemon juice
1 tsp. sugar syrup or to taste

Mix all ingredients with cracked ice in a shaker or blender and strain into a chilled cocktail glass.

APOLLO COOLER

1½ oz. Metaxa
½ oz. lemon juice
Ginger ale
Lemon slice
1 tsp. ouzo

Mix brandy and lemon juice with cracked ice in a shaker or blender and pour into a chilled highball glass. Fill with ginger ale, stir gently, and garnish with lemon slice. Top with ouzo.

APRICOT BRANDY FIZZ

2 oz. apricot-flavored brandy
Several dashes grenadine
Orange slice
Lemon peel
Club soda

Pour brandy and grenadine into a chilled Old Fashioned glass with several ice cubes, add lemon peel and orange slice, fill with cold club soda, and stir gently.

APRICOT BRANDY SOUR

2 oz. apricot brandy
1 oz. lemon juice
1 tsp. sugar syrup or to taste
Lemon slice

Mix all ingredients, except lemon slice, with cracked ice in a shaker or blender and strain into a chilled cocktail glass. Garnish with lemon slice.

APRICOT PIE

1 oz. apricot brandy
1 oz. light rum
½ oz. sweet vermouth
1 tsp. lemon juice
Several dashes grenadine
Orange peel

Mix all ingredients, except orange peel, with cracked ice in a shaker or blender and pour into a chilled Old Fashioned glass. Twist orange peel over drink and drop into glass.

APRICOT LADY

1 oz. apricot brandy
1½ oz. light rum
½ oz. lime juice
1 tsp. curaçao
1 egg white (for two drinks)
Orange slice

Mix all ingredients, except orange slice, with cracked ice in a shaker or blender, pour into a chilled cocktail glass, and garnish with orange slice.

APRICOT No. 1

2 oz. apricot brandy
1 oz. orange juice
1 oz. lemon juice
Several dashes gin

Mix all ingredients with cracked ice in a shaker or blender and pour into a chilled cocktail glass.

APRICOT No. 2

1½ oz. brandy
½ oz. gin
1 oz. orange juice
½ oz. lemon or lime juice
1 tsp. orgeat syrup

Mix with cracked ice in a shaker or blender and strain into a chilled cocktail glass.

 ## B&B

1 oz. cognac
1 oz. Benedictine

Pour into a brandy snifter and swirl until well blended.

B&B COLLINS

2 oz. cognac
½ oz. lemon juice
1 tsp. syrup or to taste
Club soda
½ oz. Benedictine
Lemon slice

Mix all ingredients, except club soda, Benedictine, and lemon slice, with cracked ice in a shaker or blender and pour into a chilled Collins glass. Fill with club soda, stir gently, and top with float of Benedictine. Garnish with lemon slice.

BALTIMORE BRACER

1 oz. brandy
1 oz. anisette
1 egg white (for two drinks)

Mix all ingredients with cracked ice in a shaker or blender and pour into a chilled cocktail glass.

BART FARRELL'S FIZZ

1 oz. brandy
1 oz. pineapple juice
½ oz. lemon juice
Several dashes maraschino
   liqueur
Club soda
Dash Angostura or orange
   bitters

Mix all ingredients, except club soda and bitters, with cracked ice in a shaker or blender and pour into a chilled highball glass. Fill with club soda, top with bitters, and stir gently.

BARTON SPECIAL

1½ oz. calvados
¾ oz. gin
¾ oz. scotch
Lemon peel

Mix all ingredients, except lemon peel, with cracked ice in a shaker or blender and pour into a chilled Old Fashioned glass. Twist lemon peel over drink and drop into glass.

BATEAUX MOUCHE

1½ oz. cognac
½ oz. Dubonnet blanc
½ oz. lemon juice
1 tsp. sugar syrup
½ oz. curaçao

Mix all ingredients, except curaçao, with cracked ice in a shaker or blender and strain into a chilled cocktail glass. Top with curaçao float.

BASIN STREET BALM

1 oz. brandy
½ oz. peach brandy
½ oz. lemon juice
1 tsp. peach schnapps or
   kirsch
Orange slice

Mix all ingredients, except orange slice, with cracked ice in a shaker or blender and strain into a chilled cocktail glass. Garnish with orange slice.

BBC

2 oz. blackberry-flavored
   brandy
Cola
Lemon slice

Pour brandy into a chilled Collins glass with ice cubes and fill with cold cola. Garnish with lemon slice.

BEACH STREET COOLER

1½ oz. brandy
½ oz. curaçao
½ oz. lemon juice
Cola

Mix brandy, curaçao, and lemon
juice with cracked ice in a shaker
or blender and pour into a
chilled Collins glass. Fill with
cold cola. Stir gently.

BELMONT PARK

1 oz. apple brandy
1 oz. apricot brandy
½ oz. gin
½ oz. orange juice
Several dashes grenadine

Mix all ingredients, except
grenadine, with cracked ice in a
shaker or blender and pour
into a chilled cocktail glass. Top
with grenadine float.

 ## BESS-ARLENE

1½ oz. brandy
½ oz. curaçao
Club soda
Dash Pernod

Pour brandy and curaçao over
ice in a chilled Collins glass and
fill with cold club soda. Add a
dash of Pernod and stir gently.

 ## BETSY ROSS

1½ oz. brandy
1½ oz. port
1 egg yolk
1 tsp. sugar syrup or to taste
Several dashes curaçao
Several dashes Angostura
    bitters
Ground nutmeg (optional)

Mix all ingredients, except nutmeg, with cracked ice in a shaker
or blender and strain into a
chilled cocktail glass. Sprinkle
with ground nutmeg, if you
wish.

 ## BETWEEN THE SHEETS

1½ oz. cognac
1 oz. light rum
¾ oz. curaçao or triple sec
½ oz. lemon juice

Mix with cracked ice in a
shaker or blender and strain into
a chilled cocktail glass.

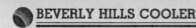 **BEVERLY HILLS COOLER**

1 oz. brandy
½ oz. Benedictine
3–4 oz. orange juice
Champagne
Gardenia or orchid (optional)

Mix brandy, Benedictine, and orange juice with cracked ice in a shaker or blender and strain into a chilled brandy snifter or Squall glass. Fill with cold champagne and garnish with a gardenia or orchid (or flower of your choice).

BIG APPLE

2 oz. applejack
½ oz. amaretto
3 oz. apple juice
1 tbsp. applesauce
Ground cinnamon

Mix all ingredients, except cinnamon, with cracked ice in a blender until smooth. Serve in a chilled parfait glass and sprinkle with cinnamon.

BLACKJACK

1 oz. blackberry brandy
1 oz. brandy
1 oz. heavy cream

Mix all ingredients with cracked ice in a shaker or blender and pour into a chilled cocktail glass.

 BOMBAY

1 oz. brandy
1 oz. dry vermouth
½ oz. sweet vermouth
½ tsp. curaçao
Dash of Pernod
Orange slice

Mix all ingredients, except orange slice, with cracked ice in a shaker or blender, pour into a chilled Old Fashioned glass, and garnish with orange slice.

BOOSTER

2 oz. brandy
1 oz. curaçao
1 egg white (for two drinks)
Pinch of ground nutmeg

Mix all ingredients, except ground nutmeg, with cracked ice in a shaker or blender and pour into a chilled cocktail glass. Sprinkle with nutmeg.

BOSOM CARESSER No. 1

1½ oz. brandy
½ oz. triple sec or curaçao
1 egg yolk
1 tsp. grenadine

Mix all ingredients with cracked ice in a shaker or blender and strain into a chilled cocktail glass.

BOSOM CARESSER No. 2

1 oz. brandy
1 oz. Madeira
½ oz. triple sec

Stir all ingredients with ice in a mixing glass and strain into a chilled cocktail glass.

 ## BOSTON BLACKIE

2 oz. blackberry-flavored
    brandy
Bitter lemon soda
Lime wedge

Add brandy to a chilled Collins glass with ice cubes and fill with cold bitter lemon soda. Stir gently and garnish with lime wedge.

BRANDANA FRAPPÉ

1½ oz. applejack or calvados
½ oz. crème de banane
½ oz. lime juice
Orange slice

Mix applejack, banana liqueur, and lime juice with plenty of cracked ice in a blender for a few seconds until slushy and pour into a chilled wine glass. Garnish with orange slice.

BRANDANA COOLER

1½ oz. brandy
¾ oz. crème de banane
½ oz. lemon juice
Club soda, chilled
Lemon wedge
Banana slice

Mix all ingredients, except club soda, lemon and banana slices, with cracked ice in a shaker or blender and pour into a chilled Collins glass. Fill with club soda, stir gently, and garnish with lemon wedge and banana slice.

BRANDIED APRICOT

1½ oz. brandy
½ oz. apricot brandy
½ oz. lemon juice
Canned or dried apricot

Mix all ingredients, except apricot, with cracked ice in a shaker or blender and strain into a chilled cocktail glass. Garnish with an apricot.

BRANDY ALEXANDER

1½ oz. brandy
1 oz. crème de cacao
1 oz. heavy cream

Mix all ingredients with cracked ice in a shaker or blender and strain into a chilled cocktail glass.

BRANDY BUCK

1½ oz. brandy
¼ oz. white crème de menthe
½ oz. lemon juice
Ginger ale, chilled
Several seedless grapes

Mix all ingredients, except ginger ale and grapes, with cracked ice in a shaker or blender and pour into a chilled highball glass. Fill with club soda, stir gently, and garnish with seedless grapes.

BRANDY CASSIS

1½ oz. brandy
¼ oz. crème de cassis or to taste
½ oz. lemon juice
Lemon peel

Mix all ingredients, except lemon peel, with cracked ice in a shaker or blender and strain into a chilled cocktail glass. Twist lemon peel over drink and drop into glass.

 ## BRANDY CHAMPERELLE

½ oz. curaçao
½ oz. yellow Chartreuse
½ oz. anisette
½ oz. cognac

Prechill all ingredients, and, in the order listed, carefully pour each into a chilled sherry glass using the bowl of a barspoon so that each floats on the one beneath it.

 ## BRANDY COBBLER

2–3 oz. brandy
1 tsp. curaçao or maraschino or peach liqueur
1 tsp. pineapple syrup or sugar syrup to taste
Orange slice
Maraschino cherry

Fill a chilled glass goblet about three-quarters full of cracked ice and add brandy, liqueur, and syrup. Stir briskly with bar spoon until glass begins to frost. Garnish with orange slice and cherry.

BRANDY CRUSTA

Spiral peel of a medium
  orange or large lemon
Lemon slice
Superfine sugar
2–3 oz. brandy
½ oz. lemon juice
½ oz. maraschino liqueur
Several dashes Angostura
  bitters
Maraschino cherry

Cut a thin, even spiral from an orange or lemon after cutting off the ends of the fruit. Rub the rim of a chilled wine goblet with lemon slice and roll rim in superfine sugar until well coated. Mix brandy, lemon juice, maraschino liqueur and bitters with cracked ice in a shaker or blender and pour into goblet that has been lined with orange or lemon spiral. Garnish with maraschino cherry.

 BRANDY DAISY

2–3 oz. brandy
Juice of ½ lemon
½ oz. raspberry syrup or
  grenadine
1 tsp. sugar syrup
Club soda
Peach slice or orange slice
Pineapple stick
Maraschino cherry
Dash Pernod or maraschino
  liqueur (optional)

Mix brandy, lemon juice, raspberry, and sugar syrup with cracked ice in a shaker or blender and pour into a chilled wine goblet and add additional cracked ice. Stir briskly until goblet is frosted. Fill with cold club soda and garnish with fruits. A dash of Pernod is sometimes used to top off drink.

BRANDY EGGNOG

2–3 oz. brandy
½ oz. sugar syrup or to taste
1 cup milk
1 egg
Freshly ground nutmeg

Mix all ingredients, except nutmeg, with cracked ice in a shaker or blender and strain into a chilled highball glass. Sprinkle with nutmeg.

 BRANDY FIX

2–3 oz. brandy
1 tsp. sugar syrup
1 tsp. water
Juice of ½ lemon

Add all ingredients to a chilled double Old Fashioned glass and fill with cracked ice. Stir until glass frosts. Serve with a straw, if you wish.

 **BRANDY FIZZ**

2–3 oz. brandy
1½ oz. lemon juice or half
  lime and lemon juice
½ oz. sugar syrup or to taste
Club soda

Mix all ingredients, except
soda, with cracked ice in a shaker
or blender and pour into a
chilled highball glass. Add additional ice cubes if necessary
and fill with cold club soda.

 BRANDY FLIP

2 oz. brandy
1 egg
1 tsp. sugar syrup or to taste
½ oz. cream (optional)
Ground nutmeg

Mix all ingredients, except nutmeg, with cracked ice in a
blender and pour into a chilled
wine glass. Sprinkle with nutmeg.

 BRANDY GUMP

2–3 oz. brandy
½ oz. lemon juice
½ tsp. grenadine

Mix all ingredients with cracked
ice in a shaker or blender and
strain into a chilled cocktail
glass.

 BRANDY JULEP

6 mint leaves
1 tsp. sugar syrup or honey
Brandy
Mint sprig
Powdered sugar

Place mint leaves in a chilled
double Old Fashioned glass and
add syrup or honey and a little
cold water. Muddle leaves until
bruised and fill glass with
shaved or finely crushed ice. Fill
with brandy and churn with a
barspoon until glass frosts. Add
more ice and brandy and churn
until well frosted. Garnish with
mint sprig and dust it with
powdered sugar.

BRANDY MANHATTAN

2 oz. brandy
½ oz. sweet or dry vermouth
Dash Angostura bitters
Maraschino cherry

Combine brandy, sweet vermouth,
and Angostura bitters in a mixing
glass with several ice cubes, stir
well, and strain into a chilled
cocktail glass. Garnish with
maraschino cherry.

BRANDY MELBA

1½ oz. brandy
½ oz. peach schnapps
¼ oz. raspberry liqueur
½ oz. lemon juice
Several dashes orange bitters
Peach slice

Mix all ingredients, except peach slice, with cracked ice in a shaker or blender, strain into a chilled cocktail glass, and garnish with peach slice.

BRANDY MILK PUNCH

2 oz. brandy
8 oz. milk
1 tsp. sugar syrup
Pinch of ground nutmeg

Mix all ingredients, except ground nutmeg, with cracked ice in a shaker or blender, pour into a chilled double Old Fashioned glass, and sprinkle with nutmeg.

BRANDY OLD FASHIONED

1 sugar cube
Several dashes Angostura
  bitters
3 oz. brandy
Lemon peel

Place sugar cube in a chilled Old Fashioned glass and sprinkle with bitters and a dash of cold water. Muddle sugar cube until dissolved. Add ice cubes and brandy. Twist lemon peel over drink and drop into glass.

BRANDY SANGAREE

½ tsp. superfine sugar
Dash water
2–3 oz. brandy
Ground nutmeg

Dissolve sugar with a little water in a chilled double Old Fashioned glass, add ice cubes and brandy. Stir well and sprinkle with ground nutmeg.

BRANDY SCAFFA No. 1

½ oz. raspberry syrup
½ oz. maraschino liqueur
½ oz. green Chartreuse
½ oz. cognac

In a sherry or parfait glass carefully pour in the ingredients,

in the exact order listed, using the round bottom of a spoon so they remain separated. This traditional recipe is similar to a pousse-café and a *champerelle*, using various ingredients poured in layers and never mixed, except by the drinker.

BRANDY SCAFFA No. 2

1½ oz. cognac
1½ oz. maraschino liqueur
Dash Angostura bitters

Mix all ingredients with ice cubes in a chilled double Old Fashioned glass.

 ## BRANDY SOUR

2 oz. brandy
1 oz. lemon juice
½ oz. orange juice (optional)
1 tsp. sugar syrup or to taste
Maraschino cherry

Mix all ingredients, except cherry, with cracked ice in a shaker or blender, strain into a chilled Whiskey Sour glass, and garnish with cherry.

 ## BRONX CHEER

2 oz. apricot brandy
6 oz. raspberry soda
Orange peel

Mix brandy and soda with ice cubes in a chilled Collins glass. Twist orange peel over drink and drop into glass.

BULL'S MILK

2 oz. brandy
½ oz. dark Jamaica rum
6 oz. milk
1 tsp. sugar syrup or to taste
Pinch cinnamon or nutmeg

Mix all ingredients, except spice, with cracked ice in a shaker or blender and pour into a chilled highball glass. Sprinkle with spice.

 ## CALIFORNIA COLA

1½ oz. brandy
½ oz. triple sec
Cola
Lemon slice

Pour brandy and triple sec over ice in a chilled Collins glass and fill with cold cola. Garnish with lemon slice.

 ## CALIFORNIA DREAMING

2 oz. apricot brandy
4 oz. orange soda
1 scoop orange sherbet

Mix with cracked ice in a blender for a few seconds until smooth. Serve in a parfait glass.

CANDY COCKTAIL

1 oz. brandy
1 oz. Galliano
Dash maraschino liqueur
2 scoops orange sherbet
Chocolate chips

Mix all ingredients, except
chocolate chips, with cracked ice
in a blender until smooth and
pour into a chilled wine goblet.
Sprinkle chocolate chips on
top.

CAPTAIN KIDD

1½ oz. brandy
1 oz. dark Jamaica rum
1 oz. crème de cacao
Orange slice
Maraschino cherry
Pineapple stick

Mix all ingredients, except orange
slice, maraschino cherry, and
pineapple stick, with cracked
ice in a shaker or blender and
pour into a chilled Delmonico
glass. Garnish with fruit.

CARROL

1½ oz. brandy
¾ oz. sweet vermouth
Maraschino cherry

Mix all ingredients, except maraschino cherry, with cracked ice
in a shaker or blender, pour
into a chilled cocktail glass, and
garnish with cherry.

CHAMPAGNE COOLER

1 oz. brandy
1 oz. Cointreau
Champagne
Mint sprigs

Pour brandy and Cointreau into
a chilled Squall glass or wine
goblet, fill with champagne,
and stir gently. Garnish with
mint sprigs.

CHAMPAGNE DREAM

Dash Pernod
½ oz. cognac
½ oz. curaçao
Dash maple syrup
Brut champagne

Rinse a large, chilled champagne tulip glass with Pernod. In
a mixing glass add several ice
cubes, cognac, curaçao, and
maple syrup and strain into
champagne tulip. Fill with cold
champagne and stir gently.

CHAMPS ELYSEES

1½ oz. cognac
½ oz. yellow Chartreuse
½ oz. lemon juice
1 tsp. sugar syrup or to taste
Dash Angostura bitters

Mix all ingredients with cracked ice in a shaker or blender and pour into a chilled cocktail glass.

CHERRY BERRY

1½ oz. blackberry-flavored
   brandy
½ oz. cherry brandy
6 oz. black-cherry soda
Maraschino cherry

Pour brandies into a tall, chilled Collins glass with ice cubes and fill with cold black-cherry soda. Stir gently. Garnish with cherry.

CHERRY BLOSSOM

1½ oz. brandy
¾ oz. cherry brandy or cherry
   liqueur
½ oz. curaçao
½ oz. lemon juice

¼ oz. grenadine
1 tsp. sugar syrup or to taste

Mix all ingredients with cracked ice in a shaker or blender and strain into a chilled cocktail glass.

CHERRY HILL

1 oz. brandy
1 oz. cherry brandy
½ oz. dry vermouth
Orange peel

Mix all ingredients, except orange peel, with cracked ice in a shaker or blender and pour into a chilled cocktail glass. Twist orange peel over drink and drop into glass.

CHICAGO

Lemon wedge
Superfine sugar
1½ oz. brandy
Dash curaçao
Dash Angostura bitters
Champagne

Moisten the rim of a chilled wine goblet with lemon wedge and roll rim in sugar until evenly coated. Mix brandy, curaçao, and bitters with cracked ice in a mixing glass and strain into goblet. Fill with cold champagne.

CLASSIC

Lemon wedge
Superfine sugar
1½ oz. brandy
½ oz. curaçao
½ oz. maraschino liqueur
½ oz. lemon juice
Lemon peel

Moisten rim of a chilled cocktail glass with a lemon wedge and dip rim in a superfine sugar until evenly coated. Mix brandy, curaçao, maraschino liqueur, and lemon juice with cracked ice in a shaker or blender and strain into cocktail glass. Twist lemon peel over drink and drop into glass.

CNOSSUS COOLER

1½ oz. Metaxa
Several dashes Angostura
  bitters
5 oz. pineapple juice
Maraschino cherry
Orange slice

Mix brandy and bitters in a chilled highball glass with several ice cubes and stir. Add pineapple juice and garnish with cherry and orange slice.

COCOA MOCHA

2 oz. coffee-flavored brandy
Chocolate soda
Cinnamon stick

Pour brandy over ice in a double Old Fashioned glass and fill with cold chocolate soda. Garnish with cinnamon stick.

COFFEE COCKTAIL No. 1

1 oz. brandy
1 oz. Cointreau
1 oz. cold black coffee

Shake with cracked ice and pour into a chilled parfait glass.

COFFEE COCKTAIL No. 2

1½ oz. brandy
¾ oz. port
Several dashes curaçao
Several dashes sugar syrup
  or to taste
1 egg yolk
Ground nutmeg

Mix all ingredients, except nutmeg, with cracked ice in a blender and strain into a chilled cocktail glass. Sprinkle with nutmeg.

 COFFEE FIZZ

2 oz. coffee-flavored brandy
2 oz. milk or half-and-half
1 egg (optional)
Cream soda
Pinch ground cinnamon

Mix brandy, milk, and egg with cracked ice in a blender and pour into a chilled Collins glass. Fill with cream soda, add additional ice, if necessary, and sprinkle with cinnamon.

COFFEE FLIP

1 oz. cognac
½ oz. port
4 oz. coffee
½ tsp. sugar syrup
1 egg
Pinch of ground nutmeg

Mix all ingredients, except ground nutmeg, with cracked ice in a shaker or blender, pour into a chilled Squall glass or wine goblet. Add additional ice, if necessary. Sprinkle with nutmeg.

 COLD DECK

1½ oz. brandy
¾ oz. sweet vermouth
¾ oz. peppermint schnapps
    or white crème de menthe

Mix all ingredients with cracked ice in a shaker or blender and strain into a chilled cocktail glass.
Note: For a Dry Cold Deck, substitute a dry vermouth in place of sweet vermouth.

 CORPSE REVIVER

1½ oz. applejack
¾ oz. brandy
½ oz. sweet vermouth

Mix with cracked ice in a shaker or blender and strain into a chilled cocktail glass.

DANISH KISS

1½ oz. applejack
1 oz. Peter Heering
1 oz. cream

Mix with cracked ice in a shaker or blender and strain into a chilled cocktail glass.

 DEAUVILLE

1 oz. brandy
¾ oz. apple brandy
½ oz. triple sec or Cointreau
½ oz. lemon juice

Mix all ingredients with cracked ice in a shaker or blender and strain into a chilled cocktail glass.

 DEPTH BOMB

1¼ oz. apple brandy
1¼ oz. brandy
Several dashes lemon juice
Several dashes grenadine

Mix all ingredients with cracked ice in a shaker or blender and pour into a chilled cocktail glass.

DONNA'S DELIGHT

1½ oz. brandy
1 oz. apricot brandy
½ oz. amaretto

Mix with plenty of cracked ice in a blender for a few seconds and pour into a chilled cocktail glass.

DOROTHY JOHNSON'S JOY

1 oz. brandy
1 oz. port
½ cup vanilla ice cream

Mix all ingredients in a blender for a few seconds until smooth and pour into a chilled parfait glass.

DOUBLE BRANDY FLIP

1 oz. brandy
1 oz. apricot brandy
½ oz. sugar syrup
1 egg
Ground nutmeg

Mix all ingredients, except ground nutmeg, with cracked ice in a shaker or blender, strain into a chilled cocktail glass, and sprinkle with nutmeg.

 EAST INDIA

1½ oz. brandy
½ oz. curaçao
½ oz. pineapple juice
Dash Angostura bitters

Mix with cracked ice in a shaker or blender and strain into a chilled cocktail glass.

ELYSEE PALACE

1 oz. cognac
½ oz. raspberry liqueur
Brut champagne
½ tsp. framboise

Stir cognac and raspberry liqueur with several ice cubes in a mixing glass until well chilled. Pour into a chilled tulip glass, fill with cold champagne, and top with a framboise float.

ESCOFFIER COCKTAIL

1½ oz. calvados
¾ oz. Cointreau
¾ oz. Dubonnet rouge
Dash Angostura bitters
Maraschino cherry

Blend calvados, Cointreau, Dubonnet and bitters with cracked ice in a mixing glass. Stir briskly and strain into a chilled cocktail glass. Garnish with maraschino cherry.

FANTASIO

1 oz. brandy
¾ oz. dry vermouth
1 tsp. white crème de cacao
1 tsp. maraschino liqueur

Mix all ingredients with cracked ice in a shaker or blender and pour into a chilled cocktail glass.

FJORD

1 oz. brandy
½ oz. aquavit
1 oz. orange juice
½ oz. lime juice
1 tsp. grenadine

Mix all ingredients with cracked ice in a shaker or blender and strain into a chilled cocktail glass.

FLAG

1½ oz. apricot brandy
Several dashes curaçao
1 tsp. crème yvette
1 oz. dry red wine

Mix apricot brandy and curaçao with cracked ice in a shaker or blender. Pour crème yvette into a chilled Old Fashioned glass, then carefully strain brandy and curaçao mixture over a barspoon so that the mixture floats on top of the crème yvette. Top with red wine float.

FOXHOUND

1½ oz. brandy
½ oz. cranberry juice
1 tsp. kummel
1 tsp. lemon juice
Lemon slice

Mix all ingredients, except lemon slice, with cracked ice in a shaker or blender, pour into a chilled Old Fashioned glass, and garnish with lemon slice.

 **FRENCH 75**

1½ oz. cognac
½ oz. sugar syrup or to taste
Juice of ½ lemon
Brut champagne
Lemon peel

Mix all ingredients, except champagne and lemon peel, with cracked ice in a shaker or blender, pour into a chilled high-ball glass and fill with cold champagne. Twist lemon peel over drink and drop into glass.

FRENCH CONNECTION

1½ oz. cognac
¾ oz. Amaretto di Saronno

Mix with ice cubes in a chilled Old Fashioned glass.

 FROUPE

1½ oz. brandy
1½ oz. sweet vermouth
1 tsp. Benedictine

Blend all ingredients in a mixing glass with several ice cubes, stir well, and strain into a chilled cocktail glass.

 FRUIT PASSION

1½ oz. brandy
½ oz. triple sec
½ oz. cherry liqueur
½ oz. lemon juice

Dash raspberry syrup or grenadine

Mix with cracked ice in a shaker or blender and strain into a chilled cocktail glass.

FUZZY BROTHER

1½ oz. brandy
½ oz. peach schnapps
4 oz. orange juice

Mix with cracked ice in a shaker or blender and serve in a chilled double Old Fashioned glass. Add additional ice, if necessary.

 GAZETTE

1½ oz. brandy
1 oz. sweet vermouth
1 tsp. lemon juice
1 tsp. sugar syrup

Mix all ingredients with cracked ice in a shaker or blender and pour into a chilled cocktail glass.

GEORGIA PEACH FIZZ

1½ oz. brandy
½ oz. peach brandy
½ oz. lemon juice
1 tsp. crème de banane
1 tsp. sugar syrup
Club soda
Fresh or brandied peach slice

Mix all ingredients, except club soda and peach slice, with cracked ice in a shaker or blender and pour into a chilled Collins glass. Fill with club soda, stir gently, and garnish with peach slice.

GINGER JONES

1½ oz. brandy
½ oz. ginger brandy
1 oz. orange juice
½ oz. lime juice
½ oz. sugar syrup or to taste
Preserved ginger

Mix all ingredients, except preserved ginger, with cracked ice in a shaker or blender and pour into a chilled Old Fashioned glass. Garnish with ginger.

GOLDEN CHAIN

1 oz. cognac
1 oz. Galliano
½ oz. lime juice
Dash yellow Chartreuse
Lime slice

Mix all ingredients, except lime slice, with cracked ice in a shaker or blender and strain into a chilled cocktail glass. Garnish with lime slice.

GOLDEN SLIPPER

1 oz. apricot brandy
1 oz. yellow Chartreuse
1 egg yolk

Mix all ingredients with cracked ice in a shaker or blender and pour into a chilled cocktail glass.

GOLF EL PARAISO

¾ oz. apple brandy
¾ oz. light rum
½ oz. orange juice
½ oz. lemon juice
¼ oz. grenadine
Orange slice

Mix all ingredients, except orange slice, with cracked ice in a shaker or blender and pour into a chilled Old Fashioned glass. Garnish with orange slice.

GOLFE JAUN

1½ oz. brandy
½ oz. maraschino liqueur
1 oz. pineapple juice
½ oz. lemon juice
½ tsp. kirsch

Mix all ingredients, except kirsch, with cracked ice in a shaker or blender and strain into a chilled cocktail glass. Top with a kirsch float.

THE GOOD DOCTOR

2 oz. coffee-flavored brandy
2 oz. half-and-half or cream
Dr. Pepper or black raspberry soda
Pinch powdered cinnamon

Mix brandy and half-and-half with cracked ice in a shaker or blender and pour into a chilled highball glass. Fill with cold Dr. Pepper and additional ice, if necessary. Sprinkle with cinnamon.

GOODNIGHT SWEETHEART COCKTAIL

1 oz. cognac
1 oz. apricot brandy
1 oz. port
1 tsp. sugar syrup or to taste
1 egg yolk
Lemon peel
Pinch of ground cinnamon

Mix all ingredients, except lemon peel and ground cinnamon, with cracked ice in a shaker or blender and pour into a chilled wine goblet. Twist lemon peel over drink and drop into glass.

GRANADA

1 oz. brandy
1 oz. fino sherry
½ oz. curaçao
Tonic water
Orange slice

Mix all ingredients, except tonic water and orange slice, with cracked ice in a shaker or blender and pour into a chilled highball glass. Fill with cold tonic, stir gently, and garnish with orange slice.

GRAND APPLE

1 oz. calvados
½ oz. cognac
½ oz. Grand Marnier
Lemon peel
Orange peel

Pour calvados, cognac, and Grand Marnier in a mixing glass with several ice cubes, stir well, and pour into a chilled Old Fashioned glass. Twist lemon and orange peels over drink and drop into glass.

GRANT PARK

1½ oz. apricot-flavored brandy
2 oz. orange juice
1 oz. lemon juice
½ oz. orgeat syrup or to taste

Mix with cracked ice in a shaker or blender and pour into a chilled cocktail glass.

GRENADIER

1½ oz. brandy
¾ oz. ginger-flavored brandy
Freshly grated ginger
Dash sugar syrup or to taste

Mix with ice cubes in a pitcher and strain into a chilled cocktail glass.

HALF MOON STREET

2 oz. brandy
1 oz. pineapple juice
½ oz. lemon juice
½ oz. sugar syrup
Several dashes lime juice
Club soda
Several dashes 151-proof
    Demerara rum
Orange slice

Mix all ingredients, except club soda, rum, and orange slice, with cracked ice in a shaker or blender and pour into a chilled Collins glass. Add several ice cubes, fill with soda and float of rum. Garnish with orange slice.

HARVARD

1½ oz. brandy
½ oz. sweet vermouth
¼ oz. lemon juice
1 tsp. grenadine
Dash Angostura bitters

Mix all ingredients with cracked ice in a shaker or blender and strain into a chilled cocktail glass.

HIGH APPLEBALL

2 oz. apple brandy
Ginger ale or club soda
Lemon peel

Pour apple brandy into a chilled highball glass with several ice cubes, fill with ginger ale, and stir gently. Twist lemon peel over drink and drop into glass.

HO-HO-KUS POCUS

1 oz. applejack
1 oz. brandy
Several dashes bourbon

Mix all ingredients with cracked ice in a shaker or blender and pour into a chilled cocktail glass.

HONEYMOON

1½ oz. apple brandy
¾ oz. Benedictine
1 oz. lemon juice
Several dashes curaçao

Mix all ingredients with cracked ice in a shaker or blender and pour into a chilled cocktail glass.

HOTEL DU CAP

1 oz. applejack
½ oz. apricot brandy
¾ oz. lemon juice
1 tsp. grenadine
Dash orange bitters

Mix all ingredients with cracked ice in a shaker or blender and strain into a chilled cocktail glass.

ICHBIEN

2 oz. calvados
½ oz. curaçao
2 oz. milk or cream
1 egg yolk
Ground nutmeg

Mix all ingredients, except nutmeg, with cracked ice in a shaker or blender and strain into a chilled Delmonico glass. Sprinkle with nutmeg.

IMPERIAL HOUSE FRAPPÉ

1½ oz. port
¾ oz. brandy
1 egg yolk
Freshly grated nutmeg

Mix port, brandy, and egg yolk with plenty of cracked ice in a blender until slushy and pour into a chilled wine glass.

INCA PUNCH

1 oz. Pisco
½ oz. triple sec
1 oz. dry red wine
1½ oz. orange juice
1½ oz. pineapple juice
Mint sprig

Mix all ingredients, except mint sprig, with cracked ice in a shaker or blender and pour into a chilled Squall glass or wine goblet. Garnish with mint sprig.

JACK-IN-THE-BOX

1½ oz. applejack
1 oz. pineapple juice
1 oz. lemon juice
Several dashes Angostura
    bitters

Mix all ingredients with cracked
ice in a shaker or blender and
pour into a chilled cocktail
glass.

JACK RABBIT

1½ oz. applejack
½ oz. lemon juice
½ oz. orange juice
1 tsp. maple syrup or to taste

Mix all ingredients with cracked
ice in a shaker or blender and
strain into a chilled cocktail
glass.

JACKROSE

2 oz. applejack
½ oz. lime or lemon juice
1 tsp. grenadine

Mix all ingredients with cracked
ice in a shaker or blender and
strain into a chilled cocktail
glass.

JANET HOWARD

2 oz. brandy
1¼ oz. orgeat syrup
Several dashes Angostura
    bitters

Mix with cracked ice in a
shaker or blender and strain into
a chilled cocktail glass.

JAPANESE

2 oz. brandy
¼ oz. orgeat syrup
¼ oz. lime juice
Dash Angostura bitters
Lime peel

Mix all ingredients, except lime
peel, with cracked ice in a shaker
or blender and strain into a
chilled cocktail glass. Twist lime
peel over drink and drop into
glass.

BARTENDER'S SECRET NO. 16

Fresh ice. No, it doesn't refer to freshening someone's glass
with additional ice. It is an important consideration, especially for the home bartender. Ice that has been kept for a long

time in a freezer not only will take on odors from meats, fish, and vegetables stored nearby but will become stale with the passage of time. You probably have experienced the flat, musty taste of water that has been stored for a long period of time in a sealed container or the unpleasant odor from an empty jar that has been closed and stored away in the back of a cupboard. Old ice can give an off-taste and odor to many mixed drinks, particularly those that require a generous amount of ice in their making. So, do as good hosts and experienced mixologists do: use fresh ice. It's the cheapest ingredient in any drink, so you might as well go first class.

JEAN LAFITE'S FRAPPÉ

1½ oz. brandy
1 oz. medium or dark Jamaica rum
½ oz. lemon or lime juice
1 tsp. orgeat syrup or Falernum
1 egg yolk

Mix with a generous amount of cracked ice in a blender for a few seconds until slushy and spoon into a chilled wine goblet.

JEAVONS HEAVEN

1 oz. cognac
1 oz. green Chartreuse

Mix with plenty of cracked ice in a blender for a few seconds and serve in a chilled cocktail glass.

JULY 4TH SALUTE

1 oz. cherry brandy
1 oz. white crème de cacao
1 oz. cream

Mix with cracked ice in a shaker or blender and strain into a chilled cocktail glass.

KAHLUA TOREADOR

2 oz. brandy
1 oz. Kahlua
1 egg white (for two drinks)

Mix all ingredients with cracked ice in a shaker or blender and pour into a chilled cocktail glass.

KATINKA'S PALINKA

2 oz. Zwack Barack Palinka
   apricot brandy
½ oz. lemon juice
1 tsp. sugar syrup or to taste
Club soda
Orange slice

Mix all ingredients, except club soda and orange slice, with cracked ice in a shaker or blender and pour into a chilled highball glass. Fill with club soda and garnish with orange slice.

KING'S PEG

2–3 oz. cognac
Brut champagne

Pour cognac into a chilled wine goblet with several ice cubes and fill with cold champagne.

KISS THE BOYS GOODBYE

1 oz. brandy
1 oz. sloe gin
¼ oz. lemon juice
1 egg white (for two drinks)

Mix all ingredients with cracked ice in a shaker or blender and strain into a chilled cocktail glass.

KUHIO KOOLER

½ cup crushed pineapple
½ oz. sugar syrup or to taste
2 oz. brandy
Several dashes raspberry
   syrup
Club soda
Lemon peel
Pineapple stick

Combine crushed pineapple and sugar syrup in a mixing glass and muddle fruit. Add brandy, raspberry syrup, and several ice cubes and stir well. Pour into a chilled highball glass, fill with club soda, and stir gently. Twist lemon peel over drink and drop in. Garnish with pineapple stick.

LA GRANDE CASACADE

1 oz. brandy
½ oz. parfait amour
½ oz. lemon juice
½ oz. orange juice
Several dashes Cointreau

Mix all ingredients with cracked ice in a shaker or blender and pour into a chilled cocktail glass.

LA JOLLA

1½ oz. brandy
½ oz. crème de banane
¼ oz. lemon juice
1 tsp. orange juice

Mix all ingredients with cracked ice in a shaker or blender and strain into a chilled cocktail glass.

LAKE COMO

1½ oz. brandy
¾ oz. Tuaca
Lemon peel

Combine brandy and Tuaca liqueur in a mixing glass with several ice cubes, stir well, and pour into a chilled Old Fashioned glass. Twist lemon peel over drink and drop into glass.

LALLAH ROOKH COCKTAIL No. 2

1½ oz. cognac
½ oz. Jamaica rum
¼ oz. sugar syrup
¼ oz. vanilla extract
1 tsp. heavy cream

Mix all ingredients with cracked ice in a shaker or blender and pour into a chilled Old-Fashioned glass.

LAYER CAKE

1 oz. crème de cacao
1 oz. brandy
1 oz. heavy cream
Halved maraschino cherry
   (optional)

Prechill all ingredients, including the Delmonico glass you will use to make this drink. Using a bar spoon, carefully pour each liquid ingredient into the glass in layers in the order listed. Cut a cherry in half and carefully place the cut-end down on cream so it floats on top.

LE CAGNARD

2 oz. brandy
½ oz. Amer Picon
Lemon peel
Orange peel

Combine brandy and Amer Picon in a mixing glass with several ice cubes, stir well, and pour into a chilled Old Fashioned glass. Twist lemon and orange peels over drink and drop into glass.

LIBERTY

1½ oz. calvados
¾ oz. light rum
Several dashes sugar syrup
Maraschino cherry

Mix all ingredients, except maraschino cherry, with cracked ice in a shaker or blender, strain into a chilled cocktail glass, and garnish with cherry.

LIANO

1 oz. cognac
½ oz. Galliano
½ oz. Grand Marnier

Mix with cracked ice in a shaker or blender and strain into a chilled cocktail glass.

 ## LOUDSPEAKER

1 oz. brandy
1 oz. gin
¼ oz. Cointreau
½ oz. lemon juice

Mix with cracked ice and strain into a cocktail glass.

 ## MALIBU MOCHA

1½ oz. brandy
½ oz. crème de cacao
Cola
Maraschino cherry

Pour brandy and crème de cacao over ice in a chilled Collins glass and fill with cold cola. Garnish with cherry.

 ## MARCONI WIRELESS

1½ oz. apple brandy
½ oz. sweet vermouth
Several dashes orange bitters

Mix all ingredients with cracked ice in a shaker or blender and pour into a chilled cocktail glass.

 ## MARGO MOORE

1½ oz. brandy
¾ oz. light rum
Several dashes curaçao
Bitter lemon soda

Pour brandy and rum over ice in a chilled Collins glass, add dashes of curaçao, and fill with cold bitter lemon soda. Stir gently.

MAYFAIR COCKTAIL

1 oz. cognac
1 oz. Dubonnet rouge
½ oz. lime juice
1 tsp. sugar syrup
Several dashes Angostura
   bitters
Orange peel

Mix all ingredients, except orange peel, with cracked ice in a shaker or blender and strain into a chilled cocktail glass. Twist orange peel over drink and drop into glass.

MÉDOC COCKTAIL

1½ oz. brandy
½ oz. Cordial Médoc
½ oz. lemon juice
Orange peel

Mix all ingredients, except orange peel, with cracked ice in a shaker or blender and strain into a chilled cocktail glass. Twist orange peel over drink and drop into glass.

MEMPHIS BELLE

1½ oz. brandy
¾ oz. Southern Comfort
½ oz. lemon juice
Several dashes orange bitters

Mix with cracked ice in a shaker or blender and strain into a chilled cocktail glass.

MERION'S CRICKET

2 oz. apricot brandy
½ oz. sloe gin
½ oz. lime juice

Mix all ingredients with cracked ice in a shaker or blender and pour into a chilled cocktail glass.

MERRY WIDOW No. 2

1½ oz. cherry brandy
1 oz. maraschino liqueur
Maraschino cherry

Mix all ingredients, except maraschino cherry, with cracked ice in a shaker or blender. Strain into a chilled cocktail glass and garnish with cherry.

MIKADO

1½ oz. brandy
Several dashes curaçao
Several dashes crème de noyaux
Several dashes orgeat syrup
Several dashes Angostura bitters

Mix all ingredients with cracked ice in a shaker or blender and pour into a chilled cocktail glass.

MONMOUTH PARK

1 oz. calvados
½ oz. white port
½ oz. apricot brandy
½ oz. lemon juice
Orange slice

Mix all ingredients, except orange slice, with cracked ice in a shaker or blender and strain into a chilled cocktail glass. Garnish with orange slice.

THE MOOCH

2 oz. apricot brandy
6 oz. lemon-lime soda
Lemon twist

Mix brandy and soda with ice cubes in a chilled highball glass. Twist lemon peel over drink and drop into glass.

MOONRAKER

1½ applejack or calvados
¾ oz. light rum
½ oz. lime juice
½ oz. orgeat syrup or Falernum to taste
Apple slice

Mix all ingredients, except apple slice, with cracked ice in a shaker or blender and pour into a chilled Squall glass. Garnish with apple slice.

MONTPARNASSE

½ oz. cognac
1 tsp. kirsch
Dash orange bitters
1 tsp. orgeat syrup
Brut champagne
¼ cup lemon or orange ice

Mix cognac, kirsch, bitters, and syrup with cracked ice in a shaker or blender and strain into a chilled Squall or large tulip glass. Fill almost to the brim with cold champagne and top with lemon or orange ice float.

 **MOON RIVER**

1½ oz. brandy
½ oz. peppermint schnapps
Lemon-lime soda
Dash grenadine

Pour brandy and schnapps over ice in a chilled Collins glass, fill with cold soda, and stir gently. Top with a dash of grenadine.

MORNING

1 oz. brandy
1 oz. dry vermouth
Several dashes Pernod
Several dashes curaçao
Several dashes maraschino
    liqueur

Several dashes orange bitters
Maraschino cherry

Mix all ingredients, except maraschino cherry, with cracked ice in a shaker or blender, pour into a chilled Old Fashioned glass, and garnish with cherry.

MOTHER SHERMAN

1½ oz. apricot brandy
1 oz. orange juice
Several dashes orange bitters

Mix all ingredients with cracked ice in a shaker or blender and pour into a chilled cocktail glass.

MUSCATEL FLIP

2 oz. brandy
4 oz. muscatel wine
¼ oz. heavy cream
1 egg
1 tsp. sugar syrup or to taste
Ground nutmeg

Mix all ingredients, except nutmeg, with cracked ice in a blender until smooth. Serve in chilled parfait glass and sprinkle with nutmeg.

NEWTON'S GRAVITY APPLE

1½ oz. apple brandy
½ oz. curaçao or triple sec
Several dashes Angostura
    bitters

Mix all ingredients with cracked ice in a shaker or blender and strain into a chilled cocktail glass.

NINE-PICK

1 oz. brandy
1 oz. Pernod
1 oz. Cointreau
1 egg yolk

Mix all ingredients with cracked ice in a shaker or blender and pour into a chilled Delmonico glass.

NORMANDY COLLINS

2 oz. calvados
½ oz. lemon juice
1 tsp. sugar syrup
1 tsp. cream
1 egg white (for two drinks)
Club soda
Lime slice
Maraschino cherry

Mix all ingredients, except club soda, lime slice, and maraschino cherry, with cracked ice in a shaker or blender and pour into a chilled Collins glass. Fill with club soda, stir gently, and garnish with lime slice and cherry.

NORMANDY GOLD

1 oz. calvados
1 oz. gin
1 oz. apricot liqueur
1 oz. orange juice
Several dashes grenadine

Mix with cracked ice in a shaker or blender and strain into a chilled cocktail glass.

OAK ROOM SPECIAL

1 oz. cherry brandy
1 oz. brandy
1 oz. crème de cacao
1 egg white (for two drinks)

Mix all ingredients with cracked ice in a shaker or blender and strain into a chilled cocktail glass.

ODD McINTYRE

1 oz. brandy
1 oz. Cointreau or triple sec
1 oz. Lillet blanc
½ oz. lemon juice

Mix with cracked ice in a shaker or blender and strain into a chilled cocktail glass.

OLYMPIC

1 oz. brandy
1 oz. curaçao
1 oz. orange juice

Mix all ingredients with cracked ice in a shaker or blender and pour into a chilled cocktail glass.

OOM PAUL

1 oz. calvados or applejack
1 oz. Dubonnet rouge
Several dashes Angostura
  bitters

Mix all ingredients with cracked ice in a shaker or blender and pour into a chilled cocktail glass.

ORIENTA POINT

1 oz. brandy
1 oz. gin
Several dashes dry vermouth
Green olive

Mix all ingredients, except green olive, with cracked ice in a shaker or blender, strain into a chilled cocktail glass, and garnish with olive.

PANCHO VILLA No. 1

1 oz. brandy
1 oz. white or gold tequila
1 oz. light rum
1 tsp. cherry brandy or cherry
  liqueur
4 oz. pineapple juice

Mix all ingredients with cracked ice in a shaker or blender and pour into a chilled wine goblet.

PAVILION CAPRICE COOLER

½ oz. honey
4 oz. grapefruit juice,
  unsweetened
½ oz. lemon juice
1½ oz. peach brandy
1 egg white (for two drinks)

Blend honey, grapefruit juice, and lemon juice with a barspoon until honey is dissolved. Pour mixture into a blender with cracked ice and add brandy and egg white and blend until smooth. Serve in a chilled Squall glass or brandy snifter.

PEACH FUZZ

1½ oz. peach brandy
½ oz. white crème de cacao
1 oz. heavy cream
1 tsp. apple schnapps

Mix all ingredients, except apple schnapps, with cracked ice in a shaker or blender and pour into a chilled cocktail glass. Top with a float of apple schnapps.

PEACHTREE SLING

1½ oz. brandy
¾ oz. peach brandy
½ oz. lemon juice
¼ oz. sugar syrup or to taste
Club soda
Brandied or fresh peach slice
1 tsp. peach liqueur

Mix all ingredients, except soda, peach slice, and peach liqueur, with cracked ice in a shaker or blender and pour into a chilled Collins glass. Fill with cold club soda and garnish with peach slice. Top off with peach liqueur float.

PEAR BRANDY FIZZ

1½ oz. pear brandy
1 tsp. lime juice
Club soda
Lemon peel
Pear strips (sliced lengthwise)

Pour brandy and lime juice in a chilled highball glass with several ice cubes, fill with club soda, and stir gently. Twist lemon peel over drink and drop into glass. Garnish with pear strips.

PETER PIPER'S PINEAPPLE POP

1½ oz. apple brandy
½ oz. framboise
½ oz. pineapple juice
Lemon-lime soda
Pineapple stick

Mix all ingredients, except soda and pineapple stick, with cracked ice in a shaker or blender and pour into a chilled Collins glass. Fill with cold lemon-lime soda and garnish with pineapple stick.

PHILADELPHIA SCOTSMAN

1 oz. apple brandy
1 oz. port
1 oz. orange juice
Club soda

Mix all ingredients except club soda with cracked ice in a shaker or blender and pour into a chilled highball glass. Fill with club soda and stir gently.

PHOEBE SNOW

1½ oz. cognac
1½ oz. Dubonnet rouge
Dash Pernod

Mix all ingredients with cracked ice in a shaker or blender and strain into a chilled cocktail glass.

PHOEBE'S SNOW MIST

1 oz. cognac
1 oz. Dubonnet rouge
¼ oz. Pernod
1 egg white (for two drinks)
Lemon peel

Mix all ingredients, except lemon peel, with cracked ice in a shaker or blender and pour into a chilled Old Fashioned glass. Twist lemon peel over drink and drop into glass.

PINK WHISKERS

1 oz. apricot brandy
½ oz. dry vermouth
1 oz. orange juice
1 tsp. grenadine
Several dashes white crème de menthe
1 oz. port

Mix all ingredients, except port, with cracked ice in a shaker or blender and pour into a chilled cocktail glass. Top with a port float.

PISCO PUNCH

3 oz. Pisco
1 tsp. lime juice
1 tsp. pineapple juice
Several pineapple chunks

Mix all ingredients with plenty of cracked ice until smooth and pour into a chilled Squall glass or wine glass.

PISCO SOUR

2 oz. Pisco
½ oz. lemon juice
½ oz. sugar syrup
1 egg white (for two drinks)
Several dashes Angostura bitters

Mix all ingredients, except Angostura bitters, with cracked ice in a shaker or blender and strain into a chilled Whiskey Sour glass. Top with several dashes Angostura bitters.

PLACE VENDOME

1 oz. gin
1 oz. Cointreau
1 oz. apricot brandy

Mix with cracked ice in a shaker or blender and strain into a chilled cocktail glass.

POLONAISE

1½ oz. brandy
½ oz. blackberry brandy or blackberry liqueur
½ oz. dry sherry
Dash lemon juice

Mix all ingredients with cracked ice in a shaker or blender and pour into a chilled Old Fashioned glass.

POOP DECK

1 oz. blackberry brandy
½ oz. brandy
½ oz. port

Mix all ingredients with cracked ice in a shaker or blender and pour into a chilled cocktail glass.

PORT BEAM

1 oz. brandy
1 oz. ruby port
½ oz. lemon juice
¼ oz. maraschino liqueur
Orange slice

Mix all ingredients, except orange slice, with cracked ice in a shaker or blender, pour into a chilled cocktail glass, and garnish with orange slice.

PRAIRIE OYSTER

1 egg
1½ oz. brandy
Several dashes Worcestershire sauce
Dash cayenne powder
Dash Tabasco sauce
Dash celery salt

Separate egg and carefully place egg yolk, unbroken, in a Delmonico glass. Add all other ingredients and drink all together with egg yolk in a single swallow.

PRINCE ALBERT'S SALUTE

2 oz. cognac
2 oz. kummel

Swirl cognac and kummel in a brandy snifter until well blended. Add ice cubes, if you wish.

PRINCE OF WALES

1 oz. brandy
1 oz. Madeira
¼ oz. curaçao
Several dashes Angostura
  bitters
Champagne
Orange slice

Mix all ingredients, except
champagne and orange slice, with
cracked ice in a shaker or
blender and pour into a chilled
Squall glass or wine goblet.
Fill with champagne, stir gently,
and garnish with orange slice.

PRINCESS MARY'S PRIDE

1½ oz. calvados
¾ oz. Dubonnet rouge
½ oz. dry vermouth

Mix all ingredients with cracked
ice in a shaker or blender and
pour into a chilled cocktail
glass.

QUAKER

1½ oz. brandy
1 oz. light rum
½ oz. lemon juice
½ oz. raspberry syrup
Lemon peel

Mix all ingredients, except
lemon peel, with cracked ice in a
shaker or blender and strain
into a chilled cocktail glass. Twist
lemon peel over drink and drop
into glass.

RADNOR HUNT

1½ oz. mirabelle
1 oz. orange juice
½ oz. lemon juice
1 tsp. sugar syrup

Mix all ingredients with cracked
ice in a shaker or blender and
pour into a chilled stirrup cup
or cocktail glass.

RAFFAELLO

½ oz. Pisco
½ oz. Galliano
½ oz. sweet vermouth
Dash Angostura bitters
Dash Grand Marnier

Mix with cracked ice in a
shaker or blender and serve on
the rocks in an Old Fashioned
glass.

RASPBERRY RICKEY

1½ oz. framboise
½ oz. lime juice
1 tsp. sugar syrup or to taste
Club soda
6 fresh raspberries

Mix all ingredients, except raspberries and club soda, with cracked ice in a shaker or blender and strain into a chilled Squall or large tulip glass. Fill with cold club soda, add ice cubes if necessary, and garnish with raspberries.

RITTENHOUSE SQUARE

1½ oz. cognac
1 oz. curaçao
½ oz. anisette
Brandied cherry

Mix all ingredients, except brandied cherry, with cracked ice in a shaker or blender, strain into a chilled Old Fashioned glass, and garnish with cherry.

ROYAL SMILE

2 oz. applejack
1 oz. gin
½ oz. lemon juice
1 tsp. grenadine

Mix with cracked ice in a shaker or blender and strain into a chilled cocktail glass.

RUSH STREET

1½ oz. brandy
½ Mandarine Napoleon
½ oz. lemon juice
Several dashes orgeat or
  sugar syrup

Mix with cracked ice in a shaker or blender and strain into a chilled cocktail glass.

SADDLE RIVER SECRET

2 oz. applejack
½ oz. triple sec
1 oz. apple juice
1 oz. cranberry juice
½ oz. lime or lemon juice
½ tsp. maple syrup or sugar
  syrup

Apple or lemon slice
½ tsp. 151-proof Demerara
  rum

Mix all ingredients, except fruit slice and rum, with cracked ice in a shaker or blender and pour into chilled Squall glass or wine goblet. Garnish with fruit slice and top with rum float.

 **SARATOGA**

2 oz. brandy
½ tsp. maraschino liqueur
1 oz. crushed pineapple or
   pineapple juice
Several dashes Angostura
   bitters

Mix all ingredients with cracked
ice in a blender and strain into a
chilled cocktail glass.

SAVOY HOTEL

1 oz. crème de cacao
1 oz. Benedictine
1 oz. cognac

Pour each ingredient carefully
into a chilled sherry glass using
the back of a barspoon so that
each ingredient floats upon the
one beneath it.

 SAVOY TANGO

1½ oz. apple brandy
1 oz. sloe gin

Combine all ingredients in a
mixing glass with several ice
cubes and stir well. Strain into
a chilled cocktail glass.

SHARKY PUNCH

2 oz. calvados
½ oz. rye whiskey
1 tsp. sugar syrup
Club soda

Mix all ingredients, except club
soda, with cracked ice in a shaker
or blender and pour into a
chilled Old Fashioned glass. Fill
with cold club soda and stir
gently.

 SIDECAR

1½ oz. brandy
¾ oz. curaçao or triple sec
½ oz. lemon juice

Mix all ingredients with cracked
ice in a shaker or blender and
strain into a chilled cocktail
glass.

SINK OR SWIM

1½ oz. brandy
½ oz. sweet vermouth
Several dashes Angostura
   bitters

Mix all ingredients with cracked
ice in a shaker or blender and
strain into a chilled cocktail
glass.

SIR RIDGEWAY KNIGHT

1 oz. brandy
¾ oz. yellow Chartreuse
¾ oz. triple sec
Several dashes Angostura
  bitters

Mix with cracked ice in a
shaker or blender and strain into
a chilled cocktail glass.

SIR WALTER RALEIGH

1½ oz. brandy
¾ oz. light rum
1 tsp. curaçao
1 tsp. lime juice
1 tsp. grenadine

Mix all ingredients with cracked
ice in a shaker or blender and
pour into a chilled cocktail
glass.

SLEDGE HAMMER

1 oz. brandy
1 oz. applejack
1 oz. dark Jamaica rum
Several dashes Pernod

Mix all ingredients with cracked
ice in a shaker or blender and
pour into a chilled cocktail
glass.

SLEEPY HEAD

3 oz. brandy
Orange peel
4–5 mint leaves
Ginger ale

Pour brandy into a chilled highball glass with ice cubes. Twist
orange peel over drink and
drop into glass. Add mint leaves,
which are slightly bruised, and
fill with cold ginger ale. Stir
gently.

SLIVOVITZ FIZZ

2 oz. slivovitz (plum brandy)
½ oz. lime juice
1 tsp. sugar syrup
Club soda
Plum slice

Mix brandy, lime juice, and
sugar with cracked ice in a shaker
or blender and pour into a
chilled highball glass. Add more
ice if necessary and fill with
cold club soda. Garnish with plum
slice.

SLOE BRANDY

2 oz. brandy
½ oz. sloe gin
1 tsp. lemon juice

Mix all ingredients with cracked ice in a shaker or blender and strain into a chilled cocktail glass.

SLOPPY JOE'S No. 2

1 oz. brandy
1 oz. port
1 oz. pineapple juice
½ tsp. triple sec
½ tsp. grenadine

Mix with cracked ice in a shaker or blender and strain into a chilled cocktail glass.

SOUTH PACIFIC

1½ oz. brandy
1 oz. gin or vodka
3 oz. grapefruit, pineapple, or orange juice
½ oz. lemon juice

Mix all ingredients with cracked ice in a shaker or blender and strain into a chilled Whiskey Sour glass.

SOUTHERN CROSS

1½ oz. brandy
½ oz. triple sec
Tonic water
Lime wedge

Pour brandy and triple sec over ice into a chilled Collins glass and fill with cold tonic water. Garnish with lime wedge.

SOUTH STREET SEAPORT

1 oz. brandy
1 oz. Madeira
¼ oz. dry vermouth
Lemon peel

Mix all ingredients, except lemon peel, with cracked ice in a shaker or blender and pour into a chilled Old Fashioned glass. Twist lemon peel over drink and drop into glass.

SPECIAL ROUGH

1½ oz. apple brandy
1½ oz. brandy
Several dashes Pernod

Mix all ingredients with cracked ice in a shaker or blender and pour into a chilled cocktail glass.

STINGER

1½ oz. brandy
1½ oz. white crème de menthe

Mix all ingredients with cracked ice in a shaker or blender and strain into a chilled cocktail glass.

STONE FENCE

2–3 oz. applejack
Several dashes Angostura bitters
Sweet apple cider

Pour applejack and bitters over ice cubes in a double Old Fashioned glass and fill with cold cider.

STRAWBERRY ROAN

2 oz. brandy
½ oz. lemon juice
½ oz. sugar syrup
1 tsp. strawberry liqueur

Mix all ingredients with cracked ice in a shaker or blender and strain into a chilled cocktail glass.

TANTALUS

1 oz. brandy
1 oz. lemon juice
1 oz. Forbidden Fruit

Mix all ingredients with cracked ice in a shaker or blender and pour into a chilled cocktail glass.

THE WHIP

1½ oz. brandy
¾ oz. sweet vermouth
¾ oz. dry vermouth
½ tsp. curaçao
Several dashes Pernod

Mix all ingredients with cracked ice in a shaker or blender and pour into a chilled cocktail glass.

333

1½ oz. calvados
1½ oz. Cointreau
1½ oz. grapefruit juice

Mix with cracked ice in a shaker or blender and strain into a chilled cocktail glass.

TORPEDO

1½ oz. calvados
¾ oz. brandy
Dash gin

Mix all ingredients with cracked ice in a shaker or blender and pour into a chilled cocktail glass.

TULIP

1 oz. apple brandy
¾ oz. apricot brandy
½ oz. sweet vermouth
½ oz. lemon juice

Mix all ingredients with cracked ice in a shaker or blender and pour into a chilled cocktail glass.

TUXEDO PARK

1½ oz. apple brandy
½ oz. white crème de menthe
Several dashes Pernod

Mix all ingredients with cracked ice in a shaker or blender and pour into a chilled brandy snifter.

VALENCIA

2 oz. apricot brandy
1 oz. orange juice
Several dashes orange bitters
Champagne (optional)

Mix all ingredients with cracked ice in a shaker or blender and pour into a chilled cocktail glass.
Note: Some recipes call for chilled champagne, in which case use a large tulip glass or a wine goblet.

VANITY FAIR

1½ oz. applejack
½ oz. cherry brandy
½ oz. maraschino liqueur
1 tsp. amaretto or crème de noyaux

Mix all ingredients, except amaretto, with cracked ice in a shaker or blender and serve in a chilled cocktail glass. Top with a float of amaretto or crème de noyaux.

VIA VENETO

1½ oz. brandy
½ oz. sambuca
½ oz. lemon juice
1 tsp. sugar syrup
1 egg white (for two drinks)

Mix all ingredients with cracked ice in a shaker or blender and pour into a chilled Old Fashioned glass.

WASHINGTON

1½ oz. brandy
1 oz. dry vermouth
½ tsp. sugar syrup
Several dashes Angostura
  bitters

Mix all ingredients with cracked
ice in a shaker or blender and
strain into a chilled cocktail
glass.

WATERBURY

2 oz. cognac
½ oz. lemon juice
1 tsp. sugar syrup
1 egg white (for two drinks)
Several dashes grenadine

Mix all ingredients with cracked
ice in a shaker or blender and
pour into a chilled cocktail
glass.

WEEP NO MORE

1½ oz. cognac
1½ oz. Dubonnet rouge
1½ oz. lime juice
Dash maraschino liqueur

Mix all ingredients with cracked
ice in a shaker or blender and
strain into a chilled cocktail
glass.

WHITEHALL CLUB

1 oz. brandy
½ oz. gin
½ oz. Grand Marnier
2 oz. orange juice
1 oz. lemon juice

½ oz. sugar syrup

Mix all ingredients with cracked
ice in a shaker or blender and
strain into a chilled parfait
glass.

WHITE WAY

1 oz. cognac
1 oz. anisette
1 oz. Pernod

Combine all ingredients in a
mixing glass with ice cubes and
strain into a chilled cocktail
glass.

WIDOW'S KISS

1 oz. applejack
½ oz. Benedictine
½ oz. yellow Chartreuse
Dash Angostura bitters
Fresh strawberry (optional)

Mix all ingredients, except
strawberry, with cracked ice in a
shaker or blender, strain into
a chilled cocktail glass, and
garnish with strawberry, if you
wish.

WILLAWA

1½ oz. brandy
¾ oz. Galliano
¾ oz. cherry brandy
¾ oz. cream
Ground nutmeg

Mix all ingredients, except nutmeg, with cracked ice in a shaker or blender and strain into a chilled cocktail glass.

YELLOW PARROT

1 oz. brandy
1 oz. Pernod
1 oz. yellow Chartreuse

Mix all ingredients with cracked ice in a shaker or blender and pour into a chilled cocktail glass.

YOKOHAMA MAMA

1½ oz. brandy
½ oz. melon liqueur
Several dashes amaretto

Mix with cracked ice in a shaker or blender and strain into a chilled cocktail glass.

ZACK IS BACK WITH THE ZWACK

2 oz. Zwack's Barack Palinka apricot brandy
Dash dry vermouth or to taste
1–2 pepperoncini or other type of medium-hot pepper

Blend brandy and vermouth in a small pitcher or mixing glass with plenty of ice and stir briskly. Pour into a chilled cocktail glass and garnish with pepperoncini or medium-hot pepper.

BOURBON, BLENDS, AND CANADIAN WHISKY

Did you ever hear of Captain Wattle?
He was all for love
and a little for the bottle.

—Anonymous

Bourbon was not the first spirit distilled in the New World, but its widespread popularity has made it the most famous American whiskey. Over the years it has won recognition and respect as a true American "original" along with the turkey, baseball, hot dogs, apple pie, and, of course, corn, which made bourbon possible. During Colonial times, rum, distilled from molasses in New England, was the big drink, mainly because it was readily available and cheap. Brandy, port, and Madeira were popular with the affluent, but beyond the means of ordinary people, since they had to be imported from Europe at great cost.

Early in the eighteenth century Scotch, Irish, and Dutch settlers began making whiskey in various parts of Maryland, Virginia, and Pennsylvania, with the result that rye and barley became important cash crops. Farmers in outlying areas soon discovered that while a horse could carry only four bushels of grain to market, it could carry two kegs of whiskey—which represented two dozen bushels of grain after its conversion into spirits. Consequently, distilling became an important part of farming. In the early days of the republic it was estimated that there were over five thousand stills operating in western Pennsylvania alone.

This tremendous whiskey output presented a tempting tax source to Alexander Hamilton, the secretary of the treasury, who was hard-pressed to pay off the debts incurred by the government when financing the American Revolution. As a result, in 1791 an excise tax was placed on whiskey production. The distiller-farmers—an independent breed—didn't like it and ruffled the feathers of more than a few tax collectors (with a little tar thrown in for good measure). President George Washington responded by sending in the militia in 1794 to show the farmers that, then as now, Uncle Sam has the last word in tax matters. The government, as every American history student learns, quickly put down the Whiskey Rebellion. Nary a shot was fired, and the principle of the federal government's right to tax the products of American enterprise was firmly established.

To evade the long arm of the tax collector, many farmers pushed west into Indian territory, and it was in southern Indiana and over the Appalachians in the bluegrass country of Kentucky that they found a haven. More important was the wonderful water supply, essential to distilling good whiskey. This was provided by a unique geological phenomenon: a vast limestone mantel that runs underground through parts of Indiana and Kentucky. The water that passes through this limestone layer is naturally filtered, and is, as they say, "as sweet as a baby's kiss." Add to this an abundance of corn (it was more plentiful than rye), and all the elements for a truly fine native whiskey were in place.

Evan Williams of Louisville is generally credited as being the first distiller in Kentucky who plied his trade fulltime, not just as a sideline. His whiskey, apparently, was not held in high esteem, however, for in 1783 he was reprimanded by the Louisville town council for bringing whiskey to an official meeting. And not only that, he received a further citation for the poor quality of the whiskey that he brought to the meeting!

Williams's whiskey probably was no worse than many. Distilling was not a precise art on the American frontier and was looked upon more as a means of preserving the harvest than a method of making a fine-flavored, aged, and mellow "sippin' whiskey." Much of the whiskey was produced haphazardly, and quality control was undreamed of in those early times. The beneficial effects of keeping spirits in wooden casks to age was well-known, but most producers were impatient to get their whiskey to market and so the "aging process" was determined by how long it took a pack horse to make the trip to town.

In the year 1789, or thereabouts, the Rev. Elijah Craig, a Baptist minister and sometime distiller, made an interesting discovery. He aged some corn whiskey in a charred oak barrel instead of the usual wooden container, which was uncharred. The resulting whiskey was not only smoother and mellower, but possessed a different flavor that was far superior to that made by traditional methods. It soon became apparent that a new name was needed for the new whiskey. The Reverend Craig lived in Georgetown, Kentucky, and since wines and spirits are frequently named for their places of origin, Georgetown was, no doubt, considered—and promptly discarded. The naming of a new product after a town named for an English monarch was not considered astute marketing, especially in those days. Why not name the new whiskey after the county in which Georgetown was located? A splendid idea. Besides, the county was named for another royal family—in France—who had aided the American cause during the Revolution. Thus, the new spirit became known far and wide as *bourbon*.

Although aging in charred oak was a boon to the finished product, other primitive methods for making distilled spirits remained, as illustrated by the manner in which alcoholic content was determined or "proved." Whiskey was mixed with gunpowder in equal proportions and ignited. If the mixture burned with a wavering yellow flame, it was too low in alcohol. If it burned rapidly with a bright blue flame, it was too strong. What was wanted was a blue flame that burned steadily, indicating to the still man that the whiskey was about 50 percent alcohol. That is, 100 proof. This is the origin of the term "proof" used to this day to indicate alcoholic content.

Today bourbon is available in varying strengths as a straight whiskey ranging from 80 to 100 proof and slightly over; as a *blend* of straight whiskies; as a sweet- or sour-mash bourbon; as a Kentucky or Tennessee bourbon; and as a regular or a bottled-in-bond whiskey. If all this seems somewhat confusing, here is a simplified explanation for the bourbon buyer:

Straight bourbon is the most common form in which this type of whiskey is marketed. There are also blended bourbons that, unlike straight bourbons, are whiskies from various distilleries, made at different times. They are labeled "blended bourbon" as opposed to "straight bourbon," which must be made during the same distilling period and at the same distillery. In a blend, by law, the age given must be that of the youngest whiskey used.

Bourbon, in whatever form, must, according to federal law, be made of a grain formula containing at least 51 percent corn (other grains usually used are barley and rye) and aged in new charred oak barrels. Bourbon can be made anywhere in the U.S., but most of it, perhaps as much as 80 percent, comes from Kentucky. Tennessee whiskey, often called "Tennessee bourbon," is straight whiskey that may be made from a mash containing at least 51 percent corn *or any other grain*. It is filtered through charcoal to give it its characteristic flavor. Some Tennessee whiskies have been promoted with a good deal of homespun kitsch, but the fact is, if it is a straight whiskey, it cannot legally contain any additives other than water. So except for the mash formula and the length of time it is aged in wood, Tennessee bourbon is like any other straight whiskey. Fine straight whiskies are produced from other grains besides corn, rye being the classic example because it was one of the first whiskeys produced in the New World. Rye whiskey has a distinctive, full-bodied rye flavor and is not to be confused with ordinary blended whiskies, which for many years in the Northeastern United States were called "ryes." True to their American Colonial roots, fine straight rye whiskies are still produced in parts of Pennsylvania and Maryland.

There seems to be much confusion in many people's minds about the terms "sour mash" and "sweet mash," the former being heavily promoted to bourbon drinkers as part of the mystique of the master distiller who employs sour mash in some arcane way to make the "real thing." These terms refer to the yeasting process. They have nothing to do with a sweet or sour taste in the finished product. Sour mash is the preferred yeasting process for making bourbon. It means that a certain proportion of the mash used must contain stillage or spent liquids (sans alcohol) that remain from the previous distillation. This is mixed with fresh mash and fermented for the new batch. Sweet mash contains no stillage from the previous distillation. In other words, it is made from scratch, with nothing remaining from the old batch. It is doubtful that anyone but a professional spirits blender could tell whether a whiskey was made with sweet or sour mash.

Many people are under the impression that the term "bottled-in-bond" is a guarantee of quality. It is not. The Bottled-in-Bond Act passed by Congress in the 1890s allowed distillers to bottle certain distilled spirits without the necessity of paying the Internal Revenue excise taxes until the product was withdrawn from the warehouse to be sold. Certain conditions prevailed. Only straight whiskies could qualify, meaning that they had to be distilled at one location, be 100 proof in strength, and be aged four years in wood. The whiskey was stored in a bonded warehouse under U.S. Treasury Department custody. There is no U.S. government certification, actual or implied, of the quality of the spirits held in bond. A poor whiskey placed in bond will undergo only a cosmetic transformation (on the label of the bottle), meaning it will change from a poor whiskey to a bonded poor whiskey.

If you count all the straight and blended bourbons on the market and add in all the private labels, it is estimated that there are about five hundred brands available to the consumer. Reading whiskey labels doesn't give the buyer a clue as to what is inside the bottle except that it is whiskey. The best way to get to know bourbon is to indulge in a program of taste testing. A good way to begin is to mix a tot of whiskey with an equal amount of water (good spring water without a pronounced mineral taste) and sample it like the professional tasters do. When you find a bourbon that you like above all the rest, stick with it.

A BOURBON CLASSIC

The most famous of the renowned classic bourbon drinks is unquestionably the Mint Julep. There are as many recipes as there are bartenders, and countless heated arguments have ensued over which recipe, hallowed by tradition and the benediction of time, will best convey—with authenticity, integrity, and professionalism—the blessings of flavor, bouquet, and well-being that are the hallmarks of a fine, aged bourbon.

Here is a recipe that was sent by an acquaintance who prides himself on the making of a good Mint Julep:

A REAL, HONEST-TO-GOD MINT JULEP

Practically everybody has heard of a Mint Julep, but few mixologists know how to concoct one properly. Mint Juleps originated in Williamsburg, Virginia, back in the seventeenth century, and the original Mint Julep has never been bettered. Here it is:

Break, and drop into a silver or pewter tankard with handle, 15 or 20 (depending on size of leaves) fresh, I repeat, fresh mint leaves. Add a scant teaspoon of granulated sugar and two tablespoons of water. Then muddle the leaves until well crushed and sugar is dissolved. Fill tankard with finely crushed ice. Pour (don't measure) enough bourbon into tankard to come to about an inch below rim. After thoroughly stirring, add crushed ice to just below rim and float thereon a teaspoon of Barbados rum. Place three or four sprigs of mint into mixture, allowing mint to protrude several inches above rim. When imbibing, shove your nose into mint and sniff and quaff at the same time. Oh boy! My mouth is watering.

I've found that the ideal main ingredient in the julep is a 90 or 100 proof, sour-mash Kentucky bourbon. Ezra Brooks is just right, and I recommend it highly. Light Mount Gay rum makes an excellent float.

If you are expecting visitors, whip up enough juleps and place them in freezer for not more than a half hour before serving. Or, if you are expecting quite a few guests, I suggest that you prepare beforehand, a mash of muddled mint leaves, sugar, and water, always adhering strictly to the proportions in the recipe. Also, save time by readying sprigs of mint to stick their noses in. If you insist on starting with a frosted tankard, all right. Personally, I can never wait for a tankard to frost, and actually it doesn't enhance the taste of the nectar one whit.

I wish to God there'd been mint on Parris Island—and bourbon.

Sincerely,
Ben Finney

BOURBON

AMALFI COCKTAIL

1½ oz. bourbon
1 oz. lemon juice
½ oz. Galliano
1 tsp. orgeat syrup
Club soda

Mix all ingredients, except club soda, in a shaker or blender with cracked ice. Pour into a chilled Collins glass. Fill with club soda.

ANCHORS AWEIGH

1 oz. bourbon
2 tsp. triple sec
2 tsp. peach brandy
2 tsp. maraschino liqueur
2 tbsp. heavy cream

Several drops of maraschino cherry juice

Mix all ingredients with cracked ice in a shaker or blender. Pour into a chilled Old Fashioned glass.

BANK HOLIDAY

½ oz. bourbon
½ oz. Galliano
½ oz. crème de cacao
½ oz. brandy
1–2 oz. sweet cream

Mix all ingredients with cracked ice in a shaker or blender and strain into a chilled cocktail glass.

BEEF AND BOURBON

1½ oz. bourbon
4 oz. beef consommé or bouillon
Juice of ½ lemon
Several dashes Worcester-shire sauce

Pinch celery seed or celery salt
Cucumber sticks (optional)

Stir all ingredients, except cucumber, with ice in a double Old Fashioned glass and garnish with cucumber sticks.

BISCAYNE MANHATTAN

1½ oz. bourbon
½ oz. sweet vermouth
2 oz. orange juice
Several dashes yellow
    Chartreuse
Orange slice

Mix all ingredients, except orange slice, with cracked ice in a shaker or blender, strain, and serve in a chilled cocktail glass. Garnish with orange slice.

BLIZZARD

3 oz. bourbon
1 oz. cranberry juice
1 tbsp. lemon juice
2 tbsp. sugar syrup

Mix all ingredients with plenty of cracked ice in a shaker or blender until drink is frosty. Serve in a chilled highball glass.

 ## BLUE GRASS BLUES

1 oz. bourbon
1 oz. dry vermouth
Several dashes Angostura
    bitters
Several dashes of blue
    curaçao
Lemon peel

Mix all ingredients, except lemon peel, in a shaker or blender with cracked ice. Serve in a chilled Old Fashioned glass. Twist the lemon peel over the drink and drop in.

 ## BLUE GRASS COCKTAIL

1½ oz. bourbon
1 oz. pineapple juice
1 oz. lemon juice
1 tsp. maraschino liqueur

Mix all ingredients with cracked ice in a shaker or blender. Strain into a chilled cocktail glass.

BOURBON A LA CRÈME

2 oz. bourbon
1 oz. dark crème de cacao
Several vanilla beans

Combine all ingredients in a

shaker or blender with cracked ice and chill in the refrigerator for one hour. When ready, mix well and strain into a chilled cocktail glass.

BOURBON BRANCA

2 oz. bourbon
1 tsp. Fernet Branca
Lemon twist (optional)

Stir bourbon and Fernet Branca with cracked ice in a chilled Old Fashioned glass. If you wish, add a twist of lemon.

BOURBON CARDINAL

2 oz. 100-proof bourbon
1 oz. grapefruit juice
1 oz. cranberry juice
½ oz. lemon juice
2 tsp. sugar or sugar syrup to taste

Generous dash maraschino cherry juice
2 maraschino cherries

Mix all ingredients with cracked ice in blender and serve in a chilled goblet.

 BOURBON COBBLER

1½ oz. bourbon
1 oz. Southern Comfort
1 tsp. peach-flavored brandy
2 tsp. lemon juice
1 tsp. sugar syrup
Club soda
Peach slice

Mix all ingredients, except soda and peach slice, with cracked ice in a shaker or blender. Pour into a chilled highball glass, add ice cubes, fill with soda, and decorate with peach slice.

 BOURBON COLLINS No. 1

1½ oz. bourbon
½ oz. lime juice
1 tsp. sugar syrup or to taste
Club soda
Lime peel (optional)

Mix the bourbon and lime juice with cracked ice in a shaker or blender. Pour into a chilled 12-oz. Collins glass and fill with club soda. If you wish, twist the lime peel and drop into the drink

 BOURBON COLLINS No. 2

2 oz. 100-proof bourbon
½ oz. lemon juice
1 tsp. sugar syrup or to taste
Several dashes of Peychaud's bitters
Club soda
Lemon slice (optional)

Mix all ingredients, except soda and lemon slice, with cracked ice in a shaker or blender. Pour into a chilled highball glass and fill with club soda. Decorate with a lemon slice, if you wish.

BOURBON COOLER

3 oz. bourbon
½ oz. grenadine
1 tsp. sugar syrup or to taste
Several dashes peppermint
    schnapps
Several dashes orange bit-
    ters (optional)
Club soda
Pineapple stick

Orange slice
Maraschino cherry

Mix all ingredients, except
soda, pineapple, orange slice,
and cherry, in a blender or
shaker with cracked ice. Pour
into a chilled, tall Collins glass
and fill with club soda. Garnish
with fruit.

BOURBON CURE

2 oz. bourbon
1 oz. Dubonnet Blanc
1 tsp. Vieille Cure
Orange peel

Mix all ingredients, except the
orange peel, with cracked ice in
a shaker or blender. Pour into
a chilled Old Fashioned glass.
Twist the orange peel over the
drink and drop in.

BOURBON DAISY

1½ oz. bourbon
½ oz. lemon juice
1 tsp. grenadine
Club soda
1 tsp. Southern Comfort
Orange slice
Pineapple stick

Mix the bourbon, lemon juice,
and grenadine with cracked ice
in a shaker or blender. Pour
into a chilled highball glass and
fill with club soda. Float Southern Comfort on top. Garnish with
an orange slice and pineapple
stick.

BOURBON MILK PUNCH

1½ oz. bourbon
3 oz. milk or half-and-half
1 tsp. honey or sugar syrup
Dash vanilla extract
Nutmeg, grated

Mix all ingredients, except the
nutmeg, in a shaker or blender
with cracked ice. Pour into a
chilled Old Fashioned glass.
Sprinkle with nutmeg.

BOURBON ROSE No. 1

1½ oz. bourbon
1 oz. triple sec
4 oz. orange juice
Grenadine

Mix all ingredients, except
grenadine, with cracked ice in a
shaker or blender and pour
into a chilled highball glass. Float
some grenadine on top.

BOURBON ROSE No. 2

1½ oz. bourbon
½ oz. dry vermouth
½ oz. crème de cassis
¼ oz. lemon juice

Mix all ingredients with cracked ice in a shaker or blender. Serve in a chilled Old Fashioned glass.

BOURBON SATIN

1 oz. bourbon
1 oz. white crème de cacao
1 oz. heavy cream

Mix all ingredients with cracked ice in a shaker or blender. Strain into a chilled cocktail glass.

BOURBON SIDECAR

1½ oz. bourbon
¾ oz. curaçao or triple sec
½ oz. lemon juice

Mix all ingredients with cracked ice in a shaker or blender and strain into a chilled cocktail glass.

BOURBON SLOE GIN FIZZ

1 tsp. sugar syrup or to taste
½ tsp. lemon juice
1½ oz. bourbon
¾ oz. sloe gin
Club soda
Lemon slice
Maraschino cherry

Pour syrup, lemon juice, bourbon, and sloe gin into a 14-oz. Collins glass, add a little cracked ice, and mix well. Add additional ice, fill with club soda, and garnish with lemon slice and cherry.

BOURBON SOUR

2 oz. bourbon
Juice of ½ lemon
½ tsp. sugar or sugar syrup
Orange slice

Mix all ingredients, except orange slice, in a shaker or blender with cracked ice. Strain into a chilled Whiskey Sour glass. Garnish with a slice of orange.

BRIGHTON PUNCH

1 oz. bourbon
1 oz. cognac
¾ oz. Benedictine
Juice of ½ lemon
Juice of ½ orange
1 tsp. sugar syrup or to taste
Club soda
Orange slice

Mix all ingredients, except soda and orange slice, with cracked ice in a shaker or blender and pour into a chilled highball or Collins glass. Fill with soda, stir gently, and garnish with orange slice.

CHAMPAGNE JULEP

Several sprigs of mint
1 tsp. sugar syrup
3 oz. bourbon
Brut champagne or dry sparkling wine.

Remove a half-dozen mint leaves from sprig and put them

in a tall Collins glass with syrup and muddle. Fill glass two-thirds full with cracked ice, pour in bourbon, and stir briskly. Add additional ice if necessary and fill with ice-cold champagne or sparkling wine. Stir gently and garnish with a large mint sprig.

CHURCHILL DOWNS COOLER

1½ oz. bourbon
1 oz. crème de banane
½ oz. triple sec
3 oz. pineapple juice
½ oz. lemon juice
Club soda
Pineapple slice
Maraschino cherry

Mix all ingredients, except soda, pineapple slice, and cherry, with cracked ice in a shaker or blender and pour into a 14-oz. Collins glass and fill with soda. Garnish with pineapple slice and cherry.

COLONEL LEE'S COOLER

1 oz. bourbon
1 oz. brandy
2 tsp. triple sec
4 oz. ginger ale

Mix the bourbon, brandy, and triple sec with cracked ice in a chilled highball glass and gently stir. Fill with ginger ale.

COMMODORE COCKTAIL No. 2

1½ oz. bourbon
¾ oz. white crème de cacao
½ oz. lemon juice

Mix all ingredients with cracked ice in a shaker or blender and strain into a chilled cocktail glass.

COOL COLONEL

1½ oz. bourbon
1 oz. Southern Comfort
3 oz. strong tea, chilled
½ oz. lemon juice
1 tsp. sugar syrup or to taste
Club soda
Lemon peel

Mix all ingredients, except soda and lemon peel, in a shaker or blender with cracked ice. Pour into a chilled, tall Collins glass, fill with soda, and twist lemon peel over drink and drop into glass.

 ## CRESCENT CITY SPECIAL

2 oz. bourbon
1 tsp. Herbsaint or Pernod
½ tsp. orgeat or sugar syrup
Several dashes Peychaud's
   bitters
Lemon twist

Stir all ingredients, except lemon twist, in a double Old Fashioned glass with ice, twist lemon peel over drink, and drop in glass.

DERBY DAY SPECIAL

1 oz. bourbon
1 oz. heavy cream
1 oz. crème de banane
Dash Grand Marnier

Mix all ingredients with cracked ice in a shaker or blender. Serve in a chilled Old Fashioned glass.

 ## A DRY MAHONEY

6 parts bourbon (2½ oz.)
1 part dry vermouth (½ oz.)
Lemon peel

Stir all ingredients, except lemon peel, with ice and strain into a chilled cocktail glass.

Twist lemon peel over drink and drop rind in glass. Serve with an ice cube or two on the side in a second glass.
Note: This is a New York ad man's version of the classic dry Manhattan.

 ## EASY SAZERAC

¼ tsp. Pernod, Herbsaint,
   or other absinthe substitute
½ tsp. sugar
1 tbsp. water
Dash Peychaud's bitters
2 oz. bourbon, rye, or blended
   whiskey
Lemon peel

Pour Pernod into a chilled Old Fashioned glass and swirl around until the inside is coated. Add the sugar, water, and Peychaud's bitters and muddle until the sugar is dissolved. Add bourbon, rye, or blended whiskey with ice cubes and stir well. Twist the lemon peel over the drink and drop in.

FATHER'S MILK

1½–2 oz. bourbon
1 tsp. sugar syrup or to taste
1 cup milk
Nutmeg (optional)

Mix bourbon and syrup with milk in a tall highball glass with cracked ice and dust with grated nutmeg. For a frothy drink, mix in blender and pour into a highball glass.

FLINTLOCK

1½ oz. bourbon
½ oz. applejack
1 tsp. lemon juice
Several dashes grenadine

Several dashes peppermint schnapps

Mix all ingredients with cracked ice in a shaker or blender. Strain into a chilled cocktail glass.

FORESTER

1½ oz. bourbon
¾ oz. cherry liqueur
1 tsp. lemon juice
Maraschino cherry

Mix all ingredients, except cherry, with cracked ice in a shaker or blender. Pour into a chilled Old Fashioned glass. Garnish with cherry.

THE FONTAINEBLEU SIDECAR

2 oz. bourbon
1 oz. curaçao or Cointreau
Juice of ½ lemon
Grand Marnier float

Mix all ingredients, except Grand Marnier, with cracked ice in a shaker or blender and pour into a chilled wine goblet. Float a teaspoon or two of Grand Marnier on top.

FRENCH TWIST

1½ oz. bourbon
1½ oz. brandy
½ oz. Grand Marnier
1 tsp. lemon juice

Mix all ingredients with cracked ice in a shaker or blender. Strain into a chilled cocktail glass.

 # FROZEN MINT JULEP

2 oz. bourbon
1 oz. lemon juice
1 oz. sugar syrup
6 small mint leaves
Mint sprig

Muddle mint leaves with bourbon, lemon juice, and syrup in a bar glass. Put all ingredients, except mint sprig, in a blender with finely crushed ice and mix at high speed for no longer than 15 seconds or until ice becomes mushy. Serve in a chilled double Old Fashioned glass and garnish with a sprig of mint.

GINZA

2 oz. bourbon
1 oz. sake
1 tsp. sugar syrup or to taste
1 tsp. lemon juice
Orange slice

Mix all ingredients, except orange, with cracked ice in a shaker or blender. Pour into a chilled cocktail glass. Garnish with orange slice.

GOLDEN GLOW

1½ oz. bourbon
½ oz. Jamaica rum
2 oz. orange juice
1 tsp. lemon juice
Falernum or sugar syrup to taste

Dash grenadine

Mix all ingredients, except grenadine, with cracked ice in a shaker or blender, strain, and pour into a chilled cocktail glass. Top with a grenadine float.

GRENOBLE COCKTAIL

1½ oz. bourbon
½ oz. framboise
½ oz. triple sec
1 oz. orange juice

1 tsp. orgeat syrup

Mix all ingredients with cracked ice in a shaker or blender. Serve in a chilled cocktail glass.

 # HAWAIIAN EYE

1½ oz. bourbon
½ oz. crème de banane
1 oz. Kahlua
3–4 oz. pineapple juice
1 oz. heavy cream
Dash Pernod (optional)
1 egg white

Pineapple slice
Cherry

Mix all ingredients, except pineapple slice and cherry, with cracked ice in a shaker or blender at high speed for 15 seconds. Pour into a chilled highball glass. Garnish with a pineapple slice and cherry.

HEARN'S COCKTAIL

¾ oz. bourbon or Irish
   whiskey
¾ oz. sweet vermouth
¾ oz. Pernod
Several dashes Angostura
   bitters

Mix all ingredients with cracked
ice in a shaker or blender. Serve
in a chilled Old Fashioned
glass.

HUNTRESS COCKTAIL

1 oz. bourbon
1 oz. cherry liqueur
1 oz. heavy cream
Dash triple sec

Mix all ingredients thoroughly
in a shaker or blender with
cracked ice. Strain and serve
in a chilled cocktail glass.

ITALIAN STALLION

1½ oz. bourbon
½ oz. Campari
½ oz. sweet vermouth
Dash Angostura bitters
Lemon peel

Stir all ingredients, except
lemon peel, with ice in a pitcher
and strain into a chilled cocktail glass. Twist lemon peel over
drink and drop into glass.

JAMAICA SHAKE

1½ oz. bourbon
1 oz. Jamaica dark rum
1 oz. heavy cream

Mix all ingredients with cracked
ice in a shaker or blender. Strain
into a chilled cocktail glass.

KENTUCKY CHAMPAGNE COCKTAIL

1 oz. 100-proof bourbon
½ oz. peach liqueur
Several dashes bitters
Champagne
Peach slice

Mix the bourbon, peach schnapps,
and bitters in a chilled wine
goblet and stir with ice cubes.
Fill with champagne. Garnish
with peach slice.

KENTUCKY COOLER

1½ oz. bourbon
¾ oz. brandy
1 oz. lemon juice
2 tsp. sugar syrup or to taste
Club soda
Barbados rum

Mix all ingredients, except soda
and rum, in a shaker or blender
with cracked ice. Pour into a
chilled 14-oz. Collins glass, add
ice, and fill with club soda.
Add a float of rum.

KENTUCKY ORANGE BLOSSOM

1½ oz. bourbon
½ oz. triple sec
1 oz. orange juice
Lemon peel

Mix all ingredients, except lemon peel, with cracked ice in a shaker or blender. Pour into a chilled Old Fashioned glass. Twist the lemon peel over the drink and drop in.

KEY WEST COCKTAIL

1½ oz. bourbon
1 oz. orange juice
1 oz. pineapple juice
1 tsp. lemon juice
Several dashes Angostura bitters
Orgeat or sugar syrup to taste

Mix all ingredients with cracked ice in a shaker or blender. Pour into a chilled Old Fashioned glass.

LITTLE COLONEL

2 oz. bourbon
1 oz. Southern Comfort
1 oz. lime juice

Mix all ingredients with cracked ice in a shaker or blender and strain into a chilled cocktail glass. If a sweeter drink is desired, add more Southern Comfort.

LOUISVILLE STINGER

1 oz. bourbon
1 oz. light rum
2 tsp. white crème de cacao
2 tsp. white crème de menthe

Mix all ingredients with cracked ice in a shaker or blender. Serve in a chilled cocktail glass.

MAN O' WAR

2 oz. bourbon
1 oz. orange curaçao
½ oz. sweet vermouth
Juice of ½ lime

Mix all ingredients with cracked ice in a shaker or blender. Pour into a chilled cocktail glass.

MANHATTAN, BOURBON

1½–2 oz. bourbon
½ oz. sweet vermouth
Dash bitters (optional)
Maraschino cherry

Pour the bourbon, vermouth, and bitters in a shaker along with ice cubes and stir. Strain into a chilled cocktail glass. Garnish with a maraschino cherry.

MILLIONAIRE COCKTAIL No. 2

1½ oz. bourbon
½ oz. Pernod
Several dashes curaçao
Several dashes grenadine
1 egg white (for two drinks)

Mix all ingredients with cracked ice and strain into a chilled cocktail glass.

MINT CONDITION

¾ oz. bourbon
¾ oz. peppermint schnapps
¾ oz. vodka
½ oz. Kahlua

Mix all ingredients with cracked ice in a shaker or blender. Serve in a chilled Whiskey Sour glass.

MIRAMAR

2½ oz. bourbon
½ oz. Benedictine

Mix ingredients with cracked ice in a shaker or blender. Strain into a chilled cocktail glass.

MISSISSIPPI MIST

1½ oz. bourbon
1½ oz. Southern Comfort

Pour bourbon and Southern Comfort into an Old Fashioned glass. Fill with crushed ice and gently stir.

NEVINS COCKTAIL

1½ oz. bourbon
½ oz. apricot liqueur
1 oz. grapefruit juice
1 tsp. lemon juice
Several dashes Angostura
  bitters

Mix all ingredients with cracked ice in a shaker or blender. Serve in an Old Fashioned glass.

NEW ORLEANS COCKTAIL

1½ oz. bourbon
½ oz. Pernod
Dash orange bitters
Several dashes Angostura
  bitters
Dash anisette
Sugar syrup to taste

Lemon peel

Mix all ingredients, except
lemon peel, with cracked ice in a
shaker or blender. Pour into a
chilled Old Fashioned glass. Twist
the lemon peel over drink and
drop in.

 ## OLD FASHIONED

1½–2 oz. bourbon, blended
  whiskey, Canadian, or rye
Dash water
Dash sugar syrup or to taste
Dash or two Angostura bitters

Mix all ingredients in an Old
Fashioned glass and add several
ice cubes (no fruit).

PADDOCK SPECIAL

2 oz. bourbon
1 oz. green crème de menthe
Juice of ½ lime
1 tsp. sugar syrup or to taste
6 small mint leaves
Club soda
Mint sprig

Add bourbon, crème de menthe,
lime juice, syrup, and mint leaves
to a bar glass and muddle
leaves well. Put into a blender
with cracked ice and mix well.
Pour into a chilled Collins glass
and fill with soda. Garnish
with mint sprig.

PADUCAH PALOOKAH

1½ oz. bourbon
½ oz. apricot-flavored brandy
Juice of ½ lime
1 tsp. sugar syrup or to taste
Dash grenadine
Lime slice
Maraschino cherry

Mix all ingredients, except lime
slice and cherry, with cracked ice
in a shaker or blender and
strain into a chilled Old Fashioned glass. Garnish with lime
slice and cherry.

PAPPARAZZI

1½ oz. bourbon
½ oz. sweet vermouth
½ oz. Fernet Branca
Several dashes anesone
  liqueur or Pernod

Mix all ingredients with cracked
ice in a shaker or blender. Strain
into a chilled cocktail glass.

POLO DREAM

1½–2 oz. bourbon
1 oz. orange juice
¾ oz. orgeat syrup or to taste

Mix with cracked ice in a shaker or blender and strain into a chilled cocktail glass.

PORT LIGHT

2 oz. bourbon
½ oz. La Grande Passion or passion fruit juice
½ oz. honey
1 oz. lemon juice
1 egg white (for two drinks)
Mint sprigs (optional)

Mix all ingredients, except mint sprigs, with cracked ice in a shaker or blender and pour into a Collins glass. Garnish with mint.

PRESBYTERIAN

2–3 oz. bourbon
Ginger ale
Club soda

Pour bourbon into a chilled highball glass, add ice cubes, and fill with equal parts of ginger ale and club soda.

PRIDE OF PADUCAH

2 oz. bourbon
1 oz. dark crème de cacao
1 oz. heavy cream
Several almonds, toasted and slivered

Mix all ingredients, except almonds, in a shaker or blender with cracked ice. Pour into a chilled Old Fashioned glass. Decorate with slivered almonds.

QUICK AND EASY MINT JULEP

Several mint sprigs
1 tsp. superfine sugar
1 tsp. water
3 oz. bourbon

Muddle mint sprigs in a double Old Fashioned glass with sugar and water until sugar is dissolved. Fill glass with finely crushed ice and add bourbon. Stir briskly with an iced tea spoon. Garnish with a mint sprig.

RED ROVER

1½ oz. bourbon
½ oz. sloe gin
½ oz. lemon juice
1 tsp. sugar syrup
Lemon slice
Peach slice (optional)

Mix all ingredients, except
lemon and peach slices, in a
shaker or blender with cracked
ice, strain and pour into a chilled
cocktail glass. Garnish with
the lemon slice and peach slice.

RODEO DRIVE RAMMER

1½ oz. bourbon
½ oz. peach brandy
½ oz. curaçao
½ oz. Jamaica rum
3 oz. orange juice
1 tsp. orgeat syrup, Falernum,
   or sugar syrup
Club soda

Pineapple slice
Maraschino cherry

Mix all ingredients, except
soda, pineapple, and cherry, with
cracked ice in a shaker or
blender and pour into a 14-oz.
Collins glass. Fill with soda,
stir gently, and garnish with pineapple and cherry.

ROUND HILL SPECIAL

1½ oz. bourbon
½ oz. Jamaica dark rum
2 tsp. orange juice
2 tsp. lemon juice
1 tsp. orgeat syrup

Mix all ingredients with cracked
ice in a shaker or blender. Strain
into a chilled cocktail glass.

ROYAL ROOST

¾ oz. bourbon or rye
¾ oz. Dubonnet rouge
Several dashes curaçao
Several dashes Pernod
Pineapple slice
Orange slice
Lemon peel
Generous dashes Peychaud's
   bitters (optional)

Mix all ingredients, except orange
and pineapple slices, lemon peel
and bitters, with cracked ice
in a mixing glass and strain into
a chilled Old Fashioned glass
with several ice cubes. Garnish
with fruit and top with bitters.

ROYAL WHISKEY SOUR

2 oz. bourbon, rye, Cana-
    dian or blended whiskey
Juice of ½ lemon
1 tsp. sugar syrup or to taste
2 brandied maraschino
    cherries

Mix all ingredients with cracked
ice in a blender until cherries are
chopped fine and pour into a
Whiskey Sour glass.

S.S. MANHATTAN

1½ oz. bourbon
½ oz. Benedictine
2 oz. orange juice

Mix all ingredients with cracked
ice in a shaker or blender and
pour into a chilled cocktail
glass.

SARATOGA FIZZ

1½ oz. bourbon
1 tsp. lemon juice
1 tsp. lime juice
1 tsp. sugar syrup or to taste
1 egg white
Club soda
Maraschino cherry

Mix all ingredients, except club
soda and cherry, with cracked
ice in a shaker or blender.
Pour into a chilled highball glass
and fill with cold club soda.
Garnish with cherry.

 THE SAZERAC

1 sugar cube
2 dashes Peychaud's bitters
Dash Angostura bitters
    (optional)
2 oz. straight bourbon, rye,
    or blended whiskey
Dash Herbsaint or Pernod
Lemon peel

Chill two Old Fashioned glasses
with crushed ice. Remove ice
from one glass and in it place
a sugar cube with a little water.
Add bitters and crush sugar
cube with a muddler until all
sugar is dissolved. Add whiskey and several ice cubes and
stir well. Empty the second
glass of crushed ice, add a
generous dash of Herbsaint and
coat inside of glass thoroughly.
Pour excess out and pour in
mixture from first glass. Twist
lemon peel over drink but do
not put into glass. Do not add
more ice unless desired.
Note: This is the classic New
Orleans Sazerac requiring two
glasses, the best straight rye or
bourbon obtainable, Peychaud's
bitters, and Herbsaint, an
absinthe substitute made in
Louisiana.

SEAGIRT COCKTAIL

1½ oz. bourbon
2 oz. grapefruit juice
1 oz. cranberry juice
½ tsp. orgeat syrup

Mix all ingredients with cracked ice in a shaker or blender. Strain into a chilled cocktail glass.

SHERRY TWIST No. 3

1½ oz. bourbon or blended
   whiskey
¾ oz. cocktail sherry
Lemon peel

Pour the bourbon or blended whiskey and sherry into a shaker with cracked ice and stir. Strain into a chilled cocktail glass. Twist the lemon peel over drink and drop in.

SMOOTH SAILING

2 oz. bourbon
2 oz. half-and-half or cream
Club soda

Mix bourbon and cream with cracked ice in a shaker or blender and strain into a chilled Old Fashioned glass. Fill with cold club soda and stir gently.

SOUTHERN GINGER

1½ oz. 100-proof bourbon
1 tsp. ginger-flavored brandy
1 tsp. lemon juice
Ginger ale
Lemon twist

Mix all ingredients, except ginger ale and lemon twist, with cracked ice in a shaker or blender and pour into a double Old Fashioned glass. Fill with ginger ale, twist lemon over drink, and drop peel into glass.

SOUTHSIDE

6 mint leaves
1 tsp. sugar syrup or to taste
Juice of ½ lemon
1½–2 oz. bourbon
Spring water

Muddle mint leaves in sugar and lemon juice, add bourbon, a little spring water, crushed ice, and muddle again. Garnish with additional mint leaves if you wish.

SPRING HOUSE SOUR

1½ oz. bourbon
½ oz. peppermint schnapps
1 tbsp. lemon juice
1 tsp. sugar syrup or to taste
Mint sprig (optional)
Maraschino cherry

Mix all ingredients, except mint and cherry, in a shaker or blender with cracked ice and pour into an Old Fashioned glass. Garnish with mint sprig and cherry.

STINGER SOUR

1½ oz. bourbon
1 tbsp. lemon juice
Several dashes peppermint
schnapps

Sugar syrup to taste

Mix all ingredients with cracked ice in a shaker or blender. Serve in a chilled cocktail glass.

SWEET AND SOUR BOURBON

1½ oz. bourbon
4 oz. orange juice
Pinch or two sugar
Pinch salt
Maraschino cherry

Mix all ingredients, except cherry, in a shaker or blender with cracked ice and pour into a Whiskey Sour glass. Garnish with cherry.

THREE–BASE HIT

1 oz. bourbon
1 oz. light rum
1 oz. brandy
2 tsp. lemon juice

Falernum or sugar syrup to taste

Mix all ingredients with cracked ice in a shaker or blender. Strain into a chilled cocktail glass.

TIVOLI COCKTAIL

1½ oz. bourbon
½ oz. sweet vermouth
½ oz. aquavit
Dash Campari

Mix all ingredients with cracked ice in a shaker or blender and strain into a chilled cocktail glass.

TROLLEY COOLER

2 oz. bourbon
Pineapple juice
Cranberry juice

Pour the bourbon into a highball glass to which ice has been added. Fill the glass with equal parts of pineapple and cranberry juices and stir.

WALDORF COCKTAIL

1½ oz. bourbon
¾ oz. Pernod
½ oz. sweet vermouth
Dash Angostura bitters

Stir with ice and strain into a chilled cocktail glass.

 ## WALLY HARBANGER

1 oz. bourbon
½ oz. Galliano
1 oz. lemon juice
1 tsp. sugar syrup
Sprig of mint (optional)

Mix all ingredients, except mint sprig, with crushed ice in a shaker or blender. Serve in a chilled Old Fashioned glass. Decorate with a sprig of mint.

 ## WARD EIGHT

1½–2 oz. bourbon
1 oz. lemon juice
1 oz. orange juice
Sugar syrup to taste
Dash grenadine

Mix all ingredients with cracked ice in a shaker or blender and strain into a chilled cocktail glass.

 ## WHIRLAWAY

2 oz. bourbon
1 oz. curaçao
Several dashes Angostura
   bitters
Club soda

Mix all ingredients, except soda, in a blender or shaker with cracked ice. Pour into a chilled Old Fashioned glass and top with club soda.

 ## THE WHISKEY HOUND

1½ oz. 100-proof bourbon
½ oz. 86-proof Demerara rum
1 oz. lemon juice
1 oz. orange juice
1 oz. grapefruit juice
1 tbsp. sugar or sugar syrup
   to taste
Dash maraschino cherry juice

Mix all ingredients with cracked ice in a shaker of blender and pour into double Old Fashioned glass.
Note: 151-proof Demerara rum may be used for the hearty drinker.

WHISPER OF A KISS

1½ oz. bourbon
¾ oz. apricot liqueur
½ tsp. lemon juice
1 tsp. grenadine

Mix with cracked ice in a
shaker or blender, strain, and
serve in a chilled cocktail
glass.

BLENDED WHISKEY

Blended whiskey is a combination of various straight whiskeys, grain spirits, and, in some cases, light whiskeys. The whiskeys and spirits are carefully selected by the blender to produce a flavorful, well-balanced, smooth, and harmonious formula that can be precisely duplicated and quality-controlled over an extended period of time on a full production basis. The blend must contain at least 20 percent straight whiskeys while the remainder may be grain neutral spirits (spirits distilled out at 190 proof or more, which are later reduced in proof for blending purposes), or grain spirits (neutral spirits that are aged in wood to produce a certain amount of mellowing and delicate flavor overtones), or light whiskeys, or any combination thereof.

Much of the whiskey that is popular today is blended. This reflects a growing trend toward lighter food and beverages of all kinds. By the term "lighter," in the popular sense, we mean not only light-bodied but less filling. It is the general desire for a lack of heaviness that explains a gradual movement in the American brewing industry away from the traditional rich, hoppy, full-bodied European-style beers and ales and toward a pale, dry, light-bodied product with high carbonation and far less intensity of flavor.

Light whiskeys, themselves a relatively recent category in distilled spirits in the U.S., are distilled at high proofs, over 160, and stored in seasoned, or used, charred oak containers. The resulting whiskey has much less flavor presence than a straight whiskey. It is valuable in making blended whiskey because it can be used to replace grain neutral spirits in the blend, thus giving more character to the finished product while still retaining a light body.

Watching a master blender at work is fascinating, and will give anyone a new appreciation of the complexities involved in developing a blended whiskey. He sits at a large, round, revolving table. Lining the edge of the table will be as many as sixty glasses. Sherry glasses are best for nosing spirits samples because their modified tulip shape concentrates the aroma. Each glass has an identification code inscribed on its foot. A watch crystal is placed on top of the glass to prevent evaporation. The blender, using nose and mouth and drawing upon a prodigious memory for all the nuances of taste and smell, proceeds to move from glass to glass, noting colors—ranging from clear through straw, fawn, sand, beige, tan, and amber to rich walnut, dark mahogany, and tobacco brown—sniffing, tasting, comparing, remembering other scents and flavors from other times. His concentration is broken only when he pauses to make notes. If he is creating a new blended whiskey, he and his assistants may check hundreds of samples from the spirits "library." The final selection for the blend, after testing many, many combinations, may comprise as many as 50 different distilled components.

The care that is taken in the blending laboratory to keep unwanted and extraneous elements from interfering with the blending process is vital, for the blender must keep his senses sharp and in tune. The glasses are all steam-cleaned to prevent a soap or detergent residue from building up. Each sample is reduced to exactly 40 proof (20 percent alcohol) by adding demineralized spring water to the whiskey. The serious whiskey drinker need not be this fastidious, but it should be noted that spring water used as a mixer (as well as to make ice cubes) will in many cases markedly improve the flavor of whiskey over a drink made with tap water. The problem of detergent residue in glasses is not relegated to the laboratory. It is evident at wine tastings, where large numbers of glasses are required, some of which have not been properly rinsed. It is also the bane of the beer drinker. Improperly washed glasses are a principle cause of beer prematurely losing its head.

Anyone can enhance his or her enjoyment of spirits by taking some cues from the professional blender. The nose is paramount in the tasting process. Some blenders say that they can tell more about a sample by smelling it than tasting it. So use your nose when trying a drink, even a mixed one. Give it a good sniff before you drink it and concentrate on the sensations and impressions your olfactory senses are sending you. Wine aficionados consider smelling essential to the appreciation of wine; so it is with whiskey. A carefully made whiskey deserves to be savored and enjoyed like a fine wine.

 ## AUNT GRACE'S PACIFIER

2 oz. blended whiskey
1 oz. raspberry syrup
Club soda

Pour blended whiskey and raspberry syrup into a chilled Old Fashioned glass and stir well. Add several ice cubes and fill with club soda.

BANDANA

1½ oz. blended whiskey
¾ oz. banana liqueur
1 tsp. lemon juice
1 tsp. orange juice

Mix all ingredients with cracked ice in a shaker or blender. Strain into a chilled cocktail glass.

BARBIZON COCKTAIL

1½ oz. blended whiskey
½ oz. Benedictine
Several dashes Cointreau
Juice of ½ lime or ¼ lemon

Mix all ingredients with cracked ice in a shaker or blender. Strain into a chilled cocktail glass.

BERRY PATCH

1½ oz. blended whiskey
1 oz. blackberry brandy
½ oz. lemon juice
½ oz. grenadine

Mix all ingredients with cracked ice in a shaker or blender, strain, and pour into a chilled cocktail glass.

BLACK HAWK

1 oz. blended whiskey
1 oz. sloe gin
½ oz. lemon juice
Maraschino cherry

Mix all ingredients, except cherry, with cracked ice in a shaker or blender. Strain into a chilled cocktail glass. Garnish with a maraschino cherry.

BLENDED COMFORT

2 oz. blended whiskey
1 oz. Southern Comfort
½ oz. dry vermouth
1 oz. orange juice
1 oz. lemon juice
¼ peach, skinned
Lemon slice

Orange slice

Mix all ingredients, except orange and lemon slices, with cracked ice in a shaker or blender. Pour into a chilled Collins glass. Garnish with a slice of orange and slice of lemon.

BLUE GRASS VELVET

1½ oz. blended whiskey
½ oz. Benedictine
2 tsp. lemon juice

Mix all ingredients with cracked ice in a shaker or blender. Strain into a chilled cocktail glass.

BOILERMAKER

1½ oz. blended whiskey
12 oz. mug or pilsener glass
of beer

Drink the whiskey straight and immediately follow with a beer chaser. Some prefer to pour the whiskey into the beer and quaff them together.

BOSS TWEED SPECIAL

1 oz. blended whiskey
1 oz. light rum
1 oz. brandy
1 oz. lemon juice
1 tsp. sugar syrup or to taste

Several dashes Angostura bitters

Mix all ingredients with cracked ice in a shaker or blender and serve in a chilled Old Fashioned glass

BOSUN'S MATE

1 oz. blended whiskey
1 oz. ruby port
1 oz. Jamaica rum
Several dashes Angostura bitters

Mix all ingredients with cracked ice in a shaker or blender and strain into a chilled Old Fashioned glass.

BOTOFOGO COCKTAIL

1 oz. blended whiskey
1 oz. sweet vermouth
Several dashes Amer Picon

Mix all ingredients with cracked ice in a shaker or blender and strain into a chilled cocktail glass.

CABLEGRAM

2 oz. blended whiskey
1 tsp. sugar syrup
½ oz. lemon juice
Ginger ale

Mix all ingredients, except ginger ale, with cracked ice in a shaker or blender. Pour into a chilled highball glass and fill with ginger ale.

CANDY PANTS

1½ oz. blended whiskey
½ oz. cherry-flavored brandy
1 tsp. lemon juice
Sugar syrup to taste
Dash grenadine

Mix all ingredients with cracked ice in a shaker of blender, strain, and serve in a chilled cocktail glass.

CHAPEL HILL

1½ oz. blended whiskey
½ oz. curaçao
½ oz. lemon juice
Orange slice

Mix all ingredients, except orange slice, with cracked ice in a shaker or blender. Pour into a chilled cocktail glass. Decorate with a slice of orange.

COFFEE EGG NOG

1½ oz. blended whiskey
1 oz. Kahlua
6 oz. milk
1 oz. heavy cream
1 tsp. sugar syrup
½ tsp. instant coffee

1 egg
Ground cinnamon

Mix all ingredients, except cinnamon, with cracked ice in a shaker or blender and strain into a chilled Collins glass. Sprinkle with ground cinnamon.

COMMODORE No. 1

1½ oz. blended whiskey
½ oz. strawberry liqueur
½ oz. lime juice
2 oz. orange juice
Dash orange bitters

Mix all ingredients with cracked ice in a shaker or blender. Strain into a chilled cocktail glass.

CONTINENTAL PERFECT

1 oz. blended whiskey
1 oz. dry vermouth
1 oz. sweet vermouth
Several dashes Angostura
   bitters
1 orange section

Mix all ingredients, except orange, with cracked ice in a shaker or blender. Pour into a chilled Old Fashioned glass. Garnish with orange section.

DANNY'S DOWNFALL

1 oz. blended whiskey
1 oz. gin
1 oz. sweet vermouth

Pour all ingredients into a mixing glass and stir with ice cubes. Strain into a chilled cocktail glass.

DELTA

1½ oz. blended whiskey
½ oz. Southern Comfort
½ oz. lime juice
½ tsp. sugar syrup
Orange slice
Fresh peach slice

Mix all ingredients, except orange and peach slices, with cracked ice in a shaker or blender. Pour into a chilled Old Fashioned glass. Garnish with orange and peach slices.

DERBY FIZZ

1½ oz. blended whiskey
1 tsp. curaçao
1 tsp. sugar syrup
1 tsp. lemon juice
1 egg
Club soda

Mix all ingredients, except club soda, with cracked ice in a shaker or blender. Strain into a chilled highball glass. Fill with club soda.

DERBY No. 2

1 oz. blended whiskey
½ oz. sweet vermouth
½ oz. white curaçao
½ oz. lime juice
Mint sprig (optional)

Mix all ingredients, except mint sprig, with cracked ice in a shaker or blender. Pour into a chilled Old Fashioned glass. Decorate with a mint sprig.

 DE RIGUEUR

1½ oz. blended whiskey
½ oz. grapefruit juice
2 tsp. honey

Mix all ingredients with cracked ice in a shaker or blender. Strain into a chilled cocktail glass.

 DINAH

1½ oz. blended whiskey
½ oz. lemon juice
1 tsp. honey or sugar syrup
½ tsp. peppermint schnapps
Mint sprig

Mix all ingredients, except schnapps and mint, with cracked ice in a shaker or blender and strain into a chilled cocktail glass. Garnish with a mint sprig and a float of peppermint schnapps.

BARTENDER'S SECRET NO. 17

Frosting glasses, mugs, or tankards is as important to the proper presentation of special drinks such as the Mint Julep as a pastry chef's ingenious decorations on a layer cake or petit four. To make your drinks look appetizing and crackling cold be sure that the glass or mug is *completely dry* on the outside, since moisture retards frosting and if the glass is wet enough it won't frost at all. For best results, place dry glasses in freezer for an hour or so before using. Metal, such as copper, pewter or silver frost best and look elegant. A note of caution: Do not hold mug with bare hand. It will melt frost. Use a glove or bar towel.

DIXIE DRAM

2 oz. blended whiskey
½ oz. white crème de menthe
¼ oz. lemon juice
½ tsp. sugar syrup
Several dashes curaçao

Mix all ingredients with cracked ice in a shaker or blender. Pour into a chilled Old Fashioned glass.

DORADO

1½ oz. blended whiskey
6 oz. orange juice
1 tsp. liquid Pina Colada mix
Several dashes grenadine
Pineapple stick
Maraschino cherry

Mix all ingredients, except fruit, with cracked ice in a shaker or blender and pour into a 10- or 12-oz. Collins glass. Garnish with fruit.

EDEN ROC FIZZ

1½ oz. blended whiskey
1 egg white (for two drinks)
½ oz. lemon juice
1 tsp. sugar syrup
1 tsp. Pernod
Club soda

Mix all ingredients, except club soda, with cracked ice in a shaker or blender. Pour into a chilled highball glass and fill with club soda.

FLAVIO'S SPECIAL

1½ oz. blended whiskey
½ oz. sweet vermouth
½ oz. Grand Marnier
Dash orange bitters

Pour all ingredients into a mixing glass with several ice cubes and gently stir. Strain into a chilled cocktail glass.

 **FRISCO SOUR**

1½ oz. blended whiskey
¾ oz. Benedictine
1 tsp. lemon juice
1 tsp. lime juice
Dash grenadine (optional)
Orange slice

Mix all ingredients, except orange
slice, in a shaker or blender,
with cracked ice and strain into
a Whiskey Sour glass. Garnish
with orange slice.

 GINGER JOLT

1½ oz. blended whiskey
¾ oz. ginger-flavored wine
Slice ginger root
Club soda

Pour whiskey and wine into a
highball glass with ice cubes.
Smash ginger root with a hammer,
mallet, or the side of a meat
cleaver and drop into drink. Fill
with club soda.

 GINGER SNAP

1 oz. blended whiskey
1 oz. ginger-flavored brandy
6 oz. cola
Several dashes lemon juice

Stir all ingredients with ice in
a 10-oz. Collins glass.

 GLOOM LIFTER

1½ oz. blended whiskey
¾ oz. brandy
½ oz. raspberry liqueur
1 tsp. sugar syrup or to taste
1 tsp. lemon juice
1 egg white (for two drinks)

Mix all ingredients with cracked
ice in a shaker or blender. Pour
into a chilled Old Fashioned
glass.

GRAPEFRUIT COOLER

2 oz. blended whiskey
4 oz. grapefruit juice
½ oz. red currant syrup
¼ oz. lemon juice
½ orange slice
½ lemon slice

Mix all ingredients, except orange
and lemon slices, with cracked
ice in a shaker or blender. Pour
into a chilled Collins glass with
several ice cubes. Garnish
with fruit slices.

GUIDO'S SPECIAL

1½ oz. blended whiskey
¾ oz. dry vermouth
1 oz. pineapple juice
Club soda
Dash sambuca

Mix all ingredients, except club soda and sambuca, with cracked ice in a shaker or blender. Pour into a chilled Collins glass with additional cracked ice. Fill with club soda and float sambuca on top.

 ## HAWAII SEVEN-O

1½ oz. blended whiskey
½ oz. amaretto
6 oz. orange juice
1 heaping tsp. Pina Colada mix

Mix all ingredients with cracked ice in a shaker or blender and serve in a 10-oz. Collins glass. Use more Pina Colada mix is a sweeter drink is desired.

 ## HENRY MORGAN'S GROG

1½ oz. blended whiskey
1 oz. Pernod
½ oz. Jamaica dark rum
1 oz. heavy cream
Ground nutmeg

Mix all ingredients, except nutmeg, with cracked ice in a shaker or blender. Pour into a chilled Old Fashioned glass. Sprinkle with ground nutmeg.

 ## HORSE'S NECK

1 lemon
2–3 oz. blended whiskey
Ginger ale

Peel the lemon in one continuous strip and place in a chilled

Collins glass. Pour in whiskey and ice cubes and squeeze a few drops of lemon juice into glass. Fill with ginger ale and stir gently.

 ## INDIAN RIVER COCKTAIL No. 1

1½ oz. blended whiskey
¼ oz. raspberry liqueur
¼ oz. sweet vermouth
½ oz. grapefruit juice

Mix all ingredients with cracked ice in a shaker or blender. Pour into a chilled Old Fashioned glass.

 ## ITALIAN SHAMROCK

1½ oz. blended whiskey
½ oz. peppermint schnapps
½ oz. amaretto
1½ oz. milk

Mix all ingredients with cracked ice in a shaker or blender, strain, and pour into a chilled cocktail glass.

JAPANESE FIZZ

2 oz. blended whiskey
¾ oz. port
½ oz. lemon juice
1 tsp. sugar syrup
Club soda
Orange peel
Pineapple stick

Mix all ingredients, except club soda, orange, and pineapple, with cracked ice in a shaker or blender. Pour into a chilled highball glass and fill with club soda. Twist orange peel over drink and drop in. Garnish with a pineapple stick.

JUNIOR LEAGUE

1½ oz. blended whiskey
1 oz. anisette
Maraschino cherry

Mix all ingredients, except cherry, with cracked ice in a shaker or blender. Strain into a chilled cocktail glass. Garnish with a maraschino cherry.

KEY BISCAYNE

1½ oz. blended whiskey
½ oz. curaçao
½ oz. sweet vermouth
Juice of ½ lime
Mint sprig (optional)

Mix all ingredients, except mint sprig, with cracked ice in a shaker or blender. Strain into a chilled cocktail glass. Garnish with a sprig of mint.

KONA COOLER

1½ oz. blended whiskey
¾ oz. white crème de cacao
6 oz. pineapple juice
Pineapple slice
Maraschino cherry

Mix all ingredients, except fruit, with cracked ice in a shaker or blender and serve in a 10-oz. Collins glass. Garnish with fruit.

LADIES' COCKTAIL

1½ oz. blended whiskey
1 tsp. anisette
Several dashes Pernod
Several dashes Angostura bitters
Pineapple stick

Mix all ingredients, except pineapple stick, with cracked ice in a shaker or blender and strain into a chilled Old Fashioned glass. Garnish with a pineapple stick.

LAWHILL COCKTAIL

1½ oz. blended whiskey
½ oz. dry vermouth
¼ tsp. Pernod
¼ tsp. maraschino liqueur
½ oz. orange juice
Dash Angostura bitters

Mix all ingredients with cracked ice in a shaker or blender. Strain into a chilled cocktail glass.

 LORD RODNEY

1½ oz. blended whiskey
¾ oz. Jamaica rum
1 tsp. coconut syrup
Dash of white crème de cacao

Mix all ingredients with cracked ice in a shaker or blender. Strain into a chilled cocktail glass.

 LOS ANGELES COCKTAIL

4 oz. blended whiskey
1 oz. lemon juice
2 oz. sugar syrup or to taste
Several dashes sweet
    vermouth

1 egg

Mix all ingredients with cracked ice in a shaker or blender and pour into chilled Old Fashioned glasses. Serves two.

 MADEIRA COCKTAIL

1½ oz. blended whiskey
1½ oz. Malmsey Madeira
1 tsp. grenadine
Dash lemon juice
Orange slice

Mix all ingredients, except orange, with cracked ice in a shaker or blender. Pour into a chilled Old Fashioned glass. Decorate with orange slice.

MANHATTAN, The Original

1½–2 oz. blended whiskey
¼–½ oz. sweet vermouth
Dash Angostura bitters
Maraschino cherry (optional)

Mix all ingredients with plenty of ice in a mixing glass or pitcher

and strain into a chilled cocktail glass. Note: Amount of vermouth should be adjusted to individual taste.
Note: See Page 330 for Manhattan variations.

BARTENDER'S SECRET NO. 18

The simplest mixer in the world—water—can make or break a drink. Heavily treated or chlorinated tap water will flatten the flavor of premium whiskey faster than you can say, "I'll have another." If you compare your favorite scotch or bourbon with tap water and a good spring water, your taste buds will quickly show you the difference. Ice cubes made with spring water are also a flavor saver, and they'll look crystal clear in your glass.

 ## MANHASSET

1½ oz. blended whiskey
¼ oz. dry vermouth
¼ oz. sweet vermouth
½ oz. lemon juice
Lemon peel

Mix all ingredients with cracked ice in a shaker or blender. Strain into a chilled cocktail glass. Twist lemon peel over drink and drop in.

MAY COCKTAIL

1½ oz. blended whiskey
¼ oz. kirschwasser
¼ oz. strawberry liqueur
May wine, chilled
Lemon slice

Mix all ingredients, except wine and lemon slice, with cracked ice in a shaker or blender. Pour into a chilled Old Fashioned glass. Fill with May wine and stir. Decorate with a slice of lemon.

MARTHA WASHINGTON

1½ oz. blended whiskey
¾ oz. cherry liqueur
1 tsp. lemon juice
Several dashes grenadine
   (optional)
Maraschino cherry

Mix all ingredients, except cherry, with cracked ice in a shaker or blender, strain, and serve in a chilled cocktail glass. Garnish with cherry.

 ## NEW ORLEANS OLD FASHIONED

½ tsp. sugar syrup
Several dashes Angostura
   bitters
2 tsp. water or club soda
1½–2 oz. blended whiskey
Several dashes Peychaud's
   bitters
Lemon peel

Combine sugar, bitters, and water or club soda in a mixing glass and stir until sugar dissolves. Add the blended whiskey along with several ice cubes, thoroughly stir, and top with Peychaud's bitters. Twist lemon peel over drink and drop in.

NEW WORLD

1½ oz. blended whiskey
½ oz. lime juice
1 tsp. grenadine
Lime peel

Mix all ingredients, except lime peel, with cracked ice in a shaker or blender. Strain into a chilled cocktail glass and twist lime peel over drink and drop in.

NEW YORKER

1½ oz. blended whiskey
½ oz. lime juice
1 tsp. sugar syrup or to taste
Dash grenadine
Lemon peel
Orange peel

Mix all ingredients, except lemon and orange peels, with cracked ice in a shaker or blender. Strain into a chilled cocktail glass and twist lemon peel and orange peel over drink and drop in.

NEW YORK SOUR

2 oz. blended whiskey
½ oz. lemon juice
1 tsp. sugar syrup or to taste
½ oz. dry red wine
½ slice of lemon

Mix blended whiskey, lemon juice, and sugar with cracked ice in a shaker or blender. Pour into a chilled Whiskey Sour glass and top with dry red wine and stir. Decorate with a slice of lemon.

NORMANDY JACK

1½ oz. blended whiskey
¾ oz. applejack or calvados
½ oz. lemon juice
1 tsp. sugar syrup or to taste

Mix all ingredients with cracked ice in a shaker or blender. Strain into a chilled cocktail glass.

OH, HENRY!

1½ oz. blended whiskey
¼ oz. Benedictine
3 oz. ginger ale
Lemon wedge

Stir all ingredients, except lemon wedge, in a chilled Old Fashioned glass with ice. Garnish with lemon wedge.

OLD ORCHARD SOUR

2 oz. blended whiskey
½ oz. lemon juice
½ oz. lime juice
1 tsp. sugar syrup or to taste
1 tsp. strawberry cordial
Club soda

Mix all ingredients, except club soda, with cracked ice in a shaker or blender. Pour into a chilled Collins glass. Fill with club soda.

ORLY BIRD

1½ oz. blended whiskey
1 tbsp. sweet vermouth
Several dashes Pernod
Several dashes cherry brandy

Mix all ingredients with cracked ice in a shaker or blender. Strain into a chilled cocktail glass.

PAINTED PONY

1 oz. blended whiskey
1 oz. Grand Marnier
¾ oz. orange juice
¾ oz. lemon juice
1 tsp. grenadine

Mix all ingredients with cracked ice in a shaker or blender, strain, and serve in a chilled cocktail glass.

PARK LANE

1½ oz. blended whiskey
½ oz. sloe gin
1 tsp. lemon juice
½ tsp. sugar syrup or to taste

Mix all ingredients with cracked ice in a shaker or blender. Strain into a chilled cocktail glass.

PEACHTREE STREET

1½ oz. blended whiskey
1 oz. Southern Comfort
Several dashes orange bitters
Maraschino cherry

Mix all ingredients, except cherry, with cracked ice in a shaker or blender. Strain into a chilled cocktail glass. Decorate with a maraschino cherry.

PERE BISE

1½ oz. blended whiskey
½ oz. Cherry Marnier
¼ oz. lemon juice
1 egg white (for two drinks)
Dash Pernod

Mix all ingredients with cracked ice in a shaker or blender. Pour into a chilled Whiskey Sour glass.

PINK ALMOND

1 oz. blended whiskey
½ oz. crème de noyaux
½ oz. orgeat syrup or amaretto
½ oz. kirsch
½ oz. lemon juice
Lemon slice

Mix all ingredients, except lemon slice, with cracked ice in a shaker or blender. Pour into a chilled Whiskey Sour glass. Decorate with lemon slice.

POIRE WILLIAM'S FIZZ

1½ oz. blended whiskey
2–3 oz. grapefruit juice
½ oz. pear brandy
Club soda

Pour all ingredients, except club soda, in a chilled highball glass with ice cubes. Fill with club soda and stir gently.

PREAKNESS

2 oz. blended whiskey
¼ oz. sweet vermouth
¼ oz. Benedictine
Dash Angostura bitters

Pour all ingredients into a mixing glass with several ice cubes, gently stir, and strain into a chilled cocktail glass.

PRINCE VALIANT

1½ oz. blended whiskey
1 tsp. white crème de menthe
  or peppermint schnapps
Dash orange bitters

Pour all ingredients into an Old Fashioned glass and stir with ice.

RATTLESNAKE

1½ oz. blended whiskey
1 tsp. lemon juice
1 tsp. sugar syrup
1 egg white (for two drinks)
Several dashes Pernod

Mix all ingredients with cracked ice in a shaker or blender. Pour into a chilled Old Fashioned glass.

RED ROOSTER

1 oz. blended whiskey
3 oz. St. Raphael, Byrhh, or
    Dubonnet rouge
Several dashes lemon juice
Lemon or orange twist

Stir all ingredients, except fruit peel, in a double Old Fashioned glass with ice. Twist peel over drink and drop in glass.

RED VELVET SWING

1½ oz. blended whiskey
½ oz. sloe gin
1 tsp. lemon juice
2 tsp. confectioner's sugar
    or to taste

Mix all ingredients with cracked ice in a shaker or blender, strain, and serve in a chilled cocktail glass.

ROSE HALL NIGHTCAP

1 oz. blended whiskey
1 oz. Pernod
1 oz. heavy cream
1 tsp. dark crème de cacao

Mix all ingredients, except crème de cacao, with cracked ice in a shaker or blender. Pour into a chilled Old Fashioned glass. Add a float of dark crème de cacao.

RUE DE RIVOLI

1 oz. blended whiskey
1 oz. dry vermouth
1 oz. Dubonnet rouge
1 oz. orange juice
½ orange slice

Combine all ingredients in a mixing glass with several ice cubes and stir thoroughly. Pour into a chilled Old Fashioned glass.

ST. CLOUD COCKTAIL

1 oz. blended whiskey
1 oz. Pernod
1 oz. cream
Ground nutmeg

Mix all ingredients, except nutmeg, with cracked ice in a shaker or blender. Pour into a chilled cocktail glass. Sprinkle with ground nutmeg.

BARTENDER'S SECRET NO. 19

Before putting a load of dirty glasses in the dishwasher, check for lipstick on the rims. A little pre-wash spray helps get rid of these stains, which a home dishwasher cannot always remove completely. Fine crystal should be hand-washed, never put into a dishwasher. If washing in hard water, a half ounce of vinegar added to your sink makes your glasses bright and shiny. Dishes and glasses washed by hand should be placed in a rack and allowed to air dry. If your fine lead crystal becomes dusty as a result of infrequent use, never polish with a cloth. It will scratch the glass. They must be washed by hand and air dried.

 ## ST. LOUIS COCKTAIL

1½ oz. blended whiskey
½ oz. Southern Comfort
1 tsp. orgeat syrup or amaretto
2 tsp. lime juice
Lime slice

Mix all ingredients, except lime slice, with cracked ice in a shaker or blender. Strain into a chilled cocktail glass. Decorate with lime slice.

 ## 7 & 7

1½ oz. Seagram's 7-Crown blended whiskey
4 oz. 7-Up soda

Pour blended whiskey into a chilled highball glass with several ice cubes. Add 7-Up and stir gently.

 ## 7 OF CLUBS

The following eight recipes were created by the author for the Seagram Distillers Company

1½ oz. blended whiskey
¾ oz. peppermint schnapps
6 oz. Coca-Cola

Stir with ice in a 10-oz. Collins glass.

 ## 7 OF DIAMONDS

1½ oz. blended whiskey
1 oz. crème de cassis
Dash lemon juice

Mix all ingredients with cracked ice in a shaker or blender, strain, and pour into a chilled cocktail glass.

 ## 7 OF HEARTS

1½ oz. blended whiskey
½ oz. amaretto
6 oz. orange juice
1 tsp. grenadine

Stir with cracked ice in a 10- or 12-oz. Collins glass or mix with ice in a shaker or blender.

7 OF SPADES

1½ oz. blended whiskey
¾ oz. amaretto
6 oz. Cola

Dash lemon juice (optional)

Stir all ingredients with cracked ice in a 10-oz. Collins glass.

 7 STINGER

1 oz. blended whiskey
1 oz. peppermint schnapps

Mix with cracked ice in a shaker or blender, strain, and serve in a chilled cocktail glass.

 7 VEILS

1½ oz. blended whiskey
1 oz. pineapple juice
1 oz. lemon juice
¾ oz. white crème de cacao
1 tsp. grenadine

Mix all ingredients with cracked ice in a shaker or blender, strain, and serve in a chilled cocktail glass.

 SHAMROCK-7

1 oz. blended whiskey
½ oz. white crème de cacao
½ oz. peppermint schnapps
1 oz. milk

Mix all ingredients with cracked ice in a shaker or blender, strain, and pour into a chilled cocktail glass.

 SHERRY & 7

1½ oz. blended whiskey
¾ oz. cocktail sherry
Maraschino cherry

Mix sherry and whiskey with cracked ice in a pitcher, strain, and serve in a chilled cocktail glass. Garnish with cherry.

 SKY CLUB SPECIAL

1½ oz. blended whiskey
½ oz. gold rum
3 oz. orange juice

Pour all ingredients into a mixing glass with several ice cubes and gently stir. Strain into a chilled cocktail glass.

SOUTHERN FIZZ

1½ oz. blended whiskey or
   bourbon
½ oz. Southern Comfort
½ oz. lemon juice
2 oz. orange juice
1 tsp. orgeat syrup

Club soda

Mix all ingredients, except club
soda, in a shaker or blender with
cracked ice and pour into a
14-oz. Collins glass. Fill up with
club soda and stir gently.

 ## STONYBROOK

1½ oz. blended whiskey
½ oz. triple sec
½ oz. crème de noyaux
1 egg white (for two drinks)
Lemon peel
Orange peel

Mix all ingredients, except
lemon and orange peels, with
cracked ice in a shaker or
blender and strain into a chilled
cocktail glass. Twist the lemon
peel and orange peel over the
drink and drop in.

 ## SUMMER FIZZ

1½ oz. blended whiskey
3 oz. grapefruit juice
1 tsp. strawberry liqueur
Club soda

Pour all ingredients, except
club soda, into a chilled highball
glass with ice cubes. Fill with
the club soda and stir gently.

 ## THE SUNSET GUN

4 oz. blended whiskey, rye,
   or bourbon
6 cloves
1 oz. curaçao
Several dashes orange bitters

Pour whiskey into a glass,
add cloves, cover, and let steep
for about an hour. Remove
cloves, pour whiskey into a shaker
or blender with cracked ice,
add curaçao, and mix well. Strain
into chilled cocktail glasses
and top with orange bitters. Return cloves to glasses or put in
some new ones.
Note: This drink is for two, to be
mixed immediately following
retreat, when the sunset gun is
fired and the flag lowered.

 ## TEMPTATION COCKTAIL

1½ oz. blended whiskey
½ oz. Dubonnet rouge
Several dashes curaçao
Several dashes Pernod
Orange peel
Lemon peel

Mix all ingredients, except fruit
peels, with cracked ice in a shaker
or blender, strain into a chilled
cocktail glass, and twist peels
over drink and drop into glass.

TOMMY LATTA

1½ oz. blended whiskey
½ tsp. dry vermouth
½ tsp. sweet vermouth
Several dashes lemon juice

Dash sugar syrup or to taste

Mix all ingredients with cracked ice in a shaker or blender and strain into a chilled cocktail glass.

TOM NEUBERGER'S TODDY

1 tsp. honey
2 oz. water
2 oz. blended whiskey
Dash maraschino liqueur
Lemon peel and cinnamon
    stick

Combine honey and water in a chilled Old Fashioned glass and stir until sugar dissolves. Add the blended whiskey and maraschino along with several ice cubes. Stir well. Twist lemon peel over the drink, drop in and garnish with cinnamon stick.

VINCENNES

1½ oz. blended whiskey
1 oz. Dubonnet rouge
½ oz. triple sec
Dash Pernod
Lime peel

Combine all ingredients, except lime peel, in a mixing glass with several ice cubes and stir thoroughly. Strain into a chilled cocktail glass. Twist lime peel over the drink and drop in.

WATERLOO

1½ oz. blended whiskey
¾ oz. Mandarine Napoleon
1 tsp. lemon juice
1 tsp. sugar syrup or to taste
Club soda
Orange slice

Mix all ingredients, except club soda and orange slice, with cracked ice in a shaker or blender. Strain into a chilled Old Fashioned glass. Top with club soda. Decorate with orange slice.

WHIPPET

1½ oz. blended whiskey
½ oz. peppermint schnapps
½ oz. white crème de cacao

Mix all ingredients with cracked ice in a shaker or blender. Strain into a chilled cocktail glass.

WHISKEY COBBLER

1 tsp. sugar syrup
1 tsp. orgeat syrup or
   amaretto
2 oz. blended whiskey
Dash curaçao
Mint sprig (optional)

Fill a large wine goblet with finely crushed ice, pour in sugar syrup, orgeat or amaretto, and churn with a barspoon until well mixed. Add more ice if necessary and pour in whiskey. Continue churning until frost begins to form on the outside of goblet. Throw in a dash of curaçao and garnish with a mint sprig.

WHISKEY CURAÇAO FIZZ

2 oz. blended whiskey
½ oz. curaçao
1 oz. lemon juice
1 tsp. sugar
Club soda
Orange slice

Mix all ingredients, except club soda and orange slice, with cracked ice in a shaker or blender. Pour into a chilled Collins glass with several ice cubes and fill with club soda. Garnish with orange slice.

WHISKEY DAISY

2 oz. blended whiskey or
   bourbon
1 tsp. red currant syrup,
   raspberry syrup, or
   grenadine
½ oz. lemon juice
Club soda (optional)
1 tsp. yellow Chartreuse
Slice of lemon

Mix all ingredients, except club soda, Chartreuse, and lemon slice, with cracked ice in a shaker or blender. Pour into a chilled highball glass. Fill with club soda, if you wish. Add a float of yellow Chartreuse and decorate with a lemon slice.
Note: Other floats are used with the daisy such as curaçao, maraschino liqueur, Grand Marnier, green Chartreuse, Benedictine, and Galliano, to name a few.

WHISKEY FIZZ

1½ oz. blended whiskey
Several dashes Angostura
   bitters
½ tsp. sugar syrup or to taste
Club soda

Mix whiskey, bitters, and sugar in a chilled highball glass with ice and fill with club soda.

WHISKEY RICKEY

1½ oz. blended whiskey
Juice of ½ lime
1 tsp. sugar syrup
Club soda
Lime peel

Mix whiskey, lime juice, and sugar in a Collins glass with cracked ice, fill with club soda, and twist lime peel over drink and drop into glass.

ZAGREB COCKTAIL

2 oz. blended whiskey
½ oz. slivovitz
1 tsp. lemon juice
1 tsp. sugar syrup
Club soda
Pineapple stick

Mix all ingredients, except club soda and pineapple stick, with cracked ice in a shaker or blender. Strain into a chilled wine glass. Fill with club soda. Decorate with pineapple.

MANHATTAN VARIATIONS

CARACAS MANHATTAN

1½ oz. blended whiskey
¾ oz. sweet vermouth
1 tsp. Benedictine
Several dashes Amer Picon
1 egg white (for two drinks)
Maraschino cherry

Mix all ingredients, except maraschino cherry, with cracked ice in a shaker or blender. Pour into a chilled Old Fashioned glass. Garnish with a maraschino cherry.

 ## DANISH MANHATTAN

1½ oz. blended whiskey
¼ oz. kirschwasser
¼ oz. Peter Heering

Mix all ingredients with cracked ice in a shaker or blender. Strain into a chilled cocktail glass.

 ## MANHATTAN, DRY

1½–2 oz. blended whiskey
¼–½ oz. dry vermouth
Dash Angostura bitters
   (optional)
Lemon peel

Mix all ingredients with plenty of ice in a mixing glass or a pitcher and strain into a chilled cocktail glass. Twist lemon peel over drink and drop into glass.

DUBONNET MANHATTAN

1½ oz. blended whiskey
1 oz. Dubonnet rouge
Maraschino cherry

Mix all ingredients, except cherry, with cracked ice in a shaker or blender. Pour into a chilled Old Fashioned glass. Garnish with maraschino cherry.

MANHATTAN COOLER

1½ oz. blended whiskey
½ oz. dry vermouth
½ oz. amaretto
2 oz. orange juice
1 oz. lemon juice

Club soda

Mix all ingredients, except club soda, with cracked ice in shaker or blender. Pour into a chilled Collins glass. Fill with club soda.

MARIA'S MANHATTAN

1½ oz. blended whiskey
½ oz. dry vermouth
½ oz. strawberry liqueur

Pour all ingredients in a mixing glass with several ice cubes and stir well. Strain into a chilled cocktail glass.

OLD-FASHIONED MANHATTAN

1½ oz. blended whiskey
1½ oz. sweet vermouth
Maraschino cherry

Mix all ingredients with cracked ice in a shaker or blender. Pour into a chilled cocktail glass. Garnish with a maraschino cherry.

PARISIAN MANHATTAN

1½ oz. blended whiskey
½ oz. sweet vermouth
Several dashes Amer Picon
Maraschino cherry

Mix all ingredients with cracked ice in a shaker or blender. Strain into a chilled cocktail glass. Garnish with a cherry.

MANHATTAN, PERFECT

1½–2 oz. blended whiskey
½ oz. sweet vermouth
¼ oz. dry vermouth
Dash Angostura bitters
  (optional)
Lemon peel or maraschino
  cherry

Mix all ingredients with cracked ice in a mixing glass or pitcher and strain into a chilled cocktail glass. Garnish with lemon peel or maraschino cherry.

ROSEY MANHATTAN

1½ oz. blended whiskey
½ oz. dry vermouth
½ oz. raspberry liqueur

Mix all ingredients with cracked ice in a shaker or blender. Strain into a chilled cocktail glass.

SWISS MANHATTAN

1½ oz. blended whiskey
½ oz. dry vermouth
½ oz. kirsch
Several dashes Angostura bitters (optional)

Mix all ingredients with cracked ice in a shaker or blender. Serve in a chilled Old Fashioned glass.

CANADIAN WHISKY

Canadian whiskies are all blends of spirits made from cereal grains such as wheat, rye, corn, and barley. By law, they must be at least three years old, though in practice, most Canadians are six years old or more. They are characterized by a delicate flavor, a very light body, and a smoothness that is brought about by aging in wood. Like American blended whiskeys, Canadians have a high level of mixability because the flavors are not strong or trenchant. Like other blended whiskeys, Canadian whiskies are referred to as "rye" in certain parts of the U.S. This is incorrect, since these blends may contain some rye, but probably not more so than that which is found in American blends. Canadian whisky, while similar to other blends, has unique qualities of its own and a pleasant, unobtrusive character that makes it particularly appealing to those who do not enjoy what they perceive to be a strong whisky taste. As a base for mixed drinks, Canadian whisky is outstanding.

BONAVENTURE COCKTAIL

1½ oz. Canadian whisky
½ oz. Cherry Marnier
½ oz. lemon juice
½ oz. orange juice

Mix all ingredients with cracked ice in a shaker or blender. Pour into a chilled Old Fashioned glass.

CANADIAN AND CAMPARI

1 oz. Canadian whisky
½ oz. Campari
1 oz. dry vermouth
Lemon peel

Mix all ingredients, except lemon peel, with cracked ice in a shaker or blender. Strain into a chilled cocktail glass. Twist lemon peel over drink and drop in.

CANADIAN APPLE

1½ oz. Canadian whisky
½ oz. calvados
1½ tsp. sugar syrup
1 tsp. lemon juice
Several pinches powdered
    cinnamon
Lemon slice

Mix all ingredients, except lemon slice, with cracked ice in a shaker or blender. Pour into a chilled Old Fashioned glass. Garnish with a slice of lemon.

CANADIAN BLACKBERRY COCKTAIL

1½ oz. Canadian whisky
½ oz. blackberry brandy
    or blackberry liqueur
½ oz. orange juice
1 tsp. lemon juice
1 tsp. sugar syrup

Mix all ingredients with cracked ice in a shaker or blender. Serve in a chilled Old Fashioned glass. If blackberry liqueur is used in place of blackberry brandy, you may want to omit sugar syrup.

CANADIAN COCKTAIL

1½ oz. Canadian whisky
½ oz. curaçao
½ oz. lemon juice
1 tsp. sugar syrup (optional)
Dash Angostura bitters

Mix all ingredients with cracked ice in a shaker or blender. Pour into a chilled Old Fashioned glass.

CANADIAN DAISY

1½ oz. Canadian whisky
½ oz. lemon juice
1 tsp. raspberry syrup
Club soda
1 tsp. brandy
Whole raspberries (optional)

Mix the Canadian whisky, lemon juice, and raspberry syrup with cracked ice in a shaker or blender. Pour into a chilled high-ball glass and fill with club soda. Add a float of brandy. Garnish with whole raspberries.

CANADIAN DOG'S NOSE

2 oz. Canadian whisky
4 oz. tomato juice, chilled
1 tsp. Worcestershire sauce
½ tsp. Tabasco sauce
6 oz. cold beer
Freshly ground black pepper
Salt

Pour the Canadian whisky, tomato juice, Worcestershire sauce, and Tabasco sauce into a shaker with ice cubes and stir well. Pour into a chilled Collins glass. Add beer while slowly stirring. Sprinkle with salt and ground black pepper.

CANADIAN HURRICANE

1½ oz. Canadian whisky
½ oz. white crème de menthe
½ oz. dry gin
Juice of ½ lemon

Mix all ingredients with cracked ice in a shaker or blender. Strain into a cocktail glass.

CANADIAN MANHATTAN

1½-2 oz. Canadian whisky
½ oz. sweet vermouth
Dash Angostura bitters
   (optional)
Maraschino cherry

Pour whisky, vermouth, and bitters into a shaker with ice cubes. Stir gently and strain into a chilled cocktail glass. Garnish with a maraschino cherry.

CANADIAN MOUNTY

1½ oz. Canadian whisky
1 oz. cranberry liqueur
1 oz. orange juice
1 tsp. lemon juice

Mix all ingredients with cracked ice in a shaker or blender. Pour into a chilled Old Fashioned glass.

CANADIAN OLD FASHIONED

1½ oz. Canadian whisky
½ tsp. curaçao
Dash lemon juice
Dash Angostura bitters
Lemon peel
Orange peel

Mix all ingredients, except lemon and orange peels, with cracked ice in a shaker or blender. Pour into a chilled Old Fashioned glass. Twist lemon and orange peel over drink and drop in.

CANADIAN PINEAPPLE FIX

1½ oz. Canadian whisky
½ oz. maraschino liqueur
½ oz. pineapple juice
½ oz. lemon juice
Pineapple stick

Mix all ingredients, except pineapple stick, with cracked ice in a shaker or blender. Pour into a chilled Old Fashioned glass. Decorate with a pineapple stick.

 ## CANADIAN STONE FENCE

1½ oz. Canadian whisky
½ oz. triple sec
2 oz. apple cider
1 tsp. sugar syrup

Mix all ingredients with cracked ice in a shaker or blender. Strain into a chilled cocktail glass.

 ## COMMONWEALTH COCKTAIL

1¾ oz. Canadian whisky
½ oz. Van der Hum
1 tsp. lemon juice
Orange peel

Mix all ingredients, except orange peel, with cracked ice in a shaker or blender. Pour into a chilled cocktail glass. Twist orange peel over drink and drop in.

CORDIAL CANADIAN

1 oz. Canadian whisky
1 oz. dry vermouth
1 oz. Cordial Médoc
Maraschino cherry

Pour ingredients into a shaker without ice and stir thoroughly. Pour into a chilled Old Fashioned glass with ice and garnish with cherry.

 ## DOG SLED

2 oz. Canadian whisky
2 oz. orange juice
1 tbsp. lemon juice
1 tsp. grenadine

Mix all ingredients with cracked ice in a shaker or blender. Pour into a chilled Old Fashioned glass.

BARTENDER'S SECRET NO. 20

Since sugar and alcohol do not readily mix, busy professional bartenders use superfine sugar or, better yet, simple sugar syrup to speed up the mixing process. A good working formula is 2 cups sugar to 1 cup water. Mix sugar with cold water in a saucepan and boil for 5 minutes or until all sugar is dissolved and the syrup is clear. Cool and bottle. It will last a considerable period of time and save considerable time in drink making, especially for a large number of guests.

 ## 8ᵉ ARRONDISSEMENT Canadian Ward Eight

2 oz. Canadian whisky
½ oz. lemon juice
½ tsp. grenadine
1 tsp. maple syrup or sugar syrup
Slice of lemon

Mix all ingredients, except lemon slice, with cracked ice in a shaker or blender. Pour into a chilled cocktail glass. Garnish with a slice of lemon.

 ## ESQUIMAUX CREME

1½ oz. Canadian whisky
1 oz. Grand Marnier
1 oz. heavy cream
1 tsp. lemon juice
1 egg
Nutmeg, grated
Cinnamon, powdered

Mix all ingredients, except nutmeg and cinnamon, with cracked ice in a shaker or blender. Pour into a chilled wine goblet and sprinkle with nutmeg and cinnamon.

 ## FROBISHER FIZZ

1½ oz. Canadian whisky
1 oz. peppermint schnapps
¼ oz. white crème de cacao
1 egg white (for two drinks)
Club soda

Mix all ingredients, except club soda, with cracked ice in a shaker or blender. Pour into a chilled double Old Fashioned glass and fill with club soda.

 ## FRONTENAC COCKTAIL

1½ oz. Canadian whisky
½ oz. Grand Marnier
Several dashes kirschwasser
Dash orange bitters

Mix all ingredients with cracked ice in a shaker or blender. Pour into a chilled cocktail glass.

HABITANT COCKTAIL

1½ oz. Canadian whisky
1 oz. lemon juice
1 tsp. maple syrup
Orange slice
Cherry

Mix all ingredients, except orange slice and cherry, with cracked ice in a shaker or blender. Strain into a chilled cocktail glass. Decorate with a slice of orange and cherry.

 ## IRISH CANADIAN SANGAREE

1 oz. Canadian whisky
½ oz. Irish Mist
½ oz. orange juice
½ oz. lemon juice
Nutmeg, grated

Pour whisky, Irish Mist, orange and lemon juices into a chilled Old Fashioned glass and stir with ice. Dust with nutmeg.

 ## IRISH MOUNTY

1½ oz. Canadian whisky
1 oz. Irish Mist
½ oz. heavy cream
Nutmeg, grated

Mix all ingredients, except nutmeg, with cracked ice in a shaker or blender. Strain into a chilled cocktail glass and sprinkle with nutmeg.

 ## LAKE LOUISE COCKTAIL

1½ oz. Canadian whisky
½ oz. amaretto
½ oz. heavy cream

Mix all ingredients with cracked ice in a shaker or blender. Strain into a chilled cocktail glass.

 ## LA RESERVE COCKTAIL

1½ oz. Canadian whisky
½ oz. yellow Chartreuse
2 oz. orange juice

Mix all ingredients with cracked ice in a shaker or blender. Strain into a chilled cocktail glass.

 ## MAMMAMATTAWA

1½ oz. Canadian whisky
½ oz. Drambuie
¼ oz. cherry brandy

Mix all ingredients with cracked ice in a shaker or blender. Serve in a chilled cocktail glass.

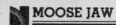MOOSE JAW

1½ oz. Canadian whisky
1 oz. apple brandy
1 tsp. grenadine or sugar
  syrup
1 tsp. lemon juice

*Several dashes peppermint
schnapps*

Mix all ingredients in a shaker
or blender with cracked ice. Pour
into a chilled Old Fashioned
glass.

MT. TREMBLANT

1 oz. Canadian whisky
½ oz. dry vermouth
½ oz. Grand Marnier
½ oz. cranberry liqueur

Mix all ingredients with cracked
ice in a shaker or blender. Strain
into a chilled cocktail glass.

THE MUSKOKA COCKTAIL

1½ oz. Canadian whisky
½ oz. scotch
1 oz. orange juice
½ oz. lemon juice
1 tsp. maple syrup or sugar
  syrup

Dash grenadine

Mix all ingredients with cracked
ice in a shaker or blender. Strain
into a chilled Whiskey Sour
glass.

OPENING No. 1

1½ oz. Canadian whisky
1 tsp. sweet vermouth
1 tsp. grenadine

Stir with ice in a pitcher or
mixing glass and strain into a
chilled cocktail glass.

QUEBEC COCKTAIL

1½ oz. Canadian whisky
½ oz. Amer Picon
½ oz. maraschino liqueur
½ oz. dry vermouth

Mix all ingredients with cracked
ice in a shaker or blender. Strain
into a chilled cocktail glass.

STE. AGATHE COCKTAIL

1½ oz. Canadian whisky
¾ oz. Cointreau
1 tsp. grenadine
½ oz. lemon juice
Lemon peel

Mix all ingredients, except lemon
peel, with cracked ice in a shaker
or blender. Strain into a chilled
cocktail glass. Twist lemon
peel over drink and drop in.

SASKATOON STINGER

2 oz. Canadian whisky
1 oz. peppermint schnapps or
    white crème de menthe
Lemon peel

Pour whisky and peppermint schnapps into a chilled Old Fashioned glass with ice cubes and stir gently. Twist lemon peel over drink and drop in.

 ## SINGAPORE COCKTAIL

1½ oz. Canadian whisky
¾ oz. sloe gin
¼ oz. Rose's lime juice
½ oz. lemon juice
Cucumber peel

Mix all ingredients, except cucumber peel, with cracked ice in a shaker or blender. Pour into a chilled Old Fashioned glass. Garnish with a cucumber peel.

 ## TROIS RIVIÈRES

1½ oz. Canadian whisky
¾ oz. Dubonnet rouge
½ oz. triple sec
Orange peel

Mix all ingredients, except orange peel, with cracked ice in a shaker or blender. Strain into a chilled cocktail glass. Twist orange peel over drink and drop in.

 ## VANCOUVER COCKTAIL

2 oz. Canadian whisky
1 oz. Dubonnet rouge
½ oz. lemon juice
1 egg white (for two drinks)
½ tsp. maple syrup or sugar
    syrup

Several dashes orange
    bitters (optional)

Mix all ingredients with cracked ice in a shaker or blender. Pour into a chilled cocktail glass.

RYE

 ## BAL HARBOUR COCKTAIL

1½ oz. rye
½ oz. dry vermouth
1 oz. grapefruit juice
Maraschino cherry

Mix all ingredients, except cherry, with cracked ice in a shaker or blender. Strain into a chilled cocktail glass. Garnish with maraschino cherry.

BLINKER

1½ oz. rye
2 oz. grapefruit juice
1 tsp. grenadine

Mix all ingredients with cracked
ice in a shaker or blender. Pour
into a chilled cocktail glass.

ELK'S OWN

1½ oz. rye
¾ oz. port
Juice of ½ lemon
1 egg white
1 tsp. powdered sugar
Pineapple stick

Mix all ingredients, except
pineapple, with cracked ice in a
shaker or blender. Pour into a
chilled Old Fashioned glass.
Garnish with pineapple stick.

FRISCO COCKTAIL

1½ oz. rye
1½ oz. Benedictine
½ oz. lemon juice
Orange peel

Mix all ingredients, except orange
peel, in a shaker or blender with
cracked ice and strain into a
chilled cocktail glass. Garnish
with orange peel.

FOX RIVER

1½ oz. rye
½ oz. dark crème de cacao
Several dashes orange bitters
   or peach bitters
Lemon peel

Mix all ingredients, except
lemon peel, with cracked ice in a
shaker or blender. Pour into a
chilled cocktail glass. Twist
lemon peel over drink and drop
in.

FRUITY OLD FASHIONED

1½ oz. rye
1 oz. sugar syrup
1 tsp. cherry juice
Several dashes Angostura or
   orange bitters
Peach slice or pineapple slice
Orange slice
Maraschino cherry

Lemon peel
Whole strawberry (optional)

Mix all ingredients, except fruit
and lemon peel, with cracked ice
in a chilled Old Fashioned glass.
Garnish with strawberry, orange
slice, and maraschino cherry.
Twist lemon peel over drink and
drop in along with strawberry.

HESITATION

1½ oz. rye
1½ oz. Swedish Punsch
Several dashes lemon juice

Mix all ingredients with cracked ice in a shaker or blender. Pour into a chilled cocktail glass.

HUNTER'S COCKTAIL

1½ oz. rye
½ oz. cherry brandy
Maraschino cherry

Pour rye and cherry brandy into an Old Fashioned glass with ice. Stir well. Garnish with maraschino cherry.

INDIAN RIVER COCKTAIL No. 2

1 oz. rye
1 oz. dry vermouth
2 oz. orange juice
Several dashes raspberry syrup

Mix all ingredients with cracked ice in a shaker or blender. Pour into a chilled Old Fashioned glass.

KUNGSHOLM COCKTAIL

1 oz. rye
1 oz. Swedish Punsch
2 oz. orange juice
½ oz. raspberry syrup

Several dashes Pernod

Mix all ingredients with cracked ice in a shaker or blender. Pour into a chilled double Old Fashioned glass.

LAFAYETTE

1½ oz. rye
¼ oz. dry vermouth
¼ oz. Dubonnet rouge
Several dashes Angostura bitters

Mix all ingredients with cracked ice in a shaker or blender. Pour into a chilled Old Fashioned glass.

LISBON COCKTAIL

1½ oz. rye
2 oz. port
½ oz. lemon juice
1 tsp. sugar syrup or to taste
1 egg white (for two drinks)

Mix all ingredients with cracked ice in a shaker or blender. Pour into a chilled Old Fashioned glass.

LORD BALTIMORE'S CUP

½ tsp. sugar syrup or
  to taste
Several dashes Angostura
  bitters
1 oz. rye
Champagne
Several dashes Pernod

Combine sugar and Angostura
bitters in chilled wine goblet.
Add rye and several ice cubes.
Fill with champagne and add
a float of Pernod.

 ## MONTE CARLO

1½ oz. rye
½ oz. Benedictine
Several dashes Angostura
  bitters

Mix all ingredients with cracked
ice in a shaker or blender. Pour
into a chilled cocktail glass.

NEW YORK

1½ oz. rye
½ oz. lime juice
1 tsp. sugar syrup
Several dashes grenadine
Orange peel

Mix all ingredients, except orange
peel, with cracked ice in a shaker
or blender. Pour into a chilled
Old Fashioned glass. Twist
orange peel over drink and drop
in.

 ## NORMANDY COOLER

1 oz. rye
1 oz. calvados
1 tsp. sugar syrup
Club soda
Lemon slice

Mix all ingredients, except club
soda, with cracked ice in a shaker
or blender. Pour into a chilled
highball glass and fill with club
soda. Garnish with lemon slice.

 ## OPENING No. 2

1½ oz. rye
¼ oz. sweet vermouth
Dash grenadine
Dash maraschino liqueur

Mix all ingredients with cracked
ice in a shaker or blender. Pour
into a chilled cocktail glass.

PERFECT RYE MANHATTAN

2 oz. rye
½ tsp. sweet vermouth
½ tsp. dry vermouth
Several dashes Angostura
   bitters
Maraschino cherry

Mix all ingredients, except cherry, with cracked ice in a shaker or blender. Strain into a chilled cocktail glass. Garnish with maraschino cherry.

PINK RYE

1½ oz. rye
Several dashes Angostura
   bitters

Fill an Old Fashioned glass with crushed ice, pour in rye, add bitters and stir well.

RED TOP

1½ oz. rye
½ oz. lemon or lime juice
1 tsp. sugar syrup
1 egg white (for two drinks)
½ oz. claret

Mix all ingredients, except claret, with cracked ice in a shaker or blender. Strain into a chilled Whiskey Sour glass. Top with claret.

ROARING TWENTIES MANHATTAN

1 oz. rye
2 oz. dry or sweet vermouth
Several dashes orange bitters

Mix all ingredients with cracked ice in a mixing glass. Serve in a chilled cocktail glass.

ROCK AND RYE COOLER

1 oz. rock and rye
1 oz. vodka
1 tsp. lime juice
Lemon-lime soda
Lime slice

Mix all ingredients, except soda and lime slice, with cracked ice in a shaker or blender. Pour into a chilled highball glass. Fill with lemon-lime soda. Garnish with lime slice.

ROCKY RIVER COCKTAIL

1 oz. rye
1 oz. apricot brandy
1 tsp. lemon juice
Sugar syrup to taste
Maraschino cherry

Mix all ingredients, except cherry, with cracked ice in a shaker or blender. Strain into a chilled cocktail glass. Decorate with maraschino cherry.

ROSE HALL RYE TODDY

1 oz. rye
1 oz. Jamaica rum
Juice of ½ lime
1 oz. sugar syrup or Falernum
   to taste

Mix all ingredients with cracked ice in a shaker or blender. Pour into a chilled Old Fashioned glass.

RYE FIZZ

1½ oz. rye
Dash Angostura bitters
Dash sugar syrup
Club soda

Combine rye, bitters, and syrup in a mixing glass. Stir well. Pour into a chilled highball glass along with several ice cubes. Fill with club soda.

RYE FLIP

1½ oz. rye
1 egg
1 tsp. sugar syrup
Ground nutmeg

Mix all ingredients, except nutmeg, with cracked ice in a shaker or blender. Strain into a chilled brandy glass. Sprinkle with ground nutmeg.

RYE MANHATTAN

1½ oz. rye
¼ oz. sweet vermouth
Maraschino cherry

Mix rye and vermouth in a mixing glass with cracked ice

and strain into a chilled cocktail glass. Garnish with cherry. For a drier drink, substitute dry vermouth in place of sweet and use lemon twist in place of cherry.

SHAKER HEIGHTS

½ oz. rye
½ oz. gin
½ oz. sweet vermouth
½ oz. brandy
Several dashes orange bitters

Mix all ingredients with cracked ice in a shaker or blender. Strain into a chilled cocktail glass.

STRØGET COCKTAIL

2 oz. rye
1 oz. Peter Heering
½ oz. lemon juice

Mix all ingredients with cracked ice in a shaker or blender and strain into a chilled cocktail glass.

TENNESSEE

2 oz. rye
1 oz. maraschino liqueur
½ oz. lemon juice

Mix all ingredients with cracked ice in a shaker or blender. Serve in a chilled cocktail glass.

 ## T.N.T. COCKTAIL No. 1

1½ oz. rye
1½ oz. Pernod

Mix both ingredients with cracked ice in a shaker or blender. Serve in a chilled cocktail glass.

WHITEHALL COCKTAIL

1½ oz. rye
½ oz. lime juice
½ oz. Benedictine
Several dashes Angostura
    bitters

Mix all ingredients with cracked ice in a shaker or blender. Serve in a chilled cocktail glass.

 ## YASHMAK

1½ oz. rye
¾ oz. dry vermouth
½ oz. Pernod
Several dashes Angostura
    bitters
Sugar syrup to taste

Mix all ingredients with cracked ice in a shaker or blender. Pour into a chilled highball glass.

IN SEARCH OF IRISH SPIRITS AND THE SCOTCH MYSTIQUE

> I've taken more good from alcohol
> than alcohol has taken from me.
> —Winston Churchill

No one knows precisely when the Irish invented whiskey, but invent it they did, and, as many an Irishman truly believes, in terms of civilized blessings this event ranks in stature with the discovery of fire and the invention of the wheel.

The art of distillation had been around for several thousand years, for Aristotle wrote of it three centuries before the birth of Christ. It was known in ancient Egypt and Mesopotamia as well as China and some other parts of the Far East, but the Saracens are generally credited with introducing distilling to the modern era. The use of the alembic (an Arabic word), which is very similar in appearance and function to the old-fashioned copper-pot still, to manufacture potable spirits eluded man until the sixth century. This is about the time when the Celts came upon their momentous discovery. The English, never ones to be shy about raising a goblet at the drop of a cork, gave the name "whiskey" to the Gaelic *uisce beatha* (meaning "water of life") after the army of Henry II returned to England in 1170 from a foray to the Emerald Isle. The expedition was undistinguished except for a protracted and enthusiastic sampling of the native distilled beverages.

Word of this golden elixir spread throughout the realm, and it ultimately became a favorite potation in royal circles. Queen Elizabeth I was known to take a tot or two, possibly through the good offices of her friend and confidant, Sir Walter Raleigh, who was presented with a puncheon of homemade whiskey by the Earl of Cork when he was en route to the New World. Even the czar of all the Russias, Peter the Great, preferred Irish whiskey over vodka and said so in no uncertain terms. "Of all the wines," he proclaimed, "the Irish is the best." By the end of the eighteenth century Ireland was awash with whiskey stills—more than two thousand according to the tax collectors, who, then as now, were not welcome in the glens and hollows of the back country.

Having invented whiskey, it follows as surely as night shall follow the day that one must have a place to drink it. The parlor wouldn't do in olden days, for that was a family room. It must be a public place and accessible to all. Enter the public house, i.e., the pub.

If the Irish didn't invent the pub, they surely turned it into a most lasting national institution. Today, throughout the length of the republic, from Malin Head in the north to Mizen Head in the south, there are reportedly some ten thousand pubs. They are very much an integral part of the cultural life and the social fabric of the land. An Irish pub, whether a bright and brassy emporium in Dublin, or a humble wayside bar at a village crossroad in Donegal or Kerry, must be experienced to be appreciated. The Irish pub is at once a haven, forum, recreation center, retreat, snack bar, and saloon, but—first and foremost—a drinking establishment. It is here you will find arrayed along the back bar, behind great ebony tap handles bearing the names Guinness Stout, Smithwick's ale, and Harp beer, the distinguished company of Irish whiskeys: Dunphy's, John Jameson, Old Bushmill's, Murphy's, Paddy, Power's, and Tullamore Dew, to name the most popular brands. Currently, Bushmills and Jameson are available in the U.S.

You also will find something else in every Irish pub: the opportunity to do exactly what you want to do. You can drink quietly, enjoy a light meal of "pub grub," read your newspaper, have a go at the dart board, or socialize. The latter, for most, is a great attraction. It is said that an Irishman won't walk across the street for a free drink, but will travel a mile or two for some good conversation. True or not, you'll find plenty of good conversation in Irish pubs without any question, for the Irish are a gregarious lot—friendly, outgoing, articulate, and loquacious, all of which is aided by a few drams of good Irish whiskey or a pint or two of Guinness.

Having frequented more than a few pubs on several visits to Ireland, I have often marveled at feeling so fit the morning after a night out in a pub. Aside from the natural stimulation of pleasant surroundings and friendly encounters, I have concluded that the care and aging that go into the making of Irish whiskey has a salutary effect (in moderate quantities, of course) on the human organism.

Irish whiskey, like scotch, is made from barley and water, but unlike scotch, the malted and unmalted barley used to make

Irish whiskey is dried in smokeless kilns, whereas the Scots dry their barley over peat fires, thus accounting for the smoky flavor of scotch. During the great potato famines of the early nineteenth century it was feared there would be a world shortage of Irish spirits by some who believed that Irish whiskey is the product of potatoes. This bit of misinformation came about, no doubt, from the fact that illicit whiskey is known in Ireland as "poteen," a name derived from the pot stills that are an essential part of the bootlegger's paraphernalia.

The basic process of making whiskey is quite simple on paper, but in practice requires considerable skill and experience. The barley, malted and unmalted (malting is achieved by allowing barley to sprout and stopping the growing process at just the right time by kiln drying), is ground along with other cereal grains such as rye, wheat, and corn, mixed with water, and cooked in huge tuns, or tanks. Then yeast is added, and the mixture is allowed to ferment for several days. The first of three distillations takes place in large pot stills after which the whiskey—raw, powerful, and crystal clear—is placed in oak casks and allowed to age from four to fifteen years. After sampling and testing when the maturation process has been completed, the whiskey is reduced in alcoholic strength by the addition of distilled water until it reaches 80 proof and allowed to "rest" for a time before being bottled. The result is a whiskey that is full-bodied, smooth, mellow, and possessed of a distinctive barley malt flavor. Irish whiskey is highly regarded by those who know and respect fine whiskey. It deserves more exposure than simply as a basic ingredient for Irish Coffee, as delectable as that worthy libation may be, for it is excellent on-the-rocks with a little water, club soda, or other mixers, and in a wide range of mixed drinks.

In and around the softly rolling, verdant counties of southern Ireland (palm trees grow in Kerry), 'tis said that soil in Tipperary and Waterford is so rich that a toothpick stuck in the sod will sprout in a fortnight. Here nature's bounty seems endless, and dairy products from Cork are legend. It was the richness of Ireland's cream that softened and smoothed out the resulting flavor of coffee, and Irish whiskey in Irish Coffee. What if, someone may have surmised, we leave out the coffee and just combine a little whiskey and cream? They did and it was delicious and a whole new liquor category began to take shape. R.& A. Bailey Co., Ltd, of Dublin found a way to homogenize spirits and cream so that after bottling it would have a reasonable shelf life without refrigeration under most climatic conditions. In the brief time since its birth in 1979, Bailey's Original Irish Cream Liqueur has rocketed to a sales level of one million cases per year, making it, according to industry sources, the number-one selling liqueur in the world.

This success story has encouraged a host of similar proprietary liqueurs made with Irish whiskey and various flavorings blended with fresh cream. All are quality products and include such brands as Carolans, the number-two Irish cream liqueur; Waterford, made by Irish Distillers International, who own and control all of the major whiskey production in Ireland; O'Darby's; and Emmett's, and, no doubt, others which have not yet crossed my lips. One thing is certain, all of the cream liqueurs seem to have an irresistible appetite appeal for many, many people, even those who are not disposed to be whisky drinkers. Perhaps therein lies the secret of its success: It tastes more like an adult milk shake than an alcoholic beverage. And apparently that's a taste that a lot of people like.

In Tullamore, very near to the geographical center of Ireland, another remarkable spiritous product is made by the Irish Mist Liqueur Company, Ltd., which in a relatively brief period of time has achieved recognition as one of the world's great proprietary liqueurs. Irish Mist is exciting to the palate and to the imagination, for it is believed by members of the Williams family, who created the liqueur from an old formula, that Irish Mist may be a re-creation of the lost heather wine of Ireland.

Now, if you don't know about heather wine you haven't been reading any Irish folklore lately. According to legend, heather wine was made from a closely guarded recipe by "the little people," or fairies. It also was said to be the favorite tonic of the Tuatha de Danann, an ancient Irish race endowed with magical powers since driven underground by the Celts, where, some say, they flourish to this day. Nevertheless, there are enough historical references, folklore notwithstanding, to convince many scholars that heather wine did indeed exist. Heather wine is alluded to in Irish song and story and records dating back to the pagan era of Irish history. And then it was gone.

The date of that disappearance is 1691, a year of great rebellion, when the "Wild Geese," the Irish nobility, fled Ireland. It is said that they took the secret of heather wine with them. Nobody really knows the whereabouts of the ancient formula. It remains a mystery. As the story goes, some of the Irish exiles later joined the army of Maria Theresa, the empress of Austria, where they served with distinction. So one fine day when the Williams family received a visitor from Austria bearing an ancient recipe purported to be the lost secret of heather wine, the pieces seemed to fit together. More important than the credibility of the visitor was the formula itself. It stood up to close scrutiny and tested out beyond all expectations. So when you quaff some Irish Mist, "the legendary liqueur," you just might be sampling Ireland's lost heather wine. In any event, the experience is a pleasant one.

Whether the real secret of heather wine has been recovered or not, I do not know, but it surely fires the imagination with another kind of spirit—the spirit of Ireland's glorious past. You sense it when you stand on the brow of the Hill of Tailte watching the sun set across the Blackwater River that runs through the gently rolling Meath countryside. Here was held the ancient festival of Aonoch Tailteann, games of strength and skill dating from prehistoric times. Close by, on the hilltop, lie the ruins of Rath Dubh, or Black Fort, built by King Tuathal. In these once great halls cups were raised high as toasts were drunk, perhaps with heather wine, to the champions of the games. Here in the valley of the Boyne, you are surrounded by jewels in the crown of Irish history: Kells, where the famous Book of Kells was written; Tara, home of ancient Irish kings; and the Hill of Slane, where St. Patrick lit the paschal fire in A.D. 433.

One can only guess what part heather wine and *uisce beatha* played in those ancient times, but one thing we do know, these spirits are very much a part of the lore and the legends of this wondrous land.

THE SCOTCH MYSTIQUE

Scotch whisky is made of grain, yeast, and water; fermented, then distilled, aged, and bottled. The process seems simple enough yet no spirit has as many subtle complexities in its making or is surrounded in as much lore and tradition. As many a traveler has found to his astonishment and delight after even a brief journey down the "Whisky Trail" in Scotland, once exposed to the Scotch whisky mystique, one may never again drink this remarkable beverage with indifference or lack of appreciation.

How, you ask, in this age of computers, lasers, and electronically controlled industry, can anything as simple as the distilling of Scotch whisky be characterized as complex? The answer is that making scotch is not complex—but it is surrounded by mystery (such as why the letter "e" is omitted from the word "whisky"). It is not what is known about the process of Scotch whisky production that is intriguing, but what is seemingly unknowable.

A case in point: Two identical casks of scotch aging in the same warehouse, one on the earthen floor, the other on a rack nearby, twelve feet above the floor, will have different characteristics when sampled at the end of the aging period. The reason is known. It has to do with air circulation, since casks of whisky "breathe" as they age. But just *how* this can have such an effect on the finished whisky is a mystery.

Then there is the Laphroaig mystery. It seems that when

some of the single-malt whisky produced by this highly respected distillery on the Isle of Islay (pronounced **eye-lay**) is put up in casks for aging, it takes on a seaweed tang in the ninth month. This completely disappears at the twelfth year, however. Some say that this is due to the sea washing against the distillery walls, but exactly *how* this affects the whisky is not so easy to explain.

Despite dedicated efforts to make surrogate scotch in other places as diverse as Asia and North America, the results have been a perfectly drinkable whisky, but lacking in those subtle qualities that would be considered attributes of a fine scotch.

There are two types of Scotch whisky: malt whisky, which is made in an old-fashioned pot still (similar to cognac) and grain whiskey, which is made in a patent or continuous still, sometimes called a Coffey still after its inventor, Aeneas Coffey. Malt whisky is made entirely from malted barley, and grain whisky is made from malted barley combined with unmalted barley and corn. The malting process involves the soaking of barley for two to three days in water and then spreading it out over a wide area so it can germinate or sprout. During this period, which lasts from eight to twelve days, the enzyme diastase is released. The enzyme makes the starch in the barley soluble so it can be converted to sugar. During the malting process the rate of germination and temperature must be carefully controlled. In some places the barley is still spread out on a malting floor and turned by hand to regulate the germination activity. In modern facilities the malting is done in boxes or drums turned by machine while temperature-controlled air is blown through the germinating grain.

At precisely the right time, the germination is stopped by drying the green malt (malted barley) in a kiln. The peat that is used to fire the kiln is responsible for the smoky taste that is a characteristic of malt whisky. The dried malt then is ground in a grist mill and poured into a huge tank or tun, where the mash is mixed with hot water. The liquid soluble starch (wort) created by the malting process is, after eight hours, drawn off from the mash tun and transferred to the fermentation vats. Here, the wort is fermented by yeast for forty-eight hours. This converts the sugar in the wort to low-strength alcohol (wash) and various by-products that are not involved in the scotch-making process. These are then filtered out.

The malt whisky is distilled twice in large copper-pot stills. The distillation process involves heating the wash mixture until it is vaporized. The vapors are collected in a condenser that is cooled by water, causing them to return to a liquid state. The pot still (similar in principle to the old alembic used by alchemists) must be emptied and recharged after each distilling cycle. In the case of grain whisky, the patent still is continuous in its operation as it is in the form of a huge column, not a pot, and thus can be charged and emptied without interfering with the distillation process.

The raw whisky is now ready for maturation in oak casks. They may be new American white oak containers, used sherry butts, or even casks that have held other spirits such as American bourbon. The whisky must age for at least three years, although most are aged longer. Malt whiskies require longer maturation than grain whiskies—as long as fourteen or fifteen years. Some blenders say that everything that can be achieved in aging is realized before the fifteenth year. For grain whiskies, six to eight years is considered optimum. When aging is complete, the whisky is ready for the most important step of all: blending.

In Scotland a master blender holds a position of high esteem considering the fact that ninety-eight percent of all whiskies produced at Scotland's 116 malt-whisky distilleries and fourteen grain-whisky distilleries are used to make *blended* Scotch whisky. While it is true there is a growing desire in the U.S. for single-malt whiskies (unblended), and storied names are appearing in American bars such as The Glenlivet, Knockando, Glenfiddich, Laphroaig, Glenmorangie, Macallan, and others, single malts account for only a tiny percentage of total scotch sales worldwide.

The blender's task is to replicate the blend in use, week in and week out, year after year. Quality control and ensuring a consistent product is of prime importance. Creating new blends is challenging and exciting, but is only a small part of the blender's job. The average blend will involve from fifteen to fifty different whiskies, since each distillery produces a whisky that has unique flavor and aroma. This individuality is one of the great aspects of the scotch mystique: how malt whiskies can vary in taste, using the very same ingredients and distilled in the same way only a short distance from one another. Since the blender and his team must sample, in some instances, four hundred casks in a single day, he must rely on his nose and his ability to remember his individual olfactory experiences, much as an accomplished composer will remember tones, chords, and melodies. As a rule, blenders do not taste the whiskies they sample, but rely entirely upon their highly educated noses.

Blending is designed to achieve a synergistic effect in the end product, meaning that the whole will be far superior to any of the individual elements it contains. To aid the blender in the task of selecting components that will "marry well" when blended, a library of spirits is carefully assembled. (Certain whiskies "fight one another," causing the temperature in the vats to rise, while some components of one whisky will cancel out the qualities of another whisky and thus cannot be used in a particular blending formula.) The library will contain samples from perhaps a hundred distilleries. In addition, it will have samples of many different blends devised by the blender and his assistants as well as samples of blends, purchased on the open market, of many competing brands of scotch. Most important is the collection of "key" malt whiskies from the most important distilleries in the various areas of Scotland, classified by the types of scotch produced in each. Lowland malt whiskies in the south of Scotland are represented by such names as Glenkinchie, Lomand, Ladyburn, and Inverleven; Islay malts by Bowmore, Bruichladdich, Legavulin, and Laphroaig; the Campbeltown malts by Glen Scotia and Springbank; the grain distilleries by such names as Cambus, Dumbarton, Girvan, and Strathclyde; and—the largest group of all—the Highland malts, with some of the most hallowed names in the long history of scotch making: Aberfeldy, Ardmore, Cardow, Dufftown Glenlivet, Craigellachie, Dalwhinnie, Glenfarclas, Glendronach, Glen Grant, Knockando, Ord, Speyside, Strathisla, Talisker, and Tormore, among many others.

When the blender goes to work he has a vast arsenal of flavors and aromas to choose from, many of which are well-known to him. In devising a blend, he strives to utilize each component in exactly the right proportion to achieve the optimum flavor, character, and balance in the finished product. A hypothetical blend might consist of the following: sixty-five percent grain whiskies made up of the products of two or three grain distilleries, and thirty-five percent malt whiskies comprised of products from ten to fifteen malt distilleries. The malts, by far the most important components in the blend, might be chosen as follows: four to six Highland malts for body, three to four Speyside malts for balance, three or four Lowland malts for lightness, and one or two Islay malts for accent.

When all of the matured whiskies are "called" from the warehouse by the blender and his staff, they will be "vatted" or mixed to exacting specifications and then returned to wood to marry for six to nine months. When the blend is checked before bottling, it will have achieved precisely the flavor, bouquet or aroma, body, and color that the blender expected. Into every bottle will go a symphonic melding of Scotland's finest—the grain, the sun, the rain, the soil, the water that coursed through Highland heather and bracken, and, finally, the yeast and wood and the coming together with all the science and art and care that man can muster.

And there will be something else that goes into every bottle of whisky—a generous portion of scotch mystique.

ABERDEEN SOUR

2 oz. scotch
1 oz. orange juice
1 oz. lemon juice
½ oz. triple sec

Mix all ingredients with cracked ice in a shaker or blender. Pour into a chilled Old Fashioned glass.

AFFINITY COCKTAIL No. 2

1 oz. scotch
1 oz. dry sherry
1 oz. port
Several dashes Angostura
    bitters
Lemon peel
Maraschino cherry

Stir all ingredients, except lemon and cherry, in a mixing glass with cracked ice and strain into a chilled cocktail glass. Twist lemon peel over drink and drop into glass and garnish with a cherry.

ARDMORE COCKTAIL

1 oz. scotch
½ oz. Cherry Marnier
½ oz. sweet vermouth
2 oz. orange juice

Mix all ingredients with cracked ice in a shaker or blender. Strain into a chilled cocktail glass.

ARGYLL COCKTAIL

1 oz. scotch
1 oz. calvados
½ oz. dry gin
1 tsp. heather honey or sugar
    syrup

Mix all ingredients, except lemon peel, with cracked ice in a shaker or blender. Pour into a chilled Old Fashioned glass. Twist lemon peel over drink and drop in.

AULD MAN'S MILK Cold

1 tsp. sugar syrup
1 whole egg
5 oz. heavy cream, or 3 oz.
    cream and 3 oz. milk
2 oz. scotch
Grated nutmeg

Beat egg separately with sugar syrup and add to a shaker or blender with cream, scotch, and cracked ice. Mix well and pour into a chilled Old Fashioned glass. Sprinkle with grated nutmeg.

BARTENDER'S SECRET NO. 21

When filling a number of glasses from the same cocktail shaker or blender, don't fill the first glass to the top and then the remaining glasses. You will usually come out short on the last glass unless you are experienced. Experts fill each glass about half full and then return to glass number one and repeat the procedure. This will insure an equal portion for everyone.

BAIRN

1½ oz. scotch
¾ oz. Cointreau
Several dashes orange bitters

Mix all ingredients with cracked ice in a shaker or blender. Strain into a chilled cocktail glass.

BALLSBRIDGE BRACER

1½ oz. Irish whiskey
¾ oz. Irish Mist
3 oz. orange juice
1 egg white (for two drinks)

Mix all ingredients with cracked ice in a shaker or blender. Strain into a chilled Whiskey Sour glass.

BALLYLICKEY BELT

½ tsp. Heather honey or to
   taste
1½ oz. Irish whiskey
Club soda
Lemon peel

Muddle heather honey with a little water or club soda until dissolved and pour in whiskey. Add several ice cubes and fill with club soda. Twist lemon peel over drink and drop into glass.

BALMORAL STIRRUP CUP

1½ oz. scotch
1 oz. Cointreau
Several dashes Angostura
   bitters

Mix all ingredients with cracked ice in a shaker or blender. Strain into a chilled cocktail glass.

BANCHORY COCKTAIL

1 oz. scotch
1 oz. medium sherry
1 tsp. lemon juice
1 tsp. orange juice
½ tsp. sugar syrup

Mix all ingredients with cracked ice in a shaker or blender. Strain into a chilled cocktail glass.

BANFF BANG

1½ oz. gin
½ oz. amontillado sherry
1 oz. scotch
Lemon peel

Mix gin and amontillado with cracked ice in a shaker or blender. Pour into a chilled Old Fashioned glass. Twist lemon peel over drink and drop in, and float scotch on top.

BARBARY COAST

¾ oz. scotch
¾ oz. light rum
¾ oz. gin
¾ oz. white crème de cacao
1 oz. cream

Mix all ingredients with cracked ice in a shaker or blender. Pour into a chilled Old Fashioned glass.

BLACKTHORN No. 1

1½ oz. Irish whiskey
1½ oz. dry vermouth
Several dashes Pernod
Several dashes Angostura
  bitters

Mix all ingredients with cracked ice in a shaker or blender. Pour into a chilled Old Fashioned glass.
Note: Sloe gin can be used in place of Irish whiskey.

BLACKWATCH

1½ oz. scotch
½ oz. curaçao
½ oz. brandy
Lemon slice
Mint sprig

Pour scotch, curaçao, and brandy into a chilled highball glass along with several ice cubes. Gently stir. Garnish with lemon slice and mint sprig.

BLOOD & SAND

¾ oz. scotch
¾ oz. cherry brandy
¾ oz. sweet vermouth
¾ oz. orange juice

Mix all ingredients with cracked ice in a shaker or blender. Pour into a chilled Old Fashioned glass.

BLUE FIRTH

1½ oz. scotch
½ oz. blue curaçao
Dash dry vermouth
Dash orange bitters

Mix all ingredients with cracked ice in a shaker or blender. Strain into a chilled cocktail glass.

BOBBY BURNS

1½ oz. scotch
½ oz. dry vermouth
½ oz. sweet vermouth
Dash Benedictine

Mix all ingredients with cracked
ice in a shaker or blender. Strain
into a chilled cocktail glass.

BONNIE PRINCE CHARLIE

1½ oz. scotch
½ oz. dry vermouth
Several dashes Pernod
Lemon peel

Mix all ingredients, except
lemon peel, with cracked ice in a
shaker or blender. Strain into
a chilled Martini glass. Twist
lemon peel over drink and drop
in.

BOW STREET SPECIAL

1½ oz. Irish whiskey
¾ oz. triple sec
1 oz. lemon juice

Mix with cracked ice in a
shaker or blender and strain into
a chilled cocktail glass.

BRAEMAR COCKTAIL

1½ oz. scotch
½ oz. sweet vermouth
½ oz. Benedictine

Mix all ingredients with cracked
ice in a shaker or blender. Strain
into a chilled cocktail glass.

BRIGADOON

1 oz. scotch
1 oz. grapefruit juice
1 oz. dry vermouth

Mix all ingredients with cracked
ice in a shaker or blender. Pour
into a chilled Old Fashioned
glass.

BUNRATTY PEG

1½ oz. Irish whiskey
¾ oz. Irish Mist, amaretto, or
   Drambuie

Stir with ice and strain into a
chilled cocktail glass or with ice
cubes in an Old Fashioned
glass.

CABER TOSS

1¼ oz. scotch
1¼ oz. gin
½ oz. Pernod

Mix all ingredients with cracked ice in a blender or shaker. Strain into a chilled cocktail glass.

CAITHNESS COMFORT

2–3 oz. scotch
½ oz. honey
½ oz. triple sec
6 oz. milk
1 oz. cream

Pinch grated nutmeg

Mix all ingredients except nutmeg in a shaker or blender with cracked ice and pour into a chilled Collins glass. Add pinch of grated nutmeg.

CAMPBELTOWN JOY

1½ oz. scotch
1 tsp. dry vermouth
½ oz. Drambuie
Dash orange bitters

Mix all ingredients with cracked ice in a shaker or blender. Strain into a chilled cocktail glass.

CELTIC BULL

1½ oz. Irish whiskey
2 oz. beef consommé or
   bouillon
2 oz. tomato juice
*Several dashes Worcester-
   shire sauce*

Dash Tabasco sauce
Freshly ground pepper

Mix all ingredients with cracked ice in a shaker or blender. Pour into a chilled Old Fashioned glass.

COCKTAIL NA MARA Cocktail of the Sea

2 oz. Irish whiskey
2 oz. clam juice
4 oz. tomato juice
½ oz. lemon juice
*Several dashes Worcester-
   shire sauce*

Dash Tabasco sauce
Pinch white pepper

Stir all ingredients well in a mixing glass with cracked ice and pour into a chilled high-ball glass.

COLLODEN CHEER

1 oz. scotch
1 oz. dry sherry
½ oz. lemon juice
½ oz. La Grande Passion

Mix all ingredients with cracked ice in a shaker or blender. Strain into a chilled cocktail glass.

CONNEMARA CLAMMER

2 oz. Irish whiskey
2 oz. clam juice
3 oz. V-8 juice
1 tsp. lime juice
Several dashes Worcester-
    shire sauce
½ tsp. horseradish

Several pinches freshly
    ground black or white
    pepper

Mix all ingredients with cracked
ice in a shaker or blender. Strain
into a chilled double Old Fashioned glass.

CORK COMFORT

1½ oz. Irish whiskey
¾ oz. sweet vermouth
Several dashes Angostura
    bitters
Several dashes Southern
    Comfort

Mix all ingredients with cracked
ice in a shaker or blender. Pour
into a chilled Old Fashioned
glass.

DINGLE DRAM

1½ oz. Irish whiskey
½ oz. Irish Mist
Coffee soda
Dash crème de cacao
Whipped cream

Pour Irish whiskey and Irish
Mist into a chilled highball glass
along with several ice cubes.
Fill with coffee soda. Stir gently.
Add a float of crème de cacao.
Top with dollop of whipped cream.

DUNDEE DRAM

1 oz. scotch
1 oz. gin
½ oz. Drambuie
1 tsp. lemon juice
Lemon peel
Maraschino cherry

Mix all ingredients, except
lemon peel and cherry, with
cracked ice in a shaker or
blender. Pour into a chilled Old
Fashioned glass. Twist lemon
peel over drink and drop in. Garnish with cherry.

DUNDEE DUNKER

2 oz. scotch
6 oz. milk
1 tsp. golden syrup or honey
Grated nutmeg
Shortbread

Mix all ingredients, except nutmeg and shortbread, with cracked
ice in a shaker or blender.
Pour into a chilled Old Fashioned glass. Sprinkle with
grated nutmeg. Dunk shortbread
in mixture as you drink it.

ERIC THE RED

1½ oz. scotch
½ oz. Peter Heering
1 tsp. dry vermouth

Mix all ingredients with cracked ice in a shaker or blender. Pour into a chilled Old Fashioned glass.

FLYING SCOT

1½ oz. scotch
1 oz. sweet vermouth
Several dashes sugar syrup
Several dashes Angostura
  bitters

Mix all ingredients with cracked ice in a shaker or blender. Pour into a chilled Old Fashioned glass.

GLASGOW

1½ oz. scotch
½ oz. crème de noyaux or
  amaretto
¼ oz. dry vermouth
½ oz. lemon juice

Mix all ingredients with cracked ice in a shaker or blender. Strain into a chilled cocktail glass.

GLENBEIGH FIZZ

1½ oz. Irish whiskey
1 oz. medium sherry
½ oz. crème de noyaux
½ oz. lemon juice
Club soda

Pour all ingredients, except club soda, with several ice cubes in a chilled highball glass and stir. Fill with club soda.

GLENEAGLES AERIE

1½ oz. scotch
½ oz. dry vermouth
½ oz. port
Dash orange bitters

Mix all ingredients with cracked ice in a shaker or blender. Strain into a chilled cocktail glass.

THE GODFATHER

1½ oz. scotch, bourbon, or
  blended whiskey
¾ oz. Amaretto di Saronno

Mix with ice cubes in a chilled Old Fashioned glass.

GRAFTON STREET SOUR

1½ oz. Irish whiskey
½ oz. triple sec
1 oz. lime juice
¼ oz. raspberry liqueur

Mix all ingredients, except raspberry liqueur, with cracked ice in a shaker or blender and strain into a chilled cocktail glass. Top with raspberry liqueur.

GRETNA GREEN

½ oz. Falernum or heather honey
1½ oz. scotch
½ oz. green Chartreuse
1 oz. lemon juice

Mix Falernum or honey with a little water until dissolved and pour into a shaker or blender with scotch, green Chartreuse, and lemon juice, and mix thoroughly with cracked ice. Strain into a chilled cocktail glass.

HARRY LAUDER

1½ oz. scotch
1½ oz. sweet vermouth
½ tsp. sugar syrup

Mix all ingredients with cracked ice in a shaker or blender. Strain into a chilled cocktail glass.

HIGHLAND FLING No. 1

1½ oz. scotch
3 oz. milk
1 tsp. sugar syrup
Nutmeg

Mix all ingredients, except nutmeg, with cracked ice in a shaker or blender. Pour into a chilled Old Fashioned glass. Sprinkle with nutmeg.

HIGHLAND FLING No. 2

1½ oz. scotch
½ oz. sweet vermouth
Several dashes orange bitters
Olive

Mix all ingredients, except olive, with cracked ice in a shaker or blender. Pour into a chilled cocktail glass. Drop in olive.

HIGHLAND MORNING

1 oz. scotch
¾ oz. Cointreau
3 oz. grapefruit juice

Mix all ingredients with cracked ice in a shaker or blender. Pour into a chilled Old Fashioned glass.

INNISFREE FIZZ

2 oz. Irish whiskey
1 oz. lemon juice
1 oz. curaçao
½ tsp. sugar syrup or to taste
Club soda

Mix all ingredients, except club soda, with cracked ice in a shaker or blender. Strain into a chilled wine goblet and fill with club soda.

INVERCAULD CASTLE COOLER

1½ oz. scotch
1 oz. Benedictine
Ginger ale

Pour scotch and Benedictine into a chilled highball glass, add several ice cubes, and fill with ginger ale. Stir gently.

INVERNESS COCKTAIL

2 oz. scotch
½ oz. lemon juice
1 tsp. orgeat syrup
1 tsp. triple sec or curaçao

Mix all ingredients, except triple sec, with cracked ice in a shaker or blender and strain into a chilled cocktail glass. Top with a float of triple sec or curaçao.

IRISH BUCK

1½ oz. Irish whiskey
Lemon peel
Ginger ale

Pour Irish whiskey into chilled highball glass with cracked ice. Twist lemon peel over drink and drop in. Add ginger ale.

IRISH FIX

2 oz. Irish whiskey
½ oz. Irish Mist
½ oz. lemon juice
½ oz. pineapple syrup or pineapple juice
Orange slice
Lemon slice

Mix all ingredients, except fruit slices, with cracked ice in a shaker or blender and pour into an Old Fashioned glass. Garnish with fruit slices.
Note: If pineapple juice is used in place of pineapple syrup, add a little sugar syrup to taste.

IRISH KILT

1 oz. Irish whiskey
1 oz. scotch
1 oz. lemon juice
1½ oz. sugar syrup or to taste
Several dashes orange bitters

Mix all ingredients with cracked ice in a shaker or blender and strain into a chilled cocktail glass.

IRISH RAINBOW

1½ oz. Irish whiskey
Several dashes Pernod
Several dashes curaçao
Several dashes maraschino
    liqueur
Several dashes Angostura
    bitters

Orange peel

Mix all ingredients, except orange peel, with cracked ice in a shaker or blender. Pour into a chilled Old Fashioned glass. Twist orange peel over drink and drop in.

IRISH SHILLELAGH

1½ oz. Irish whiskey
½ oz. sloe gin
½ oz. light rum
1 oz. lemon juice
1 tsp. sugar syrup
2 peach slices, diced
5–6 fresh raspberries

Maraschino cherry

Mix all ingredients, except berries and cherry, with cracked ice in a shaker or blender. Pour into a chilled Old Fashioned glass. Garnish with raspberries and cherry.

J.J.'S SHAMROCK

1 oz. Irish whiskey
½ oz. crème de cacao (white)
½ oz. crème de menthe (green)
1 oz. milk

Mix in a shaker or blender with cracked ice and serve in a chilled cocktail glass.

JAPANESE FIZZ No. 2

2 oz. scotch
2 oz. dry red wine
½ oz. lemon juice
1 tsp. sugar syrup
Club soda
Pineapple spear

Mix all ingredients, except club soda and pineapple, with cracked ice in a shaker or blender. Pour into a chilled highball glass and fill with club soda. Decorate with pineapple.

KERRY COOLER

2 oz. Irish whiskey
1½ oz. medium sherry
1 oz. orgeat syrup
½ oz. lemon juice
Club soda
Lemon slice

Mix all ingredients, except club soda and lemon slice, with cracked ice in a shaker or blender. Pour into a chilled highball glass and fill with club soda. Garnish with lemon slice.

KILDRUMMY

1½ oz. scotch
½ oz. sweet vermouth
Several dashes orange bitters
Several dashes Pernod

Mix all ingredients with cracked
ice in a shaker or blender. Pour
into a chilled Old Fashioned
glass.

KINSALE COOLER

1½ oz. Irish whiskey
1 oz. Irish Mist
1 oz. lemon juice
Club soda
Ginger ale
Lemon peel

Mix Irish Mist, whiskey and
lemon juice with cracked ice in a
shaker or blender. Pour into a
chilled Collins glass. Fill with
equal parts of club soda and
ginger ale. Stir gently. Twist
lemon peel over drink and drop in.

KISS ME AGAIN

1½ oz. scotch
Several dashes Pernod
1 egg white (for two drinks)
Orange slice

Mix all ingredients, except orange
slice, with cracked ice in a shaker
or blender and pour into a
chilled cocktail glass.

LOCH LOMOND

1½ oz. scotch
½ oz. sugar syrup
Several dashes Angostura
  bitters

Mix all ingredients with cracked
ice in a shaker or blender and
pour into a chilled cocktail
glass.

LOCH NESS

1½ oz. scotch
1 oz. Pernod
¼ oz. sweet vermouth

Mix all ingredients with cracked
ice in a shaker or blender. Pour
into a chilled Old Fashioned
glass.

MAMIE TAYLOR

3 oz. scotch
½ oz. lime juice
Ginger ale
Lemon slice

Pour scotch and lime juice in a
chilled Collins glass with several
ice cubes. Fill with ginger ale
and gently stir. Garnish with
lemon slice.

MIAMI BEACH COCKTAIL

1 oz. scotch
1 oz. dry vermouth
1 oz. grapefruit juice

Mix all ingredients with cracked ice in a shaker or blender. Strain into a chilled cocktail glass.

THE MINCH

1½ oz. scotch
1 tsp. peppermint schnapps
Club soda
Peppermint stick or candy cane (optional)

Mix all ingredients, except club soda and stick, with cracked ice in a shaker or blender. Pour into a chilled Old Fashioned glass. Fill with club soda. Decorate with peppermint stick or candy cane.

MODERN No. 2

3 oz. scotch
Several dashes Jamaica rum
Several dashes Pernod
Several dashes lemon juice
Several dashes orange bitters
Maraschino cherry

Mix all ingredients, except maraschino cherry, with cracked ice in a shaker or blender. Pour into a chilled Old Fashioned glass. Decorate with cherry.

MONTROSE MILK

2 oz. scotch
6 oz. chocolate milk
1 tsp. curaçao
Grated chocolate

Mix all ingredients, except chocolate, with cracked ice in a shaker or blender. Pour into a chilled double Old Fashioned glass. Sprinkle with grated chocolate.

MORNING GLORY

1 oz. scotch
1 oz. brandy
½ tsp. sugar syrup
Several dashes curaçao
Dash Pernod
Several dashes Angostura bitters
Club soda
Powdered sugar

Mix all ingredients, except club soda and powdered sugar, with cracked ice in a shaker or blender. Pour into a chilled Collins glass. Fill with club soda. Wet a barspoon with water and roll in a little powdered sugar. Use this spoon to stir the drink before serving.

MORNING GLORY FIZZ

2 oz. scotch
¼ oz. Pernod
½ oz. lemon juice
1 tsp. sugar
1 egg white (for two drinks)
Dash Peychaud's bitters
Club soda
Lemon slice

Mix all ingredients, except club
soda and lemon slice, with cracked
ice in a shaker or blender. Pour
into a chilled Collins glass.
Fill with club soda. Decorate with
fruit slice.

PADDY COCKTAIL

1½ oz. Irish whiskey
¾ oz. sweet vermouth
Several dashes Angostura
    bitters

Mix all ingredients with cracked
ice in a shaker or blender. Serve
in a chilled cocktail glass

PARKNASILLA PEG LEG

1½ oz. Irish whiskey
1 oz. coconut syrup
3 oz. pineapple juice
1 tsp. lemon juice
Club soda

Mix whiskey, coconut syrup,
and fruit juices in a shaker or
blender with cracked ice and
pour into a chilled highball glass
along with several ice cubes.
Fill with club soda. Stir gently.

PERTH COCKTAIL

2 oz. scotch
½ oz. lemon juice
1 tsp. sugar syrup
Several dashes curaçao
Dash amaretto

Mix all ingredients with cracked
ice in a shaker or blender. Pour
into a chilled cocktail glass.

PRESTWICK

1½ oz. scotch
½ oz. sweet vermouth
Several dashes orange
    curaçao
Several dashes Drambuie
Orange peel

Mix all ingredients, except
Drambuie and orange peel, with
cracked ice in a shaker or
blender. Pour into a chilled Old
Fashioned glass. Twist orange
peel over drink and drop in. Top
with float of Drambuie.

PRINCE EDWARD

1½ oz. scotch
½ oz. Lillet blanc
¼ oz. Drambuie
Preserved orange slice

Mix all ingredients, except orange slice, with cracked ice in a shaker or blender. Pour into a chilled Old Fashioned glass. Garnish with orange slice.

PRINCES STREET

1½ oz. scotch
1 egg white (for two drinks)
1 tsp. sugar syrup
1 tsp. curaçao

Mix all ingredients with cracked ice in a shaker or blender. Strain into a chilled cocktail glass.

THE PURPLE HEATHER

1½ oz. scotch
½ oz. crème de cassis
Club soda

Mix scotch and crème de cassis in a highball glass with ice and fill with club soda.

P.V. DOYLE

1½ oz. Irish whiskey
¾ oz. green crème de menthe
1 oz. heavy cream
Maraschino cherry

Mix all ingredients, except maraschino cherry, with cracked ice in a shaker or blender and pour into a chilled cocktail glass.

PYEWACKET'S REVENGE

1½ oz. scotch
6 oz. cola
Lemon peel

Pour scotch into a chilled double Old Fashioned glass along with several ice cubes. Fill with cola and stir gently. Twist lemon peel over drink and drop in.

REMSEN COOLER

2–3 oz. scotch
1 tsp. sugar syrup
Club soda
Lemon peel

Pour scotch and sugar syrup into a chilled Collins glass along with several ice cubes. Fill with club soda. Thoroughly stir. Twist lemon peel over drink and drop in.
Note: For a gin Remsen Cooler, substitute gin for scotch and ginger ale for club soda.

RING OF KERRY

1½ oz. Irish whiskey
1 oz. Bailey's Irish Cream
½ oz. Kahlua or crème de
    cacao
1 tsp. shaved chocolate

Mix all ingredients, except
shaved chocolate, with cracked
ice in a shaker or blender.
Strain into a chilled cocktail glass.
Sprinkle with shaved chocolate.

 ## ROB ROY

1½–2 oz. scotch
½ oz. sweet vermouth
Dash orange bitters (optional)
Maraschino cherry

Pour all ingredients, except
cherry, into a mixing glass along
with several ice cubes. Stir
well. Strain into a chilled cocktail glass. Garnish with cherry.

 ## ROB ROY Dry

1½–2 oz. scotch
½ oz. dry vermouth
Dash Angostura bitters
    (optional)
Lemon peel

Stir all ingredients, except
lemon peel, with ice in a mixing
glass and strain into a chilled
cocktail glass. Twist lemon peel
over drink and drop into glass.

ROYAL DEESIDE

1 oz. scotch
1 oz. brandy
1 oz. Parfait Amour
Several dashes Pernod
Several dashes orange bitters

Mix all ingredients with cracked
ice in a shaker or blender. Pour
into a chilled Old Fashioned
glass.

ROYAL ROB ROY

1½ oz. scotch
1½ oz. Drambuie
¼ oz. dry vermouth
¼ oz. sweet vermouth
Maraschino cherry

Mix all ingredients, except
cherry, with cracked ice in a
shaker or blender. Strain into
a chilled cocktail glass and
decorate with cherry.

 ## RUSTY NAIL

1½ oz. scotch
1 oz. Drambuie

Pour ingredients into a chilled
Old Fashioned glass along with
several ice cubes. Stir.

SCOTCH BUCK

2–3 oz. scotch
¼ oz. lime or lemon juice
Ginger ale
Lime or lemon wedge

Mix scotch and lime juice with cracked ice in a mixing glass and pour into a chilled highball glass. Fill with ginger ale and garnish with fruit wedge.

SCOTCH COOLER

3 oz. scotch
Several dashes white crème
  de menthe
Club soda

Pour scotch and crème de menthe into a chilled highball glass. Stir. Add several ice cubes. Top with club soda.

SCOTCH FLIP

2 oz. scotch
1 egg white
½ oz. sugar syrup
Club soda

Mix all ingredients, except club soda, with cracked ice in a shaker or blender. Pour into a chilled Old Fashioned glass. Add club soda and stir gently.

SCOTCH HOLIDAY SOUR

2 oz. scotch
1 oz. Cherry Marnier
1 oz. lemon juice
½ oz. sweet vermouth
1 egg white (for two drinks)
Lemon slice

Mix all ingredients, except lemon slice, with cracked ice in a shaker or blender. Strain into a chilled Whiskey Sour glass. Garnish with lemon slice.

SCOTCH JULEP

6–8 mint leaves
1 oz. Drambuie
2 oz. scotch
Mint sprig

Muddle mint leaves, Drambuie, and a little water together in a

chilled double Old Fashioned glass. Fill with finely crushed ice and add scotch. Muddle again and add more scotch and more ice if you wish. Garnish with mint sprig.

SCOTCH MIST

1½–2 oz. scotch
Lemon peel

Pour scotch into a chilled Old Fashioned glass filled with crushed ice. Twist lemon peel over drink and drop into glass.

SCOTCH ORANGE FIX

2 oz. scotch
½ oz. lemon juice
1 tsp. sugar syrup
1 tsp. curaçao
Orange peel cut in a long
    spiral

Mix all ingredients, except
curaçao and peel, with cracked
ice in a shaker or blender and
pour into a double Old Fashioned glass. Add orange peel
and additional ice. Top with
curaçao.

 ## SCOTCH SANGAREE

1 tsp. heather honey or to
    taste
1½ oz. scotch
Lemon peel
Club soda
Grated nutmeg

Mix heather honey and a little
water or club soda in a double
Old Fashioned glass until
honey is dissolved. Add scotch
and a lemon twist, ice cubes,
and fill with club soda. Sprinkle
grated nutmeg over top.

 ## SCOTCH SMASH

6 mint leaves
Heather honey or sugar syrup
2–3 oz. scotch
Orange bitters
Mint sprig

Muddle honey or sugar with
mint in a double Old Fashioned
glass and fill with crushed ice.
Add scotch and mix well with a
barspoon. Add additional ice
and scotch if desired. Top with
orange bitters and a mint sprig.

 ## SCOTCH SOUR

1½ oz. scotch
½ oz. lemon juice
1 tsp. sugar syrup
Orange slice
Maraschino cherry

Mix all ingredients, except orange
slice and maraschino cherry,
with cracked ice in a shaker or
blender. Strain into a chilled
Whiskey Sour glass. Garnish
with orange slice and cherry.

SCOTTISH COBBLER

1½ oz. scotch
½ oz. pineapple syrup, sugar
    syrup, or honey
½ oz. curaçao
Mint sprigs

Mix all ingredients, except
mint, with cracked ice in a shaker
or blender. Strain into a chilled
Old Fashioned glass and garnish
with mint sprigs.

SCOTTISH HORSE'S NECK

1 lemon, peeled in long
   spiral
2–3 oz. scotch
½ oz. sweet vermouth
½ oz. dry vermouth

Place lemon peel in a chilled

Collins glass with one end of
peel hanging over rim. Pour in
scotch, sweet and dry vermouths.
Fill glass with cracked ice.
Stir well and let stand for a few
minutes before drinking.

SECRET

1½ oz. scotch
Several dashes peppermint
   schnapps
Club soda

Mix all ingredients, except club
soda, with cracked ice in a shaker
or blender. Pour into a chilled
Old Fashioned glass. Fill with
club soda.

SERPENT'S TOOTH

¾ oz. Irish whiskey
1½ oz. sweet vermouth
½ oz. kummel
¾ oz. lemon juice
Several dashes Angostura
   bitters
Lemon peel

Mix all ingredients, except
lemon peel, with cracked ice in a
shaker or blender. Pour into a
chilled Old Fashioned glass. Twist
lemon peel over drink and drop
in.

SHAMROCK No. 1

1½ oz. Irish whiskey
¾ oz. dry vermouth
1 tsp. green Chartreuse
1 tsp. green crème de menthe

Stir all ingredients with plenty
of ice in a pitcher and strain into
a chilled cocktail glass.

SHAMROCK No. 2

1½ oz. Irish whiskey
1½ oz. green crème de menthe
2 oz. heavy cream
Maraschino cherry

Mix all ingredients, except
cherry, with cracked ice in a
shaker or blender. Pour into a
chilled Old Fashioned glass. Garnish with maraschino cherry.

SHAMROCK No. 3

1½ oz. Irish whiskey
¾ oz. green crème de menthe
4 oz. vanilla ice cream

Mix all ingredients in a blender
at high speed until smooth. Pour
into a chilled wine goblet.

SHETLAND PONY

1½ oz. scotch
¾ oz. Irish Mist
Dash orange bitters (optional)

Mix all ingredients with cracked ice in a mixing glass and strain into a chilled cocktail glass.

SKIBBEREEN TONIC

2 oz. Irish whiskey
Tonic water
Lemon peel

Pour Irish whiskey into a chilled Old Fashioned glass with several ice cubes. Fill with tonic water. Twist lemon peel over drink and drop in.

SKYE SWIZZLE

¾ oz. scotch
¾ oz. Jamaica rum
¾ oz. dry gin
1 tsp. lime juice
Several dashes sweet
   vermouth

Several dashes cherry brandy
Maraschino cherry

Mix all ingredients, except maraschino cherry, with cracked ice in a shaker or blender. Pour into a chilled Collins glass. Garnish with cherry.

SPIRIT OF SCOTLAND

2 oz. scotch
¾ oz. Drambuie
¼ oz. lemon juice

Mix all ingredients with cracked ice in a shaker or blender and strain into a chilled cocktail glass.

STIRLING SOUR

1½ oz. scotch
½ oz. lime juice
1 tsp. sugar syrup or to taste
Several dashes Cointreau

Mix all ingredients with cracked ice in a shaker or blender. Pour into a chilled cocktail or Whiskey Sour glass.

STONEHAVEN

1½ oz. scotch
½ oz. Cointreau
½ oz. sweet vermouth
2 tsp. lime juice

Mix all ingredients with cracked ice in a shaker or blender. Pour into a chilled Old Fashioned glass.

THISTLE

2 oz. scotch
1 oz. sweet vermouth
Several dashes Angostura
  bitters

Mix all ingredients with cracked
ice in a shaker or blender. Strain
into a chilled cocktail glass.

 ## TIPPERARY

1 oz. Irish whiskey
1 oz. sweet vermouth
½ oz. green Chartreuse

Combine all ingredients with
several ice cubes in mixing glass.
Stir well and strain into a
chilled cocktail glass.

 ## TRILBY No. 2

¾ oz. scotch
¾ oz. sweet vermouth
¾ oz. parfait amour
Several dashes Pernod
Several dashes Angostura
  bitters

Mix all ingredients with cracked
ice in a shaker or blender. Pour
into a chilled Old Fashioned
glass.

URQUHART CASTLE

1½ oz. scotch
Several dashes dry vermouth
Several dashes Cointreau
Several dashes orange bitters

Mix all ingredients with cracked
ice in a shaker or blender. Pour
into a chilled Old Fashioned
glass.

WHISKEY MAC

2 oz. scotch
2 oz. ginger wine

Mix all ingredients with cracked
ice in a shaker or blender. Pour
into a chilled Old Fashioned
glass.

 ## WICKLOW COOLER

1½ oz. Irish whiskey
1 oz. Jamaica dark rum
½ oz. lime juice
1 oz. orange juice
1 tsp. Falernum or orgeat
  syrup
Ginger ale

Mix all ingredients, except ginger ale, with cracked ice in a
shaker or blender. Pour into a
chilled Collins glass. Fill with
ginger ale.

MONTEZUMA'S LEGACY: TEQUILA

Ay, Chihuahua!
—Uttered by an American friend in a
Mexican *cantina* upon taking his first drink
of straight tequila with lime and salt.

Legend has it that in ancient times a Toltec of royal blood discovered a miraculous potion in the heart of the great spiked maguey plant. He called it "honey water" (*aguamiel* in Spanish), for when it was fermented and imbibed, it produced a wondrous effect. (The sap or juice of the maguey is still referred to as *aguamiel* when making pulque, a fermented, mildly alcoholic beverage consumed fresh, like draft beer, in Mexico, where it is extremely popular.) To win favor with the king, he prepared a flask of this magic brew and dispatched his young and beautiful daughter, Princess Xochitl, to present this gift at the royal court. History does not tell us what the king thought of the gift, but he apparently was quite taken with Xochitl, who soon became Queen Xochitl and bore him a son.

From these auspicious beginnings have come pulque, which is probably the first alcoholic beverage to originate in the New World, and later, after the Spanish conquistadors imported the art of distillation, mescal, and its more refined cousin, tequila.

The reputation that tequila once had among the uninitiated as a raw, harsh beverage is undeserved. It probably resulted from tourists being subjected to cheap, unaged mescals or other forms of *aguardientes* distilled from coconuts, cane, corn, or pineapple. The alcoholic content of most tequila runs from 80 to 86 proof, which puts it in a class with most whiskeys, rum, gin, and vodka.

The subtle and elusive flavor of tequila perhaps accounts for its growing popularity in the U.S. Pungent and faintly yeasty, it defies more precise description, but marries well with other spirits and liqueurs and almost any kind of fruit juice. It is especially good with citrus fruits and does wonders for tomato juice, thus providing a proper foundation for a smashing Bloody Mary and similar concoctions employing the tomato.

As you might have guessed, most tequila is produced in and

around the town of Tequila, about thirty-five miles from Guadalajara in the state of Jalisco. It is distilled from the juice that is extracted from the heart of the *agave tequilana weber* or so-called "blue agave," which is just one of the more than four hundred varieties of the agave or maguey plant. Of this extensive plant category only a few types of maguey may used to produce mescal and only one, the *agave tequilana*, is used to make tequila.

In the area surrounding the town of Tequila—a strictly delimited zone, the boundaries of which are specified by the Mexican government—some forty to fifty distillers or *tequileros* cultivate the blue agave and make tequila. After a ten-year growing process, the heart of the agave is harvested and roasted in huge steam ovens. The hearts are then shredded, the juice pressed out, and sugar added for a four-day period of fermentation. After a double distillation (needed to bring the alcoholic content up to the proper level), the white spirit is ready for drinking, without further processing, like gin or vodka. A part of the production will be set aside and aged in wooden casks from a period of a few months to as long as seven years. During this period the tequila takes on a yellow or golden color and is marketed as *tequila añejo*. The older *añejos* command premium prices and are worth it to the tequila connoisseur since the aging process gives them a smooth, mellow finish comparable to fine old bourbon or cognac.

Whether you take tequila neat with salt and lime in the classic Mexican style or use it to build a zippy cocktail or a tall, refreshing summer cooler, tequila deserves knowing. The creative mixologist will find a challenge in devising tequila drinks because of its elusive and unique flavor characteristics, but the rewards and satisfaction are great, especially when you hit upon the right flavor combination resulting in a delicious recipe that is unlike any other.

THE "MEXICAN ITCH"—THE ORIGINAL TEQUILA TOT

No one who has reached his majority should be deprived of the opportunity to quaff a hearty peg of tequila *cantina*-style with coarse salt and fresh lime at least once. It is a moving experience, especially if one has a tender gullet. Here follows a memorable experience on the part of a Mexicophile companion on a journey of discovery south of the border:

"Tequila estilo Pancho Villa, por favor," croaks my hot and thirsty friend through parched throat as he swaggers up to the bar in the local *cantina*. The fact that a gringo from New York City would have the audacity to order Mexico's national spiritous drink "Pancho Villa style" naturally evokes a smile from the *cantinero* as he serves up a shot of white, unaged tequila, a wedge of lime, and coarse kitchen salt. Sometimes a glass of *sangrita*, a peppery mixture of tomato and orange juice, hot chiles, onion, and divers seasonings, is proffered as a chaser.

Now begins the venerable ritual of the "Mexican Itch." As an empathetic and rapt audience of local hombres watches appreciatively, my friend grasps the wedge of lime between the thumb and forefinger of his left hand, places a pinch of salt in the fleshy depression near the thumb on the back of the same hand, and with his right hand carefully lifts the shimmering glass of tequila until it is at eye level. Then, with the graceful, fluid motion of a matador executing a flawless *veronica* in the *corrida de toros*, the salt is deftly licked, the tequila is quaffed, and the lime is sucked, all of which is followed by a zesty draught of sangrita.

"Ay Chihuahua!" exclaims my friend as he gasps for air. The effect of this assault on the gullet is pronounced and instantaneous. The shock quickly passes, however, and is gradually replaced by a warm, pervasive sensation of well-being, a glow that suffuses the whole man as earthly cares begin to fade.

A more genteel version of the basic lime-tequila-salt combination (sans *sangrita*) is to be had in the Margarita, the major differences being that a pony of triple sec is added and the ingredients are mixed, with ice, in a cocktail shaker or blender instead of in the stomach. The effect is not as dramatic as when taking tequila neat, but it is pleasant and satisfying nevertheless.

Tequila's full potential as a key ingredient in the creation of a host of tempting drink recipes has yet to be fully exploited. One thing is evident: The Mexican Itch, a good-natured reference to the classic method of imbibing tequila, could spread rapidly beyond the borders of Mexico. If it follows the route of vodka, it promises to become epidemic. As to the cure for this contagious malady, there alas is none—only temporary remission.

Once you have the "Itch," as everyone in Mexico knows, you have it for life.

ACAPULCO CLAM DIGGER

1½ oz. tequila
3 oz. tomato juice
3 oz. clam juice
½ tsp. horseradish
Several dashes Tabasco
    sauce
Several dashes Worcester-
    shire sauce

Dash of lemon juice

Mix all ingredients thoroughly in a double Old Fashioned glass with cracked ice. Garnish with lemon slice. Clamato juice may be used in place of clam and tomato juice.

BERTA'S SPECIAL

In the lovely old silver city of Taxco you may have the good fortune to come upon a famous watering place known as Bertita's Bar, renowned for a drink named after Bertha, the proprietor—who, some say, was the progenitor of the ubiquitous Margarita. In any event, the Bertha or Berta Special (also known as the Taxco Fizz) is a mighty fine way to relax after a silver shopping tour of the city.

2 oz. tequila
Juice of 1 lime
1 tsp. sugar syrup or honey
Several dashes orange bitters
1 egg white
Club soda
Lime slice

Mix all ingredients, except soda, in a shaker or blender with cracked ice and pour into a 14-oz. Collins glass. Fill with club soda, stir gently, and garnish with a lime slice if you wish.

BLUE SHARK

1 oz. white tequila
1 oz. vodka
¾ oz. blue curaçao

Mix all ingredients with cracked ice in a shaker or blender, strain, and serve in a chilled cocktail glass.

 BRAVE BULL

1½ oz. white tequila
¾ oz. Kahlua
Lemon peel

Mix all ingredients, except

lemon peel, with cracked ice in a shaker or blender and pour into an Old Fashioned glass. Twist lemon peel over drink and drop into glass.

 BUNNY BONANZA

1½ oz. tequila
1 oz. applejack
½ oz. lemon juice
1 tsp. simple syrup or maple syrup
Generous dash triple sec or curaçao

Lemon slice

Mix all ingredients with cracked ice in a shaker or blender and serve in a chilled Old Fashioned glass. Garnish with lemon slice.

BARTENDER'S SECRET NO. 22

A little salt goes a long way with some people, who find it interferes with their ability to taste certain essential flavors. A mixture of equal parts of salt and sugar instead of salt alone is a very palatable solution for any drink recipe that specifies a coating of salt on the rim of the glass.

CAFE DEL PRADO

1 tsp. instant coffee
2 tsp. instant cocoa
1½ oz. tequila
Whipped cream
Powdered cinnamon or
    nutmeg

Put coffee and cocoa in a mug and fill with boiling water. Add tequila, mix well, and top with whipped cream. Grate a little cinnamon or nutmeg on top.

CAN CAN

1½ oz. white tequila
½ oz. dry vermouth
4 oz. grapefruit juice
½ tsp. sugar syrup or to taste
Orange slice

Mix all ingredients, except orange slice, in a shaker or blender with cracked ice and pour into a double Old Fashioned glass. Garnish with orange slice.

¡CARAMBA!

1½ oz. white tequila
3 oz. grapefruit juice
1 tsp. sugar or to taste
Club soda

Mix all ingredients, except soda, in a shaker or blender with cracked ice, pour into tall highball glass, and top with club soda.

CAROLINA

3 oz. gold tequila
1 oz. cream
Generous tsp. grenadine
Generous dashes vanilla
    extract
1 egg white (for two drinks)

Powdered cinnamon
Maraschino cherry

Mix all ingredients, except cinnamon and cherry, in a shaker or blender with cracked ice, and pour into a chilled cocktail glass.

CHANGUIRONGO

1½ oz. tequila
Orange, lemon-lime, ginger
    ale, or other flavored soda
Lemon or lime wedge

Put ice cubes in a tall highball or Collins glass, pour in tequila and soda, stir gently, and garnish with fruit wedge.

CHAPALA

1½ oz. tequila
¾ oz. orange juice
¾ oz. lemon juice
½ oz. grenadine or to taste
Generous dashes triple sec
Orange slice

Mix all ingredients, except orange, with cracked ice in a shaker or blender, pour into an Old Fashioned glass, and garnish with orange slice.

CHAPULTEPEC CASTLE

1½ oz. tequila
1 oz. Grand Marnier
4 oz. fresh orange juice
Orange slice

Mix all ingredients in a shaker or blender with cracked ice and pour into a double Old Fashioned glass. Garnish with an orange slice if you wish.

CHERRY COCO

1½ oz. tequila
¾ oz. coconut cream
1 oz. lime or lemon juice
1 tsp. maraschino liqueur

Mix all ingredients in a shaker or blender with cracked ice and pour into a chilled Whiskey Sour glass or champagne tulip glass.

COCO LOCO

1 coconut, topped
1 oz. tequila
1 oz. gin
1 oz. light rum
1 oz. pineapple juice
½ fresh lime
Falernum or simple syrup to
    taste

Open fresh coconut by sawing off the top, taking care not to spill out the coconut water. Add some cracked ice to the coconut and pour in all the liquid ingredients. Squeeze lime over drink and drop in husk. Stir well, adding a little additional cracked ice if necessary.

DANIEL DE ORO

1½ oz. tequila
Orange juice
Damiana

Put some ice cubes in a tall Collins glass, pour in tequila, and fill with orange juice. Top with a float of Damiana.
Note: This is a specialty of the Su Casa Restaurant in Chicago.

EL CID

1½ oz. tequila
1 oz. lemon juice or lime juice
½ oz. orgeat syrup
Tonic water
Grenadine
Lime slice

Pour tequila, juice, and syrup into a tall Collins glass and mix well. Add cracked ice and fill with tonic. Top with a dash or two of grenadine and decorate with lime slice.

 EL TORO SANGRIENTO The Bloody Bull

1½ oz. tequila
3 oz. tomato juice
3 oz. beef consommé or
    bouillon
Dash lemon juice
Several dashes Worcester-
    shire sauce

Pinch celery salt (optional)
Pinch white pepper

Mix all ingredients with cracked ice and serve in a double Old Fashioned glass.

ESMERALDA

1½ oz. tequila
Juice of 1 lime
1 tsp. honey
Dash Angostura bitters
    (optional)

Mix all ingredients in a shaker or blender with cracked ice, strain, and pour into a chilled cocktail glass.

FROSTBITE

1½ oz. white tequila
½ oz. white crème de cacao
¾ oz. blue curaçao
2 oz. cream

Mix all ingredients with cracked ice in a shaker or blender and pour into a chilled cocktail glass or Whiskey Sour glass.

 FROZEN MARGARITA

1½ oz. tequila
½ oz. triple sec
1 oz. lemon or lime juice
Salt or sugar/salt mixture (see
    Bartender's Secret No. 22)
Lime slice

Use 1½ to 2 cups of cracked ice for each drink. Add ice, tequila, triple sec, and juice to blender and mix for 5 to 10 sec-

onds until slushy and firm (not watery) and pour into large chilled cocktail glass or wine goblet, the rim of which has been rubbed with lime juice and coated with salt. Garnish with lime slice. *Note:* Because of the large amount of ice used to make a frappé-style drink, larger glasses than would be used for a regular recipe are needed.

GENTLE BEN

1 oz. white tequila
1 oz. vodka
1 oz. gin
3 oz. orange juice
1 tsp. sloe gin (optional)
Orange slice

Mix all ingredients, except sloe gin, in a shaker or blender and pour into a double Old Fashioned glass. Float sloe gin on top of drink and garnish with an orange slice if you wish.

GENTLE BULL

1½ oz. tequila
¾ oz. coffee liqueur
¾ oz. cream

Mix all ingredients with cracked ice in a shaker or blender and pour into a chilled cocktail glass.

GRAPESHOT

1½ oz. tequila
¾ oz. curaçao
1 oz. grape juice

Mix all ingredients with cracked ice in a shaker or blender, strain, and pour into a chilled cocktail glass.

GRINGO SWIZZLE

2 oz. tequila
½ oz. crème de cassis or to taste
1 oz. lime juice
1 oz. pineapple juice
1 oz. orange juice
Ginger ale

Mix all ingredients, except ginger ale, in a shaker or blender with cracked ice and pour into a 14-oz. Collins glass. Add more ice if needed and fill with ginger ale.

GUADALAJARA

1½ oz. tequila
2–3 oz. grapefruit juice
1 tsp. almond extract
Dash lime juice
Dash triple sec or curaçao
Mint sprigs (optional)

Mix all ingredients, except mint, in a shaker or blender and pour into a chilled wine goblet. Garnish with mint.

 **HOT PANTS**

1½ oz. tequila
¾ oz. peppermint schnapps
¾ oz. grapefruit juice
½ tsp. grenadine or to taste

Mix all ingredients in a shaker or blender with cracked ice, strain, and pour into a chilled cocktail glass. You may frost the rim of the glass with salt or salt/sugar mixture if you wish (see *Bartender's Secret 22*).

 MARGARITA

1½ oz. tequila, white or gold
½ oz. triple sec
Juice of ½ large or one small lime
Coarse salt

Mix tequila, triple sec, and lime juice with cracked ice in a shaker or blender with plenty of cracked ice. Rub rim of a chilled cocktail glass with a piece of cut lime and dip the rim of the glass in a saucer of salt until it is evenly coated. Strain and pour Margarita mixture into glass and garnish with a thin slice of lime.

 MATADOR

1½ oz. tequila
3 oz. pineapple juice
1 oz. lime juice
½ tsp. sugar syrup or to taste

Mix all ingredients with cracked ice in a shaker or blender, strain, and pour into a chilled cocktail glass.

Note: There are many variations of this drink. Some use honey, grenadine, coconut syrup, or triple sec as a sweetener, but they are all based on the pineapple/lime juice combination.

MEXICAN BULL SHOT

1½ oz. tequila
¾ oz. lime or lemon juice
4–6 oz. beef consommé
Generous dashes Worcestershire sauce

Pinch celery salt or celery seed

Mix all ingredients with ice in a double Old Fashioned glass and garnish with a lime wedge.

MEXICAN COFFEE

1½ oz. tequila
Kahlua or sugar syrup to taste
Strong hot black coffee
Whipped cream

Mix tequila and sweetener in a large mug, pour in hot coffee, and top with a generous dollop of whipped cream.

MEXICAN PEPPER POT

1½ oz. tequila
Dr Pepper
Lime wedge

Put ice cubes in a highball or
Collins glass, pour in tequila,
and fill with soda. Squeeze
lime over drink and drop husk
into glass.

 ## MEXICAN TANGERINE

1½ oz. gold tequila
1 oz. Mandarine Napoleon
½ oz. grenadine
Juice of 1 small lime

Mix all ingredients in a shaker
or blender with cracked ice,
strain, and pour into a chilled
cocktail glass.

MEXICOLA

1½ oz. tequila
Cola
Lemon twist

Put ice cubes in a tall highball
glass, add tequila and cola, stir
gently, and garnish with lemon
twist.

MOCKINGBIRD

1½ oz. tequila
¾ oz. white crème de menthe
Juice of ½ lime

Mix all ingredients with cracked
ice in a shaker or blender, strain,
and serve in a chilled cocktail
glass.

 ## MONJA LOCA Crazy Nun

1½ oz. tequila
1½ oz. anisette

Fill an Old Fashioned glass
with finely crushed ice, pour in

tequila and anisette, and swizzle
with a spoon, muddler, or
swizzle stick. Use less anisette
for a drier drink.

MONTEZUMA

1½ oz. tequila
1 oz. Madeira
1 egg yolk

Mix all ingredients in a shaker
or blender with cracked ice,
strain, and pour into a chilled
cocktail glass.

MUCHACHA APASIONADO

1 oz. tequila
1 oz. La Grande Passion
Juice of ½ lime
½ tsp. amaretto
Dash grenadine

Mix all ingredients in a shaker or blender with cracked ice, strain, and serve in a chilled cocktail glass. Garnish with a lime slice if you wish.

PEACHTREE MARGARITA

1½ oz. tequila
1 oz. DeKuyper Peachtree Schnapps
Juice of 1 lime
Salt

Mix all ingredients with cracked ice in a shaker or blender, strain, and pour into a chilled cocktail glass that has been rimmed with salt, or use a salt and sugar mixture *(see Bartender's Secret No. 22)*

PIERRE MARQUES CODLER

1½ oz. Olé tequila
½ oz. Strega
2 oz. cranberry juice
1 oz. pineapple juice

Fill a tall Collins glass with cracked ice, add ingredients, and stir well. You may mix in a shaker or blender if you wish.

PIÑA

1½ oz. tequila
3 oz. fresh pineapple juice
1 oz. lime juice
1 tsp. honey or sugar syrup
Lime slice

Mix all ingredients with cracked ice in a shaker or a blender and serve in an Old Fashioned glass. Garnish with lime slice.

PIÑATA

1½ oz. gold tequila
1 oz. banana liqueur
1 oz. lime juice

Mix all ingredients with cracked ice in a blender or shaker, strain, and pour into a chilled cocktail glass.

PRADO

1½ oz. tequila
½ oz. maraschino liqueur
¾ oz. lemon or lime juice
1 egg white (for two drinks)
1 tsp. grenadine

Maraschino cherry

Mix all ingredients in a shaker or blender with cracked ice and serve in a Whiskey Sour glass. Garnish with a maraschino cherry.

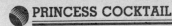 **PRINCESS COCKTAIL**

1 oz. tequila
1½ oz. La Grande Passion
Juice of ½ lime
Lime slice

Mix all ingredients with cracked ice in a shaker or blender, strain, and pour into a chilled cocktail glass. Garnish with a slice of lime.

ROSITA

1½ oz. tequila
1 oz. Campari
½ oz. dry vermouth
½ oz. sweet vermouth
Lemon or orange twist

Put some cracked ice into a double Old Fashioned glass, add all ingredients except fruit peel, and stir until well mixed. Squeeze fruit peel over drink and drop into glass.

 ROYAL MATADOR

Whole pineapple
3 oz. gold tequila
1½ oz. framboise
Juice of 1 lime
1 tsp. orgeat syrup or amaretto

Remove top from pineapple and reserve with leaves intact. Carefully scoop out pineapple, being careful not to puncture the shell, which will be used to serve this

drink. Place pineapple chunks in a blender and extract as much juice as possible or use a juice extractor. Strain pineapple juice and return to blender, adding tequila, framboise, lime juice, syrup, and cracked ice. Mix well and pour into pineapple shell, adding additional ice if needed. Replace top and serve with straws. Makes two drinks.

 SANGRITA

Another favorite way of drinking tequila in Mexico is *con sangrita*, which means the tequila is tossed off neat and the sangrita is drunk as a chaser. Sangrita is traditionally a peppery mixture of tart oranges, tomato juice, onion, hot chilies, and other seasonings, which you can make to your own taste or buy bottled in stores that specialize in Mexican foods. Sangrita can also be used to make the spiciest Bloody Mary you've ever put a lip to.

2 cups tomato juice
1 cup orange juice
2 oz. lime juice
1–2 tsp. Tabasco sauce or to taste
2 tsp. finely minced onion

1–2 tsp. Worcestershire sauce
Several pinches white pepper
Celery salt or seasoned salt to taste

Blend well, strain, and chill in refrigerator. Yields about 3½ cups.

SAUZALIKY

1½ oz. tequila
3 oz. orange juice
Dash lime or lemon juice
½ ripe banana

Mix all ingredients with cracked
ice in a shaker or blender and
pour into a wine goblet.

 ## SENORA LA ZONGA

1½ oz. tequila
1 oz. white crème de cacao
2 oz. evaporated milk
Dash vanilla extract
Dash orgeat syrup (optional)
Dash maraschino cherry juice

Mix all ingredients with cracked
ice in a shaker or blender and
pour into a chilled Whiskey
Sour glass or a wine goblet. Almond extract may be used in
place of orgeat syrup.

SLOE CABALLERO

1 oz. tequila
1 oz. sloe gin
1 oz. lime juice

Mix all ingredients in a shaker
or a blender with cracked ice,
strain, and pour into a chilled
cocktail glass.

 ## SNEAKY PETE

Some poorly made mescals—poor relations to tequila—were
called "Sneaky Pete" because in addition to possessing the
flavor characteristics of a good belt of battery acid, some of
the delayed effects were memorable in the intensity of their
manifestations and their reluctance to depart. Here is a civilized recipe using tequila and the popular tequila-pineapple-
lime combination that is the basis of many recipes.

4 oz. tequila
1 oz. white crème de menthe
1 oz. pineapple juice
1 oz. lime or lemon juice
Lime slices

Mix all ingredients, except lime
slices, in a shaker or blender with
cracked ice, strain, and pour into
chilled cocktail glasses. Garnish
with lime slices. Makes two
drinks.

BARTENDER'S SECRET NO. 23

No one has ever devised a simple way to divide the raw white
of an egg into two equal parts. When egg white is called for in
a drink, one egg white can be overwhelming for a single

recipe. Smart bartenders use *one* egg white for *two* drinks. "But my customer only ordered one drink," you say. Make two anyway. Somebody will drink the second one—maybe you at the end of your shift.

STEAMING BULL

1½ oz. tequila
3 oz. beef consommé or bouillon
3 oz. tomato juice
Generous pinches celery salt or celery seed
Generous dashes Worcestershire sauce
½ tsp. lemon juice (optional)

Heat all ingredients in a saucepan except tequila. Stir well and heat to boiling point. Heat a mug by rinsing with boiling water, pour in tequila, and fill to the brim with contents of saucepan.

STRAWBERRY MARGARITA

1½ oz. tequila
½ oz. triple sec
½ oz. strawberry schnapps or strawberry liqueur
1 oz. lime juice
5–6 fresh or frozen strawberries (optional)

Mix all ingredients, except strawberries, in a shaker or blender with cracked ice and pour into a wine goblet. Garnish with strawberries. Rim of glass may be frosted with salt or salt/sugar mixture (see Bartender's Secret No. 22).

SUBMARINO

1 oz. tequila in glass jigger
1 large mug or stein of beer

Fill mug with cold beer within several inches of the rim and drop jigger with tequila into the mug. Some prefer to simply pour the tequila into the beer while others drink the tequila straight and follow it with a beer chaser.

TEQUILA COLLINS

1½ oz. white tequila
1 oz. lemon juice
Sugar syrup to taste
Club soda
Maraschino cherry

Put several ice cubes in a 14-oz. Collins glass, add tequila, lemon juice, and sweetener. Stir well, fill with club soda, and garnish with cherry.

TEQUILA COMFORT

1½ oz. tequila
1½ oz. Southern Comfort
3 oz. orange juice

Mix all ingredients with cracked ice in a shaker or blender and pour into a Whiskey Sour glass.

TEQUILA GIMLET

1½ oz. tequila
1 oz. Rose's lime juice
Lime wedge

Pour tequila and lime juice into an Old Fashioned glass with ice cubes, stir well, and garnish with lime wedge.

TEQUILA GHOST

1½ oz. white tequila
¾ oz. Pernod
½ oz. lemon juice

Mix all ingredients in a shaker or blender with cracked ice, strain, and pour into a chilled cocktail glass.

TEQUILA ICE COFFEE

1½ oz. tequila
1 tsp. sugar or to taste
Dash lime or lemon juice
Strong black coffee

Add tequila, sugar, and fruit juice to a highball glass and fill with cracked ice and black coffee. Stir and serve.

TEQUILA MANHATTAN

1½ oz. gold tequila
Several dashes sweet
  vermouth
Lime slice

Mix tequila and vermouth with cracked ice in a shaker or blender, strain, and pour into a chilled cocktail glass and garnish with lime slice.

Note: Some prefer a sweeter drink, and vermouth should be adjusted to individual taste. Dry vermouth may be used in place of sweet vermouth or vermouths may be used in combination to make a "perfect" Tequila Manhattan.

⬤ TEQUILA MARIA

1½ oz. tequila
4 oz. tomato juice
Juice of ¼ lime
½ tsp. fresh grated
  horseradish
Generous dashes Worcestershire sauce
Generous dashes Tabasco
  sauce

Generous pinch white pepper
Generous pinch celery salt or
  celery seed
Generous pinch tarragon,
  oregano, or dill

Stir all ingredients with cracked
ice and pour into a chilled double
Old Fashioned glass.

TEQUILA OLD FASHIONED

1 lump sugar
Several dashes Angostura
  bitters
1½ oz. gold tequila
Lemon twist

Place sugar cube in Old Fashioned glass and saturate with
bitters. Muddle until sugar is

dissolved, add ice, tequila, and a
jigger or two of water. Stir
well and garnish with lemon
twist.
Note: An interesting variation
is to add an ounce of lime
or lemon juice and enough
additional sugar to sweeten to
your taste.

TEQUILA ROSA

1½ oz. white tequila
¾ oz. dry vermouth
Dash grenadine
Lemon peel

Mix all ingredients, except
lemon twist, with cracked ice in
a shaker or blender, strain,
and pour into a chilled cocktail
glass. Twist lemon peel over
drink and drop into glass.

TEQUILA RUSSIAN STYLE

1 bottle of tequila
Orange peel

Pour a bottle of tequila into a
large, wide-mouthed container or
decanter. Carefully remove the
zest (the colored, outside part of
an orange peel) of a selected
orange with an unblemished skin.
With patience, the entire outside of the peel can be cut off

in a single, unbroken spiral,
leaving the white, inner part of
the peel on the orange. Gently
force the zest into the container
of tequila, seal, and let stand
for several days. The flavored
tequila can then be used to make
any drink calling for tequila,
or tossed off straight, as the
Russians drink vodka.

TEQUILA SOUR

1½ oz. tequila
1 oz. lime juice or lemon
  juice
1 tsp. confectioner's sugar or
  to taste

Mix all ingredients in a shaker
or blender with cracked ice,
strain, and pour into a chilled
cocktail glass.
Note: This is also called a Tequila Daiquiri.

TEQUILA STINGER

1½ oz. gold tequila
¾ oz. white crème de menthe

Mix ingredients in a shaker or
blender with cracked ice, strain,
and pour into a chilled cocktail glass.

Next to the Margarita, the most popular tequila mixed drink is
the Sunrise, which is essentially tequila, orange juice, and
grenadine, which provides the "sunrise." Another version is
made without orange juice with crème de cassis substituted in
place of grenadine.

 ## TEQUILA SUNRISE No. 2

1½ oz. tequila
Generous dash Cointreau or
  triple sec
Juice of ½ lime
Club soda
½ oz. crème de cassis
Lime slice

Mix tequila, cassis, and lime
juice in a tall Collins glass with
cracked ice. Fill with soda and
top off with orange liqueur. Garnish with lime slice and stir
gently.

TEQUILA SUNRISE The Original

1½ oz. tequila
Juice of ½ lime
3 oz. orange juice
¾ oz. grenadine
Lime slice

Mix all ingredients, except

grenadine and lime slice, in a
shaker or blender with cracked
ice and pour into a tall Collins
glass with additional ice if
needed. Slowly pour in grenadine. Do not stir. Garnish with
lime slice.

TEQUILA TEA

1½ oz. tequila
Hot tea
Lemon slice
Sugar to taste (optional)

Pour tequila into a large mug,
fill with tea, and garnish with
lemon slice.

TEQUINI

2 oz. white tequila
Dash dry vermouth or to taste
Pepperoncini, olive, or lemon
   twist

Stir tequila and desired amount
of dry vermouth in a pitcher with
plenty of ice, strain, and pour
into a chilled cocktail glass. Garnish with pepperoncini, olive,
or lemon twist.

TIJUANA CHERRY

1 oz. tequila
1 oz. Peter Heering
Juice of ½ lime or lemon

Mix all ingredients with cracked
ice in a shaker or blender, strain,
and serve in a chilled cocktail
glass.

T.N.T (Tequila 'N' Tonic)

1½ oz. tequila
Tonic water
Lime wedge

Put ice cubes in a highball or
Collins glass, pour in tequila,
and fill with tonic. Garnish
with lime wedge.

TOREADOR

1½ oz. tequila
½ oz. crème de cacao
2 tbsp. whipped cream
Cocoa powder

Mix tequila and crème de cacao
in shaker or blender with cracked
ice, strain, and pour into a chilled
cocktail glass or goblet. Top
with whipped cream and sprinkle
a little cocoa over the top.

TORRIDORA MEXICANO

1½ oz. tequila
¾ oz. coffee-flavored brandy
Juice of ½ lime

Mix all ingredients with cracked
ice in a shaker or blender, strain,
and pour into a chilled cocktail glass.

ZORRO

1½ oz. tequila
1 oz. slivovitz
1 oz. lime juice or lemon
   juice
1 tsp. sugar syrup or to taste

Mix all ingredients in a shaker
or blender with cracked ice and
pour into a chilled cocktail
glass.

THE FLAVORFUL WORLD OF LIQUEURS

Double, double, toil and trouble;
Fire burn and cauldron bubble.
—Macbeth

The flavorful world of liqueurs and cordials has its origins in the ancient lore of drugs and medicines. The use of roots, barks, seeds, herbs, spices, fruits, flowers, and other flora has been the basis of assuaging human ills since the beginning of civilization, long before the art of distilling was known. The discovery of the technique of distilling probably had the same impact on the pharmacology of the Middle Ages as the discovery of antibiotics in the twentieth century had on modern medicine.

We tend to look upon distilling in terms of beverage alcohol, but the production of such spirits as brandy, vodka, and whiskey was actually only one of the many benefits of this new technique. The still provided the basis of modern chemistry by making it possible to extract many new compounds derived from natural sources. Even in medieval times distilling made possible a thriving perfume industry as well as greatly improved paints and varnishes. It also provided a practical method of preserving the extracts of fruits, herbs, and other biological substances long before the invention of refrigeration or reliable canning and bottling methods.

It was only natural that in medieval times people looked upon alcohol as a highly valuable medicine. The restorative effects of brandy were well-known. Of greater importance, medicines that were perishable could be kept for extended periods when alcohol was used in their preparation. Distilled compounds were also in vogue for other reasons: as tonics, disease preventives, love potions, and aphrodisiacs. More than a few experimenters hoped to produce a distillate that would eclipse every other medicine made heretofore: an elixir of life.

Many of our present-day liqueurs and cordials (the names are used interchangeably) were created in the continuing search for new medicines. Gin (though not a liqueur) is a good example. It was first made by Franciscus de la Boe, also known as Dr. Sylvius, a professor at the University of Leyden (Leiden). Looking for new medicines to combat tropical diseases contracted by sailors on Dutch East India Company ships, he steeped some juniper berries in alcohol, thus stumbling on a rudimentary gin. Called *jenever* in the Netherlands, the name was shortened to "gin" when it was distilled in England. Curaçao is a well-known liqueur that was created as a preventive against scurvy. In the seventeenth century it was not known that this malady was caused by a nutritional deficiency, but ship doctors noticed that when fresh fruit supplies ran out, sailors began getting sick. It was believed that the dried peel of curaçao oranges processed with alcohol and given to the seamen when fresh oranges were not available might turn the trick. It didn't (they were on the right track, since oranges are a natural source of vitamin C, the lack of which was causing all the trouble) but, according to all accounts, curaçao liqueur was a big hit on board.

Today, liqueurs have limited medicinal value, although many people swear that certain liqueurs can settle an upset stomach or, as a digestive aid, relieve an overly full one. Instead they are valued for their contributions to the flavor combinations in a vast range of mixed drinks. Liqueurs also are excellent flavor enhancers in cooking, and every chef has a repertoire of spirits that are used for flambé dishes, ice cream toppings, pastries, sorbets, puddings, sauces, ragouts, pâtes, souffles, dessert crepes, game dishes, and fruits.

Liqueurs traditionally have been made by *infusion* (steeping flavoring agents in water, like making tea), *maceration* (steeping flavoring agents in alcohol for an extended period until most of the flavor has been extracted), and *distillation* (mixing flavoring agents with alcohol and distilling them together in a pot still). *Percolation*—similar to percolating coffee—is another, more modern method. Spirits are percolated or dripped through flavoring agents for long periods until optimum flavor and fragrance extraction is completed. All liqueurs are sweetened by various means and must, by law, contain at least 2.5 percent sugar by weight. Most liqueurs contain considerably more than that, the amount varying according to the formulas used by individual distillers.

Improvements are constantly being made in the state of the art. For instance, we have seen the recent ascendence of a whole new category of cream liqueurs, which are produced in a variety of flavors. A technical breakthrough made it possible for the distiller to homogenize dairy cream with alcohol, yielding a stable end product requiring no refrigeration (at least not in temperate climes) with fairly long shelf life. Another improvement in the process of extracting flavors from various botanicals has brought forth a new wave of schnapps liqueurs, which are characterized by a very natural, intense fruit flavor and fragrance. These innovations are self-evident and significant, and consumers were quick to respond. As this is being written, there is little doubt that new taste experiences are being researched and developed for a vast audience of thirsty and appreciative consumers.

The many different types and brands of liqueurs and cordials are divided into two important categories. The first encompasses the full range of *generic* products. This category, which probably accounts for less than half of all liqueurs on the market, includes all of the basic flavors from whatever source that can be made by any distiller. Some of the most popular generic liqueurs are crème de cassis (black currants), crème de cacao (cocoa and vanilla), crème de menthe (peppermint), triple sec (oranges), crème de café (coffee), sloe gin (sloe berries), and many more. This group also includes the fruit-flavored brandies such as peach-flavored brandy, apricot-flavored brandy, cherry-flavored brandy, etc. These brandies are made in the U.S. and by law are sweetened (2.5 percent or more sugar). They should not be confused with the clear brandies distilled in Europe, such as kirschwasser, which contain no sweeteners. Both the so-called "true" brandies (framboise, mirabelle, fraise, kirsch and others) and the flavored brandies are used extensively in mixed drinks. There is often confusion between liqueurs and brandies. A cherry liqueur, a cherry brandy, and a cherry-flavored brandy are all really quite different. The liqueur is quite sweet with a low alcoholic content (approximately 48 to 60 proof); a cherry brandy such as kirsch is not sweet at all and has a high alcoholic content (approximately 86 to 100 proof), and a cherry-flavored brandy may have a trace of sweetness with a medium-high alcoholic content (approximately 70 proof or more). In Europe, however, there are cherry brandies that are sweetened and look and taste exactly like a cherry liqueur and bottled at a relatively low (48 proof) alcoholic level. Therefore it pays to read labels and make tasting notes when liqueurs are concerned.

The second major category of liqueurs are *proprietary* brands such as Benedictine, Chartreuse, Drambuie, Grand Marnier, Cointreau, and Irish Mist, to mention but a few of the most famous names. All proprietary specialty liqueurs are made from formulas that are trade secrets, many of them closely guarded family recipes that have been handed down through many generations. Some of these liqueurs have become legendary, surrounded by colorful histories and lore. Benedictine is made from a closely guarded recipe created by Benedictine monks in 1510. Chartreuse, still made by the Carthusian brothers in France, originated in 1605. Drambuie, "Prince Charles Edward's Liqueur" is reputed to be made from a recipe that Bonnie Prince Charlie gave to a retainer in gratitude for loyal services rendered in 1745 after the battle of Culloden Moor. Irish Mist may be very close to a recreation of the lost recipe for Irish heather wine, which disappeared from Ireland after the Rebellion of 1691 when much of the Irish nobility fled the country. Liquore Galliano was created in the late 1800s and named after Major Giuseppe Galliano, a hero of the Italo-Abyssinian War. And then there is Southern Comfort, a bourbon-based invention of a St. Louis bartender who discovered that peach liqueur seemed to have a real affinity for whiskey.

Almost every proprietary brand has an interesting story regarding its origins and development, and new stories are being written as new creations are brought into the marketplace.

Liqueurs are fascinating because they come to us from an ancient heritage, a bridge to the past. They are a part of the unending search for medicines to make life bearable, or love potions and aphrodisiacs to make life enjoyable, or the elusive elixirs of life to make it ageless. But even in ancient times, liqueurs were revered for another vital and practical function: to provide the means to enhance and improve all manner of food and drink. And so, liqueurs and cordials, even in this modern age, whatever the time or the season, give us a world of flavors at our fingertips.

ABBOT'S DELIGHT

1½ oz. Frangelico
3 oz. pineapple juice
½ small ripe banana, peeled and sliced
Several dashes Angostura bitters

Mix all ingredients with cracked ice in a blender until smooth and pour into a chilled parfait glass.

ACAPULCO JOY

1½ oz. Kahlua
1 oz. peach brandy
Large scoop vanilla ice cream
½ ripe banana, peeled and sliced
Pinch ground nutmeg
· Maraschino cherry

Mix all ingredients, except nutmeg and maraschino cherry, in a blender until smooth and pour into a chilled wine goblet. Sprinkle with ground nutmeg and garnish with cherry.

ADIRONDACK SUNDAE

1½ oz. peppermint schnapps
½ oz. crème de cacao
Several dashes maraschino
   liqueur

Scoop chocolate ice cream

Mix all ingredients in a blender
until smooth and serve in a chilled
parfait glass.

 ## AKRON, OH!

1 oz. Droste Bittersweet
   Chocolate
1 oz. peppermint schnapps
1 oz. white crème de cacao
Dash curaçao

Mix all ingredients, except
curaçao, with cracked ice in a
shaker or blender, pour into a
chilled cocktail glass, and top
with a curaçao float.

 ## ALABAMA SLAMMER

1 oz. amaretto
1 oz. Southern Comfort
½ oz. sloe gin
Dash lemon juice

Mix amaretto, Southern Comfort,
and sloe gin in a chilled highball
glass with ice and add a dash
of lemon juice. Stir well.

 ## ALFONSO SPECIAL

1½ oz. Grand Marnier
¾ oz. gin
1 tsp. dry vermouth
1 tsp. sweet vermouth

*Several dashes Angostura
   bitters*

Mix all ingredients with cracked
ice in a shaker or blender and
strain into a chilled cocktail glass.

AMSTERDAMER

1½ oz. advocaat egg liqueur
1½ oz. cherry brandy

Mix all ingredients with cracked
ice in a shaker or blender and
pour into a chilled cocktail glass.

 ## ANTOINE'S TRIUMPH

1½ oz. Praline liqueur
¾ oz. CocoRibe
½ oz. dark Jamaica rum
1 oz. whipped cream
1 tsp. chocolate shavings
1 tsp. grated coconut

Mix spirits with cracked ice in a
shaker or blender and pour into a
chilled Delmonico glass or parfait
glass. Top with generous helping
of whipped cream and sprinkle
with chocolate shavings and
grated coconut.

 **APASSIONATA**

1½ oz. La Grande Passion
¾ oz. amaretto
4 oz. grapefruit juice
Red maraschino cherry
Green maraschino cherry

Mix all ingredients, except mar-

aschino cherries, with cracked ice in a shaker or blender and pour into a large chilled goblet. Garnish with red and green cherries.
Note: Created by the author for Carillon Importers Ltd.

 APPLE PIE

1½ oz. DeKuyper Apple Barrel Schnapps
1½ oz. DeKuyper Cinnamon Schnapps
Orange slice

Pour apple and cinnamon schnapps into a chilled cocktail glass with cracked ice and garnish with orange slice.

 ARCTIC JOY

1 oz. peppermint schnapps
1 oz. white crème de cacao
1 oz. light cream

Mix all ingredients with cracked ice in a shaker or blender and strain into a chilled cocktail glass.

 ARNAUD'S DELIGHT

1½ oz. Praline liqueur
1 oz. light rum or vodka
2 oz. cream
½ oz. coconut cream

Mix all ingredients with cracked ice in a blender until smooth and pour into a chilled parfait glass.

 AVERY ISLAND

1½ oz. sloe gin
¾ oz. Southern Comfort
5 oz. orange juice
Orange slice

Mix all ingredients, except orange slice, with cracked ice in a shaker or blender and pour into a chilled Collins glass. Garnish with orange slice.

BARTENDER'S SECRET NO. 24

White rings and other blemishes on wooden tabletops caused by alcoholic beverage spills can usually be removed by the rapid application of a little first aid. Try rubbing the area with a cloth moistened with camphorated oil or turpentine. Some have found that sprinkling salt over the stain and rubbing with a cloth saturated with lemon oil is effective. Or you can flood the area with lemon oil, let stand for a few hours, and wipe off. Prompt action is important. Wood surfaces defaced by old stains must usually be refinished.

 ## BALLYLICKEY DICKIE

1½ oz. amaretto
1 oz. Irish cream
1 scoop vanilla ice cream
1 oz. slivered almonds
Pinch ground nutmeg
Pinch powdered cinnamon
Maraschino cherry

Mix all ingredients, except spices and maraschino cherry, in a blender until smooth and pour into a chilled wine goblet. Sprinkle with ground nutmeg and powdered cinnamon, and garnish with cherry.

BANANA ITALIANO

1 oz. Galliano
½ oz. crème de banane
1 oz. cream

Mix all ingredients with cracked ice in a shaker or blender and strain into a chilled champagne glass.

BARBELLA

2 oz. Cointreau
1 oz. sambuca

Mix all ingredients with cracked ice in a shaker or blender and pour into a chilled cocktail glass.

BARRACUDA No. 1

½ oz. Galliano
1 oz. gold rum
1 oz. pineapple juice
¼ oz. lime juice
¼ oz. sugar syrup
Champagne
Lime slice
Maraschino cherry
Pineapple shell, carved out
  (optional)

Mix all ingredients, except champagne, lime slice, and maraschino cherry, with cracked ice in a shaker or blender, pour into a fresh pineapple shell or a Hurricane glass, and fill with champagne. Stir gently and garnish with fruit.

 ## BARRACUDA No. 2

1 oz. Benedictine
1 oz. gin
2 oz. grapefruit juice

Mix with cracked ice in a
shaker or blender and serve in a
chilled cocktail glass.
Note: Created by the author
for Benedictine Whitbread
Enterprises Inc.

 ## BEE STING

1 oz. Benedictine
1 oz. bourbon
½ oz. lemon juice
2 oz. orange juice

Mix with cracked ice in a
shaker or blender and pour into a
chilled Delmonico glass.
Note: Created by the author
for Benedictine Whitbread
Enterprises, Inc.

BELGRADE BELT

1 oz. Grand Marnier
1 tsp. quetsch plum brandy
1 tsp. orange slice
Lemon slice

Combine all ingredients, except
lemon slice, in a mixing glass,
stir, and pour into a chilled
deep-saucer champagne glass
packed with cracked ice. Garnish
with lemon slice.

BEVERLY'S HILLS

1½ oz. Cointreau
½ oz. cognac
¼ oz. Kahlua

Mix all ingredients with cracked
ice in a shaker or blender and
strain into a chilled cocktail
glass.

 ## BIJOU MEDICI

½ oz. Grand Marnier
½ oz. Galliano
½ oz. gin
1½ oz. cream

Mix all ingredients with cracked
ice in a shaker or blender and
strain into a chilled cocktail
glass.

BLACKJACK

1 oz. kirsch
½ oz. brandy
1 cup cold black coffee

Mix all ingredients with cracked
ice in a shaker or blender and
pour into a chilled wine glass.

BLANCHE

1 oz. Cointreau
1 oz. curaçao
1 oz. anisette

Mix all ingredients with cracked ice in a shaker or blender and strain into a chilled cocktail glass.

BLUE ANGEL

½ oz. blue curaçao
½ oz. crème de violette
½ oz. brandy
½ oz. lemon juice
½ oz. cream

Mix all ingredients with cracked ice in a shaker or blender and strain into a chilled cocktail glass.

BLUE BAR COOLER

½ oz. yellow Chartreuse
½ oz. cognac
Lemon-lime soda
Orange slice

Mix all ingredients, except soda and orange slice, with cracked ice in a shaker or blender, strain into a chilled Squall glass or wine goblet, fill with lemon-lime soda, and stir gently. Garnish with orange slice.

BLUE COOL

1½ oz. peppermint schnapps
¾ oz. blue curaçao
Lemon-lime soda
Lemon wheel

Combine peppermint schnapps and curaçao in a chilled highball glass with several ice cubes and stir well. Fill with cold lemon-lime soda and stir gently. Slice lemon wheel half way through and slip over rim of glass.

BLUE LADY

1½ oz. blue curaçao
½ oz. white crème de cacao
½ oz. light cream

Mix all ingredients with cracked ice in a shaker or blender and pour into a chilled cocktail glass.

BOURBON DELUXE

2 oz. bourbon
1 oz. Praline liqueur

Pour ingredients into a chilled Old Fashioned glass with several ice cubes and stir gently.

BRYN MAWR COLLEGE COOLER

1½ oz. Malibu or CocoRibe
½ oz. dark Jamaica rum
Dash lime or lemon juice
Dash orgeat syrup
Scoop butter-pecan or rum-
    raisin ice cream

Maraschino cherry

Mix all ingredients, except
maraschino cherry, in a blender
until smooth. Serve in a chilled
parfait glass or wine goblet.
Garnish with cherry.

 ## BUBBLING PASSION

1½ oz. La Grande Passion
Brut champagne or sparkling
    wine
Lemon peel

Pour La Grande Passion into a

chilled champagne flute or goblet and fill with ice-cold champagne. Twist lemon peel over
drink and drop into glass.
Note: Created by the author for
Carillon Importers Ltd.

CADIZ

¾ oz. blackberry liqueur
¾ oz. amontillado sherry
½ oz. triple sec
½ oz. cream

Mix all ingredients with cracked
ice in a shaker or blender and
pour into a chilled Old Fashioned glass.

CAFÉ KAHLUA

2–3 oz. Kahlua
1–½ oz. gold Jamaica rum
2 oz. cream
Cinnamon stick

Mix all ingredients, except cinnamon stick, with cracked ice in
a shaker or blender, pour into
a chilled Old Fashioned glass,
and garnish with cinnamon stick.

CAFÉ LIGONIER

¾ oz. crème de cacao
¾ oz. cognac
1 cup cold black coffee
Cinnamon stick

Mix all ingredients, except cinnamon stick, with cracked ice in
a shaker or blender and pour
into a chilled highball glass.
Garnish with cinnamon stick.

 ## CAFE ROMANO

1 oz. sambuca
1 oz. Kahlua
1 oz. cream

Mix all ingredients with cracked
ice in a shaker or blender and
strain into a chilled cocktail
glass.

CALM VOYAGE

½ oz. Galliano or Strega
1 oz. light rum
½ oz. passion fruit syrup
½ oz. lemon juice
1 egg white (for two drinks)

Mix all ingredients with cracked ice in a blender until smooth and pour into a chilled champagne tulip glass.

CAPE COD COOLER

2 oz. sloe gin
1 oz. gin
5 oz. cranberry juice
½ oz. lemon juice
½ oz. orgeat syrup
Lime slice

Mix all ingredients, except lime slice, with cracked ice in a shaker or blender and pour into a chilled Collins glass. Garnish with lime slice and add extra ice if necessary.

CAP MARTIN

1 oz. crème de cassis
½ oz. cognac
1 oz. pineapple juice
Orange slice

Mix all ingredients, except orange slice, with cracked ice in a shaker or blender and strain into a chilled cocktail glass. Garnish with orange slice.

CAPRI

1½ oz. white crème de cacao
1½ oz. crème de banane
1 oz. cream

Mix all ingredients with cracked ice in a shaker or blender and strain into a chilled cocktail glass.

CARA SPOSA

1 oz. coffee-flavored brandy
   or Tia Maria
1 oz. triple sec
½ oz. cream

Mix all ingredients with cracked ice in a shaker or blender and strain into a chilled cocktail glass.

CARLOS PERFECTO

1½ oz. Kahlua
1½ oz. Spanish brandy
Cream

Mix all ingredients, except cream, with cracked ice in a shaker or blender, pour into a chilled Old Fashioned glass, and top with float of cream.

CHARLOTTESVILLE, VA.

1½ oz. Southern Comfort
½ oz. Pernod
2 oz. orange juice
1 oz. lemon juice

Mix all ingredients with cracked ice in a shaker or blender and strain into a chilled cocktail glass.

CHARTREUSE COOLER

1½ oz. yellow Chartreuse
4 oz. orange juice
½ oz. lemon or lime juice
Bitter lemon soda or lemon-
    lime soda
Orange slice

Mix all ingredients, except soda and orange slice, with cracked ice in a shaker or blender and pour into a chilled Collins glass. Fill with bitter lemon or lemon-lime soda, stir gently, and garnish with orange slice.

 ## CHERRY-M COLADA

1½ oz. Cherry Marnier
1 oz. light rum (optional)
1 oz. coconut cream
4 oz. pineapple juice

Mix all ingredients with cracked ice in a shaker or blender and pour into a chilled double Old Fashioned glass.
Note: Created by the author for Carillon Importers Ltd.

 ## CHERRY-M DAIQUIRI

1 oz. Cherry Marnier
1 oz. light rum
Juice of ½ (large) lime

Mix all ingredients with cracked

ice in a shaker or blender and strain into a chilled cocktail glass.
Note: Created by the author for Carillon Importers Ltd.

 ## CHERRY-M SOUR

1½ oz. Cherry Marnier
¾ oz. Bombay gin
Juice of ½ lemon

Mix all ingredients with cracked

ice in a shaker or blender and strain into a chilled cocktail glass.
Note: Created by the author for Carillon Importers Ltd.

 ## CHERRY TART

1½ oz. Cherry Marnier
¾ oz. white crème de cacao
1 oz. light cream

Mix all ingredients with cracked

ice in a shaker or blender and strain into a chilled cocktail glass.
Note: Created by the author for Carillon Importers Ltd.

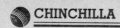

CHINCHILLA

1 oz. Benedictine
1 oz. triple sec
1 oz. light cream

Mix all ingredients with cracked ice in a shaker or blender and strain into a chilled cocktail glass.
Note: Created by the author for Benedictine Whitbread Enterprises, Inc.

CHOLULA

1 oz. Benedictine
½ oz. Kahlua
¾ oz. cream

Mix with cracked ice in a shaker or blender and strain into a chilled cocktail glass.
Note: Created by the author for Benedictine Whitbread Enterprises, Inc.

CHRYSANTHEMUM

1½ oz. Benedictine
1 oz. dry vermouth
Several dashes Pernod
Orange peel

Stir everything, except orange peel, with ice cubes in a mixing glass and strain into a chilled cocktail glass. Twist orange peel over drink and drop into glass.
Note: Created by the author for Benedictine Whitbread Enterprises, Inc.

COCONUT COVE

1½ oz. CocoRibe
½ oz. lime juice
1 tsp. orgeat syrup or Falernum
½ ripe banana, peeled and sliced
Scoop vanilla ice cream

Mix all ingredients with cracked ice in a blender until smooth and pour into a chilled parfait or Squall glass.

CORAL GOLD

1 oz. Cointreau
1 oz. gold Barbados rum
½ oz. peppermint schnapps

Mix all ingredients with cracked ice in a shaker or blender and strain into a chilled cocktail glass.

CORDIAL MÉDOC CUP

1 oz. Cordial Médoc
½ oz. cognac
1 oz. lemon juice
1 tsp. sugar syrup or to taste
Brut champagne
Orange slice

Mix all ingredients, except champagne and orange slice, with cracked ice in a shaker or blender and pour into a chilled wine goblet. Fill with champagne, stir gently, and garnish with orange slice.

CORTINA CUP

2 oz. Strega
½ oz. peppermint schnapps
  or white crème de menthe
1 oz. orange juice
1 oz. lemon juice
½ tsp. Pernod
Orange slice

Mix all ingredients, except Pernod and orange slice, with cracked ice in a shaker or blender and strain into a chilled wine goblet. Float Pernod on top and garnish with orange slice.

COZUMEL CUP

1½ oz. crème de banane
1½ oz. white crème de menthe

Pour ingredients into a chilled Old Fashioned glass with several ice cubes and stir well.

CULROSS

1 oz. apricot-flavored brandy
1 oz. light rum
1 oz. Lillet blanc
½ oz. lemon juice

Mix with cracked ice in a shaker or blender and strain into a chilled cocktail glass.

CURAÇAO COOLER

1½ oz. blue curaçao
1 oz. light rum
5 oz. orange juice
1 oz. lime juice
Orange peel

Mix all ingredients, except orange peel, with cracked ice in a shaker or blender and pour into a chilled Collins glass. Twist orange peel over drink and drop into glass.

# DALE'S HERSHEY

1 oz. Vander Mint
1 oz. peppermint schnapps
½ oz. curaçao
Large scoop chocolate ice
    cream
1 tbsp. whipped cream
1 tsp. finely chopped Hershey
    chocolate kisses

Mix all ingredients, except whipped cream and chocolate kisses, in a blender for a few seconds until smooth. Top with whipped cream and garnish with chopped Hershey chocolate kisses.

DANISH SNOWBALL

2 oz. Peter Heering
6 bing cherries, pitted and
    chopped
Large scoop New York cherry
    ice cream

Combine Peter Heering and chopped cherries in a mixing glass and pour over ice cream, which has been placed in a chilled sherbet or wine glass.

DORCHESTER NIGHT CAP

1 oz. Galliano
1 oz. brandy
1 tsp. white crème de menthe

Stir all ingredients in a mixing glass with cracked ice and strain into a chilled brandy snifter filled with several ice cubes. Serve with a straw.

DUCHESS

1 oz. Pernod
1 oz. dry vermouth
1 oz. sweet vermouth

Mix all ingredients with cracked ice in a shaker or blender and pour into a chilled cocktail glass.

EAST SIDE

1 oz. amaretto
1 oz. light rum
½ oz. Malibu or CocoRibe
1 oz. cream
1 tsp. toasted, shredded
    coconut (optional)

Mix all ingredients, except toasted, shredded coconut, with cracked ice in a blender until smooth, pour into a chilled wine goblet, and sprinkle with shredded coconut.

ERMINE TAIL

1 oz. sambuca
½ oz. cream
Pinch instant expresso coffee
  powder

Pour sambuca into a pony glass
and, using the back of a spoon,
carefully pour cream into glass
so it floats. Dust top with powdered coffee.

FERRARI

2 oz. vermouth
1 oz. amaretto
Lemon twist

Pour vermouth and amaretto
into a chilled double Old Fashioned glass with ice cubes,
stir well, and add lemon twist.

FESTIVAL

¾ oz. crème de cacao
1 oz. apricot brandy
¾ tsp. cream
1 tsp. grenadine

Mix all ingredients with cracked
ice in a shaker or blender and
pour into a chilled cocktail
glass.

FOREIGN AFFAIR

1 oz. sambuca
1 oz. brandy
Lemon peel

Mix all ingredients, except

lemon peel, with cracked ice in a
shaker or blender and strain
into a chilled cocktail glass. Twist
lemon peel over drink and drop
into glass.

FRED FERRETTI'S DELIGHT

1 oz. grappa
1 oz. Strega
1 oz. orange juice
1 oz. lemon juice
Lemon peel

Mix all ingredients, except
lemon peel, with cracked ice in a
shaker or blender and strain
into a chilled cocktail glass. Twist
lemon peel over drink and drop
into glass.

FRIAR TUCK

2 oz. Frangelico
2 oz. lemon juice
1 tsp. grenadine
Orange slice

Mix all ingredients, except orange
slice and maraschino cherry,
with cracked ice in a shaker or
blender, pour into a chilled Old
Fashioned glass, and garnish
with orange slice.

FRISCO

1½ oz. Benedictine
1½ oz. bourbon
Lemon peel

Stir Benedictine and bourbon with ice cubes and strain into a chilled cocktail glass. Twist lemon peel over drink and drop into glass.

FUZZY FRUIT

1½ oz. DeKuyper Peachtree
  Schnapps
Grapefruit juice, chilled

Pour schnapps into a chilled highball glass with several ice cubes and fill with grapefruit juice.

FUZZY NAVEL

1½ oz. DeKuyper Peachtree
  Schnapps
Orange juice, chilled

Pour schnapps into a chilled highball glass with several ice cubes and fill with orange juice.

GALATOIRÉS GLORY

2 oz. Southern Comfort
1 oz. cognac
½ oz. lemon juice
Several dashes grenadine

Mix all ingredients with cracked ice in a shaker or blender and pour into a chilled cocktail glass.

GALWAY GLADNESS

¾ oz. peppermint schnapps
¾ oz. Tia Maria
¾ oz. Bailey's Irish Cream
¾ oz. cream

Mix all ingredients in a blender for a few seconds until smooth and pour into a chilled wine goblet with several ice cubes.

GEORGIA PEACH

1½ oz. DeKuyper Peachtree
  Schnapps
¾ oz. white crème de cacao
1 oz. cream
Peach slice

Mix all ingredients, except peach slice, with cracked ice in a shaker or blender, strain into a chilled cocktail glass, and garnish with fruit slice.

GLAD EYES

1½ oz. Pernod
½ oz. peppermint schnapps

Mix all ingredients with cracked ice in a shaker or blender and pour into a chilled cocktail glass.

GLOOM CHASER

1 oz. Grand Marnier
1 oz. curaçao
½ oz. lemon juice
¼ oz. grenadine

Mix all ingredients with cracked ice in a shaker or blender and pour into a chilled cocktail glass.

GOLD CADILLAC

2 oz. Galliano
1 oz. white crème de cacao
1 oz. cream

Mix all ingredients with cracked ice in a blender for 10 seconds and strain into a chilled cocktail glass.

GOLDEN DRAGON

1½ oz. yellow Chartreuse
1½ oz. brandy
Lemon peel

Stir Chartreuse and brandy with ice cubes in a mixing glass and strain into a chilled cocktail glass. Twist lemon peel over drink and drop into glass.

GOLDEN DREAM No. 1

1½ oz. Galliano
1 oz. Cointreau
1 oz. orange juice
1 tsp. cream

Mix with cracked ice in a shaker or blender and strain into a chilled cocktail glass.

GOLDEN DREAM No. 2

1 oz. Irish cream
1 oz. Cointreau
1 oz. crème de banane
1 oz. cream
Orange slice

Mix all ingredients, except orange slice, with cracked ice in a blender, strain into a chilled Whiskey Sour glass, and garnish with orange slice.

THE GRAND, GRAND COCKTAIL

1 oz. Cherry Marnier
1 oz. Grand Marnier
1 oz. cream or scoop vanilla
 ice cream
Dash Bombay gin (optional)

Mix all ingredients with finely

cracked ice in a blender and strain into a chilled cocktail glass. If ice cream is used, use generous scoop and mix in a blender for only a few seconds so mixture is slightly slushy.
Note: Created by the author for Carillon Importers Ltd.

GRAND HOTEL

1½ oz. Grand Marnier
1½ oz. gin
½ oz. dry vermouth
Dash lemon juice
Lemon peel

Mix all ingredients, except lemon peel, with cracked ice in a shaker or blender and pour into a chilled cocktail glass. Twist lemon peel over drink and drop into glass.

GRASSE SUNSET

1½ oz. Pernod
¾ oz. Cointreau
½ oz. lime juice

Mix all ingredients with cracked ice in a shaker or blender and pour into a chilled cocktail glass.

GRASSHOPPER

1 oz. green crème de menthe
1 oz. white crème de cacao
1 oz. light cream

Mix all ingredients with cracked ice in a shaker or blender and strain into a chilled cocktail glass.

GREEN CHARTREUSE NECTAR

½ oz. green Chartreuse
1 oz. apricot schnapps

Combine all ingredients in a chilled Old Fashioned glass with several ice cubes and stir well.

HALLEY'S COMFORT

1½ oz. Southern Comfort
1½ oz. peach schnapps
Club soda

Pour Southern Comfort and peach schnapps into a chilled Old Fashioned glass with several ice cubes and top with club soda.

 **HARVARD YARD**

1 oz. gin
¾ oz. peppermint schnapps
½ oz. cranberry liqueur
Dash triple sec
Orange slice

Mix all ingredients, except orange slice, with cracked ice in a shaker or blender, strain into a chilled cocktail glass, and garnish with orange slice.

 HOME COMING

1½ oz. amaretto
1½ oz. Irish cream

Mix all ingredients for a few seconds with cracked ice in a shaker or blender and strain into a chilled cocktail glass.

HONG KONG SUNDAE

1 oz. Galliano
½ oz. Cointreau
Scoop orange or lemon sherbet

Mix all ingredients in a blender until smooth and pour into a chilled parfait glass.

HOOPLA

¾ oz. Cointreau
¾ oz. Lillet blanc
¾ oz. brandy
¾ oz. lemon juice

Mix all ingredients with cracked ice in a shaker or blender and pour into a chilled cocktail glass.

ICE BOAT

1 oz. peppermint schnapps
1 oz. vodka

Combine all ingredients in a mixing glass with several ice cubes, stir well, and strain into a chilled brandy snifter filled with crushed ice.

 IMPERIAL KIR

2 oz. crème de cassis
1 oz. kirsch
Champagne, sparkling wine, or white wine

Mix all ingredients, except champagne or wine, with cracked ice in a shaker or blender and pour into a large wine goblet. Fill with cold champagne or wine and stir gently.

IL PARADISO

1 oz. Tuaca
1 oz. curaçao
1 oz. cream

Mix all ingredients with cracked ice in a blender for a few seconds and strain into a chilled cocktail glass.

ITALIAN PACIFIER

1½ oz. white crème de menthe
Several dashes Fernet Branca

Pour crème de menthe into a chilled sherry glass packed with cracked ice and float Fernet Branca on top.

IXTAPA

1½ oz. Kahlua
½ oz. tequila

Stir ingredients in a mixing glass with cracked ice and serve in a chilled cocktail glass.

JACARANDA

1 oz. Haitian rum
½ oz. peppermint schnapps
1½ oz. mango nectar
½ oz. cream
1 tsp. peach schnapps

Mix all ingredients, except peach schnapps, with cracked ice in a shaker or blender and pour into a chilled cocktail glass. Top with peach schnapps.

JOANNA WINDHAM'S JOY

1 oz. Southern Comfort
½ oz. gold tequila
6 oz. orange juice
Maraschino cherry
1 tsp. raspberry syrup

Mix all ingredients, except maraschino cherry and raspberry syrup, with cracked ice in a shaker or blender and pour into a chilled Collins glass. Garnish with cherry and float raspberry syrup on top.

JOHNNIE'S COCKTAIL

1½ oz. sloe gin
¾ oz. curaçao or triple sec
1 tsp. anisette

Mix all ingredients with cracked ice in a shaker or blender and pour into a chilled cocktail glass.

KAHLUA HUMMER

1 oz. Kahlua
1 oz. light rum
½ cup vanilla ice cream

Mix all ingredients in a blender until smooth and pour into a chilled parfait glass.

KAISER KOLA

1½ oz. kirschwasser
Cola
Lime wedge

Pour kirschwasser into a chilled highball glass with several ice cubes. Fill with cold cola and stir gently. Squeeze lime wedge over drink and drop into glass.

KAMIKAZE

1 oz. triple sec
1 oz. vodka
1 oz. lime juice

Mix with cracked ice and strain into a chilled cocktail glass.

KIRSCHWASSER RICKEY

1½ oz. kirschwasser
½ oz. lime juice
Lemon-lime soda
Several pitted black cherries, speared on cocktail toothpick

Pour kirschwasser and lime juice into a chilled highball glass with several ice cubes and fill with lemon-lime soda. Stir gently and garnish with speared black cherries.

KISS ME QUICK

2 oz. Pernod
½ oz. curaçao
Several dashes Angostura bitters
Club soda

Mix all ingredients, except club soda, with cracked ice in a shaker or blender and pour into a chilled brandy snifter. Fill with club soda and stir gently. Add additional ice if necessary.

KOWLOON

1 oz. Grand Marnier
1 oz. Kahlua
2–3 oz. orange juice
Orange slice

Combine all ingredients, except orange slice, in a mixing glass, stir well, and pour into a chilled wine glass with plenty of cracked ice. Garnish with orange slice.

KREMLIN COCKTAIL

1 oz. Tia Maria or crème
  de cacao
1 oz. vodka
1 oz. cream

Mix all ingredients with cracked
ice in a blender for a few seconds until smooth and pour
into a chilled cocktail glass.

 ## LA BOMBA

1 oz. light rum
½ oz. curaçao
½ oz. anisette
½ oz. apricot brandy
½ oz. lemon juice
Pineapple stick or slice

Mix all ingredients, except
pineapple stick or slice, with
cracked ice in a shaker or
blender, pour into a chilled cocktail glass, and garnish with
pineapple.

 ## LA CONDAMINE

2 oz. Pernod
1 oz. gin
1 tsp. anisette
1 egg white (for two drinks)
Club soda

Mix all ingredients, except club
soda, with cracked ice in a shaker
or blender and pour into a
chilled highball glass. Fill with
cold club soda and stir gently.

 ## LA GRANDE AFFAIRE

1½ oz. La Grande Passion
1 oz. Crème de Grand
  Marnier

Mix all ingredients briefly but
briskly with cracked ice in a
shaker or blender and strain into
a chilled cocktail glass.
Note: Created by the author for
Carillon Importers Ltd.

 ## LA GRANDE PASSION COCKTAIL

1½ oz. La Grande Passion
1 oz. Grand Marnier
Juice of ½ lemon
Sugar to taste (optional)

Mix all ingredients with cracked
ice in a shaker or blender and
strain into a chilled cocktail
glass.
Note: Created by the author for
Carillon Importers Ltd.

LADY LOVERLY'S CHATTER

1½ oz. mirabelle or quetsch
½ oz. maraschino liqueur
2 oz. orange juice
1 oz. lemon juice

Mix all ingredients with cracked ice in a shaker or blender and strain into a chilled cocktail glass.

 ## LAS HADAS

1 oz. sambuca
1 oz. Kahlua
Several coffee beans

Stir sambuca and Kahlua in a mixing glass with cracked ice and pour into a chilled wine goblet. Add additional ice if necessary and float coffee beans on top of drink.

 ## THE LEAF

1 oz. melon liqueur
½ oz. white rum
2 oz. half-and-half

Mix all ingredients in a blender and pour into an Old Fashioned glass with several ice cubes.

 ## LEE KRUSKA'S BANANA COOLER

1½ oz. gold rum
1 oz. crème de banane
½ oz. 151-proof rum
4 oz. pineapple juice
1 oz. orange juice
½ oz. orgeat syrup

½ ripe banana, peeled and
   sliced
Lime slice

Mix all ingredients, except lime slice, with cracked ice in a blender until smooth and pour into a chilled Collins glass. Garnish with lime slice.

 ## LEMONADE MODERNE

1½ oz. sloe gin
1½ oz. sherry
2 oz. lemon juice
1 oz. sugar syrup or to taste
Club soda
Lemon peel

Mix all ingredients, except club soda and lemon peel, with cracked ice in a shaker or blender and pour into a chilled highball glass. Fill with club soda and stir gently. Twist lemon peel over drink and drop into glass. Add additional ice cubes if necessary.

LIEBFRAUMILCH

1½ oz. white crème de
    cacao
1½ oz. heavy cream
Juice of 1 lime

Mix all ingredients with cracked
ice in a shaker or blender and
strain into a chilled cocktail
glass.

LOLLIPOP

¾ oz. Cointreau
¾ oz. kirsch
¾ oz. green Chartreuse
Several dashes maraschino
    liqueur

Mix all ingredients with cracked
ice in a shaker or blender and
pour into a chilled cocktail
glass.

LONDON FOG

½ oz. white crème de menthe
½ oz. anisette
Scoop vanilla ice cream

Mix all ingredients with cracked
ice in a blender for a few seconds and pour into a chilled
parfait glass. Do not overmix.

LOWER DARBY

1 oz. melon liqueur
1 oz. cream
Several dashes triple sec
Pinch of ground nutmeg

Mix all ingredients, except nutmeg, with cracked ice in a shaker
or blender and strain into a
chilled cocktail glass. Sprinkle
with ground nutmeg.

LOVE

2 oz. sloe gin
1 egg white (for two drinks)
½ oz. lemon juice
Several dashes raspberry
    syrup or grenadine

Mix all ingredients with cracked
ice in a shaker or blender and
pour into a chilled cocktail
glass.

MACARONI

1½ oz. Pernod
½ oz. sweet vermouth

Mix all ingredients with cracked
ice in a shaker or blender and
pour into a chilled cocktail
glass.

MAHARANI OF PUNXSUTAWNEY

1 oz. brandy
½ oz. crème de noyaux or
   amaretto
½ oz. kirsch
¼ oz. orgeat syrup
1 oz. lemon juice

Lemon slice

Mix all ingredients, except
lemon slice, with cracked ice in a
shaker or blender, pour into a
chilled cocktail glass, and
garnish with lemon slice.

MALIBU BUBY

2 oz. Malibu
1 oz. gold Barbados rum
2 oz. orange juice
1 oz. lime juice
Several dashes curaçao
Maraschino cherry

Mix all ingredients, except
maraschino cherry, with cracked
ice in a shaker or blender, strain
into a chilled wine glass, and
garnish with cherry.

MANDARIN

1 oz. Grand Marnier
½ oz. Cherry Marnier
2 oz. orange juice
1 oz. lemon juice
Several dashes orange flower
   water

Mix all ingredients with cracked
ice in a shaker or blender and
pour into a chilled cocktail
glass. Sprinkle a little additional
orange flower water on top, if
you wish.

MARBELLA CLUB

1 oz. Grand Marnier
3 oz. orange juice
1 egg white (for two drinks)
Several dashes peach or
   orange bitters
Champagne
Maraschino cherry

Mix all ingredients, except
champagne and maraschino
cherry, with cracked ice in a
shaker or blender and strain
into a chilled wine goblet. Fill
with cold champagne, stir
gently, and garnish with cherry.

MARIE ANTOINETTE

1 oz. Kahlua
1 oz. crème de banane
Club soda

Mix all ingredients, except club
soda, with cracked ice in a shaker
or blender, pour into a chilled
cocktail glass, and top with float
of cold club soda.

MARMALADE

1 oz. Benedictine
¾ oz. curaçao
2 oz. orange juice

Mix with cracked ice in a shaker or blender and strain into a chilled cocktail glass.
Note: Created by the author for Benedictine Whitbread Enterprises, Inc.

 # MARTINIQUE

1 oz. Benedictine
1 oz. light rum or Martinique rum
4 oz. pineapple juice

Mix with cracked ice in a shaker or blender and pour into a chilled highball glass with ice cubes.
Note: Created by the author for Benedictine Whitbread Enterprises, Inc.

 # MARY LYONS FIZZ

Brut champagne
Several dashes green Chartreuse
Several dashes cognac

Pour all ingredients into a chilled champagne tulip glass and stir gently.

 # MAURA'S COFFEE

1 oz. Irish cream
½ oz. Irish whiskey
5 oz. iced black coffee
1 oz. heavy cream

Mix all ingredients in a blender with a tablespoon of cracked ice until smooth and pour into a chilled wine goblet.

MAZATLÁN

1 oz. white crème de cacao
1 oz. light rum
½ oz. coconut cream
1 oz. cream

Mix all ingredients with cracked ice in a shaker or blender and pour into a chilled cocktail glass.

McCLELLAND

2 oz. sloe gin
1 oz. curaçao
Several dashes orange bitters

Mix all ingredients with cracked ice in a shaker or blender and strain into a chilled cocktail glass.

MELON PATCH

1 oz. melon liqueur
½ oz. triple sec
½ oz. vodka
Club soda
Orange slice

Combine melon liqueur, triple sec, and vodka in a chilled highball glass with several ice cubes and stir. Fill with club soda, stir gently, and garnish with orange slice.

MIAMI MELONI

1 oz. melon liqueur
1 oz. light rum
1 oz. cream

Mix all ingredients with cracked ice in a shaker or blender and strain into a chilled cocktail glass.

MIDORI SOUR

2 oz. melon liqueur
1 oz. lemon juice
1 tsp. sugar syrup

Mix all ingredients with cracked ice in shaker or blender and strain into a chilled Whiskey Sour glass.

MINTY MARTINI

2 oz. gin or vodka
1 oz. peppermint schnapps
Orange or lemon peel

Combine all ingredients, except peel, in a mixing glass with ice cubes, stir well, and strain into a chilled cocktail glass. Twist peel over drink and drop into glass.

MOBILE BAY

1½ oz. Southern Comfort
1 oz. gin
1 oz. grapefruit juice
1 tsp. lemon juice

Mix all ingredients with cracked ice in a shaker or blender and pour into a chilled Old Fashioned glass.

MOCHA MINT

¾ oz. Kahlua or coffee-
    flavored brandy
¾ oz. crème de menthe
¾ oz. crème de cacao

Mix all ingredients with cracked ice in a shaker or blender and strain into a chilled cocktail glass.

MODERN No. 1

¾ oz. Scotch
1½ oz. sloe gin
Several dashes Pernod
Several dashes grenadine
Several dashes orange bitters

Mix all ingredients with cracked ice in a shaker or blender. Pour into a chilled Old Fashioned glass.

MOONGLOW

1 oz. Benedictine
1 oz. white crème de cacao
1 oz. cream

Mix with cracked ice in a

blender until smooth and serve in a chilled cocktail glass.
Note: Created by the author for Benedictine Whitbread Enterprises, Inc.

MOONSHINE COCKTAIL

1 oz. Galliano
¾ oz. white crème de cacao
¼ oz. orange juice
1 oz. vanilla ice cream

Mix all ingredients with cracked ice in a shaker or blender and pour into a large, chilled cocktail glass.

MORGAN'S FAIR CHILD

1 oz. melon liqueur
½ oz. amaretto
Scoop vanilla ice cream
1 tbsp. whipped cream
Maraschino cherry

Mix all ingredients, except whipped cream and maraschino cherry, in a blender until smooth and pour into a chilled parfait glass. Top with whipped cream and garnish with cherry.

MORNING CALL

1 oz. peach schnapps
½ oz. white crème de cacao
2 oz. orange juice
1 egg white (for two drinks)
Maraschino cherry

Mix all ingredients except maraschino cherry, with cracked ice in a shaker or blender, strain into a chilled cocktail glass, and garnish with cherry.

MOULIN ROUGE

1½ oz. sloe gin
½ oz. sweet vermouth
Several dashes Angostura
  bitters

Mix all ingredients with cracked ice in a shaker or blender and pour into a chilled cocktail glass.

MOUNTAIN STRAWBERRY BREEZE

1½ oz. DeKuyper Mountain
  Strawberry Schnapps
1 oz. grapefruit juice
1 oz. orange juice
Orange slice

Combine strawberry schnapps,
grapefruit and orange juices in a
chilled highball glass with several ice cubes, stir, and garnish
with orange slice.

 ## THE MYSTERY COCKTAIL

1 oz. Ricard
1–2 oz. La Grande Passion
Lemon peel

Mix all ingredients, except
lemon peel, with cracked ice in a
shaker or blender and strain
into a chilled cocktail glass. Twist
lemon peel over drink and drop
into glass.
Note: Created by the author for
Carillon Importers Ltd.

 ## NIGHTINGALE

1 oz. crème de banane
½ oz. curaçao
1 oz. cream
1 egg white (for two drinks)
Maraschino cherry

Mix all ingredients, except maraschino cherry, with cracked ice
in a shaker or blender, strain
into a chilled cocktail glass, and
garnish with cherry.

NINETEEN PICK-ME-UP

1½ oz. Pernod
¾ oz. gin
Several dashes sugar syrup
Several dashes Angostura
  bitters
Several dashes orange bitters
Club soda

Mix all ingredients, except club
soda, with cracked ice in a shaker
or blender, pour into a chilled
highball glass, and fill with club
soda. May be made as a cocktail
by omitting soda.

NORTHERN LIGHTS

1½ oz. Yukon Jack Canadian
  liqueur
4 oz. cranberry juice
4 oz. orange juice

Mix all ingredients with cracked
ice in a shaker or blender and
pour into a chilled highball
glass. Add several ice cubes if
necessary.

NUTCRACKER

1½ oz. DeKuyper Hazelnut
   Liqueur
1½ oz. DeKuyper Coconut
   Amaretto
1½ oz. heavy cream

Mix all ingredients with cracked
ice in a shaker or blender and
strain into a chilled cocktail
glass.

NUTTY COLADA

2–3 oz. amaretto
1 oz. gold rum (optional)
1½ oz. coconut syrup or to
   taste
2 oz. pineapple juice
Pineapple slice

Mix all ingredients, except
pineapple slice, with cracked ice
in a blender until smooth, pour
into a chilled Squall glass or a
Collins glass, and garnish with
pineapple slice.

OSTEND FIZZ

1 oz. kirsch
1 oz. crème de cassis
Club soda
Lemon peel

Stir kirsch and crème de cassis

with ice cubes in a highball or
Collins glass until thoroughly
mixed and fill with cold club
soda. Twist lemon peel over
drink and drop into glass.

PACIFIC PACIFIER

1 oz. Cointreau
½ oz. crème de banane
½ oz. light cream

Mix all ingredients with cracked
ice in a shaker or blender and
pour into a chilled Old Fashioned glass.

PADDY'S DERIVATION

1½ oz. Irish cream
½ oz. apricot brandy
½ oz. Irish whiskey
Maraschino cherry

Mix all ingredients, except
maraschino cherry, with cracked
ice in a shaker or blender, strain
into a chilled cocktail glass, and
garnish with cherry.

PALM BEACH POLO SPECIAL

1 oz. peppermint schnapps
1 oz. crème de banane
1 oz. light cream

Mix all ingredients with cracked
ice in a shaker or blender and
pour into a chilled Whiskey
Sour glass.

PAPPY McCOY

1 oz. Jeremiah Weed Bourbon
    liqueur
½ oz. tequila
½ cup orange juice

Mix all ingredients with cracked
ice in a shaker or blender and
serve in a chilled Delmonico
glass.

 PARKNASILLA PALMS

2 oz. Irish cream
½ oz. Cointreau
Orange peel

Mix all ingredients, except orange
peel, with cracked ice in a shaker
or blender for a few seconds
and strain into a chilled cocktail
glass. Twist orange peel over
drink and drop into glass.

THE PASHA'S PASSION

1½ oz. Pistacha
1 oz. crème de menthe

Mix all ingredients with cracked
ice in a shaker or blender and
strain into a chilled cocktail
glass.

PASSION COLADA

1½–2 oz. La Grande Passion
4 oz. pineapple juice
1–2 oz. coconut cream,
    depending on sweetness
    desired
1 oz. light rum (optional)
Pineapple stick
Maraschino cherry

Mix all ingredients, except
pineapple stick and maraschino
cherry, with cracked ice in a
shaker or blender and pour into a
chilled double Old Fashioned
glass. Garnish with pineapple
stick and cherry.
Note: This may be made very
easily by using any of the
popular prepared Pina Colada
mixes in place of coconut cream
and pineapple juice. Created
by the author for Carillon
Importers Ltd.

PASSION SHAKE

3 oz. La Grande Passion
1 cup whole milk
1 ripe banana, sliced
½ pint vanilla ice cream
Grated nutmeg

Mix La Grande Passion, milk,
and banana in a blender with a
little cracked ice until banana
is liquified. Add ice cream and
blend for just a few seconds so
ice cream is mushy. Serve in
chilled parfait or sherbet glasses.
Makes 2 drinks.
Note: Created by the author for
Carillon Importers Ltd.

PEACH BANG!

1 oz. Southern Comfort or
   peach brandy
1 oz. peach schnapps
2 oz. peach nectar or juice
   from ½ cup ripe peaches,
   crushed
Dash lemon juice

1 oz. cream
Brandied peach slice
   (optional)

Mix all ingredients, except
peach slice, with cracked ice in a
shaker or blender, pour into a
chilled cocktail glass, and garnish
with brandied peach slice.

 PEACHES AND CREAM

1½ oz. DeKuyper peachtree
   Schnapps
2 oz. half-and-half or milk

Mix all ingredients in a shaker
or blender and pour into a chilled
Old Fashioned glass with several
ice cubes.

 PEACHTREE TONIC

2 oz. DeKuyper Peachtree
   Schnapps
Tonic water
Orange slice

Pour schnapps into a chilled
Collins glass with several ice
cubes, fill with cold tonic water,
and stir gently. Garnish with
orange slice.

 PERNOD COCKTAIL

½ oz. water
Several dashes sugar syrup
Several dashes Angostura
   bitters
2 oz. Pernod

Fill an Old Fashioned glass
half full with crushed ice, add
water, syrup, and bitters and
stir well. Add Pernod and stir
again.

PERNOD FLIP

1½ oz. Pernod
1 oz. heavy cream
½ oz. orgeat syrup or sugar
   syrup to taste
1 egg
Pinch ground nutmeg

Mix all ingredients, except nutmeg, with cracked ice in a blender
until smooth and pour into a
chilled wine goblet. Sprinkle with
ground nutmeg.

PERNOD FRAPPÉ

1½ oz. Pernod
½ oz. anisette
Several dashes Angostura
   bitters

Mix all ingredients with cracked
ice in a shaker or blender and
strain into a chilled cocktail
glass.

PERSIAN MELON

1½ oz. melon liqueur
⅔ oz. Pistacha
1 tsp. lime juice
Ginger ale
2 blanched pistachio nuts
   (optional)

Combine all ingredients, except
ginger ale and pistachio nuts,
in a chilled highball glass with
several ice cubes and stir well.
Fill with cold ginger ale, stir
gently, and garnish with pistachio
nuts.

PEUGEOT

1½ oz. Cointreau
¾ oz. calvados
2 oz. orange juice

Mix all ingredients with cracked
ice in a shaker or blender and
strain into a chilled cocktail
glass.

PICON

1 oz. Amer Picon
1 oz. sweet vermouth

Mix all ingredients with cracked
ice in a shaker or blender and
pour into a chilled cocktail
glass.

PICON FIZZ

1½ oz. Amer Picon
¼ oz. grenadine
Club soda
½ oz. cognac

Pour Amer Picon and grenadine
into a chilled highball glass, add
several ice cubes and stir well.
Fill with cold club soda, stir
gently, and float cognac on top.

PICON ORANGE

2 oz. Amer Picon
2 oz. orange juice
Club soda

Mix Amer Picon and orange
juice with cracked ice in a shaker

or blender and pour into a
double Old Fashioned glass. Fill
with club soda and stir gently.
Add additional ice cubes if
necessary.

PICON SOUR

1½ oz. Amer Picon
½ oz. lemon juice
1 tsp. sugar syrup or to taste

Mix with cracked ice in a
shaker or blender and strain into
a Whiskey Sour glass.

 ## PIMLICO SPECIAL

1½ oz. brandy
½ oz. amaretto
½ oz. white crème de cacao

Mix all ingredients with cracked
ice in a shaker or blender and
pour into a chilled cocktail
glass.

 ## PINA KOALAPEAR

2 oz. DeKuyper Harvest Pear
    Schnapps
1 oz. CocoRibe
1 oz. cream
Pear slice

Mix all ingredients, except pear
slice, with cracked ice in a shaker
or blender, pour into a chilled
cocktail glass, and garnish with
pear slice.

 ## PINK SQUIRREL

1 oz. crème de noyaux
1 oz. white crème de cacao
1 oz. cream

Mix all ingredients with cracked
ice in a shaker or blender and
strain into a chilled cocktail
glass.

A PASSEL OF POUSSE-CAFÉS

The Pousse-Café is the multilayered wedding cake of the
mixed-drink world. A skillfully made Pousse-Café, consisting
of as many as seven differently colored layers of liqueurs,
each floating on the one beneath it and served in a tall, slim,
stemmed glass, is a spectacular drink creation. It requires
patience, a precise knowledge of the specific gravity or rela-
tive weight of each ingredient to be used, and a steady hand.
A simple miscalculation (all liqueurs of the same type may not
weigh exactly the same from brand to brand because proof or
alcoholic content, the amount of sugar used, and flavoring
agents will vary from one distiller to another), an ingredient
poured too hurriedly, or a jarred glass, and all is lost. The
rainbow magic of a Pousse-Café in the making can, in a trice,
turn into an expensive disaster. For this reason it is consid-

ered poor form to order this drink in a busy bar and if you do, don't be surprised if the bartender demurs.

A variety of Pousse-Café recipes follow, and none should be regarded as completely fail-safe for the reasons given above. It is suggested that you test any Pousse-Café concoction that you intend to serve to guests; it will be time well spent because you will need to practice the delicate business of pouring each liquid ingredient down the side of a tilted glass or over the back of an inverted barspoon or down the length of a stirring rod. A pony or Pousse-Café glass is traditionally used. The old-fashioned ones only had a capacity of two ounces or less. If you can find a larger size, so much the better. They make a better looking presentation of liqueurs, and if you plan to build a Pousse-Café of the seven-layer type, you will need a big glass. Pousse-Café recipes always list ingredients in descending order, meaning that the heaviest liquids appear at the top of the list and should be poured into the glass first. Amount of each ingredient used depends upon the size of the glass and the number of different spirits called for in your recipe. As a rule, a teaspoon or ¼ ounce is standard.

ANGEL'S KISS

Crème de cacao
Crème yvette
Prunelle
Rich cream

Layer ingredients, one on top of the other in the order given in a Pousse-Café glass. For pouring instructions, see Bartender's Secret No. 25.

 ## ANGEL'S TIT

Crème de cacao
Maraschino liqueur
Rich cream
Maraschino cherry

Layer ingredients, one on top of the other in the order given in a pony glass. Chill for a half hour before serving and garnish with a cherry. See Bartender's Secret No. 25 for pouring instructions.

 ## A CLASSIC POUSSE-CAFÉ

Raspberry syrup (or
    grenadine)
Crème de cacao
Maraschino liqueur
Curaçao
Crème de menthe (green)

Parfait Amour
Cognac

Layer ingredients one on the other in the order given, using a large liqueur glass or a Pousse-Café glass. For pouring instructions, see Bartender's Secret No. 25.

COPENHAGEN POUSSE-CAFÉ

Crème de banane
Peter Heering
Cognac

Layer ingredients, one on top of the other in the order given in a pony glass. For pouring instructions, see Bartender's Secret No. 25.

OLD GLORY

½ oz. grenadine
½ oz. heavy cream
½ oz. crème yvette

Carefully pour each ingredient

in the order listed into a large pony glass so that each liqueur floats on the one preceding it. See Bartender's Secret No. 25 for pouring methods.

POUSSE L'AMOUR

½ oz. maraschino liqueur
1 egg yolk (unbroken)
½ oz. Benedictine
½ oz. cognac

Layer ingredients, one on top of the other in the order given in a Pousse-Café glass. For pouring instructions see Bartender's Secret No. 25.

RUE DE LA PAIX POUSSE-CAFÉ

Benedictine
Curaçao
Kirschwasser

Layer ingredients, one on top of the other in the order given in a pony glass. For pouring instructions, see Bartender's Secret No. 25.

ST. MORITZ POUSSE-CAFÉ

Raspberry syrup
Anisette
Parfait Amour
Yellow Chartreuse
Green Chartreuse
Curaçao

Cognac

Layer ingredients in the order given, one on top of the other in a Pousse-Café glass. For pouring instructions, see Bartender's Secret No. 25.

SAVOY POUSSE-CAFÉ

Crème de cacao
Benedictine
Cognac

Layer ingredients, one on the other in a pony or Pousse-Café glass. For pouring instructions, see Bartender's Secret No. 25.

STARS AND STRIPES No. 1

Grenadine
Maraschino liqueur
Parfait Amour

Layer ingredients, in the order given, one on top of the other in a pony glass. See Bartender's Secret No. 25 for pouring instructions.

STARS AND STRIPES No. 2

Crème de cassis
Green Chartreuse
Maraschino liqueur

Layer ingredients in the order given in a pony glass, one on top of the other. See Bartender's Secret No. 25 for pouring instructions.

QUEEN ELIZABETH WINE

1½ oz. Benedictine
¾ oz. dry vermouth
¾ oz. lemon or lime juice

Mix all ingredients with cracked ice in a shaker or blender and strain into a chilled cocktail glass.

RAINBOW ROOM

1½ oz. Cointreau
1 oz. brandy
½ oz. peach schnapps

Mix all ingredients with cracked ice in a shaker or blender and strain into a chilled cocktail glass.

RANCHO MIRAGE

1 oz. blackberry brandy
1 oz. gin
1 oz. crème de banane
1 oz. cream

Mix all ingredients with cracked ice in a shaker or blender and strain into a chilled cocktail glass.

RED DANE

2 oz. vodka
1 oz. Peter Heering

Combine all ingredients in a mixing glass with several ice cubes, stir, and strain into a chilled cocktail glass.

REPULSE BAY SPECIAL

1½ oz. crème de banane
½ oz. peach schnapps
½ oz. grenadine
1½ oz. orange juice

1½ oz. cream

Mix all ingredients in a shaker or blender with cracked ice and strain into a chilled wine glass.

RHETT BUTLER

1½ oz. Southern Comfort
½ oz. lime juice
1 tsp. curaçao
1 tsp. lemon juice
1 tsp. sugar syrup

Mix all ingredients with cracked ice in a shaker or blender and strain into a chilled cocktail glass.

RICARD FLORIDIAN

1½ oz. Ricard
1 tsp. amaretto, crème de noyaux, or orgeat syrup
4 oz. grapefruit juice

Mix all ingredients with cracked ice in a shaker or blender and pour into a chilled Old Fashioned glass.
Note: Created by the author for Carillon Importers Ltd.

RIC-O-CHET

1½ oz. Ricard
1 oz. cognac
Champagne or sparkling wine

Pour Ricard and cognac into a

large chilled wine goblet, add several ice cubes, and stir until cold. Remove ice cubes and fill with ice-cold sparkling wine.
Note: Created by the author for Carillon Importers Ltd.

RICARD ROSE

¾ oz. Ricard
1½ oz. dark rum
4 oz. cranberry juice

Mix all ingredients with cracked

ice in a shaker or blender and pour into a chilled Old Fashioned glass or wine goblet.
Note: Created by the author for Carillon Importers Ltd.

BARTENDER'S SECRET NO. 25

When making Pousse-cafes, master bartenders usually pour liquid *slowly* over the back or round bottom of a bar spoon that is held inside the glass very near the previous ingredient that has been poured. A stirring rod may be used in place of a spoon. Other bartenders prefer to pour liquid very slowly down the inside of the glass or down a glass stirring rod. Any agitation or rush of liquid will cause the layers to mix, at which point one must begin again. However, patience and adroit spoon-handling can produce a multi-hued libation fit for an empress.

 ## RICARD SATIN

3 oz. Ricard
2 oz. Bombay gin
1 egg white
1 oz. cream (optional)
Sugar syrup to taste

Mix all ingredients with cracked ice in a shaker or blender and strain into a chilled cocktail glass. Makes 2 servings.
Note: Created by the author for Carillon Importers Ltd.

RIVER CLUB

¾ oz. peppermint schnapps
¾ oz. Kahlua
¾ oz. white crème de cacao

Mix all ingredients with cracked ice in a shaker or blender and pour into a chilled cocktail glass.

 ## ROLLS ROYCE No. 2

1 oz. Cointreau
1 oz. cognac
1 oz. orange juice

Mix all ingredients with cracked ice in a shaker or blender and pour into a chilled cocktail glass.

 ## ROMAN HOLIDAY

½ oz. amaretto
½ oz. sambuca
½ oz. blackberry brandy
1½ oz. light cream

Mix with cracked ice in a blender and strain into a chilled cocktail glass.

 ## ROMAN SNOWBALL

2–3 oz. sambuca
5 coffee beans

Fill a large tulip glass half full of finely crushed ice and pour in

Sambuca. Add coffee beans and serve with a straw. Chew beans after they have been steeped in Sambuca for a few minutes.

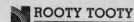

ROOTY TOOTY

2 oz. DeKuyper Old Tavern
   Rootbeer Schnapps
4 oz. orange juice

Mix all ingredients with cracked
ice in a blender until smooth and
pour into a chilled Old Fashioned glass.

RUBY FIZZ

3 oz. sloe gin
1 oz. lemon juice
1 tsp. sugar syrup
1 tsp. grenadine
1 egg white (for two drinks)
Club soda

Mix all ingredients, except club
soda, with cracked ice in a shaker
or blender and pour into a
chilled highball glass. Fill with
club soda and stir gently.

RUM DUM

1 oz. Barbados rum
½ oz. crème de cacao
½ oz. peppermint schnapps
½ oz. cream
1 tsp. maraschino liqueur

Mix all ingredients, except
maraschino liqueur, with cracked
ice in a shaker or blender, strain
into a chilled cocktail glass, and
top with maraschino liqueur.

ST. THOMAS SPECIAL

1½ oz. light rum
¾ oz. Peter Heering
½ oz. cream

Mix all ingredients with cracked
ice in a blender and pour into a
chilled cocktail glass.

SAN FRANCISCO

1 oz. sloe gin
1 oz. dry vermouth
1 oz. sweet vermouth
Several dashes Angostura
   bitters
Several dashes orange bitters

Maraschino cherry

Mix all ingredients, except
maraschino cherry, with cracked
ice in a shaker or blender and
pour into a chilled cocktail glass.
Garnish with cherry.

SATIN GLIDER

1 oz. peppermint schnapps
1 oz. white crème de cacao
½ oz. sambuca
1 oz. cream

Combine all ingredients with
cracked ice in a shaker or blender
and pour into a chilled cocktail
glass.

SCARLETT O'HARA

1½ oz. Southern Comfort
1½ oz. cranberry juice
½ oz. lime juice

Stir with cracked ice in a mixing glass and strain into a chilled cocktail glass.

 ## SCHIEDAM SALUTE

1 oz. advocaat egg liqueur
2 oz. Genever gin
1 oz. orange juice
½ oz. lemon juice
1 tsp. Galliano

Mix all ingredients with cracked ice in a shaker or blender and strain into a chilled Delmonico glass.

SENOR MÉDOC

1½ oz. Cordial Médoc
¾ oz. amontillado sherry

Stir ingredients in a mixing glass with ice cubes and pour into a chilled Old Fashioned glass. Add additional ice cubes if necessary.

SLOE GIN COCKTAIL

1½ oz. sloe gin
½ oz. dry vermouth

Mix all ingredients with cracked ice in a shaker or blender and strain into a chilled cocktail glass.

 ## SLOE GIN FIZZ

2–3 oz. sloe gin
½ oz. lemon juice
1 tsp. sugar syrup or to taste
Club soda
Lemon slice

Mix sloe gin, lemon juice, and syrup with cracked ice in a shaker or blender and pour into a chilled Collins glass. Fill with cold club soda and garnish with lemon slice. Stir gently.

SLOE SCREW

1½ oz. sloe gin
Orange juice

Pour sloe gin into a chilled Old Fashioned glass with several ice cubes, fill with orange juice, and stir.

SNOW JOB

2 oz. pear schnapps
1 oz. heavy cream or half-and-half
Pinch ground cinnamon

Mix all ingredients, except cinnamon, with cracked ice in a shaker or blender, and sprinkle ground cinnamon on top.

 ## SOMBRERO

1½ oz. Kahlua
1 oz. cream

Pour Kahlua into a chilled Old

Fashioned glass with several ice cubes, then using the back of a spoon, carefully pour in cream so that it floats.

 ## SPINNAKER

1 oz. Benedictine
1 oz. gin
4 oz. orange juice

Mix with cracked ice in a shaker or blender and pour into a

chilled double Old Fashioned glass with ice cubes.
Note: Created by the author for Benedictine Whitbread Enterprises, Inc.

 ## SOUTH BEND

1½ oz. Irish cream
1½ oz. Frangelico
1 oz. orange juice
1 oz. cream

Mix all ingredients with cracked ice in a shaker or blender and pour into a chilled parfait glass.

 ## SOUTHERN STIRRUP CUP

1½ oz. Southern Comfort
¾ oz. light rum or gin
2 oz. cranberry juice
2 oz. grapefruit juice
½ oz. lemon or lime juice
Club soda
Mint sprigs

Mix all ingredients, except soda and mint, with cracked ice in a shaker or blender and pour into a chilled silver mug. Fill with cold club soda and stir gently. Garnish with mint sprig.

STRAWBERRY COMFORT

1½ oz. Southern Comfort
½ oz. strawberry liqueur or strawberry schnapps
Lemon slice

Stir Southern Comfort and

strawberry liqueur or schnapps in a mixing glass with several ice cubes and pour into a chilled Old Fashioned glass. Add additional ice cubes if necessary. Garnish with lemon slice.

STREGA DAIQUIRI

1 oz. Strega
1 oz. light rum
½ oz. lemon juice
½ oz. orange juice
½ tsp. orgeat syrup or to
  taste
Maraschino cherry

Mix all ingredients, except
maraschino cherry, with cracked
ice in a shaker or blender, strain
into a chilled cocktail glass, and
garnish with cherry.

STREGA FLIP

1½ oz. Strega
¾ oz. brandy
1 oz. orange juice
½ oz. sugar syrup
½ oz. lemon juice
1 egg
Pinch ground nutmeg

Mix all ingredients, except nutmeg, with cracked ice in a shaker
or blender and pour into a
chilled highball glass. Sprinkle
with ground nutmeg.

STREGA SATIN

1½ oz. Strega
1 oz. vodka
2 oz. orange juice
Large scoop vanilla ice cream

Mix all ingredients in a blender
until smooth and pour into a
chilled parfait or sherbet glass.
Serve with a straw.

SUISSESSE

1½ oz. Pernod
½ oz. anisette
1 egg white (for two drinks)
Several dashes cream
  (optional)

Mix with cracked ice in a
shaker or blender and strain into
a chilled cocktail glass.

SUMATRA PLANTER'S PUNCH

1 oz. Swedish Punsch
1 oz. gold rum
2 oz. pineapple juice
1 oz. lime juice
1 tsp. 151-proof Demerara rum

Mix all ingredients, except
Demerara rum, with cracked ice
in a shaker or blender and
pour into a chilled Old Fashioned glass. Top with 151-proof
Demerara rum.

SUMMERTIME

1 tsp. white crème de menthe
  or peppermint schnapps
1 tsp. green crème de menthe
Scoop vanilla ice cream

Mix all ingredients in a blender
for a few seconds until smooth
and pour into a chilled parfait
glass. Do not overmix.

SUNDOWNER

1 oz. Benedictine
1 oz. light or gold rum
4 oz. orange juice

Mix with cracked ice in a shaker
or blender and serve in a chilled
highball glass with ice cubes.
Note: Created by the author
for Benedictine Whitbread
Enterprises, Inc.

SWEDISH LULLABY

1½ oz. Swedish Punsch
1 oz. Cherry Marnier
½ oz. lemon juice

Mix all ingredients with cracked
ice in a shaker or blender and
strain into a chilled cocktail
glass.

TAPPAN ZEE TOT

2 oz. blackberry brandy
1 oz. blackberry liqueur
½ oz. lime juice

Mix all ingredients with cracked
ice in a shaker or blender and
strain into a chilled cocktail
glass.

TAWNY RUSSIAN

1 oz. DeKuyper Coconut
  Amaretto
1 oz. vodka

Pour all ingredients into a
chilled double Old Fashioned
glass with several ice cubes
and stir well.

TIGER TAIL

1½ oz. Pernod or Ricard
4 oz. orange juice
Dash triple sec
Lime wedge

Mix all ingredients, except lime
wedge, with cracked ice in a
shaker or blender, pour into a
chilled Delmonico glass or wine
glass, and decorate with lime
wedge.

TIVOLI TONIC

2 oz. Peter Heering
½ oz. lemon or lime juice
Tonic water
Lime slice

Pour liqueur and lemon or lime juice into a chilled highball glass and stir well. Add several ice cubes, fill with cold tonic water, and stir gently. Garnish with lime slice.

TRICYCLE

2 oz. triple sec
3 oz. orange juice
2 oz. cream

Mix all ingredients with cracked ice in a shaker or blender and strain into a chilled wine goblet.

TRI-NUT SUNDAE

Large scoop vanilla ice cream
1 oz. Pistacha
1 oz. Frangelico
1 oz. amaretto

Put ice cream in a large chilled goblet or sherbet glass. Pour liqueurs individually on different parts of the ice cream.

TUACA COCKTAIL

1 oz. vodka
1 oz. Tuaca
½ oz. lime juice

Mix all ingredients with cracked ice in a blender or shaker and strain into a chilled cocktail glass.

TUACA FLIP

3 oz. Tuaca
1 oz. cream (optional)
½ tsp. sugar syrup
1 egg
Pinch of ground nutmeg

Mix all ingredients, except ground nutmeg, with cracked ice in a shaker or blender, strain into a chilled cocktail glass, and sprinkle with nutmeg.

TURKEY TROT

2 oz. Wild Turkey bourbon
   liqueur
1½ oz. Wild Turkey
Lemon peel

Pour bourbon liqueur and bourbon into a chilled Old Fashioned glass with several ice cubes and stir well. Twist lemon peel over drink and drop into glass.

TYPHOON BETTY

1 oz. Cherry Marnier
½ oz. kirschwasser
½ oz. ginger-flavored brandy
1 piece preserved ginger
   (optional)
Maraschino cherry

Mix all ingredients, except preserved ginger and maraschino cherry, in a shaker or blender and pour into a chilled cocktail glass with plenty of cracked ice. Garnish with ginger and cherry speared together on a cocktail toothpick.

VELVET HAMMER

1 oz. Cointreau
1 oz. white crème de cacao
1 oz. heavy cream

Mix all ingredients with cracked ice in a shaker or blender and strain into a chilled cocktail glass.

VICTORY

1½ oz. Pernod
¾ oz. grenadine or raspberry
   syrup
Club soda

Mix all ingredients, except club soda, with cracked ice in a shaker or blender, pour into a chilled highball glass, and fill with club soda. Stir gently.

VIKING

1½ oz. Swedish Punsch
1 oz. aquavit
1 oz. lime juice

Mix all ingredients with cracked ice in a shaker or blender and pour into a chilled cocktail glass.

VILLANOVA VICTORY CUP

1 oz. light rum
1 oz. strawberry liqueur
½ oz. kirschwasser
1 oz. orange juice
1 tsp. lemon juice
Large strawberry (optional)

Mix all ingredients, except strawberry, with cracked ice in a shaker or blender, strain into a chilled cocktail glass, and garnish with strawberry.

WALDORF

2 oz. Swedish Punsch
1 oz. gin
1 oz. lemon juice

Mix all ingredients with cracked ice in a shaker or blender and pour into a chilled cocktail glass.

WALLY HARVBANGER No. 1

1½ oz. Galliano
1½ oz. dark Jamaica rum
1 oz. orange juice
1 oz. pineapple juice
½ oz. lime juice
Pineapple stick

Mix all ingredients, except pineapple stick, with cracked ice in a blender until smooth, pour into a chilled Squall glass or brandy snifter, and garnish with pineapple stick.

WESTCHESTER EYE-OPENER

1½ oz. Benedictine
½ oz. cognac
1 egg
1 oz. cream

Mix all ingredients, except cream, with cracked ice in a shaker or blender and strain into a chilled cocktail glass. Top with float of cream and stir gently several times.

WETZLAR COFFEE

1 oz. kirsch
½ oz. crème de cacao
1 oz. cream
1 cup cold black coffee
1 egg white (for two drinks)

Mix all ingredients with cracked ice in a shaker or blender and pour into a chilled highball glass.

WHITE LADY No. 1

1½ oz. gin
¾ oz. Cointreau
¾ oz. lemon juice

Mix with cracked ice in a shaker or blender and strain into a chilled cocktail glass.

WHITE LADY No. 2

1½ oz. Cointreau
½ oz. brandy
¼ oz. white crème de menthe

Mix all ingredients with cracked ice in a shaker or blender and strain into a chilled cocktail glass.

WHITE LADY No. 3

1½ oz. gin
¼ oz. cream
1 tsp. sugar syrup or to taste
1 egg white (for two drinks)

Mix with cracked ice in a blender and strain into a chilled cocktail glass.

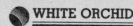 ## WHITE ORCHID

1½ oz. Benedictine
1½ oz. light cream

Shake well with cracked ice
and strain into a chilled cocktail
glass.
Note: Created by the author for
Benedictine Whitbread Enterprises, Inc.

WHITE VELVET

1½ oz. sambuca
1 tsp. lemon juice
1 egg white

Mix all ingredients with cracked
ice in a blender at medium speed
for 20 seconds and strain into
a chilled cocktail glass.

YELLOW CHARTREUSE NECTAR

¾ oz. yellow Chartreuse
¾ oz. apricot schnapps

Combine all ingredients in a
chilled Old Fashioned glass with
several ice cubes and stir well.

 ## YELLOWJACKET

1 oz. Benedictine
1 oz. vodka
4 oz. orange juice

Mix with cracked ice in a
shaker or blender and pour into a
chilled Collins glass with ice
cubes.
Note: Created by the author
for Benedictine Whitbread
Enterprises, Inc.

YODEL

2 oz. Fernet Branca
3 oz. orange juice
Club soda

Pour Fernet Branca and orange
juice into a chilled double Old
Fashioned glass with several
ice cubes, fill with club soda,
and stir gently.

 ## ZIHUATENEJO

1 oz. Galliano
1 oz. light rum
4 oz. orange juice
Scoop vanilla ice cream

Mix all ingredients in a blender
until smooth and pour into a
chilled Squall glass or wine
goblet.

WONDROUS WAYS WITH WINE

Sine cerere et libero friget venus.
(Without bread and wine love grows cold.)
—Old Roman saying

Americans are discovering what our ancestors in wine-producing countries learned hundreds of years ago: that wine is a marvelous mixer, a delightful and satisfying ingredient for all manner of libations for social drinking and special occasions. A great bourgeoning interest in wine has taken place in the U.S. in recent years. We have learned much about wine, and most important, we have learned to be comfortable with it and to enjoy it for what it is: a wholesome, natural, satisfying beverage that, when taken in moderation, of course, can be most beneficial in the pursuit of happiness and the enjoyment of life.

Here we are concerned with the everyday use of wine as an important ingredient in the "new mixology"—the creative approach to drink making—rather than the lore and traditions of grand crus and rare vintages. Wines of various kinds are adding a new dimension to cocktails, coolers, punches, and party drinks—an area of the beverage world ordinarily considered, with some notable exceptions, to be the domain of distilled spirits. This is a relatively recent point of view, however, for wine has been used in Europe since ancient times as a base ingredient in numerous drink recipes. Indeed, a number of recipes in this chapter are inventions from the eighteenth and nineteenth centuries, and some of the punch recipes in Chapter 12 had their origins in ancient Greece and Rome.

From the earliest times, wine has been flavored and sweetened in many ways. Sometimes this was done to improve the taste of a poor wine, but more often it was done to preserve the vintage from premature spoilage. Feasts and special religious and state occasions required something special in the way of food and drink. Then as now, new culinary creations were in order to commemorate a coronation, the wining of a battle, or a great wedding feast. One of the oldest accounts of a punch was given by Daniel, who described a dinner given by Belshazzar, the king of Babylon, for four hundred guests. The liquid refreshment included red wines, "a heady brew of barley and a wine of date palms stiffened with honey." (*Daniel* 5:1). In ancient Greece, Hippocrates, the father of medicine, originated a concoction consisting of wine sweetened with honey and flavored with spices such as cinnamon, which became known in various forms as Hippocras, a popular drink during the Middle Ages. In the *Iliad*, Homer describes a feast given by Nestor to celebrate his return from the Trojan wars. He writes that Hekemede, a lady of the house, prepared a punch made of Pramian wine (believed to be rather heavy and sweet, not unlike a ruby port) by mixing it with grated goat cheese, a sprinkling of barley, and accompanied with a raw onion to be eaten with the drink.

Many of today's fortified wines, such as sherry, port, and Madeira, as well as the so-called apéritif or aromatized wines, such as Dubonnet, Byrrh, and St. Raphael, have their roots in the flavored wines of old. Glühwein, a staple of aprés-ski hot drinks, is simply a modern-day Hippocras. And that German favorite, May Wine (*maiwein*), flavored with woodruff, an aromatic herb, follows the venerable tradition of flavoring wines with spices, herbs, fruits, and flowers. Most modern punches, flavored with fruits, and fruit-based liqueurs such as curaçao, spices, and sweetened with flavored syrups like orgeat or honey, are based upon ancient recipes. Sangria is a good example.

The modern mixologist looks upon wines ranging from table wines, dessert wines, and sparkling wines to highly flavored apéritif and specialty wines as important ingredients in the full spectrum of mixed drinks. Many of the wine cocktails and coolers in this chapter are simply recycled concoctions from recent times: the "Art Deco" drinks of the roaring Twenties and the Thirties; the Belle Epoque libations of the last part of the 1800s, and the hearty grogs of the American colonial period. Other recipes are new innovations using wine as a basic and significant ingredient. Champagne (or comparable, good-quality sparkling wine) appears in many recipes. What could possibly be a better foundation for a refreshing tall drink or an elegant cocktail? The French showed us the way, and we are indebted to them.

They not only invented champagne, but taught us not to be afraid to mix it with other things that make good drinks.

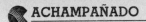 ACHAMPAÑADO

3–4 oz. dry vermouth
½ tsp. sugar syrup
Juice of ¼ lime
Club soda

Pour vermouth into a chilled collins glass with several ice cubes, add sugar syrup, lime juice, and stir until sugar syrup is dissolved. Fill glass with cold club soda and stir gently.
Note: Vermouth and vermouth drinks such as the Achampañado are quite popular in many South American countries.

 ADDINGTON

2 oz. dry vermouth
2 oz. sweet vermouth
Club soda
Orange peel

Pour vermouths into a chilled Collins glass with several ice cubes, stir, and fill with club soda. Twist orange peel over drink and drop into glass.

 ADONIS COCKTAIL

3 oz. fino sherry
1 oz. sweet vermouth
Dash orange bitters
Orange peel

Mix sherry, vermouth, and bitters in a small pitcher with ice and strain into a chilled cocktail glass. Twist orange peel over drink and drop into glass.

AFFINITY COCKTAIL

1 oz. sweet vermouth
1 oz. dry vermouth
1 oz. scotch
Several dashes Angostura
   bitters
Maraschino cherry

Stir vermouths, scotch, and bitters in a mixing glass with ice cubes and strain into a chilled cocktail glass. Garnish with a cherry.

ALFONSO COCKTAIL

2 oz. Dubonnet rouge
1 tsp. curaçao or sugar syrup
   to taste
Several dashes Angostura
   bitters
Brut champagne
Lemon peel

Prechill all ingredients and pour Dubonnet, curaçao or syrup, and bitters into a chilled wine goblet and fill with champagne. Stir gently and garnish with lemon peel.

 AMERICANO

2 oz. sweet vermouth
2 oz. Campari
Club soda
Orange peel

Mix vermouth and Campari in
a mixing glass with ice and strain
into an Old Fashioned glass.
Add several ice cubes and club
soda. Twist orange peel over
drink and drop into glass.

ANY PORT IN A STORM

3 oz. ruby port
1 oz. cognac
1 oz. lemon juice
1 tsp. maraschino liqueur
Club soda

Mix port, cognac, maraschino,
and lemon juice with cracked ice
in a blender or shaker and
pour into a chilled Collins or
highball glass. Add additional
ice if necessary and fill glass
with cold club soda.

 APPETIZER

2–3 oz. Dubonnet rouge
Juice of 1 orange

Mix with cracked ice in a
blender or shaker and strain into
a chilled cocktail glass.

ARUBA COOLER

3 oz. dry vermouth
1½ oz. curaçao
Club soda

Pour dry vermouth and curaçao
into a chilled highball glass with
several ice cubes, fill with
club soda, and stir gently.

 AZZURRA

3 oz. Cinzano Bianco
½ oz. triple sec
Tonic water
Lemon peel

Pour Cinzano and triple sec
into a chilled highball glass
with several ice cubes and
stir well. Fill with cold tonic
water and stir gently. Garnish with a lemon peel.
Note: Created by the author for
Cinzano and the *Azzurra*,
Italy's entry in the America's
Cup trials at Newport, Rhode
Island.

BAHIA

1½ oz. amontillado sherry
1½ oz. dry vermouth or sweet
   vermouth
½ tsp. Pernod or Herbsaint
Several dashes Peychaud's
   bitters, orange bitters,
   or Angostura bitters

Stir briskly with cracked ice in
a pitcher or mixing glass and
strain into a chilled cocktail
glass.

BAMBOO COCKTAIL

2 oz. fino sherry
2 oz. dry vermouth
Several dashes Angostura
   bitters

Stir with ice in a mixing glass
and strain into a chilled cocktail
glass.

BLACK PRINCE

1 oz. blackberry-flavored
   brandy
Dash lemon or lime juice
Brut champagne

Pour brandy into a chilled tulip
glass, add lemon or lime juice,
and fill with cold champagne.

BLACK VELVET

½ pt. Guinness stout
½ pt. champagne

Prechill stout and champagne
and pour carefully into a chilled
highball or Collins glass. Stir
gently so as not to lose the fizz.

BOB DANBY

2–3 oz. Dubonnet rouge
1 oz. brandy
Orange slice

Stir Dubonnet and brandy with
several ice cubes in a mixing
glass and strain into a chilled
cocktail glass. Garnish with
orange slice.

BOCUSE SPECIAL

½ oz. crème de cassis
½ oz. framboise
Brut champagne

Mix cassis and framboise briskly
with several ice cubes in a mixing glass and strain into a
chilled tulip glass. Fill with cold
champagne and stir gently.
Note: This is a favorite of the
renowned French chef, Paul
Bocuse.

BONSONI

3 oz. sweet vermouth
1 oz. Fernet Branca
Lemon or orange peel

Stir vermouth and Fernet Branca briskly with ice cubes in a mixing glass and strain into a chilled cocktail glass. Twist lemon peel over drink and drop into glass.

THE BROKEN SPUR

3 oz. white port
½ oz. gin
½ oz. sweet vermouth
1 egg yolk
½ tsp. anisette
Grated nutmeg

Mix all ingredients, except nutmeg, with cracked ice in a blender and strain into a chilled cocktail glass. Sprinkle with a little grated nutmeg.

B.V.D.

1 oz. Dubonnet, St. Raphael, or Byrrh
1 oz. dry vermouth
1 oz. light rum
Orange peel

Mix all ingredients, except orange peel, with cracked ice in a small pitcher and strain into a chilled cocktail glass. Twist orange peel over drink and drop into glass.

BYCULLA

1 oz. sherry
1 oz. port
1 oz. Stone's ginger wine
1 oz. curaçao

Mix with ice cubes in a small pitcher and strain into a chilled cocktail glass.

BYRRH CASSIS

2–3 oz. Byrrh
1 oz. crème de cassis
Club soda

Mix Byrrh and cassis in a chilled wine goblet with several ice cubes and fill with club soda.

CANARIE D'OR

1 oz. cognac or armagnac
Brut champagne
½ oz. yellow Chartreuse

Prechill all ingredients and pour cognac into a chilled tulip glass. Fill with cold champagne and float yellow Chartreuse on top.

CHAMPAGNE BLUES

Brut champagne
Blue curaçao
Lemon peel

Prechill champagne and curaçao.
Pour champagne into a chilled
tulip glass and add curaçao to
taste. Twist lemon peel over drink
and drop into glass.
Note: Created by the author for
Nan and Ivan Lyons, writers of
Champagne Blues and *Someone
Is Killing the Great Chefs of
Europe.*

CHAMPAGNE COCKTAIL

1 sugar cube
Several dashes Angostura
  bitters, orange bitters, or
  Peychaud's bitters
Champagne
Lemon or orange peel
  (optional)

Put a sugar cube in a chilled
champagne tulip glass and
saturate it with bitters. Fill with
cold champagne and stir gently.
Garnish with lemon peel if
you wish.

CHAMPAGNE CUP

½ oz. cognac
½ oz. curaçao
Brut champagne
Orange slice
Mint sprig

Pour cognac and curaçao into
a chilled large wine goblet, add
a cube of ice, and fill with
cold champagne. Stir gently and
garnish with orange slice and
mint sprig.

CHAMPAGNE CRUSTA

1 large orange
1 oz. cognac or armagnac
½ oz. kummel
½ oz. lemon juice
½ tsp. sugar syrup or to taste
Orange bitters
Brut champagne

Select a large orange with an
unblemished peel. Carefully
remove peel by cutting it so that
you have a long, continuous spiral
of the zest (outer peel) of the
orange. Place this in a large,
chilled balloon glass or wine
goblet. Mix brandy, kummel,
lemon juice, and syrup in a
shaker or blender with cracked
ice and strain into glass.
Sprinkle generously with bitters
and fill with cold champagne.

CHAMPAGNE NAPOLEON

½ oz. Grand Marnier
½ oz. curaçao
½ oz. maraschino liqueur
Several dashes rosewater
Brut champagne

Pour Grand Marnier, curaçao, and maraschino into a mixing glass with several ice cubes and stir briskly. Strain into a chilled tulip glass, sprinkle with rosewater, and fill with cold champagne.

CHOCOLATE COCKTAIL

3 oz. ruby port
1 oz. yellow Chartreuse
1 egg yolk
1 tsp. grated chocolate

Mix all ingredients, except chocolate, with cracked ice in a blender or shaker and strain into a chilled cocktail glass. Sprinkle with grated chocolate.

CHRYSANTHEMUM COCKTAIL

2 oz. dry vermouth
1½ oz. Benedictine
Several dashes Pernod
Orange peel

Stir vermouth and Benedictine briskly with cracked ice in a mixing glass and strain into a chilled cocktail glass. Sprinkle with Pernod and stir gently. Twist orange peel over drink and drop into glass.

COFFEE COCKTAIL No. 3

3 oz. ruby port
1 oz. cognac
1 egg yolk
½ tsp. sugar syrup
Dash curaçao
Grated nutmeg

Mix all ingredients, except nutmeg, with cracked ice in a blender or a shaker and strain into a chilled Delmonico glass.

CORONATION COCKTAIL No. 3

1 oz. sweet vermouth
1 oz. dry vermouth
1 oz. calvados or applejack
Several dashes apricot
   liqueur or apricot brandy

Stir briskly with cracked ice in a mixing glass and strain into a chilled cocktail glass.

COUNTRY CLUB COOLER

4 oz. Lillet blanc or dry
  vermouth
1 tsp. grenadine
Club soda or ginger ale
Orange peel

Pour Lillet and grenadine into a
chilled Collins glass, stir well,
and add several ice cubes. Fill
glass with cold soda and garnish with an orange peel cut into
a long spiral.

 ## DEATH IN THE AFTERNOON

1½ oz. Pernod
Brut champagne

Pour Pernod into a mixing glass
with several ice cubes and stir
briskly. Add Pernod to a chilled
tulip glass and fill with cold
champagne. Stir gently.

Note: This was purported to be a
favorite of Ernest Hemingway's
when he lived in Paris in the
1920s. It is said that he rotated
Pernod as an additive with
cognac or green Chartreuse; all
calculated to put a little extra
bite into the champagne.

DIABOLO

1½ oz. white port
1 oz. dry vermouth
Dash lemon juice
Lemon peel

Mix port, vermouth, and lemon
juice with cracked ice in a shaker
and strain into a chilled cocktail glass. Twist lemon peel over
drink and drop into glass.

 ## DUBONNET FIZZ

3–4 oz. Dubonnet rouge
½ oz. cherry brandy
2 oz. freshly squeezed orange
  juice
1 oz. freshly squeezed lemon
  juice
Club soda or champagne

Mix Dubonnet, brandy, and
juices with cracked ice in a shaker
or blender and strain into a
chilled Collins glass. Add several
ice cubes and fill with club
soda or champagne.

 ## DUCHESS COCKTAIL

1 oz. dry vermouth
1 oz. sweet vermouth
1 oz. Pernod
Orange slice

Stir vermouths and Pernod
briskly with ice cubes in a mixing glass and strain into a
chilled cocktail glass. Garnish
with an orange slice.

DUPLEX COCKTAIL

2 oz. dry vermouth
2 oz. sweet vermouth
Several dashes orange bitters

Stir briskly in a mixing glass
with cracked ice and strain into a
chilled cocktail glass.

 ## FRENCH 75

1 oz. lemon juice
½ oz. sugar syrup or to taste
1½ oz. cognac
Brut champagne

Mix lemon juice and syrup
with several ice cubes in a chilled
Collins glass until syrup is dissolved, add cognac, and fill with
cold champagne. Stir gently.
Note: Some recipe books specify

gin in place of cognac for this
drink. It may be palatable, but it
is *not* a French 75. The French
75 was so named by American
doughboys during World War I
(after the renowned French Army
field piece with a bore diameter
measuring 75 millimeters), who
found cognac and champagne
very enjoyable and readily
available.

 ## GENERAL HARRISON'S EGG NOG

1 whole egg
1 cup hard cider
1 tsp. sugar syrup or to taste

Mix all ingredients with cracked
ice in a blender and pour into a
chilled highball glass.

 ## THE GRAND SCREWDRIVER

Juice of 1 orange
1 oz. Grand Marnier
Brut champagne

Mix orange juice and Grand
Marnier with cracked ice in a
blender or shaker for a few

seconds to chill, strain into a
chilled large wine goblet, and
fill with cold champagne. Do not
add ice.
Note: This drink is at its grandest
when all ingredients are crackling cold.

GRAND SLAM

1½ oz. Swedish Punsch
1 oz. sweet vermouth
1 oz. dry vermouth

Stir all ingredients briskly with
ice in a mixing glass and strain
into a chilled cocktail glass.

GREEN ROOM

2 oz. dry vermouth
¾ oz. brandy
Several dashes curaçao
Orange peel

Stir vermouth, brandy, and curaçao briskly in a mixing glass with ice and strain into a chilled cocktail glass. Twist orange peel over drink and drop into glass.

IMPERIAL HOUSE BRACER cold

2 oz. port
1 oz. cognac
1 egg yolk
¾ oz. cream
Grated nutmeg

Mix all ingredients, except nutmeg, with cracked ice in a blender or shaker and strain into a chilled cocktail glass. Top with a sprinkle of nutmeg.

INCA COCKTAIL

1 oz. amontillado sherry
1 oz. dry vermouth
1 oz. sweet vermouth
1 oz. gin

1 tsp. orgeat syrup or sugar
    syrup to taste
Several dashes orange bitters

Mix with cracked ice in a blender or shaker and pour into a chilled Delmonico glass.

J.P. FIZZ

3 oz. Dubonnet rouge
1 oz. gin or brandy
½ oz. curaçao
Club soda
Orange or lemon slice

Stir Dubonnet, gin, and curaçao in a mixing glass with cracked ice and strain into a chilled Collins glass. Add several ice cubes and fill with cold club soda. Stir gently and garnish with orange slice or lemon slice.

KIR

½ oz. crème de cassis
5 oz. dry white wine

Prechill cassis and wine and mix together in a chilled wine glass.

KIR ROYALE

½ oz. crème de cassis
5–6 oz. brut champagne

Mix cassis and cold champagne gently in a chilled champagne tulip glass.

LE COQ HARDY CHAMPAGNE COCKTAIL

1 sugar cube
Dash Angostura bitters or
    orange bitters
1 drop Fernet Branca
1 drop Grand Marnier
1 drop cognac
Brut champagne
Orange peel

Place sugar cube in a chilled champagne tulip glass and saturate it with bitters, Fernet Branca, Grand Marnier, and cognac. Fill with cold champagne. Garnish with a small strip of orange zest (the outer, colored part of the peel, not the white).

LITTLE BISHOP

2 oz. fresh orange juice
1 oz. lemon juice
1 tsp. sugar syrup or to taste
Dry red wine
½ oz. dark Jamaica rum
Orange slice

Mix orange juice, lemon juice, and syrup with cracked ice in a shaker or blender and strain into a chilled highball glass. Add an ice cube or two, fill with wine, and top with a float of rum. Garnish with an orange slice.

THE MAHARAJAH'S BURRA-PEG

1 sugar cube
Several dashes Angostura
    bitters
1–2 oz. cognac
Brut champagne

Saturate a sugar cube with bitters and put into a chilled

balloon glass. Add chilled cognac and fill with cold champagne. Stir gently.
Note: This is also known as the King's Peg and the Russian Cocktail. Some prefer this drink sans sugar and bitters.

MARAGATO SPECIAL

1 oz. dry vermouth
1 oz. sweet vermouth
1 oz. light rum
1 oz. lemon juice
½ oz. lime juice

½ oz. sugar syrup or to taste
Dash kirsch

Mix with cracked ice in a blender or shaker and strain into a chilled wine glass.

BARTENDER'S SECRET NO. 26

Most wine books tell you to chill white wines and sparkling wines but to serve red wines at room temperature. The "room temperature" generally referred to is that which is found in Europe and especially England. Americans consider 72 degrees to be an acceptable room temperature. In England, 50 degrees or thereabouts is probably somewhere near the norm. A red wine served at 50 degrees will generally taste more sprightly than the same wine served at 72 degrees. A good sommelier knows that putting a *little* chill on even a distinguished red wine definitely makes it more palatable.

 ## MIMOSA

6 oz. brut champagne
3 oz. fresh orange juice

Prechill orange juice and champagne and mix together in a

chilled wine goblet. Proportions of wine and juice may be adjusted for individual tastes. If drink needs more chilling, add an ice cube or 2 tbsp. cracked ice.

NINETEEN

3 oz. dry vermouth
½ oz. gin
½ oz. kirsch
Several dashes Pernod
Several dashes sugar syrup
    or to taste

Mix all ingredients with cracked ice in a shaker or blender and strain into a chilled cocktail glass.

 ### PACIFIC PALISADES

1½ oz. Campari
1 oz. orange juice
Brut champagne

Mix Campari and orange juice in a chilled wine goblet with an ice cube and fill with cold champagne.

PANTOMIME

2 oz. dry vermouth
1 egg white (for two drinks)
Several dashes orgeat syrup
Dash grenadine

Mix all ingredients with cracked ice in a blender and strain into a chilled cocktail glass.

 ## PHILOMEL COCKTAIL

2½ oz. amontillado sherry
1½ oz. St. Raphael
1 oz. light rum
1½ oz. orange juice
Pinch ground cayenne or
    white pepper

Mix all ingredients, except cayenne, with cracked ice in a blender or shaker and strain into a chilled wine goblet. Sprinkle with ground cayenne.

PICON COCKTAIL

2 oz. Amer Picon
2 oz. dry vermouth

Stir briskly with ice in a mixing glass and strain into a chilled cocktail glass.

PIZZETTI

1 oz. cognac
2 oz. orange juice
2 oz. grapefruit juice
Brut champagne

Mix cognac and fruit juices in a blender or shaker with cracked ice and strain into a chilled wine goblet. Fill with cold champagne and stir gently.
Note: From the Hotel de la Poste, Cortina, Italy

BARTENDER'S SECRET NO. 27

Spare the fizz. And if the fizz comes from champagne or other good sparkling wine made by the time-honored *méthode champenois* (a natural way of making sparkling wine with a second fermentation in the bottle), all the more reason to preserve it. All mixologists should use care when using a sparkling wine in the making of mixed drinks, and especially punches, to stir the mixture gently so as not to dissipate the sparkle. And for the same reason, all swizzle sticks, those destructive devices no doubt invented by die-hard Prohibitionists to take the joy out of drinking champagne, should be seized and burned or otherwise obliterated. For this reason, a warning notice should be printed on every sparkling wine label:

> PLEASE SPARE THE SPARKLE
> Don't stir out in minutes
> what it took months of
> work by master winemakers
> to put into this bottle.

PORT MILK PUNCH

3–4 oz. ruby port
1 cup milk
1 tsp. superfine sugar or
   honey to taste
Grated nutmeg

Mix port, milk, and sugar with cracked ice in a blender and strain into a chilled Collins glass. Sprinkle with nutmeg.

PORT SANGAREE

5 oz. port
1 tsp. sugar syrup or to taste
Grated nutmeg

Mix port and syrup with several
ice cubes in a large chilled wine
goblet until syrup dissolves.

Sprinkle with a little nutmeg.
Note: A Sangaree, a gentle
concoction popular in a bygone
era, is basically any wine,
sweetened to taste, served with
or without ice and topped with
grated nutmeg.

PORT SNORT

2 oz. tawny port
2 oz. sloe gin
Lemon slice

Stir port and sloe gin briskly
with cracked ice in a mixing
glass and strain into a chilled
cocktail glass. Garnish with a
lemon slice.

PUENTE ROMANO SPECIAL

2–3 oz. cream sherry
¾ oz. brandy
1½ oz. orange juice
1 oz. heavy cream
Dash curaçao

Mix all ingredients with cracked
ice in a blender or shaker and
strain into a chilled Delmonico
glass.
Note: Created by the author for
the Puente Romano, Marbella,
Spain.

RACE CUP COCKTAIL

1 oz. sweet vermouth
1 oz. tequila
3 oz. grapefruit juice

Mix all ingredients with cracked
ice in a shaker or blender and
strain into a chilled cocktail
glass.

RAYMOND HITCHCOCKTAIL

3 oz. sweet vermouth
2–3 oz. fresh orange juice
Several dashes orange bitters
Slice of pineapple

Mix vermouth, juice, and bitters
with cracked ice in a shaker or
blender and strain into a chilled
Old Fashioned glass. Garnish
with pineapple slice.

REFORM COCKTAIL

2 oz. fino sherry
1 oz. sweet vermouth
Several dashes orange bitters

Stir with ice in a mixing glass
and strain into a chilled cocktail
glass.

RHINE WINE SPRITZER

4 oz. rhine, Mosel, or
  Johannisberger riesling
  wine
Club soda or mineral water
Lemon or lime peel (optional)

Pour cold Rhine wine into a
chilled wine goblet or highball
glass with several ice cubes,
and fill with cold club soda or
sparkling mineral water. Twist
lemon peel over drink and drop
into glass.
Note: This is the original Spritzer,
but it can be made with any
wine of your choice, a little ice,
and sparkling water. The name
comes from the German word
"spritzig," meaning fizzy, bubbly,
and lively, which is what a
well-made Spritzer should be.

RITZ FIZZ

4 oz. sauterne, barsac, or
  other sweet white wine
2 oz. dry vermouth
½ oz. kirsch
½ oz. peach-flavored brandy
½ tsp. orgeat syrup or sugar
  syrup to taste
Club soda
Orange peel

Combine sauterne, vermouth,
kirsch, brandy, and syrup with
ice cubes in a mixing glass.
Stir well and pour into a large
chilled wine goblet or large
brandy snifter. Fill with club soda
and garnish with an orange
peel cut in a long spiral.

ROY HOWARD

2–3 oz. Lillet blanc
1 oz. brandy
1 oz. orange juice
Several dashes grenadine

Mix all ingredients with cracked
ice in a shaker or blender and
strain into a chilled cocktail
glass.

SANCTUARY

2 oz. Dubonnet rouge
1 oz. Amer Picon
1 oz. Cointreau
Lemon peel

Stir Dubonnet, Amer Picon, and
Cointreau in a mixing glass with
ice and strain into a chilled
cocktail glass.

BARTENDER'S SECRET NO. 28

How do you open a bottle of champagne? By removing the wire
fastener and foil that covers the crown of every champagne

bottle and twisting the cork until it can be pulled out of the bottle. Right? Wrong. Experienced sommeliers and bartenders know that the easy way to open a bottle of champagne is to hold the cork in one hand and *turn the bottle* with the other. Try it, it works. Place the bottle upright on the bar or table and use a bar towel to get a firm grip on the cork, hold tightly and slowly turn the bottle with your other hand.

 ## SATIN'S WHISKERS COCKTAIL

1½ oz. sweet vermouth
1½ oz. dry vermouth
1 oz. gin
½ oz. Grand Marnier
3–4 oz. fresh orange juice
Dash orange bitters

Mix with cracked ice in a blender or shaker and strain into a chilled wine glass.

 ## SHERRY AND EGG

1 whole egg
Amontillado sherry

Carefully break an egg into a chilled wine glass, leaving the yolk intact. Fill with slightly chilled sherry.

Note: Other wines such as such as port and Madeira may also be used. And some prefer spirits such as brandy and whiskey, which were popular combinations in the nineteenth century.

 ## SHERRY COBBLER

Several dashes curaçao
Several dashes pineapple
    syrup or sugar syrup
4 oz. amontillado sherry
Lemon peel
Pineapple stick
Mint sprig (optional)

Fill a large chilled wine goblet with crushed ice, add curaçao and syrup, and churn the glass

with a barspoon. Then add sherry and churn until a frost appears on the outside of the glass. Add more ice, if necessary. Twist lemon peel over drink and drop into glass. Garnish with pineapple stick and mint sprig. *Note:* Cobblers may utilize fortified wines such as port, sherry, and Madeira; table wines, both red and white; dessert wines such as sauterne and all spirits.

SHERRY EGG NOG

3–4 oz. amontillado sherry
1 whole egg
1 cup milk
1 tsp. superfine sugar or
    brown sugar to taste
Grated nutmeg

Mix sherry, egg, milk, and sugar in a blender with cracked ice and strain into a tall Collins glass or wine goblet chilled in the refrigerator. Top with a sprinkling of nutmeg.

SHERRY SHANDY

2–3 oz. amontillado sherry
Several dashes Angostura or
    orange bitters (optional)
Ginger beer or ginger ale
Lemon slice

Mix sherry and bitters in a highball glass with several ice cubes, fill with cold ginger beer, and garnish with a lemon slice.

SHERRY SOUR

3 oz. fino sherry
1 oz. lemon juice
1 oz. orange or grapefruit juice
½ oz. sugar syrup or to taste
Maraschino cherry

Mix all ingredients, except cherry, with cracked ice in a shaker or blender and pour into a chilled Whiskey Sour glass. Garnish with a cherry.

 ## SHERRY TWIST No. 1

3 oz. amontillado sherry
1 oz. Spanish brandy,
    cognac, or armagnac
1 oz. dry vermouth
½ oz. curaçao
Several dashes lemon juice
Pinch ground cinnamon

Mix all ingredients, except cinnamon, with cracked ice in a shaker or blender and strain into a chilled Delmonico glass. Top with ground cinnamon.

 ## SHERRY TWIST No. 2

3 oz. amontillado sherry
1½ oz. bourbon or blended
    whiskey
½ oz. curaçao
3 oz. fresh orange juice
½ oz. lemon juice

3 whole cloves
Pinch cayenne or ground
    white pepper

Mix all ingredients with cracked ice in a blender or shaker and strain into a chilled Old Fashioned glass or a wine goblet.

SHIP COCKTAIL

3 oz. amontillado or fino
  sherry
¾ oz. blended whiskey
¾ oz. light rum
1 tsp. sugar syrup or to taste
Several dashes orange bitters

Several dashes prune juice
  or prune syrup

Mix all ingredients with cracked
ice in a shaker or blender and
strain into a chilled cocktail
glass.

SONOMA CUP

3 oz. dry white wine
½ oz. Cointreau
3 oz. orange juice
Club soda

Mix all ingredients, except club
soda, with cracked ice in a shaker
or blender and pour into a
chilled Collins glass. Fill glass
with cold club soda and stir
gently.

SOUL KISS

1 oz. Dubonnet or St. Raphael
1 oz. dry vermouth
1 oz. sweet vermouth
1 oz. orange juice

Mix with cracked ice in a
blender or shaker and strain into
a Delmonico glass.

SOUTHERN CHAMPAGNE COCKTAIL

1 oz. Southern Comfort
Dash Angostura or orange
  bitters
Brut champagne
Orange peel

Prechill all ingredients and
pour Southern Comfort into a
chilled tulip glass, add bitters,
and fill with champagne. Twist
orange peel over drink and drop
into glass.

SOYER AU CHAMPAGNE

2 tbsp. vanilla ice cream
Several dashes curaçao
Several dashes maraschino
  liqueur
Several dashes cognac
Champagne
Orange slice
Maraschino cherry

Put vanilla ice cream into a
chilled wine goblet or large
champagne flute and mix with
curaçao, maraschino, and cognac.
Fill goblet with cold champagne
and stir gently. Garnish with
orange slice and maraschino
cherry.

SPION KOP

2 oz. Dubonnet rouge
2 oz. dry vermouth
Orange peel

Stir Dubonnet and vermouth in a chilled Old Fashioned glass with ice cubes. Twist orange peel over drink and drop into glass.

STRAIGHT LAW COCKTAIL

2 oz. fino sherry
1 oz. gin
Lemon peel

Mix gin and sherry with ice in a small pitcher and strain into a chilled cocktail glass. Twist lemon peel over drink and drop into glass.

TEMPTER COCKTAIL

2 oz. port
2 oz. apricot-flavored brandy

Stir with ice in a mixing glass and strain into a chilled cocktail glass.

THIRD RAIL

2–3 oz. dry vermouth
Several dashes curaçao
Several dashes peppermint
   schnapps
Lemon or orange peel

Stir vermouth, curaçao, and schnapps briskly with ice cubes in a mixing glass and strain into a chilled cocktail glass. Twist fruit peel over drink and drop into glass.

TINTON COCKTAIL

2 oz. port
2 oz. applejack or calvados

Stir with ice in a mixing glass and strain into a chilled cocktail glass.

TINTORETTO

¼ cup pureed pears
1 oz. pear brandy
Brut champagne
Mint sprig (optional)

Puree a ripe pear using a sieve and spoon puree into a chilled balloon glass. Add brandy and cold champagne and a little cracked ice, if you wish (otherwise, prechill all ingredients). Garnish with a small mint sprig.

TROLLHAGEN SPECIAL

1 oz. B&B liqueur
Brut champagne
Orange peel

Prechill B&B and pour into a chilled balloon glass. Fill with cold champagne and stir gently. Twist orange peel over drink and drop into glass.

 ## TUXEDO

2–3 oz. fino sherry
½ oz. anisette
Several dashes maraschino
  liqueur
Several dashes Angostura
  bitters, orange bitters,
  or Peychaud's bitters

Mix with ice in a small pitcher and strain into a chilled cocktail glass.

 ## VERMOUTH CASSIS

3 oz. dry vermouth
1 oz. crème de cassis
Club soda

Mix vermouth and cassis with ice cubes in a chilled highball glass and fill with cold club soda.

 ## VICTOR COCKTAIL

1½ oz. sweet vermouth
¾ oz. brandy
¾ oz. gin
Orange peel

Mix vermouth, brandy, and gin with cracked ice in a shaker or blender and strain into a chilled cocktail glass. Twist orange peel over drink and drop into glass.

WALTZING MATILDA

3–4 oz. dry white wine
1 oz. gin
1½ oz. passion fruit juice
¼ tsp. curaçao
Club soda, ginger ale, or
  lemon-lime soda
Orange peel

Mix wine, gin, passion fruit, and curaçao with cracked ice in a shaker or blender and pour into a chilled Collins glass. Add several ice cubes and fill with cold soda. Stir gently and twist orange peel over drink and drop into glass.

WEEP NO MORE

1½ oz. Dubonnet rouge
1½ oz. cognac
1½ oz. lime·juice
Dash maraschino liqueur

Mix all ingredients with cracked
ice in a shaker or blender and
strain into a chilled cocktail
glass.

 WHISPERS OF THE FROST

1 oz. ruby port
1 oz. fino sherry
1 oz. straight bourbon or
    straight rye whiskey
½ tsp. sugar syrup or to taste
Lemon peel

Stir port, sherry, bourbon, and
syrup with cracked ice in a mixing
glass until syrup is dissolved
and strain into a chilled cocktail
glass. Twist lemon peel over
drink and drop into glass.

WINE COLLINS

4 oz. Madeira, port, or
    marsala
½ oz. lime juice
Lemon-lime soda
Maraschino cherry

Pour wine and lime juice into
a chilled Collins glass and stir
with several ice cubes. Fill
glass with cold lemon-lime soda,
stir again, and garnish with a
cherry.

WINE LEMONADE

Juice of large lemon
½ oz. sugar syrup or to taste
4 oz. dry or sweet, red, rosé,
    or white wine
Club soda
Lemon slice
Maraschino cherry

Pour lemon juice and syrup
into a chilled Collins glass and
stir until syrup is dissolved.
Add wine and fill glass with cold
soda. Stir gently and garnish
with lemon slice and a cherry.

BARTENDER'S SECRET No. 29

Vermouth is a popular, complex, aromatized wine with a relatively high alcoholic content (16 to 18 percent) that is indispensable to the making of many mixed drinks. If you buy a bottle of
either sweet or dry vermouth and let it stand in your liquor
cabinet for weeks after it has been opened, you will find the
subtle flavor overtones that vermouth can impart to drinks will

have disappeared. Store opened bottles of vermouth in your refrigerator. Unless you use a great deal vermouth, buy the 375 ml bottle instead of the 750 ml size. It takes up less space in the refrigerator and, no doubt, will be used up before it becomes stale.

WYOMING SWING COCKTAIL

2 oz. sweet vermouth
2 oz. dry vermouth
3–4 oz. fresh orange juice
1 tsp. orgeat syrup or sugar
   syrup to taste
Orange slice

Mix with cracked ice in a blender or shaker and serve in a chilled highball glass. Add additional ice cubes if needed and garnish with an orange slice.

YELLOW RATTLER

1 oz. dry vermouth
1 oz. sweet vermouth
1 oz. gin
2–3 oz. fresh orange juice

Mix with cracked ice in a blender or shaker and serve in a chilled wine glass.

ZANZIBAR

2–3 oz. dry vermouth
1 oz. gin
¾ oz. lemon juice
1 tsp. sugar syrup or to taste
Several dashes orange bitters
Lemon peel

Mix all ingredients, except lemon peel, with cracked ice in a blender or shaker and strain into a chilled Delmonico glass. Twist lemon peel over drink and drop into glass.

HOUSE SPECIALTIES FROM THE WORLD'S GREAT BARS

> There is nothing by which so much
> happiness has been produced as by
> a good tavern or inn.
> —Samuel Johnson

Good bartenders make good bars. And accomplished chefs fulfill the same role for restaurants. In both instances, the patrons may be glamorous, the decor may be stunning, and the service cheerful and competent, but if what is served is dreary, skimpy, and poorly made, many customers may come and go but few will ever become regulars. The professionalism required to operate a successful bar is detailed in the first chapter of this book. Here we are concerned with bartenders who are not only professional but also creative. Like their counterparts in the kitchen, they frequently devise a recipe that is unique (whether it be original or simply an innovative way of preparing a standard recipe) and which in time becomes a popular, widely acclaimed speciality of the house.

The cocktail is an American invention, and the mixologists who devised mixed drinks that have become classics are all a part of an American tradition. It is a creative tradition that has spread to every continent. Even in the most unlikely places, a traveler can stumble upon a small bar where an enterprising bartender has created a very special (and often a very good) house libation that is served with justifiable pride.

It was not always so, of course. A century ago, with the exception of a few of the more elegant restaurants in large cities, the American drinking scene was pretty much relegated to what was drawn from a keg or poured from a bottle. Early mixologists like Jerry Thomas, the legendary "professor" who created the spectacular Blue Blazer and is credited by many historians as the originator of the Manhattan and the Martinez, the forerunner of the Martini, helped lay the foundation for a gradual change in American tastes toward more genteel, more flavorful drinks. Others followed and made their contributions: Harry C. Ramos, who was renowned in New Orleans at the turn of the century for his creation, the Ramos Gin Fizz. The drink became so popular that on a busy night Harry would have as many as thirty shaker boys, who would pass ice-cold shakers down the line, each giving it a good buffeting as it passed by. And in New York, tales are still told about Johnnie Solon, head barman at the old Waldorf-Astoria, who created many concoctions such as the Bronx cocktail for the likes of J.P. Morgan, Jimmie Walker, and Buffalo Bill Cody. (When offered a drink by an admirer, Cody invariably would reply, "Sir, you speak the language of my tribe.")

In the Roaring Twenties an enterprising Scot from Dundee, Harry MacElhone, opened Harry's New York Bar in Paris. It quickly became known as a hangout for American expatriates such as F. Scott Fitzgerald, Ernest Hemingway, and George Gershwin, who wrote parts of his *An American in Paris* on the downstairs piano. Harry's also served American-style hot dogs and American cocktails such as some of Harry MacElhone's own inventions, including the Sidecar, the White Lady, and Death in the Afternoon, reputed to be a great favorite of Ernest Hemingway's. It was at this very bar that Fernand Petiot is credited with inventing the Bloody Mary.

Around the corner from Harry's New York Bar and just a short walk down the Rue de la Paix is Place Vendôme and the venerable Ritz Hotel. The bars in the Ritz also were creating American-style cocktails in the 1920s, and "style" is the right word for them. Beginning with inventions such as the Mimosa (champagne and orange juice) and Hemingway's Special (lime, bourbon, and a dash of Pernod), the Ritz bars have offered elegant and unusual refreshment to the rich and famous through the years, and the bartenders who created these inspired potations have become legends. Barmen like Frank Meyer, Georges (Sheuer) and Bertin (Jean Bernard Azimont) had an international following, and their handiworks still fill the drink menu at *Les Bars du Ritz*.

About the same time, an American bartender, Harry Craddock, took up residence at London's Savoy Hotel and made its American Bar a source of brilliantly conceived and executed original cocktails. He later compiled *The Savoy Cocktail Book*, a bibber's bible that has become a classic. His successor, Joe Gilmore, another inventive mixologist, carried on the Craddock tradition, devising many interesting new concoctions that helped make the Savoy famous.

The late Trader Vic (Victor Bergeron) was an indefatigable inventor of new and exciting drinks. He changed the drinking habits of the country (with his contemporary Don the Beach-comber of Hollywood) and made exotic "Polynesian-style" rum drinks the rage in the 1940s and '50s. Trader Vic was proud of his prowess as a mixologist and enjoyed being called a "saloon keeper." Some of his famous drink inventions are the Mai Tai, the Fog Cutter, the Scorpion, and the Tortuga. Creativity in food and drink propelled Trader Vic's from a small Oakland, California, bar (originally known as "Hinky-Dinks") to a large food-products company and a chain of twenty restaurants world-wide grossing in excess of $50 million a year.

The basis of selecting the establishments and recipes that appear here was not predicated upon size, success, or reputation, although all of these factors, of course, played a part. The primary consideration is creative, imaginative, innovative mixology; and a house policy of serving expertly made drinks. Apologies are in order for the very fine watering places, bartenders, and original recipes that could not be included due to space limitations. One fact, however, became quite obvious as the research for this chapter progressed: the number of good bars creating and promoting special house drinks is growing and would in itself form the basis for a valuable drink-recipe book.

AL CAPONE

1½ oz. brandy
¾ oz. Marsala
Dash Drambuie

Mix with cracked ice in a shaker or blender and strain into a balloon glass.
Note: Created by Raffaele de Martinis of the Cavalieri Hilton International, Rome.

ALOHA

1 oz. dark Jamaica rum
1½ oz. Myers's rum cream liqueur
½ oz. Rose's lime juice
2 oz. pineapple juice
2 oz. orange juice
1 oz. coconut syrup or to taste
Small scoop vanilla ice cream
Pineapple stick

Mix all ingredients, except pineapple stick, with cracked ice in a blender and pour into a chilled Hurricane or Collins glass. Do not overmix. Garnish with pineapple stick.
Note: From the Kahala Hilton Hotel, Honolulu.

ANATOLE COFFEE

½ oz. Courvoisier
½ oz. Tia Maria
½ oz. Frangelico
Cold black coffee
Whipped cream
Chocolate shavings

Mix all ingredients, except whipped cream and chocolate, with a little cracked ice in a blender and pour into a chilled wine goblet. Top with whipped cream and sprinkle with shavings scraped from a bar of chocolate with a knife.
Note: From Loews Anatole Hotel, Dallas.

THE ANNABELE SPECIAL

1½ oz. Benedictine
⅓ oz. dry vermouth
⅓ oz. lime juice

Mix with cracked ice in a shaker or blender and strain into a chilled cocktail glass. Proportions may be varied for individual tastes.
Note: From Annabele's, London.

AZTEC

1 oz. gin
½ oz. cherry brandy
1 oz. Pina Colada mix
1 oz. orange juice
Pineapple slice
Maraschino cherry

Mix all ingredients, except pineapple and cherry, with cracked ice in a shaker or blender and serve in a double Old Fashioned glass. Garnish with fruit.
Note: From the Arizona Biltmore, Phoenix.

BATH CURE

1½ oz. dark Jamaica rum
1½ oz. brandy
1½ oz. vodka
2 oz. light Puerto Rican rum
1 oz. Puerto Rican gold rum
1 oz. 151-proof rum
½ oz. lime juice
1 oz. orange juice
1 oz. pineapple juice
1 oz. lemon juice
½ oz. grenadine
1 tsp. sugar syrup or to taste
Red, blue and, green
   vegetable coloring
Lime slice
Maraschino cherry

Mix all ingredients, except lime slice and cherry, with cracked ice in a blender and strain into a 14- or 16-oz. double Old Fashioned-style glass that has been frozen in a mold of shaved ice. Decorate sides of ice mold with red, blue, and green vegetable coloring. Garnish with lime slice and maraschino cherry and serve with two straws.
Note: From the Pump Room, Ambassador East Hotel, Chicago.

BELLINI

3 oz. pureed peaches
Dash lemon juice
Maraschino liqueur to taste
Brut champagne

Puree ripe peaches in a blender

and spoon into a large, chilled
wine goblet. Sprinkle with
lemon juice and sweeten with
maraschino liqueur. Fill with
ice cold champagne.
Note: From Harry's Bar, Venice.

BOLSHOI PUNCH

1 oz. vodka
¼ oz. light rum
¼ oz. crème de cassis
Juice of 1 lemon
1–2 tsp. sugar syrup or to
   taste

Mix all ingredients with cracked
ice in a shaker or blender and
strain into a chilled cocktail
glass.
Note: From the Russian Tea Room,
New York.

BOSSA NOVA

1 oz. light Puerto Rican
   rum
1 oz. Galliano
¼ oz. apricot brandy
3 oz. pineapple juice
1½ oz. lemon mix
Pineapple slice
Maraschino cherry

Mix all ingredients, except
pineapple slice and cherry, with
cracked ice in a shaker or
blender and pour into a chilled
Squall glass or a ten-pin pilsener
glass. Garnish with pineapple
slice and cherry.
Note: From the Sonesta Beach
Hotel, Key Biscayne, Florida.

THE "BOSS McCLURE" COCKTAIL

1 oz. cognac
1 oz. gin
½ oz. orange curaçao
½ oz. apricot liqueur
Lemon twist

Mix all ingredients, except
lemon twist, with cracked ice in
a shaker or blender and strain
into a chilled cocktail glass.
Garnish with lemon twist.
Note: From the Vista International
Hotel, Washington, D.C.

CAMEL PUNCH

1 oz. dark rum
¾ oz. vodka
½ oz. cherry brandy
½ oz. apricot brandy
3 oz. pineapple juice
1 tbsp. diced assorted fruits

Mix all ingredients, except
fruits, with cracked ice in a
shaker or blender and strain into
a chilled pilsener glass. Add
additional ice cubes if necessary
and garnish with diced fruits.
Note: From the Petra Forum Hotel,
Petra, Jordan.

CANGREJO COCKTAIL

2 oz. light rum
1 oz. Dubonnet rouge
½ oz. Campari
½ oz. lime juice
Sugar syrup to taste
Pineapple slice

Mix all ingredients, except pineapple, with plenty of cracked ice in a blender and pour into a double Old Fashioned glass.
Note: From the Cartagena Hilton, Cartagena, Colombia.

THE CARIBE PIÑA COLADA

2 oz. dark rum
8 oz. light rum
2 oz. heavy cream
5 oz. coconut cream
10 oz. pineapple juice
Pineapple spears

Mix all ingredients with crushed ice in a blender for 10 seconds and serve in chilled Hurricane glasses or Poco Grande glasses. Garnish with pineapple spears. Makes 4 drinks.
From the Caribe Hilton International, San Juan, Puerto Rico.
Note: The Piña Colada was invented by Ramón "Monchito" Marrero in 1958 at the Caribe Hilton.

CARNEGIE COCKTAIL

1¼ oz. scotch
1 oz. Bailey's Irish Cream
3½ oz. cranberry juice
Orange slice
Mint sprig

Mix scotch, Irish cream, and cranberry juice with cracked ice in a shaker or blender and pour over ice cubes in a chilled highball glass. Garnish with orange and mint.
Note: Created by Joseph Reilly, Hotel Inter-Continental, New York, New York.

COLE PORTER

1½ oz. gin
3 or 4 small plum tomatoes, cooked and chilled
Dash Angostura bitters
Dash Worcestershire sauce
Dash lemon juice

Mix all ingredients with cracked ice in a blender until smooth and pour into a chilled Old Fashioned glass.
Note: From the Waldorf-Astoria Hotel, New York.

COMET COCKTAIL

1 oz. rum
¾ oz. Chambord
¾ oz. strawberry liqueur
2–3 oz. sweet-and-sour mix
1 small scoop vanilla ice
   cream

Mix all ingredients in a chilled blender bowl until smooth and creamy. Do not overmix. Pour into a chilled wine goblet.
Note: From the Sandpiper and Tradewinds Resort Hotels, St. Petersburg Beach, Florida.

CORPSE REVIVER

¾ oz. white crème de menthe
¾ oz. brandy
¾ oz. Fernet Branca

Mix with cracked ice in a shaker or blender and strain into a chilled cocktail glass.
Note: This is a hangover straightener created by Joe Gilmore, Savoy Hotel, London.

CROCODILE

1 oz. rum
1 oz. blue curaçao
2 oz. orange juice
3 oz. sweet-and-sour mix
Dash orgeat syrup

Mix all ingredients with cracked ice in a shaker or blender. Pour into a chilled Old Fashioned glass.
Note: From Loews Anatole Hotel, Dallas, Texas.

CROWN JEWEL

1½ oz. light rum
½ oz. crème de noyaux
1¼ oz. lemon juice
1 oz. coconut cream
1 egg white (for 2 drinks)
Fresh whole strawberry

Mix all ingredients, except strawberry, with cracked ice in a blender until smooth, pour into a chilled wine goblet, and garnish with strawberry.
Note: From the Fairmont Hotel, San Francisco.

CUPID'S BOW

½ oz. Peter Heering
5 oz. brut champagne

Pour Peter Heering into a chilled tulip glass and fill with cold champagne.
Note: From the Drake Hotel, Chicago.

DERBY DAIQUIRI

3 oz. light rum
2 oz. orange juice
1 oz. lime juice
1 oz. sugar syrup

Mix all ingredients with cracked ice in a shaker or blender and strain into a chilled wine glass. *Note:* From the Mai-Kai Polynesian Restaurant, Fort Lauderdale, Florida.

DESERT BREEZE

1 oz. gin
1 oz. blue curaçao
1 oz. coconut cream
½ oz. lemon juice
Lemon-lime soda
Pineapple stick

Mix all ingredients, except soda and pineapple, with cracked ice in a shaker or blender and serve in a tall, chilled chimney glass. Fill with soda and garnish with pineapple. *Note:* From the Camelback Inn, Scottsdale, Arizona.

EAST WINDS DELITE

2 oz. gold rum
½ oz. Galliano
1 oz. orange juice
½ oz. lime juice
Sugar syrup to taste
Dash Grenadine

Mix with cracked ice in a shaker or blender and pour into a chilled Collins glass. *Note:* From East Winds Inn, Castries, St. Lucia.

FIVE-LEGGED MULE

1½ oz. gin
1 oz. Dubonnet rouge
1 oz. dry vermouth
Dash lemon juice
Dash grenadine

Mix all ingredients with cracked ice in a shaker or blender and strain into a chilled cocktail glass. *Note:* From the Hotel Muehlebach, Kansas City.

FOUQUET'S PICK-ME-UP

1 oz. Grand Marnier
½ oz. kirsch
2 oz. orange juice
Brut champagne
Orange slice

Mix Grand Marnier, kirsch, and cold orange juice with cracked ice in a large, chilled wine goblet. Fill with ice-cold champagne, stir gently, and garnish with an orange slice. *Note:* From Fouquet's restaurant, Paris.

FRANGIPANI

1¼ oz. dark rum
1¼ oz. Frangelico
½ oz. anisette
2½ oz. pineapple juice
Dash lime juice

Mix all ingredients with cracked ice in a shaker or blender. Pour into a chilled Squall glass or Poco Grande glass.
Note: From Marriott's Sam Lord's Castle, Barbados.

FROSTED ROMANCE

1 oz. Chambord
¾ oz. white crème de cacao
2 scoops vanilla ice cream
Whipped cream

Mix all ingredients, except

whipped cream, in blender until smooth and creamy. Do not overmix. Serve in a chilled balloon glass and top with whipped cream.
Note: From the Drake Hotel, Chicago.

FROZEN PEACHTREE ROAD RACE

1¼ oz. peach schnapps
1¼ oz. vodka
2 oz. peach puree
2 oz. orange juice
Cranberry juice

Mix all ingredients, except cranberry juice, with two cups of

crushed ice in a blender at high speed for a few seconds and serve in a chilled Collins glass. Top with a cranberry juice float. Serve with straws.
Note: From the Ritz-Carlton, Atlanta, Georgia.

GOLDEN HORNET

1½ oz. gin
½ oz. amontillado sherry
½ oz. scotch
Lemon peel

Pour gin and amontillado sherry in mixing glass with several ice

cubes, stir well, and pour into a chilled Old Fashioned glass. Top with scotch and twist lemon peel over drink and drop into glass.
Note: From the Playboy Club, New York.

GOLDEN TULIP

1 oz. vodka
½ oz. apricot brandy
½ oz. curaçao
½ oz. orange juice
½ oz. lemon juice
Orange slice
Maraschino cherry

Mix all ingredients, except orange and cherry, with cracked ice in a shaker or blender and strain into a chilled cocktail glass. Garnish with orange slice and cherry.
Note: Created by Gerry Kooyman, Hotel Pulitzer, Amsterdam.

GOOD AND PLENTY

1 oz. vodka
1 oz. Kahlua
Dash anisette
½ scoop vanilla ice cream

Mix all ingredients in a blender for a few seconds until smooth.

Do not overmix or drink will become watery. Pour into a chilled wine goblet.
Note: From the Bonaventure Inter-Continental Hotel and Spa, Ft. Lauderdale, Florida.

GREEN FANTASY

1 oz. vodka
1 oz. dry vermouth
1 oz. melon liqueur
Kiwi slices

Mix all ingredients, except kiwi, with plenty of crushed ice until drink is frappéed. Serve in a chilled balloon glass and garnish with kiwi slices.
Note: From the Vista International Hotel, New York.

GRITTI SPECIAL

3 oz. Cinzano dry vermouth
2 oz. Campari
1 oz. Chinamartini or Punt e Mes

Mix well with ice cubes in a pitcher and strain into a chilled wine goblet.
Note: From the Gritti Palace, Venice.

HANDLEBAR

1½ oz. scotch
¾ oz. Drambuie
½ oz. Rose's lime juice

Mix with cracked ice in a shaker or blender and strain into a chilled cocktail glass.
Note: From the Oak Room Bar, Hotel Plaza, New York.

THE HARPOONER

1½ oz. light Puerto Rican rum
1½ oz. Trinidad rum
1½ oz. light Jamaica rum
1½ oz. Haitian rum
1 oz. crème de cacao
½ oz. brandy
4 oz. pineapple juice
2 oz. lime juice

Dash Angostura bitters
Dash 151-proof Demerara rum

Mix all ingredients, except Demerara rum, with cracked ice in a blender and pour into a chilled double Old Fashioned glass. Top off with Demerara rum.
Note: From the Crown Point Hotel, Tobago.

HEAVENLY SPIRITS

1 oz. vodka
½ oz. amaretto
¼ oz. triple sec
¼ oz. Galliano
2 oz. orange juice

Mix all ingredients with cracked ice in a shaker or blender and strain into a chilled cocktail glass.
Note: From the Heaven Restaurant, Pittsburgh.

HOT PINT

4 oz. blended whiskey
4 eggs
4 tbsp. sugar or to taste
1 qt. ale, heated

In each of 4 heat-proof mugs add 1 oz. whiskey, 1 egg, and sugar to taste. Stir well and pour in ale, heated almost to boiling point. Continue stirring to prevent egg from curdling. Hot ale is traditionally poured into mug from a height to make the drinks frothy. Makes 4 servings.
Note: From the Al Ain Inter-Continental Hotel, Abu Dhabi, United Arab Emirates.

ICE CREAM COLADA

1½ oz. light rum
½ oz. banana, melon, or
    strawberry liqueur
2 scoops vanilla ice cream
3 oz. coconut cream
1 oz. heavy cream
4 oz. crushed pineapple
1 tsp. shredded coconut

Mix all ingredients, except shredded coconut, in a blender until smooth, pour into a chilled wine goblet, and sprinkle with coconut.
Note: From the Boca Raton Hotel and Club, Boca Raton, Florida.

JERRY'S CHRISTMAS COCKTAIL

1½ oz. Irish whiskey
1 oz. Irish Mist
1 oz. lemon juice
1 egg white (for two drinks)
Ground nutmeg
Orange slice

Mix all ingredients, except nutmeg and orange, with cracked ice in a shaker or blender and pour into a chilled Delmonico glass or a wine glass. Sprinkle with nutmeg and garnish with orange slice.
Note: Created by Jerry Fitzpatrick, Gresham Hotel, Dublin.

JUNGLE BIRD

1½ oz. dark rum
¾ oz. Campari
4 oz. pineapple juice
½ oz. lime juice
½ oz. sugar syrup or to taste
Maraschino cherry
1 lime slice
1 orange slice
Orchid (optional)

Mix all ingredients, except cherry, orange and lime slices, and orchid, with cracked ice in a shaker or blender and serve in special ceramic-bird container or use a chilled Hurricane glass. Garnish with cherry, orange and lemon slice, and an orchid. *Note:* From the Kuala Lumpur Hilton, Kuala Lumpur, Malaysia.

KENYA SIKU KUU

1 oz. Kenya white rum
1 oz. Cointreau
2 oz. passion fruit juice
Orange slice
Maraschino cherry
Mint sprig

Mix rum, Cointreau, and passion fruit juice with cracked ice in a shaker or blender and serve in a chilled cocktail glass. Garnish with orange, cherry, and mint. *Note:* From the Mount Kenya Safari Club, Nanyuki, Kenya. Siku Kuu means "Christmas."

KEVIN'S COFFEE

¾ oz. Jamaica rum
¾ oz. Grand Marnier
¾ oz. Tia Maria
Hot black coffee
Whipped cream
Pinch of powdered cinnamon

Mix spirits and coffee together in a large mug or Irish coffee glass, top with whipped cream and a pinch of cinnamon. *Note:* This can be served as a

cold drink. Mix spirits and cold black coffee in a blender with a little cracked ice and pour into a Squall glass or a large wine goblet. Add more ice cubes if needed, top with generous serving of whipped cream, and sprinkle with powdered cinnamon. From the Allendale Bar & Grill, Allendale, New Jersey.

THE KISS

1½ oz. vodka
¾ oz. chocolate-cherry liqueur
¾ oz. heavy cream
½ fresh strawberry

Mix all ingredients, except strawberry, with cracked ice in a shaker or blender and strain into a chilled cocktail glass. Garnish with strawberry. *Note:* From the Grand Hyatt Hotel, New York.

KOKONOKO

1½ oz. tequila
¾ oz. La Grande Passion
1 oz. pineapple juice
½ oz. coconut syrup or to
    taste

Mix all ingredients with cracked
ice in a shaker or blender and
pour into a chilled Squall glass
or a Poco Grande glass. Garnish
with pineapple and orange
slices, if you wish.
Note: From the Kahala Hilton,
Honolulu.

LADY DI

1 oz. Benedictine
½ oz. tequila
1 oz. cream
½ tsp. orgeat syrup or to
    taste

Mix with cracked ice in a
blender and pour into a chilled
cocktail glass.
Note: Created by L. Baril, Hotel
Inter-Continental, Paris.

LADY KILLER

1 oz. gin
½ oz. apricot brandy
2 oz. passion fruit juice
2 oz. pineapple juice
Orange peel

Mix all ingredients, except orange
peel, with cracked ice in a shaker
or blender and strain into a
chilled cocktail glass. Garnish
with orange peel.
Note: From the Kronenhalle,
Zurich.

LA PEROUSE DISCOVERY

1 oz. Tuaca
¾ oz. Kahlua
4 oz. black coffee
Whipped cream
Chocolate shavings

Blend all ingredients, except
whipped cream and chocolate,
with a little cracked ice in a
shaker or blender and pour into a
chilled parfait glass. Top with
a generous portion of whipped
cream and sprinkle with chocolate shavings scraped from a
chocolate bar with a kitchen
knife. This drink may also be
served hot in a mug or Irish
Coffee glass.
Note: From the Maui Inter-
Continental Wailea, Kihei,
Maui, Hawaii.

BARTENDER'S SECRET NO. 30

Glass, metal, wood, or plastic, it makes no difference. When
moisture forms on the outside of a glass and flows down onto

the coaster, the coaster sticks to the glass and usually ends up on the floor or in your lap. You can easily make the best stick-proof coaster in the world by cutting circles out of carpet swatches or scraps (a carpet store is the place to go) and gluing them to conventional coasters. Try it. It really works.

LODGE FIZZ

1½ oz. gin
½ oz. lemon juice
1 tsp. crème de noyaux
1½ oz. half-and-half
1 tsp. sugar syrup
Club soda

Mix all ingredients, except soda, with cracked ice in a shaker or blender and serve in a chilled Collins glass. Fill with cold club soda and stir gently.
Note: From the Lodge at Pebble Beach, Pebble Beach, California.

LONG ISLAND ICED TEA

½ oz. gin
½ oz. vodka
½ oz. white tequila
½ oz. white rum
¼ oz. white crème de menthe
3 oz. sour mix
Cola
Lemon wedge
Mint sprigs (optional)

Mix all ingredients, except cola, lemon, and mint, with cracked ice in a blender and pour into a tall, chilled Collins glass. Fill glass with cold cola, stir gently, and garnish with lemon wedge and mint sprigs.
Note: From the United Nations Plaza Hotel, New York.

MANDARIN PUNCH

1½ oz. dark Jamaica rum
½ oz. mandarine liqueur
2 oz. orange juice
2 oz. pineaple juice
Orange slice
Maraschino cherry

Mix all ingredients, except orange

slice and cherry, with cracked ice in a shaker or blender and pour into a chilled highball glass. Add additional ice cubes and garnish with orange slice and cherry.
Note: From the Captain's Bar, Mandarin Oriental Hotel, Hong Kong.

MANSION SMOOTHIE

1 oz. Bacardi Light
½ oz. amaretto
¼ oz. Kahlua
¼ oz. Peter Heering
Pinch ground nutmeg

Mix all ingredients, except nutmeg, with cracked ice in a shaker or blender and pour into a chilled cocktail glass. Sprinkle top with ground nutmeg.
Note: From the Mansion on Turtle Creek, Dallas.

MARQUIS ROYAL

4½ oz. champagne
¾ oz. Chambord
¼ oz. Cointreau
Fresh raspberry

Combine all ingredients, except raspberry, in a chilled flute champagne glass. Decorate with raspberry.
Note: From the New York Marriott Marquis Hotel, New York.

THE MAYFAIR SPRITZER

4 oz. white wine (your
   favorite)
2 oz. club soda
Several dashes Campari

Pour chilled white wine into a chilled Collins glass, add several ice cubes and cold soda. Add several dashes of Campari and stir gently.
Note: From the Mayfair Regent Hotel, New York.

MELANCHOLY BABY

1½ oz. gold rum
1 oz. crème de banane
¾ oz. wild strawberry liqueur
3 oz. pineapple juice
Lime slice

Mix all ingredients, except lime slice, with cracked ice in a shaker or blender and strain into a chilled tulip or parfait glass. Garnish with lime slice.
Note: From Pinehurst, Pinehurst, North Carolina.

MEXICAN HOP

1½ oz. coffee-flavored brandy
2 oz. Irish cream
Pinch ground nutmeg or
   cinnamon

Mix with cracked ice in a shaker or blender and pour into a chilled Old Fashioned glass. Sprinkle with spice.
Note: From Innisbrook, Tarpon Springs, Florida.

MIAMI WHAMMY

1½ oz. light rum
1½ oz. Nassau Royale
Orange slice

Add rum, liqueur, and ice cubes to a mixing glass, stir briskly, and strain into a chilled cocktail glass. Garnish with orange slice.
Note: From the Omni Hotel, Miami.

MIDORI MARGARITA

1 oz. tequila
1 oz. Midori
1 oz. sweet and sour mix
Watermelon ball
Cantaloupe ball

Mix all ingredients, except
melon balls, with cracked ice in
a shaker or blender. Pour into
a chilled cocktail glass, the rim
of which has been moistened
with lemon juice and rolled in
salt. Garnish with melon balls
skewered on toothpicks.
Note: From the Mansion on Turtle
Creek, Dallas.

MIMI COCKTAIL

1 oz. gin
½ oz. apricot brandy
½ oz. cognac
1 egg white (for two drinks)
Dash grenadine
Lemon juice
Powdered sugar

Mix gin, apricot brandy, cognac,
egg white, and grenadine in a
shaker or blender and pour into
a chilled cocktail glass, the rim
of which has been dipped in
lemon juice and rolled in
powdered sugar.
Note: From the Hotel George V,
Paris.

MOUNT FUJI

1½ oz. gin
½ oz. lemon juice
½ oz. heavy cream
1 tsp. pineapple juice
1 egg white
Several dashes maraschino
  liqueur or cherry brandy
Maraschino cherry

Mix all ingredients, except maraschino cherry, with cracked ice
in a shaker or blender and
pour into a chilled Old Fashioned glass. Garnish with
cherry.
Note: From the Imperial Hotel,
Tokyo.

MUDSLIDE

1 oz. vodka
1 oz. Kahlua
1 oz. Bailey's Irish Cream

Mix with cracked ice in a
shaker or blender and serve in a
chilled cocktail glass.
Note: From the Allendale Bar &
Grill, Allendale, New Jersey.

BARTENDER'S SECRET NO. 31

From time to time you will come across recipes that specify
so-called bar mixes such as sweet-and-sour and similar lemon-
lime combinations containing a sweetener and sometimes egg

white to make a drink with a foamy head. Bar mixes come in powdered as well as liquid versions. They have one great advantage in that they offer an instantly ready drink mix that yields consistent results when making drinks for a large number of people. And, obviously, they fulfill a need when on a camping trip or an extended cruise on a small boat and fresh fruit is not available. For home drink-making, even for fairly large groups, fresh or frozen fruit juices are undeniably the best choice.

MYSTIC COOLER

1½ oz. vodka
½ oz. orange juice
½ oz. pineapple juice
½ oz. grapefruit juice
½ oz. crème de banane
1 tsp. grenadine
Lime slice

Mix vodka and fruit juices in a shaker or blender with cracked ice and pour into a chilled Collins glass. Float crème de banane on top and gently add float of grenadine. Top with lime slice.
Note: From the Royal Sonesta Hotel, New Orleans.

NUMERO UNO

1 oz. vodka
Juice of ½ lime
Sugar syrup to taste
Brut champagne
Mint sprig, slightly bruised

Mix vodka, lime, and sugar with cracked ice in a blender and strain into a chilled tulip champagne glass. Fill with cold champagne and garnish with mint sprig.
Note: From La Caravelle, New York.

PALM COURT SPECIAL

2½ oz. Stolichnaya vodka
1 tbsp. Rose's lime juice
1 tbsp. fresh lime juice
Several dashes Cointreau

Mix all ingredients well in a mixing glass with cracked ice and strain into a chilled cocktail glass.
Note: From the Palm Court, Plaza Hotel, New York.

PAPERBACK The Publisher's Special

1 oz. Lillet blanc
1 oz. gin
1 oz. framboise

Blend with ice in a mixing glass and strain into a chilled cocktail glass.
Note: Created by Joe Gilmore, Savoy Hotel, London.

PEAR SOUR

2 oz. pear brandy or pear
  schnapps
1 oz. lemon juice
½ oz. sugar syrup or to taste
Brandied pear slice or canned
  pear slice

Mix all ingredients, except pear slice, in a shaker or blender with cracked ice and strain into a chilled cocktail glass. Garnish with pear slice.
Note: From the Four Seasons, New York.

THE PETRIFIER

2 oz. cognac
2 oz. gin
2 oz. vodka
2 oz. triple sec
½ oz. Grand Marnier
Several dashes Angostura
  bitters
Grenadine to taste
Ginger ale
Orange slice
Maraschino cherry

Mix all ingredients, except ginger ale, orange slice, and cherry, with cracked ice in a shaker or blender and pour into a large goblet, beer schooner, or tankard, that has been well chilled. Add additional ice if necessary and fill with cold ginger ale. Garnish with orange slice and cherry.
Note: Created by Andy MacElhone, Harry's New York Bar, Paris.

PINK APRICOT SOUR

1½ oz. apricot-flavored
  brandy
Juice of ½ lemon
½ oz. grenadine
Orange slice
Maraschino cherry

Mix all ingredients, except orange slice and cherry, in a blender with cracked ice and pour into a chilled balloon glass. Garnish with orange slice and maraschino cherry.
Note: From Ye Cottage Inn, Keyport, New Jersey.

PINK PANTHER No. 1

2 oz. gin
2 oz. apple juice
4 oz. grapefruit juice
Dash grenadine (or enough
  to make a pink drink)
Mint sprigs

Mix all ingredients, except mint, with cracked ice in a shaker or blender and strain into a wine goblet that has been well chilled. Garnish with mint sprig.
Note: From the Sign of the Dove, New York.

PIRATE'S PASSION

1 oz. dark rum
½ oz. gin
1¼ oz. La Grande Passion
2 oz. orange juice
2 oz. pineapple juice
Dash grenadine

Mix all ingredients with cracked ice in a shaker or blender. Pour into a chilled Squall glass or a Poco Grande glass.
Note: From Marriott's Sam Lord's Castle, Barbados.

POINSETTIA

½ oz. Cointreau or triple sec
3 oz. cranberry juice
3 oz. brut champagne

Prechill all ingredients, including glass. Mix Cointreau and cranberry juice in champagne glass and pour in champagne.
Note: From Windows on the World, New York.

PUTTING GREEN

¾ oz. gin
1 oz. melon liqueur
1½ oz. orange juice
1½ oz. lemon juice
Green cherry
Orange slice

Mix all ingredients, except green cherry and orange slice, with cracked ice in a shaker or blender. Pour into a frosted Collins glass. Garnish with cherry and orange slice. This drink may also be served frozen or as a mist.
Note: From the Colonnade Hotel, Boston.

RACQUEL WELCH

¾ oz. Tuaca
¾ oz. amaretto
¾ oz. white crème de cacao
Several dashes sweet cream

Mix all ingredients with cracked ice in a shaker or blender. Pour into a chilled wine glass.
Note: Created by Bru Danger of the "21" Club, New York.

RAYON VERT

2 oz. dry vermouth
1 oz. Izzara
1 oz. blue curaçao
Dash orange curaçao
Dash framboise

Mix with cracked ice in a blender and strain into a chilled cocktail glass.
Note: From Hotel du Palais, Biarritz, France.

RAZ-MA-TAZZ

1½ oz. brandy
2½ oz. raspberry liqueur
2½ cups French vanilla ice
   cream, softened
Fresh raspberries

Mix all ingredients, except

fresh raspberries, in a blender
until smooth. Pour into chilled
parfait or sherbet glasses. Garnish with fresh raspberries.
Makes 2 servings.
Note: From the Hyatt Regency
Atlanta.

RED ROCK CANYON

1½ oz. vodka
¼ oz. crème de cassis
¼ oz. peach brandy
¼ oz. Cointreau
Several dashes Campari
Maraschino cherry
Orange slice

Mix all ingredients, except
Campari, maraschino cherry, and
orange slice, with cracked ice
in a blender and pour into a
chilled Collins glass. Top with
Campari float. Garnish with
cherry and orange.
Note: From Caesar's Palace, Las
Vegas.

REGISTRY SUNSET

½ oz. Amaretto
½ oz. Grand Marnier
½ oz. crème de banane
Dash sweet and sour mix
Dash pineapple juice
Pineapple wedge
Fresh orchid

Mix all ingredients, except
pineapple wedge and orchid, with
cracked ice in a shaker or blender
and strain into a chilled cocktail
glass. Garnish with pineapple
wedge and a fresh orchid.
Note: From the Registry Resort,
Scottsdale, Arizona.

REMINGTON FREEZE

1½ oz. Chambord
2 scoops vanilla ice cream
8 raspberries

Mix all ingredients, except 2
raspberries, with cracked ice in a

blender until smooth. Pour into
a chilled wine glass and garnish
with raspberries. *Do not overmix
or drink will become watery.*
Note: From the Remington on
Post Oak Park, Houston.

RITZ SPECIAL

2 oz. cognac
2 tsp. kirsch
2 tsp. sweet vermouth
2 tsp. crème de cacao

Mix with cracked ice in a
shaker or blender and strain into
a chilled cocktail glass.
Note: From the Hotel Ritz, Paris.

RITZ SPECIAL PICK-ME-UP

¾ oz. cognac
¾ oz. Cointreau
4 oz. orange juice
Brut champagne

Mix all ingredients, except champagne, with cracked ice in a blender and pour into a chilled balloon glass. Fill with cold champagne and stir gently. *Note:* From the Hotel Ritz, Paris.

ROSALIE

½ oz. gin
½ oz. Grand Marnier
½ oz. Cointreau
½ oz. Campari
Dash grenadine

Mix with cracked ice in a shaker or blender and strain into a chilled cocktail glass. *Note:* Created by Fridrich Lechner, Hotel Inter-Continental, Zagreb, Yugoslavia.

ST. GREGORY COCKTAIL

1 oz. apple brandy
½ oz. B&B
1 tsp. triple sec
½ oz. sweet and sour mix
Lime slice
Lemon slice

Mix all ingredients, except lime and lemon slices, with cracked ice in a blender for two seconds. Strain into a chilled cocktail glass. Garnish with fruit wheels. *Note:* Created by Sam Aronis, Fairmont Hotel, San Francisco.

SCOTTISH SUNSET

1 oz. scotch
1 oz. coconut rum
½ oz. Grand Marnier
4 oz. orange juice
1 oz. grenadine
Lime slice
Orange slice

Mix all ingredients, except lime and orange slices, with cracked ice in a shaker or blender and pour over ice cubes in a chilled highball glass. Garnish with lime and orange wheels. *Note:* Created by Gene Ciesielski, Hotel Inter-Continental, Hilton Head, South Carolina.

SCRATCH

Dash Salignac
Dash cranberry juice
Dash vodka
Champagne, chilled
Raspberry eau-de-vie
Lemon peel

Combine Salignac, cranberry juice, and vodka in chilled champagne glass. Fill with champagne and add float of raspberry brandy. Twist lemon peel over drink and drop into glass. *Note:* From the Scratch Restaurant, Santa Monica, California.

SEA PINE'S STRAWBERRY FREEZE

1½ oz. light rum
2 oz. orange juice
1 oz. coconut cream or to
taste
4 large strawberries

Mix in a blender with cracked
ice until smooth and pour into a
chilled brandy snifter. Garnish
with a strawberry
Note: From Sea Pines Plantation,
Hilton Head, South Carolina.

747

1 oz. bourbon
½ oz. vodka
½ oz. Galliano
½ oz. white crème de cacao
1 oz. half-and-half

Mix with cracked ice in a
blender and strain into a chilled
wine goblet.
Note: From La Costa Hotel and
Spa, Carlsbad, California.

SNOWFLAKE

2 oz. Galliano
1 oz. white crème de cacao
3 oz. cream
3 dashes Pernod
Orange slice
Maraschino cherry

Mix all ingredients, except orange
slice and cherry, with cracked
ice in a blender and pour into a
large, chilled brandy snifter.
Garnish with orange slice and
maraschino cherry.
Note: From the Warwick Hotel,
Philadelphia.

SPUMONI COFFEE

½ oz. Galliano
½ oz. Tuaca
½ oz. crème de cacao
1 cup hot black coffee
1 tbsp. whipped cream
Shaved chocolate

Mix liqueurs with steaming
hot coffee in a large, heatproof
mug, top with whipped cream,
and sprinkle with chocolate shaved
from your favorite chocolate bar.
Note: From the Panorama Room,
Portland Hilton, Portland.

STRAWBERRY MIMOSA

3½ oz. orange juice
3–4 large fresh strawberries
3½ oz. brut champagne

Mix orange juice and strawberries with a little shaved ice in
a blender until smooth. Pour
into a chilled wine goblet and
add cold champagne. Stir gently
so as not to lose the bubbles.
Note: From the New York Hilton,
New York.

TAHOE JULIUS

1½ oz. vodka
3 oz. orange juice
1 oz. half-and-half
1 egg
1 tsp. sugar syrup or to taste

Mix with cracked ice in a blender until smooth and strain into a chilled Squall glass or wine glass.
Note: From Harrah's Hotel and Casino, Lake Tahoe, Nevada.

TOASTED ALMOND

1½ oz. Kahlua
1 oz. amaretto
1½ oz. cream or half-and-half
Pinch ground nutmeg or
   cinnamon

Mix all ingredients, except spice, with cracked ice in a shaker or blender and strain into a chilled cocktail glass. Sprinkle nutmeg or cinnamon on top.
Note: From Windows on the World, New York.

TORTUGA

½ lime
1½ oz. 151-proof Demerara
   rum
1 oz. sweet vermouth
1½ oz. orange juice
1 oz. lemon juice
Dash curaçao
Dash crème de cacao
Dash grenadine
Mint sprig

Squeeze lime into a blender with cracked ice and add all other ingredients, except mint sprig, and serve with ice in the biggest glass you can find. Garnish with spent lime shell and mint sprig.
Note: From Trader Vic's, San Francisco.

TROPICAL DECEMBER

1 oz. Mandarine Napoleon
1 oz. gin
½ oz. blue curaçao
4 oz. orange juice
2 oz. guava juice
2 oz. mango juice
Splash tonic water
Orange slice
Maraschino cherry
Mint sprig

Mix all ingredients, except tonic water, orange slice, cherry, and mint in a shaker or blender with cracked ice and pour into a tall, chilled Collins or iced tea glass. Top with a splash of tonic and garnish with orange slice, cherry, and mint sprig.
Note: From the Hotel Inter-Continental Kinshasa, Zaire.

VICTOR'S SPECIAL

1 oz. bourbon
1 oz. Grand Marnier
1 oz. lime juice
½ oz. sugar syrup or to taste
Dash grenadine
Lemon wedge
Pineapple slice or stick
Maraschino cherry

Mix all ingredients, except lemon wedge, pineapple, and cherry, with cracked ice in a shaker or blender and serve in a chilled wine goblet. Garnish with lemon wedge, pineapple, and cherry.
Note: From the Taj Mahal Inter-Continental Hotel, Bombay.

VIKING COCKTAIL

1 oz. vodka
1 oz. Grand Marnier
1 oz. Campari or Cinzano
  Bitter
Dash lemon juice

Mix all ingredients with cracked ice in a shaker or blender and strain into a chilled cocktail glass.
Note: Created by Bjarne Eriksen of the Hotel Viking, Oslo.

VOUVRAY SUMMER APERITIF

3 oz. vouvray wine
6 large strawberries
Dash grenadine

Place 5 strawberries (reserve 1 strawberry for garnish) and vouvray in a blender with 3 oz. of cracked ice, add a dash of grenadine, and blend until smooth. Pour into a chilled champagne glass or wine glass and garnish with whole strawberry.
Note: From the Jefferson Hotel, Washington, D.C.

WAILEA TROPICAL ITCH

1 oz. blended whiskey
1 oz. dark Jamaica rum
½ oz. curaçao or triple sec
1 oz. orange juice
Dash Angostura or orange
  bitters
Pineapple stick
Maraschino cherry

Mix all ingredients, except pineapple and cherry, with cracked ice in a blender and pour into a chilled Hurricane glass. Garnish with pineapple stick and maraschino cherry.
Note: From the Wailea Beach Hotel, Maui, Hawaii.

WHITE GHOST

1¼ oz. Frangelico
¾ oz. white crème de cacao
¼ oz. Chambord
2 oz. heavy cream
Fresh raspberry

Mix all ingredients, except raspberry, with cracked ice in a blender until smooth. Pour into a chilled cocktail glass. Garnish with fresh raspberry.
Note: From the New York Marriott Marquis Hotel, New York.

WINDJAMMER

1½ oz. Jamaica rum
1½ oz. light rum
1½ oz. white crème de cacao
6 oz. pineapple juice
1 oz. heavy cream
Grated nutmeg

Mix all ingredients, except nutmeg, with cracked ice in a shaker or blender and pour into a double Old Fashioned glass. Sprinkle with grated nutmeg.
Note: From the Coral Harbor Restaurant, Nassau.

WINDSOR ROMANCE

¾ oz. mint-chocolate liqueur
¾ oz. amaretto
¾ oz. gin
¾ oz. passion fruit juice

Mix all ingredients with cracked ice in a shaker or blender and strain into a chilled cocktail glass.
Note: Created by Peter Dorelli, Savoy Hotel, London. Concocted in honor of the wedding of the Prince and Princess of Wales.

YELLOWFINGERS

1 oz. blackberry brandy
1 oz. crème de banane
½ oz. gin
½ oz. heavy cream

Mix with cracked ice in a shaker or blender and strain into a chilled Old Fashioned glass.
Note: Created by Louis Pappalardo, Bull and Bear Bar, Waldorf-Astoria Hotel, New York.

ZAPATA

1 oz. tequila
½ oz. Campari
Juice of 1 orange

Mix all ingredients with cracked ice in a shaker or blender. Pour into a chilled champagne goblet.
Note: Created by Bru Mysak of the "21" Club, New York.

PUNCHES:
THE TIMELESS
ALLURE OF THE
FLOWING BOWL

> There, gentlemen, is my champagne and my
> claret. I am no great judge of wine and I give
> you these on the authority of my wine
> merchant; but I can answer for my punch,
> for I made it myself.
>
> —Lord Pembroke

The punch bowl is the original community cocktail. And punches
traditionally have been festive, culinary showpieces, concocted
with great care and pride. The flowing bowl of a long past,
more gracious era was the center of the party; the hub of a
golden circle of family and friends; and perhaps the expression, "proud as punch," reflected the importance of the custom and circumstances of punch making and serving. Punches
were never intended to be labor-saving devices or a means of
do-it-yourself dispensing of refreshments for the multitude.
Nor were they devised as a stratagem whereby a small amount
of wines and spirits sufficient for the few could be stretched to
serve the many. Unfortunately, punches have become equated
with drab, uninspired drinks served on such auspicious occasions as the crowning of the new basketball queen or the
dedication of the new department of sanitation incinerator and
solid-waste compactor. We have all suffered from episodes of
dreary liquid boredom or stomach-wrenching, acidic assaults
from concoctions that were unfit for human consumption. It is
our purpose here to provide some simple rules, which, if followed, will produce exemplary punches, together with a collection of good punch recipes, both modern and traditional,
that have achieved gratifying results. (And see chapter fourteen for nonalcoholic punches.)

The word "punch" is reputed to be a derivative of the Hindustani word *pānch*, meaning "five" (as in *panchāmrit*, a mixture of five ingredients), which is believed to be the basis for the "Rule of Five," the traditional means of making a punch. However, it is doubtful if the word "punch" originated in the Far East. As Congreve put it so memorably, "To drink is a Christian diversion, unknown to the Turk or the Persian." Some historians believe the name is of English origin and is a contraction of the word "puncheon," a small cask holding about eighty gallons of liquid. Mariners stored their wines and spirits in puncheons, and seamen in the British Navy in particular were often served their rum rations from these or similar small casks.

Liberally applied, the Rule of Five is summed up in the axiom: "One sour, two sweet, three strong, four weak," with the fifth element being spices and other flavorings. In olden times, this may have been a good working formula, but tastes change and so perhaps this has gone the way of the equal-parts-of-gin-and-vermouth Martini. The Rule of Five, whether or not applied literally, embodies a valid idea: balance. Good drink recipes must have balance as every professional mixologist knows. Anyone can have a go at making a new drink whether by the glass or by the bowl, but if the ingredients are not properly balanced, the results will be undistinguished, flat, and moribund. And it follows, the more ingredients, the more essential—and critical—the task of achieving balance. The Rule of Five is simply an effort, albeit arbitrary and inflexible, to produce a formula for balance in a punch.

Here follow the rules of punch making gleaned from many sources and put to test on many occasions. It is mostly just common sense based upon an old-fashioned idea that your guests deserve the best and a good host's primary responsibility is to see that this comes to pass.

THE RULES OF THE BOWL

1. A punch may be made in an engraved bowl of gold or cut crystal or English bone china. For entertaining the more elegant, the better. For outdoor entertaining, a stockpot, kettle or other large cooking container; wooden bucket, a cut-down keg or steel drum, or even a hollowed-out ice cake will fill the bill, depending upon the theme of the party. Be sure the bowl is large so it can be properly chilled with a large cake of ice. For hot punches, a heatproof bowl is essential since an acceptable hot punch must be served piping hot, just as a cold punch should be served crackling cold. Since proper presentation is important in culinary

matters, if you do not have the right kind of punch bowl, borrow one from a friend or rent one from a caterer.

2. Use only the finest ingredients, the freshest fruits and the best spices and mixers. Do not for a moment think that a substandard whisky or wine will go unnoticed in the punch bowl because of the presence of many other ingredients. Each part, however small, contributes to or detracts from the whole. By the same token, stock enough supplies so that you will have adequate refills for the punch bowl. If the weather is hot, be guided by the old adage: generously estimate the amount of ice you think you need and get three times as much.

3. Planning the right type of punch is as important as planning the party. A light, not too authoritative punch is in order for a graduation party that many people of all age groups will be attending. Powerhouse mixtures such as Fish House Punch should be reserved for a small group of experienced drinkers who understand the perils of strong, seductively tasty potations. A summertime punch should be designed to be refreshing and thirst-quenching, whereas a cold weather concoction should be bracing and stimulating. If the group is made up of adults and teenagers, a second, nonalcoholic punch should be made. A well-made nonalcoholic punch can be just as appetizing and refreshing as the other kind.

4. For cold punches, all ingredients should be chilled in advance, including the punch bowl itself. If large ice cakes are not available, slabs of ice made by freezing water in milk cartons will do, or you can remove the dividers in your ice trays and make small slabs this way. *Ice cubes are out for punches.* They melt too quickly and create unwanted dilution. Fruit juices should be squeezed in advance and strained before using. It is important that your punch be clear, not murky. Do not fill the bowl with whole fruit. It does nothing for the punch but get in the way of serving and drinking. A few orange or lemon slices are sufficient. Remember that sugar and alcohol don't mix readily, so it is advisable to add fruit juices and other nonalcoholic ingredients with your sweetener first to make certain the sweetener is dissolved. Alcoholic beverages go in about an hour before the guests arrive to prevent excessive evaporation. Sparkling wines and mixers such as club soda and ginger ale are added just before serving and stirred into the punch gently to preserve carbonation.

5. The crucial point in the party will come when much of the punch has been drunk, much of the ice has melted, and it is recycling time. This does *not* mean getting more punch from

the pantry and dumping it into the bowl; it means *renewing the bowl* by removing it from the table for a thorough rinsing, a filling of fresh ice, and preparing the punch as you did the first time around. If you have two punch bowls you can rotate, fine; otherwise your guests will have to wait a few minutes until the new punch (with clean cups) is brought in. It will be worth the wait, for everything will be fresh and clean and sparkling. The second serving will taste exactly like the first, if not better, and your guests will be the first to notice they are getting top-shelf treatment. This will do wonders for your reputation as a party-giver.

6. Punch cups are important for a crucial reason: you must know exactly how much you can put in them for serving purposes so you can estimate how much punch you will need for your guests. Generally, a punch cup serving is reckoned to be four ounces, since the traditional punch cup is smaller than a tea cup. For purposes of standardization, unless otherwise specified, all servings in this chapter will be four ounces.

7. Estimating the number of servings, and therefore the amount of punch makings you will need, is important since running out of food or beverages at a party is an affront to your guests and brands you as a poor planner or a niggardly host. Caterers who are pretty good at counting the house estimate that the average guest will consume between two and three cups. Some, of course, will have only one drink and others will have four or more. The important thing to remember is *no party-giver should expect to come out even.* You should plan, as insurance, to have food and beverages left over. For every quart of punch you will get about 8 4-ounce servings and about 8½ servings from a liter. A gallon of punch will yield 32 servings. There will actually be slightly more due to ice meltage, but this is not exactly a plus, since ice meltage and dilution should be held to a minimum. A watery punch is unforgivable. If you have punch left over, fear not, if it contains a nominal amount of alcohol; it will keep for several weeks in a tightly sealed container in your refrigerator.

If you will but follow the rules of the bowl, your punches will be legendary, you will be lionized, and your guests will love coming to your parties.

APPLEJACK PUNCH

2 750-ml. bottles applejack or
  calvados
1 pt. light rum
1 pt. peach-flavored brandy
1 pt. lemon juice
1 cup brandy
½ cup maple syrup or sugar
  syrup to taste
2 l. lemon-lime soda or 1 l.
  lemon-lime soda and 1 l.
  club soda

½ red apple thinly sliced

Prechill all ingredients and
pour applejack, rum, peach
brandy, brandy, lemon juice, and
maple syrup into a chilled
punch bowl with a large cake of
ice. Stir well, adjust sweetness, and pour in soda. Stir gently
and garnish with apple slices.
Makes about 45 servings.

 ARIZONA SUNSHINE

1 l. light rum
1 qt. vanilla ice cream
1 qt. cold black coffee

Mix all ingredients in a chilled
punch bowl and ladle into
punch cups. Makes about 24 cups.

 ARTILLERY PUNCH

1 l. straight rye, bourbon,
  or blended whiskey
1 l. dry red wine
1 l. strong black tea
1 pt. dark Jamaica rum
1 pt. orange juice
1 cup brandy
1 cup gin
1 cup lemon juice

4 oz. Benedictine
Sugar syrup to taste
Lemon peels

Prechill all ingredients and
put into a chilled punch bowl
with a large cake of ice. Stir
well, adjust sweetness, and
garnish with a few lemon peels.
Makes about 40 servings.

ASCOT CUP

2 750-ml. bottles red
  Bordeaux or California
  cabernet sauvignon
1 pt. fino sherry
½ cup cognac
½ cup curaçao
½ cup raspberry syrup
½ cup lemon juice
1 oz. framboise or raspberry
  liqueur
2 qt. club soda or 1 bottle
  each club soda and
  champagne

Orange and lemon slices,
  thinly sliced

Prechill ingredients and, except
for club soda or champagne
and fruit slices, put everything
in a chilled punch bowl and stir
well. Add a cake of ice and
just before serving, gently stir in
club soda or champagne. Garnish with a few orange and lemon
slices. Makes about 37 servings.

AZTEC PUNCH

4 l. tequila
4 qt. grapefruit juice
2 qt. tea
1 cup lemon juice
1-2 cups orgeat or simple
   syrup
1 cup curacao

1 oz. Angostura bitters
   (optional)
1 tsp. ground cinnamon

Chill all ingredients and mix
in a large punch bowl with a
cake of ice. Yields about 90
5-oz. servings.

 ## BALLSBRIDGE BRACER PUNCH

2 750-ml. bottles Irish whiskey
½ pt. peach-flavored brandy
1 pt. fresh lemon juice
½ cup maple syrup or honey
   to taste
2 l. club soda or ginger ale
   or 2 750-ml. bottles
   champagne
Sliced brandied peaches
   (optional)

Prechill all ingredients and
pour whiskey, brandy, lemon
juice, and syrup (which has
been dissolved in a little water)
into a chilled punch bowl and
mix well. Add a large cake of ice
and just before serving, pour
in club soda or ginger ale or
champagne or any combina-
tion thereof (i.e. half soda, half
ginger ale; half soda, half
champagne, etc.) depending on
the strength desired. Slice some
brandied peaches thinly and put
one slice in every cup of punch.
Makes about 37 servings.

 ## BALTIMORE EGG NOG

12 eggs
2 cups superfine or
   confectioner's sugar
1 pt. cognac
1 cup dark Jamaica rum
1 cup peach brandy or
   Madeira
3 pt. milk
1 pt. cream
Grated nutmeg

Separate eggs and beat yolks
with sugar until thick and gradually stir in cognac, rum, and
peach brandy (some recipes specify Madeira in place of peach
brandy), milk, and cream. Keep
in refrigerator until well chilled.
In another bowl, beat egg whites
until stiff. When ready to serve,
transfer egg-yolk mixture to a
chilled punch bowl and carefully fold in whites without beating or stirring. Makes about 28
servings.
Note: Do not put any ice into the
punch bowl.

BENGAL LANCER'S PUNCH

1 l. dry red wine
3 oz. gold Barbados rum
3 oz. curaçao
½ cup lime juice
½ cup pineapple juice
½ cup orange juice
2 oz. orgeat syrup or sugar
   syrup to taste
1 750-ml. bottle champagne

1 pt. club soda
Lime slices

Prechill all ingredients and
put everything, except champagne
and soda, in a chilled punch bowl
with a cake of ice and stir well.
Immediately before serving, add
champagne and soda and stir
gently. Garnish with a few lime
slices. Approximately 24 servings.

 ## BOMBAY PUNCH

12 lemons
Sugar to taste
1 750-ml. bottle cognac
1 750-ml. bottle medium-dry
   sherry
½ cup maraschino liqueur
½ cup curaçao
4 750-ml. bottles brut
   champagne
2 l. club soda

Squeeze juice from lemons and
sweeten to taste with sugar in a
chilled punch bowl with a large
cake of ice. Add cognac, sherry,
maraschino, and curaçao and
stir well. Immediately before
serving, add cold champagne and
club soda. Stir gently to preserve
carbonation. Makes about 58
servings.

BOURBON PUNCH

2 l. straight Kentucky bourbon
1 pt. fresh orange juice
1 cup peach-flavored brandy
1 cup fresh lemon juice
⅔ cup orgeat syrup or sugar
   syrup to taste
2 qt. club soda or 2 750-ml.
   bottles champagne
12 maraschino cherries

Prechill all ingredients and,
excepting club soda or champagne, put everything into a
chilled punch bowl, stir well,
and check sweetness. When
ready to serve, add club soda or
champagne, stir gently, and
garnish with maraschino cherries.
Makes about 42 servings.

BARTENDER'S SECRET NO. 32

Ice cakes for large punch bowls may not be easy to come by,
but you can make your own by removing the separater inserts
in your ice trays and freezing solid slabs of ice. This works
well and three or four slabs will cool your punch very nicely.

BRANDY PUNCH

12 lemons
4 oranges
Superfine sugar
½ cup grenadine or raspberry
  syrup
1 cup curaçao
2 750-ml. bottles cognac
1 750-ml. bottle champagne
  or club soda

Squeeze juice from fruit and pour into a chilled punch bowl with ice cake. Add sugar and stir until sugar is dissolved. Add grenadine, curaçao, and cognac. Stir well and just before serving, add cold champagne and stir gently. Spiral peels from your oranges make a good garnish. Makes about 30 servings.

 BUDDHA PUNCH

1 pt. Rhine wine or riesling
1 cup light rum
1 cup orange juice
½ cup lemon juice
½ cup Cointreau
½ oz. kirschwasser
1 oz. sugar syrup or to taste
Several dashes Angostura
  bitters (optional)

1 750-ml. bottle sparkling
  Mosel or champagne
1 lime thinly sliced

Prechill all ingredients and put into a chilled punch bowl, excepting sparkling wine and lime slices, which will be added just before serving. Mix well and add a large cake of ice. Makes about 17 servings.

BURGUNDY PUNCH

2 750-ml. bottles red Burgundy
1 pt. orange juice
1 cup port
1 cup cherry brandy
½ cup lemon juice
1 oz. sugar syrup or to taste
1 l. club soda (optional)

Orange slices

Prechill all ingredients and pour into a chilled punch bowl with a cake of ice. Stir well and garnish with a few orange slices. If soda is used, add just before serving and stir gently. Makes about 22 servings.

 CARDINAL PUNCH

2 750-ml. bottles dry red wine
1 pt. cognac
1 pt. Jamaica gold rum
3 oz. sweet vermouth
½ cup sugar syrup or to taste
1 750-ml. bottle brut
  champagne
2 l. club soda
Sliced oranges

Prechill all ingredients and put red wine, cognac, rum, ver-

mouth, and sugar syrup in a chilled punch bowl with a cake of ice. Mix well and check sweetness. Pour in cold champagne and club soda and stir gently. Garnish with a few thinly sliced orange peels. Makes about 46 servings.
Note: Some prefer more champagne than club soda, so feel free to adjust quantities to suit your taste.

CELEBRITY PUNCH

1 750-ml. bottle gold rum
1 750-ml. bottle gin
1 l. grape juice
1 pt. orange juice
2 l. ginger ale
Small jar maraschino cherries
6 orange slices

6 lemon slices

Pour chilled spirits and fruit juices into punch bowl with large cake of ice and stir well. Gently stir in ginger ale and jar of cherries, including juice. Garnish with fruit slices. Makes about 43 4-oz. servings.

 ## CHAMPAGNE PUNCH

1 cup cognac
1 cup maraschino liqueur
1 cup curaçao
½ cup sugar syrup or to taste
2 750-ml. bottles brut
    champagne
1 l. club soda (optional)

Prechill all ingredients and

pour cognac, maraschino liqueur, curaçao, and syrup into a chilled punch bowl with a cake of ice and stir well. Just before serving, add champagne and stir gently. Add cold club soda to reduce potency and increase the fizziness, if you wish. Makes about 19 servings.

 ## DAVID EISENDRATH'S "FAMILY DRINK"

½ gal. blended pineapple-
    grapefruit juice
1 l. gold rum
1½ cups lemon juice
1½ cups Falernum

Mix well with ice in a blender

and serve in chilled Old Fashioned glasses or mix without ice and store in a gallon jug in the refrigerator. Mixture will keep well for an extended period of time if tightly sealed. Makes 30 servings.

 ## DAVID O'WACHSMAN'S IRISH PUNCH

2 750-ml. bottles Irish whiskey
½ pt. triple sec or curaçao
1 pt. fresh lemon juice
½ pt. fresh orange juice
¼ cup raspberry syrup or
    grenadine
¼ cup sugar syrup or honey
    to taste
1 750-ml. bottle champagne
1 l. club soda
Fresh mint sprigs

Prechill all ingredients and pour whiskey, Cointreau, lemon juice, orange juice, raspberry syrup, and sugar syrup into a chilled punch bowl with a cake of ice and mix well. Just before serving, pour in champagne and club soda and stir gently. Garnish with mint sprigs. Makes about 37 servings. Note: For a weaker punch, use 2 bottles of soda. For a special occasion, you may want to use 2 bottles of champagne and no soda at all.

THE DEVIL'S CUP

1 cup cognac
½ cup lemon juice
2 oz. green Chartreuse
2 oz. yellow Chartreuse
2 oz. Benedictine
2 oz. sugar syrup or to taste
2 750-ml. bottles brut
   champagne
1 l. club soda

Prechill all ingredients and pour cognac, lemon juice, liqueurs, and syrup into a chilled punch bowl with a cake of ice. Mix well and check sweetness. Add cold champagne and club soda just before serving and stir gently. Makes about 27 servings.

DRAGOON PUNCH

2 small lemons, thinly sliced
¼ cup superfine sugar
1 l. ale
1 l. porter or a mixture of ½
   beer and ½ stout
1 cup amontillado sherry
1 cup brandy
2 750-ml. bottles champagne

Prechill all ingredients. Put a cake of ice in a chilled punch bowl, cover ice with lemon slices, and cover lemons with a thin coating of sugar. Bruise lemons with a muddler or a heavy serving spoon. Add ale and porter or beer and stout mixture, sherry, and brandy and stir well. Just before serving, stir in champagne gently. Makes about 34 servings.

DUBONNET PUNCH

1 750-ml. bottle Dubonnet
   rouge
1 pt. gin or vodka
½ cup curaçao
Juice of 6 limes
1 pt. club soda
Lime peel cut in a spiral
Orange slices cut thin

Prechill all ingredients and add Dubonnet, gin or vodka, curaçao, and lime juice to a chilled punch bowl and mix well. Adjust sweetness by adding more curaçao. Just before serving, add club soda and stir gently. Garnish with lime peels and a few orange slices. Makes about 17 servings.

BARTENDER'S SECRET NO. 33

Some punches, while flavorful, well-balanced, and hearty, like Fish House Punch, are simply too strong for protracted drinking. The solution is obviously to extend or dilute the mixture so the high alcoholic content is spread out over more servings. Instead of disturbing the flavor or balance by adding, say, more fruit juice, experienced bartenders opt for club soda. The sparkle adds to the punch and does not interfere with the basic recipe. If done with care (so as not to make the punch watery), this is a practical way to keep your guests from having an abbreviated evening.

EAST OF SUEZ

1 qt. hot tea
1 lemon, sliced thin
2 oz. lime juice
1 cup superfine sugar
½ pt. Batavia arak or
   Swedish Punsch
½ pt. triple sec or curaçao
1 pt. dark Jamaica rum
1 pt. cognac

Put tea, lemon slices, lime juice, and sugar into the flaming pan of a chafing dish and simmer over direct heat until all sugar is dissolved. Add arak, triple sec, and rum. Heat but do not boil. Warm some cognac in a ladle by keeping it partially submersed in the hot punch, ignite, and pour blazing into chafing dish. After a few moments, extinguish flames, then pour in remainder of cognac. Makes about 20 servings.

 ## EGG NOG Basic

12 eggs
2 cups superfine sugar
1 pt. cognac
1 pt. dark Jamaica rum
3 pt. milk
1 pt. cream
Grated nutmeg

Separate eggs and beat yolks and sugar together until thick. Stir in cognac, rum, milk, and

cream, and chill in refrigerator until needed. Just before serving, transfer egg mixture from refrigerator to a chilled punch bowl. Beat egg whites until stiff and carefully fold whites into the egg nog without beating or stirring. Sprinkle the top with nutmeg. Makes about 28 servings. *Note:* Do not put any ice in the punch bowl.

 ## EGG POSSET

6 egg yolks
½ cup sugar or to taste
½ tsp. ground cinnamon
½ tsp. ground nutmeg
½ tsp. ground cloves
1 750-ml. bottle dry red wine

Beat egg yolks well with sugar and spices. Heat wine in a saucepan, bring to a simmer, and pour into egg mixture, stirring constantly. Serve in warmed cups. Makes 6 servings.

ENGLISH BISHOP No. 1

6 large oranges
Brown sugar
Whole cloves
3–4 cinnamon sticks
1 750-ml. bottle gold Barbados
rum or dark Jamaica rum
½ gallon apple cider
Grated nutmeg

Dampen outside of oranges and coat with brown sugar, then stud each orange with about a dozen cloves. Place in a roasting pan and put in the broiler of a medium oven (350°) and brown well until juice begins to seep out of oranges. Quarter oranges and place in a heatproof punch bowl. Add cinnamon sticks and sprinkle a little more brown sugar on oranges. Pour in rum that has been warmed in a pan, ignite, and set ablaze for a few seconds. Extinguish by pouring in hot cider. Stir well and sprinkle with nutmeg. Makes 24 servings.

Note: Some prefer a piece of orange with their punch, in which case a larger cup may be needed with teaspoons.

 ENGLISH BISHOP No. 2

6 large oranges
Brown sugar
Whole cloves
3–4 cinnamon sticks
2 750-ml. bottles ruby port
1 cup cognac

Prepare oranges in oven as in the recipe above and place in the flaming pan of a chafing dish over direct heat. Add cinnamon sticks and port, cover, and simmer gently for 15 minutes, but do not boil. Pour in cognac (except for an ounce or two) gently so that it stays on top of wine mixture. Remove one orange, put into a ladle, and douse with several ounces of cognac, ignite, and lower blazing into pan, which in turn will ignite the contents of the chafing dish. After a few moments extinguish with the lid of the pan. Makes about 16 servings.

Note: Some will want portions of orange with their punch, in which case a large cup may be needed and teaspoons provided.

 ENGLISH CHRISTMAS PUNCH

2 750-ml. bottles dry red wine
3 cups strong tea
Juice of 1 large orange
Juice of 1 lemon
1 lb. superfine sugar
1 750-ml. bottle dark Jamaica
rum

Heat wine, tea and fruit juices in a chafing dish or saucepan, but do not boil. This punch may be served from the chafing dish or transferred to a heatproof punch bowl. Put sugar into a large ladle and saturate with rum. If ladle is not large enough for all the sugar, put remainder in punch bowl. Ignite rum in ladle and pour blazing into punch. Stir well, extinguish flames, and then pour remainder of rum into punch. Stir again and serve. Makes about 27 servings.

FIRESIDE PUNCH

1 pt. strong hot black tea
1 cup fresh orange juice
½ cup fresh lemon juice
Brown sugar, maple syrup,
   or honey to taste
4 oz. curaçao
1 750-ml. bottle dark Jamaica
   rum

In a chafing dish or saucepan
put in hot tea, fruit juices, and
sugar, syrup, or honey, and
mix well until sweeteners are
dissolved. Add curaçao and
rum and heat, but do not boil.
Stir well and serve in warmed
mugs. Makes slightly more than
14 cups.

FISH HOUSE PUNCH The Original

¾ lb. sugar or to taste
2 l. spring water
1 l. freshly squeezed lemon
   juice
½ cup peach brandy
1 l. cognac
2 l. dark Jamaica rum

Dissolve sugar in spring water, stir in lemon juice, and add
peach brandy, cognac, and
rum. Check sweetness and pour
into a chilled punch bowl with
a cake of ice. Makes about 52
servings.
Note: This is America's most venerable punch from the State in
Schuylkill club of Philadelphia,
established in 1732. There are
many variations of the original
recipe, but it remains unsur-
passed. Yes, George Washington
drank here.

GUARDSMEN'S PUNCH

1 qt. green tea
1 cup brown sugar
Peel of 1 lemon
2 oz. port
1 750-ml. bottle scotch
1 cup cognac

Simmer tea, sugar, and lemon
peel in the flaming pan of a
chafing dish over direct heat
until all sugar is dissolved. Add
port and scotch and heat, but
do not boil. Add all cognac to the
pan, except several ounces for
flaming. Pour reserved cognac
into a ladle and warm by partially immersing in hot punch.
Ignite cognac and pour blazing into pan. After a few moments, extinguish flame with
pan lid. Makes about 17 servings.

HARVARD PUNCH

1 l. blended whiskey
1 pt. brandy
1 cup Grand Marnier or triple sec
1 cup orange juice
½ cup lemon juice
½ cup orgeat or sugar syrup to taste
2 750-ml. bottles champagne or 2 l. club soda or ginger ale
Orange and lemon slices

Mix all ingredients, except champagne or soda and fruit slices, in a large, chilled container or punch bowl, cover, and chill in refrigerator for one hour. When ready to serve, add a large cake of ice to bowl and pour in champagne or club soda or ginger ale, stir gently, and garnish with a few orange and lemon slices. Makes about 32 servings.

HOLIDAY PUNCH

1 l. gin
½ cup curaçao
5 cups orange juice
1½ cups lemon juice
2 oz. grenadine
1 l. lemon-lime soda
4 lemon slices
4 orange slices

Pour chilled gin, curaçao, fruit juices, and grenadine into a punch bowl with a cake of ice. Stir well, add soda, and stir again gently. Garnish with fruit slices. Makes about 32 servings.

JACK-THE-GRIPPER

1 750-ml. bottle applejack or calvados
Juice of 3 lemons
¼ cup maple syrup, honey, or sugar syrup
1 oz. ginger-flavored brandy
½ oz. Angostura bitters (optional)
Cinnamon sticks
Lemon peel
Boiling water

Heat applejack, lemon juice, and syrup in the flaming pan of a chafing dish over direct heat. Stir until syrup is dissolved. Add brandy, bitters, cinnamon, and a few pieces of lemon peel. Stir well and ignite. After a few moments, extinguish flames by adding a little boiling water or use pan lid. Makes about 8 servings.

JEFFERSON DAVIS PUNCH

12 750-ml. bottles Bordeaux
  or dry red wine
2 750-ml. bottles oloroso sherry
½ l. brandy
1 pt. freshly squeezed lemon
  juice
1 cup dark Jamaica rum
1 cup maraschino liqueur
5 l. club soda
5 l. ginger ale

Prechill all ingredients and
pour red wine, sherry, brandy,
lemon juice, rum, and maraschino into a punch bowl, cover,
and refrigerate for 8 hours.
When ready to serve, put in a
large ice cake and pour in
cold soda and ginger ale. Stir
gently and garnish with a little fruit, if you wish. Makes about
186 servings.

J.P.'S PUNCH

2 qt. orange juice
1 qt. pineapple juice
1 cup lime juice
2 ripe bananas, peeled and
  sliced thin
2 oz. grenadine or raspberry
  syrup
1 750-ml. bottle dark Jamaica
  rum
1 l. gold Puerto Rican rum
12 Maraschino cherries

Pour orange and pineapple
juice into a chilled punch bowl
with a large cake of ice. Put lime
juice, bananas, and grenadine
into a blender and mix until
bananas are creamy. Pour into
punch bowl with Jamaica rum
and Puerto Rican rum and stir
well. Garnish with maraschino
cherries. Makes about 42 servings.

KENNETH BOLES' SHOOTING MIXTURE

3 750-ml. bottles cherry
  wine
1½ 750-ml. bottles cherry
  brandy
1 750-ml. bottle brandy

Mix all ingredients and refrigerate for several hours, covered,
before serving. Shooting mixture may be stored in bottles in a
cool place for future use. Makes
40 servings.
Note: This wonderful restorative,
designed to aid and comfort
those who climb about on the
cold and desolate moors of the
Scottish Highlands in foul weather,
is the invention of Kenneth Boles,
a stalwart outdoorsman, guide,
and good companion.

KRAMBAMBULI PUNCH

2 750-ml. bottles dry red
  wine
2 oranges
2 lemons
1 cup superfine sugar or to
  taste
1 pt. dark Jamaica rum
1 pt. Batavia arak or
  Swedish Punsch

Pour wine and the juice of oranges
and lemons into the flaming pan
of a chafing dish and heat
over direct flame until mixture is
hot. Add sugar and stir until
dissolved. Put a little rum and
arak into a long-handled ladle,
warm by partially submerging in
wine mixture, ignite, and pour
flaming into chafing dish.
Extinguish flames after a few
moments and add remainder of
rum and arak. Makes about 24
servings.

LA PALOMA PUNCH

1 l. tequila
½ cup maraschino liqueur
½ cup peach brandy
1 16-oz. can pineapple chunks
  with juice
2 l. lemon/lime soda
1 750-ml. bottle sparkling
  wine or champagne

Chill all ingredients in refrigerator and mix in a large punch
bowl with a cake of ice. Add
sparkling wine last and stir in
gently. Yields about 35 servings.

MICHEL ROUX PUNCH

1½ cups La Grande Passion
1 cup Grand Marnier
1 cup Absolut vodka or
  Bombay gin
1 cup Marnier-La Postolle
  Cognac
2 750-ml. bottles Champagne
  de Venoge Brut
1 l. club soda (optional)
1 orange sliced thin

Prechill all ingredients and
pour La Grande Passion, Grand
Marnier, Absolut vodka or Bombay
gin, and Marnier-La Postolle
Cognac into a chilled punch bowl
with a cake of ice. Stir well
and add cold champagne and
some club soda, if you wish.
Stir gently. Makes about 30
servings.

MULLED CLARET

2 oz. honey or sugar syrup
    to taste
1 750-ml. bottle red Bordeaux
1 pt. ruby port
1 cup brandy
6 whole cloves
Several cinnamon sticks,
    broken
½ tsp. grated nutmeg
Lemon peel

Dissolve honey with a cup of
water in the flaming pan of a
chafing dish over direct heat.
Pour in Bordeaux, port, brandy,
and add spices and lemon
peel. Heat over low flame, but do
not boil. Stir from time to time
and serve when hot. Makes 13
servings.

 ## MYRTLE BANK PUNCH

½ pt. fresh lime juice
½ cup maraschino liqueur
¼ cup orgeat syrup or
    Falernum to taste
1 oz. raspberry syrup or
    grenadine
1 750-ml. bottle 151-proof
    Demerara rum

Mix lime juice, maraschino,
orgeat syrup, and raspberry syrup
with cracked ice in a blender
and pour into a chilled punch
bowl with a cake of ice. Pour
in Demerara rum and mix well.
Makes about 10 servings.

BARTENDER'S SECRET NO. 34

When flaming punches in a large container such as a chafing
dish or a heat-proof punch bowl, it is necessary to have a lid
handy to extinguish the flames in the container. In the case of
a large punch bowl for which no securely fitting lid is available, make a cover using two layers of very heavy institutional
aluminum broiling foil that is shaped so it will cover the bowl
tightly. In no instance should any punch mixture be flamed for
more than a few seconds because it allows too much alcohol to
burn away. Make certain a lid is close by before the flaming
process begins, since this is the only method for quickly extin-
guishing the flames in a container without damaging the
contents.

NEGUS

1 large lemon
6–8 sugar cubes
Boiling water
1 cinnamon stick
1 nutmeg, crushed
6 whole cloves
Several dashes lemon juice
  (optional)
1 750-ml. bottle port, Madeira,
  sherry, or dry red or white
  wine

Rub all of the zest (outside peel) off a lemon until only the white, inner peel shows, using as many sugar cubes as necessary. Put sugar cubes in a warmed pitcher and add enough boiling water to completely dissolve sugar. Add spices, some lemon juice, if you wish, and wine. Mix well and when ready to serve, pour in 2 cups of boiling water. Makes about 10 servings.

Note: This "mull" (heated with hot water instead of a red-hot flip iron) was named for Colonel Francis Negus, who presumably enjoyed this daily "after his morning walk." He lived during the reign of Queen Anne.

OLD COLONIAL HOT TEA PUNCH

1 l. dark Jamaica rum
1 pt. brandy
3 pt. hot tea
1 pt. fresh lemon juice
½ cup honey, orgeat syrup or
  sugar syrup to taste
3 oz. curaçao
½ lemon, thinly sliced

Mix rum, brandy, hot tea, lemon juice, honey or syrup, and curaçao in a saucepan and stir until honey or syrup is completely dissolved. Check for sweetness, and when cool, pour into a chilled punch bowl with a large cake of ice. Garnish with lemon slices. Makes about 30 servings.

OLD-FASHIONED WHISKEY PUNCH

1 l. blended whiskey
1 pt. dark Jamaica, gold
  Jamaica, or Barbados
  gold rum
1 pt. fresh lemon juice
1 pt. black tea, chilled
1 cup orgeat syrup or sugar
  syrup to taste
4 oz. curaçao
1 750-ml. bottle champagne
  brut

6 each, thin orange and
  lemon slices

Mix all ingredients, except champagne and fruit slices, in a punch bowl, cover, and chill for several hours in the refrigerator. When ready to serve, put a large ice cake in punch, add champagne, stir gently, and garnish with fruit slices. Makes about 30 servings.

OLD NAVY PUNCH

Juice of 4 lemons
Meat of 1 fresh pineapple or
    canned pineapple
1 750-ml. bottle dark Jamaica
    rum or Demerara rum
    (90 proof)
1 pt. cognac
1 pt. peach-flavored brandy
    or Southern Comfort

Sugar syrup, orgeat syrup, or
    Falernum to taste
4 750-ml. bottles brut
    champagne

Put lemon juice, pineapple,
rum, cognac, brandy, and syrup
in a prechilled punch bowl
and mix well. Add large ice cake
and immediately before serving, pour in champagne and stir
gently. Makes about 45 servings.

OLD OXFORD UNIVERSITY PUNCH

1 cup brown sugar
2 qt. boiling water
1 pt. lemon juice
1 750-ml. bottle cognac
1 750-ml. bottle 151-proof
    Demerara rum
Cinnamon sticks and whole
    cloves (optional)

Dissolve brown sugar with boiling water in the flaming pan of a

chafing dish and then add
lemon juice and cognac. Heat,
but do not boil. Pour in Demerara
rum, reserving several ounces for
flaming. Warm remainder of
rum in a ladle, ignite, and pour
into chafing dish. After a few
moments, extinguish flames with
pan lid. Garnish with cinnamon sticks and whole cloves, if
you wish. Makes 33 servings.

 ## PARK AVENUE ORANGE BLOSSOM

2 qt. fresh orange juice
6-oz. jar maraschino cherries
3 750-ml. bottles brut
    champagne

Pour cold orange juice and
cherries (with juice) into a pre-

chilled punch bowl with a large
cake of ice. Stir well and add
cold champagne and stir gently.
Serve in chilled 8-oz. champagne
tulip glasses. Makes about 24
6-ounce servings.

BARTENDER'S SECRET NO. 35

The making of tea for punches is important. You may get by
with a teabag sloshed about in a cup of tepid water when
making a cup of "Old Herbal Dreadful" tea for your aunt, but a
liter or so of that very same tea can ruin a beautiful punch.
Tea in punch is a balancer and a binder. It smooths out the
punch and holds the disparate elements together. A strong tea
is often called for in punches (green or black are usually

specified, black being the odds-on favorite since it is "seasoned" or fermented after picking while green tea is dried immediately after harvesting), but that does not mean bitter and overbrewed. On the other hand, a weak, bland tea does nothing for a punch except dilute it. To make a proper cup of tea, scald out a teapot, add a rounded teaspoon of tea leaves for each cup and fill pot with spring water just brought to a brisk boil. After three minutes of steeping—and *not more* than 5 minutes at the outside—stir tea and strain into cups. Remember, when a recipe calls for strong tea, it means fully brewed, but not harsh and bitter from oversteeping.

PENNSYLVANIA HUNT CUP PUNCH

1 cup gold Puerto Rican, Barbados, Haitian, or Martinique rum
½ cup dark Jamaica rum or Rhum Negrita
½ cup Malibu or CocoRibe
½ cup peach brandy
Juice of 6 lemons
Juice of 1 large orange
Juice of 1 tangerine (or substitute another orange)
6 oz. can of pineapple juice or ¾ cup fresh pineapple juice

6–8 oz. Falernum or sugar syrup to taste

Mix all ingredients in a large container and allow to stand in the refrigerator, *tightly covered,* overnight. Serve in a chilled punch bowl with a large cake of ice. Makes about 12 servings. *Note:* Created by the author for tailgate luncheons that precede this outstanding annual steeplechase and turf-racing event for charity.

PICCADILLY PUNCH

2 large lemons
12 whole cloves
2 cinnamon sticks
¼ tsp. grated nutmeg
1 cup superfine sugar
2 cups hot water or (optional) ruby port
1 750-ml. bottle cognac

Slice peel from lemons, stud with cloves, and place into the flaming pan of a chafing dish along with juice. Add cinnamon

sticks, nutmeg, sugar, and hot water and simmer until all sugar is dissolved. Warm some cognac in a ladle, ignite, and pour blazing into chafing dish. Extinguish and then pour remainder of cognac into pan. Stir and serve. Makes about 11 servings.
Note: Some recipes call for port in place of hot water, in which case the lemon juice and sugar would have to be adjusted for individual tastes.

PRINCE'S (PRINCESS'S) PUNCH

1 750-ml. bottle Benedictine
1 750-ml. bottle cognac
½–1 pt. fresh lemon juice,
    depending upon tartness
    desired
2 oz. sugar syrup or to taste
4 750-ml. bottles champagne
½ lemon thinly sliced
10 maraschino cherries

Prechill all ingredients and
put Benedictine, cognac, lemon
juice, and sugar syrup into a
chilled punch bowl. Mix well and
adjust sweetness. Just before
serving, gently stir in champagne and garnish with lemon
slices and cherries. Makes about
42 servings.
Note: The secret of this punch is
to use just the right amount
of lemon juice, adding more lemon
juice and sugar syrup as needed
until the balance is just right.

QUEEN ANNE'S SHRUB

1 pt. lemon juice
Grated zest (outer peel) of 2
    lemons
2 lbs. sugar or to taste
2 750-ml. bottles brandy
2 750-ml. bottles dry white
    wine
Several strips of lemon peel
Mint sprigs (optional)

Clean out a large container
with a tight-fitting lid with boiling water. In a small mixing
bowl combine lemon juice, zest,
and sugar and stir until sugar
is dissolved. Pour into large container with brandy and 1 bottle of wine, reserving the other.
Seal the container and store in
a cool place for 5 or 6 weeks. To
serve, strain shrub into a
chilled punch bowl with a cake of
ice, add second bottle of white
wine, and garnish with long strips
of lemon peels and several
mint sprigs. Makes about 30
servings.

REGENT'S PUNCH

1 750-ml. bottle Rhine wine
2 750-ml. bottles Madeira
1 750-ml. bottle curaçao
1 750-ml. bottle cognac
1 pt. dark Jamaica rum
1 pt. tea
3 cups orange juice
5 oz. lemon juice
½ cup sugar syrup or to taste
3 750-ml. bottles champagne
2 l. club soda

Prechill all ingredients and
mix in a chilled punch bowl with
ice cake, reserving champagne
and club soda until just before
serving. When ready to serve,
add champagne and soda and
stir very gently. Makes approximately 83 servings.

ROMAN PUNCH

1 750-ml. bottle Haitian,
   Martinique, or Barbados rum
1 750-ml. bottle brut
   champagne
½ cup curaçao
1 cup lemon juice
¾ cup orange juice
1 tbsp. raspberry syrup or
   grenadine or to taste

Whites of 10 eggs
Orange peels

Mix all ingredients, prechilled,
except egg whites and orange
peels, in a chilled punch bowl
with an ice cake. Check sweetness.
Beat egg whites until fairly stiff
and gently stir into punch.
Garnish with a few orange peels.
Makes about 20 servings.

 ST. CECELIA SOCIETY PUNCH

6 limes, sliced thin
4 lemons, sliced thin
1 small ripe pineapple,
   skinned, cored, and sliced
   thin
1 cup superfine sugar
1 750-ml. bottle cognac
1 750-ml. bottle peach brandy
1 qt. iced tea
1 pt. dark Jamaica rum
1 cup curaçao
4 750-ml. bottles brut
   champagne
2 l. club soda

Place sliced limes, lemons,
and pineapple in a large pot
with a lid that fits securely.
Spread sugar evenly over the
fruit and muddle until sugar is
pounded or pressed into the slices.
Pour in cognac, cover, and let
stand for 24 hours. Pour the entire contents of the pot into a
chilled punch bowl containing a
large cake of ice. Add chilled
peach brandy, tea, rum, and
curaçao, and stir well. Just
before guests arrive, gently stir
in cold champagne and club
soda. Check sweetness and serve.
Makes about 70 servings.

 SANGRIA Basic

2 750-ml. bottles dry red
   wine
3 oz. curaçao
2 oz. brandy (optional)
Juice of 1 orange
Juice of 1 lemon or lime
4 oz. sugar syrup or to taste
1 l. club soda (optional)
6 each thin orange and lemon
   slices
1 fresh or brandied peach
   sliced thin (optional)

Prechill all ingredients and
mix wine, curaçao, brandy, fruit

juices, and sugar syrup until
well blended and strain into a
chilled punch bowl with a cake
of ice or serve from chilled pitchers. Add club soda, if you
wish, and garnish with orange
and lemon slices. A fresh or
brandied peach may be added to
the punch. Makes 24 servings.
Note: Sangria is basically wine
flavored with fresh fruits and
sweetened to taste. Spirits are
often added for flavor and soda
may be used to provide fizziness.
There are many recipes and
variations.

SANGRIA Blonde

2 750-ml. bottles chablis,
　Mosel, Rhine wine, or
　California Johannisberg
　riesling
2–3 oz. curaçao
1 oz. kirschwasser
½ cup orange juice, freshly
　squeezed
2 oz. lemon or lime juice
2 oz. sugar syrup or to taste

1 l. club soda
½ orange sliced thinly

Prechill all ingredients and
pour in wine, curaçao, kirsch,
and fruit juices and let steep
for 30 minutes with a cake of ice.
Just before serving, pour in
soda, stir gently, and garnish
with orange slices. Makes
about 25 servings.

SANGRIA Champagne

1 750-ml. bottle riesling
　wine
1 generous cup grapefruit
　sections
2 oz. gin
1 oz. triple sec
1 oz. maraschino liqueur or
　sugar syrup to taste
3 oz. grapefruit juice
Several dashes lime juice
1 750-ml. bottle champagne
1 lime, sliced thin
Mint sprigs (optional)

Prechill all ingredients and mix
riesling, grapefruit, gin, triple
sec, maraschino liqueur,
grapefruit and lime juices, in a
chilled punch bowl with a cake
of ice. Check sweetness and add
more lime juice if too sweet or
more maraschino or triple sec if
too tart. Pour in champagne
and stir gently. Garnish with
lime sections and mint sprigs.
Makes about 16 servings.

SANGRIA Mexican

4 oz. gold tequila
1 bottle dry red wine
1 orange sliced
1 lemon sliced
1 lime sliced
2 oz. curaçao
1 fresh peach, peeled,
　quartered, and studded
　with cloves

2–3 cinnamon sticks
Club soda or sparkling wine
　(optional)

Mix all ingredients, except
peach, cinnamon, and soda or
sparkling wine, in a punch
bowl in which has been placed a
cake of ice. Add peach and
cinnamon and soda or sparkling
wine if more dilution is required.
Makes 8 servings.

SEWICKLEY HEIGHTS GUN CLUB PUNCH

1 qt. pineapple juice
1 qt. grapefruit juice
1 qt. orange juice
1 l. dark Jamaica rum
1 pt. gold rum
1 6-oz. jar maraschino cherries
1 qt. lemon-lime soda
½ tsp. powdered cinnamon

Pour pineapple, grapefruit, and orange juice into a prechilled punch bowl with a large cake of ice. Add Jamaica rum and mix well. Take cup of gold rum and the entire contents of a jar of cherries and mix in a blender until cherries are chopped fine and pour into punch bowl with remainder of gold rum. Stir well and just before serving, add lemon-lime soda and stir gently. Sprinkle with powdered cinnamon. Makes about 40 servings.

 ## SHAMROCK PUNCH

2 750-ml. bottles Irish whiskey
½ pt. Irish Mist
1 pt. fresh lemon juice
½ cup honey or sugar syrup
    to taste
2 750-ml. bottles champagne,
    or 1 bottle champagne
    and 1 bottle club soda
Fresh shamrocks or clover

Prechill all ingredients and pour whiskey, Irish Mist, and lemon juice into a chilled punch bowl with a cake of ice. Add honey after dissolving it in a cup with a little warm water and mix well. Immediately before serving, pour in champagne and stir gently. Garnish with a few fresh shamrocks. Makes about 33 servings.
Note: For a less potent punch, use club soda in place of champagne.

 ## SHANGHAI PUNCH

2 qt. hot black tea
1 750-ml. bottle cognac
1 pt. curaçao
1 pt. dark Jamaica or
    Demerara rum
2 cups lemon juice
1½ oz. orgeat syrup
1 oz. orange flower water
Orange peel
Lemon peel
Cinnamon sticks

Mix all ingredients, except orange and lemon peels and cinnamon sticks, in the flaming pan of a chafing dish over direct heat and bring to simmering. Serve steaming in mugs with a garnish of orange and lemon peel and a stick of cinnamon. Makes about 35 servings.
Note: This *is* from Shanghai and was popular with the White Russian colony before World War II.

SHERRY TWIST PUNCH

1 750-ml. bottle amontillado
  sherry
1 pt. Spanish brandy or
  armagnac
½ pt. dry vermouth
½ pt. curaçao
Juice of 1 lemon
Ground cinnamon

Prechill all ingredients and
mix (except for cinnamon) in a
chilled punch bowl with a cake of
ice. Sprinkle powdered cinnamon
over punch. Makes about 15
servings.

SVEN'S GLÖGG

½ gal. dry red wine
1 pt. port
½ cup dry vermouth
1 cup blanched almonds
1 cup seedless raisins
¼ cup dried bitter orange
  peel
4 cinnamon sticks
1½ tbsp. cardamom seeds
1 tbsp. whole cloves
1 tsp. aniseed
1 tsp. fennel seed
⅔ cup granulated sugar
1 pt. vodka
1 pt. cognac
1 pt. rye whiskey or blended
  whiskey

Pour red wine, port, and vermouth
into a large bowl. Add almonds
and raisins. Put orange peel,
cinnamon sticks (broken), cardamom, cloves, aniseed, and fennel
seed into a cloth bag and add it
to the wine mixture. Cover and let
stand overnight. Transfer all
ingredients from bowl to a
saucepan and heat over a low

flame. Add sugar to taste and
allow to simmer for a few
minutes, but do not boil. Remove
from heat, add vodka, cognac
and rye, cover pan, and heat
until punch reaches boiling
point. Remove cloth bag and pour
punch into the flaming pan of
a chafing dish (or a warmed
heat-proof punch bowl); cover
and heat over a low fire. Just
before serving, put an ounce or
two of warmed cognac in a long-
handled ladle, ignite, remove lid
(be sure to stand away from
chafing dish) and pour flaming
liquid into punch. Allow to blaze
for a few moments and extinguish
by covering with lid. Serve in
cups with spoons. Be sure to put
a helping of almonds and raisins
into each cup along with the
glogg. Makes about 33 servings.
Note: Glögg is traditionally served
with ginger snaps and is a
great favorite in Sweden during
the Christmas season. Every
family has a treasured recipe for
this festive punch. This is one
of them.

BARTENDER'S SECRET NO. 36

No professional chef or experienced cook would dream of serving a soup, sauce, or other made-from-scratch recipe without
tasting it during the course of preparation. All recipes are

subject to change and modification depending on the nature of the available ingredients and the taste preferences of the one who is doing the cooking. Complicated punches and other mixed drinks are no different. They must always be checked for flavor before serving (unless you have made the recipe many times) and especially for sweetness. If a punch turns out to be too sour or too sweet despite the fact that you have followed the recipe assiduously, adjustments should be made until you are satisfied with the results.

TOM AND JERRY

12 eggs
2½ lbs. superfine sugar
1½ tsp. ground cinnamon
½ tsp. ground cloves
½ tsp. ground allspice
¼ tsp. cream of tartar
4 oz. dark Jamaica rum
1 l. bottle brandy, bourbon, or rum
Boiling water, milk, or coffee

Separate eggs. Beat yolks with 2 tbs. sugar (reserving remainder for the whites), ground cinnamon, cloves, and allspice until they are smooth and creamy, then add rum gradually, stirring constantly. In another bowl, beat egg whites with a pinch of cream of tartar until soft peaks form, then beat in remainder of sugar until peaks stiffen. Carefully fold whites into yolks. This batter is the basis of individual servings. When ready to serve, scald out a Tom and Jerry mug or other heatproof container and put a ladleful of the batter into a cup. Add 2 oz. of brandy or bourbon or rum or any combination that suits your taste (i.e. half brandy and half rum), fill with boiling water or milk and sprinkle with nutmeg.
Note: This recipe is based on the original created by the famous mixologist, Jerry Thomas, and adjusted to modern tastes. Sugar and other ingredients may be varied.

TRADER VIC'S TIKI PUNCH

1 pt. Cointreau or triple sec
1 pt. gin
¾ cup fresh lime juice
4 750-ml. bottles champagne

Prechill all ingredients and pour Cointreau, gin, and lime juice into a chilled punch bowl with a cake of ice. Mix well, let stand an hour, and check sweetness, adding more lime juice or Cointreau to suit your taste. Just before serving, add champagne and stir gently. Makes about 35 servings.

VICTORIA PARADE PUNCH

1 750-ml. bottle blended
   whiskey, scotch, or bourbon
1 750-ml. bottle dark Jamaica
   rum
1 750-ml. bottle Benedictine
1 750-ml. bottle cherry brandy
1 pt. Darjeeling tea
1 cup orange juice
4 oz. lemon juice

4 oz. sugar syrup, pineapple
   syrup, or Falernum
Orange and lemon slices

Chill all ingredients and mix
together in a large punch bowl
with a cake of ice. Stir well,
adjust sweetness, and serve.
Makes about 33 servings.

WASSAIL BOWL

1 cup brown sugar
2 tsp. grated nutmeg
2 tsp. powdered ginger
3 cinnamon sticks, broken
½ tsp. mace
6 whole cloves
6 allspice berries
3 750-ml. bottles Madeira,
   sherry, port, or Marsala
6–8 eggs
1 cup cognac or gold rum
4 baked apples, cored but
   not skinned

Put sugar and spices in a
saucepan or the flaming pan of a
chafing dish over direct heat
and add a cup or two of water.

Bring to a boil and stir well
until all sugar is dissolved. Add
wine and heat, but do not boil.
Separately, beat egg yolks and
egg whites and fold together,
then pour eggs into a warmed,
heat-proof punch bowl. Add
the hot wine mixture to the punch
bowl a little at a time, stirring
constantly until all wine has been
blended with the eggs. Stir
briskly and add cognac. Stir again
and add baked apples. Makes
about 28 servings. Put a bit of
baked apple into each cup.
Note: This traditional English
Christmas punch can be made
with wine, beer, cider, ale, or
any combination thereof.

WOODCHOPPER'S PUNCH

1 l. fresh lemon juice
1 pt. maple syrup
6 cinnamon sticks or 1 tsp.
   powdered cinnamon
2 750-ml. bottles straight rye,
   bourbon, or Canadian
   whisky

Simmer lemon juice, maple syrup,
and cinnamon in a saucepan
until maple syrup is dissolved.
Stir well and check sweetness.
Pour in whisky, mix well, and
serve in warmed mugs. This
punch may also be served cold
in a pitcher or a punch bowl with
ice. Makes about 25 servings.

XALAPA PUNCH

2 l. hot, strong black tea
Zests (outside peel) or 2 large
oranges, grated
1½ cups sugar syrup or honey
to taste
1 750-ml. bottle gold rum
1 750-ml. bottle applejack or
calvados
1 750-ml. bottle dry red wine
12 thinly sliced orange and
lemon sections

Pour hot tea into a saucepan
with orange zest (only the colored
peel of the orange, not the
white) and let steep until tea
cools. Add sugar or honey and
mix thoroughly until dissolved.
Stir in spirits and wine and
chill in refrigerator, covered, for
an hour or two before serving
in a chilled punch bowl with a
cake of ice. Garnish with orange
and lemon sections. Makes about
40 servings.

YARD OF FLANNEL

1 l. ale
4 eggs
3 tbsp. superfine sugar or to
taste
½ tsp. ground nutmeg
½ tsp. ground ginger,
cinnamon, or allspice
½ cup Martinique, Haitian,
gold Jamaica, or other
aromatic rum
Boiling water

Heat ale in a saucepan over
low heat. In a small bowl, beat
eggs with rum, sugar, and spices
and pour into a pitcher that has
been rinsed with boiling water.
In a second pitcher, also rinsed
with boiling water, pour hot ale
from the saucepan and very gradually add to egg mixture, stirring constantly until well blended.
Before serving in heated mugs,
pour mixture from one pitcher to
another until frothy. Makes 4
servings.

ZOMBIE PUNCH

2 750-ml. bottles gold Puerto
Rican rum
1 750-ml. bottle dark Jamaica
rum
1 pt. 151-proof Demerara rum
1 pt. curaçao or triple sec
1 pt. lime juice
1 pt. orange juice
1 cup lemon juice
1 cup papaya juice or pineapple juice
1 cup passion fruit juice or
La Grande Passion
½ cup grenadine

2 oz. Pernod
Pineapple slices

Mix all ingredients well in a
chilled punch bowl, add a large
cake of ice, and let stand for
several hours in a cool place or
in your refrigerator. Garnish with
a few thin pineapple slices.
Makes about 42 servings.
Note: Fruit-juice proportions depend upon the freshness and
availability of tropical fruits. Feel
free to adjust quantities to suit
your taste.

HOT DRINKS: THE FIRE SPIRITS

When you and I went down the lane
  with ale mugs in our hands,
The night we went to Glastonbury
  by way of Goodwin Sands.
            —G. K. Chesterton

You have made your last run down the mountain. It is dusk
and you have begun to feel the pervasive, penetrating cold
despite your vigorous activity on the ski slopes. In the main
hall of the lodge a great fire roars in the hearth, and as you
and your companions begin to thaw out in front of the fire a
waiter appears holding a tray of steaming mugs. "What is it?"
you ask as you deftly lift one from the tray and to your lips in
a quick, sweeping motion. Suddenly the heady aroma of spirits
and spices assails your nose and you take a sip of the burning
liquid. The waiter answers your question, but you do not hear.
The burning sensation has cascaded down your throat, and
your whole being is suffused with what seems to be a
bourgeoning wave of warmth and, at the same time, a soothing sensation of glorious relaxation and well-being.

You have fallen under the spell of the fire spirits, an unfail-
ing antidote for cold that has restored life to body and spirit for
all manner of men and women from ancient times. Hot drinks
are well-known for their restorative properties and it is no
secret in cold countries that hot alcoholic beverages are consumed with gusto and great regularity. In olden days, hot
drinks were indeed the original "central heating." The Colonial tavern in America was a good example. The taproom was
the social center dominated by a great fireplace and a cheerful, blazing fire that had an important function aside from
providing heat and light on cold, wintry nights. In the fireplace were kept the flip irons or loggerheads (also called
"hotties" and "flip dogs," but not "pokers," as pokers were
designed for fire tending, not drink making), which were used
to mull the drinks that were served in large mugs, tankards,

bowls, cups, or whatever would survive a sudden dose of heat. Wines, spirits, beers, ales, and divers mixtures known by such names as "Kill-Divil," "Rattle Skull," and "Whistle-Belly Vengeance" were regularly "frothed" using a red-hot flip iron. The resulting burnt flavor was highly prized by our Colonial forebears.

Few of these hot potations have survived the passing of the years except for the name "flip" (derived from "flip iron") and the recipe itself: a mix of wine or spirits, beer or ale, eggs, sugar, cream, and spices which lives on, though without the use of beer or ale, and which may be served hot or cold. Another hand-me-down is the phrase "being at loggerheads," which alludes to disputes and spirited debates during which opponents would use loggerheads to make their point. Many early American inns and taverns were centers of discourse, for they fulfilled the functions of meeting place, public forum, social club, restaurant, and town saloon.

Modern hot libations are no longer mulled with a flip dog but flamed instead. (No doubt, as this is being written, some enterprising pub owner is preparing to feature hot drinks heated with a red-hot iron and they'll become the rage!) To the uninitiated, blazing drinks may seem to be the pursuit of fools who are (1) showing off; (2) burning up good spirits to no worthy end; and (3) taking a chance on starting a fire or injuring someone. There is, of course, an element of truth in all of these assertions, depending on who is doing the drink making and under what circumstances.

There is a certain amount of show in any pyrotechnical display, especially at the bar or your dining table, but if that were the only purpose—a spectacle—then it probably wouldn't be worth the effort. Proper flaming of drinks adds flavor that cannot be achieved by conventional methods: sugar and syrups are carmelized; essential oils from citrus peels are ignited; butter, spices, and flavorings are enhanced; and spirits undergo chemical changes that can produce new and intriguing flavors. Not all recipes for flamed drinks yield optimum results. This is a matter of experimentation and experience. In any event, the flaming process should last no more than ten or fifteen seconds, so the amount of alcohol that is burned away is negligible. A far more important consideration is safety. Fire is not a toy to be played with by the inexperienced, the foolhardy, or the inebriated. See Bartender's Secret No.31 for detailed safety rules on how to flame drinks for festive, flavorful, *and* harmless enjoyment.

ABERDEEN ANGUS

½ oz. lime juice
½ oz. heather honey
Boiling water
2 oz. scotch
1 oz. Drambuie

Put lime juice and honey into

a heat-proof mug, add a little
boiling water, and stir until
honey is dissolved. Add scotch.
Warm Drambuie in a small
ladle, ignite, and pour blazing
into mug. Fill with boiling water
and stir.

 ## ADULT HOT CHOCOLATE

1 cup hot chocolate
1½ oz. peppermint schnapps
1 generous tbsp. whipped
  cream

Pour hot chocolate and schnapps
into a warmed mug and stir well.
Top with whipped cream.

 ## ALHAMBRA ROYALE

1 cup hot chocolate
1 piece orange peel
1½ oz. cognac
1 tbsp. whipped cream
  (optional)

Fill cup nearly full of hot
chocolate and add orange peel.
Warm cognac in a ladle over hot
water, ignite, and pour blazing
into cup of chocolate. Stir well
and top with whipped cream, if
you wish.

APPLE BARREL APRÈS-SKI TODDY

1½ oz. DeKuyper Apple
  Barrel Schnapps
1 oz. brandy
1 cup apple cider or apple
  juice
1 tsp. honey or to taste
Cinnamon stick

Mix all ingredients in a saucepan
and heat until simmering, but
do not boil. Pour into a mug
that has been rinsed in boiling
water.

 ## BEACHCOMBER'S BRACER

1 tsp. honey or sugar syrup
Dash lemon juice
Boiling water
1 oz. bourbon or rye
1 oz. light Jamaica rum
1 oz. curaçao
Dash Angostura bitters

Dissolve honey with lemon
juice and a little boiling water in
a heat-proof mug and add bourbon, rum, curaçao, and a dash of
bitters. Fill mug with boiling
water and stir well.

THE BLACK STRIPE

2 tsp. molasses or honey
Boiling water
Lemon peel
Cinnamon stick
2–3 oz. dark Jamaica rum
Ground nutmeg

Dissolve molasses in a heat-proof mug with a little boiling water. Add lemon peel and cinnamon stick and more boiling water. Float rum on top and blaze for a few seconds, if you wish. Stir to extinguish flames and top with a sprinkling of nutmeg.

 ## BLUE BLAZER

4 oz. scotch
4 oz. boiling water
2 tsp. sugar
2 small lemon peels

Pour scotch into one warmed mug and boiling water into the other. Ignite scotch, and while blazing, pour back and forth between the two mugs. Extinguish and serve drink in two mugs. Add 1 tsp. sugar to each mug, stir well, and garnish with lemon peels. Makes two drinks.
Note: Professional bartenders attempting to make this drink are cautioned to practice with cold water first to avoid scalding themselves and innocent bystanders at the bar.

CAFÉ AMARETTO

1 cup hot, strong black
   coffee
1 oz. amaretto
½ oz. cognac
1 tbsp. whipped cream

Pour amaretto into coffee and stir well. Float cognac on top, using the back of a spoon, and top with a generous portion of whipped cream.

 ## CAFÉ BRÛLOT Basic

Several cinnamon sticks
8 whole cloves
4–5 sugar cubes, depending
   on sweetness desired
Outer peel (zest) of ½ orange
Outer peel (zest) of ½ lemon
4 oz. cognac
1 pt. strong hot black coffee

Place all ingredients, except cognac and coffee, in a *brûlot* bowl or chafing dish. Soften sugar cubes with a little water and mash them into orange and lemon peels with a muddler. Add warmed cognac and mix well with other ingredients in bowl. Ignite and blaze for a few seconds and pour in hot coffee. Ladle into demitasse cups. Makes four servings.

CAFÉ BRÛLOT GRAND MARNIER

2 sugar cubes
2 cinnamon sticks
8 whole cloves
Outer peel (zest) of ½ orange
Outer peel (zest) of ½ lemon
Small piece of vanilla bean
3 oz. Grand Marnier
2 oz. cognac or dark rum
1 pt. hot, strong black coffee

Put all ingredients, except spirits and coffee, in a *brûlot* bowl or a chafing dish. Moisten sugar cubes with a little water and mash into orange and lemon peels with a muddler or heavy spoon. Add warmed Grand Marnier and cognac and mix well. Place a small sugar cube in a ladle and add a tbsp. of cognac that has been warmed. Ignite and pour blazing into bowl. After a few seconds pour in coffee and stir. Makes four demitasse servings.

CAFÉ DIABLE

2 cinnamon sticks
8 whole cloves
6 whole coffee beans
2 oz. cognac
1 oz. Cointreau
1 oz. curaçao
1 pt. hot, strong black coffee

Place all ingredients, except coffee, in a chafing dish or *brûlot* bowl and warm over low, direct heat. Ignite and blaze for a few seconds and pour in coffee. Mix well. Makes four demitasse servings.

CAFÉ DIANA

6 oz. Southern Comfort
½ tsp. lemon juice
4 minced maraschino cherries
2 tsp. maraschino cherry juice
½ tsp. ground ginger
1 large segment cocktail orange preserved in syrup
2 tsp. cocktail orange syrup
8 whole cloves
Several pinches powdered cinnamon
Several pinches powdered nutmeg

4 cups hot, strong black coffee
4 small cinnamon sticks

Put all ingredients, except hot coffee, in the flaming pan of a chafing dish and stir well. When heated (do not boil), ignite and blaze for a few seconds. Pour in hot coffee, stir well, and serve in warmed cups with cinnamon sticks. Makes four servings.

CAFÉ DORN

1 pt. hot, strong black
  coffee
4 pieces lemon peel
4 pieces orange peel
4 cinnamon sticks
12 whole cloves
Honey or sugar syrup to taste
1½ oz. Benedictine
1½ oz. kummel
1½ oz. dark Jamaica rum
7 oz. cognac

4 tbsp. whipped cream

Mix coffee, fruit peels, spices,
honey, Benedictine, kummel, rum,
and 3 oz. of cognac in a saucepan or chafing dish and bring to
a simmer. Do not boil. Ladle
into warmed mugs or cups and
add 1 oz. of cognac to each
cup. Top with a generous tablespoon of whipped cream. Serves
four.

CAFÉ JEAVONS

1 tsp. coconut syrup
Hot black coffee
1 oz. dark Jamaica rum
1 oz. cognac
Orange peel
1 generous tbsp. vanilla ice
  cream
Pinch ground cinnamon

Pour coconut syrup and hot
coffee into a large, heat-proof
mug that has been rinsed with
hot water. Stir until syrup is
dissolved. Add rum, cognac,
orange peel, and ice cream
float. Sprinkle with cinnamon.

CAFÉ NAPOLEON

2 tbsp. honey
Outer peel (zest) of ½ orange
1 tsp. lemon juice
2–3 cinnamon sticks
8 whole cloves
4 cups hot, strong black coffee
2 oz. B&B liqueur
1 oz. kummel
1 oz. gold rum
1 oz. cognac
Whipped cream
Grated nutmeg

Put all ingredients, except spirits,
whipped cream, and nutmeg, into
the flaming pan of a chafing
dish over direct heat and bring to
a simmer, but do not boil. Add
B&B, kummel, and rum and stir
well. Warm cognac in a ladle
over hot water, ignite, and pour
blazing into chafing dish. Stir
and serve in large cups or mugs,
top with whipped cream, and
sprinkle with nutmeg. Makes four
servings.

BARTENDER'S SECRET NO. 37

Serving a hot drink in a cold glass is as bad as serving hot
food on a cold plate. Glasses used for hot beverages should be

rinsed in hot water so they are thoroughly warmed before serving. Actually, the best container for a hot drink is a china cup, and better still is an earthenware mug because it holds the heat longer. When pouring very hot drinks into cups and glasses, be sure to place a spoon in the container to prevent cracking. Silver, pewter, and copper mugs should be used with care in the service of very hot drinks. The excellent heat conductivity of these metallic containers can cause minor burns to the lips and mouth.

 ## CAFE ROYALE No. 1

4 sugar cubes
1 pt. hot, strong black coffee
4 oz. 100-proof bourbon

Place sugar cube in each of 4 warmed demitasse cups and fill almost full of hot coffee. Carefully float 1 oz. of bourbon in each cup, ignite, and flame for a few seconds. Stir with spoon to extinguish the flames. Serves four.

 ## CAFE ROYALE No. 2

4 sugar cubes
1 pt. hot, strong black coffee
4 oz. cognac

Place sugar cube in each of 4 demitasse cups that have been rinsed with boiling water. Fill each cup nearly full with hot coffee and carefully float an ounce of cognac in each cup. Ignite, flame for a few seconds, and stir with a spoon to extinguish the flames. Serves four.

CAFÉ WELLINGTON

½ cup whipping cream
¼ tsp. instant coffee
2 tsp. coconut syrup
1 oz. light rum
Hot black coffee

Blend whipping cream with instant coffee until it stands up in stiff peaks. In a heat-proof cup add coconut syrup and a little coffee and stir until syrup is dissolved. Add rum and stir well while filling cup with more coffee. Top with whipped cream. Whipped-cream mixture is sufficient for from four to six cups of coffee.

CAPETOWN COFFEE

1 cup hot black coffee
1 tbsp. coconut cream or to
  taste
1½ oz. bourbon, rye, or
  blended whiskey
1 tbsp. whipped cream

In a warmed mug put hot coffee
and coconut cream and stir until
cream is dissolved. Add whiskey,
stir, and top with whipped cream.

CHARTREUSE CHOCOLATE KISS

½ oz. green Chartreuse
1 cup hot chocolate
1 heaping tbsp. whipped
  cream
Chocolate shavings

Pour Chartreuse into a warmed,
heat-proof mug, fill with hot
chocolate, and garnish with
dollop of whipped cream and
chocolate shavings.

CHOKLAD PRINS BERTIL

1 cup hot chocolate
1½ oz. Grand Marnier or
  triple sec
½ oz. cognac (optional if
  triple sec is used in place
  of Grand Marnier)
1 heaping tbsp. whipped
  cream

Scald a heat-proof mug with
boiling water and fill with
steaming hot chocolate. Add
Grand Marnier or triple sec
and cognac and stir well. Top
with whipped cream.
Note: Created by the author for
H.R.H. Prince Bertil of Sweden.

COFFEE GROG

1 tsp. butter
1 tbsp. brown sugar or 1 tsp.
  coconut syrup
Grated nutmeg
12 whole cloves
4 cinnamon sticks
4 small slices lemon peel
4 small slices orange peel
1 cup dark Jamaica rum
Hot, strong black coffee
Whipped cream (optional)

Cream butter with brown sugar
and several pinches of nutmeg
and into each of 4 flameproof
mugs add some of the butter-
sugar mixture, 3 cloves, and 1
each cinnamon stick, lemon peel,
orange peel, and 2 oz. of rum.
Stir well and ignite and blaze for
a few seconds. Pour in coffee
and stir well. Top with whipped
cream, if you wish. Makes four
servings.
Note: Be sure to warm rum in
advance so it will flame.

COFFEE ORLOFF

¾ oz. vodka
¾ oz. Tia Maria
1 cup hot black coffee
¾ oz. Crème de Grand
   Marnier

Scald a large cup or mug with
boiling water and add vodka, Tia
Maria, and steaming black coffee.
Stir well and carefully float
Crème de Grand Marnier on top.

 COMFORTABLE COFFEE COCKTAIL

1½ oz. Southern Comfort
1 oz. Kahlua
Several dashes orange bitters
Lemon peel
Orange peel
Pinch powdered cinnamon

In a saucepan, heat 2 oz. of
water and all other ingredients,
except cinnamon, to the simmering point. Pour into a warmed,
heat-proof mug and sprinkle
with powdered cinnamon.

DOWN EAST HOT BUTTERED RUM

2 tsp. brown sugar
1 cup apple cider
Cinnamon stick
4 whole cloves
1 piece lemon peel
2 oz. gold label rum
Small pat butter
Grated nutmeg

In a warmed, heat-proof mug,
add sugar and a little cider that
had been heated to the boiling
point. Stir until sugar is dissolved and add cinnamon,
cloves, lemon peel, and rum. Fill
with hot cider, stir, and top
with butter and grated nutmeg.

FLAMING HOT BUTTERED RUM

1 tbsp. brown sugar
Cinnamon stick
Lemon peel or orange peel
Whole cloves
Boiling water
2–3 oz. dark Jamaica rum
Pinch of sugar
½ oz. 151-proof Demerara rum
Pat of butter
Grated nutmeg

Rinse a large, heat-proof mug
with boiling water, add sugar,

cinnamon stick, and a lemon or
orange peel studded with cloves.
Pour in enough boiling water
to dissolve sugar and stir in rum.
Fill mug with boiling water
and place pat of butter on top of
drink. Warm Demerara rum in
a ladle, into which you have put
a pinch of sugar, by partially
immersing the bowl in hot water.
Ignite rum and pour blazing
into mug. Add a little additional
butter, if you wish, and sprinkle with nutmeg.

FLAMES OVER JERSEY

2 oz. applejack or apple
    schnapps
4 oz. apple cider or apple
    juice
Pinch ground cinnamon
Pinch ground nutmeg
¼ baked apple
½ oz. 151-proof Demerara rum

Into the flaming pan of a chafing dish or saucepan, put all ingredients except Demerara rum, and heat over a low flame until apple is warmed through (do not boil). Just before serving, warm Demerara rum in a ladle over hot water, ignite, and pour blazing into pan. After a few seconds extinguish flame with pan lid and serve in a warmed mug or wine goblet with a spoon.

FUZZY NUT

1½ oz. DeKuyper Peachtree
    Schnapps
½ oz. amaretto
5 oz. hot chocolate
Marshmallow or whipped
    cream
Pinch ground cinnamon

Combine Peachtree Schnapps, amaretto, and hot chocolate in a warm mug and stir. Garnish with marshmallow or dollop of whipped cream and sprinkle ground cinnamon on top.

 GINGER PEACHY TOM AND JERRY

1 egg
½ oz. orgeat syrup or to taste
Pinch ground ginger
Pinch ground cinnamon
1 oz. peach-flavored brandy
1 oz. light rum or cognac
1 oz. milk
1 oz. cream
Pinch ground nutmeg

Beat egg yolk in a small bowl, add orgeat syrup, ground ginger and cinnamon, and blend well. Beat egg white separately in a small bowl until stiff, carefully fold yolk mixture into white, and spoon egg mixture into a large, warmed mug. Combine peach brandy, rum or cognac, milk, and cream in a small saucepan, heat, and pour into mug while stirring constantly. Sprinkle with topping of ground nutmeg.

 GLÜHWEIN

5 oz. Madeira or dry red
    wine
Lemon peel
Orange peel
Small cinnamon stick, broken
Several whole cloves

Pinch of ground nutmeg
1 tsp. honey or to taste

Heat all ingredients in a saucepan and stir until honey is dissolved. Do not boil. Serve in a warmed, heat-proof mug.

GOLDEN GROG

¾ oz. straight rye or bourbon
¾ oz. gold Jamaica or
   Barbados rum
¾ oz. Cointreau
1 tsp. orgeat syrup or
   Falernum to taste
Boiling water

Cinnamon stick
Lemon or orange slice

Put rye, rum, Cointreau, and syrup into a warmed, heat-proof mug, fill with boiling water, and stir well. Garnish with cinnamon stick and lemon or orange slice.

GOODNIGHT SWEETHEART HOT MILK PUNCH

1 tsp. superfine sugar
1 cup milk
1 oz. dark Jamaica rum
1 oz. cognac
1 oz. gin or vodka
Dash Angostura bitters
Grated nutmeg

Dissolve sugar in milk and heat in saucepan. When milk is hot, add rum, cognac, gin, and bitters. Heat again and stir well. Pour mixture into a blender and mix at high speed. Pour into a mug that has been rinsed with boiling water and top with a sprinkling of nutmeg.

GRINGO GROG

1 tsp. brown sugar or to
   taste
3 whole cloves
Cinnamon stick
Boiling water
2 oz. tequila
Pat of butter
Grated nutmeg

Rinse out a heat-proof mug with boiling water, add brown sugar, cloves, cinnamon, and pour in enough boiling water to dissolve sugar. Add tequila and fill mug with boiling water. Top with butter and sprinkling of nutmeg.

HIGHLAND HOT MILK PUNCH

2 oz. scotch
1 oz. Drambuie
½ oz. sugar syrup or to taste
1 whole egg, beaten
1 cup milk
Pinch powdered cinnamon

Heat all ingredients, except cinnamon, in a saucepan over low heat, stirring from time to time to prevent milk from scorching. Rinse a heatproof mug with boiling water and fill with hot punch. Sprinkle cinnamon on top.

HOT APPLE BANG!

1 oz. applejack
1 oz. apple schnapps
4 oz. apple cider or apple juice
½ oz. maple syrup or sugar syrup to taste
Several whole cloves
Slice of baked apple (optional)
Cinnamon stick
Pat butter
Grated nutmeg
Lemon slice

Rinse a heat-proof mug with boiling water, add applejack, schnapps, cider, and maple syrup that has been heated (but not boiled) in a saucepan, and stir well. Stud baked apple with cloves and add to mug with cinnamon stick. Add additional hot apple cider, top with butter and nutmeg, and garnish with lemon slice.

HOT BENEFACTOR

1 tsp. sugar syrup or to taste
2 oz. Jamaica rum
2 oz. dry red wine
Lemon slice
Grated nutmeg

Add syrup to saucepan with a little hot water and stir until sugar is dissolved. Add rum and wine, and heat until it begins to simmer. Serve in warmed, heat-proof mug with lemon slice and a sprinkling of grated nutmeg.

HOT BRANDY FLIP

2 oz. brandy (rum, whiskey, or gin may be used)
1 whole egg
1 tsp. sugar syrup or to taste
Grated nutmeg

Mix all ingredients, except nutmeg, in a blender and pour into a saucepan. Heat gently and pour into a warm Delmonico glass and sprinkle with nutmeg.
Note: Some recipes call for 2 to 4 oz. of milk, which may be used for those liking a longer drink.

HOT BRICK TODDY

¼ tsp. powdered cinnamon
1 tsp. sugar syrup
1 pat butter
Boiling water
2 oz. bourbon, rye, Canadian, or blended whiskey

In an Old Fashioned glass that has been rinsed in hot water, add cinnamon, syrup, and butter and enough boiling water to combine ingredients. Add whiskey and fill with boiling water.

HOT BULL

2 oz. vodka or tequila
3 oz. tomato juice or V-8 juice
3 oz. beef consommé or bouillon
Several dashes Worcestershire sauce
Several dashes Tabasco sauce
Dash lemon juice
Pinch celery seed or celery salt
Dash white pepper

Heat all ingredients in a saucepan until steaming, but do not boil. Serve in a warmed, heatproof mug.

HOT BUTTERED BOURBON

1½ oz. bourbon
1 oz. Wild Turkey bourbon liqueur
6 oz. apple cider or apple juice
Cinnamon stick
Pat of butter
Pinch ground nutmeg
Pinch ground ginger

Heat bourbon, bourbon liqueur, and apple cider or juice in a saucepan and pour into a warmed mug. Add cinnamon stick and butter and stir. Sprinkle with ground nutmeg and ginger.

HOT BUTTERED RUM Basic

1 generous tbsp. brown sugar
1 cinnamon stick
Lemon peel
6 whole cloves
Boiling water
2–3 oz. dark Jamaica rum
Pat of butter
Grated nutmeg

Rinse a large mug with boiling water and add brown sugar, cinnamon stick, and a lemon peel studded with cloves. Pour in a little boiling water and stir until sugar is dissolved. Add rum and fill with boiling water. Stir, then place pat of butter on top of drink, and sprinkle with grated nutmeg.

HOT BUTTERED SOUTHERN COMFORT

2 oz. Southern Comfort
½ oz. curaçao
Whole cloves
Cinnamon stick
Orange or lemon slice
Pat of butter
Grated nutmeg

Heat all ingredients, except butter and nutmeg, in a saucepan with a cup of water, stir well, and pour, steaming, into a mug that has been rinsed with boiling water. Top with butter and a sprinkling of nutmeg.

HOT DAMN!

1 egg yolk
1 tbsp. superfine sugar
6 oz. milk
1 oz. brandy
1 oz. dark Jamaica rum
½ oz. crème de cacao
Grated nutmeg

Beat egg with sugar and stir in milk. Put brandy, rum, and crème de cacao into a saucepan over low heat and add egg mixture, stirring constantly until hot. Pour into a warmed mug and top with grated nutmeg.

HOT EGGNOG

1 egg
Pinch of salt
1 tbsp. superfine sugar
1 cup hot milk
2–3 oz. warm brandy
Pinch ground nutmeg

Place egg and salt in a mixing bowl and beat until egg is thick; add sugar and beat until blended. Add hot milk and brandy, mix well by hand or in a blender, and pour into a warmed mug that has been rinsed in hot water. Sprinkle with ground nutmeg.

 ## HOT KENTUCKY TODDY

Honey or sugar syrup to
    taste
Dash orange bitters
4 whole cloves
2–3 oz. bourbon
Lemon slice

Boiling water
Grated nutmeg

Put all ingredients, except nutmeg, in a warmed, heat-proof mug and fill with boiling water. Stir well and sprinkle with nutmeg.

 ## HOT MILK PUNCH Basic

2–3 oz. whiskey, gin, rum,
    brandy, or vodka
1 cup milk
1 whole egg (optional)
1 tsp. sugar syrup or to taste
Pinch powdered nutmeg, cin-
    namon, or allspice

Heat all ingredients, except spice, in a saucepan over low heat, stirring regularly to make

certain milk does not scorch. When piping hot, pour into a heat-proof mug that has been rinsed in boiling water and top with nutmeg or spice of your choice.
Note: If glasses are used, be certain to warm them in advance and keep a long spoon in the glass when pouring in hot liquid to prevent cracking.

HOT NAIL

2 oz. scotch
1 oz. Drambuie
Dash lemon juice
Lemon slice
Orange slice
Boiling water
Cinnamon stick

Pour Drambuie, scotch, and
lemon juice into a warmed mug,
add lemon and orange slices
and boiling water. Garnish with
cinnamon stick.

HOT PASSION

1½ oz. La Grande Passion
1 cup hot black coffee
1 oz. Crème de Grand Marnier

Pour La Grande Passion into a
steaming cup of black coffee and
gently spoon on Crème de
Grand Marnier so it floats on top.

HOT PORT FLIP

3 oz. port, Madeira, or
  Marsala
1 egg
1 tsp. superfine sugar
2 oz. heavy cream
Pinch grated nutmeg

Heat wine in saucepan, but do
not boil. Beat egg with sugar in a
bowl using a whisk, blend in
cream, and pour into saucepan
with wine, stirring constantly.
Serve in a warmed mug and
sprinkle with nutmeg.

HOT TEA GROG

1 oz. dark Jamaica rum
1 oz. cognac
½ tsp. honey or to taste
Several cloves
Cinnamon stick

Pinch grated nutmeg
1 cup hot tea

Mix all ingredients together in
a saucepan, heat, and pour into
a warmed mug.

HOT TEA TODDY

1½ oz. gold rum
½ tsp. honey or to taste
Pinch powdered cinnamon
Lemon slice or orange slice
1 cup hot tea
Candied ginger

Heat all ingredients, except
ginger, in a saucepan until
steaming hot and pour into a
warmed cup or mug. Garnish
with a large piece of candied
ginger.

HOT TODDY Basic

2-3 oz. whiskey, brandy,
    rum, gin, or vodka
1 oz. sugar syrup or to taste
4 whole cloves
Generous pinch powdered
    cinnamon
Lemon slice
Boiling water
Grated nutmeg
Cinnamon stick

Warm a mug or Old Fashioned
glass and add all ingredients,
except nutmeg, and fill with
boiling water. Stir and top with
grated nutmeg. Garnish with
cinnamon stick, if you wish.
Note: Any type of whiskey, rum,
or brandy will make a good
toddy. It is a matter of personal
preference. Measurements are
approximate, depending on how
strong, sweet, or spicy you
want your toddy to be.

IMPERIAL HOUSE BRACER Hot

2 egg yolks
3 oz. cream or half-and-half
3 oz. ruby port
2 oz. cognac
Grated nutmeg

Beat egg yolks and beat in
cream. Gradually mix in port,
using a whisk, and then add
cognac. Heat in a saucepan over
low heat, stir well, and serve
in warmed wine goblets or mugs.
Sprinkle with grated nutmeg.
Makes two servings.

INDIAN SUMMER

Pinch confectioner's sugar
Pinch powdered cinnamon
2 oz. apple schnapps
5 oz. hot apple cider
Cinnamon stick

Wet the rim of a heat-proof
mug and roll in a mixture of half
cinnamon and half sugar. Add
warmed apple schnapps and mix
in mug with hot apple cider.
Garnish with cinnamon stick.

IRISH COFFEE Basic

Hot black coffee
1 tsp. sugar syrup or super-
    fine sugar
1½ oz. Irish whiskey
1-2 tbsp. whipped cream

Rinse a wine glass or goblet
with hot water, add a little hot
coffee and sugar, and stir until

sugar is dissolved. Add whiskey,
fill with hot coffee, allowing
room for topping. Cover with a
generous amount of whipped
cream. Do not stir. Sip coffee
through whipped cream.
Note: Some recipes call for heavy
cream—unwhipped—as a top-
ping. This is a matter of individual taste.

JACK'S APPLE

2 oz. applejack
4 oz. hot apple cider
1 tsp. honey
Pinch ground nutmeg
Pinch ground cinnamon
Slice baked apple

Heat applejack and cider in a saucepan and stir in honey until dissolved. Pour into a warmed, heat-proof mug and sprinkle with ground nutmeg and cinnamon. Garnish with baked apple slice.

JAMAICA COFFEE

½ oz. cognac
½ oz. Tia Maria
½ oz. dark Jamaica rum
Hot black coffee
1 heaping tbsp. whipped
   cream
Pinch ground cinnamon
Pinch ground ginger

Warm cognac, Tia Maria, and rum in a saucepan, ignite, and pour quickly into a warmed, heat-proof mug. Fill with hot coffee, top with whipped cream, and sprinkle top with cinnamon and ginger.

JERSEY FLASH

1 tsp. honey or sugar syrup
4 whole cloves
Pinch cinnamon
Lemon peel
2 oz. gin
Hot apple cider or apple juice
Grated nutmeg

Rinse out a heat-proof mug with boiling water and add honey, cloves, cinnamon, lemon peel, and a little boiling water to dissolve honey. Pour in warmed gin, ignite, blaze for a few seconds, and fill mug with hot cider. Sprinkle with grated nutmeg.

JERSEY TODDY

1 tsp. honey
Boiling water
Several dashes Angostura
   bitters
2–3 oz. applejack or calvados
Lemon peel
Cinnamon stick

Put honey in a warmed, heat-proof mug and add enough boiling water to dissolve honey. Add bitters, apple jack, and fill with boiling water. Garnish with lemon peel and cinnamon stick.

KENT'S CORNERS HOT CUP

5 oz. cider
2 oz. dark Jamaica rum
1 oz. maple syrup or to taste
½ tsp. lemon juice
Cinnamon stick

Heat all ingredients in a saucepan and bring to boiling point, but do not boil. Serve in a warmed mug.

THE LOCOMOTIVE

6 oz. dry red wine
½ oz. curaçao
½ oz. maraschino liqueur
(optional)
½ oz. honey or sugar syrup
to taste
1 egg
Lemon slice
Ground cinnamon

In the flaming pan of a chafing dish (or a saucepan) mix red wine, curaçao, maraschino, and honey until honey is dissolved. Gradually warm wine over direct heat (but do not boil), stir in a lightly beaten egg, and bring to a simmer. Pour into a warmed, heat-proof mug, add lemon slice and pinch of cinnamon.

LONDON DOCK

½ oz. honey or sugar syrup
1½ oz. dark Jamaica rum
1½ oz. dry red wine
Lemon peel
Cinnamon stick
Grated nutmeg

Dissolve honey with a little boiling water in a heat-proof mug. Add remainder of ingredients, except nutmeg, and fill mug with boiling water. Top with grated nutmeg.

MEXICAN COFFEE

1 oz. Kahlua
½ oz. tequila
Hot black coffee
1 generous tbsp. whipped
cream
Pinch ground cinnamon

Pour Kahlua, tequila, and hot coffee into a warmed mug or Irish coffee glass, stir well, and top with whipped cream and a sprinkling of cinnamon.

BARTENDER'S SECRET NO. 38

How is the best way to flame drinks? Answer: *safely.* As everyone knows, alcohol is a flammable substance. What many people do not know is that when alcohol is warmed it begins to vaporize, and this vapor is very flammable indeed. For this reason, alcohol used for all flambé food dishes and flaming hot drinks must be warmed or it will not ignite unless the proof is very high (100 to 151). Professionals always treat alcohol with respect. *Here are some safety rules:* Do not use large amounts of alcohol to flame drinks. A scant ounce is sufficient. When heating spirits in a saucepan or chafing dish, stand well back and do not bend over to look into the pan. When igniting spirits in a brightly lit room, it is best to dim the lights because the flames from alcohol are almost invisible in daylight. Do not place uncorked bottles of spirits near any open flame. Never pour spirits from a bottle into a flaming dish (fire may blow back). Never flame anything in a large pan or chafing dish with people sitting at the table (it could spill over). Instead, do your flaming on a cart or serving table. And never flame anything near draperies, curtains, or in the vicinity of party decorations such as paper bunting, streamers, and other flammable festoons, trimmings, and table coverings.

 ## MIKE GILL'S GROG

1 750-ml. bottle Haitian or
  Martinique rum
1 pt. orange juice
1 cup brandy
½ cup kummel
½ cup Benedictine
½ cup lemon juice
½ cup Falernum or honey to
  taste

1 cup canned pineapple,
  cubed with juice
1 liter spring water

Mix all ingredients in a saucepan and heat until simmering. Serve in warmed mugs with a pineapple cube. Makes about 26 servings.

 ## MRS. CAHILL'S IRISH COFFEE

Hot, strong black coffee
2 oz. Irish whiskey
½ oz. Kahlua or Irish Mist,
  depending on sweetness
  desired
Orange peel
1–2 tbsp. whipped cream

Rinse a wine goblet, mug, or a beer schooner with hot water and fill, leaving room at the top, with hot coffee. Stir in whiskey and Kahlua or Irish Mist. Add a slice of the outer zest of an orange peel and top with a generous serving of whipped cream.

MULLED ALE

1 cup ale
Small piece whole ginger
1 pat butter (optional)
1 tsp. sugar
1 or 2 eggs (depending on
    richness desired)

Put ale, ginger, butter, and
sugar into a saucepan and heat
to the boiling point, but do not
boil. In a bowl, beat the eggs

with a tablespoon of cold ale
and pour into saucepan. Pour ale
mixture back and forth between two saucepans to froth,
return to heat, and serve hot
in a warmed mug.
Note: The alternative method of
preparation is to plunge a red-
hot poker or flip iron into a large
tankard containing this mixture.

 MULLED CIDER

2 oz. gold Jamaica, Barbados,
    or Haitian rum
Dash Angostura bitters
4 whole cloves
Cinnamon stick
Pinch ground allspice
1 tsp. honey or sugar syrup
    to taste
1 cup apple cider or apple
    juice
Lemon twist

Heat all ingredients in a saucepan and strain into a warmed
mug.
Note: An alternative method of
making this drink is to put all
ingredients into a tankard and
froth by plunging a red-hot
poker into the mixture.

 MULLED CLARET

5 oz. red Bordeaux
1 oz. port
¾ oz. brandy
Pinch ground cinnamon
Pinch grated nutmeg

Several whole cloves
Lemon peel

Heat all ingredients in a saucepan (do not boil) and pour into a
warmed mug.

PEDRO MacDONALD'S CUP

1½ oz. scotch
2 oz. cream or oloroso sherry
½ tsp. lemon juice
1 tsp. sugar syrup or honey
    to taste
Several dashes Angostura
    bitters

Several dashes orange bitters
Cinnamon stick
Orange peel

Heat all ingredients with 2 oz.
of water in a saucepan and pour
into a heatproof mug.

PUERTO BANUS BRUNCH SPECIAL

1½ oz. light rum
1 oz. cream sherry
4 oz. orange juice
1 tsp. honey or to taste
Several dashes Angostura or
    orange bitters

Cinnamon stick
Orange slice

Heat all ingredients, except
orange slice, and pour into a
warmed mug or Old Fashioned
glass. Garnish with orange slice.

 ## ROCK & RYE TODDY

3 oz. rock & rye
Dash Angostura bitters
Lemon slice
Cinnamon stick
Boiling water
Grated nutmeg

Rinse a heatproof mug with hot
water and add rock & rye, bitters,
lemon slice, and cinnamon stick.
Fill with boiling water and stir
well. Sprinkle with grated nutmeg.

 ## RUMFUSTIAN

2 egg yolks
1 tsp. sugar or to taste
1 cup ale
2 oz. gin
2 oz. sherry
Cinnamon stick
Several whole cloves
Lemon peel
Grated nutmeg

Beat egg yolks in a bowl with
sugar. In a saucepan, bring ale,
gin, sherry, cinnamon, cloves,
and lemon peel to the boiling
point (but do not boil), then
pour in egg mixture, stirring
briskly with a whisk. Serve in
a warmed mug and top with
grated nutmeg.

 ## SHEILA GOODMAN'S GINKEN SOUP

1½ cups canned or home-
    made chicken soup
1 oz. gin
Pinch white pepper
½ tsp. chopped parsley

If canned or packaged, prepare
soup according to directions, heat
in a saucepan, and add gin
when simmering, but do not boil.
Add pepper and parsley, and
serve piping hot in a large mug.

BARTENDER'S SECRET NO. 39

Piping hot drinks are much to be desired, especially when
there is a chill in the air. Drinks can be made with boiling hot

ingredients as long as they are *nonalcoholic*. Wines and spirits should never be boiled. Why let all the zip in your drink go up in steam? Also, many liqueurs and almost all wines do not stand up well to high heat and develop an off flavor. Care should be taken when heating alcoholic ingredients over an open flame. Use small quantities and a low flame. Spirits are volatile materials that can ignite and flare up, causing singed hair and eyelashes, and in some cases minor burns.

 ## ST. VINCENT HOT BUTTERED RUM

1 tbsp. brown sugar
Small lemon peel or orange
    peel
Whole cloves
Cinnamon stick
2 oz. dark or gold Jamaica
    rum
1 oz. crème de cacao
Pat butter
Grated nutmeg

Put brown sugar into a warmed, heat-proof mug with peel studded with cloves and cinnamon stick. Pour in a little boiling water and stir until sugar is dissolved. Add rum, crème de cacao, and fill with boiling water. Stir and top with butter and grated nutmeg.

SKI LIFT

1 oz. DeKuyper Peachtree
    Schnapps
½ oz. CocoRibe
5 oz. hot chocolate
Marshmallow or whipped
    cream
Pinch ground cinnamon

Combine schnapps, coconut rum, and hot chocolate in a warm mug and stir. Garnish with marshmallow or dollop of whipped cream and sprinkle cinnamon on top.

 ## SKIER'S TODDY

1 cup hot chocolate
¾ oz. Kahlua, Tia Maria, or
    crème de cacao
¾ oz. triple sec
Several marshmallows or
    whipped marshmallow
    topping

Rinse out a large mug with boiling water, add steaming hot chocolate, and stir in liqueurs. Top with marshmallow.

SLALOM STEAMER

½ oz. package hot cocoa
   mix
½ tsp. instant coffee
Boiling water
1½ oz. gold Puerto Rican,
   Barbados, or Jamaica
   rum
Ground cinnamon or nutmeg

Add cocoa mix and coffee to a
warmed mug and fill almost to
the top with boiling water. Stir
in rum and mix well. For a richer
drink use milk instead of water.
Sprinkle with ground cinnamon
or nutmeg.

STEAMING MARY

2 oz. vodka
5 oz. tomato juice or V-8 juice
1 tbsp. hot barbecue sauce or
   to taste
½ tsp. lemon juice
Several dashes Tabasco
   sauce
Pinch white pepper

Small pat butter
Pinch ground or chopped dill

Heat vodka, tomato juice, barbecue sauce, lemon juice, Tabasco,
and white pepper in a saucepan
to a simmer, but do not boil.
Pour into a warmed mug and top
with butter and a sprinkling of
dill.

TOM AND JERRY Individual

1 egg
½ oz. sugar syrup or to taste
1 oz. dark Jamaica rum
1 oz. cognac
Grated nutmeg

Separate egg and beat the
yolk and white individually. Fold
white and yolk together, add

syrup, and put into a warmed,
heat-proof mug. Add rum and
cognac and fill with boiling water.
Sprinkle with grated nutmeg.
Note: Some recipes call for
additional spices such as ground
cinnamon, cloves, and allspice.
This is a matter of individual
taste.

VESUVIO

1 cup hot strong black
   coffee
1 oz. sambuca
1 sugar cube

Fill warmed cup with hot coffee
and, using an inverted teaspoon,

carefully float half of the sambuca
on top of the coffee. Place
a sugar cube in a spoon and
pour remainder of sambuca into
spoon. Ignite and dip blazing
spoon into cup. Let cup flame
for a few seconds and stir
coffee to extinguish flames.

WINDJAMMER

Peel of half a large orange
Brown sugar
2 oz. gold Jamaica or
*   Barbados rum*
1 oz. rock & rye
1 oz. curaçao
Lemon peel
Boiling water

Cut orange peel in a thin spiral, moisten, and coat with brown sugar. Place spiral in a heat-proof mug, add about ½ oz. of warmed rum and flame until sugar is carmelized. Add remainder of rum, rock & rye, curaçao, and lemon peel, fill with boiling water, and stir well.

 ## WINTER PASSION

1 oz. La Grande Passion
1 cup hot tea
Milk or cream (optional)

Add La Grande Passion to hot tea and add milk or cream, if you wish. Stir and serve.

GOOD DRINKS SANS SPIRITS

With a little creative planning and care,
the nonalcoholic drink can be just
as appetizing and satisfying as any other
kind of liquid refreshment
that you serve to your guests.
                                    —John Poister

A good drink has nothing to do with how big it is, how strong
it is, or how much alcohol it contains—whether a big slug, just
a little, or none at all. The recipes in this chapter have been
carefully researched and tested. Many are all good, meaning
that the recipes produce predictable results, are flavorful, refreshing, and satisfying. They can be served at any social
occasion with pride and will taste just as good sans spirits as
the alcoholic kind. Artistry in drink making should not be
relegated only to alcoholic drinks. There are times when, for
whatever reason, anyone may choose to have light, nonalcoholic refreshment in place of conventional cocktails, wine, or
beer. Rather than restricting the nondrinking guest to soda
pop, tea, or coffee, the considerate host will provide a selection of imaginative, well-made, flavorful beverages without
alcohol that will be appropriate to the occasion and do honor
to the nonimbibing guest.

Time was when the selection of fruit juices was limited to
lemon, lime, grapefruit, pineapple, and orange; and not always
fresh, but canned or frozen. Today with greatly improved transportation from tropical growers and streamlined distribution
to the market, the resourceful host will find a large selection
of tropical fruits that were rarely seen in the U.S. just a few
years ago. Freezing and canning methods have also improved
greatly, so that exotic fruits, which are quite acceptable for
drink-making purposes, may be had out of season. Party plan-
ners will find that many alcoholic coolers, party drinks, and
punches are excellent even when the alcohol is omitted.

With a little creative planning and care, the nonalcoholic

drink can be just as appetizing and satisfying as any other kind of liquid refreshment that you serve to your guests. This includes attention to proper glassware and attractive garnishes as well as the other essentials of good mixology.

Gone are the days when the well-meaning host would say, "Oh, just have one" to the nonimbibing guest. However well intended, this is misdirected hospitality and unnecessary. Instead the nondrinker should be presented with a good drink sans spirits that will make other, drinking guests exclaim, "That looks great. I'll have one!"

AILEEN PETERSON'S CIDER CUP

1 cup fresh apple cider
1 cup hot tea
1 tsp. brown sugar or to taste
Dash orange juice
Dash lemon juice
Pinch powdered cinnamon
Pinch grated nutmeg

2 cinnamon sticks

Mix all ingredients, except cinnamon sticks, in a saucepan over low heat and bring to a simmer. Serve in warmed mugs and garnish with cinnamon sticks. Makes two servings.

APRÈS TENNIS BRACER

1 oz. canned frozen orange
    juice concentrate
Ginger ale
Orange slice

Spoon orange juice concentrate

into a 10-oz. glass and fill with cold ginger ale. Add an ice cube or two, if you wish, and garnish with orange slice. Stir gently.

ARYAN

½ cup plain yogurt
½ cup cold spring water
2 tsp. dried mint leaves or
    fresh mint, finely chopped
Pinch salt

Mix all ingredients in a blender until smooth and serve in a chilled goblet. Add several ice cubes, if you wish.

BANANA MILK SHAKE

1 cup whole milk
1 small ripe banana or a half
    of a medium-size banana
2 scoops vanilla, butter pecan,
    or coconut ice cream
Powdered cinnamon or grated
    nutmeg

Mix all ingredients, except cinnamon or nutmeg, in a blender and pour into a 10-oz. glass. Sprinkle top with cinnamon or nutmeg.

 BLACK COW

Root beer
2 scoops vanilla ice cream
Root beer

Put scoops of ice cream into a chilled 12- or 14-oz. glass and fill with cold root beer. Stir gently and serve with a spoon.

BREAKFAST EGGNOG

1–2 oz. frozen orange juice concentrate or 2–3 oz. fresh orange juice
¾ cup whole milk or skim milk, very cold
1 egg

Powdered cinnamon or grated nutmeg

Mix all ingredients, except spice, in a blender until smooth and foamy. Pour into a chilled goblet and sprinkle with cinnamon or nutmeg or both.

BUTTERMILK BOUNTY

1 tsp. honey
1 cup buttermilk
¼ cup ripe banana, thinly sliced
¼ cup ripe pear, peeled and chopped
Pinch powdered cinnamon

Dissolve honey with a little buttermilk in a cup and pour into a blender. Add remaining milk, banana, and pear. Blend until smooth and pour into a chilled wine glass. Sprinkle with cinnamon.

CAFÉ VIENNOISE

1 cup cold strong black coffee
1 oz. heavy cream
1 tsp. chocolate syrup
½ tsp. powdered cinnamon
Pinch grated nutmeg

Mix coffee, cream, chocolate, and cinnamon in a blender until smooth and pour into a Squall glass or a wine goblet. Sprinkle with nutmeg.
Note: This elegant coffee is often served with a generous topping of whipped cream.

A CALF SHOT

6 oz. beef consommé or bouillon
½ oz. lemon juice
Several dashes Worcestershire sauce or to taste
Several pinches celery salt or celery seed

Several pinches white pepper

Stir well with ice cubes in a mixing glass and pour into a chilled Old Fashioned glass. Add additional ice cubes if necessary.

CARIBBEAN CELEBRATION PUNCH

1 cup pineapple, chopped
1 cup orange sections
1 cup grapefruit sections
1 package frozen straw-
  berries, thawed
1 pt. orange juice
1 cup grapefruit juice
1 cup papaya juice
1 cup guava juice
1 cup passion fruit juice
1 6-oz. jar maraschino cherries
2 l. ginger ale
1 l. lemon-lime soda
1 l. club soda
1 banana, thinly sliced
1 lime, thinly sliced

Prechill all ingredients and mix pineapple, orange and grapefruit sections in a blender; add strawberries and orange juice until fruit is pulverized but still chunky. Remove and set aside. Then mix grapefruit, papaya, guava, passion fruit juices and maraschino cherries in a blender until cherries are pulverized. Pour into a chilled punch bowl and mix in fruit from the first blending and stir well. Chill with a large cake of ice. Just before serving, gently stir in ginger ale and soda. Garnish with thinly sliced banana and lime. Makes about 55 servings.

CHERRY VELVET

Several scoops New York
  cherry or vanilla ice cream
¼ cup cream or half and half
6 maraschino cherries
1 tbsp. maraschino cherry
  juice

Mix all ingredients in a blender for a few seconds until cherries are pulverized and serve in a chilled goblet.

CHOCOLATE MALTED

1 cup whole milk
2 scoops chocolate ice cream
¼ cup chocolate syrup
2 generous tbsp. malt powder

Mix in a blender until smooth and pour into a chilled 10-oz. glass with straws.

CREAMSICLE

Several scoops vanilla ice
  cream
1 cup fresh orange juice
1 tsp. orgeat syrup or almond
  extract

Mix all ingredients in a blender for a few seconds until smooth and serve in a chilled goblet.

DOWN EAST DELIGHT

½ cup fresh orange juice
2 oz. grapefruit juice
2 oz. cranberry juice
1 oz. orgeat syrup or honey
  to taste
Maraschino cherry

Mix all ingredients, except cherry, with cracked ice in a blender or shaker and pour into a chilled Old Fashioned glass. Garnish with a cherry.

EGG NOG FOR ONE

1 whole egg
2 tsp. superfine sugar
Pinch salt
Several dashes vanilla extract
1 cup milk
Grated nutmeg or powdered
  cinnamon

Beat egg with sugar and salt until well blended and smooth, and spoon into a chilled highball glass. Add vanilla and a little cold milk and stir briskly. Add remainder of milk, stir again, and top with nutmeg or cinnamon. *Note:* Ice is not used in the making of this drink, so make certain all ingredients are prechilled.

FISHERMAN'S CUP

2–3 oz. tomato juice
2 oz. clam juice
2 oz. sauerkraut juice
½ tsp. horseradish
Several dashes Tabasco
  sauce
Several dashes Worcester-
  shire sauce
Dash lemon juice

Stir all ingredients with several ice cubes or mix with cracked ice in a shaker or blender and pour into a chilled highball glass. *Note:* This is an excellent party punch. Increase quantities, mix well in a chilled punch bowl, taste for seasoning, and chill with a large cake of ice.

FLORIDA PUNCH

2 qt. fresh orange juice
1 qt. fresh grapefruit juice
2 l. ginger ale
1 cup fresh lime juice
1 cup orgeat syrup or sugar
  syrup to taste
½ cup grenadine

Chill all ingredients in advance and mix in a chilled punch bowl with a large cake of ice. Makes about 46 servings.

▚ GARDEN CUP

1½ cups buttermilk
¼ cup ripe avocado, mashed
¼ cup cucumber, peeled, seeded, and finely chopped
1 tsp. onion, finely chopped
1 tsp. parsley, finely chopped

Pinch celery salt or to taste
Pinch white pepper

Mix all ingredients in a blender until smooth and serve in chilled wine goblets or parfait glasses. Makes two drinks.

GENTLE SEA BREEZE

½ cup cranberry juice
½ cup grapefruit juice

Mix in a blender until foamy and pour into a 12-oz. glass with several ice cubes.

GINGER PEACHY SHAKE

1 cup milk
¼ cup fresh or frozen peaches, sliced thinly or chopped
2 scoops peach or vanilla ice cream
¼ tsp. powdered ginger
¼ tsp. powdered cinnamon
Whipped cream (optional)

Mix peaches with a little milk in a blender until peaches are pulverized, add remainder of milk, ice cream, and spices. Blend for a few seconds until mixture is smooth and pour into a tall, chilled glass. Top with a mound of whipped cream, if you wish.

ICE-BREAKER PUNCH

1 6-oz. can frozen orange juice
1 6-oz. can frozen grapefruit juice
1 6-oz. can frozen pineapple juice
1 qt. ginger ale
1 qt. lemon-lime soda
½ cup liquid Pina Colada mix or to taste
½ tsp. powdered cinnamon
½ tsp. grated nutmeg
1 small ripe banana, thinly sliced

Prepare frozen fruit juices according to instructions on cans and pour into a chilled punch bowl with a large cake of ice. Gently stir in ginger ale and lemon-lime soda and sweeten to taste with Pina Colada mix. To make blending easier, dilute Pina Colada mix with a little fruit juice or water before mixing in punch. Sprinkle punch with cinnamon and nutmeg to taste and garnish with banana slices. Makes about 35 servings.

GINGER SNAPPER

2 oz. orange juice
2 oz. grapefruit juice
2 oz. cranberry juice
1 tbsp. ginger marmalade
½ tsp. freshly grated ginger
Orange slice

Mix all ingredients, except orange slice, with cracked ice in a shaker or blender until marmalade is dissolved and pour into a chilled Old Fashioned glass or tumbler. Add additional ice, if you wish, and garnish with orange slice.

 JOHN'S JUICE

3 cups fresh orange juice
1 tbsp. liquid Pina Colada mix

Mix in an electric blender until Pina Colada mix is dissolved and chill in the refrigerator until cold.

JONES BEACH COCKTAIL

5 oz. beef consommé or bouillon
3 oz. clam juice
Juice of ½ lemon or lime
½ tsp. horseradish
Several dashes Worcestershire sauce

Pinch celery salt or celery seed

Mix all ingredients with cracked ice in a shaker or blender and serve in a chilled highball glass with ice cubes.

JUNGLE COOLER

4 oz. pineapple juice
2 oz. orange juice
1 oz. liquid Pina Colada mix
½ oz. passion fruit juice
Pineapple slice

Mix all ingredients, except pineapple slice, with cracked ice in a blender or shaker and pour into a tall, chilled Collins glass. Garnish with a pineapple slice.

KEYPORT COCKTAIL

5–6 oz. clam juice
1 oz. seafood cocktail sauce or to taste
½ oz. lemon juice
Several dashes Tabasco sauce
Several dashes Worcestershire sauce

Several pinches celery salt
Lemon slice

Mix all ingredients, except lemon slice, with cracked ice in a shaker or blender and strain into a chilled Old Fashioned glass. Garnish with a lemon slice.

THE LONE PRAIRIE OYSTER

1 tsp. Worcestershire sauce
½ tsp. cider vinegar
1 tsp. cocktail sauce (red)
Several dashes Tabasco
   sauce
Pinch celery salt
Pinch cayenne
Dash Angostura bitters
   (optional)
1 egg yolk

In a chilled wine goblet, mix all ingredients, except egg yolk, with a spoon until well blended. Carefully add egg yolk to glass so that it is unbroken.
Note: The contents of entire glass are to be swallowed in one gulp without breaking the egg yolk.

MILKMAID'S COOLER

¾ cup buttermilk
¾ cup tomato juice
Dash lemon juice
Pinch white pepper
Pinch dried basil
Dash Worcestershire sauce
   (optional)

Prechill all ingredients and mix in a blender until smooth. Serve in a tall, chilled Collins glass.

MOCHA COFFEE

½ cup strong black coffee
½ cup hot chocolate
1 tbsp. whipped cream
Pinch powdered cinnamon,
   grated nutmeg, and grated
   orange peel

Combine coffee and chocolate in a warmed mug, stir, top with a generous spoonful of whipped cream, and sprinkle with pinch of cinnamon, nutmeg, or orange peel.

MULLED CIDER

2 cinnamon sticks, broken
12 whole cloves
1 tsp. allspice berries
½ gallon apple cider
½ cup brown sugar or to
   taste
Dried apple rings
Whole cinnamon sticks

Put broken cinnamon sticks, cloves, and allspice into a cheesecloth bag and place in a saucepan with cider and brown sugar. Stir and heat over a low flame and simmer for a few minutes until spice flavors have an opportunity to dissipate. Remove spice bag and ladle into warmed cups in which you have put an apple ring and a cinnamon stick. Makes 16 servings.

ON TO OMSK!

5 oz. beet borscht
½ tsp. lemon or lime juice
½ tsp. horseradish
Several dashes Tabasco
   sauce or to taste
Several dashes Worcester-
   shire sauce

2 tbsp. plain yogurt or sour
   cream

Stir all ingredients, except yogurt, with cracked ice in a mixing glass and strain into a chilled Old Fashioned glass. Top with yogurt or sour cream.

 ORANGE FLOWER COOLER

3 oz. orange juice
3 oz. grapefruit juice
1 tsp. maraschino cherry juice
6 maraschino cherries
½ tsp. orange flower water

Mix all ingredients with cracked ice in a blender until cherries are pulverized and pour into a chilled goblet or Collins glass. Add additional ice, if necessary.

 ORANGE JUICE SUPREME

6 oz. fresh orange juice
2–3 preserved cocktail orange
   sections with syrup
1 tsp. orange marmalade
Several dashes lime or lemon
   juice
Several dashes raspberry
   syrup or grenadine

Mix with cracked ice in a blender or shaker until orange sections are pulverized and marmalade is dissolved. Pour into a tall, chilled highball or Collins glass. Add additional ice, if you wish.

ORGEAT COCKTAIL

1 oz. lemon juice
¾ oz. orgeat syrup or to taste
1 egg white
Maraschino cherry

Mix with cracked ice in a blender or shaker and strain into a chilled cocktail glass.

PALM GROVE COOLER

2 oz. orange juice
1 oz. guava juice
1 oz. grapefruit juice
1 oz. pineapple juice
½ oz. lime juice
½ oz. grenadine
1 small, ripe banana
Several dashes Angostura
    bitters
Club soda

Pineapple slice
Maraschino cherry

Mix all ingredients, except
soda, pineapple slice, and cherry,
with cracked ice in a blender and
pour into a tall, chilled Collins
glass and fill with cold club
soda. Stir gently and garnish
with pineapple slice and
maraschino cherry.

PLANTER'S PAUNCH

2 oz. pineapple juice
2 oz. orange juice
1 oz. lime or lemon juice
1 oz. coconut syrup or to
    taste
1 oz. passion fruit juice
½ oz. grenadine
6 maraschino cherries
Club soda

Pineapple slice
Orange slice

Mix all ingredients, except
soda, orange slice, and pineapple
slice, with cracked ice in a
blender until cherries are crushed.
Pour into a chilled Collins
glass. Add cold club soda an stir
gently. Garnish with pineapple
slice and orange slice.

PLUM JOY

Juice of 2 plums
½ cup cold water
1 oz. lemon juice
½ oz. sugar syrup or to taste
2 tbsp. plum jelly
Lemon-lime soda

Mix all ingredients with cracked
ice in a blender and strain into a
large Collins glass. Fill with
lemon-lime soda, stir gently, and
add additional ice if necessary.

PONY'S NECK

1 large lemon or orange
Ginger ale
½ tsp. lime juice
Dash Angostura bitters
    (optional)
Maraschino cherry

Carefully peel the outer layer
(zest) of a lemon or orange in a
thin, unbroken spiral that is
then fitted into a highball or
Collins glass with one end
hooked over the rim of the glass.
Add several ice cubes and fill
with cold ginger ale. Stir in lime
juice and bitters gently, and
garnish with a maraschino cherry.

POOR SUFFERING BUSTARD

Dash Angostura bitters
6 oz. ginger beer
1 tsp. Rose's lime juice
Cucumber slice
Lemon slice
Mint sprig

Swirl bitters around a chilled Old Fashioned glass and empty. Add several ice cubes, fill with cold ginger beer, and garnish with cucumber, lemon and mint. Stir gently.

RASPBERRY-MA-TAZZ

5 oz. pineapple juice
12 raspberries or 6 strawberries
1 small, ripe banana
Grated nutmeg

Mix all ingredients, except nutmeg, with cracked ice in a blender and pour into a chilled highball glass. Sprinkle with grated nutmeg. Add additional ice, if necessary.

RASPBERRY SODA

¼ cup frozen or fresh raspberries
2 scoops raspberry sherbet, raspberry ice, or vanilla ice cream
Creme soda, lemon-lime soda, or club soda
Whipped cream
Whole raspberry

Blend raspberries with several tbsp. sherbet in a blender until pulverized. If frozen raspberries are used, be sure to add some of the syrup. Pour into a chilled 12-oz. glass, add remainder of sherbet, fill with cold soda, stir gently, and garnish with a topping of whipped cream dotted with a whole raspberry.

ROYAL CHOCOLATE-NUT SHAKE

½ cup chunky peanut butter
½ cup chocolate syrup
1 cup whole milk
2 scoops chocolate, vanilla, or butter pecan ice cream
Whipped cream (optional)

Mix peanut butter and chocolate syrup with a little milk in a blender until mixture is smooth. Add remainder of milk and ice cream and mix for a few seconds until smooth. Top with mound of whipped cream, if you wish.

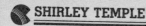# SHIRLEY TEMPLE

4 oz. ginger ale
1 tsp. grenadine
Orange slice
Lemon peel
Maraschino cherry

Pour ginger ale and grenadine into a chilled wine glass with an ice cube and stir gently. Garnish with orange slice, lemon peel, and maraschino cherry.

STEPPES SHAKE

½ cup diced, ripe cantaloupe
½ cup sliced, ripe banana
½ cup plain yogurt
1 tsp. sugar syrup or honey
   to taste
Several dashes lemon juice

Mix all ingredients in a blender until smooth and pour into a tall, chilled Collins glass or large wine goblet.
Note: Other fruit combinations may be used. If honey is used as a sweetener, dissolve it with a little water before putting into blender.

SUNSET COOLER

½ cup cranberry juice
2–3 oz. fresh orange juice
Dash lemon juice
Ginger ale
Lemon slice

Mix cranberry juice, orange juice, and lemon juice with cracked ice in a shaker or blender and strain into a tall, chilled Collins glass. Add several ice cubes and fill glass with cold ginger ale. Garnish with lemon slice.

T. M. HUNT'S CUP

½ cup fresh orange juice
2 scoops vanilla ice cream
Several dashes vanilla extract
1 tsp. honey or sugar syrup
   to taste
1 egg (optional)
Pinch powdered cinnamon
Pinch grated nutmeg

Mix cold orange juice, ice cream, vanilla, honey, and egg in a blender until honey is dissolved and mixture is smooth but not watery. Pour into a chilled Collins glass or large goblet and sprinkle with cinnamon and nutmeg.
Note: Honey will mix more easily if you dissolve it with a little milk or water in a cup before adding to blender.

TRANSFUSION

3 oz. grape juice
6 oz. ginger ale
Several dashes lime juice
Lime slice

Pour grape juice and ginger ale into a chilled highball glass with several ice cubes, add lime juice, stir gently, and garnish with lime slice.

VICAR'S COFFEE

1 cup strong black coffee
½ tsp. orgeat syrup
Several pinches powdered
  cinnamon
1–2 scoops chocolate ice
  cream
Whipped cream
Grated nutmeg

Put cold coffee, syrup, cinnamon, and ice cream into a blender and mix for a few seconds until smooth but not watery. Serve in a chilled wine goblet and top with a generous mound of whipped cream and sprinkle with nutmeg.

VIRGIN MARY

6 oz. tomato juice or V-8
  juice
1 tsp. dill, chopped
1 tsp. fresh lemon juice
¼ tsp. Worcestershire sauce
Several pinches celery salt
  or celery seed

Pinch white pepper
Several dashes Tabasco
  sauce

Stir all ingredients well in a mixing glass and pour into a chilled highball glass with several ice cubes.

YE COTTAGE COCKTAIL

3 oz. tomato or V-8 juice
3 oz. clam juice
Several dashes Tabasco
  sauce
Several dashes Worcester-
  shire sauce
½ tsp. lemon juice
Fresh dill, finely chopped (or
  dried dill may be
  substituted)

Mix all ingredients, except dill, with cracked ice in a shaker or blender and pour into a chilled Old Fashioned glass or a highball glass. Top with chopped dill.
Note: This is a refreshing drink at any time of the day or night. Some will want to add a jigger of vodka, but it is just as good without.

GLOSSARY

Abbot's Bitters See Chapter 1 under *Bitters*.

Abricotine The proprietary name for an apricot liqueur made by the French house of Garnier.

Absinthe An anise-flavored, high-proof liqueur now banned due to the alleged toxic effects of wormwood, which reputedly turned the brains of heavy users to mush.

Advocaat A bottled egg nog mixture made with brandy and eggs that originated in the Netherlands. Also spelled Advockaat.

Afri-Koko A chocolate-coconut cordial made in the West African county of Sierra Leone.

Aguardiente "Burning water" and well named for this generally high-powered, low-quality, brandy-like spirit popular in parts of Spain and South America.

Airelle An eau-de-vie made from the red mountain cranberry (see *Myrtille*).

Amaretto A generic cordial invented in Italy and made from apricot pits and herbs, yielding a pleasant almond flavor.

Amer Picon See Chapter 1 under *Bitters*.

Anesone The ouzo of Italy; an anis-based absinthe substitute.

Angostura Bitters See Chapter 1 under *Bitters*.

Anisette A very sweet, anise-based generic liqueur. That produced by the firm of Marie Brizard is generally considered to be an outstanding example of this cordial.

Applejack Sometimes called apple brandy, this spirit, distilled from apples, is aged in wooden barrels like whiskey (see *Calvados*).

Apéritif See Chapter 1 under *Mixology*.

Apricot Brandy Rarely made as an eau-de-vie, this spirit is usually available in the U.S. as apricot-*flavored* brandy.

Apry An apricot cordial made by the firm of Marie Brizard.

Aquavit See Chapter 3 under *Flavored Vodkas*. Also spelled Akvavit.

Armagnac See Chapter 5.

Amontillado An amber, medium-dry sherry often possessing a nutty flavor and excellent as an apéritif or mixed-drink ingredient.

Asbach Uralt An excellent German brandy, similar to cognac, and matured in oak barrels.

Arak (Also Arrack and Arrak) A generic term that refers to various spirits made in parts of the Pacific, Southeast Asia, and the Middle East. See *Batavia Arak.*

Aurum A fine, golden orange liqueur from Italy.

B&B A mixture of cognac and Benedictine, yielding a drier product than Benedictine alone.

Barack Palinka An outstanding eau de vie distilled from apricot fruit and stones by the Austrian firm of Zwack.

Barbados rum See Chapter 4.

Batavia Arak A rich, pungent, aromatic rum made from malted rice and molasses and aged in barrels like cognac in Indonesia.

Bacardi See Chapter 4.

Benedictine A venerable, complex, aromatic herbal liqueur invented by a Benedictine monk in the early sixteenth century, but now purely a commercial enterprise and generally recognized to be one of the world's top five proprietary liqueurs.

Bergamot A brandy-based liqueur made in Germany from bergamot, a very flavorful citrus fruit.

Bitters See Chapter 1 under *Bitters.*

Blackberry Popular as a cordial and as a flavored brandy in the U.S.

Blended whiskey See Chapter 6.

Boker's Bitters See Chapter 1 under *Bitters.*

Boonekamp See Chapter 1 under *Bitters.*

Borovicka A Czechoslovakian juniper brandy that bears a greater resemblance to gin than brandy.

Bourbon See Chapter 6.

Bronte An English herbal liqueur made of fruits and spices, also known as Yorkshire liqueur.

Byrrh An aromatic apéritif wine from France with overtones of orange and quinine.

Calisay A liqueur specialty from Barcelona used for flavoring and as a *digestif* with strong quinine overtones.

Caloric Punsch See *Swedish Punsch.*

Calvados One of the most important eaux-de-vie distilled from the apples of Normandy and considered the quintessential apple brandy, especially that classified *Calvados du Pays d'Auge.*

Campari A popular Italian bitter apéritif with a brilliant red hue and strong quinine underpinnings.

Canadian whisky See Chapter 6.

Cerise See *Kirschwasser*.

Certosa Liqueurs of various colors and flavors faintly reminiscent of Chartreuse distilled by an order of monks near Florence, Italy.

Chartreuse One of the royal family of great proprietary liqueurs, this complex formulation in green and yellow versions has been made by the Carthusian monks near Grenoble since 1605.

Cherry liqueurs Like orange liqueurs, these are usually compounded with fruit, flavorings, and sweeteners. A few outstanding names include Cherry Marnier (France), Peter Heering (Denmark), DeKuyper (The Netherlands), Cheristock (Italy), Rocher Cherry Brandy (France), Grant's Morella Cherry Brandy (England), Cerasella (Italy), and Wisniak (Poland). Maraschino liqueur, like cherry cordials, is made by many distillers, but the world's largest producer of maraschino is the Luxardo firm of Torreglia, Italy.

China-Martini See Chapter 1 under *Bitters*.

Chocolate liqueurs Crème de cacao, a very popular, generic chocolate liqueur available in the traditional cocoa color or clear for mixed drinks, is manufactured by many producers worldwide including such famous names as Bols, DeKuyper, Garnier, Marie Brizard, and Hiram Walker. There are also speciality chocolate liqueurs such as Vandermint and Royal Mint-Chocolate Liqueur, mint-chocolate mixtures; Sabra, a chocolate-orange cordial from Israel; Marmot from Switzerland with little pieces of chocolate in the liqueur; Droste Bittersweet Chocolate Liqueur, and chocolate-coconut combinations such as Afri-koko and Choclair. Some distillers like Hiram Walker market a line of flavored chocolate cordials using orange, raspberry, cherry, and other fruits.

Coffee liqueurs Crème de mocha or crème de cafe are generic coffee-based liqueurs made by a number of producers. Specialty proprietary brands like Kahlua from Mexico and Tia Maria from Jamaica have become famous. Other specialties included Pasha Turkish Coffee Liqueur, Gallwey's Irish Coffee Liqueur, and Coffee Espresso from Italy.

Chouao An area in Venezuela reputed to grow some of the world's finest cocoa beans, which explains why the name is sometimes used on crème de cacao labels.

Cognac See Chapter 5.

Cointreau A famous proprietary brand of triple sec that is popular straight and as a versatile ingredient for many mixed drinks.

Coing A rare eau-de-vie made from quince.

Cordial Médoc A complex, proprietary liqueur produced in Bordeaux, France, with a brandy base and overtones of raspberry, orange, cacao, and other flavorings.

Crème liqueurs The prefix *crème* indicates that sugar is basic to these formulations that encompass a full spectrum of flavorings. Here are a few:

Crème de almond (almond)
Crème de banane (banana)
Crème de cacao (cocoa-vanilla)
Crème de cassis (black currants)
Crème de celeri (celery)
Crème de d'anana (pineapple)
Crème de menthe (peppermint)
Crème de noisette (hazelnuts)
Crème de noyaux (bitter almond)
Crème de mocha (coffee)
Crème de rose (vanilla and roses)
Crème de thé (tea)
Crème de vanilla (vanilla beans)
Crème de violette (violets)
Crème de yvette (violets)

Curaçao An intense orange liqueur made from the peels of green oranges from the island of Curaçao. In clear, orange, and blue colors.

Cynar An aromatized wine from Italy flavored with the artichoke.

Cuarenta y Tres A brandy-based proprietary liqueur from Spain containing 43 ingredients with a hint of vanilla. Also known as Licor 43.

Damiana A French proprietary liqueur specialty.

Danziger Goldwasser Originally made in Danzig by the firm of Der Lachs (established 1598) and popularly known as *eau-de-vie de Danzig*, Goldwasser is characterized by little bits of gold leaf that float around in the bottle and a spicy, citrus flavor.

Demerara rum See Chapter 4.

Drambuie Drambuie, the great proprietary liqueur of Scotland made of scotch and heather honey, is considered to be one of the top five world-class formulations. Reputed to have been Bonnie Prince Charles's own family recipe.

Dubonnet A famous aromatized wine of French origin, available in red and white with a flavor base of quinine. Now made in the U.S.

Eaux-de-vie Literally "waters of life," which was once used to describe all distilled spirits, but now generally encompassing only clear distillates such as the fruit brandies made in Europe (i.e., framboise, kirsch, mirabelle, calvados, quetsch, etc.).

Estomacal-Bonet A Spanish liqueur similar to the specialty of the Basque country, Izzara.

Falernum See Chapter 1 under *Flavorings and Sweeteners.*

Fernet Branca See Chapter 1 under *Bitters.*

Fino A light, dry, fragrant sherry type usually drunk cold.

Fior d'Alpe An Italian proprietary liqueur instantly recognizable by a twig in the bottle festooned with rock-candy crystals. Made from a venerable herbal recipe.

Fleurs d'Acacia An Alsatian eau-de-vie made from acacia flowers.

Forbidden Fruit An American creation, one of the few grapefruit liqueurs.

Fraise The French word for strawberry generally refers to the clear eau-de-vie fruit brandy, but may also designate a liqueur (*crème de fraise*).

Framboise Usually denotes an eau-de-vie made from raspberries, but can also be used to identify a liqueur made from raspberries (*crème de framboise*).

Frangelico A proprietary liqueur with a pronounced hazelnut flavor.

Framberry A brand name for a raspberry liqueur produced by the Alsatian firm of Dolfi.

Galliano A sweet, spicy, herbal liqueur popular taken neat and as a mixed-drink ingredient. Named in honor of an Italian war hero, Major Giuseppe Galliano.

Genever See Jenever.

Gentiane An eau-de-vie made from gentian root.

Gilka A famous German name long associated with kummel, a liqueur with a distinctive caraway-cumin flavor. The Dutch firm of Bols in The Netherlands also claims to have fathered this spirit in the sixteenth century.

Gin See Chapter 2.

Glayva A Scottish proprietary liqueur with a scotch-whisky base similar to Drambuie.

Goldwasser See *Danziger Goldwasser.*

Grand Gruyere An herbal liqueur from Switzerland.

Grand Marnier One of the top five world-class proprietary liqueurs with a distinctive curaçao-cognac flavor that is highly prized by connoisseur, chef, and mixologist.

Grappa A popular Italian pomace brandy made from grape, pulp, skin, and seeds that are the residue from the wine press after the juice has been extracted (see *Marc*).

Groseille Currants, both red and white, which are sometimes made into an eau-de-vie.

Herbsaint An absinthe substitute similar to Pernod made in New Orleans.

Hollands gin See *Jenever*.

Himbergeist A German eau-de-vie, literally "spirit of raspberry."

Houx A rare and expensive eau-de-vie made from holly berries in Alsace.

Irish cream liqueur A popular sweet, rich liqueur made with cream, Irish whiskey, and sweeteners homogenized into a well-balanced cordial. Bailey's began it all, quickly followed by other brands such as Carolan's, Dunphy's, Emmet's, O'Darby's, St. Brendan's, Waterford, and others.

Irish Mist This excellent proprietary liqueur, like Drambuie, utilizes heather honey and has a similarly legendary provenance, believed by some to be a recreation of Ireland's lost heather wine dating back to the pre-Christian era. A spicy, sweet concoction with an Irish-whiskey base.

Irish whiskey See Chapter 7.

Izzara The liqueur of the Basques; an herbal mixture with an armagnac base and, like Chartreuse, available in both green and yellow versions.

Jaegermeister See Chapter 1 under *Bitters*.

Jenever A distinctive spirit, not at all like London or dry gin, with a malty flavor that is very popular in The Netherlands, where it originated in the seventeenth century (also spelled *Genever* and known as Schiedam or Hollands gin).

Kahlua Mexico's famous *licor de café*, sweet, rich, flavorful, and well balanced.

Kirsch (Also *kirschwasser*) A trenchant eau-de-vie made from cherries and distilled by producers in a large area around the Rhine where Germany, France and Switzerland share common borders.

Kümmel An old, generic liqueur available in both dry and sweet versions, made with caraway, cumin, coriander, and various other herbs. Some distinguished brands include Allasch, Bolskümmel, and Gilka.

La Grande Passion A fine proprietary specialty liqueur made in France by Marnier-Lapostolle, the firm that makes Grand Marnier. Pronounced passion-fruit flavor with an armagnac base.

Lakka A liqueur made from the Arctic cloudberry by the firm of Marli in Turku, Finland.

Lillet A popular French apéritif wine that is available in red and white versions.

Liqueur d'Anis An aniseed liqueur such as anisette.

Liqueur d'Or An herbal specialty liqueur produced by the firm of Garnier and similar to yellow Chartreuse in flavor and character.

Licor 43 See *Cuarenta y Tres*.

Lochan Ora A proprietary liqueur made of Scotch whisky, honey, and various herbs. Similar to Drambuie.

Madeira Fortified wines from the Portuguese island of Madeira, blended, like sherry, using the *solera* system so that young wines are blended with older ones in successive stages to achieve consistent quality. Madeiras range from very dry to very sweet and are as highly prized in the kitchen as they are drunk as an apéritif or as a dessert wine.

Malaga A sweet, fortified wine from southern Spain.

Mandarine Napoleon A medium-sweet, well-balanced tangerine liqueur with a cognac base. Made in Brussels.

Manzanilla The driest of all sherries, which is made in the area surrounding Sanlucar de Barrameda in the "Sherry Triangle" of southern Spain.

Maraschino A sweet liqueur made from Marasca cherries, which grow in Dalmatia bordering on the Adriatic Sea (see *Cherry liqueurs*).

Marc A pomace brandy from France, principally from Burgundy, similar to grappa, which comes from Italy. The grape skins, stems, and pulp that are used to make this eau-de-vie give it a characteristic woody taste.

Marsala A robust, Madeira-like, fortified wine from Sicily ranging from dry to very sweet with a distinctive flavor that makes it excellent for cooking as well as drinking.

Mastikha An anise-based liqueur from Greece.

Mazarine A proprietary liqueur from the house of Cusenier from a seventeenth century recipe. Suggestive of yellow Chartreuse with a spicy, herbal flavor.

Mead A honey wine of ancient origins that is still made in England, parts of Europe, and the U.S.

Mesimara A liqueur made from the wild Arctic bramble by Marli of Turku, Finland.

Metaxa A popular Greek brandy that has been sweetened to give it a liqueur quality.

Midori A muskmelon- or cantaloupe-flavored liqueur from the Japanese house of Suntory.

Mirabelle A popular eau-de-vie distilled from the yellow plum.

Mistra Italian ouzo, an anise-based liqueur.

Moscato A fortified wine made from the Muscat grape in various countries such as Italy, Spain, and Portugal.

Mûre An eau-de-vie made from the blackberry or mulberry.

Myrtille An eau-de-vie made from the whortleberry or hurtleberry (also bilberry), a large species encompassing several varieties. Sometimes referred to as airelle.

Ojen A Spanish, anise-based, absinthe-type liqueur sans wormwood, which has been banned from spiritous beverages.

Okolehao A distillate of rice, taro root, and molasses from Hawaii that is guaranteed to loosen up the luau.

Oloroso A rich, sweet sherry type that is popular as an after-dinner drink.

Orgeat A syrup with a pronounced almond flavor, which makes it a good sweetener for desserts and mixed drinks.

Ouzo An anise-based, sweet liqueur that is the national spiritous drink of Greece.

Parfait Amour The elixir of "perfect love" is a sweet, perfumed liqueur with hints of flowers, spices and fruit, and a mauve color that apparently had great appeal to women in the nineteenth century.

Pasha A Turkish coffee liqueur.

Pastis A French generic term for all anise-based, absinthe-type liqueurs.

Pastis de Marseilles A proprietary anise-based liqueur from the city of the same name.

Peppermint schnapps An intensely mint-flavored liqueur that is lighter and less sweet than older mint-based liqueurs such as crème de menthe.

Pernod A famous, proprietary absinthe-type liqueur from France without the wormwood ingredient that was a part of the original absinthe formula.

Persico A peach liqueur with overtones of almond and other fruits and flavorings made by the Dutch firm of Bols.

Peter Heering A famous proprietary cherry liqueur from Denmark with a rich, full-bodied, intense cherry flavor. Formerly known as Cherry Heering. The name was changed to afford better copyright protection for the brand.

Pimento Dram A Jamaican specialty liqueur, this spicy, zesty, tropical elixir is made from the flower buds of the pimento tree.

Pineau des Charentes A *mistelle* (grape juice to which sufficient alcohol has been added to stop fermentation) from the cognac area in France, prized as an apéritif.

Pisco An unusual brandy from Muscat wines made in and around Ica, Peru, on the coastal desert south of Lima. Made famous as the main ingredient in Pisco Punch.

Pistàchà A pistachio-flavored liqueur produced by Cointreau, Ltd. in the U.S.

Poire Williams An exceedingly fine eau-de-vie made from the Williams or Bartlett pear.

Port (Porto) Port or Porto (*Vinho do Porto*), its official designation, is the great fortified wine of a strictly controlled area of the Douro region of Portugal. Port has been used as a generic term to describe port-type wines wherever they may have been produced, but since 1968, only wines produced in Portugal may use the Porto appellation.

Praline A New Orleans liqueur that recreates the butter-pecan-brown-sugar-vanilla flavor of the traditional praline candy.

Prunelle The French name for the sloeberry, source of sloe gin, which can also be made into a delightful eau-de-vie. The sloeberry is not a berry but a wild plum and, for the record, sloe gin is not a gin, but a very fruity liqueur that is the base of the sloe gin fizz.

Punt e Mes A famous proprietary apéritif wine from Milan with intriguing orange-quinine flavors.

Quetsch An eau-de-vie made from the purple plum.

Quinquina An apéritif wine with a quinine flavor base.

Raki A Turkish liqueur with a sweet licorice flavor.

Raspberry See *Framboise*.

Ricard A popular French *pastis* with a pronounced anise-licorice flavor in the absinthe tradition.

Rock and Rye A generic liqueur made with whiskey, whole fruits, and sweetened with rock-candy crystals. Sometimes taken as a hot toddy to alleviate cold symptoms.

Roiano A proprietary Italian liqueur made from various herbs with an anise-vanilla-spice flavor reminiscent of Galliano.

Rum See Chapter 4.

Rye whiskey See Chapter 6.

Sabra A chocolate-orange liqueur from Israel.

Sake A unique Japanese brewed beverage that is not a rice wine as some mistakenly suppose, and not a spirit since it is not distilled. It is nevertheless a versatile product that may be drunk hot or cold or used to make mixed drinks such as a vodka or gin Martini.

Sambuca An anise-like Italian liqueur, but not made with aniseed, but the elder *Sambucus nigra*. Traditionally drunk after dinner with coffee beans.

Schiedam gin See *Jenever*.

Schnapps The word "schnapps" (from the German word *schnappen*, meaning "snap") refers to a tot of .vodka, gin, brandy, or other spirit. In Scandinavia the word is *snaps* and almost always means akvavit. Today in the U.S., the term has taken on a new meaning to identify a whole new generation of intensely flavored, sweet, inexpensive liqueurs of moderate strength (22 to 30 per cent alcohol by volume). The DeKuyper brands of Appelbarrel schnapps and Peachtree schnapps, while not the first in the U.S. market, are generally credited with launching the "schnapps sweep" due to technical breakthroughs that yielded a fresh rather than "cooked" fruit flavor. Other flavors such as cola, cinnamon, root beer, cranberry, butterscotch, strawberry, hazelnut, apricot, and other types proliferated from a number of distillers, making the schnapps category an overnight success.

Scotch See Chapter 7.

Sherry One of the classic fortified wines produced in a restricted area known as the "Sherry triangle" that surrounds the city of Jerez de la Frontera in the south of Spain between Seville and Cadiz. Sherry ranges in color from straw to dark amber and in taste from very dry (Manzanilla) to very sweet, which is designated a cream sherry. All sherries exported from Spain are blends using the *solera* method (i.e., maturing young wines by blending them with older wines in successive stages to achieve predictable quality and consistency).

Slivovitz A plum brandy similar to quetsch, aged in wood, but classified as an eau-de-vie. Made in Yugoslavia and some other parts of eastern Europe.

Sloe gin a sweet, fruity liqueur made from the sloe berry or wild plum (also called prunelle and blackthorn) that is popular mainly in mixed drinks.

Sommer Garden A proprietary liqueur from Odense, Denmark, purported to be the world's first after-dinner liqueur without sugar (it is sweetened with saccharin).

Southern Comfort A popular proprietary liqueur from St. Louis used extensively in mixed drinks and often described as a peach whiskey.

Steinhager A unique German gin made exclusively from juniper berries that are crushed, fermented, distilled, and then redistilled with grain neutral spirits. Its name comes from the Westphalian town of Steinhagen. It is also known by its generic name: wacholder.

Stonsdorfer See Chapter 1 under *Bitters*.

Strawberry See *Fraise*.

Strega A sweet, spicy, proprietary liqueur from Italy reputed to be made from over 70 ingredients.

Sureau An eau-de-vie from Alsace made from elderberries.

Swedish Punch This sweet, spicy liqueur is popular in Sweden, especially during the winter months due to its legendary warming qualities, hence the name: Caloric Punsch. The predominant flavor is Batavia arak, an aromatic rum from Indonesia.

Tequila See Chapter 8.

Tia Maria A venerable coffee liqueur from Jamaica with a pleasant aroma and overtones of tropical spices in its flavorings.

Triple sec A generic liqueur made by many producers, varying in its orange flavor, aroma, and sweetness. Made from sweet and bitter oranges, this clear liqueur is probably best characterized by the Cointreau brand.

Tuaca An Italian, brandy-based, proprietary liqueur with the suggestion of many flavors such as vanilla, citrus, almond, coconut, orange, and cocoa among others.

Van Der Hum A brandy-based tangerine liqueur made in South Africa from Dutch origins.

Vandermint A "liquid after-dinner chocolate mint" perhaps best describes this proprietary liqueur from The Netherlands.

Verveine du Velay A French herbal liqueur made from plants of the genus *Verbena*. Popular as a *digestif*.

Vieille Cure A complex, aged liqueur of the herbal type from Bordeaux, reputedly made from over 50 ingredients and available in yellow and green suggestive of Chartreuse.

Vodka See Chapter 3.

Whiskey liqueurs Drambuie, Irish Mist, Glayva, and Lochan Ora are examples of whiskey liqueurs made with Scotch and Irish whiskey bases. American whiskey liqueurs include Wild Turkey Liqueur made from bourbon; and George M. Tiddy's Canadian Liqueur and Yukon Jack, both made from Canadian whiskies.

Wishniak (Wisniak) A wild cherry liqueur that originated in Poland and is now made in other parts of eastern Europe.

INDEX